Rose
Of The Flats

To Eileen,
Enjoy!

Dario Addario

DARIO ADDARIO

PAGE PUBLISHING, INC.
Conneaut Lake, PA

First originally published by Page Publishing 2020

ISBN 978-1-68456-953-3 (pbk)
ISBN 978-1-68456-954-0 (digital)

Printed in the United States of America

Introduction

Cascade Flats, New Hampshire, 1957

Not only was my brother small, he was so unruly, people said. He hated to be controlled by others. Pigheaded, they called him, a high school literature teacher who became a royal pain in the ass to those who tried to keep him in his place.

"Regular people," my brother used to call them.

Having come from Cascade Flats, he seemed different to them, somehow, as well as smaller. He had given them the impression of being gentle and humble, and they in turn had given him the opportunity to serve them, to instill in the suggestible minds of youth the values which have made them, the regulars, what they are. But just one year after he had begun teaching, he proved to them how perverse he really was by doing something colossally stupid.

He married Rosie—actually married her.

That was five years ago.

As I sit here at the kitchen table, I'm distracted by the grunts and groans coming out of him at the big oak chair where I have him tied. I've placed him at the other end of the table facing the window of the porch so he can watch heavy snow descending slowly. It's been another long winter. If he's capable of boredom, he's lost interest in the snow. He seems to prefer sitting in sunlight, but I'm not sure. I'm not sure of anything anymore. I have faith in Rosie, though. She has spent the last two years, day and night, trying to get him to respond to us. I've persuaded her to go out of the house for a while, but she feels guilty leaving him.

3

Writing this was originally her idea, to introduce us and to provide some of the background that had prompted him to begin this manuscript, his third unfinished book, I think. He'll never write again, or teach. That part of his life ended two years ago, when he was twenty-five, the victim of an accident, according to official reports. Rosie's brother, who had been there, says otherwise. My brother can't tell us; he doesn't speak. I have to keep one eye on him, because when he squirms in the chair, he tends to slide under the ropes. I've put a piece of rope around his waist, through the slats, and tied the ends at the back of the chair. Another piece of rope is across his small chest, under his right arm. He lost his left arm somewhere in Korea. He lost his legs here, on the home front. And he lost his mind. Damage to his brain has been irreparable. Rosie refuses to put him in a nursing home and insists that we can give him better care and attention and comfort here at home, tranquilizing him with pain-killing drugs. She made a fuss about leaving him but has taken her three children to the ice skating rink. They, too, demand her attention and love, and she tries to make their lives secure, even happy. I don't know where she gets her strength. Without her, my own life, I feel, would have drained out of me long ago. Last Christmas, the way she admonished me for spoiling the kids by giving them too much, made me feel so good I almost cried. I used to think of her as a lamb. When she married my brother, I, the big brother, would have to assure them of my support, I thought, as though they couldn't get along without it.

Anyone who knows her, really knows her, loves her. She's always willing to listen to problems of others, in spite of her own, and is genuinely concerned about the oppression of others, telling me that life is too precious to waste on hate. A year ago last December, after giving birth to her third child and faced with the loss, virtually, of my brother, she was concerned over the fate of Rosa Parks who had refused to give up her seat on a bus to a young white man, way down in Montgomery, Alabama. When I callously remarked that we had our own problems right here, she smiled at me.

My mother, too, loved her; she really did, but when she heard that Rosie had officially become part of the family, my mother became sick to her stomach, afraid of how regular people would react to us. Anyone, I thought, who had ever met Rosie had to be brainless and heartless not to understand why my brother was so attracted to her. Seldom has nature put so much into the creation of any being. She was formed from a perfect mold, almost. Intelligent, gentle, with a deep sense of family loyalty, she's also sensually graceful without being pretentious or stuck on herself. Except for a few light splotches on her arms, her flesh is sleek and naturally bronzed and her face exquisitely slender with high cheekbones and long forehead, and eyes as black as olives. She smiles easily, as though small compliments touch her deeply, and her smile is enough to melt the bleakness within me. And the way she sticks by my brother, and endures, has inspired me, a beer-guzzling skeptic who had almost lost faith in the human race. Every morning, she helps me bathe him, dresses the kids, gets us breakfast, and cleans the house. We shave him daily with an electric razor and cut his hair about once a month while he struggles with us. We bathe him every afternoon and change his clothes, and at night we bathe him again and then lay him down in a crib and pull the sides up. Sometimes, during the night, we have to change his sheets and bathe him again. Rosie has so much love in her, so much courage, yet so much anguish. This morning when he seemed to gaze at his reflection in the bathroom mirror, his daughter, at three years old, stared at him and asked us if her father knew who he was. Rosie choked back her tears and hugged her. I'm not saying she's perfect. Sometimes she's exhausted and depressed and doesn't restrain her tears and almost blames herself for our situation, as though she's ashamed of who and what she is; and I get so damn angry I feel like shaking her. "What gives others the right to condemn you?" She sees through their alleged superiority, but sometimes certain distortions, instilled in us in childhood through the irrationality of others toward us, persist even as we mature.

To know something doesn't always mean controlling it. I've discovered that one truth, after almost three decades. I, who had known almost everything about nearly everything just a few years ago, suddenly feel lost and confused, like her. Regular people, I've observed, have a construct of the world into which everything fits neatly, making life simple, making everything either black or white, never both at the same time, otherwise life would be complex and would require so much thinking from us that understanding it would be too difficult. I envy them, especially their ease in blaming victims for their circumstances. Rosie and I are lost souls in the mountains. She can't provide the answers to our situation. Regular people have. Their answer is so simple, I wonder why we haven't considered it: put my brother in a nursing home, and put his children up for adoption. They're certain that Rosie and I are committing adultery. After all, we're in a situation that would tempt even them. Anyway, whatever she is, she's genuine, everything, almost, that any intelligent person should admire in another: the woman my brother loved, the ideal wife, almost, and the loving mother of his children—but she's a nigger.

Now, I don't mean that in a derogatory sense. Well, hell, you know what I mean, don't you? To think of her as inferior to regular Americans is only normal. Isn't it? I mean, since regular people feel that way, those who don't are as dumb as my brother was. All the old sayings must mean *something*, don't they? "What am I, black?" had to originate somewhere.

Regular people think I'm biased, just because she's related to me. Well, maybe I am. I admit that sometimes I tend to forget their labels, and they have to remind me of what Rosie is, of her great grandparents as contented slaves singing spirituals in those cotton fields away, and of her ancestors as savages dancing to primitive beats of drums until civilization with its high standards here in the land of the free came to them as a blessing, giving them the cheapest mode of transportation to a new life, and incorporating them into a sort of welfare system under the guidance of superiors. Their progress, from paganism to salvation, was willed, by God! But the white man's burden, like children, must be kept under control.

When I remind Rosie that God has given her natural rhythm, she laughs at me, imagining herself, probably, trying to dance the jitterbug. She has a fascinating laugh. Her dark eyes light up and her gentle lips part, radiating warmth from the core of her being. Everything about her is fascinating, and I enjoy hugging her. She's petite. When she wraps a kerchief around her face, she looks like a black Madonna; in a bathing suit, everyone, including women, stares at her body.

But regular women resent her, and they ask me if she enjoys eating watermelon and fried chicken. Well, she does. So do they. But that's different, I guess. She also enjoys eating spaghetti, and steak, and lobsters, and hot dogs and apple pie. That seems strange, I know.

Even Minnie Birch, with whom I was madly in love, my English teacher in high school, a regular American from Boston, a sophisticated lady and all, once told another teacher that Rosie's a little nigger twerp trying to worm her way into white society by marrying into a family that was almost white. Minnie meant mine. Her ancestors, she once told me, had come on *The Mayflower*. Mine had probably come in shrimp boats, I told her. We're little people.

Minnie has told me that there had never been any problems with prejudice here in the White Mountains until my brother married Rosie. "Now that I think about it," I said, "you're right." I've never actually known anyone to admit being prejudiced. Sometimes some people preface their derogatory remarks by saying, "I'm the last person in the world who's prejudiced," so I guess they know what they're talking about. Christians (Catholics and Protestants) hate each other's guts, and Jews are restricted from certain resort areas here in New Hampshire, but those aren't real problems. Anyway, a healthy amount of prejudice, like a certain amount of sex, makes us feel good. Some people don't know when I'm bullshitting, but stop and think of the benefits of looking down at those below, at the natural losers, and laughing like hell at them.

There's enough prejudice around today, for all of us, although it's not always perfect. Rosie still becomes bewildered by tourists, sometimes, who give the impression that they've seen a lot of blacks and know a lot more about them than she does and want to know what the hell she's doing here in New Hampshire anyway. When she tells them she was born here, they look at her as though she's nuts. Those same people go out of their way to get tanned to look more like her.

Some people say that prejudice is learned; others say it's natural. I don't know, but to me neither theory makes any sense. For example, jungle people who let their women go around showing off their naked breasts are obviously stupid. They ain't got any notions of modesty and morality, unaware that in this country we pay to look at breasts of naked women, that it's a good way of getting our rocks off and of boosting our economy. But among jungle people such a commercial enterprise wouldn't succeed, and they probably think we're crazy. Jungle people simply aren't aware of the commercial value of naked breasts nor of our free enterprise system because they don't know any better. So I'm reluctant to say that their prejudice against us is learned, because to me, learning means acquiring insight. I mean, to them sex is probably just something natural, not a spectacular form of entertainment. Their lack of awareness indicates, to me, that their prejudice isn't learned. And I doubt that it's natural, because prejudice against us Americans just doesn't seem natural. Their prejudice stems from not understanding our culture from our point of view. So, to say that their ignorance is learned doesn't make sense to me.

But ignorance can be perpetuated through our institutions, because we can be trained, like Pavlov's dog, to react in certain ways to certain conditions. We mustn't confuse training with learning, though, as we do sometimes in our educational establishments. To make prejudice flourish (and I think we've done a pretty good job), all of our institutions have to support each other in perpetuating the stereotyped images of all aliens and in promoting the image of regular people, the way our schools promote Dick and Jane, and the movies promote Tarzan, lord of the jungle, who, as every kid in this country knows, is a real Dick, and the way comic books promote Sheena, queen of the jungle, with her long golden hair, and everything else, the nocturnal object of my fantasies when I was a kid and used to stare at her swinging on a vine clenched between her white thighs, and pretend I was her mate. Tarzan had Jane. But I had Sheena.

Our most influential institution, the entertainment industry, has been doing a good job upholding our traditions, showing how blacks are useful as servants and entertainers, with minstrel shows using blacks, sometimes, to impersonate whites impersonating comical darkies, and with hilarious cartoons of Little Black Sambo. That diminutive darkie is a cute little bugger. Cute as a pup. How would you like to own him as a pet? But knowing what we do about the birds and the bees, the thought of Sambo growing up and dangling his ding-dong at dainty Jane makes you want to puke, doesn't it? That's worse than imagining Snow White getting banged by the bashful dwarf.

Now, suppose, if you can, that Snow White sees in the little guy the image of God. Such a grotesque picture puts a hell of a strain on the imagination, I know. She'd be a prime candidate for the nut house, right?

So, before my brother married Rosie, I warned him how regular people would react to a son of theirs. Not only would he be dark, he'd be small. Certainly not the type of Dick that Jane's folks have in mind. My brother got upset with me. But, hell, I hadn't invented the damn rules.

And he got upset when he had been expected to give up teaching. He had known the rules, but he had the gall to break them, reminding others, as though they needed reminding, of his smallness. If he couldn't marry someone socially acceptable, Minnie told me, he should have resigned himself to loneliness.

Such a teacher, especially during the Korean police action, or whatever the hell it was, was obviously a commie. The damn fool had declared his own war in the mountains of New Hampshire, just north of Mt. Washington, and nine months after he had married Rosie, he was wallowing in muddy trenches in Korea. But whose fault was that?

He had thought, as a teacher, he would be exempt from the draft. Not *him*! I mean he was *dangerous*. His marriage to Rosie, in seventeen of our states, was actually a crime. If he had been in Russia, he'd have to conform. So why the hell couldn't he conform in *this* country? What right did he have to oppose the system? Love it the way it is, or get the hell out. But he was determined to come back, to change things. That's the way he was. You just couldn't reason with him.

After Rosie showed me the unfinished script, I said, "It's too bad he never had a chance to finish it." And she said, "Let's finish it for him." She was serious. "Hell," I said, "I'm an insurance man, not a damn writer." But she, a college grad who went to the University of New Hampshire, is as adamant as my brother was, especially when her eyes reflect the fire in her soul.

During the past two years, we've been working on his script, but I don't know where it ends. "We'll know when we come to it," Rosie said, full of confidence. I've become obsessed by this damn script, forgetting, even, my goal of making piles of money to become as good as regulars. I haven't sold them any insurance in months. I've thought of a "going out of business" sale to get rid of my damn apps.

My brother used prejudice as a metaphor to examine relationships, but began his script in the middle of the story, when he married Rosie, and used fictitious names of people and places. After I read it, I said, "I don't like the way I'm portrayed." She smiled. And I'd use our own names, I told her, and I wouldn't refer to Cascade Flats as Erebus, as he did, not even metaphorically, in spite of the similarities. After all, the flats is our home. "I'm going to write a lengthy introduction," I warned her, "breaking most of the damn rules of narration, probably, telling about some of the people and events that affected us before you married." An effective story, any trained insurance man will tell you, has to be kept simple; but this one isn't simple. Our story, I told her, had begun long ago. I think it goes all the way back to Adam and Eve who had begotten Cain who had said to Abel, "Hell, if I can't be number one, I ain't playing."

Cascade Flats, with forty or so weary looking houses lined up along the west bank of the Androscoggin River, contains French Canadians and Italians mostly, whose primary existence is in serving the biggest paper mill in the Northeast. Rosie and her folks had lived here until the second world war. Her brother Nicola and I, older than she by more than three years, used to eat and sleep at each other's houses. Sometimes we called him Nick, which Italians pronounced Neegaw. His father's my godfather, so Nick and I have been related since birth, the year before the stock market had crashed. As kids, we had known very little of the outside world and presumed it was a marvelous place, like a tremendous movie created by God.

And then the war came.

That winter, a squad of Negro soldiers arrived, right here in Cascade, between the flats and the hill, where the waiting room of the old trolley stop had been converted into barracks. Unless you've lived here, in a godforsaken little hole in the mountains, separated from the rest of humanity, you can't imagine the curiosity they aroused and the fear they inspired, like aliens from another planet, turning limbo into a seething turmoil. Some people were friendly, inviting them into warm homes and feeding them, but most folks were wary. Some even warned us that the soldiers would inflict the evil eye on us, but hey, the same folks, my father said, had said the same thing about Jews, of whom he knew something, having been descended from Hebrews. But I'll talk about that later.

Cascaders, incidentally, never used the word "colored" in reference to people, not until television became popular. So, back then, Nick and I were unaware of the term. We visited the soldiers once. We were a little scared at first, but they turned out to be friendly, letting us examine their army gear and laughing and joking with us, and then I yelled, "Hey, Neegaw, look at dis bayonet!" and the soldiers stared at me, and one of them asked us if we were colored. We thought he meant Calabrese (which sounds like "colorbraze"), who are Italians from Calabria, the toe of Italy. I'm not, but Nick, surprised, said, "How did you know?" And the soldier said, "Well, that ain't hard to guess. You sure look colored. How do folks here treat you all?" Nick shrugged, saying, "Pretty good." And the soldier said, "Well, I'll be damned!" And wrinkling his brow, he said to me, "You look almost white enough to pass." "Pass what?" I asked. And he laughed. They all laughed.

Anyway, when we went home and told my father how friendly the nigger soldiers were, he told us to never use that word again because it was a derogatory term. They were kids, he said, caught up in the war like the rest of us, but they'd be forced back into invisibility again. Neither Nick nor I understood. We went to Nick's house, and he told his father we had visited the nigger soldiers, and his father yelled, "I don't want to hear that word, ever again, from either of you." From the tone of his voice, we knew he really meant it, but hell, folks young and old called them nigger soldiers, which sounded natural, like calling Italians wops, and his father said that wop's a derogatory term, too, and that if he'd ever hear either of us saying it again, he'd wash our mouths out with soap.

That was the winter when our training in racism had really begun. Under what we had called people, there are subspecies, which are separate, as in "separate but equal rights," and qualitatively different from regular people. So, in order to distinguish better blood from worse, it's important to our society to officially identify us from birth. According to law, apparently, race is determined by the lowest form of blood. So Nick is colored. It says so right on his birth certificate. He's officially stuck with the natural limitations of his race even though his father had graduated from Howard University and School of Medicine and had returned to the flats to care for his people, as he called us.

And if the war hadn't come to this neck of the woods, Ben John, as we call his father, would still be trying to cure us of our sicknesses. So the war had precipitated a confrontation with a situation that had been ignored until then.

Though the war for us had barely begun, the soldiers disappeared, suddenly, like the way they had arrived, and Nick and I didn't get a chance to learn anything from them, but folks who knew all about them said that they hadn't been created like regular people, that they had been misplaced heathens from jungles who couldn't endure our cold climate.

Now, I'm not sure that these same folks would go so far as to agree with the enemy, wholeheartedly. During the war, radio and movies were telling us that the Nazi version of the master race was full of baloney. The Three Stooges made a movie, and Spike Jones a recording, which poked fun at the Fuehrer and his dupes who didn't know any better, rushing to destruction like moths into a roaring fire. After all, if Hitler would conquer the whole world, he'd murder or enslave the rest of us who didn't belong to his master race.

But we Americans didn't have to worry, not with God on our side. The brown bomber, Joe Louis, an American Negro, we were reminded, had knocked the Hun to hell in the very first round. Now, we, the people of the United States, Americans all, red, white, and otherwise, were in the same boat, and we would unite under God to keep it afloat, regular people up front, navigating, and the rest of us in back, paddling.

"Joe Louis," a commentator in a newsreel said, "is a credit to his race." "Which race does he mean?" Nick asked me. He was obviously thinking of the human race as a whole. And then he said, as though suddenly seeing the light, "I guess he means Friday should always obey Robinson Crusoe."

After the soldiers had become invisible (much sooner than even my father had expected) their spirits haunted the flats, and Nick and Rosie and their folks were driven out.

The war, I thought, had changed us. My father disagreed. "The war," he said, "didn't rear itself up from a vacuum."

And he argued with others. He told them that the cold climate was in their heads, that they had become infected with negrophobia, which destroyed their perception and made them see others as threatening. "But dey ain't like us, dem!" I had never seen my father become so angry. Some folks called him a bleeding heart, which I couldn't understand, because, to me, it conjured up the image of Le Sacre Coeur. But my father wasn't Christian. I don't mean that he had anything against the teachings of Christ. Hell, he let my mother bring me up in her religion. The folks who called him a bleeding heart must have thought of him as a messiah, I thought; and then I remembered that Jesus was really Hebrew, not French.

Anyway, through the years, I've learned that the climate isn't peculiar to our region, that it's a normal condition throughout our civilization. Before the war, the people of Cascade Flats hadn't known any better, because, being such ignorant foreigners, they had respected any educated person who could read and write for them, especially a doctor who could cure them of sickness without charging anything when they couldn't afford it.

Maybe the war hadn't actually changed us, but it sure as hell brought out a lot of hostility, especially in my little brother Dante. Some folks began calling him Napoleon, after the little wop who had become a French tyrant. "Dat liddle guy, ees tough, im."

But he was such a scrawny runt that, before the war, folks used to have a lot of fun with him, calling him peewee or half-pint. In the grocery store they would pick him up and sit him on the scale to see if he could make the arrow go all the way around. They'd tell him not to stand on cracks between floorboards or he'd disappear. If a wind was blowing, they'd tell him to hurry home or he'd fly away. They'd wrap a hand around his wrist, which was so tiny that the tips of their fingers would easily touch. "Ay, lookid dis!" When we played baseball, and my brother would come to bat, they would chant: "Joe, Joe, Di Maggio!" and laugh like hell. Folks never got sick of the same old jokes, as though their imaginations had been frozen; and the kids, of course, imitated them, and my brother would just seem to shrink even more. To make him feel better, my mother would tell him that he was a smart, cute little kid, that someday he'd be somebody. "Good things," she'd tell him, "come in small packages." But if he were so damn smart, I thought, he would have known that she was bullshitting, trying to protect him, especially from regular girls who like big things in a real man, as in the saying, "That's real big of you."

And then, when the war came, like the proverbial shit hitting the fan, all the hostility in his tiny body erupted. Until then, folks used to say how cute he and little Rosie were together, with her pigtails and bronze flesh against his fair skin and blue eyes, but when the soldiers appeared, kids, in spiteful tones, began calling her a little nigger, and my brother began lashing out at them with his tiny fists. All the kids were bigger than he, but he didn't care. He became proof that small people are, by nature, pugnacious. He became a hell of a scrapper. He'd get so damn mad, tears would stream down his face, and he'd never stop punching. A sledgehammer wouldn't have stopped him. He'd keep on fighting no matter how much punishment he was taking. He was too damn stupid to admit defeat. The more he'd get hit, the more determined he'd become. Even grownups had difficulty stopping him. He'd lash out at anyone. Being almost two years older than he was and almost twice his size, a damn good fighter with a wicked punch, I'd step in, afraid he'd get hurt, and threaten to beat the hell out of him if he wouldn't stop fighting, but he wasn't afraid of me. I'd get mad and call him a dumb little shit, and I'd finally grab his arms and tell him I was sorry I called him that, and I'd hug him and kiss his wet cheeks, and he'd forgive me. I'd take out my handkerchief and wipe the tears from his face and tell him to blow his nose into my handkerchief. Whenever I did that, he knew I really loved him. And then I'd look at Rosie who'd be crying, too, and I'd put my arms around her and let her blow her nose into the same handkerchief. And then she'd press herself between Dante and me, and I'd feel pretty good.

I'd glare at the other kids and wonder why in hell they wouldn't let Rosie and Dante alone and just let them be together; but growing up, I thought, meant adjusting to the world, conforming to conventional rules, and pretending, to some extent, anyway, to follow the expectations of others. But even then, I somehow knew that Dante was too stubborn to yield.

As his big brother, my job was to take good care of him, which I usually did, but he was such a pain in the ass when I wanted to smoke or make out with a girl that I'd tell him to get lost, and he'd say, "Why?" And I'd say, "Cause I say so, dat's why." And he'd say, "Whachew goin to do?" And I'd say, "You're too damn small to know." And he'd shrug and walk away. To me he was always too small to know, and I'd always have to set a good example for him, but "Do as I tell you, kid, not what I do."

Fighting, for him, though, sure as hell paid off. Others began to respect him, and I didn't have to feel so sorry for him or ashamed that the runt was my brother.

Whenever he'd get into a fight, though, my father would say to me, "Your job is to watch your little brother. What's wrong with you, anyway?" Whenever my brother did anything wrong, I was blamed; whenever he did anything right, I was ignored, and he was praised. Very early in life I discovered that justice is blind.

My father's razor strap used to hang by the bathroom sink, and he'd pretend that the strap was for sharpening his razor, but I knew damn well what its primary function was. He had never threatened Dante with it, though, probably because he was so damn small. But he sure as hell wasn't fragile.

His smallness, sometimes, appealed to certain women. At school, when we would fight, the nuns would whack our fists with a thick ruler, and then they'd make us stay after school at least an hour to pray, and then they'd hand us a note for our parents to sign, and we'd have to return it the next morning before classes and promise to make every effort to get along with others. They would even make us fighters shake hands to seal the promise. But when the war came, and all the hostility in Dante emerged, the nuns actually blamed others! They saw him as a little crusader fighting evil. The way Minnie Birch later put it: the nuns were encouraging him to be a nigger lover. But the nuns, after all, didn't know any better. They were affected by an innocent look in his eyes, the look of a little old man, full of pathos.

After school, they would invite him and Rosie into their kitchen, and they'd have a grand old time, making fudge or taffy; and he'd come home with a bag of it. He loved the nuns. Hell, I would have loved them, too, if they had treated *me* like that.

In spite of the respect he had gained, Dante hated to fight, as though he'd never feel big enough to enjoy the manly arts. He wouldn't pluck a flower, even, he was such a sentimentalist. The way animals seemed to sense in him a deep feeling for all living things made me think of Francis of Assisi. Instead of being interested in war movies or wanting to join the boy scouts to wear the uniform and to march in patriotic parades like a red-blooded American boy, he read sentimental books about animals, such as Bambi, which were bad influences on an impressionable kid like Dante. He hated to see, for example, the normal kids playing war games and shooting at birds and squirrels and chipmunks. He'd even take wounded animals home to make them well again. Most of them died, of course. I tried to warn him that nature is cruel. To survive, I told him, a little guy like him had to convince others, always, of how hard he was deep down, otherwise, he'd end up like a lamb on the altar. But Dante didn't always listen to me, in spite of my wisdom, which came to me naturally.

Looking back now on our childhood, it's easy to see where the seeds of his character had fallen, to see how a little guy like him must have had an incurably twisted ego to disregard the traditional barriers of society and to refuse to accept discrimination as a normal condition.

Some folks thought that Dante would become a priest. I remember once when a nun had approached my mother in church and actually told her that Dante was destined for the priesthood, that she prayed for him always. Nuns and drunks, I noticed, felt the same way about him. Drunks used to invite him into the beer joint where no other kids were ever allowed, and the old Italian woman who owned it would smile at him and serve him free root beer and potato chips. The rest of us kids would steal little green apples from a tree in front of her smelly joint, making enough noise that she'd come screaming out at us in Italian. She'd never scream at Dante, though. Anyway, the drunks, who enjoyed communing with my little brother, told him that someday he'd be Pope, he was that smart. One of the drunks said, "Why not become a millionaire?" And another drunk said, "You don tink da Pope's a millionaire?"

My mother, a Jansenist like *her* mother, had absolutely no doubts whatsoever that he had been chosen by God Almighty to serve in the priesthood. She almost had a nervous breakdown that winter after the war had broken out and he was getting into so many fights.

A few days before Nick and his folks moved away, they had supper at our house. That was on a Sunday, I remember, because we had home-made spaghetti and meatballs. Sunday was the day when our families got together with the other families and drank wine and talked and played cards sometimes, but that particular Sunday was gloomy. Our mothers were preparing supper during the afternoon, and they were so jittery that our fathers told us to stay out of the kitchen. The night before, on a cold, windy March night, while Nick and his family had been asleep, the window of their front room shattered. Among pieces of glass on the floor was a rock with a note tied to it. The note read: "Get out, niggers! Go home!"

We ate in silence that evening. My mother's hands were shaking. Her face seemed paler than usual, and the skin under her eyes was red. People used to say that she was the most attractive woman in the flats. She was small and fragile looking, but not thin, and compared to my father and me, her skin seemed almost white. That winter, she looked anemic. Her black hair was dull. As she was clearing the table and carrying dishes to the sink, a plate dropped and shattered, and sauce splattered the floor.

Nick's mother, Anna, told my mother, who was fighting back tears, to sit in the living room. Anna cleaned the floor, cleared the table, and after she washed the dishes, Nick and I wiped them.

After we put the dishes away, Nick and I began a game of checkers at the table while Rosie and Dante were watching. The grownups, in the living room, were speaking in low tones.

After a while my father told us to join them. The four of us barely entered the room, stopped, and looked at them. My mother and Anna were sitting on the couch on the other side of the room, their legs crossed. Ben John was on a soft chair to our left, and my father, holding a glass of red wine, was sitting to our right, closest to us. He held the glass up. A strip of paper with the word "wine" was taped to the glass. "Do you know what this is?" he asked, pointing to the word.

"Wine," we said.

"Is it wine, or is it the word for wine?"

"The word."

"Where's the wine?"

"In the glass," Dante and Rosie answered.

Nick and I looked at each other.

"How do you know," my father asked, "this isn't vinegar?"

Nick and I almost laughed, but my father looked at us sternly.

"This word is a label. Do you know what labels are?"

We stared at him.

"Of course," I said. "Words that tell what's inside of something."

He turned the glass around. The word "vinegar" was taped to the other side of the glass.

"Does this label change what's inside this glass?"

We shook our heads.

He took a sip.

"Tastes like wine."

Ben John crossed his ankles, removed his spectacles, and wiped the lenses on his wool sweater. He seemed to be studying us. All of them were.

"People," he said, "label each other. They do it to understand certain things about certain people. Sometimes the labels are helpful. People call me doctor because I treat the sick. They give me other labels, too, and think they know what I am, what's inside of me. People want to know your labels. Do you know what yours are?"

We nodded.

"Italian," Nick said, "and Negro and French."

"Are you American?"

"Of course."

"What's that mean?"

Nick shrugged.

"Your mother's Italian. What does that mean?"

We looked at her. Next to my mother, Anna wasn't much bigger, but she was darker.

"She was made in Italy," Rosie said.

The grownups grinned at her.

"Does that mean anything else to you?" Ben John asked.

"She speaks Italian."

"So do I, but I'm not Italian."

"You have an Italian nose," Rosie said.

The grownups laughed.

Before the war, Ben John used to say, "It grew this big after I married Anna."

He put his glasses on again.

Compared to my father, who was taller than average, but slim, my godfather was a giant with a low, soft voice.

"You're right, sweetheart," he said, holding his arm out to Rosie and Dante. "Why don't you two kids sit on the floor here. We have something important to discuss." They sat upon the dark red rug, leaned back against the chair, and snuggled against his legs. "Maybe you've heard some people say that Italians are bad because they're the enemy."

His saying that surprised me because Nick and I, in our first year in high school a few miles away, had been called nigger wops, and we had been expelled from school several times for fighting. We were a problem, some people said.

"Labels don't change what's inside of us," Ben John said. "When I treat a sick person, labels don't make much difference. Inside, people are all the same; only the labels are different, but they don't tell me much about the person, not what's deep inside. There are some people who feel that if you don't have the same labels as they have, that there's something wrong with you. Do you think there's anything wrong with being Italian?"

"No," we said, but I wasn't really sure of that.

"You're the same now as you were before the war. You haven't changed. Labels don't change you. Do you think there's anything wrong with being Negro?"

"No." But I wasn't sure of that, either.

"Sometimes some Americans forget what freedom and justice mean."

And then he told us about the laws of segregation.

"Some people outside the flats believe in segregation. They've been coming here and causing trouble. It's not going to end until we move away."

Ben John and my father tried to explain the differences within the human race, but the distinctions, they said, were not always clear.

My father reached down to the floor on the other side of his chair and picked up a thin magazine, which looked like our school paper. He opened it, folded back some pages, turned it around on his knees, and showed us an outline of a man containing black and white pictures of men of various races, from snow white at the top, to charcoal black at the bottom. "Some people," my father said, "compare races to the parts of a human body. Here at the head," he said, pointing to the drawing, "representing the brain, the eyes, the ears, and the mouth of the human race, is this man." He pointed to him. "'Tall, with fair skin,'" my father quoted from the text, "'blond hair, blue eyes, long head, very intelligent and highly civilized, characterized by his love of independence and logical reasoning.' And here, in the middle of the body, as you can see, is this man. 'Short in stature, with olive skin, dark hair and eyes, relatively long head, characterized by his love of art and impulsive emotions.' And all the way down, at the feet, is this man. The person who put this paper together apparently feels that everything he says here is true. Like Hitler, he wants us to think that all the people in the world should always be controlled by a super race, which, he says, is pure white. Nature, he says, has made us that way, and we should accept it. Everyone, knowing his place in life, he says, would be happy. The person who wrote this has been coming into the flats with others at night and causing trouble for Ben John and his family."

"Who?" I asked.

My father looked at Ben John.

"We can't prove it," Ben John said.

"The biology teacher in your school."

"Shackle? Mister Shackle?"

"Has he said anything to either of you?" my father asked Nick and me.

"No," we said.

"He probably knows more about biology than I do, but that doesn't make him right. Ben John has studied biology, too."

My father looked at him again.

Ben John said, "He tells people I can't face the truth, because I'm Negro, but he doesn't tell them that he believes his theories because he wants to feel superior."

"He's confusing people," my father said, and paused, and looked at my mother.

(From that evening, to my junior year in high school, when Jed Shackle became my biology teacher, I couldn't figure out to what part of that human body I belonged. I knew I didn't belong to the head. I was hoping I belonged to the heart, but that was only wishful thinking. According to Jed Shackle, I was lower than that. The highest place left for me was the generative organ. So, that explains my personality. To the eyes of the body, my place was probably considered nasty. But what would the rest of the body do without me?)

My father sighed.

"When we've visited your mother's grandfather, have you ever noticed how dark he is?"

I nodded.

The son of runaway slaves from Louisiana, he lived on a farm in Quebec. He was in his nineties then and had entertained Nick and me that past summer with fascinating stories of slavery in his childhood.

"Do you know what race he is?" my father asked.

I shrugged, saying, "Black."

My father looked at my mother again. She looked at me, then at Dante. Closing her eyes, she wiped them with her fingers.

Ben John said, "In this country, according to the laws, which will probably change, because such laws change with the times, if someone is partially black, even an eighth, and in some states, a sixteenth, or less, that person is legally black. When I filled out the birth certificates on you and Dante, under race I put down white, but if certain people find out about you, they'll change your label to black."

"Ben John and his family," my father said, "are being forced to leave. We'd be forced to leave, too, and so would your grandmother, if certain people find out her father is black."

On the morning they had planned to leave, Rosie became sick, snow was falling, and they almost postponed their journey. They'd be going all the way down to Louisiana to live among relatives. To us kids, Louisiana sounded too distant ever to reach, especially by an automobile loaded down with whatever they could cram into it. The rest of their belongings had been sold. The night before, Dante and I had stayed with them, and Ben John, playing a banjo, had sung "O Susanna" to cheer Rosie, who couldn't be cheered; and then, as though relinquishing his most prized possession, he had given me the banjo. "Take care of this, for me, your goomba." Their furniture was gone. Even their telephone, one of the few in the flats, which others had felt free to use, anytime, was gone. That night we had slept on blankets on the floor. In the morning, my father came, saw the misery in Rosie, and told Ben John that if he wanted her to stay to finish the school year, she could stay with us, and we would take her to Louisiana. Her eyes lit up, and then she turned to her father. He agreed. She embraced him, kissing him, turned, and dashed to my father and hugged him. By noon, the snow stopped, and the sun came out, and Nick and his folks left.

I couldn't wait for the school year to end. We'd be taking the train all the way down to the other end of this country, travelling through strange worlds; and when I told other kids, they envied me. Around here, the only ones we knew who had the privilege of travelling so far were servicemen. The word quickly spread, and a reporter from The Berlin Reporter came to our house.

Now, Berlin (which rhymes with Merlin) isn't just a little hole in the ground like the flats; it's a city, the only one between central New Hampshire and Quebec, a city with a main street with five and ten cent stores and movies and a lot of houses and streets and even an airport and everything else that a regular city has, plus the biggest ski jump in the whole world. Berlin is big enough to have its own newspaper, which comes out every week.

The reporter wanted to take pictures of Rosie and Dante. My father sat at the kitchen table, motioned the reporter to sit, and then wrote something, which stated in English and in French that a humanitarian doctor who had lived here the past thirty-three years, the lifetime of Christ on earth, and who had served the people, often without pay, had been forced from his home and community by a bunch of bigots who had condemned him because, in their judgment, something of his genesis is somehow morally defective.

The reporter read it. "I guess you want us to print this." My father nodded. "That's no problem. But I think, to be more effective, you should be more specific in stating that racial prejudice is the issue." And my father said, "Until now, it's never been an issue, not here in the flats."

"But now it is!"

My father stared at him, grabbed the sheet of paper, and added that, in the last century, three sons of a black slave woman had become priests, that one of them, James Healy, had become bishop of Portland, Maine, and that his brother Patrick had become president of Georgetown University; if race had been an issue, my father wrote, the Church would have committed a sin against humanity. The condemnation of Dr. Benjamin Jourdan was our disgrace, and our loss was severe. Depravity, obviously, lay in us who project it onto him and his family, sacrificing them in atonement for our sins. "Ben John, as we call him," my father concluded, "which means 'good morning' in Italian, not only bears the dignity of his black African heritage, but he is a devout Catholic who is raising his children in the best tradition of his partially French ancestry."

The reporter, after reading it, grinned at my father. The population of Berlin is mostly French, as French as Quebec.

The reporter took pictures of Rosie and Dante, and a few days later a photo of them appeared on the front page of the paper, and they became celebrities for a day in the Berlin area, where most people had already known who Ben John and my father were, because my father was politically active and was trying to unionize the mill workers. His statement was printed under the photograph, in English and in French. But the following week, in a letter to the editor, someone, whose name had been withheld, called my father a commie agitator who was trying to dupe the French. "If he thinks they're so blind and wants them to believe that the negro heritage is so wonderful, why is he hiding his own and refusing to admit publicly that he's a Jew? Most communists in this country are Jews who are stirring up unrest among negroes and instigating them to commit their dirty work in a concerted effort to destroy our country." And so forth and so on. It was a low blow, especially since we were at war, but I didn't understand, then, everything that was going on. The editor had mentioned the letter to my father, who had given his consent to publish it, saying he knew who the writer of the letter was. Hell, he wouldn't tell me who it was.

Anyhow, when summer vacation finally came, my mother, who was a very practical woman, said that Dante and I couldn't go to Louisiana, that the trip was too expensive. Only my father and Rosie would go. I protested. "I told everybody I was going. I'd be too embarrassed not to! How can I face people?"

My father said, "The experience will be good for them. They'll learn more about this country in a few days than they'll ever learn in school."

"We can't afford it." Amen. She had spoken. Looking back, I know now what she meant.

I should never have shown her some of the letters Nick had written. He had difficulty adjusting to the laws of segregation. He lived in what folks down there called nigger town, a row of shanties, and had to go to an outhouse to take a crap. He wasn't allowed in some places where regular people went, but he went to special places marked "for colored" just for people like him, he wrote. Like colored movies, for example. And a colored church. He had even gone to a colored funeral at a colored graveyard; and he went to a colored school where he was learning that everything was really black and white.

Nick attended a Catholic high school and was taught that, though his religion didn't approve of the laws of segregation and discrimination, he was bound, as a good citizen, to obey the laws of his society; but folks here in the flats thought that segregation laws couldn't apply to Catholic institutions anywhere, that such laws were perverse as all hell, that they were downright Protestant. (Folks here, under certain circumstances, can be pretty damn liberal.) Anyway, Nick figured that if the temple of God would become unrestricted, white Christians would retaliate against them. There was a clan of some sort, which sounded like kook clucks, who kept what they called undesirables in place by threatening them. The kook clucks were suspected of having burned the church that Nick attended.

Sunday services were held outside while a new church was being built, but on that Christmas Eve, Ben John wanted to take the family to midnight Mass, as he had each year, so Nick and Rosie and their mother (who was "colored" because Italians were also "colored" in Louisiana) and grandmother piled into the car, and Ben John drove them into town, to the "white" church. They entered, and occupied the back pew, but as the church was filling to near capacity, an usher motioned them to stand at the back. Even the grandmother, an arthritic in her seventies, who walked with a cane, had to stand during the hour and a half celebration of their Savior.

Communion, Nick had thought, transcended superficial differences and united the faithful. Communion, however, in the "white" church, was allowed to Nick and his family only after the others had been served, for the others, apparently, were served by their own savior, created in their image.

Christ had died. He was born again. Not a kike, though, not this time.

Modern saviors, Nick wrote me, had been created in the image and glory of the super race. Superman for instance, who had come from a distant heaven to save us "faster than a speeding bullet, more powerful than a locomotive" had a thing about rushing into telephone booths and pulling his clothes off. What was he, really? And The Lone Ranger galloping out of the pages of yesteryear from out of the sunset had hid his identity. What was he? Hell, I knew what he was. Him great savior, keemo sabby; him bringum civilization wherever him go.

But Nick wrote me an interesting story of The Lone Ranger's faithful companion Tonto, the noble savage, who, like a pet dog, had always obeyed his master, which was natural, Nick wrote, for an Indian like Tonto. Anyway, one day they were attacked by the bad ones, the nonconformists. To protect themselves, they jumped down from their horses and took cover in a gully. The Lone Ranger looked up to assess their situation. There were Indians to the front of them, Indians to their left, to their right, and behind them. And The Lone Ranger said, "We're in big trouble, Tonto." And the red man said, "What you mean 'we,' pale face?"

The world war had lasted all through my years in high school. Back then, in Berlin, most of the people, including salesclerks, couldn't understand English, so French was spoken in all the stores. During the past ten years, Berlin has changed to English, due, I suspect, not only to education, but to movies and popular television shows such as *The Mickey Mouse Club* and wrestling matches. But French seemed so damn natural to us that, before I entered high school, I was unaware of the attitude of regular people towards the French. Here, in Cascade, in our grammar school on the hill, St. Benedict's, which is on the boundary of Berlin and Gorham, we were taught in both languages, but English was spoken by nuns with French accents. In every classroom there was a picture of the Sacred Heart of Jesus with the inscription on it: "For God and Country." The nuns had impressed upon us the importance of loving our country and to demonstrate our good citizenship as Americans to the Anglo Protestants, who were so skeptical of us Catholics, to prove to them that we were as patriotic, or even more so, as they were.

In the flats, which is really part of the town of Gorham (which is English speaking), some of us speak French, Italian, and English, but our English dialect seems to amuse outsiders who are struck by its peculiarity. Our English has a French flavor of Yankee spiced with Italian. While other people imbibe soft drinks, we paisans let our kids bib de sody; while children of others play marbles, our kids shoot de clams. While others use the toilet, so do us in de flats, ere, but it's a softer toilette, interchangeable with bughouse. (For years, I had thought that "bughouse" was a derivation of an Italian word that sounded like "buckhaus" because all the Italians here used that word, but when I was in Italy and said to my host, "*Devo andare al buckhaus,*" he stared at me, bewildered. I had to go *where?* In desperation, I pointed to my rear end. "*Cacca?*" he asked. Hell, I had thought that was an English word. Anyway, I found out later that bughouse derived from English. I don't know why the Italian immigrants here had adopted that particular word, but since the outhouse was in back of the house, they went to the buckhaus.)

And here in Cascade, we're Catlics, us, not Prodiztenz. In high school, some of the teachers made fun of our dialect, but I noticed that they couldn't understand French or Italian. "This is America," they'd say; "speak English, only English." So, when I'd remember where I was, I'd speak their English. "Canucks," they would tell us, "can speak English if they really want to." After all, anyone, even little kids, could speak English, it's so natural, so why wouldn't the French? They weren't, apparently, very patriotic, even though they pretended to respect our flag, rising to their feet and saluting it, even in the Berlin Theater whenever the flag was shown on the screen. Regular people don't do that, though, so it was a dumb thing to do. The French, after all, didn't know any better. Just to show how dumb they really were, at sporting events, the people of Berlin would even applaud visiting teams whenever they'd make good plays. I guess that's why Mark Twain said that when man was created, he was placed somewhere between the angels and the French.

Our high school, which we in the flats called Protestant, is four miles south of here, in downtown Gorham. My first day in the damn school a smart ass kid asked me, "What's the three best years in a Frenchman's life?" Before I had a chance to think about it, he said, "The first grade" and started to chuckle. I tell *you*, mister, that was the last time he got funny with *me*. The blood from his nose squirted all over the place. When the principal kicked me out, I said, "Well, I ain takin no shit from Prodizten school kids." And he said the school wasn't Protestant; it was public. And I said, "What's de diffrenze?" And he said it wasn't a religious school. "I know," I said;

"it's Prodizten." And he insisted it wasn't. "Den how come you make us pray in Prodizten?" And he said, "That's the law."

I never held that against nice Protestant girls, though. I liked them. A lot. Especially the ones who believed in sin but not in hell, like Minnie Birch. In my senior year, when she arrived, I was even willing to become a minister, like my father's cousin, Giuseppe Valentino, who changed his name to Joe Valentine and became a theology professor at Yale, where I went to college until my father died. By becoming a minister, I'd be able to save Minnie Birch. That's what she told me.

Here in the flats, a Protestant is a curiosity; a minister is truly a phenomenon. Back then, whenever my father's cousin would visit, I'd brag about him to the other kids. "Yous wanna see a *real* Prodizten? I got one in de ouse."

Although my father, who, in following the tradition of my grandmother, was a Jew, reminding me of Le Sacre Coeur, but wasn't really a blind follower of any particular organized religion, praying with as much devotion in a church as in a synagogue, had believed that truly religious people were seeking ultimate values, he had also believed that intolerant people, who demanded that everyone else follow only the particular beliefs of those same intolerant people, who claimed that their way was the only path to the kingdom of God, were suspended in ignorance, breeding suspicion and fear and hate, and separating us ultimately from God and from each other. The words of St. Augustine: "Love, and do what you will" was his guide, the meaning of which, I confess, still eludes me. One of the few who knows anything about his theology is Ben John, who remembers him as having commanded respect, even from those who feared and hated him, although why anyone should have feared and hated him seems strange to us who revere his memory.

My mother used to say that he had the heart of a lamb. She actually believed that he was created without sin, that he was as pure as the first man, before Adam had taken the forbidden fruit, and that she was his first, and only, woman. She saw Dante, I guess, as someone as pure as my father. I hate to tell you how she saw *me*.

My father had promised her to raise Dante and me in the Catholic faith but made her promise that we'd be allowed to examine our beliefs. She was, as I've stated, a very practical woman and felt that he was an easy idealist who needed her to keep him down to earth. We went to church regularly, and occasionally my father, who told us how Catholicism had come from Judaism, took Dante and me to a little synagogue in Berlin.

(I met a kid there, Max, who was my age but couldn't understand Italian and was surprised I couldn't understand Yiddish, so I taught him some choice words like *va fa in culo,* which sounds like bah fun ghoul, and he taught me some, like schmuck. We would have taught each other a lot more, I'm sure, if he hadn't moved away.)

My mother and father, as opposite as night and day, were as complimentary, I guess.

My father was called Amad, and sometimes Amo, for Amadeus, his real name, which sounded more reverent in Latin than in Italian, I guess. My mother was called Toni. He used to say that a lot of her beliefs were more Jewish than his. (He probably meant, I think, she had, as some of his predecessors had done, anthropomorphized the Supreme Being, because it was easier for her to relate to a He rather than to an It.) She believed in a wrathful God constantly at war with the devil, whom my father called Asmodeus, "spirit of anger." My mother believed that the devil was actual, not symbolic; my father called the devil a personification of spiritual depravity, the deprivation of good. He believed in an ontological Good from which life emanated, through which we could transcend our illusions and become one with Life.

My mother believed that we were created in the image of God ("Thou hast made him a little lower than the gods") but that, due to the flesh, the instrument of the devil, depravity was the natural condition of man (a radical departure from Judaism in spite of, "I was born guilty, a sinner when my mother conceived me"), which could be overcome only through divine intervention; my father believed that her devil had been created by fanatics who had inculcated the doctrine of depravity into others who had carried it with them not only into New England but into Quebec, where, almost three hundred years later, she had been raised with the deep belief in the devil and in hell and in the uncertainty of seeing God, for "many are called, but few are chosen." The doctrine of depravity, he told her, was a departure from the official teachings of her own religion; a doctrine that was a misinterpretation of divine revelation by puritanical men who had created a god in their own image, a god who reflected their own fears and their own level of development; a doctrine that was taught in American churches and schools but was alien to most Italians who perceived all of nature, including human nature, as the creation of the Divine Being and was, therefore, good.

My mother believed that spirit and flesh were separate entities, and that good and evil could be determined by antagonistic forces of nature manifested in a dualism of man; my father believed in the oneness of nature, that the evil side of man was not governed by a nature separate from his good side, not any more than night and day were governed by two separate natures.

My mother believed that all accidents and disasters, including wars, were in accordance with the will of God; my father thought that was a contradiction. She accepted contradiction as a matter of faith and felt that reason was unreliable; reason, to him, was the guide to faith. And the business of warfare and other evil acts he attributed not to the will of God, but to ignorance and greed.

My mother believed that to get anywhere in this life, one had to be independent with an instinct for business, that she had the ability to make enough money to insure our survival, but that my father didn't have any sense for business, in spite of what regular people said about Jews; my father definitely agreed in her ability to survive.

During the depression, she and my father's only sister, Maria, had sold so much homemade beer and wine and liqueur that others had to help them produce enough to supply the demand, making sure that the Berlin area wouldn't go dry during that period of prohibition. And during the war, when the gasoline shortage had forced the only filling station in the flats to close, my mother bought it and converted it into a restaurant.

My father, who usually worked in the woods, would help in the restaurant in the evenings when he was needed; otherwise, he'd be in the front room of the house, his library. Before he died, he had almost five hundred books and had such a fantastic memory that he could discuss each one in detail, and he kept only the books that were worth reading several times. My mother, though she had shared some of his interests, didn't always understand him, or try, not after she had become busy earning a good living for us.

After ten years of school in Canada, she had moved with her family to the flats a year after a public elementary school had been built here, before the construction of the Catholic school on the hill; and one teacher, who had spoken only English, had taught all the grades, divided into three groups: beginners, intermediates, and my father and Ben John. My mother, sixteen then, nearly four years older than my father, had been placed in the school as a beginner, and he had been assigned to her as tutor and translator. She was bright, the teacher said, for a French girl. My father pulled her up, and at the end of the school year, they graduated from the eighth grade.

Sometimes, in the evenings, he had gone to her house, and they had sat at the kitchen table and had worked on their assignments while her mother had sat in a rocker and had watched them, like an archangel, armed with rosary beads clenched in her fists.

After graduation, my mother was expected to marry and bear children, so, in spite of her protests, marriage was arranged through her mother to a friend of the family, a thirty year old illiterate farm hand in Quebec who moved to the flats to work in the mill.

I had known since childhood that her first husband, through whom she was childless, had died, and that she was over thirty when she married my father, who, being Jewish, had never been accepted by her mother.

And, being the smart shit that I was, way back in grammar school, I figured out that I had been born prematurely, by at least three months. Unlike my little brother who was woefully ignorant of the facts of life back then, I knew that our mother and father had fooled around with each other, even before their wedding day. But, until recently, I hadn't known their circumstances.

Anyway, during the first few years of her first marriage, while her husband was at work, my mother continued to have my father tutor her.

If she and Ben John hadn't encouraged him to remain in high school, he would have quit, because the system, he felt, frustrated intellectual growth and curiosity. Ben John said the problem was that he had surpassed the teachers. My father was more interested in Plato than in Penrod, Ben John told me.

My mother shared my father's interests in books he had loaned her. He performed parts of *Huckleberry Finn* for her, emphasizing the satire, and made her laugh when he read Jim and Huck discussing the French.

She was fascinated by *Madame Bovary*, which he had loaned her in his senior year. "Do you think," she asked, teasing him, "I'm like Emma?" They were sitting at her kitchen table under a crucifix where he could see a statue of the Virgin on a bedroom bureau. When he replied, "I imagine her as beautiful, almost as beautiful as you," she smiled softly, stirred by his desire for her. "Beautiful?" she murmured. "Can such a woman be beautiful, inside?" He pulled a sheet of paper from his pocket, unfolded it, and read: "Like the statue of Venus, her body is graceful, creating an illusion of motion, soft and sensual; her flesh as smooth as ivory, as soft as spring snow falling upon evergreens in the darkness of night; her face, delicate, exquisitely sculptured; and her eyes, dark blue, almost black, like her raven hair." Her dark blue eyes were absorbing him. "I wrote it," he said, "last night." "For me?" she whispered. "I wrote it out of desperation. A statue is not a living being. And spring snow is cold, delaying the warmth of new life." She stared at him. "You're infatuated with me, attracted to an older woman, to the forbidden fruit." But infatuation, she knew, was nothing compared to his anguish, to the knot that bound him to the depths of her being, to their desperate desire, detestable to the spirit, she felt. Yet, from the day they had met, to the day he died, she knew he was devoted to her. She called him "mon ami" and told him, back then, that he was so young, so pure, too pure to want her, to follow her into the woods, where she picked berries and fed him a few, one at a time, yet he seemed so much older, even older than she.

I never would have known of their secret life if she hadn't written a memoir in a notebook nearly a hundred pages long and had locked it in a large jewelry box, which Rosie and I had recently discovered, a few months after my mother had died. She had written it in French. I was astonished by the writing, as though it had been written by someone else, by a different woman, "a deeply passionate, introspective woman," said Rosie. "Her writing is fascinating," she said. "I can't believe she actually wrote this; I just can't believe it!" Some of the passages are detailed, and colorful, in spite of her puritanical upbringing. I wondered why she had written it. "Not for anyone else to read," said Rosie. "She wrote it not only to cope with her conflicts, but to preserve her feelings of certain moments, to possess them for the rest of her life."

My mother had written: "He is so innocent, even in our desperate need, and I will lose him, I know; I will have him, here, on paper, only, to read in loneliness. If the fulfillment of our love is not to be, the agony and the sweetness of our longing I will keep before me, through time and distance. He is a rare jewel, a brilliant star in the distant darkness of blackest, coldest night, whose distant touch penetrates the night and melts my flesh, enkindling a fire in my womb. But shall we yield, losing ourselves in each other, letting the fire consume us, and losing our souls in the eternal fires of damnation? Or must we always deny each other? I pray, to subdue the desires of the flesh, but my prayers go unanswered. God, why are we tempted to the limits of our strength? Am I doomed to everlasting damnation, to struggle in hell in this world and into the next?"

Each night she prayed, but prayers, she wrote, were not enough to ward off the evil spirits of darkness who, taking the form of her beloved to deceive her, descended upon her in her sleep.

"He, with the heart of a lamb, does not know the mystery of evil in the natural state, for he was created without sin. Yes, without sin! Shall I yield to the dictate of my womanhood rather than to the dictate of virtue? To take him is to have him fall with me into adultery."

She wasn't much older than I am now (I'm almost thirty) when she had ended her memoir, writing until giving me birth, "giving," she wrote "scandalmongers an excuse to gloat." There, her memoir ends, nearly fourteen years after she had begun it, ending it abruptly, as though she had finally found a limited peace in a relatively stable, even conventional, life. Until we read her memoir, we hadn't known the years of anguish my mother had endured; we had known only what, for her, had followed, the anguish she had to endure on behalf of my father and Dante.

She never mentioned any names nor made direct references to her husband, except once, maybe, when she wrote: "Monsieur died." That was followed by, "During the wake and the funeral, others were shocked by my impropriety: I had refused to shed any tears." And folded between the pages was a sheet of paper on which a long paragraph was written in English, undated and unsigned.

> *While I was walking along the bank of the river, I suddenly saw old lady LaPan in her chicken coop. I dropped quickly against the slope, into tall weeds between a bush of flowering lilacs and a chokecherry tree. The other kids said she was a witch who would curse us with her evil eyes if we'd let her get close enough. Not that we ever did. The only times we'd ever see her was when she'd sit on her upstairs porch and lean over the railing and rave at us in French. I had never expected to see her outside, especially on this balmy, misty morning with light rain falling. She was dressed in black, like a nun. It couldn't have been anyone else, not in the LaPan coop. As she was pouring feed from a bucket into the trough, a rooster was sneaking up behind her, stretched his neck and flapped his wings, and was about to peck her. She turned quickly and shoved her black, longlaced shoe against him. He squawked "aaawk!" and ran off. I couldn't be sure she was laughing at him, but it sounded that way. She pushed open the gate of the coop, stepped onto the mushy ground of her yet unplanted garden, and instead of hooking the gate, she left it open and moved towards me. I could see her*

clearly on the other side of the garden, but I didn't think she could see me, even as she walked slowly towards the lilac bush. Above her long dress, a black bonnet framed her pumpkin face. She approached the lilac bush and turned slightly away from me, to an opening on the bank, stopped, and looked down into the fast flowing river. She removed her bonnet, letting long silvery hair cascade over her thin body, held it by the brim, and tossed it underhand over the water. A breeze lifted it, and it glided towards the middle of the river, landed softly on a wave, and bobbed up and down as it moved with the flow. Old lady La Pan looked up, over the river, to the mountain, which walled us in from the outside world. And then she sat on the bank, removed her shoes and stockings, stood up, and tossed them into the water. She turned towards me, grabbed a stem of lilacs, snapped it from the bush, held the lilacs to her nose, and walked to the middle of the garden plot. She raised her dress up to bony knees, exposing pale, thin calves, and wiggled her toes in the muddy soil. She began to hum and to stomp her feet, splattering mud, as though she were doing a clog dance. And then, drawing closer to me and gazing in my direction, she stopped. The air grew softer, almost still, and warm rain was trickling down my face. As I felt the roar of the river rushing behind me, she waved the lilacs, their fragrance filling the air, and she spread her arms, like wings, and spun herself around several times. Suddenly she stopped. Pushing the branches of the lilacs aside, she stood between the flowers and the chokecherry tree and looked directly at me. Leaves were covering part of her face, but as her dark blue eyes were gazing into mine, I could see that she was smiling. And in that moment, as

raindrops fell softly into my eyes, I saw a beautiful
woman, and I heard her voice. "Bon jour, garcon."

As I stared at the paragraph, Rosie said, "You know who wrote this, don't you?"

"Who?"

"Your father."

For at least a year, my mother was required, as a widow in mourning, to wear black, from her head to her toes, and to discourage any suitors during that period, but one rainy day, later that spring, while she was planting her garden, "He, my beloved, suddenly appeared on the river bank, his eyes caressing my body, wet from the rain that made my black dress cling to my flesh. As we stood, silently gazing at each other, drops of rain were rolling down my face, running down my neck, falling between my breasts and running down my belly and down my inner thighs as his desire penetrated the inside of me. And my womb was throbbing. Quivers darted up my body, into my breasts, to the tips of my nipples. But, consumed by a sudden fear, and trembling, I turned away quickly from him and closed my eyes. I took a deep breath to dispel my sudden anxiety, yet, longing for the security of his embrace, I waited for him to touch me. Nothing happened. I turned back. He had disappeared."

Later that summer, early one morning, she went deep into the woods, knowing he would be there, because she had told him the day before that she'd be picking strawberries at the ledge near the top of the ridge. After she had arrived there, she waited eagerly, having picked a few handfuls of berries and dropping them into a gallon bucket tied to her waist, but she wasn't interested in picking berries. Determined to overcome her anxieties and to submit to their desires, she had arranged a rendezvous with him at the ledge. She would persuade him to take her to the other side of the mountain, to a cabin he had built for himself. And she was determined that they would spend the day together in the cabin.

Under her long, black dress, the thinnest she had, she was wearing nothing.

Finally, he appeared, but immediately he told her to hurry back down the mountain because a rainstorm was coming. She looked up, seeing dark clouds over them, but, smiling, she pushed the bucket to her hip, drew close to him, put her hands on his sides, saying, "I came here to be with you, mon ami, unless you have another woman in your cabin," and nudged the front of his body with hers. He responded, embracing her. "Have you suddenly gone crazy?" he asked affectionately. And she said, "Not suddenly, no!" A few, barely perceptible drops of moisture touched their flesh, and he told her to hurry, to follow him to the cabin. And as they were scampering up the mountain, near the top, a strong wind above them began to blow, bringing sprinkles. When he reached the top of the ridge, he stopped and looked back at her. "It's coming!" He clasped her hand and pulled her to the top, and he held her by the waist, holding her to his side. Facing the wind, they saw sheets of rain moving across a narrow valley and approaching them rapidly. "Are you too tired to run anymore?" Breathing heavily, she smiled and shook her head. And as they were running down the slope, heavy rain began pouring on them.

When they came to the bottom of the hill, to a stream running rapidly in the downpour, he stopped again and waited for her. He was drenched. But he was smiling at her, the rain splattering his face. She leaned against him, and, together, they began to laugh. Suddenly, as he touched the front of her, lightly, the warmth of his hand on her breast sent a current through her body, into her womb. "And, at that very moment, I would have lain with him, with my beloved, upon the wet earth, in the torrential rain." But he continued moving, and she followed him, running beside the stream, and after a while, he stopped again, turned to her and pointed to a small log shelter partially hidden by the leaves of trees beating rapidly in the wind and rain. He grasped her hand and pulled her, and, dashing over the wet ground, they approached a door. Quickly, he pushed it open, pulled her inside, and slammed the door behind them. And, breathing heavily, they leaned together against it. Hearing the wind blowing and the rain splattering against the cabin, they laughed. He put his hands on her head and rubbed it, trying to push the water from her hair, and then he cupped her face and kissed her on the mouth. "Although his shirt was wet from the rain, the heat of his body penetrated my flesh, stirring the deepest part of me, and I felt the determination of my desire penetrating his own flesh, my desire feeding his desire and arousing him. And I felt the hardness of his body pushing into me, as though trying to penetrate me, now, with our clothes still on. And again, my womb was throbbing." But he withdrew his mouth from hers, abruptly, and he pulled her to the front of a huge stone fireplace and sat her on an orange crate as he prepared to build a fire.

The cabin was dim with two small windows. A small bed, neatly made, its head against the middle of the back wall opposite the fireplace, occupied a large portion of the room, small and cozy. In almost no time, her beloved had built a blazing fire. She had removed the bucket from her waist and had placed the berries, soaked in rainwater, on the floor, and she had taken off her shoes. After he had lit the fire, her beloved removed his shirt and his shoes and socks, and standing close to the fire, water dripping from his trousers, he told her to stand beside him, closer to the fireplace. Standing next to him, the dress sticking to her flesh, she felt naked. His eyes, she noted, were glancing at her breasts, her nipples, and his desire was boldly obvious.

She said, "I'm freezing," and made herself shiver.

"Take off your dress."

Putting her hands to the top of the dress, she said, "My hands are cold. Would you unbutton my dress for me?"

As he began to unbutton it, she said softly, "I'm not wearing anything under my dress."

Without saying anything, gazing at her breasts and emitting soft sighs, he unbuttoned her dress, separating it slowly as his eyes absorbed her flesh. After undoing each button, he would look into her eyes.

"My determination, enhancing his, my own desire feeding his, the fire in him burned within me, within the deepest, most tender part of me, making it hard and intense, throbbing with unrestrained passion, with anticipation I had never felt before."

He suddenly knelt before her, kissing her belly. His warm hands, on her hips, pulling her against him, moved slowly up her flesh and touched her breasts, squeezing them. She clasped the back of his head, holding his face to her belly, and she began pushing herself against him, making no effort to subdue the sounds of her deep breathing.

His hands, on her shoulders, were pushing the top of her dress away from her, and, quickly, her dress dropped to the floor. He stood up, pushed his trousers and shorts down, and "as we stood together, completely naked, in front of the roaring flames, I looked upon him with a craving so deep within me, seeing the magnitude of his own desire, the splendor of his manhood, directed at me, that every part of me cried out to feel every part of my beloved, to feel him, now, and as we caressed, I waited no longer.

"Dripping down my thighs, now, were not the drops of rain, but warm juices from inside of me, deep inside of me. And without shame, I touched him, fondling his manhood. And pulling it against me, I urged him to enter, to come inside of me.

"'Now! Take me! Now!'

"He lifted me off my feet and carried me quickly to the bed, and he lay me upon his bed, and, finally, I felt him entering me, my beloved, entering me, not as in a dream this time, but in reality, coming into me, my beloved, for the very first time, coming into me, deeply, and filling me with himself."

I was flabbergasted; I could hardly breathe.

"Wow!" Rosie said. "I've never thought of your mother as, well, as so damn passionate!"

"Well," I grumbled, "talk about purple prose!"

"Oh, Tonio! She recorded this for herself!"

In his script, Dante portrayed her as conventional, which, as our mother, she certainly was, especially when Dante married Rosie. "I think I understand her better now," Rosie said, "especially her fears. If your father had been alive when Dante and I were married, he would have made the situation easier for all of us."

There's a similarity, a connection, between the circumstances of his death and of Dante's "accident."

Every spring, the river north of the mill, becomes jammed with huge chunks of ice between the logs, and log rollers, with hooks at the end of poles, walk out on the logs and clear them. That's what my father was doing when someone from a car on the highway apparently took a shot at him with a shotgun. The log that he was standing on was struck, and splinters flew up, and my father, losing his balance, fell into the river while the car sped away.

A logger pulled him out by hooking his jacket, but he had been crushed between logs and died minutes later.

The logger, who spoke only French, tried to tell the police investigator about the shot, but the policeman assumed, apparently, that a car had backfired, coincidentally, at the time of the incident.

5

My father had graduated from high school at seventeen during the first world war. "The Great War," people had called it back then, the war that would end all wars. He joined the army, went to France, saw enough combat to wish it upon no one, turned eighteen shortly after the war had ended, returned home, briefly, and returned to Europe, to Italy, to his native village in the mountains of Abruzzo, which he and his family had left eight years earlier, and then went to college in Rome, staying with his mother's parents who had descended from Hebrews (*Ebrei*, in Italian) and lived near the River Tiber, within walking distance of the Vatican.

My Italian grandfather, whom I call Tattone for "grandfather" in his native dialect, is Dante Valentino, for whom my brother Dante was named. (I was named after my mother's grandfather, Antoine, the runaway slave.) The elder Dante had entered the priesthood, although, as he later discovered, God had not called him into it, and he had been granted a special dispensation, and subsequently he had married my grandmother Rosa, my Nonna, for whom Rosie was named.

My father's genealogy hasn't set well with my other grandmother, my grandmere, whom I call Meme, who is a devout Catholic. Well, Catholic, anyway. Tattone calls her a Jansenist, which, he says, is closely related to the Calvinists.

He has often said that there were two Catholic religions: that of inquiring minds constantly striving for deeper understanding, and

45

that of closed minds in which everything was either black or white, the popular, but superficial, religion, which was still being taught, at least here in America, by our parish priests and nuns, and which, like anything else that was so popular, was so difficult to replace by official teachings, because, in the popular versions, especially in Jansenism, which had spread from France to Ireland to America following the Protestant Reformation, everything was concrete, literal, such as actual flesh burning in actual fire in a physical place called Hell, not ever symbolic, not figurative, not analogous, not metaphorical, not even metaphysical or mystical or spiritual, but made religion so much easier to understand, especially for those who were supposed to teach it, who, like most teachers in our public schools, seldom encouraged questions, but simply expected obedience as from sheep following shepherds, underestimating people as rational beings, and presenting a view so narrow, so restrictive, so smothering, and so alien to the Italian spirit, he would say, that no true Italian, being so damn stubborn, could accept, but, he would add sometimes, smiling, at least it gave those Catholics something to rebel against when they would use their intelligence and try to satisfy their desire to know.

When I was in the eighth grade, he had been confronted by my teacher once, who was quite strict and commanded obedience to her, but being such a gentle old man, he had responded in a manner that had not offended her, not directly, anyway. Maybe, like the rest of us, especially us guys, he respected her as soon as he saw her. She was young and attractive, especially for a nun, I thought. Even I liked her, sometimes.

I was supposed to meet him right after school to visit a sick old man on the hill, near the school. Tattone was waiting for me outside to make sure I would go with him, but after the other kids had left and I hadn't shown up, he went into the school to look for me. As he entered my classroom, the nun immediately told him in French that she was keeping me after school because I had said something vulgarly to another kid, and I told him in Italian that she was unjust to me, because, although I had told the kid in Italian to go hang himself by his balls, neither the kid nor the nun had understood what I had said, and therefore she had no right to detain me. In French, he told me I was rude to be speaking in Italian in front of the nun; speak either in English or in French so that she could understand. That encouraged her, I think, especially since she had seen him and my grandmother attend church, to ask him if he had truly been a priest. He said he still was, and that she must have known that he would be a priest for the rest of his life. Yes, she said she knew, but she had thought that he might have been excommunicated. No, he was Catholic, still. He had met with the Pope who had granted him a special dispensation. And then she asked if his wife was Catholic, too. No, she was Hebrew. Consternation crossed her face. She would pray for his wife, she said, but, surely, he knew that in the eyes of God, she was not really his wife. She was, he assured her. They had been married in the Church, he said, by another priest in Rome. The way she was looking at him, I thought she was going to say she'd pray for all Italian priests. She didn't, but she asked him why Italians were not good Catholics. After a brief silence my grandfather replied, "Surely, some of them are. Many saints are Italian, such as Francis of Assisi, and Thomas Aquinas, and the old Pope who had granted me a dispensation was a very devout Catholic." She had meant the Italian immigrants. "Why don't they attend church more often?" They did, where there were Italian churches. "But why don't they go here?" Because this church wasn't Italian. But it was the same Mass; they could still celebrate the Mass, here, in Latin. Still, the Italians felt out of place, here, in this church. Why should they? Most Italians, he told her, did not share her belief that nature, having been created by God, was inherently evil; on the contrary, all creation, especially of human nature, including sex (sex especially, I thought), was good, very good, but the doctrine of depravity made them feel they were in a church different from the one they knew in Italy. Unlike the nun, we Italians did not believe that celebrating life to the fullest was somehow evil. Occasionally, he admitted, an Italian, such as Savonorola, troubled by excessive desires of the flesh, had been attracted to depravity, but a healthy, compassionate person should pity him. But surely, she said, looking at him in disbelief, he knew that we had been born in the state of original sin; as a priest, he had to be aware, especially as a priest, that through the nature of our flesh, we were strongly attracted to evil!

"Sister," he said with profound sympathy, "I prefer to think that you, such a strong and attractive young woman, who has chosen this vocation, are strongly attracted to God, but, if like Savonorola, you are troubled by excessive desires through the nature of your flesh and are attracted to evil, you should seek the help of a compassionate priest, at least."

Her mouth opened, but no words came out. I thought she was going to ask him to help her, but my presence, I guess, prevented her. Or maybe she knew he was not attracted to evil.

Our interpretation of original sin, he told her, was different than hers: to us, it didn't mean we were naturally attracted to evil; it simply meant, as it meant to the Hebrews, that we hadn't developed our potentials, the *amore*, the *imago dei* in each of us, our divinity, and, as such, not having perfected ourselves, in exercising our free wills, we were prone to making mistakes, to sin, which means, in Hebrew, to miss the mark, which was not quite the same as saying we were inclined, through our nature, to evil, but, if those mistakes were harmful, they were not good, they were sinful, and the first, or original, sin was depicted in the story of Adam and Eve, who, in choosing to eat the forbidden fruit and not knowing the consequences of their action, though they were tempted by the serpent, by their curiosity to know, they had the alternative not to eat the fruit, but, thinking it might be good, they ate from the tree of life, and then they knew good and evil and were expelled from Paradise, in the same way that a person who, in committing, as he is bound to do, sin for the first time, must be held responsible, because he is the agent of his actions even though he acted in ignorance, for evil is bred by ignorance, but God has also endowed us with intelligence, expecting us to use it, to think, to know; that's what made us truly human, that, and our ability to love.

She said that too much thinking could drive a person crazy, that some things were not worth thinking about, and that we were better off not knowing the other things. "Besides," she said, "we can always rely on the authority of others who were created to do our thinking for us."

I thought she made a lot of sense.

Tattone told her that in order to understand their differences, she should read the French priest, Calvin, then she should read the Italian priest, Aquinas.

Like many of the other countries in Europe, France, he told her, had become a Protestant country, almost, three hundred years ago, especially when the Huguenots rebelled against annexation by the Duke of Savoy, and had they succeeded, she would have been a Protestant now, probably, but with her same beliefs, so she shouldn't feel harshly toward the Protestants, because Calvin, and the German priest, Luther, and all the other Catholic priests who had led the Protestant movement, had tried to reform the Church from within, but the political leaders of their respective countries had seized that opportune moment to separate themselves from the political influences of Rome, because the Church was dominated by us Italians who thus had power over the leaders of those other countries, even though our own country had been fragmented and ruled by those same political leaders of those other countries. So, he said, the Protestant movement was as political as it was religious, embracing nationalism. But don't blame the Protestants. Blame us Italians. After all, we Italians, as she well knew, he said, were an awfully stubborn bunch of thickheads to deal with. On that note, leaving her more bewildered than enlightened, we left.

Later, one evening, I told Meme, who was rocking in her chair in her living room, about the confrontation. The nun, surely, had put him in his place. No, I said; I thought it was the other way around. She said he had the devil behind him, whispering in his ear. After all, what could a corrupt priest know about religion? I didn't know, but Tattone seemed to know more than the nun did. So did the devil!

Then she asked me what my own thoughts were on the subject of religion. I knew she wanted to know if Tattone had been an influence on me, a bad influence, and I never even wanted to think that of him. I loved them all, my whole family, so much, that to see the harshness of Meme towards my paternal relatives was very painful to me. She was separating her own self, I felt, from part of me, which was also, therefore, part of herself, of which she seemed unaware, having built a barrier that excluded them and prevented her from knowing and enjoying them as I had, and I felt badly, not so much for myself, but for her.

I told her that part of me knew that part of nature was good, and that part of me saw part of nature as so mixed up that it could never be good, not completely. And although I didn't know what the hell I was talking about, she exclaimed, "*Tres bien*, Antoine!"

And she said she knew what I meant, that I was so wise for someone my age, and that she was so proud and happy that I was her grandson. She knew, of course, that there was good in nature, for even some Italians, such as Francis of Assisi, were good, and that the best things in nature, colorful birds, baby animals, flowers, fruits, and trees displayed the glory of God and were put on this earth for the enjoyment of mankind, but she also knew there was, in the deepest part of nature, in the darkest hearts of men, unquestionably, a terribly evil force. Just look at the cruelty of white Americans! They were possessed, obviously, she said, by the devil. Such cruelty could never be explained otherwise. How else could anyone, especially the English, some of whom even attend church and call themselves Christian, profess that slavery is the will of God?

Like the nun, I thought, she made a lot of sense. And although I wanted to pat myself on the back for the wisdom she thought I had, I really knew I couldn't take all the credit for it. I had acquired much of my wisdom from serious comic books, gangster and cowboy movies, and dramatic radio programs, especially one on Sunday afternoons. Listening very intently to a deep voice coming from the radio, I could feel it penetrating me: "Who knows what evil lurks in the hearts of men? The Shadow knows! Ha, ha, ha."

That thought was so damn scary, no wonder Italians didn't want to believe it.

But the notion that evil lurked in the hearts of men was all around us, so I knew that there had to be something to it. Could so many people, like my Meme and the nun, be so wrong?

I stood up, approached Meme who began rocking harder in her chair, embraced her, and bid her good evening. Just as I was leaving, she invited me to supper the next day. I couldn't immediately think of any excuses to refuse, so, reluctantly, I accepted.

When I was a kid, I hated to eat supper at her house, because afterwards she'd make me kneel with her and say the rosary, all of it, and if I'd try to sneak out, she'd get mad at me and call me a Protestant.

She went through moods when she wouldn't allow any smoking or drinking in her house, which she, a dainty woman, ruled like a queen, looking very dignified with her silvery hair, covered by a shawl, sometimes, draping her dark face. And my grandpere, Pepe, would sneak to Tattone's house and help him drink his wine, and Pepe would return to his own house, feeling pretty good, singing French and Italian songs, and Meme would yell at him, until he'd finally wave his hands at her and tell her to be quiet. She wouldn't speak to him for days and would come to our house and complain to my mother how terrible the old man was, carousing with that corrupt Italian priest married to a Jew.

Meme thought that Jews had horns growing out of their heads and had hoofs for feet. She really believed that. No kidding. Hell, that's not something to joke about. She used to tell me I had Jew's feet, almost. My toes are webbed. To me, they seemed natural. Skin between two toes. No big deal. And sometimes, pretending to pat me on the head, I knew she was feeling for signs of any horns. And when I tried to tell her that Nonna didn't have horns or hoofed feet, she thought, "What does the kid know, anyway?" She told me that my Nonna had always kept her hair wound like a huge turban, and covered her feet with pointed shoes so I couldn't see her horns and hoofs. My Nonna would refuse to show them to me, even if I'd beg her, Meme said.

And I said, "I bet she would!"

Meme embarrassed the hell out of me once when she forced me to make a junkman show her his feet. Before the war, when we were paid for our junk, every Saturday morning a junkman would come walking beside an old mare pulling a wagon down the road of the flats. Kids would say, "Here comes the Jew," but to them, "Jew" was simply another word for "junkman." They assumed that people were either Catholic or Protestant, that my Italian grandmother, not Protestant, had to be Catholic. It was only logical, they thought. Whenever I tried to enlighten them, they thought I was bullshitting them, just because I kidded them about other things. When I told them Jesus was a Jew, they said he was a carpenter. When I told them Protestants are Christians, too, that originally they were protesting Catholics, the kids knew better and thought I was only trying to confuse them.

Anyway, during the week, we looked for rags and stuffed them into potato sacks, and we gathered scrap metal for Saturday mornings. Usually I made a quarter, which was pretty good, considering that cowboy pictures at the Saturday matinee in the Berlin Theater cost ten cents. One morning, another junkman, whom none of us had seen before, showed up, a little earlier than usual, not with a horse and wagon, but with a pickup truck. He was short and bow-legged and wore a shabby derby. While he was weighing sacks, I suddenly had a brilliant idea that would make me a lot more money.

I took my sack of rags behind Meme's house, to the potato bin in her garage, put some of the rags into three other sacks, dropped chunks of wood into the middle of the rags, tied the tops of the sacks, and dragged them to the front of the house, and waited for the junkman to weigh them.

Finally, he picked up one of my sacks, seemed a little surprised by the weight, but placed the neck of the sack on a hook of a scale and watched the damn pointer leap up to almost twice the usual weight. He did the same with my other three sacks. After he weighed the few scraps of metal I had, he reached into his deep pocket, withdrew a role of dollars, peeled one off, placed it in my waiting palm, and added three quarters.

I shoved the money into my pocket, turned, and ran off, laughing like hell.

When the other kids asked me how come the rags weighed so much, I told them about the wood. Now, I had enough sense to know that sooner or later the junkman would discover the wood, and that he'd at least be suspicious of any more sacks weighing too much, but apparently the other kids were thinking only of the opportunity to make more money, because the following Saturday morning they gathered at the side of the road and had ten times as many sacks as usual. When I tried to tell them how crazy they were, they wouldn't listen. When the pickup truck pulled up, I went into Meme's house to watch from a window, because I thought if the junkman would recognize me, he'd think I had instigated a conspiracy against him.

He lifted the first sack, dropped it, took out a jackknife, and slit the middle of the bag open. Sure enough, he pulled out a chunk of wood. "You kids ain't pullin the wool ova my eyes again. If you want ya money, take the damn wood out, right naow." And the kids opened their sacks and began to remove the wood.

Meme noticed me looking out the window. She, too, looked out.

"Antoine," she said, "tell him I want to see him."

"Why, Meme?"

"Never mind. You tell him."

I hated to have the junkman see me, but I sighed, went to the front door, opened it, and yelled at him, "Hey, junkman, my granmudda wanna see you!"

He looked at me.

"In de ouse," I said.

He approached the house, walked slowly up the few steps, onto the porch, and stopped.

"Come inzide."

Meme, trying to act dignified in her long black dress, sat in her rocking chair on the other side of the living room. She put on her spectacles, smiled, and looked very intelligent.

The junkman, slowly, reluctantly, his eyes darting around, stepped inside.

My grandmother spoke in French. I translated.

"Take off ya at," I said, pointing to his shabby derby.

He removed it.

Meme stared at his head, which was as bald as an eggshell.

Frowning, she said, "Tell him to remove his boots."

"Does she wanna sell some junk?" he drawled.

"She says, take off de boots."

"Huh?" He looked at Meme. "I didn't mean to track up ya floah, mam," he said, raising his voice as though she were hard of hearing and could understand English if it were loud enough, and then he went down on one knee, placed the derby on the floor, unlaced one of his leather boots, and removed it. His white wool sock had a hole at the end of his big toe, and when he saw Meme staring at it, he seemed embarrassed. He removed the other boot and then stood up.

"Tell him to remove his stockings."

"Take off de socks."

"The socks?"

"Yeah."

"But my socksa clean."

He turned to Meme and raised his voice again. "My socksa clean, mam. Put em on jes this monnin." He lifted his right foot, the one with the hole in the sock, and showed it to Meme. "See?"

She leaned down and peered at his foot, and then she looked up at me and said, "How does he expect me to see through his stocking?"

"She says, take off ya socks."

He shrugged, but then he bent down and removed his socks.

Meme, gawking at his feet, exclaimed, "Where are his hoofs?"

I didn't dare ask him.

While he was standing there, barefooted, and wondering, perhaps, what I was saying, I told Meme the Berlin Jews spoke a language I couldn't understand. My father, who knew the Hebrew service, called it Yiddish, which even he didn't understand. Meme thought all Jews could understand each other, but I reminded her that although Catholics follow the Mass in Latin, not all Catholics speak the same language. She respected my intelligence, she said. I told her that the other junkman, who couldn't speak English, spoke Yiddish, and that I couldn't understand him.

"But you seem to understand this one."

I turned to him.

"Do you speak Yiddish?"

"Huh?"

"Yiddish. Do you know Yiddish?"

"What's *that*?"

"Do you know what schmuck is?"

"Huh?"

Hell, I wouldn't have said it if I had thought he knew.

I told Meme he couldn't understand Yiddish.

"So? Neither does your father, you said. That doesn't make this junkman any less of a Jew. Does it?"

"But if he's a Jew, I would have noticed him in the synagogue. They all greet me there. The other junkman, the one with the long hair and beard, even greets me when he comes here to collect my junk."

I turned to the junkman again.

"Shalom."

No response.

"Shalom aleichem!"

"Sorry," he said, "I don't parlay French."

"He doesn't even know the Hebrew greeting. He's not a Jew."

"What is he?"

"Do you speak udda languages?"

"Jes English."

"Do you go to church?"

"Huh? Well, sometimes," he drawled. "Yep," he said and turned to Meme and spoke in a loud voice again. "I'm a Christian, mam, an honest Christian."

"He's English," I said to Meme, "Protestant."

Her dark face grew so livid, I thought she was going to throw up.

"What's he doing in my house! Tell him to leave! At once!"

"You gotta go now."

He didn't understand.

"But what about the junk she wants to sell?"

"She ain got nuttin. She wanna see your feet, dat's all."

"My feet?"

"Yeah, ya feet."

He stared at me, looked down at his feet, and then turned to Meme again.

"You people are crazy!"

Quickly, he picked up his derby, socks, and boots, and scrambled out of the house, muttering, "Crazy," as he rushed barefooted across the porch and down the steps, toward the kids who were staring at his feet. "Crazy. Crazy damn fools! All of you!" He went directly to his truck, climbed into the cab, and sped away, leaving the kids standing there with their junk.

Meme was disappointed. She would go to her grave, she said, without ever seeing the horns and hoofs of a Jew.

I told my father what had happened. I even promised to pay the money back to the junkman.

A few days later, my mother, with the help of Pepe and the local priest, who's French, brought Meme and Nonna together in our house, and Nonna showed her feet, which aren't even webbed, to Meme, and then Nonna unwound her long white hair and let it flow down her body, and invited Meme to feel her head for the horns. Meme seemed embarrassed. She seldom admits to making mistakes, but she admitted it then and almost cried. Hell, no one is perfect, not all the time. Nonna embraced her. And then we each had a glass of wine. Nonna raised her glass, saying "*Paix!*" And, clicking our glasses together, the priest said, "Shalom!" Nonna responded, "Shalom ale-ichman!" At that moment, I knew a barrier had been removed, and I felt a lump in my throat. After a few minutes, anyone would have thought that my grandmothers had always been friendly, especially when Meme insisted on pouring Nonna another glass of wine. To this day, they are still friendly.

Anyway, the following Saturday, the Jewish junkman returned to the flats. After he paid the other kids for their junk, I gave him mine. He grabbed my arm. "Valentino!" He said something in Yiddish and pointed to my sneakers, and then he pointed to the hoofs of the mare and laughed. None of us kids had even seen him smile before, much less laugh. After he weighed my junk, he offered me a dollar bill. Back then, during the depression, that was a lot of money for a kid to get for junk. My heart was splitting because I had to refuse it. I waved my hands, saying that was too much. He shoved the money into my pocket and said, "Shalom," and said something that indicated, I thought, that he owed me something for getting rid of the other junkman. And then he pointed to the back of the mare and invited me to ride it, but I was afraid. I didn't belong up there. I knew I'd fall off, making a fool out of myself, but Dante was willing to ride it. The junkman hoisted him onto the mare, and my little brother sat up straight, as though he had always belonged there, and as we kids followed, the mare carried him to the end of the flats and back again, to the gate of the mill, a distance of not much more than half a mile, all told, but the event seemed spectacular. And, when he left, the junkman said, "Shalom aleichem," and waved at us. From that day, until the war came, the Jew with his old mare was our one and only junkman.

And then the pickup truck, painted red, white, and blue, returned, not to the flats, but to the school on the hill, where we were expected to bring our junk and to give it out of patriotic duty, not for money.

The war, as I've stated, brought a lot of changes.

Most of the mill closed. One section began manufacturing (believe it or not) gas masks for the military. The younger mill workers were called into the service, and many of the older ones went to Portland to work in the shipyard. Gone for the duration. Some would never return. People were issued ration stamps to buy most of the essentials, such as meat, coffee, sugar, and gasoline. And on cars, the top halves of headlights were painted black to dim the lights just in case enemy planes flew over, which I don't think any of them ever had. The whistle in the mill would blow several times to indicate air raid alerts (only drills), and older men from Gorham, with white helmets, would stroll proudly up and down the sidewalk and order us inside. And at night, during air raids, called blackouts, all lights had to be off. Unlike the "police action" that would follow in Korea, everyone took part in the war back then. And we kids became too sophisticated for cowboy pictures and went to see real war movies for adults. According to the movies, gorgeous women fell head over heels in love with guys in uniforms; and the war was a splendid adventure, a morality play, with lots of laughs. At Christmas, with even Santa wearing a helmet, beebee guns became popular gifts for kids to practice shooting, killing birds and other small animals, but I was too old at thirteen for kid games, and too young for adulterate pleasures. I'd have to wait four more years for the official opportunity to have excited women falling all over me. My father gave me war novels, such as *All Quiet on the Western Front* and *Johnny Got His Gun*, which took the fun and glory out of war, and I had to go to more war movies to remind myself that the greatness of man was woven with the glories of war, that to the victor went the spoils to honor his greatness, and to the vanquished, disgrace. In the spring of my senior year, the master race was facing disgrace, and the impudent mites of the rising sun were getting squashed under the might of our invincible greatness. And then, my father's two youngest brothers, Moses and Joseph, were both killed in the war.

After it ended, my Nonna was informed that some of her relatives, among millions of other people, had been put into concentration camps by the Nazis and had been tortured and killed.

People said it could never happen here, not in the Berlin area.

6

When I was a junior in high school, and Shackle became my biology teacher, my father, who had become a member of the school board, directed my attention to a two volume geography text, which had been used in public schools during the last century. It's called *Morse's Universal Geography*, by a doctor of divinity, Jedidiah Morse, the Calvinist "Minister of the Congregational Church in Charlestown," (Massachusetts) and the father of Samuel, the inventor. The title page also indicates that the text contains "Sixty-three Maps; by Arrowsmith and Lewis." (I immediately thought of Sinclair Lewis, author of *Arrowsmith,* and of *Elmer Gantry*, the evangelist who wanted "to keep all foreigners, Jews, Catholics, and negroes in their place, which was no place at all, and let the country be led by native Protestants, like Elmer Gantry.")

In his section on Europe, Jedidiah Morse wrote that the French were "vain and incapable of moderation, jealous, irritable, unmeaning in their professions, loose in their principles, and inclined to intrigue." The Spanish were even worse; they were "short and thin; complexion is olive; credulous, superstitious, and bigoted, revengeful. One of the most striking national manners and customs is the common practice of adultery." And the Portuguese were "in stature, inferior to the Spaniards; complexion is swarthy."

In Canada, "The French are extremely ignorant and superstitious and blindly devoted to their priests. Many are sunk far below the aborigines; but in the consequence of the emigration from England

and the United States, an increasing spirit of industry, and the establishments of schools and Christian Churches, morals are improving."

And in Louisiana, "The majority of the population are Roman Catholics," but, "A change for the better is confidently expected."

I enjoyed studying geography of the past century, especially from the Jedidian view, as my father called it, meaning, I suppose, the ability to capture, in a few words, the essence of a people and to know everything about them simply by identifying their labels.

My father thought that the Jedidian view, to some extent, was still being taught; and at a school board meeting, he raised the question: "Should public school teachers impose their views, including their labels, on others, even on Americans from different backgrounds, or should teachers try to stimulate the minds of all students and challenge them to think and to form their own views and values to make society better than it is?"

My father had been influenced by Plato and thought that education was a process of emerging from ignorance, but thought that our present educational system sometimes led from one cave into another.

Some of the board members agreed with him; others argued that our educational system should continue to enforce conformity to their views. An associate of Shackle said, "Foreigners should learn how to be American and not try to tell us how to run our own country."

An American, my father was told, conformed to the views and values of the original Americans. "In Rome, do as the Romans do, if that's where you want to be, but here, in America, do as we Americans do. Nobody asked foreigners to come here; they should be damn grateful we let them in and thankful they're not still living in their own countries."

Shackle, I'm sure, knew he had adversaries on the school board, but I have to admit that he gave me excellent grades, because he knew I was an avid learner, especially in his version of biology.

In the first lesson of the year, he approached biology by stating: "You must believe either in evolution, which makes you an atheist, or in the creation. If you want to believe your grandparents were swinging by their tails from trees, seeing the way some of you act and talk, I can believe it." He paused, looked at the regular kids on one side of the room, then looked at us kids from Cascade whom he had assigned to the other side, sneered, and then looked back to the other kids who were snickering. "Personally, I believe in the creation of Adam and Eve, because my own ancestry has been traced all the way back to them."

According to Shackle, intelligent beings had come into existence six thousand years ago, as evidenced by the findings of art on cave walls that had appeared suddenly at that time, and by the skeletons of early homo sapiens who were tall and fair and more intelligent than most people today. Unfortunately, some of the superior people had mixed with others, diluting the purity and intelligence of some of the higher species. Breeding with inferior beings was in opposition to the divine will, to the progress of the superior race, and was, as Shackle put it, the original sin. He called it miscegenation, which was the taking of the forbidden fruit, the only fruit that was forbidden to early man who had been created in Paradise, over which he had been given dominion, but through his disobedience, the taking of the forbidden fruit, the spilling of his seeds into lower species, he saw his nakedness, the animal he had created in himself, and he became ashamed, knowing evil, and, expelled from Paradise, he wandered over the face of the earth for several centuries, settling, each according to his own kind, into the various nations of this day, but many of the inferior races, like animals, were wandering, still, and are known today as nomads and immigrants.

Inspired by this knowledge, I devised a test in my junior year to compare the knowledge of students who were studying biology to those who hadn't. I told them to list the top five nationalities in order of their superiority, and then to list the bottom five and to state the reasons for their selections.

I tried to test Dante, who was a year behind me in school, but he wouldn't take the test and said I was crazy. As he watched others take it, he wanted to know how I had developed such a brainstorm. When I showed him the passages from Jedidiah, Dante said, "Damn!" He seldom used vulgar language, but he resorted to it then.

"To think that school kids were actually fed this acrimonious crap!" I told him he wasn't taking the Jedidian view in the right spirit, that he had to learn how to distinguish between the attitude of superior people and the bigotry of others, that if he would only let his eyes be opened, he would see what others see and expect from us. "By using this simple test, you can learn their rules. Don't use it among the French, though; they'll cheat. They'll try to peak at the answer sheet. And they'll flunk the test, anyway, and argue like hell." Dante said I sounded scary sometimes, and that people would take me seriously. "I'm serious! Do you know why God saved Robinson Crusoe from the shipwreck and let the Portuguese crew perish?"

Oddly enough, I discovered that the students who hadn't yet studied biology had the same knowledge of people as the biology students had. And, what really surprised me was that the kids in both groups had only listed European nationalities, even in the bottom five. They hadn't even, the kids told me, thought of the rest of the population, as though, I thought, the rest weren't really human enough to even be considered. So, Shackle wasn't teaching something that regular kids hadn't already known. I guess he was trying to educate us kids from the flats.

So, by the time I was in my senior year, I was pretty well educated.

And in my senior year, after Minnie Birch had arrived from Boston and had become my English teacher, we felt something special between us. But in his script, Dante wrote about it as an absurd situation, not as a serious attempt by a mature and intelligent young man in love with a mature and sophisticated woman to find meaning in this absurd world.

Jedidiah wrote that "New Englanders are generally tall, stout, and well built." "Tall" and "stout" doesn't describe Minnie, but "well built" does. And New England women "generally have fair, fresh and healthy countenances, mingled with much female softness and delicacy. Those who have had the advantages of a good education, and they are numerous, are genteel, easy, and agreeable in their manners, and are sprightly and sensible in conversation." That's a perfect summarization of Minnie Birch.

In the classroom, she always wore prim and proper garments, a long skirt and a jacket, usually, read daily from the Bible, flowed gracefully between her desk and mine, and pressed a red eraser tip of a pencil, sometimes, to her voluptuous lips while gazing at me with her soft green eyes. Her light brown hair was rolled up and pinned back, showing her graceful neck, but in the privacy of her small house way out in the woods, she let her hair down, letting it fall like honey over her shapely body, as smooth as alabaster. She awakened my desires for the best things in life, taking me under her wings and lifting me out of myself. And I put my trust in her, holding back nothing, confessing, even, to the black strains of my ancestry. Minnie was more than sympathetic; she was fascinated, she said, and assured me that I had the ability to become a regular person. And she admitted, rather proudly, that her own ancestry wasn't exclusively pure white. "One of my own ancestors was actually an American Indian, a beautiful young princess, my grandmother once told me." So, by adhering to proper standards, I, too, could reach her level, achieving regularity with her, sharing her judgment of others and discriminating between superior and inferior traits of various ethnic groups. Who knew more about being American than Minnie Birch? She could accept Negroes and Jews, she said, since they weren't a problem in this neck of the woods. "But Catholics have no place in our free society."

She told me that I was a pilgrim, in progress, emerging from the flats, from "the valley of the shadow of death" as she put it; and I felt myself rising up to her. Was it just a coincidence that, the summer before, the cousin of my father, a doctor of divinity, had come to the flats to free me? Was it just a coincidence that after he had said to me, "A good education will give you the freedom and opportunity to rise up in this country," that Minnie Birch entered my life? "Freedom," she said to me, "is the way of life we have inherited from my ancestors, the first settlers in America." (She didn't mean the Indians.) And she made me aware that, in being identified with the flats, there would be less freedom and opportunity for me. I didn't want to be left out. Like my cousin, I thought, I could change my labels. Minnie impressed upon me how important it was to write down the proper nationality, race, and religion on all application forms. Nationality,

I thought, was my biggest obstacle, but Minnie said I could simply write down American. Thanks to Ben John labeling me white on my birth certificate, race was no obstacle. And under religion, I could simply write down Christian. Minnie asked me what my denomination was. "Transcendentalism, I think. I admire Emerson and Walt Whitman." (I didn't mention Thoreau because the name is French.) She was impressed, until a few years later when Shackle told her my father was a Jew; but that was after I had left Yale and had returned to the flats to work in the restaurant after my father had been killed.

Jedidiah wrote that New Englanders were strict in their observance of religious laws. "The supposed severity with which these laws are composed and executed, together with some other traits in their religious character, have acquired for New Englanders the name of a superstitious, bigoted people. But all persons are called superstitious by those who are less conscientious, and less disposed to regard religion with reverence, than themselves." Jedidiah called "their venerable ancestors, the first settlers of New England." And: "Strangers are received and entertained among them with a great deal of artless sincerity, and friendly, plain hospitality." (Yeah, and "Good fences make good neighbors." Right, Robert Frost? Yeah, right. When our most celebrated and misstated New Hampshire poet laureate wrote that line, is that what he really meant?

Our state symbol, The Old Man of the Mountains, is a natural carving, an imposing profile of a rugged face jutting out from a massive rock formation near the top of a mountain. It's the inspiration for our state motto: "Live free, or die."

Minnie Birch was the woman I had planned to marry, to live free, or die with. I wasn't going to be stuck with a woman of the flats, not I.

I knew she wasn't perfect, that she wasn't always a good judge of people. As much as I loved and respected her, I had difficulty, as her student, persuading her to let me demonstrate my affection, because she said she was practically engaged to a soldier who was fighting for our country. Her love for him had been rooted in patriotism, just like in the movies. And I knew I didn't stand a chance against him. But after Germany had surrendered, someone wrote her a sad letter, informing her that he had failed to tell her, in the heat of preparing for war, of his wife back home, way out in California, Minnie told me. She was upset, but I was there, in her house in the woods, to alleviate some of her pain. That moment, I thought, marked the beginning of a deep and abiding love. Minnie called it "sweet, but it should never have happened, not with a student of mine." I said I didn't mind, not a bit. And I didn't. I was truly in love with her.

Dante thought I was infatuated with her.

"You're infatuated with all attractive women," he said.

His portrayal of me in this script isn't very flattering, characterizing me, his own brother, who had always protected him as kids, as another Elmer Gantry; but I'm not, believe me, anything like that supercilious hypocrite who thought of himself as so damn superior. I'm much more intelligent and humble. Minnie even told me so. Anyway, *Elmer Gantry*, she said, is trash. She also said that Sinclair Lewis, like Mark Twain, is downright atheistic and vulgar, poking fun at good Christians.

Although swarthy skin, according to regular people, is an indication of intellectual and moral inferiority, I'm an exception, Minnie told me; and I knew, even before I had met her, that women saw dark men as sexy, as in "tall, dark, and handsome," so I didn't mind being dark. "You have beautiful dark skin," Minnie told me. And she told me I was handsome. "Two out of three ain't so bad," I told myself. She admired my dimple in my masculine chin, which made me look older and wiser than I actually was. Sometimes, as I'd admire myself in a mirror, I'd practice smiling infectiously (which helped me later as an insurance man). My hair is black and curly, and my eyes are dark brown. And sexy. Minnie told me that my eyes looked deep inside of her, stirring her with my animal magnetism. Not that I went around bragging about it; after all, it was merely an accident of nature, something with which I was endowed. Minnie said that the animal in me excited her. Obviously, we were made for each other.

By the time I had graduated from high school, I had learned that women got aroused by the animal they sensed in certain men, and that genteel women, overwhelmed by inner turmoil, trembled in anticipation of what such men might do to them. I had noticed that in the movies. When such a woman was suddenly seized by such a man, the audience would stop chomping on their popcorn and would stare at the screen, knowing damn well that the woman would struggle at first, while irresistible passion in her surged. That's why, I thought, guys flocked to the beaches to become dark. They, too, wanted to be sexy.

But I ended up short of becoming sexually superior in stature by an inch. Six feet was the minimum height of the sexually ideal male, so I had to learn to live with borderline inferiority and to make the most of my other assets. As a basketball player in high school, I was expected to get the ball to the center, who grabbed most of the glory because he scored more than I did. That was, I thought, an indication of things to come. Minnie told me I'd continue to grow, but I didn't; and then she refused to marry me. She said I was too young. Too young, hell. The dream man was tall, dark, and handsome. Not old. Besides, I've never been more than seven years younger than she. A man, I informed her, reached his sexual peak at nineteen; a woman, at thirty. In an ideal situation, I told her, she was actually too young for me.

When my brother had stopped growing (if you could have called it that) he was half a foot shorter than I, and slim. He has brown curly hair. And his eyes are dark blue. Life used to glow from those eyes. The nuns used to see Jesus emanating from them, because his eyes seemed so intense with compassion. But, was Jesus short, like him? Not in any of the movies I ever saw. The nuns, apparently, weren't aware of all of the inherent deficiencies of little people. I mean, how many little guys become successful insurance men, or politicians? Or sexy movie stars? In the beer joint, the drunks used to speak of him, in spite of his smallness, as intellectually superior, because his eyes seemed so alert, but the drunks weren't always aware that inferior genes have always been dominant over superior genes, in the same way that the animal in us has always been stronger than the intellect. In high school, some of the girls used to call him cute, because his eyes seemed so soft. Regular guys, especially the basketball players, were flabbergasted. "What in hell do they see in that little shit?" they asked me, because they thought I knew a lot about girls. I hated to admit ignorance. I said, "It's the animal in him. He appeals to them the same way puppies do. To a little guy like him, they want to give. But from regular guys like us, they want to take." Not only did the players believe it, they even convinced me that I had, somehow, uttered a profound truth.

"If a girl has to choose between a regular guy and a puppy," I told them, "she'll take the guy anytime. Just look at Snow White. Even though she had a tender spot for little guys, when the charming prince showed up, she went for the real thing. It brought her back to life. That's why girls want to be cheerleaders. We basketball players excite them." My bits of wisdom gave the guys more confidence in themselves and made us a better team, I thought. "Girls have the same urges we do, but our rules won't let them admit it, because we want to keep them in suspense, covering sex up in mystery. And we really want them to resist us, not give in too easily, or seem too eager, not at first; we want them to make the chase exciting, and that's what they really want, too, because when they finally give in, it really means something, and they put everything into it. That's what makes us superior to other people. When sex is nothing more than a natural function, it's not as exciting. That's why it's the forbidden fruit."

"Catholics," one of the players said enviously, "know a lot more about sex than we do."

The others agreed with him.

"How the hell do you figure that?" I asked them.

"Catholics," they said, "are horny."

The summer before my senior year in high school, after the invasion at Normandy, a year before the world war would end, Nick and his folks moved out of Louisiana, having lived there more than two years, and moved to New York City, to Harlem. That first week in August, when they visited Cascade, they invited me to go back with them, and to stay with them for three weeks. I was terribly excited to be in the biggest city of the world my first time ever, with a population of almost nine million, and during the first few days, Nick took me to all the famous sites. I was impressed by the Statue of Liberty. She reminded me of her symbolic meaning even though her torch was out for the duration of the war, until "the lights go on again all over the world." And I was impressed by the Empire State Building, the tallest building in the world, as I stood on its roof near its very top and looked out over the city. And I was impressed by the span of the George Washington Bridge as Nick and I walked along the sides of it, all the way to the other end and back. I was particularly impressed by signs right on the bridge that read: "In case of air raid drive off bridge." As I leaned against the rail and looked way down at the water below, I said, "Holy shit, that's a sure way of getting killed!"

And on that first Sunday, Nick took me to a church in East Harlem, because Ben John had told us a fascinating history of the church. More than fifty years ago, it had been built by Italian immigrants. When they had arrived in this country, they had not been welcomed, not even by the Irish, who were mostly Catholic. If the

Italian immigrants wanted to participate in their religious services, they had been restricted to the basements of American Catholic churches. Excluded from American Catholicism, groups of Italians sometimes celebrated feasts in residences of paisans where an Italian priest would conduct a Mass. One group, residing in East Harlem, decided to build a church for themselves, and so, after long working hours on their own jobs, they devoted their time and labor and skills, and their money, to constructing a building that they called La Chiesa della Madonna de Monte Carmelo. One of the laborers, who had migrated from Calabria, had been a great uncle to Nick. Despite the fact that they had built their own church, which is now recognized as the first Italian church in America, they had been restricted, still, to the basement, until just a little more than twenty years ago when an Italian priest finally was made the pastor. Attending Mass in Our Lady of Mount Carmel Church, where the priest gave his sermon in Italian, was really inspiring to both Nick and me. Nick said, "This feels almost like being in Italy. Come to think of it, the Italians were the original builders not only of this building, but of the Catholic Church!"

After Mass, he told me he wanted to study for the priesthood. The previous year, in Louisiana, he had applied to several seminaries but was discouraged after he had been rejected by all of them, even though his school grades had been excellent. He couldn't understand it; all through school, priests and nuns had encouraged him to enter the priesthood. A month before he had moved here, he had met a Negro priest who had studied and had been ordained in Rome, because, the priest had told him, not many American seminaries admitted Negroes; there was as much prejudice even among Catholics in this country, the priest had said, as there was in the rest of the population, although Catholics would deny that. As soon as the war would end, Nick said, he would go to Rome; he would fulfill his dream of ending segregation by, as he put it, "bringing all people together through divine love and finding, ultimately, the happiness for which we were created." Having met the Negro priest was a sign, he thought, of his destiny. Such talk embarrassed me and made me feel sorry for him. I couldn't imagine going through life being celibate, but he felt he had a calling. It wasn't too late to save him, I thought, or at least give him half a chance. And I told him that ever since I had arrived here in New York, five days ago, I was hoping to get friendly with some of those damn good looking chicks we were seeing all over the city. He grinned at me. Anyway, we were having a great time being together again, especially in such a famous city that we had heard so damn much about.

While we were in East Harlem, we did something that some people, though, might think was a little crazy; we were talking to each other in Italian to see how the people there would react, and, to be perfectly honest, to avoid any confrontations, letting them know that we, too, were Italian, although the people spoke in different dialects. Some of them were flabbergasted and were gaping at us, especially at Nick, and asked us politely if we were Italian. Nick, pretending that his English wasn't fluent, would answer, "Si, we come a here mo den tray year ago to see," and he'd turn to me. "*Come si dice fratelli?*" I'd say, "Bruddas." And he'd say, "Bruddas, ma de war, she come, an we no can go buck to Italia." They were very friendly and interested in us, and we had a hell of a lot of fun, even though we didn't meet any good looking girls.

But a few days later, in a diner in Harlem early one evening in the middle of the week, while we were having coffee and hamburgers, two attractive girls, one of them, extraordinarily attractive, like a movie star, came in and sat in a booth across the aisle from us. They were wearing bright red dresses with plunging necklines that showed off their voluptuous bosoms. Colorful beads, which they were fingering almost constantly, hung down their dark flesh, drawing my attention to their breasts. I kept exchanging glances with the girl facing me, the really good looking one. Nick and I had planned to go to the movies later. "Do you want," I asked him in Italian, rather loudly, "these girls to go to the movies with us?" And he answered in Italian, "No, I don't think so. They look like they want to go dancing in an expensive place. Anyway, they're much older than we." And I said, "But they don't know that; we seem older than our years." We were sixteen; we could pass for twenty. Nick said, "I don't know. Maybe they want us to buy them drinks someplace." And I said, "They're looking at us; I think they're interested. Let's speak to them, but not in good English." Nick, smiling, said, "I understand."

Our conversation was making them stare at us, and the one directly across from me, facing Nick, suddenly asked, "You're not speaking Spanish, are you?"

"Io?" Nick said, pointing to himself and acting surprised that she had noticed him.

"Yeah, you and your friend."

"You spikka despanish?"

"No, not me, but I know what it sounds like."

"No, no, we no spikka despanish; we, italiani; we spikka de taliano."

"Eyetalian?"

"Si, eyetalian."

"Honey, you sure don't look eyetalian."

"Wad eyetalian looka lak?"

"Not like us colored folks!"

"I no unnerstun."

"Where are you from?"

"Italia," he said emphatically, as though she should have known.

"Italia?"

"Si, Italia. Italy. Me an heem," he said, pointing to me, "come a here mo den tray year ago, ma de war, she come, an we no can go buck."

They were staring in disbelief but were obviously interested.

"I never knew colored folks came from Italy."

"Colored folks?"

"Yeah, you know; dark like us."

"Ah, si, many colored folks in Italia."

She turned to her companion, the really nice looking one.

"Did you know that?"

"No, I thought we all came from Africa."

"Africa," Nick said, "si, Africa, near Italia. Many africani, many year in Italia, mo den two tousand year."

"I'll be damned!" the girl directly across from me said, then she suddenly stood up, asked if they could sit with us, and before

71

we could answer, she slid onto my seat and pushed herself against me, forcing me to move over. The other one, whom I could hardly restrain myself from ogling, stood up, reluctantly, I thought, and as Nick moved over, making a space for her, she sat next to him. She was looking at the other girl, and, feeling my eyes on her, she looked at me, modestly, and smiled a little.

Their dresses were tight. I was wondering why they were dressed so provocatively, but, I thought, this wasn't New Hampshire; this was the sophisticated and liberal Big City, where people got all dressed up to enjoy the night life. And I was enjoying it, too, feasting my eyes on the extraordinarily attractive girl facing me and wishing she had sat next to me.

The girl next to me asked one question after another, and Nick did the answering, but I was wondering what the hell he was talking about. I guess we were supposed to be wealthy aristocrats who had come to New York for a vacation but were stuck here now for the duration, and we were afraid of getting caught by the authorities, and that's why we were in Harlem, hiding among people who looked more like us. He didn't tell them any of that directly, only through implication. I thought he sounded too vague and evasive, but they seemed to understand and were fascinated.

Finally, I said, "We payga some a ting fo you mangiare?"

The girl beside me clasped my thigh, pushed her warm leg against mine, and said, "Honey, we'll munjaray all night long if you pay."

She began rubbing the inside of my thigh, and I pushed her hand away. It was a reflex. She grinned at me. Nick, unaware of what was happening to me, asked them, "You wanna eat some a ting?"

"We'll have a coffee and a hamburger," the one beside me said, then she lit a cigarette.

"Wad you call?" I asked.

She blew smoke into the air, her dark brown eyes squinting into mine, and said, "Whatever you like, honey. What about you?"

"Tonio. He Nick."

The waitress stopped at our table.

Nick held up two fingers, and said, "Due caffe, due humbugga."

"Humbugga?"

The girls snickered.

"Two coffees," the girl next to me said, and two hamburgers."

While we were waiting for their order, I asked, "Wad you lak tonight? Maybe," I said, swaying my shoulders, "go dunce?"

"Look, honeybunch, we can dance at our place."

Again, she reached down and thrust her hand between my thighs, and my body almost jerked out of the seat.

"If you got the money, honey, we got the time."

"Mannaggia," Nick said, "sono puttane!"

Damn, they're whores!

I said, "Everting, togetter, hava maybe five dollar."

"Five dollars!"

She withdrew her hand.

I looked at Nick.

"Andiamo," he said.

But I wanted to stay, thinking I could charm them.

I put my hand on the girl's knee, but she pushed it away immediately and said, "Sorry, hon."

"You," I said, forming a ring with my left hand below the surface of the table and then inserting the index finger of my other hand into the ring and pushing it in and out, "do lak a dis, fo money?"

"Don't get any funny ideas."

"No unnerstun, me."

Silence began to engulf us.

The girl facing me finally spoke: "What do you guys do?"

"Nutting," I said, gazing at her and trying not to show my disappointment in her.

"I mean, to make money."

"Nutting."

"But how do you live?"

"Ah," I said, shrugging my shoulders, "non gude. No make a de mucha money. Washa de deeshes, some a time, ma no mucha de money. Washa de floor. Tings lak a dat. No eat much. Non much pipple we know. Nick an me, we, how you say, we wait. Maybe de war, she finita, an we go bucka home."

"You mean, you're broke? And you can't even get back home?"
I could see sympathy in her eyes.

"You no lak Nick an me? Maybe you no lak italiani."

"I like you a lot! You're interesting, and you seem like very nice guys. Better than most Americans."

"Ah, tank a you, tank a you too much. Nick an me, we lak too much to, how you say, be amici, amici, talk widda you, to," I stammered, "to spik, to, to talk togedder, an maybe, maybe to, togedder, see movie, an tings lak a dat, togedder."

"You mean, be friends?"

"Ah, si, friends! Amici."

"Amici," she said, smiling.

"Si, amici."

"Why not? I'd like that."

"Ah, gude, gude! Today ees, ah, how you say, importante. Today Nick an Tonio make amici. Tutti amici," I said, making a circle in the air with my hand.

"I like that," she said with a broad smile. "Tutti amici."

"Ah, gude, gude! Wad we calla you? You name."

"I'm Jessie, and she's Madeline. Mad, for short."

"Ah, Jessie, bella."

"Jessica."

"Ah, Jessica. I lak too much. An," I said to the girl next to me, "Madeline, I lak. Tonight, we guda friends. No?"

"But tonight we have to work," Madeline said, and she took a puff from her cigarette.

"No," I pleaded, "non tonight; tonight importante. We talk, do tings, togedder."

"Not tonight," Madeline insisted. "We can't afford it. Besides, if we don't work, our boss will kill us."

"She means our pimp."

"Pimp?"

"Jessie, for godsake!"

"Well, that's what he is. Tonio, do you know what a pimp is?"

"De boss?"

"Yeah, the boss."

"De boss, he keel a you?"

Jessie smiled.

"No. She means he'll get mad at us."

"Ah, datsa no gude."

She looked at Madeline and said, "We could use a night off."

"We're working tonight."

"Ah," I said dejectedly, "too bud. Tonight importante, fo me. Tonight I am born." I sighed heavily. "Ma non tonight," I said, waving my hands a lot to communicate; "much year ago, tonight, in Italia, I am born."

"Buon compleanno," said Nick, smiling a little.

"Grazie. Ah, Nick, he forget, I tink, tonight I am born."

"No, no, I no forget. Tonight, I payga everting, de caffe, de humbugga, everting, an now we go to de movie. Andiamo."

"Aspetta."

"You mean," Jessie said, "this is your birthday?"

"Ah, birtay! Si, me birtay."

"Well, happy birthday, Tonio!"

"Happy birthday," said Madeline.

"How do you say it in eyetalian?" asked Jessie.

"Buon compleanno."

"Buon compleanno, Tonio."

I could see deep warmth in her dark eyes.

"Ah, datsa nize. Grazie. Tank a you. You spikka taliano now. I tich a you."

"I did, didn't I?" she said proudly.

"Ma, hoppy me, ma non too hoppy. Me guda friends, here, now, right a here, ma tonight I no see dem. Joosta Nick an me. Why?"

"It's his birthday," Jessie pleaded with Madeline.

"Don't go crazy on me, girl."

"Go crazy? Whoza go crazy?"

"Oh, don't pay any attention to her, Tonio. How old are you?"

I sure as hell didn't want to tell her I was only sixteen, so I said, "Old? No old, me."

"No, I mean, your age. What's your age?"

"No unnerstun, me."

75

"Me," she said, pointing to herself, "almost eighteen, eighteen years, and Mad, here, is nineteen, nineteen years. You understand years?"

"Si," I said, nodding, thinking that they were much younger than they looked.

Then she repeated her age, showing me her fingers to indicate the numbers.

"Si, si, capito."

"And you?" she asked.

"Wad you tink?"

"Twenty," she said without any hesitation, showing me the numbers on her fingers.

"Certo! Gude! Twenty," I said, extending my fingers, "tonight. An you, when ees, as you say, de hoppy birtay?"

"My birthday?" She smiled. "As a matter of fact, my birthday is just four days," she said, showing me four fingers, "from now, this Sunday. I'll be eighteen. And we don't work Sundays. Maybe," she said, looking at me deeply, "we could celebrate our birthdays together." She looked at Madeline. "I think we should."

But Madeline seemed reluctant to become involved with us aliens, especially since we were illegal and this was wartime.

She said, "I already have plans for Sunday," and she stubbed her cigarette into the ashtray.

Nick said, "Me, too."

Jessie looked at me with her warm eyes.

"Well, Tonio, do you want us to get together this Sunday? Just you and me?"

"I lak! Too much, I lak. Ma I no hava de money."

"You don't need any money."

"Wadda we do?"

"Whatever you want. I'm treating."

The waitress brought their coffees and hamburgers and asked if we wanted anything else. Jessie said she'd pay for everything and that we could order whatever we wanted, so Nick and I each ordered another coffee and hamburger. Then she wrote down her name and address and telephone number and gave me the slip of paper.

Madeline asked, "You're not giving him the address of the club, are you?"

"No, my apartment."

"What's gotten into you, girl?" She turned to me. "She's never done that before, not for anyone else, as far as I know, excepting her mom and me."

"I no unnerstun."

"Giving you her address and inviting you there. She's trusting you!"

"I know I can trust you, Tonio. You'll be there Sunday, won't you?"

"I be dere. Certo!"

She usually slept until noontime, so she was hoping I'd be there between two and two thirty, and we could spend the rest of the day together, and the whole night, she said.

"De night? Alla de night?"

"I'll be free."

"Free? I know id no costa me nutting, lak you say. But alla de night?"

She smiled.

"Free means I don't have to work, free to do what I want."

I looked at Nick.

"I unnerstun," he said.

But how in hell would he explain my absence to his folks?

"Is it okay?" Jessie asked.

"Si," said Nick, "ees okay."

"Good. It's settled then. I'll see you Sunday, Tonio."

I thought about her on the streets, and suddenly I was concerned about her safety, and somehow I was able, in the fractured speech that was making me feel phony now, to express my concerns. But she said she never worked the streets. They worked in an exclusive club for men where they were protected by bouncers, and where the drinks were very expensive. They put on a floorshow and sang and danced, and they mingled with the customers to induce them to buy more drinks. And the girls usually drank ginger ale but pretended they were drinking hard liquor for which the customers paid.

Madeline was reluctant to talk about their work, so Jessie said softly, "I'll tell you all about it later." And smiling, she said, "I'm glad you're worried about me."

After we left them, dusk was settling, and on the way to the movies, I asked Nick what he thought. He wasn't sure. Our little joke, he thought, had gotten out of control. "I really think she's attracted to you, and I know you're attracted to her. Hell, that's easy to see why. But what do we know about her? We know what she does for a living. That doesn't mean she's not a good person. Hell, this isn't Cascade. Compared to here, Cascade is a paradise. The poverty here is so damn miserable, it's hopeless, and her lifestyle only makes conditions worse, but she probably sees it as her only escape." He shook his head. "You don't know what you're getting into. But I know you're intrigued by the situation."

"Yeah, I am."

"So what can I say? You shouldn't get involved with her, but knowing you, you're going to play with fire."

"Well," I muttered, "I'm curious."

"And attracted to her. And you're going to get burnt. A plunge into hell. And like a damn fool, like you, I share your curiosity, but from a safe distance."

"What are you going to tell your folks, about Sunday night?"

"You've made some new friends here, and they invited you to stay overnight."

"I hope they don't get mad at me."

"Why should they?"

"Because they feel responsible for me."

"In a few more months, we'll be old enough to fight in the war. Shouldn't we be responsible for ourselves?"

"Well, I'll give you Jessie's address and phone number, just in case your folks get worried."

Nick looked at the address. His mouth opened in astonishment. She was living in his neighborhood.

"Well, at least you won't have far to go," he said.

That Sunday afternoon, on August twentieth, at quarter of two, it took me less than five minutes to walk from his place, down the street, climb three flights of her apartment building, and walk down a narrow hallway to her apartment. I tapped on the door, waited a few seconds, and the door opened.

She greeted me with a big smile.

8

"Hi, Tonio. Come in. My mom's on the phone. Be with you in a minute. You're early. I wasn't expecting you so soon."

"I come too early?"

"That's okay. I'm glad you're here. Look around if you want."

She went to the other end of the room, near =a window, and picked up a phone that was on a small table in a corner. Except for her bright eyes, she seemed like a different person. She wasn't wearing a tight, sexy dress. And she seemed younger, somehow, and fresher. Dark curly hair draped her shoulders and flowed onto a blue dress with patches of various colored flowers. It was an ordinary summer dress that hung to her calves, but she made it look pretty. Like most casually dressed girls, she wasn't wearing any stockings because they were scarce during the war. And she wasn't wearing beads or any other jewelry, not even a ring or a wristwatch. She wasn't using any cosmetics, not even lipstick.

"It's Tonio, Mama; he's here already, so I have to hang up soon."

We were in a living room with a couch on my left and a soft chair on my right and a radio and a record player and a bookcase stacked mostly with phonograph records. It was a small living room, but it was cozy.

"Yes, Mama, I told you. He's from Italy, and he's colored. But you can't tell anyone about him, Mama, because if he gets caught here, they'll lock him up."

On the other side of a doorway on my left, I could see a kitchen table against another window. I stepped into the doorway and peaked inside. It was a narrow kitchen, but neat and adequately equipped. A pot of coffee was percolating on the stove.

"No, he's never been in the club. You're embarrassing me, Mama!"

On the other side of the living room, a doorway led to another room, very small, which was her bedroom. And a door to my left, between the bedroom and the living room, led to a toilette, which had a bathtub with a shower curtain and a shower.

As I stepped into the living room again, she said, "Goodbye, Mama. I love you." And she placed the phone on its cradle. "Mothers," she sighed, then she stared at me. "You, you don't even know if," and she began to stammer, "if your, your own mother," she said, "or anyone else, in your, your family, if they," her voice dropped to a whisper, "well, if, you know." Drawing close to me, her bottom lip began to quiver. "Tonio," she said, her voice so low, I barely heard her, and she leaned against me, pushing her body against mine, and embraced me. "I'm sorry, hon, really sorry."

I was speechless. Suddenly I became aware of how much I had deceived her, and I felt rotten.

She was a whore, that's true, but she wasn't just a whore. That label was beginning to fade, and she was Jessica, a human being with feelings the same as mine, maybe even deeper, and warmer, and more compassionate, I felt.

"I give you some a ting," I said, reaching into my pocket, "fo you birtay. Non much, ma some a ting."

It was a bracelet with "Jessica" inscribed on it.

"Tonio! You shouldn't!"

"You no lak."

"I love it! Oh, it's beautiful! But you shouldn't be splurging your money on me."

"Splurging?"

She could see it was pretty cheap.

"Buying me gifts you can't afford."

She slipped it onto her left wrist, stared at it momentarily, then looked up at me, and smiled, her bright eyes becoming moist. Her eyes were expressive, dark and beautiful, and filled with so much emotion, with such tenderness, that I felt them pulling me inside of her.

"I'm deeply touched," she said, very softly.

She was gazing into me, and I could feel love inside of her, deep inside of her, filling me with a warmth I had never felt before.

"Do you mind," she whispered, "if I kiss you?"

And I enjoyed her sensual mouth against mine and the heat of her body penetrating me. I didn't kiss her passionately, I didn't think, not my best or wettest, the way I kissed when I tried to make out, yet it felt more deeply stimulating, somehow.

She withdrew her mouth slowly from mine and said tenderly, "That was nice. I've never been kissed like that before."

I stared at her.

"It's true. It's the best kiss I've ever had."

"Me, too."

"Our birthday gifts to each other," she said, hugging me again.

And I felt the warmth of her entire being penetrating mine.

She held my hands and said, "The coffee is ready. Do you want something to eat now?"

"No, you eat."

"All I want, now, is a cup of coffee. I've bought beer for you, and wine. What would you like?"

"Joosta caffe, fo now."

She pulled me into the kitchen, next to the table, and told me to sit. She went to a cupboard, pulled out two saucers and two cups, placed them on the table, went to the stove, turned off the flames, brought the coffee pot to the table, and poured the coffee. Her kitchen, she said proudly, was fairly modern, nothing like the kitchen in the tenement flat in which she had lived just a month ago. And she even had a refrigerator now, not an ice box, she said. And she opened the refrigerator door and wanted me to look inside, so I stood up, approached her, and looked inside. "Nize," I said, not knowing what else to say. Smiling, she pulled out a quart of milk.

As I sat at the table again, she asked me if I wanted cream in my coffee. I nodded. She pulled the cover of the milk bottle off, then poured cream into my coffee. She placed the cover on the bottle again, shook the bottle, removed the cover again, and poured milk into her cup. Then she sat next to me, our legs almost touching under the table. She put a spoonful of sugar into her coffee and stirred it. As I was putting sugar into mine, she said, "I'm happy, really happy, because you're here. As soon as you walked in, the whole apartment brightened up." I looked at her quizzically. "It did! It really did," she said, grinning. "I hope you don't mind that I told my mom about you. I told her that you're an interesting person, that there's something about you that I like, very much."

We became silent as she seemed to study me. Not that I was uncomfortable. Actually, just being there with her, in her own little apartment, just the two of us sipping hot coffee together, made me feel great. And I could feel my ego swelling tremendously, because, for some reason, she was being so damn nice to me. But I wished the hell I had never deceived her, and I knew I couldn't tell her the truth, not now. She'd think I had intentionally made a fool out of her, and that would have been more cruel than the deception itself.

As I looked at her, I was wondering what she was expecting from me. Could she be lonely? But how could a girl like her, who looked so damn nice, be lonely? No, she couldn't be lonely, not a girl like her. And she certainly wouldn't want a guy like me for sex, not just for sex, not in her situation, not when she could choose from so many others who, I'm sure, would gladly spend a lot of money just to be seen with her. So, why was she being so damn nice to me? Was she feeling sorry for me, for some poor lonely schmuck who was stuck in a strange place?

"What would you like to do?" she asked, suddenly pushing her leg against mine. She leaned towards me a little, her dark eyes looking into mine, intently. "Anything special?"

I have to admit that on the way here, I was thinking of getting laid; not just getting laid, but getting laid by this beautiful girl, but now I wasn't feeling so horny; I guess I felt that I was exploiting her by deceiving her.

"You're so beautiful," I murmured, so fascinated by her eyes, by the depth of her warmth, that I momentarily forgot my accent. Almost immediately, I became frightened that I had exposed myself, but she blushed, lowered her eyes, and took a sip of coffee. Fortunately, my voice had been very soft and so low that she hadn't detected any difference in my speech, not immediately, anyway, and I resumed talking. "Mo beautiful den befoe, de udder night. Oh, you beautiful den, too much beautiful, an now, mo beautiful, mo, how you say, I dunno, me, ma, mo beautiful, an I lak, now, be widda you too much. I lak, lak a dis, sit, an talk widda you."

"I mean, later," she said, smiling. "Is there anything you want to do?"

"Wad you wand?"

"Whatever you want. We can stay here, if you like, or go out; and tonight, we can eat in a nice restaurant, then go to a movie, or we can stay right here."

"Wad mo guda fo you?"

"I'm treating. Remember?"

"Si, ma tonight, you gotta eat some a ting. No?"

"Si, and you gotta eat some a ting, yes," she said, grinning. "And I'm an excellent cook. I'd like to show you just how good I am."

"Datsa nize! Stay here, I lak, joosta you an me."

"I'm glad. I was hoping you'd say that, because I'm planning a special birthday party for just the two of us tonight, a candlelight dinner with red wine and soft music from the victrola. You probably noticed my collection of records. I even have some eyetalian music, too. And for dinner, I was thinking either of steak, real beefsteak, thick and juicy, not horsemeat, or fried chicken, because I make a special batter for fried chicken, or, you can have both, if you want, with fried potatoes, or mashed, if you prefer, with thick gravy, and sweet peas; and for dessert, well, I'm not going to tell you. It's a surprise."

She touched my knee and pressed her leg against mine again.

"You some a ting, you; you special gal."

She was smiling at me and, with her warm hand stroking my knee, arousing me.

Why in hell did nature create the sexual desire in guys to be so damn obvious when, at times like this, I wanted to hide it? It was as though that greedy little tyrant had a mind of its own, betraying me at the worst times. I had no control over it, even though something else in me, maybe my conscience, made me feel that screwing her wasn't right, somehow, because I was deceiving her.

"Do you mind if I have a cigarette?"

That surprised me, and I said, "Sorry, me, I no hava cigarette."

Since the supply to civilians back then was limited, I didn't smoke much.

She laughed, then said, "I have plenty of cigarettes. I was wondering if my smoking would bother you. It bothers my mom. I can't smoke when she's around."

"I smoke, some a time, when I hava dem. Id okay widda me."

"You do? Well, we can share mine."

She stood up, went to a cupboard, opened it, pulled out two packs of cigarettes, a lighter, and a clean ashtray. She opened one pack, placed it between us on the table, and pushed the other pack towards me.

"Smoke mine for now, and keep the other pack for yourself for later."

Now she thought I was too damn poor even to buy myself cigarettes, and the deception was only getting deeper. Besides, I hated it when someone was always bumming cigarettes from you because he was too damn cheap to smoke his own unless he was forced to. I felt too damn proud to bum cigarettes from her, but she must have sensed that, because she put two cigarettes in her mouth, lit both of them, handed me one, and said, "I want to share whatever I have with you, Tonio. It makes me feel good. Really."

We became silent again for a few moments.

Then, with the cigarette in her left hand, she leaned against me and slid her right arm over my thigh, and, with her hand grasping my knee again and holding it against hers, said, "I want to know all about you. Tell me about Italy and your family."

I inhaled deeply, and after I blew the smoke out, I said, reluctantly, "In Italia ees me parenti," but not wanting to perpetuate the lie any more than I had to, I said, "an to tink a dem, id breaka me heart." And I shook my head.

"I'm sorry," she answered, barely above a whisper. "Let's talk about something else."

"Talk aboud you. I lak, some a time, go to de club, me, an see you dunce an sing. I betcha you gude."

She pulled her arm away.

"No, Tonio," she said rather harshly, "I couldn't take it, seeing you there."

"I no unnerstun."

"The club isn't any place for a guy like you. If I ever saw you there, I think I'd die."

"I no go, den; nevva."

"I want us to be amici, to be together, but I don't want you to have anything to do with that other part of me, not ever."

I was perplexed.

"Befoe I come a here, I know aboud dat udder parta you. I come joosta de same. Why you tink I come a here?"

"Why, Tonio? Why did you come here?"

"To see you, talk wid you, be guda friend."

"Because you're lonely; you're homesick."

"Notta now, widda you. De guda friend, ees take de bud wid de gude. If he no take a de bud, he no friend."

She puffed on her cigarette and was studying me, but could she see my confusion and conflicts? I had come here not only wanting sex with her, but expecting it, and now the tyrant in me, feeling the guilt, finally, running all the way down there, had retreated into its hiding place, wherever that was.

I took a sip of coffee, puffed on the cigarette, and asked, "Why you invite me here? To talk, no? Maybe, you talk, an I unnerstun, a leettle."

Hell, everybody, I thought, wanted understanding. Well, maybe not everybody, all the time. But I felt she did. She knew I already knew about the part of her that she didn't want me to have anything to do with. So why had she invited me here? Obviously, she wanted me to accept her in spite of what I already knew. Acceptance, that's what she wanted. Suddenly I thought: she wanted love; she wanted to be loved. Hell, that's what I really wanted, too, in spite of what I already knew about her.

"Why did I invite you here?" she asked, as though she were asking herself. "That's what Mad asked me. Why do you think I invited you here, Tonio?"

"I tella you befoe; to talk, be friends."

"Why should we be friends?"

"Why? Cause I lak a you, an you lak a me, I tink. Why we lak, I dunno. We lak. Datsall I know, me."

"That's exactly what I told Mad!"

"Wad you tell her?"

"I told her I invited you here because I like you, that I have a good feeling about you.

She asked me why, and I said I didn't know; I just did."

"I tink I know wad we wand, you an me. In Italia, itsa call amore. Itsa mean," I said, groping for the right words.

"Amore," she said softly. "I know what that means, Tonio."

"Ma itsa no mean," I said, actually getting a little angry thinking about it and raising my voice, "some a ting, how you say, some a ting lak, lak, focka dis ting an focka dat ting. No. In italiano, amore ees a nize; itsa no mean focka everting an everbody."

She was staring at me but didn't reply.

"Guys payga de money to focka de gals. Dats amore?"

I had gotten carried away, forgetting she was a whore, or trying to repress the fact, perhaps, and using it suddenly to hurt her, and I slapped myself on the forehead.

"Sorry, me, sorry. I spikka too much. Bigga mout, me!"

"I know what you mean."

"Ah, si, you know, bigga mout, me, too much."

"No, I meant I know what you mean about, well, about what amore doesn't mean."

"Amore, itsa come from de heart," I said gently, pointing at my chest, "from inzide, too much inzide."

"We call it love."

"Love. Si. Datsa why I come here, why you invite me. No?"

She drew a puff from her cigarette while I waited for her answer.

"Si," she finally said, very softly.

"Ma love, amore, itsa no mean," I said, shaking my head a little and leaning towards her, "you wanna me focka you. No?"

"No, it's completely different." Then, tilting her head suddenly, she stammered, "Well, but that, that depends, Tonio, on, on, well, on how you mean it." She flicked ashes into the tray. "I mean, well, love, to me, means, well, it means, it means, making love."

"Ma, making love itsa no mean fock."

"Well," she said, her voice dropping, "that depends."

She drew a deep puff.

And I felt the little tyrant stir, sticking its head out of its hiding place, but I quickly suppressed it.

"An fock, in de club, itsa mean love?"

"No!" she cried, shaking her head. "That has nothing to do with love!" She sighed. "Mad said I shouldn't have said anything about the club. I wish, now, I hadn't. I know I told you I'd tell you about it. I don't know what I was thinking. But I know I didn't want to deceive you." She puffed on the cigarette, blew smoke out, and squished the cigarette into the ashtray. "I guess I thought, at the time, we could just get together casually to celebrate our birthdays, but that's not how I really feel, not then, either."

"Wadsa mean, casually?"

I, too, put my cigarette out.

"That's not important now. I have to tell you about the club, because I know what you must already think."

"Me? I dunno, me, wad I tink."

"Whatever you think, can't be any good; it's probably even worse than the reality, so I might as well tell you." She sighed again, heavily, as though she were trying to find, deep within her, the courage to tell me. "I told you about mingling with the customers, getting them to spend their money. That's what we do. Dine and dance with them. Then we take them upstairs, to bed. We pick the customers we want, the ones who will pay us the most. They're called patrons. Sometimes they ask for certain girls, but we can refuse. That gives them more incentive to pay us more, to get the girls they want. I guess you can say we go to the highest bidders. We don't use our real names. I'm called Ruby. Nobody in the club, not even the boss, knows my real name or address, except Mad, and I don't know anything about the private lives of any of the others who work in the club, not even the boss, especially not the boss, not his name; he's only called Boss. It's as though, well, as though in the club, we're not really people, just mannequins, just, well, like dummies behind store windows, not human beings, not people who have real lives, because nobody in the club knows anything else about us. There are certain rules the patrons have to abide by. They have to behave like gentlemen. Most of them have been going there a long time, mostly big business and professional men, and they abide by the rules. I don't do any kissing, and I don't touch any of their private parts. They know that. All I'm required to do," she said, pausing, "is, well, lay back, on the bed, and, and let them, well, let them do it to me. Nothing else. Do you understand what I'm saying?"

I thought she was trying to tell me that what she did wasn't quite as degrading as what other whores did, but she was speaking of herself as just another whore, a commodity in a commercial establishment, spreading her legs and laying herself open to heartless whoremongers and letting the damn slobs abuse her, reducing her to a brainless and soulless slab of meat, a piece of ass. Just a piece of ass!

"You letta guys focka you, fo de money."

Turning away, she lowered her head.

She was in pain, as though I had stabbed her.

"You lak wad you do?"

"Of course not!" she snapped. "You think I like being a, a whore? It's contemptible!"

"Den why you do dat?"

"Why! Why does anyone need to survive? I didn't want to talk about it; I didn't want to spoil our birthdays!"

Tears began running down her face.

"Ees okay. I tella you befoe, I take de bud wid de gude, cause I lak a you; I lak a you too much."

"Why do you say you like me so damn much?"

"I tella you befoe, I dunno why, ma some a ting I feel, inzide, cause inzide you ees amore; si, amore, love," I said, waving my hands in frustration and hindered by the role I was forced now to accept, "love inzide you, in you eyes, in you heart, in alla you, I feel inzide me, make a me warm, make a me warm, inzide."

"You're attracted to me, physically."

"I no unnerstun."

"That means you just want, well, you want to," she stammered, "to, well, to fuck me."

"No, no! I no wanna focka you!" I said, reacting quickly to my guilt.

Tears were making her dark eyes glow.

"Well, maybe, maybe not just that. Maybe you don't mean, well, just that."

"Ma, fock eesa fock. No?"

"No, Tonio. It doesn't always mean the same thing. When a man and a woman love each other, I mean, really love each other, what do they want to do?"

"If day love, day love."

"And you said you came here for love. That means, to me, anyway, you want to, well, you want us to make love together."

"Si, ma datsa no mean I going focka you."

"You mean you won't go all the way with me because, because I'm a, a whore?"

"No! No! You no unnerstun!"

"You said you, well, that you like me, very much."

"Si. Inzide you ees love; ees bigga den fock. Inzide me, fo you, ees love, amore, bigga den fock."

She was gazing at me, again, with her penetrating, irresistible look, stirring feelings not only of tenderness, deep inside of me, but of sorrow and anger.

"Knowing what I do, must be, well, painful to you."

"Si, pain. An inzide you, too much pain. No?"

"That's why I said I don't want you to have anything to do with that part of me."

"Ma, dat parta you eesa parta you, joosta de same, an I feela dat parta you. Some a you pain, I take inzide me. Some a time, de pain, she make a me say bud tings, make you hurt mo. Ma, de guda parta you make a me feela gude. Too gude."

I touched her face gently and brushed away a teardrop.

"Tonio," she whispered, her eyes filling with more tears and drawing me inside of her.

She reached up and put her hand on my face.

"I think you really mean it."

She reached up with her other hand, cradling my face, and urged me to kiss her again.

I pressed my mouth against hers and closed my eyes, letting the pleasurable sensation of her kiss envelope me. It was a long kiss, which became intense, and feeling the passion swelling in me, I no longer wanted to resist it. I enjoyed the fervor of her own feelings penetrate my whole being, and I let my passion respond to her, feeling her lips moving beneath mine, and feeling her mouth sucking mine. After her lips stopped moving, I opened my eyes. Hers was closed. Slowly, her mouth withdrew from mine, and opening her eyes, she looked into mine as though feeling my own feelings.

"I've never met anyone like you. You're a good person, Tonio, really good," she said, stroking my face.

Then her hand dropped casually onto my lap, where she suddenly felt the obviousness of my desire. Startled, she looked down at me. Then she looked up at me again, quickly, and I became so damned mortified, I wanted to vanish.

"No, non too gude, me, ma de heart," I said, putting my hand on my chest, "ees gude, wid amore, bigga den down dere."

Her face lit up into a big smile, and she stared at me.

After a little while, still smiling, she said, "You're embarrassed, Tonio."

The only thing I could think of saying was, "Wadsa mean dat?"

"It means, well, it means, you have a big heart." She chuckled a little. "And it means you really want to make love to me, but you don't want me to see you like this. You're ashamed. You're ashamed because you can't hide your real feelings."

I stared at her.

"Tonio, don't be ashamed, not for wanting to make love to me. I want you. I want to go all the way with you. That means, well," she said softly, "I want you to fuck me."

My whole body quivered, and I gasped, "Ma eez no right,"

"I don't understand. Why not?"

"Eez no right," I said weakly.

"Haven't you ever, well, made love? All the way, I mean."

I had to think about it quickly. How could I, as a foreign kid, stranded and broke, explain any affairs?

"You haven't, have you!"

I looked at her sheepishly, not knowing what to say.

"That explains it! Why you said you don't want to, well, to go all the way with me. Tonio," she said, gently, "it's okay to feel this way about me. It's how I want you to feel. I feel the same way, about you. That's part of amore. You're right. Amore is bigger than fuck, but it includes it. You understand what I'm saying?"

"Ees okay?"

"Si, ees okay," she said smiling; "fo you ees okay, ony fo you."

"Ma notta now, righta now. You mak a me crazy. I no wanna feel lak a dat now."

"I understand, but we both know, now, how we really feel about each other. And I'm glad you've never, well, made love, all the way. When we do, it'll be something special, for both of us, a special gift to share on our birthdays."

"You wanna nudda cigarette?"

"You're really something," she said, and she kissed me again, gently.

As I lit two cigarettes, my hands trembled.

She touched my hand briefly and said, "Tonio, you don't have to be embarrassed, not with me, or worried. I know how you feel. And that makes me happy. And, yes, there is love, amore, much love inside of me, just for you."

As I gave her a lit cigarette, I said, "Ay, we have alla day an alla de night; we take plenta de time. No?"

"Si, we have alla day an alla de night; we take plenta de time."

"You make a funny me, de way I spik?"

"Si," she grinned, "I make a funny you, de way you spik, cause I lak a de way you spik; I lak everting aboud you."

I drew a deep puff.

After a brief silence, and my composure returned, I said, "Tella me mo aboud you."

"Are you sure? I don't want to upset you again. I've just realized that what you know about me, about what I do, is one thing, but my telling you about it, well, it makes it, well, it makes it seem more real, somehow. To you, I mean. And I don't want anything else to spoil this day. I wish I knew what to tell you."

"De guys payga too much?"

"I told you, I pick the customers who pay the most."

"You de bess lookin gal in de club?"

"All the girls are very attractive, of all races, and they're all sexier than I am."

"No, datsa no true!"

"Well, anyway, I usually get the customers I want. I prefer older, more mature men, because they're easier to manage. They have to pay a hundred dollars downstairs, at a desk near the lounge, before they're permitted to go upstairs. They pay for a room, just like in a hotel. A hundred dollars a night. Half of that, fifty dollars, is my commission."

"Fifty dollar?"

"That's only for the room. The minimum is a hundred dollars to, well, to sleep with me."

"To focka you."

I don't know why in hell I had said that. It was a stupid thing to say. And hateful.

She stared at me.

"Tonio, I don't want to upset you anymore."

"Ees okay," I murmured.

"No, it's not okay, not if it upsets you."

"I tella you, ees okay," I said, and puffed on the cigarette.

"That's how I make enough money to live in a place like this. I could never make enough, before, to even survive."

"I unnerstun, I tink."

But she knew I didn't.

I gazed at the top of her dress, at the bulge of her bosom, and felt the urge to uncover her breasts.

I lay my cigarette in the ashtray, reached out, and touched the top button.

Slowly, I unbuttoned it; and then, separating the dress a little, I uncovered the top of her bosom where her flesh began to rise. I moved my hand down to the next button, unbuttoned it, and opened her dress more until I uncovered the deep separation between her breasts just above the top of her white bra. As I was gazing at the rise of her bosom, she said, "Touch me if you want." And I touched her flesh delicately, as though feeling something very tender, like the petal of a flower. "Beautiful," I murmured. And I undid the next button, pushed her dress apart, and uncovered the front of her bra.

She was smiling.

But I suddenly thought of her exposing herself, and of letting the slobs in the club defile her, and my urge dissipated. I tried, for a moment, to think of something as beautiful as her, something beautiful that had been touched, and had been contaminated, by man, but I couldn't think clearly; all I could think of, at the time, was the poverty I had seen in squalid tenement flats in nearby neighborhoods, which had filled me with pity. And I buttoned her dress, covering her again.

I picked up my cigarette, took another puff, exhaled the smoke, then squashed the butt into the ashtray.

She didn't say anything, putting her cigarette out, too, but she was looking at me and wondering, probably, what I was thinking and feeling.

Impulsively, I lit another cigarette.

"Seriously," she finally said, "we should do something about, well, about your, your problem. In my bed. Together, letting nature take its course. Afterwards, you'll be relaxed. And we can spend the rest of the day just relaxing with each other. We can pretend we're on a vacation together, somewhere romantic, away from the rest of the world."

I was tempted, very tempted. I told myself that sooner or later we'd probably go to bed together anyway, so I might as well do it now, but knowing that she thought I was someone else was bothering me, still, and jumping into bed with her so quickly, before she could know anything about the real me, just didn't seem right, not with her, anyway. Somehow, that's the way I felt about her. I liked her too much to deceive her in any way. I knew she was feeling sympathy for the guy she thought I was and that she thought she was falling in love with him. I almost told her the truth, right then and there. But if I told her I was just a kid from New Hampshire who was there, already, on vacation, on summer vacation, from high school, I knew damn well that would only shatter the dream, which I had created for her, a dream that was fulfilling her deep need to love and be loved.

I tried to put myself in her place. If I were her, would I want to get into bed with a guy just to satisfy my sexual urge? Somehow, I didn't think so. Maybe I'd want to satisfy him because I thought I loved him, but then, if I'd find out later he was only using me to satisfy himself, his physical desire, that he was only pretending to be someone I wanted to love, I'd feel terribly hurt. I'd feel betrayed.

And, I thought, a heartless bastard like that would only make me feel dirtier. He had taken advantage of me, of my vulnerability, of my desperate need to be loved, because, to him, I'm just a whore!

I sighed deeply.

Taking her hand and putting it on my knee, I asked, "Why you wanna going bed widda me? Joosta fo me, o fo you, too?"

That seemed to surprise her.

Smiling, she squeezed my knee and replied, "No, not just for you; for me, too. For both of us, Tonio."

"Ma fo love, o joosta fo fock?"

"For love. But fuck is part of it, part of love, or it should be, with you, at least. I know that for a lot of people, it has nothing to do with love. But, when a man and a woman love each other, one of the ways of showing love is through, well, through touching each other. We have many words for touching. Sometimes we call it sex. Sex is natural, something we're supposed to respect and to use the way God intended us to use it, as a way of expressing and sharing our love, as a precious gift, as a way of bringing new life into being and of passing it down to our children, one generation after another, something that, in itself is good, really good, but, like so many other things that are good, we abuse it (and you don't have to remind me that I'm guilty of that, too, because I know how guilty I am), we twist sex into something bad, into something dirty, and then, not even making love really means making love; it has nothing to do with love."

"Why you tink we do dat? We take some a ting gude, an den it no gude."

"Why? I think that's like asking why we don't love. I've often thought about that. There are probably a lot of reasons, most of which I'll never know, but I know that when we don't love, we can't see things, especially good things, the way they really are. We get confused, and we distort things. And that prevents us from under-standing, from knowing, especially from knowing each other, keep-ing us apart. And everything becomes a threat to us. In your present situation, you must have experienced some of that. I mean, when you're desperate, down and out, everything in life, even the good things, can become scary, and when we feel threatened, we tend to hate. And when we hate, we make everything even worse; we take something good and twist it into something bad. And then we feel even more threatened. And everything just keeps getting worse. We get more confused and more disturbed. I think that's one of the rea-sons people do such bad things."

I was staring at her and feeling very tender towards her.

"Tonio, I've never met anyone who wants to talk about the same things I like to talk about," she said, squeezing my hand, "not until now."

"I lak talk widda you."

"And I like talking with you, too; I really do."

"Tella me some a ting. Wad you tink aboud a guy, lak a me, payga de money fo sex de gal?"

She seemed startled.

"I don't even want to think about it! Why would you pay to, to do that?"

"No me, no. Some udder guy, lak a me, ma notta me."

"Tonio, I know how you feel, but I can't change my circumstances. I would if I could, especially now, especially for you. But I can't."

"No, no, I talk aboud de guys dat payga de money."

"You mean, the guys in the club? How do I feel about the guys in the club?"

"Si."

"I feel nothing. That's the honest to God truth, Tonio. You don't have to worry about how I feel about them," she said, squeezing my hand again. "You're wondering if I enjoy, well, doing it. Aren't you?"

"I wanna unnerstun, me. Make a believe de gal, she going to a guy, payga de money an wanna heem focka her. How you tink de guy feel?"

"That depends on what kind of guy he is."

"Nize a guy, lak a me."

"Tonio, a nice guy like you wouldn't like it. Some of the girls enjoy, well, whoring, I guess, for all kinds of reasons, pretending they're making love to a guy who's a sexy movie star or something, or maybe the girls enjoy controlling the men and having power over them, or maybe some of the girls even do it because they hate themselves and want to degrade themselves as punishment, but that doesn't mean all whores enjoy being whores, that they're doing it just for the fun of it. Most of them are just like anyone else who has to work to make money, wishing they could do something else for a living. Some of them even have steady boyfriends, and some of them, like Mad, don't even want boyfriends, because they don't believe in love anymore. Most of them would quit if they had enough money. The prostitute in the Bible, Mary Magdalene, to whom Jesus said, 'Go, and sin no more,' must have found another way to earn a living. Most girls would rather have sex for enjoyment, not for work."

"Ma eef I sex you, you tink you lak?"

"Of course I would!"

"Ma eef I payga you de money, you no lak?"

"No, of course not."

"Ma eesa sex joosta de same. Wadsa differenz?"

"You know the difference, Tonio. And you know you wouldn't enjoy it, either, not for money."

"Ma de guys in de club, dey lak sex de gals. No?"

"You're not like the guys in the club. Suppose a woman offered you money just to, well, do it to her, how would you feel?"

"Ma datsa wad I aska you befoe, how you tink de guy feel."

"There are guys who do that for a living. We call them gigolos. You wouldn't like doing what they do. Would you?"

"I no tink I lak, no. Ma I tink de gal payga de money cause she no beautiful lak a you; no guy wanna sex her."

I put my cigarette out.

"So she's willing to pay."

"Ma, make a believe she beautiful, lak a you. Why she payga me de money, I dunno, me, ma she payga me joosta de same. Wad you tink den, ay? You tink I no lak sex de gal, beautiful, lak a you?"

"Do you think you'd like it?"

"Ma datsa wad I aska you. Wad you tink?"

"If you were desperate enough and needed money, you would probably do it to her. But do you think you'd enjoy doing it?"

"I aska *you* wad *you* tink!"

"If I offered you money to, well, to fuck me, you wouldn't like it."

"Huh? I no believe you say dat!"

"Wanting to make love to me, is not the same as fucking me for my money."

"Ma, eef you payga de money, you wanna me focka you. No?"

"Of course. That's why I'd pay you."

"An eef you wanna me focka you, an I wanna focka you, an you payga de money, you tink I no lak focka you?"

"Which is it, Tonio, wanting to make love to me, or doing it for the money?"

"Huh?"

She wasn't arguing logically, I thought.

I sighed, thinking of a reply.

"No, no, we no talk aboud love now, aboud amore; we talk aboud de gal payga de money an de guy focka de gal fo de money. You no tink de guy lak focka beautiful gal cause she payga de money?"

"I thought we were talking about *you*."

"Aboud me, si," I said, nodding, "okay, we talk aboud me, aboud me an aboud you," I was saying while nodding, stalling, thinking of a logical rebuttal. "Okay, we talk aboud me an you."

For emphasis, I was speaking with my right hand, bending my fingers and pressing them against my thumb.

"Ay, eef you payga me de money to make a love widda you," I said, shaking my hand, "you tink I no lak a de money? An eef I lak a de money, you tink I no lak mak a love widda you eef you payga me de money?"

She was staring at me, thinking.

I had her trapped, now, I thought, in a logically foolproof argument, and she would be forced to admit, logically, at least, that if a guy like me would enjoy sex with a beautiful girl like her, especially if she would pay him, she would be forced to admit that they would also enjoy it if their roles were reversed. But I wasn't absolutely sure of my argument. Other guys my age had it all figured out differently. They thought it was normal for guys to enjoy sex, and if a guy didn't enjoy it, there was something wrong with him. But they thought it was just the opposite with girls. Normal girls didn't like sex, and if a girl liked sex, there was something wrong with her. Such thinking didn't sound logical to me, but I didn't know if those other guys were just simple minded or whether they had learned a profound truth that had somehow eluded me.

I waited for her answer.

Still staring at me, she finally said, "If I paid you to do it, you really think you'd enjoy fucking me?"

She sounded as though she expected me to say yes, so, with uncertainty, I answered, "I tink, maybe, I lak."

"Really?" she asked, and paused a little, studying me with those deep, dark eyes. "You think you'd really enjoy it, even if I paid you?"

"Si, too much."

"Okay, then," she smirked, leaning against me and thrusting her hand against my crotch. "I'll pay you fifty dollars to fuck me, right now."

I became speechless and gaped at her in disbelief.

"Well, Tonio, is fifty dollars enough? If you satisfy me, I'll give you another fifty. Okay? A hundred dollars! To fuck me. Right now. Let's go! What are you waiting for?"

Suddenly, she unzipped my fly. Quickly, I pushed her hand away, and I zipped up.

"You see?" she said triumphantly, grinning. "You lost! You can't enjoy it with a woman like that!"

I was at loss for words.

"I know what you're thinking. You think guys would be tickled pink just to, well, to fuck me. And if I were even willing to pay them, they'd like it even more. But I'm right about you; you're not like other guys. I know you better than you even know your own self. You want more than fuck. You said it yourself. And you said it beautifully. Amore is bigger, much bigger. And that's what you and I both want. Amore. But it's not something that can be bought. If a woman offered you money to make love to her, you know that isn't love. A lot of men in the club brag about how they can buy anything they want, especially women, because every woman has her price, they think. I know I'm taking advantage of them, that I'm just as guilty of abusing sex as they are, but they try to impress me by how rich they are, how they can easily afford me. And, from what they tell me about their experiences with other women, with even their own wives, they think they can always buy love. Their beautiful wives married them, I guess, because these men are rich. And many of the men say they're happily married and have happy families. But why do they go to the club? You asked me how I feel about guys who, well, pay to fuck. How do you think you'd feel about a woman, even a beautiful looking woman, who says she's happily married but pays you to fuck her? What really concerns me is that I could be doing the same thing. Deceiving myself. I can see in others how that blinds them to, well, the truth, especially the truth about themselves. They don't even seem to know that they're even looking for something.

They exist, pretending that they're living, pretending that they can always buy what they really need. And I don't want that to happen to me. Yet, when I look back to where I was, to the endless struggle to survive, to barely survive, I see how that, too, blinds us."

She paused.

"I've never talked to anyone else like this."

"Ma I lak."

"I think too much. Maybe we should just exist without even thinking about it."

"I dunno, me."

"I can't believe I'm not just dreaming about you. I enjoy your company, Tonio, so much," she said, touching my knee again. "You make me feel, well, comfortable, to want to talk with you."

"Talk den. Tella me mo aboud de club."

"Are you sure?"

"Si, I wanna know tings; I wanna know aboud pipple."

"I can't tell you much about people, not about the good side. You could tell me a lot more."

"Meee? Inzide you ees gude, too much, mo den inzide me, ma I wanna know de bud side. Everbody hava bud side. No?"

"You have a bad side, Tonio?"

"Io? No, oh, no, no! San Antonio, me."

She grinned.

"You're really something. Tell me about your bad side."

"Ay, don be crazy. No, no, you tella me de budda side."

She shrugged.

"Well, like what?"

"De guys. In de bed, wad day do?"

"You know what they do."

"Ma, day go crazy? Focka you alla de night? Wad?"

She glared at me.

Damn! I had done it again. Talking before thinking about her feelings, again.

"Me," I said, feeling badly and wishing I could take back what I had said, "in de bed widda you, I go pazzo. How you say, go crazy in de bed? I dunno, me, ma in italiano, I say, molto appassionato."

"Molto appassionato?"

"Si, molto appassionato."

"Very passionate!"

"In de bed widda you, I go crazy."

"You mean, you'd get terribly excited."

"I dunno, ma you make a me molto appassionato."

She smiled.

"Terribly excited is the same as molto appassionato," she said, putting her hand on my knee. "When you say I'd make you molto appassionato, you're saying that I'd make you very passionate."

"In de bed, you make a me very passionate, alla de night, I tink."

"You really think so?"

"I tink so."

"Tonio, it's never like that, really. A man's excitement doesn't last long, and then he just wants to sleep."

"No! I dunno, me, ma pipple tella me dat you get, ah, how you say, de inzide, she go: bang! Bigga bang!"

"You mean, an orgasm."

"Orgasm. Ees nize, de orgasm?"

"Well, that's why men do it, I suppose."

"An de gal, no? De orgasm. De bigga bang."

"I really can't tell you. I know that girls have orgasms, too, but I've never had one."

"No?"

"Tonio, I hope you don't expect to, well, to get molto appassionato for long, because, well, it doesn't last long. A few seconds, maybe even a minute or so, and then it's over."

"Widda you?"

"I'm afraid, now, that you're going to be terribly disappointed."

"Whadsa mean, dat?"

"Disappointed means, well, you won't like it, the sex, because it won't be as exciting as you expected."

"Huh? No lak sex, widda you? You tink you lak sex me, ma I no lak sex you? I no unnerstun."

"Well, you'll enjoy it, at first, touching me and getting molto appassionato, but then, quickly, the bang, and it's over."

"You no hava bigga bang? Nevva?"

"Never."

She lit a couple of cigarettes and gave me one.

"De guys, in de bed widda you, day toucha you. How a you feel?"

She took a puff, exhaled, and said, finally, "I can't really describe my feelings. My body goes, well, almost numb. Being in bed with a, well, with a customer doesn't mean anything, except money. I don't really think about what we're doing. When I do, I feel disgust. I have to turn my mind off. To a customer, I'm only a toy, something to play with, not a real person. A man and a woman, in the same bed, but they're not together, not connected, not even real to each other. I know that sounds strange. Somehow, I feel disconnected, separated, even, from my own body, as though I'm observing someone, someone who isn't me, who isn't even real. I can't explain it."

"Lak some body you no lak, an you say, datsa notta me. You go away, in you head; you spirito go away, an de gal, in datta body, notta you. An de guy, he toucha de body, ma de body notta you. You feel nutting. Nutting, lak, lak, you dead; you spirito gone away, an you feel nutting."

"That's exactly how it is!"

Drawing another deep puff from her cigarette, she stared at me, exhaled, and said softly. "I feel good, really good, just talking with you."

And, for a little while, we became silent.

As Jessica stood up, went to the stove, and turned on the flames to reheat the pot of coffee, she told me she needed to make enough money to support her mother and two younger sisters who had moved into the next apartment. Last month, when her mother had first seen the apartment, she had become so overwhelmed with emotion, she wept, and Jessica, embracing her, had told her that from now on their circumstances would improve.

"You madre, she know aboud de club an everting?"

"Of course not," she said, standing in front of the stove. "Not everything. She knew I hadn't suddenly inherited a fortune from a rich uncle, so I told her I sing and dance and do odd jobs at a very expensive night club."

After she poured us each another cup of coffee, she sat next to me again and took her cigarette from the ashtray.

"De club, eet looka nize?

"It looks like an expensive hotel, which it actually is, and very exclusive."

"Exclusive?"

"It's a private club, for paying members only, who call themselves patrons. They call the club a charitable, a sort of religious, organization, because it contributes money to charitable causes. That's what I've been told, anyway."

She hadn't been there long enough to really know much more about it. She did tell me, reluctantly, however, because she hadn't wanted, she said, to upset me even more, that all of the patrons were white.

"Some of the girls who've worked in other places say we're lucky to be there, because the money's so good, and none of us are required to do anything more than, well, the basic thing. But it's still a whorehouse. Some of the girls, especially the ones who only work part time, won't even admit that we're really prostitutes. That means whores. We're called entertainers," she smirked. "Our patrons, after all, are very elegant gentlemen who would never get caught dead in a whorehouse. Anyway, some day I'll have enough money to provide a decent life for all of us. The first thing I wanted was to get us out of the flat. So, here we are. We've made it this far. I know what it feels like, Tonio, being broke. It must even feel worse for you, because you, well, you had money, and then all of a sudden, you were trapped in a strange country, always afraid of getting caught, and broke, away from your own home and family, for so long, not even knowing what's happened to any of them."

"Ma some a day, de war, she finita, an I go bucka home."

"Someday," she said dreamily, "the war will end," and she put her cigarette out.

My hypocrisy was making me feel like shit.

I drew a deep puff.

"Righta now," I said, stubbing the butt in the ashtray, "I don wanna tink aboud de war. I wanna tink aboud you."

"About me," she said, smiling. "To live this moment, together. At least we have each other, for now. And right now, I don't want to think about anything else, either; I want to think only about you. I know I shouldn't feel the way I do about you. I should feel, for your sake, that I want the war to end soon. I should want you to be home with your loved ones. But I'm glad you're here. I'm glad you came to this country when you had. If you hadn't, you probably would have been in the eyetalian army, fighting in the war, and you would have been away from home, anyway, and God knows what might have happened to you."

"Si, boom boom in de war. Much pipple die."

"And I never would have met you. So, I'm glad you're here."

"Here, oggi, ma domani, gone."

"Here today, gone tomorrow. I understand. And when you get back to Italy, you'll probably get married and raise a family."

"I dunno, me."

"Do you have a girlfriend in Italy?"

"No, I nevva hava gal friend, no place."

"I don't believe you," she said, smiling, as though she really did and was pleased.

"Ah, one gal friend, I have, here. You believe?"

"I believe you."

"An you? You hava boyfriend?"

"Yes, I have a boyfriend," she said, grinning, and took a sip of coffee. "But I've never had a boyfriend, not before today."

"I don believe! Beautiful gal lak a you?"

"That's the truth, Tonio. Honest to God. I've never actually made love; I can only imagine it, actually making love, making love, with you. I don't mean just, well, you know. I mean, loving you, kissing and caressing each other for real, for love. I've never experienced it; so, like you, I'll be experiencing it for the very first time."

She reached up, with both hands, held my face, and leaned against me. And we kissed again, a long kiss, which aroused me, again.

Putting her hand on my lap, she said, "I think it's marvelous. A man and a woman, becoming molto appassionato, just by kissing each other. I was going to say a boy and a girl, but with you I feel like a woman with her man. Imagine what it would be like in bed, Tonio, you and me, together."

I heaved a deep sigh, removed her hand, and took a sip of coffee.

"Tonio, I just want you to know that no one else has ever made me feel like this, that you excite me as much as I excite you, just by touching each other. And since this has never happened to me before, I can't explain it. But we were attracted to each other instantly, as though we suddenly felt, well, connected, somehow. I don't know why, and right now, I don't care why. All I know is that I've never felt this way before. It's like a dream, a marvelous dream, a dream that we both know won't last much longer, that we have to live, now, while we have it. And I think it's marvelous that we both feel the same way. Don't you?"

"Si, ma dis eesa nize, talka togetter. No?"

"Yes, you know it is, just being together. You, too, make me feel warm inside. Maybe that's why, when we just touch each other, we become molto appassionato."

Suddenly I thought of her having a husband, someday, and children, and I wondered how she would feel, looking back, if we would make love. I knew I would never regret it, that I would remember her fondly, always. But how would she feel? Would she feel she had been impetuous, fulfilling a dream that had only been a dream, that she would regret having made love to me, a stranger who had entered her life so briefly?

"Some a day, you getta marito an hava bambini."

"Bambini. That must mean children. I used to dream about getting married and having children. But, now, I'm too, well, ashamed to imagine myself as a mother. Besides, I don't expect any man to ever marry me, not now, not if he knew about me, and if he didn't know, I'd always worry that he'd find out. Sometimes, even now, I worry about getting seen outside the club by anyone associated with it."

Feeling her pain deeply, I said, "Amore, love, ees to take de bud wid de gude. No?"

"You mean, if a man loved me, he'd take the bad with the good?"

"Si."

"You think a man could really love, well, someone like me?"

"Certo! Si."

"You think he could ever love me enough to want me be the mother of his children?"

"Si, I know, me," I said with deep feeling.

"I can't really expect that."

"No? Den you tink I no can love alla you, huh? Dat I no come here cause, cause I wanna you love. You tink I lie!"

She stared at me.

"No, Tonio. I know you came here for love, and that's why I want you here, for love. But even if we fell madly in love with each other, and I know I could, easily, well, our situation, it's, it's, well, hopeless. We want to be together; we want amore, now, but we both know it's temporary."

"Wadsa mean dat?"

"It means," she said, softly, "it's only for now."

"How you know dat?"

"I know," she whispered.

"You wrong."

Her eyes were penetrating mine again as she said, "I can't expect more than I have now, right now. Tonio, do you really feel that I should, well, hope for more? With you, I mean. When the war's over. Do you really think that?"

"Si, I tink dat," I said, with painful longing. "Ma now ees importante. No?"

"Si, now ees importante, yes! We can live our dream, Tonio; we can live our dream together, now, right now."

Suddenly, I asked myself, "What in hell are you saying?" I had gotten caught up in the role I was playing. It had become real, even to *me*! And in just nine more days, I'll be leaving for home. Then what?

She looked at the bracelet, touched it, smiled, and then she stood up, grasped my face, and with her bright eyes looking into mine, she leaned down and kissed me on the mouth again. And then she said, "You know I'm in love with you, Tonio."

I didn't know what to say.

She pulled my head against her and held my face to her bosom.

I put my hands on her hips and let myself enjoy her softness and warmth.

"I know this seems crazy, because this is so sudden, and because our situation is so hopeless, but under these circumstances, which are, well, so crazy, I know, now, there's a reason why we've met, but before you came here, I didn't know what to expect. I was so anxious to see you, I became nervous and a little worried about my feelings for you. I've thought about you during the past few days, waiting to see you again, and I asked myself why I felt so attracted to you. Mad tried to convince me that I was fantasizing about you, and that

I was going to get burnt, even after I had told her that all I wanted was your friendship. But just before you showed up, I thought I was hoping for too much, wanting us to be amici, wanting to trust my feelings for you. But I never expected you to, well, to love me, not the way I used to dream about it. And, now, after talking with you for a little while, you're even more than I had hoped for. I've never been in love before, but I am now; I'm in love with you. Actually, I knew it as soon as I saw you, but I wasn't expecting you to feel the same way. I knew you were attracted to me, but I wasn't sure why. I'm sure, now, that something brought us together, for the time being, at least, because this is the time in our lives when we need each other the most. We want to be together; we want amore, now, to accept what life is giving us, to live this moment, together."

She lifted my face, and the affection glowing in her eyes filled the deepest part of me, stirring my deepest feelings, not only my passion, but something deeper, which I had never felt before, something much more tender.

She bent down a little, parted her lips, and placed her mouth on mine. Holding her hips, I pushed myself up while we were kissing, and I held her against me. Then I felt her hands moving down my back until she was holding my hips against hers. And the front of her, responding to my own body, began pushing into me. I knew she could feel the hardness of my desire pressing against her and stimulating her own desire, but I knew she could also feel, within a deeper part of me, the softness of my amore, which, I suddenly felt, had created the outward hardness, a manifestation of my deepest feelings in a physical form. I knew she could feel my softness, because I could feel her softness, deep within her. Never before had I ever felt this way. In the past, I had felt only the obvious but superficial hardness of my own desire. And now I felt like a different person, that something good, really good, in me had been awakened. Something very tender. And, withdrawing my mouth slowly from hers, I looked at her, at the deep softness emanating through her eyes.

"Tonio, let's sit on the couch."

Leaning against each other, we went into the living room.

As I sat near the end of the couch, she sat next to me, pushed her shoes off with her feet, curled her legs up, leaned against me, and urged me back until my head and shoulders rested in the corner, against the arm of the couch. And she tucked her head under my chin and put a hand on my lap.

"Nevva befoe I feel lak a dis, appassionato down dere, ma in here," I said, tapping my chest as she raised her head and looked at me, her face over mine, "ver warm, ver soft. Nevva befoe I feel lak a dis. You believe?"

She smiled.

"Yes, I believe, because I feel the same way, and I've never felt like this before, either."

"Ees amore, si?"

"Si, ees amore."

And her mouth touched mine again, gently, her lips brushing my lips. And I kissed her again, closing my eyes. Her leg slid over mine, and I could feel her thigh pushing between my own thighs. When the kiss ended, I opened my eyes, and, slowly, I unbuttoned her dress, the top button first, then the next, and the next one, all the way down, and as I was separating her dress more and more, I was gazing at the smoothness and beauty of her dark flesh opening up to me gradually. She, propping herself up with her arm against the back of the couch, was looking down at me, smiling. I pulled the hem at the bottom of her dress, pulled it up over her folded knees, and after I undid the last button, she, kneeling over me, clasped my face and held it to her bosom above the top of her bra. I slid my hands over her waist, under her dress, and up her back, until I felt the tiny hook at the back of her bra. And while I was kissing her below her neck and trying to unfasten the bra, something was telling me I was going too far, but something else was telling me that rejecting her would be worse than deceiving her. And I wasn't really pretending to be someone else, anyway, not on purpose; I was really the same I she thought I was. So I was a little younger than she thought. So what? And what difference did it really make where I came from? I was still I, Tonio. Embellished, a little, maybe. And "It's only for now," she had said, "to live this moment together." And although my fingers were trembling, I finally unhooked her bra.

She laughed a little.

"Why you laugh?"

"I'm sorry, Tonio, I didn't mean to laugh. It's just that the trouble you were having unhooking my bra struck me as amusing."

"You lak make a funny me, huh?"

She laughed, louder, then she held the back of my head, placed her mouth on mine, and kissed me, fervently.

While we were kissing, I slid my hands across her back, to the sides of her, and felt the roundness of her breasts. Then I pushed my hands under her bra and, cupping her flesh, began to squeeze her a little.

Moaning pleasantly, she withdrew her mouth from mine and gazed at me again.

I pushed the bra up to her neck, and I looked at her breasts swaying over me.

"Beautiful," I murmured, surprised by her nipples, which were jutting out so rigidly, and, with my index finger, I touched the tip of a nipple and wiggled it.

Her face was beaming.

I pushed myself all the way onto the couch, and I eased her down on her back so that I could get on top of her.

She spread her legs apart, taking mine between hers; and pressing my hips into hers, I kissed her on the lips again, passionately. And then I pushed myself down her sleek body, clasped one of her breasts, kissed it, and then took it into my mouth and began sucking it.

I felt her hands on the back of my head, holding me to her breast.

While I was sucking on it, I placed a hand on her other breast and began to stroke it.

Suddenly her body stiffened.

"Tonio, stop!"

I stopped.

"You're getting me too excited. You have to stop, unless you want to, well, unless you want to make love to me now, all the way, because you're getting me molto appassionato."

"All de way. Si, si!"

"Well, don't you think we should take off all our clothes first?" she said, smiling.

"Ah, si! Take off de clodes. Certo."

"Why don't we go in the bedroom? We'll be more comfortable in bed."

"Okay."

I stood up, took her hand and pulled her up, too. And as we walked across the room, I looked at her beautiful body draped by her opened dress. She was wearing tight, white panties. And as I was feasting my eyes on her thighs, on the sleekness of her legs, and on the voluptuousness of her naked breasts, I suddenly felt that I had become so damned aroused I wouldn't be able to prolong the act long enough to satisfy her. After all this time of talking about making love with each other, I could already feel my hardness swelling almost to the breaking point, and I was afraid I'd be a big disappointment to her, in spite of what she had told me about the slobs in the club. I wanted it to be completely different for her. I wanted her to feel the real thing. With *me*. So I sure as hell didn't want to think that the only damn big thing she'd feel in bed with me was her disappointment.

We crossed the threshold into her small bedroom, and as we approached the side of the bed, she withdrew from me, and then she pulled the covers down to the foot of the bed. With her back to me, her dress and her bra dropped to the floor. As I was admiring the back of her, she quickly pushed her panties down, uncovering her round buttocks, and she crawled to the other side of the bed, pulled a sheet over her, turned onto her stomach, hugged a pillow, and looked at me affectionately, smiling a little.

Still standing at the side of the bed, I took off my shirt. I pulled my side of the sheet down, uncovering her shoulders, then I sat on the bed, took off my shoes and socks, stood up, and pushed my trousers down. I sat again, took off my shorts, lifted the sheet, lay back on the bed, and pulled the sheet up to my waist. It was warm in her bedroom, so I don't know why I covered myself with the sheet. Maybe I still didn't want her to see how great my desire was.

She drew closer to me but didn't touch me, and turned onto her side, looking at me, and I turned onto my side, facing her, and, without touching each other, just looking, I could see in her beautiful face her deep affection.

"I lak look a you. I feel inna you de amore."

"And I like looking at you, too. I can also feel the love, inside of you. I can feel it flowing into me and making me feel, well, warm inside, nice and warm. I've never felt this way before."

I put my hand on her hip, feeling her smooth flesh curving upwards into her buttock, and drew myself against her, and, stroking her hip, I kissed her on the mouth, which felt so soft and so yielding. Her arm was under my shoulder as she held me against her, and as her flesh and mine pressed together, her breasts yielded against me. Then I pushed her shoulders down, urging her to lie on her back, and as we continued kissing, I lay on top of her. Moving myself down slowly on her body, I began kissing her breasts, then, cupping my hands on her breasts, I was kissing her belly. After a while, I lifted my head and looked down at her beautiful body, and although I was filled with passion, I felt that the softness in me had actually become stronger than the hardness of my desire. I could hardly believe it, I was so surprised, and for some reason, I felt proud of myself. I was looking at her as I would look at a beautiful sunrise, or a beautiful flower opening itself, or anything else that was beautiful, except that she was more beautiful than anything else I had ever seen, arousing my deepest feelings more than anything else ever had. And I knew, somehow, that I'd be able to prolong my passion now, because the hardness of my desire had emanated from the softness of my amore for her, and, although I had given myself up to the exhilaration of making love to her, of arousing our deepest feelings, my softness, I felt, transcended the hardness, making me feel very tender inside. And as I caressed her belly, I felt her body lifting up to mine, her pubis pushing against my chest and urging me to enter her. Her hands were on my shoulders, holding me against her, and her breathing became deeper and louder, and she began to moan, undulating her hips. I pushed myself up a little, kissing her breasts again, then I moved my lips up her neck, to the side of her face, kissed her ear, and moved my mouth slowly over her face until my lips touched hers again. Her lips parted, and her mouth opened, sucking on mine. And I tried to push my hardness into her, but, somehow, I wasn't able to penetrate her opening. I looked at her face. Her eyes were half shut, and she seemed to be pleading with me to enter her. Her bottom lip began quivering, and I could feel her desire; and in her eyes, I could see it, imploring me to enter her now. I reached down and felt her opening, and for a few moments, I poked my finger inside of her, just long enough to guide my hardness into her. And as I pressed it against her, what really surprised me was that her opening felt so damn narrow. And I wondered why I was so surprised. It was because, I thought, I knew she was a prostitute. For a few moments, I had thought of her only as Jessica, a beautiful girl filled with love, but suddenly I had reminded myself that she was a whore, because, without even thinking about it, I had expected the opening of her vagina to be bigger. It was my own prejudice that had created that impression. Thinking of her as a whore again had weakened my desire, and I was being so damn unfair to her, to her who had opened herself up to me, who trusted me, who had so much love in her, and who was giving me that love, because she had so much faith in me. And I didn't want anything, now, especially my prejudice, to spoil our making love together. And, knowing that the tenderness deep inside of me was still powerful enough to sustain the protuberance of my desire, I pushed my hardness into her, and I pushed again, and again, and each time I pushed deeper, she groaned, until, finally, I felt myself all the way inside of her, and her arms tightened around my shoulders, and she let out a soft moan. "Tonio, you feel so good!" And, slowly, at first, I began to move inside of her. And then another strange thing happened to me. I became aware that I wasn't even trying to satisfy my own desire as much as I was concentrating on satisfying hers. In the past, without even thinking about it, I had only wanted to satisfy myself, taking, and never really giving; now I was giving myself, completely, using my hardness to gratify her own desire, more so than trying to satisfy my own. And I became aware of her feelings, of her reactions to my hardness stroking the inside of her. I could feel the inside of her contracting, her desire swelling, intensifying. And suddenly, her body tightened, squeezing my hardness within her, so much that I was unable to move. Holding me tightly, she groaned. And after a little while, she began to relax, and I decided that since she had already reached a climax, I would withdraw from her and would try again a little later, but as I began to pull back, the inside of her contracted again, squeezing me and holding me in her. And I remained in her, feeling her inside moving and pulling on me and sending pleasurable sensations into my groin. Slowly, I began to move inside of her again, but her body quivered, and then, after I stopped, she heaved a deep sigh. Her eyes were closed, and she seemed so serene, so beautiful, her dark face adorned by a mass of pitch black hair spread against the white pillow. As I withdrew from her, she opened her eyes, and I lay on my side, facing her.

"Tonio," she said softly, gazing at me, "that was so nice! It felt even greater than I had imagined it would, much greater. I actually had an orgasm! I could feel the inside of me throbbing like crazy, until it felt like, well, like my whole body was exploding into yours. You must have felt it, too, it was so, well, so strong. The bigga bang! I wonder if you enjoyed it as much as I did."

"Certo! I enjoy, ver much, everting, de bigga bang, an everting."

She touched my face, saying, "I wish you had stayed inside of me a little longer, though. I enjoyed that, too, just feeling you inside of me."

"Ma I go inzide you again, subito."

"What do you mean?"

"I no finito, non fo now."

"You're not finished for now?"

"No. We make a love some mo."

"Some more?"

"Si, when you wanna."

"You don't mean," she said, almost laughing, "right now, do you?"

"Certo, in due o tre minuti."

"But you don't think you can feel molto appassionato, again, so soon, do you?"

"Ay, widda you? You no tink I feel appassionato? I tella befoe, in de bed widda you, I go crazy."

She smiled.

"But I don't expect you to feel appassionato again, so soon."

"Ay, when I toucha you, I feel appassionato. How a you feel?"

"Peaceful, deliciously peaceful."

"Ma, eef a you no wanna, I do nutting. Notta now."

"Okay," she said, grinning, "I want to, but if you don't get so excited again, that's okay, too. We have the rest of the day and all night together, just you and me."

I kissed her on the mouth, not a passionate kiss, but a long, tender kiss, and I could feel her responding, the desire stirring in her again. And as I continued stroking one breast, I placed my lips against the one close to my mouth and began sucking on her again. I felt her nipple recovering its rigidity. And I slid a hand down her belly, to the lower part of her abdomen, stroking her, lower and lower. I pushed my hardness against her hip, and, wrapping my leg over hers, I stroke the inside of her, feeling her become more succulent, and as I continued stroking her, she began lifting her hips against my hand. After a little while, after her breathing became heavier, I withdrew my hand, and I slid my body on top of hers. She spread her legs apart, taking me between her thighs. And, while fondling her breasts, I kissed her on the mouth, passionately. To my surprise, as I pushed my hardness against her, I felt her opening easily this time, taking me into her again. I felt her undulating, pulling me deeper into her, and I felt my hardness penetrating her. She was making soft moans as I was thrusting myself into her. And this time, I thought, after having given myself, I would also have the pleasure of taking. I was filled with the passion, now, that I had told her I would feel, because I no longer had to be concerned, now, with disappointing her. After a while, I stopped momentarily, and I slid my hands down, from under her shoulders to her hips, and I tried to push my hands under her to hold her hips against me. She looked down to see what I was doing, then she lifted herself, and I slid my hands under her, and

I held her buttocks tightly, pressing myself into her, and feeling my hardness striking deep inside of her. Her eyes were closed, and she was moaning again, moaning louder each time I thrust myself into her. And then, holding and squeezing me within her, she suddenly cried out, "Oh, shit! You feel good! You feel so damn good!" And my body tightened around hers. And, as though our insides were bursting, we felt each other coming together.

We were clinging to each other, so tightly, that we felt that never again would we be, or would want to be, separate, not ever.

And I felt my hardness shooting my sperm into her, several times, and after a little while, my erection began melting within her.

And I closed my eyes, feeling the softness.

She groaned.

I looked at her face.

Suddenly, I became scared.

She seemed unconscious. She had gone into a deep swoon, I thought. Her head was hanging back, drooped over the edge of the pillow, and her eyes, not completely shut, were rolled back. Something was wrong, very wrong.

Frightened, I held her face.

"Jessica! Jessica!"

Slowly, as I held my breath, her eyes opened, and, in a trance, she looked at me. As I exhaled, emitting a long, slow breath, she put her arms around my neck. I lifted her head a little, and as I propped the pillow up under her head, she held my face against hers and murmured, "I'm here, Tonio; I'm here, with you, and there isn't only me anymore. We're together, now."

She closed her eyes again, holding me.

And for a long while, we were silent.

And I, too, closed my eyes again, and as I lay on top of her, inside of her, holding her and enjoying the feeling of being together, I, too, let myself be taken up into a tranquil state in which there wasn't only me anymore. Never before had I felt that way. Never before had I even known of such a feeling. It felt as though time did not exist, that there was only now, and that we were bound together, somehow, through something greater than anything I could understand, because, through her, having penetrated her, having penetrated me, was an emanation of something so soft, so gentle, and so caressing, yet so absolutely powerful, that I could only marvel at the source of the feeling that had been created in me.

"Tonio, you feel so good!"

The inside of her pulled on me again, and squeezed me within her.

"You came inside of me, deep inside of me, and I will feel you inside of me, always."

She seemed, somehow, to grow even more beautiful, more radiant.

"What do I call the man I love, in eyetalian?"

"Caro mio."

"Caro mio. Hmm, I like that, caro mio."

"An I calla you, cara mia."

"Cara mia. I like being your cara mia. How do you say, 'I love you'?"

"Ti amo."

"Ti amo, Tonio. That sounds so beautiful!"

The soft inside of her was melting into little waves that were rippling through me, not arousing me, but soothing me. Then, cupping her face, I said, "I wanna you be madre de me bambini. You, madre; much love inzide you."

"Oh, Tonio," she cried out, holding me tightly, "if only things were different!"

And tears began to roll down her face.

With my hands, I tried to wipe her tears away.

"I love you so much, Tonio! Ti amo. Ti amo, Tonio, caro mio."

I kissed her eyelids, tasting her salty tears.

And we became silent again, for a long while, until finally, she said, "You will always be with me, Tonio, I know that now. No matter what happens to either of us, you are part of me now, the deepest part of me."

And, now, as I write this, on a snowy January afternoon in the White Mountains of New Hampshire, almost twelve and a half years after that August afternoon in Harlem, Jessica is still very much inside of me, even though I had become a married man. Well, sort of. Married, I mean.

Jessica was a major influence on me, even though Dante doesn't mention her in his script. In all of the other women I have ever had a relationship with, I was looking for Jessica, wanting to experience that same feeling I had shared with her. I don't believe that only one woman has been ordained by nature to fulfill the love of any one man; there are probably thousands of women right here in New Hampshire who could satisfy my need for love, but finding just one, well, that was something else. Anyway, I've always thought that love was simply an act of the will. Just look at arranged marriages. I've read somewhere that they work better than marriages based on romance. Besides, when I had left Jessica, I had left one world and had been returning to another that was familiar. In Harlem, I actually was, in some ways, a foreigner. And I had to adapt, again, to my own world, to look ahead, not backwards, but having left Jessica had been terribly painful. The deepest part of me had been wrenched away when I had left her that summer, and the void has only been filled when we have come together, which, during these past years, has been too seldom.

When we were together, we didn't usually discuss her "work" or didn't even think about it; we were simply together, enjoying the peace and tranquility we gave each other, and we experienced the feeling of floating, just floating, together, not towards, or away from, anything, but feeling that we were where we both wanted to be: together, at least for the time being.

Togetherness, I've thought, during any particular time in any particular place is, by definition, at least, temporal and, therefore, relative. But that's not to say that the *feeling* of togetherness evaporates, because, when we were actually together, time and place did not seem to exist, not for either of us. Jessica had been the only person other than Rosie with whom I have shared that experience. But before I had even reached my seventeenth birthday, I had assumed that I would have shared that experience, again, with another woman, long before now. Anyway, that's what I had expected.

Looking back, I have to admit that fear of how others would react to me had influenced my thinking. Although "love conquers fear" was the way Jessica and I felt together, I knew that, after I had left her, the opposite was also true, that fear prevented love from growing and could eventually destroy it.

She had expressed my own feelings when she had said, "This is so extraordinary! I've never been so close to anyone before. It's as though, I don't know, but, well, I can't describe the feeling, but I feel as though we've always been together, as though, well, we're sharing something I couldn't even have imagined, it's so extraordinary. And I know you feel the same way, because I can't possibly feel this way, this strongly about us, all by myself. I feel your own feelings flowing into mine. It feels so good!" She laughed a little. "I used to wonder what it would be like to love someone. This is so much more than I could possibly have imagined!"

I've never felt that close even to Minnie Birch, someone white, sophisticated, and all that, a regular American. There was always something, an enigmatic something, that kept Minnie and me separate, in spite of our desires.

Maybe *togetherness* isn't the right word, because Jessica and I had never stopped desiring each other, not even when we felt we were together. So, what did we desire, Jessica and I? Something we already had? We had actually discussed that. We had felt so natural, so comfortable, being together, that we discussed our deepest feelings. So, when I asked her what it was that we desired, and she said, "To be together," I said we were. She thought about it. "To be together, always." But desiring to be together always meant we weren't together always. Were we, then, together only temporarily? She laughed. "We know we're together now, and we both want to remain together, always."

But if we were together now, shouldn't our desire be satisfied, temporarily, at least? I compared our desire to the craving for food when one was hungry. After one was fully satisfied, the desire no longer persisted. "I know what you mean. You've satisfied me; yet, my desire for you persists. But what do you mean by desire?"

We had decided that our desire was to love each other more. Maybe we do that through knowing each other better. I had never felt that desire, not until then, when I had begun to know her. "I know. I've never felt that desire, either, until now. Although we feel we're together now, our desire for each other still persists. Maybe that means our love for each other is growing towards something. I mean, maybe we're being guided towards something, towards, well, whatever it is we still desire."

And I told her I had thought that love was simply an act of the will, but I didn't feel that way with her. I felt there was already something inside of me, deep inside of me, of which I had never been aware, something not of my own making, something that had been created in me, and was emerging, growing, as though she, Jessica, were, somehow, raising it up.

"I know. I have the same feeling, about you. Through you, I feel that, well, my feeling of separateness, especially the feeling of my own separateness, from my own body, isn't real anymore. I can't explain it, Tonio, but I feel, now, that, well, that the separateness was never real, that it was only, well, an illusion, a distortion, and that, through you, through loving you, I'm overcoming my feeling of separateness, knowing, somehow, that we've always been connected, and I'm beginning to see things, now, really seeing things, especially good things, the way they really are, the way we're supposed to see them. Is that the way you feel, too?"

I did. And I said I wondered how often people experience what we were sharing together, now.

"I don't know, but if they do, it seems to me that everyone should be much happier. Anyway, no matter what happens to either of us now, we will always have this, together. Strangely enough, there are people who would say that what we're doing, now, loving each other like this, is sinful. But one thing I know, now, that having met you, sharing this with you, I will never be the way I was. Through you, I will always be a better person. I know that! And I want you to know that, too!"

Since then, in my relationships with other women, something has always been missing, something that would have overcome any feelings of separateness. Although I had wanted so desperately to retain that desire I have experienced with Jessica, perhaps, after all, it couldn't be willed, at least, not *just* willed; it had to grow spontaneously and naturally from within my deepest self, shared, and therefore nurtured by the profoundest desires of the woman with whom I was relating. Not even with Minnie Birch, much less with the woman whom I had actually married, had I ever felt in her the desire for togetherness, for a lasting union. To Minnie, and especially to the woman I had married, togetherness seemed to imply the loss of one's individuality, not as the fulfillment, the enhancement of one's individuality.

Although my relationship with Jessica had been based on a deception, I had thought, it had become more real than my other relationships with girlfriends. But how could it, unless it had been based on something else?

During that first night with Jessica, she had asked me where Nick and I were staying.

Reluctantly, I told her we were staying in the basement of a squalid tenement, in a small room that was very cheap to rent. I was describing a room with a dirty sink and rusty pipes, with its foul odors, and with cockroaches and rats scurrying around, a place I had been in a week or so before when Ben John had taken Nick and me there one afternoon while he was visiting some of his patients. Ben John and another doctor ran a small clinic in the neighborhood, and sometimes, in the afternoons and evenings, they made their rounds in nearby tenements. Nick, working sometimes in the clinic, had accompanied his father on the visits. Not too far away was a huge hospital, St. Luke's. I had asked Nick why his father wasn't working there, and he said his father had applied there, but the hospital had a policy that excluded Negroes, in spite of the shortage of doctors, then, during the war. In the room I was describing to Jessica, lived a sick old man with a couple of other old guys. The filthy sink was low and deep, like an old washtub. Against a brick wall was a fragile look-ing folding table with three folding chairs beside it, and against the other walls were two cots and a battered old couch with the springs sticking up. Above the table, a little light, near a low ceiling, came from a small opened window looking onto the street. I thought a black cat darted past my feet. It was a huge rat. I had thought the flats I had been in were bad. I couldn't wait to get the hell out of this one.

I whispered to Nick, "Where do they cook?" He whispered, "In a kitchen they share with other tenants, but they usually eat in a small church a couple of blocks away." A few moments later, I whispered, "Where do they go to the bughouse?" He whispered, "They piss in the sink." Where do they shit? There was a toilet bowl in a closet at the end of a hallway on another side of the basement. Did I need to go? Hell, no! When we were leaving, one of the old guys asked, "How much we owe you, doctor?" One dollar. Ben John had to charge them at least a dollar so that they could maintain their dignity. If they had a dollar, they'd pay him then and there; if not, he'd put it on their charge account, he said.

I wouldn't tell Jessica the address, because, I told her, I never wanted her to visit me there.

"Live here! With me! Together! Until the war ends."

I told her I didn't want the police to find me hiding here, because she'd be in trouble.

"I'm not worried about getting into trouble! Besides, we're not at war with Italy, not anymore."

That was true. Ten months ago, after surrendering to the allies, Italy had declared war on Germany, but by then the Germans had occupied most of Italy. Just two months ago, Rome had been taken by the allies. Now the fighting continued north of Rome. Actually, there were two Italian governments, one in the northern part, still under Mussolini and his fascists, controlled by the Germans, and one in the southern part, under the new government. So, the Italians were actually involved, now, in a civil war. Lettomanoppello, the village my father was from, was currently under the new government, but we hadn't resumed communication, yet, with any of my relatives, there, nor in Rome. I told Jessica that if I'd get caught here by the police, I had no idea what they would do to me, or to her. She didn't give a damn, she said. She knew that if our situations had been reversed, I'd do the same for her.

"I feel a lot of pain inside of you, Tonio. Don't think about our situation right now. Just enjoy this, you and I, together. There isn't only me anymore. Maybe that's why our desire is so strong. We won't let anything defeat us. We're together, now, and we give strength to each other. Nothing, nothing, is going to hold us down, not even the damn war!"

My desire for her had manifested itself in its physical form, but my passion wasn't only a strong sexual desire; it was a response to my deeper feelings for her.

"You make me very happy," she said "And I can see that I make you happy, too, and that makes me even happier. This is the greatest time of my life. No one could ever ask for a happier birthday. And it's because you're here, with me. I'll cherish this time for the rest of my life. My eighteenth birthday! You have made me a woman."

But when the time would come for me to leave her, to return to Cascade, what excuse, I had wondered, could I invent? But she, ironically, had solved my predicament. And when we parted, she had assumed that Nick and I were returning to Italy on an Italian ship from New York. Well, in a way, she was almost right. Nick and I would go to Italy, but we wouldn't get there for another year, after we would complete high school.

A few days before I left her, Jessica and I and Nick had been walking towards Fifth Avenue when we noticed two Italian sailors who seemed lost. We knew they were Italian sailors because on the front of their round caps, which matched their navy blue uniforms, was the word "Italia." They were looking at a piece of paper with an Italian name and an address written on it. Nick asked them if they were from Italy. They were both from Calabria, within thirty miles from his grandfather Giovanni's hometown. When I told them my father came from Abruzzo, one of them said he had relatives in Chieti, about ten miles from Lettomanoppello. We took them to the address they had been trying to find, but that was on the east side of Fifth Avenue. We had a lengthy and animated conversation with them, and we must have asked each other a hundred questions. Jessica couldn't understand what we were saying, so Nick and I translated some of it. While we were passing a restaurant, one of the sailors asked us what a sign in the window of the restaurant meant. We looked at it: "No Italian Spoken Here We Speak Only American." Nick told them to ignore it. It was early in the evening, and people were sitting outside and watching pedestrians walk by. The person they were looking for, an older man with a bar handle moustache, happened to be sitting on the sidewalk in front of a tenement flat. He was an uncle to one of the sailors, an older brother to the sailor's mother. The eyes of the old man filled with tears. Obviously, they had never met before. The man insisted that we all go inside, upstairs to his flat, to drink wine and to meet the rest of the family. In Italian, Nick thanked him profusely but said we were on our way someplace, that we were simply helping the sailors, because they had gotten lost on the west side where we lived. The man, who seem bewildered, asked Nick how he learned to speak Italian, and Nick said that his mother was Calabrese. From Calabria? Where? Ah, he knew the area well! And then Nick said his father was a doctor, and he wrote down the address of the clinic. Before we left them, Jessica suggested that perhaps Nick and I would be permitted to return to Italy with the sailors. They would be sailing out of New York in six days.

So, during the last three days, Jessica took time off from her work to devote her time to me. During our last night together, I promised her that as soon as I'd have an opportunity I would mail her a letter from Italy. And I did. It was a long letter, which I mailed from Rome a year after I had left her.

I didn't know how to tell her about Minnie Birch, who was my English teacher during my senior year, but I told her about the terrible living conditions in Italy and about how busy the people were in the reconstruction of the sites. I told her I couldn't mail anything except in dire emergencies. But I also told her, of course, that I was finishing high school, that I was studying English, and that I was planning to return soon to the United States, and that I was hoping to go to college there.

In May, Germany surrendered.

And in early July, while the war with Japan continued, my father had somehow been able to take me and Nick on an Italian merchant ship as workers. Several times, before the war, my father had worked his way on a ship to Italy.

And Nick had somehow obtained a letter of introduction and a recommendation from the archbishop of New York, Francis

Spellman (who later would become cardinal), to present to the Pope, a personal friend, Eugenio Pacelli.

We had taken the ship from Portland, and after we landed at Naples, we took a train to Rome, where my father inquired about his grandparents, who had died during the war. They had taken refuge in the Vatican until the Germans evacuated Rome, and they returned to their apartment in Trastevere.

After three days in Rome, an elderly Italian priest, who knew my father and my grandfather, embraced us cordially and took us into the Vatican. He gave us a tour. We followed him up a very narrow passageway where we had to lean to our right to climb the stairs. And then we were outside, near the top of the dome, looking over the city. When we returned below, the priest actually introduced us to Pope Pio, Eugenio Pacelli, a slim, amiable man with dark eyes behind thick round glasses. He spoke with us for almost a half hour, and he seemed particularly pleased with Nick who wanted to study for the priesthood. He asked Nick if he had ever been pained by discrimination in the United States. Nick admitted he had, even by other Catholics, especially in Louisiana. The priest who had introduced us told the Pope that my father's grandparents, who were Hebrew, had been granted sanctuary here during the occupation. And my father thanked the Pope.

Nick became enrolled in college to begin his studies for the priesthood in autumn.

And, finally, we went to Abruzzo, to Lettomanoppello, to a small farm at the foot of the village and stayed with my great grandmother for ten days. She was a hundred and one years old, and her mind was still acute. My great grandfather had died almost four years earlier. Tattone's youngest sister, a widow, was living there with two attractive, but unmarried daughters. After they had overcome their shyness, they kidded Nick about becoming a priest. "God must be testing you," I said to Nick.

At least half of the people of the village told me that we were, somehow, related, and just about everyone had a close relative living in America. Many asked me if I knew their relatives in Portland,

Boston, and in New Jersey. And they asked me if all of the Americans are wealthy.

In spite of their poverty, every day while we were there was a feast day. We never ran out of food and wine, and we partied until late almost every night. Our presence had been a special occasion, I know, and continuous partying is not the norm here, but I surmise that Italians, here, more so than in Cascade Flats even, celebrate life whenever a slim opportunity presents itself. Puritanism is not an Italian phenomenon.

When we returned to Rome, I mailed several long letters to Jessica, and I told her not to reply, because I would be in New York soon to see her.

While we were returning home on the ship, Japan had surrendered, so I had missed the great celebration at home at the end of the war, but before starting college, when Jessica and I came together again, we had our own celebration, just the two of us. And ever since then, she has been my closest friend and confidante.

I've told her about Minnie Birch, finally, and about the woman to whom I had been duped into marrying, a teacher, who had become pregnant, had become abandoned, and had subsequently convinced me that the offspring was mine.

This introduction, Rosie insists, is not only too long, but should not include Jessica, because she has no part in Dante's script. But had Dante finished it, I think she would have been included. And, I told Rosie, I have no ideas on how to finish this narrative. She feels that, somehow, we'll both know when we come to it.

ROSE OF THE FLATS

by

Dante Valentino

Part One

Summer, 1952

They were, neither of them, black nor white, yet both.

At twilight, on Sugar Mountain, deep in the woods of the White Mountains of New Hampshire, he, in a white shirt tucked inside dark blue suit pants, was carrying a suitcase; and she, in pink slacks and a pink blouse hanging to her hips, was carrying a purse, swinging from her shoulder. She was following him, weaving between trees, ducking under low limbs, and pushing aside branches of shrubs. Shaded from sunlight, the forest was cool, but warm enough, on the first day of summer, for mosquitoes to be attracted to them. They approached the back of their log hut, barely visible through the trees, and followed the side of it, to a small clearing near a brook, which was dammed with boulders and thick sticks, forming a pool between two huge rocks on a sandy shore. The sun, unseen from the bottom of a slope, cast an orange glow at the edge of the sky. He approached the door, stepped onto a wide board, pulled the latch up, and pushed the door open. He dropped the suitcase, turned, and looked at her, and as she brushed against him, he grabbed her hand.

"Don't you want me to carry you over the threshold?"

She turned to him, her eyes as dark as olives shining from her bronze face, and grinned.

"Dante, you're kidding."

"I thought it was customary."

"Since when have you become conventional?"

"It's supposed to be romantic."

131

She laughed softly, put her hands on his narrow shoulders, drew her mouth to his, and pressed against him, her body almost the size of his, small and slim. His lips, compared to hers, were thin, and his flesh, much lighter, his nose, bigger, with a higher bridge. And his eyes were blue. His hair was dark brown and wavy; hers was black, high and thick, covering her ears and curving back at her nape, displaying the slenderness of her neck.

"Dante," she said, "that was hardly a romantic kiss."

"Not romantic with mosquitoes buzzing my ears."

He bent down, lifted her, carried her over the threshold, and said, "Behold our home! For this summer, anyway."

"You've made the bed!"

"Of course. You didn't think I'd bring you into a messy home."

He was about to release her, but she clung to him.

"On the bed, Dante."

"According to the movies, the groom carries the bride over the threshold, and she says, 'Oh, darliiing, this is sooo lovely!' But he doesn't take her to the bed."

"In the movies, they have twin beds. Where's yours?"

She grinned, dimples forming in her cheeks, as he carried her to the bed and eased her down. She clasped his head and pulled him down on top of her, but he leaped back.

"The door's open," he said.

"So?"

"Mosquitoes will be swarming in."

He went to the doorway, picked up the suitcase, closed the door, approached the bed, and looked down at her.

As she dropped the purse to the floor, she smiled at him and said, "How long are you going to stand there holding the suitcase?"

He dropped it.

"I'm thinking of changing into something comfortable," he said.

"Me too."

She unbuttoned the top button of her blouse and said, "Do you want to undress me?"

"It won't embarrass you?"

He got on the bed, sat beside her, and looked down at her. She grinned.

"I didn't say I'd let you."

"I've been wanting to undress you for years."

"Why didn't you?"

"You wouldn't let me."

"You never tried."

"Oh, yes, I have. Many times. But your hands always grabbed mine, like a reflex."

"Well, now's your big chance. I promise I won't stop you. I'll even undress you," she said, sitting up, "while you undress me."

She began unbuttoning each button of his shirt, uncovering his undershirt, then she yanked his shirt up from his pants.

"I thought you'd undress me at the same time," she said, undoing the last button of his shirt. He put his hands on her blouse and began to unbutton it, slowly.

"Why have you stopped?" he asked.

"Your arms are in the way."

"Sorry."

He let his arms hang by his sides.

"Aren't you going to take my blouse off?"

"My shirt, first."

She smiled, tugged on a sleeve, pulled it off, tugged on the other one, and pulled off his shirt, dropping it on the floor.

"Now, my blouse."

"My undershirt, next."

"My blouse, first."

"Do you feel a little foolish?"

"Do you?"

"A little."

"Like a kid playing a silly game?"

"Yeah," he said, nodding.

"And you're not enjoying it?"

"That's what makes me feel foolish. The kid in me, enjoying it."

"Does it embarrass you?"

He hesitated before answering, "No."

"It does."

"No."

"Then why do you feel foolish?"

"Does that necessarily mean I'm embarrassed?"

"You're the English teacher. You should know."

"It implies it, but it doesn't necessarily include embarrassment, always."

"You idiot. I love you."

"You expect me to be romantic, talking like this? And I thought you were trying to be sexy!"

"I am!"

"Sexy?"

"Trying, I mean."

"Ah, you are the one who's embarrassed!"

"No, I'm not!" she said, pulling his undershirt up. "Dante, I can't pull it off without your cooperation!"

He grinned, bent his head down and raised his hands up,

Quickly, she pulled off his undershirt, flung it to the floor, and said in a low, guttural tone, "Okay, you savage beast, off with my blouse!" And she pushed her shoulders back and thrust her bosom forward.

Still grinning, he unbuttoned her blouse, slowly, looking into her eyes to observe her reaction, but she was looking back at him, without blinking, determined not to reveal her embarrassment. He undid the last button, parted her blouse, and uncovered her waist. He stared at her bosom bulging over her white bra.

She quickly removed the blouse and tossed it aside, saying, "Now, unhook my bra."

Gingerly, he brushed her breasts with his fingertips.

"The hook, you sexy animal, is in back."

"You really are a sexy woman. You're the sexiest woman I've ever seen."

"And, how many sexy women have you ever seen? Naked, I mean, and in bed."

"I don't know. I've never counted."

"I'm going to make sure you forget about all the rest of them. After this, you're not going to even want to think of another woman, ever again. That's not just a promise."

He chuckled, put his arms around her, and touched the hook of her bra.

She leaned forward and kissed him on the mouth as he tried to unhook her bra, and when he finally did, she pushed herself back a little to let him look at her.

He was gawking at her breasts but said nothing.

"Dante, remove the bra!"

Without speaking, he slowly pulled the bra away from her, and he dropped it to the floor.

"Control yourself, Dante. Don't get carried away."

"I'm speechless, Rose. You're beautiful! Everything about you is so beautiful! I'm a lucky guy. I've never been able to believe how fortunate I've always been, just, well, just having you with me like this. I really think you're the most beautiful woman in the world. And I'm so damn lucky now, to have you for my wife!"

She was blushing, took his hands and held them to her breasts, and he squeezed them a little. She raised her mouth to his, and as they kissed, she leaned back and pulled him down on top of her, his naked belly pressing against hers. After a long kiss, he moved his mouth down and kissed her neck, then her shoulder, and slowly brushed his lips over her breasts, and as he began to suck on a nipple, she clasped his face and held him against her, and she waited, expecting him to pull down her slacks.

"I almost forgot," he said, suddenly withdrawing.

"What?"

"The champagne. I left it in the car."

"Save it for tomorrow."

"I bought it for tonight."

He went to the suitcase, pulled out a green polo shirt, slipped it over him, and went out.

She sat up. By the time he'd get to the car and back, he'd be gone fifteen minutes. She sighed, propped the pillows up, and sat against them.

She was determined not to become embarrassed by their naked-ness and their sexual desires. She had decided that she would excite his desires by letting him know that she, too, had been anticipating the ecstasy of coming together with him sexually.

This cabin, where they had spent some of the happiest times of their childhood together, was the ideal place for their honeymoon, small and cozy, and isolated.

A huge rock hearth, which she faced, took up most of the front wall. To the right of it, at the corner, was the door, and over a crude table with orange crates beside it, was a window overlooking the clearing to the brook, and against the opposite wall was a dry sink with shelves containing dishes and silverware. And near the bed was a bureau. The small bed, with the head against the back wall, occu-pied the middle of the cabin. Between the front of the bed and the fireplace, she and Dante used to sleep beside each other, each in a sleeping bag. His father, and his brother Tony, and her brother Nick, and she and Dante would roast hot dogs and marshmallows, and then they'd take turns telling stories. Dante was still telling stories, writing them.

One evening, eleven years ago, when she was almost eleven, and the others were outside, she and Dante were sitting together in front of the fire and began poking each other, and then he started tickling her, and she sank back, against the floor, laughing. Lying beside her, he said, "I'm going to kiss you," and she, still laughing, was shaking her head as his lips touched her face. He held her face still and kissed her on the mouth, quickly, and then he laughed with her. But as they were gazing at each other, they stopped laughing. She was anticipat-ing another kiss, but he seemed reluctant.

She asked softly, "Why did you do that?"

"I don't know. I just felt like it."

"Do you feel like doing it again?"

He hesitated before answering, "I don't know. I'm thinking about it."

"Well, you'd better not."

"Why not?"

"Because, we shouldn't be doing that."

"Why not?"

"That wasn't a real kiss, anyway. The next time, it might be real."

"It's not a sin, you know."

"A real kiss could be an occasion for sin."

"Who says?"

"Sister Therese. You wouldn't give me a real kiss, anyway."

"Why not?"

"You'd be too afraid."

"Of course not!"

"I dare you!"

As he planted his mouth on hers, giving her a long, firm kiss, she lay still, enjoying a warm feeling flowing through her.

He sat up, and he stared at her.

After a brief silence, she sat up, too, and asked, "Well, did you like it?"

"Did you?"

"I asked you first."

He nodded,

And then they burst out laughing together.

That was the summer before the war, before she and her family moved away from New Hampshire. She smiled, now, thinking of that kiss and imagining that she was still feeling it: their first intimate kiss. And, during the past few years, although they had become aware of how much they had excited the desires in each other, especially when they had been alone together, they had hardly spoken of it. There had been times when she had not wanted him to stop, when their desire had become excruciating, but he had, somehow, always found the strength to stop. The day she had moved away from New Hampshire, and they had embraced so hard, as though they were afraid they would never be together again, she had said, "I don't want you to kiss anybody else, not like we do," and he replied. "I've never wanted to. And I don't want you to, either."

They had always felt closer to each other than to anyone else, closer than brother and sister, as though they had always been part of each other, and they had even spoken of each other as the other half. Her friends had wondered what their "man" would look like, but not she. She knew. She had always known. But to let him see her utterly naked, the first time, would probably feel strange. And though she had seen his slim body, often, almost naked, in swimming trunks, he, too, would probably feel strange the first time she'd see him fully naked. She smiled. She would enjoy his nakedness. He, too, then, would enjoy hers. Why, then, should they feel strange? But she shouldn't expect them to shed their inhibitions immediately, not completely, anyway. Maybe the champagne would help suppress their inhibitions and free their libidos. Maybe Dante really knew what he was doing, providing the atmosphere for a romantic setting. This wasn't as though they were parking in a car now and were free to finally go all the way; this was a date to be celebrated for the rest of their lives. This was their first night of marriage, but there was no need to consummate their union quickly, to get it over with; they must savor each moment of this night, slowly. To be sexually appealing to him, she shouldn't even be thinking of their super egos; she should simply be herself, letting her body follow its nature. But how could she, when nature now felt so strange? She grinned at the paradox.

However, their sexual embarrassment would be the least of their problems. People who didn't know them saw her as black and him as white, though her mother, like his father, was Italian, and his great grandfather, like hers, had been a black slave. Tomorrow they would face his mother, who, with fair skin and blue eyes, was afraid to admit to white Americans her black ancestry. His own grandmother had passed down her fear of white Americans to her children. In the United States there were no laws, she had impressed on them, to protect them from the madness of whites. Anyone who was partially black was deemed black. Not white. Not even partially. And although not all whites were heartless, you could never know which of them could ever be trusted. "Always remember," Dante's Canadian grandmother would say to his mother, Antoinette, "that in the United States, it is bad enough to be French; it is much worse to be black." Dante's mother, who had prayed faithfully to St. Anthony of Padua, her patron saint, to protect her sons from white Americans, had believed that God had created Dante for the priesthood. And she, Rose, was bound as a Catholic, to encourage him. His mother, they knew, would accuse Rose of dissuading him if he would refuse to join the priesthood. His mother, even though she had always been like another mother to Rose, and loved her, had said that for Dante to marry Rose had been inconceivable. His mother could easily pass for white, but Rose could never pass. And she and Dante both knew that his mother's fears had been warranted. His father had been murdered by racists. Last year when Dante had finally told his mother that with or without her approval, he was definitely marrying Rose, his mother, trembling, had cried out: "People will destroy you! Both of you!" And she refused to participate in any of the wedding plans or to attend the wedding.

Dante had taught high school for one year while she had finished college. The week after she had graduated from the University of New Hampshire, Dante, without telling anyone in his family, went to New York. And they were married.

The door opened, and he entered.

"That was quick," she said.

"I just remembered that when we stopped to eat, I put the champagne in the suitcase so I wouldn't forget it in the car." He pulled the bottle out. "I didn't even notice it when I opened the suitcase," he muttered, and dashed out again.

She, grinning, stood up, went to the window, and saw him squatting, sinking the bottle into the pool. He stood up, waved his hands over his head to keep mosquitoes away, turned, and ran back to the cabin, his slim body moving gracefully.

She sat on the bed again as he entered.

"My hand is cold from the water," he said, approaching her. He sat on the bed. "You don't want me to touch you, not right now."

"Let me warm it for you," she said, placing his hand between her thighs. "It's nice and warm down here. Can you feel the heat?"

She squeezed her thighs together.

"Why don't I light a fire in the fireplace?"

"Why don't we light a fire down here?" she said, putting her hand on his crotch.

"The sun's going down. It's going to be cold in here in a little while. I was thinking of sitting in front of the fireplace and sipping champagne."

"And after we've consumed some champagne, will we consummate our marriage?"

He smiled, shyly.

"After all," she said, "our marriage won't be complete until we, well, you know."

"But we have all night."

"All night!"

"I mean, we don't have to rush into it. We have all night to, well, to build up to it."

"Aren't you even thinking about it?"

"Of course, I am! That's all I'm thinking about. I just keep looking at you and getting more excited with anticipation, and I want to prolong this feeling. I want this night to last a long time."

"Are you sure you haven't done this before?"

He laughed.

"I'm only doing this," he said, "for the experience, you know, so I can write about it."

"You schmuck!"

They became silent for a few moments.

"I was just thinking," she said, "that if we don't consummate our marriage and then we make love for the rest of the night, then we'll be committing fornication. We'll be committing a mortal sin, Dante."

"I've never thought of that. At least we won't be committing adultery because neither of us is really married yet. Before we do anything else, though, we should talk about it. And maybe you should cover yourself so we won't yield to temptation."

"You don't think you can restrain yourself, at least for a while longer, until we consummate our relationship?"

"I don't know. What about you?"

"Dante, you're staring at me! Don't you dare touch me!"

"How can I possibly resist?"

"Light the fire."

"I'm trying," he said, rubbing his hand against her crotch.

"In the fireplace!"

"I'm trying!"

"In the other one! And then open the bottle of champagne."

After he had lit a fire, she went to the bureau, pulled out a heavy blue blanket, unfolded it in half, spread it on the floor in front of the hearth, placed two orange crates between the bed and the blanket, took two pillows from the bed, and propped them against the orange crates. She sat on the blanket, leaned back against a pillow, stretched her legs, and crossed her ankles.

The fire crackled as flames ascended, shooting burning cinders against a screen.

Dante was standing to the side, looking at the fire.

"Well," she said, "here we are, Dante and Rose Valentino. I like the sound of our name."

He looked at her and smiled.

"When are you going to open the champagne bottle?"

"In a few more minutes. Give it time to get cold."

They became silent.

Even though the sun hadn't gone down yet, flames were beginning to reflect through the room.

"Dante, are you staring at me, at my, well, at my breasts?"

"Of course, I am. What's mine is yours, and what's yours is mine. And I'm admiring what's mine, seeing them for the first time. You've been looking at them for the past few years. You're used to seeing them; I'm not."

"Well, if you're so interested, why don't you sit beside me where you can not only see them better, but touch them if you want?"

He sat beside her.

"My hands are still cold," he said.

She grinned.

"Do you remember," she asked, "when we used to tell stories in front of the fire?"

"Of course."

"That was nice, wasn't it?"

"Yeah."

"Do you remember when you kissed me, really kissed me, for the first time?"

"I remember."

"I remember everything about that night. How you tickled me and then kissed me. And I asked you why. Do you remember what you said?'"

"Of course," he answered softly, touching her knee. "I said I wanted to."

"You made me feel like your girl friend."

"You were. You always were. I could never imagine life without you. You've always been part of me, the best half. Without you, there's nothing."

"And that's the way I've always felt about you, especially since that first kiss."

"We were just little kids."

"But it made me feel even closer to you. Imagine if we had been older, as we are now, and alone together, all night long."

"And married."

"And married, as we are now. Well, here we are, eleven years later. Alone together. All night. We can do whatever we feel like doing. What do you feel like doing?'

"I think you know. What do you feel like doing?'

"Whatever you want. You can do whatever you want with me. And after you do it, and I ask you why you did it, you'll say, 'I wanted to.'"

His hand moved from her knee, up her leg, to the inside of her thigh.

"Your hand is getting warmer, Dante."

"Not warm enough yet."

"If you pull my slacks off, you'll feel the heat. Remember, what's mine is yours. You can't see what's yours with the slacks covering it; you can't even touch it. These," she said, cupping her breasts, "were created for our babies, although I'll let you play with them if they give you pleasure, but this down here," she said, putting her hand over his and pushing it against her, "was created special, just for you, to keep you warm and secure and happy."

He was speechless, staring at her.

"Am I embarrassing you?" she asked.

"No, of course not. I'm intrigued."

"Why?"

"You're surprising me. I thought I would have to be slow and easy and gentle with you on our wedding night."

"You think I'm a prude."

"No! You're less of a prude than I am. It's just that we're in uncharted waters, and I want to navigate slowly because I'm not sure of myself. I know you have a lot of faith in me, more than I have in myself. But if I disappoint you on our very first night, I'd never forgive myself."

"Oh, you lovable idiot! Kiss me, hard!"

She clasped him, tightly, holding him against her, and pulled him down on top of her, and he felt the passion in him and the tenderness deep inside of him surging through him.

She smiled at him.

"I love you," he said.

"I know. I love you, too."

"It's starting to get dark out. I'll get the champagne."

He kissed her again, tenderly, withdrew, stood up, and went out the door.

She sat up again and waited, certain now that neither of them would be disappointed. They had married so quickly after her graduation, she thought, because neither of them had wanted to wait any longer to make love to each other. And now, finally, they were free to be together, to really experience all of the joys, as well as the agonies, of conjugal love.

He returned quickly, put another chunk of wood into the fire, twisted a corkscrew into the top of the bottle, pulled and twisted the cork from the bottle, making a pop, poured some of the champagne into a mug on the floor, placed the bottle down, offered the mug to her, and sat beside her. She took a few quick sips, and returned the mug to him.

After a while, she said, "It's getting warm in here."

"Too warm?"

"A little. Why don't you take off your shirt?"

"Okay," he said, and pulled off his polo shirt.

"Are your hands cold?"

"Yeah. The brook is ice cold."

While he was holding the mug, she put her hands on his chest, rubbed it, leaned against him, and raised her mouth to his. And he kissed her gently. And then, after slowly brushing her lips down his chest and across his belly, she put her head on his lap.

"In church this morning," she said, "you seemed so calm, so sure of yourself."

"Stunned. By your beauty."

"I was trembling."

"All I saw was you, moving gracefully down the aisle."

"God knows how nervous I was, until I saw you standing at the altar and looking at me with such confidence. A serene feeling came over me. There stood Dante, my Dante, waiting for me. Waiting for me, to take me home with him!"

"You were beaming. The beautiful Rose!"

"I know."

"You know?"

"That I was beaming," she grinned.

"And beautiful. Women were staring at you, envying your beauty. And men were staring in admiration."

"Oh, you idiot!" she said, and laughed a little, moving her cheek against his lap. She felt his desire stirring. Startled, her face lifted slightly as she looked down and saw a bulge at the side of his inner thigh. She turned her face away from his and pressed her lips against the bulge, feeling it rise up. Against his dark blue suit pants, the protrusion was actually growing bigger. She touched it, moving her fingers over it. It felt, she thought, like a bone that was suddenly growing there. Her impulse was to look at it, uncovered. And she raised her head, looked at the belt that was holding his pants up, and, since his passion had been aroused, she decided to unbuckle his belt quickly before he could stop her. That surprised him, probably, she thought. Then she undid the button of his fly. As she turned to see his reaction, his hand touched her back and began to rub it. He was staring at her. She grinned at him, saying, "Your hand is nice and warm now, and I can feel you getting hot." She unzipped his fly, looked down again, saw his blue underpants, and thrust her hand inside. Then she touched the protrusion. "It's hot! Take off your pants!" Fondling it, she was trying to pull it out gently where she could see it. She heard the mug touching the floor, and suddenly he grabbed her shoulders and pushed her down on her back, and before she even realized what he was doing, he was on top of her, pressing her against the wood floor. And, just as suddenly, he stopped.

He groaned, as though he were in pain.

Without saying anything, he rolled onto his back, lying beside her and stared into space.

They were silent for a long while.

Finally, she asked gently, "Dante, what's wrong?"

"What's wrong? You don't know what's wrong? You don't know what's wrong with the guy here, beside you? I can't even control my urges long enough to even begin to make love to you, much less to satisfy you!"

"Well, I must have gotten you too excited."

"Too excited! What are you supposed to do? You did what you should have done. You're great! You got me excited. But me, I fucked up. Pardon my French."

She grinned at him.

"Do you expect to be perfect, on your first attempt?"

"Well, maybe not perfect, but since it's a natural thing, I expected to be good enough to satisfy you, to experience with you the eternal bliss of nirvana, to feel the earth move, and to feel the big bang of the cosmos applauding us while a choir of angels sang of love, but I didn't even hear the wind blow, and the big ding dong of desire evaporated like a fart. A silent one."

She grinned again.

"If you were perfect," she said, "I'd be disappointed."

"Disappointed!"

"I'd know you'd been practicing. And if you had been practicing, that means with someone other than me."

"I think most guys are under the impression that women want men with experience."

"I don't know about other people, but I want us to experience our lovemaking together and to grow in our relationship. We have the rest our lives to improve ourselves. And our first night together hasn't even started. It's not even nighttime yet."

"But I feel as though I've done something sordid. After years of having restrained myself, of smothering the fire inside, of hearing dirty jokes about the flesh, the ignobility of copulation, or fucking, as we call it, my superego has always emerged, even in my dreams, in the solitude of my dreams, at the moment of anticipation, of making love to you, my superego has always emerged, waking me up from the dream to censure my desires. How, how can I be intimate with you, with anyone, while my spirit struggles constantly with my flesh?"

"Dante, make love to me in Italian!"

"In Italian?"

"Si, in italiano," she said, sitting up. "Making love! Creating new life!"

He stared at her.

"Making love in Italian," she said, "is beautiful. Bella! Free yourself from all the dirty words associated with making love in English. Make love to me in Italian, caro mio. That's amore."

"Amore," he murmured.

"Your mother wants you to be a priest, but her religion isn't even Catholic. It's Jansenism, a harsh, strict religion." It had been influenced by Calvin, a French priest who had established Puritanism. His ideas had spread into England and Ireland and into Canada and the United States and had promoted the belief that human nature is depraved and that sex is sordid, due to original sin. "But that belief isn't Italian, Dante. In Italian, sex is good. It's beautiful! Love! Emanating from God, not the devil. But American Catholics don't see us as good Catholics, because most Italians can't accept their version. Let's free ourselves from all the dirty labels of our sexual nature and retrieve our Italian roots and enjoy sex together."

The sun was setting, and when darkness descended, they roasted marshmallows and talked into the night, sitting on the blanket on the floor in front of the fire.

"You're so damn beautiful!"

She blushed.

"People are the only creatures that blush," he said.

"Or needs to, as Mark Twain said."

"You have beautiful legs, sleek and tawny."

"I guess it'll take a while longer for me to get over my embarrassment of being naked."

"You're doing fine."

"And you seem to be doing fine, too."

"Thanks to you, and the champagne seems to help."

"Is there more?"

He poured more into the mug, emptying the bottle, and gave her the mug.

"You're really amazing," he said. "No matter what, you always maintain your dignity."

She took a drink, returned the mug to him, and said, "Dante, you keep staring at me!"

"Are you embarrassed? Shall I close my eyes?"

"You make me feel, well, naked."

"I enjoy looking at you. I don't think I'll ever get tired of looking at you. The rose, blooming, unfolding to the heat of the fire. The beautiful Rose opening to the depths of her own warmth."

"You are the fire."

"I am the thorn of the rose."

She pushed herself up, knelt against him, and brushed her fingers through his curly hair, ruffling it "You said you couldn't even control your urges, but whenever we went parking, you always did. You always restrained yourself, for my sake. So, I can't complain, not now, not after you've waited so long. Maybe," she said, rubbing his belly and moving her hand down, "well, maybe, it won't get so hard this time to control."

"If you continue doing that, it'll get hard enough to control."

"Continue like this, you mean?" She reached down and touched him, stimulating his desire again. "It feels strange, feeling it like this, feeling it growing hard and big again. This feels daring, touching you like this, seeing this thing grow excited again."

He cupped one of her breasts, eased her down, and began sucking on a nipple.

"I love you," she murmured.

"I don't want to disappoint you again."

"You're not capable of disappointing me."

She placed her hands at the back of his head and held him against her.

Sucking on one breast, he cupped the other and squeezed it.

"Your hands are hot, Dante. They feel good."

"Your body is exquisite. You should never be ashamed or embarrassed by the nakedness of such a beautiful body."

"Your nakedness," she said, "is beautiful. Your body is slim and graceful."

"I have the body of a boy. You have the body of a voluptuous woman."

"I like your body. It's sensuous."

He cupped her breasts, raising them into opulent mounds. She closed her eyes, letting sensational pleasures surge through her, and emitted soft moans. She felt his mouth caressing her, moving down her belly as his hands moved down her sides, stroking her hips. He pushed himself up again, and his mouth was on hers. While kissing her, he moved his body to one side, and his hand slid down, touching her between the thighs. His mouth was sucking on hers while he was exploring her vagina, and then his finger went inside of her, hurting her a little.

"Dante, why don't we continue this in bed?"

"Okay," he murmured, releasing her.

As she went to the bed, bringing the pillows, he went to the fire, put another large chunk of wood in it, turned, and saw flames reflecting on her naked body.

"Beautiful," he murmured, as he lay beside her.

She turned to her side, facing him.

"Making love," he said, "might be painful for you, the first time, unless your hymen's been broken."

"You don't have to try to talk me out of it, you know."

As he lay on his back, she placed her thigh over his, put an arm over his waist, pressed her breasts against his chest, and kissed him on this lips. He grasped her hips and pulled her on top of him. As they continued kissing, he was rubbing her buttocks and pressing her against him, making her feel his hardness underneath her. She lifted her mouth from his, slid her hands under his shoulders and pushed herself against him. "Your hands are hot," she said. "Your whole body is warm and hard. You feel good, Dante." And she began to undulate her hips against his hardness. Suddenly, he lifted her and turned her onto her back, and he was on top of her, his thighs between hers, and was pressing his hardness against her. He was trying to enter her. While reflections of flames were dancing through the cabin, he was probing her, awkwardly, unable to find her opening. He withdrew a little, letting his body slide to the side of her, but he kept one leg between her thighs. He kissed her on the mouth again and slid his hand down, trying to feel her opening. She put her own hand on the lower part of his abdomen and moved it down until she felt his hardness. While he was probing her, she was touching him.

"Rose," he whispered, "take me inside of you."

As he positioned himself over her, she spread her thighs more, lifted her head a little, looked down, and gently placed his protrusion against her vagina. He pressed himself against her. He was entering her, slowly, then she felt a slight pain. He stopped. "It doesn't hurt," she said. He pushed again, slowly, penetrating a little deeper. He began rocking against her, pushing gently, then withdrawing a little, and pushing again. He had lost, she thought, the intensity of his desire, because he thought was hurting her.

"How does it feel?" he asked.

"It feels good."

"Does it hurt a little?"

"No. It feels strange, but it doesn't hurt."

"Strange? How?"

"I don't know, feeling you inside of me. It feels strange, but it feels good."

"Are you sure it doesn't hurt?"

"Dante!"

They became silent.

He rocked his hips against her, exerting more force. After a little while, she felt him penetrating deeper into her. She clung to him as he rocked against her, and she felt herself lifting to him, his hands under her hips pulling her against him as he thrust his hardness deeper into her. And, as though a barrier between them had suddenly ruptured, the inside of her began unfolding, quivering with delicate movements that pulled him into her, squeezing him within her. And everything inside of her began bursting. Her entire being was about to explode. She gasped.

"Have you," he asked hesitantly, "well, you know, finished?"

"What?"

"Did you finish?"

"Yeah," she muttered, "I think so."

"What do you mean?"

"Yeah, I did."

"You sound disappointed."

"I got frightened. Everything inside of me was bursting."

"You mean, you were having an orgasm."

"I think so, but I wasn't expecting that."

"So far, this hasn't been pleasant for you."

"Oh, you idiot," she said squeezing him. "The next time, I'll know what it is, and I'll enjoy it."

He turned and lay beside her.

"How do you feel now?" he asked.

"I don't know how to answer that. I was enjoying most of it, especially towards the end. I didn't want you to stop. You really excited me, until the climax. What about you?"

"Well, there's no question that you excite me. The only problem is in my ability to control it."

"You lost control once in your life, after years of restraint. And I was the one who did it to you!"

"I have a lot to learn yet."

"We'll enjoy learning together. We're going to have a good marriage."

"When I was young, I didn't want to believe that my own mother and father had ever done this."

She laughed.

"That's the Jansenist in you."

"I was sure my mother was a virgin."

She laughed again.

"I'll learn how to make love to you." he said. "I promise."

"I love you, schmuck, the way you are now."

At nine in the morning, while Joy was sitting at the kitchen table and writing in a notebook and pretending, thought Tony, to be another Jane Austen, he lit a cigarette, and not saying anything, because she'd accuse him of distracting her, he opened the door, stepped onto the back porch and walked down a few steps, onto a paved driveway under brightness of summer solstice, crossed the driveway, approached the steps of a back door of his family's restaurant, unlocked it, and went inside. Fifteen minutes later, the telephone rang. "Don't get your water hot," he muttered as it kept ringing. From a storage room in back, he entered the kitchen, wiped his hands against his apron, went to the phone on a wall next to a pair of swinging doors to the dining room, and answered the phone.

"Pizza Corner."

"Hello, Tonio!"

"Dante, you little shit. Where the hell are you?"

"Did you have a busy night?"

"You know damn well Friday's a busy night, that I could have used your help."

"Are you alone?"

"Yeah, I'm alone, mixing the dough. Where the hell are you?"

"With Rose, in New York. We're married."

"You're what?"

"Married."

"Married? What the hell are you talking about?"

"We got married a few minutes ago. We're at her folks' house right now"

"You got married without telling us first?"

"I didn't want to listen to Ma making a fuss."

"For crysakes. She would have made a big fuss, but she would have gotten over it, and we could have been there, having a big celebration now. What the hell am I suppose to tell her?"

"Tell her I married Rose. That's why I'm calling."

"You schmuck."

"My wife wants to say hi to you."

Her soft voice came through the phone: "Hi, Tonio."

"Rosie! Is it true what he said?"

"It's true."

"Well, congratulations. That makes me your big brother now, so I can give you hell whenever you step out of line."

She laughed a little.

"We'll see you tomorrow, Tonio."

"I'm going to get drunk tonight, for all of us."

There was a pause.

"Who's there?" he asked.

"Just my folks and Nick. We had a small wedding."

"Hey, let me speak to Nick."

Her brother came to the phone.

"Hey, Tonio, you horny wop! How's the pizza business? Still rolling in dough?"

"Nick, you pious bastard! How's Italy?'

"Great!"

"How long will you be here? And when are you getting ordained?"

"Until September. And I won't be ordained for another year."

"When you coming to the flats?"

"In a couple of weeks."

"We'll have to have a few drinks together, for Rosie and Dante."

"Good enough."

"Hey, the sexiest femme fatale in Berlin is dying to meet you. I guarantee she'll make you forget all about studying for the priesthood."

"Same old Tony. When are you going to change?"

"What the hell for?"

"You're an old married man now."

"Married men have to have fun, too."

"I heard that your wife has you wrapped around her little finger."

"Bullshit! She used to be a teacher, but I'm her boss now."

"I'll see you in a couple of weeks."

"Okay. I'll tell la femme to get ready for you. She doesn't speak much, but her body does a lot of communicating."

"I bet she's never met anyone as crazy as you."

"Probably not. She hasn't met you, yet."

"You damn fool. You're going to burn in hell."

"Well, you know what Mark Twain said. Heaven for climate, but hell for society. Hey, Nick, I'll see you then, in a couple of weeks."

"I'll be there."

"Let me speak to Dante again."

Dante returned to the phone.

"Anybody here know you're married?"

"No. I called you to prepare them."

"Well, thanks a lot."

"You can handle it. That's what big brothers are for."

"Life might get a little rough for you, sometimes, you know."

"C'est la vie."

"Well, I'll see you when you get here. Put Rosie back on the phone." She came to the phone again. "Hey, Rosie, I have my lips all puckered up for you."

"See you tomorrow."

"Okay. Hang up now so I can start getting drunk."

The phone clicked.

He hung up, pushed through the swinging doors, entered the dining room, walked up to the jukebox, inserted a quarter into the slot, pushed it in, and pressed six selections at random. While the jukebox blared, he returned to the kitchen, took a couple of shots of whiskey and several gulps of beer. He wouldn't tell his mother about the marriage until tomorrow morning. He would need her to help him tonight. He'd upset her in the morning, before she'd go to church. Yeah, before church, and then she could complain to God.

At four, when the restaurant opened, his mother, and his wife Joy, and his aunt Maria came in, but he didn't say anything about Dante and Rose.

On a busy night, with the pizza oven opening and closing, the kitchen would become hot even on a cold winter night, and he would usually drink a couple of quarts of cold beer. On that Saturday night, the kitchen became hot as hell, and he drank almost twice as much, including several shots of whiskey. By midnight, he would make over a hundred pizzas. He'd sprinkle flour onto a board, place a ball of dough on it, flatten it out with a rolling pin, drop a tin plate on the dough, cut the dough around the rim of the plate, toss the excess into a tub, scoop tomato sauce with a ladle, spread the sauce over the dough, gather shavings of provolone, drop a mound of the cheese onto the dough, spread a generous amount of whatever ingredients had been ordered, and sprinkle the pie with oregano. His pizzas were never greasy; he didn't use any olive oil, except a small amount in the kettle of sauce. And he didn't use mozzarella cheese, because it would become too stringy when it was cooked, and it didn't have the rich flavor of the more expensive provolone. He'd lift the board, open the oven door, place the board on the bottom of the oven and slide a peel, a flat shovel, under the dough and push it into the oven, close the door, and would let it bake at least ten minutes. Occasionally, before he'd start making another pizza, he would stop, grab a towel under the counter and wipe his brow, and then he'd take a drink of cold beer.

"Hey," Joy had snarled, "slow down on the beer, and you don't need whiskey; it makes you sweat more."

At first, he had ignored her, until she whacked his shoulder and grumbled, "You're going to get drunk!"

"How often have you seen me get drunk?"

"Often enough."

"Just leave me alone and tend to the customers."

"You're getting drunk!"

"For crysakes!"

"Who the hell do you think you're talking to?"

"To you, dammit!"

"Don't talk to your wife like that!" his mother, washing a stack of trays, cried out. "You should be ashamed of yourself. Your father never talked to me like that."

"Shit," he muttered, but not loud enough for his mother to hear.

"What did you say?" Joy growled.

"Nothing."

"Your brother," his mother said, "should be here helping you."

"He's not as stupid as I am," he grumbled, low enough that only Joy heard him.

He poured himself a shot of whiskey.

"Don't drink any more!" Joy yelled.

He swallowed it down.

"Passive aggressive," she muttered, drawing close to him so no one else could hear, "prick!"

Fire darted from her eyes, and she turned away.

He lit a cigarette.

Black John, Rose's grandfather, had entered the restaurant and had ordered a small pizza and a beer. He was from Calabria, the toe of Italy, and was a husky man with olive skin, like Tony's.

Tony pushed through the swinging doors and approached the booth where Black John was sitting. He had a barhandle moustache and wore a red bandana around his neck. When Dante was young, Black John would pinch his cheeks and grin, saying how beautiful he was: "Come sei bello!" and would give him a dime.

"Ay, paesano," Tony said in Italian, "your granddaughter married today."

"My granddaughter? Rosa?"

"How many you have?"

"No," he said, shaking his head.

"You think I invent a story like that?"

"If she marries, she tells me."

"They do not want my mother to know. They called me this morning. They will be here tomorrow."

"Whom she married? Dante?"

"Certainly."

"We need to celebrate! Drink a beer with me."

"Not now. My mother does not know yet. We celebrate tomorrow."

"Give everybody a beer or a glass of wine. I pay for everybody."

Tony returned to the kitchen and told Joy to serve beer or wine to anyone who wanted a drink and to charge it to Black John.

"Is he drunk?"

"Why don't you ask him?"

"We can't give anyone wine, you damn fool, not in the restaurant, even if it's free. We'd lose our license. You must be just as drunk as he is."

She asked Black John if he was drunk.

He laughed.

When he left, he gave Joy an extra ten dollars.

"You gave me ten dollars too much," she told him as he was walking away.

"Buona sera."

By midnight, Tony was exhausted, and his shirt was wet from sweat.

While the women cleaned up, he staggered out the back door, wobbled across the driveway, entered the house, ignored the baby sitter in the front room, went into the toilette, urinated, walked through the kitchen, into his bedroom, took off his clothes, and plopped into bed. He was asleep by the time Joy entered.

He slept until seven, when the baby, a little more than five months old, woke him up. Tony stood up, staggered half asleep across the kitchen and into the other bedroom where Joy was sleeping soundly, and he went to the crib, pushed the side down, unpinned a soiled diaper from the crying baby, lifted the baby's legs and wiped the feces from his buttocks and crotch, dropped the diaper into a tin box, carried the baby to the bathroom sink and dampened a washcloth with warm water, and cleaned the baby, who sprang an erection.

"Don't pee in my face, Rusty."

He returned the baby to the crib, sprinkled powder on the baby, and then he put another diaper on him.

The baby was smiling and reaching up.

"Do you know what your Uncle Dante did yesterday? He married Rosie. She's your aunt now."

The baby gurgled.

"Yeah," Tony cooed, "that's what your uncle did. You don't object, do you? But your grandmother will. She's going to throw a fit when I tell her."

He pulled the side of the crib up, went into the kitchen, took a baby milk bottle from the refrigerator, put it in a pot of water on the stove, and warmed the milk.

After a few minutes, he removed the bottle from the pot, went into the bedroom, and placed the nipple of the bottle into the baby's mouth and watched the baby suck on it contentedly, but Joy, he thought, should be breastfeeding the baby. That's why nature gave females teats, filling them with milk to nourish their young. Not only would the baby be more content, he thought, so would the mother. He looked down at her. She was sleeping soundly. He was tempted to get into bed and snuggle up to her, but he knew how she resented him for taking advantage of her, of arousing her when she felt she had no control over her body. She would feel as if he had stripped her of her dignity, as though she were no better than a bitch in heat.

He turned away from her, went into the bathroom, showered, shaved, returned to his bedroom, dressed, entered the kitchen again, put coffee on, and prepared batter for pancakes. He noticed Aunt Jemima on the package of pancake mix. "Crysakes."

He went into the other room again where Joy was still sleeping. The baby, too, had returned to sleep, and Tony removed the bottle, placing it to the side of Rusty's face.

Joy groaned as she turned in bed and pushed the covers away from the upper part of her body. She was lying on her back, her pajama top unbuttoned, exposing part of her voluptuous bosom. He sat on the bed, close to her, and gazed at her, at the fullness of her breasts. The temptation to touch her was irresistible, and he slid his hand under the pajama top and began to fondle her breast, and then he lay beside her, his face close to hers. Her eyes opened.

"You're so damn sexy, the sexiest woman ever, the goddess of goddesses."

"Stop!"

He withdrew his hand, slowly, moving the tip of his finger over her nipple.

Whenever she became excited, her dark blue eyes lit up. Her lush, flaxen hair spread over the pillow was beautiful, framing a smooth, fair complexion of an inscrutable face with a sensual mouth.

"It's after eight. Breakfast is almost ready. Your favorite. Pancakes."

She sighed.

"We're going to have company later."

"What?"

"Dante and Rosie. They were married yesterday."

Her eyes opened wide.

"And we're going to have to tell my mother."

"Good luck," she said, grinning.

"Help me to tell her. You know how to handle her."

"Are you kidding?'

"You have a way with her. When we argue, whose side does she always take?"

"That's because she knows what a shithead you are."

"We're going to have to tell her before they get here. I wonder if they were married in church."

"You know damn well they were. And your mother will be forced to recognize their marriage."

She grinned again.

"You think it's amusing, don't you?"

"It's ironic."

Tony, having married Joy outside of the Catholic Church, had been accused by his mother of living in sin. Joy, she had insisted, had been an innocent victim who had not known better. He was the one, having been brought up in the faith, who should have known better. And although Rusty had been baptized in St. Benedict's Church, because Joy had agreed to appease his mother, she still insisted that Tony marry Joy by a priest. "I'm not marrying her again, for crysakes. Once is enough." And his mother had told others, "She's a good woman even if she's not Catholic yet. It's my son who's the stubborn one, but she'll straighten him out, you just wait and see. They're practically married now, you know."

"She'll have to accept Rosie sooner or later," Tony said, "but she'll never accept her the way she's accepted you."

"She's accepted me, all right, as long as I keep licking her ass."

"Well, at least you know how to handle her."

Joy frowned.

"I wonder if Rosie's pregnant," mused Tony.

"You demented shit! Don't compare Dante to you."

"Be realistic."

"He didn't marry her because she's pregnant."

"How the hell would you know?"

"He hasn't been screwing her. He's not like the rest of you shitheads. And even if he has been screwing her, so what? Who are you to judge?"

"I'm not judging, for crynoutloud."

"He has feelings for her, deep feelings, not like you. The only feelings you've ever had is between your legs."

"And you, you married me because you fell in love with me, right?"

"You know damn well why we got married."

"To make a beautiful baby like Rusty."

His hair was bright red, and his complexion was light, and his eyes, bright blue.

Tony bent over to kiss her, but she pushed his face aside.

"I'm just trying to be affectionate."

"All you want is a cheap thrill. To you, I could be any woman in the world."

"You're not. You're the woman next to me. The woman I married."

"A good piece of ass."

"Well, that too. But, for you, it was love at first sight. Right? Because you couldn't wait to make love that first time together."

"And all you wanted was to fuck me."

"Why in hell are we fighting?"

"Because you expect me to give you what you want whenever you want it, never considering my own needs. I do all the giving, and you do all the taking."

He shook his head.

"And you don't enjoy the sex," he said sarcastically, "because you're just giving, not taking, as though taking drags you down to my level. You cling to me, and you groan, but not out of sexual gratification. Of course not. You do it only for me, sacrificing yourself. Well, take, for crysakes; don't just give. Take, and admit how much you enjoy it."

Whenever he had been able to touch her, stimulating her desires, her body, her voluptuous body, would be seething until everything within her would erupt, enveloping them in waves; and she would lose herself in a flood of ecstasy, almost losing consciousness, sinking deep within herself, and taking him with her. And afterwards, when she would cool down, she would call their act "blind forces of nature, devouring us." And he would call it "a creative act, an affirmation of life together, a transformation, like the phoenix emerging from the ashes." But his words, she had said, were as sacrosanct as shit on snow. "You would have felt the same thrills with any other woman. You just happen to be in the same bed with me at the same time."

They had met a little over a year ago when she had come into the restaurant with Minnie Birch, one of his former English teachers. Minnie had introduced her as Joy Russell, a new teacher who had started that past year, which would finish in two more months. Less than two weeks later, by chance, he met her again on Main Street in Berlin, and he took her to a café. He told her that he had been busy every day in the restaurant except on Sundays, so his social life had been limited. That Sunday, in May, he had planned to spend a few hours in his cabin in the woods to get it ready for summer. She asked if he wanted company.

The ground was still covered by snow around the cabin. She had been wearing casual shoes, and her feet had become wet, so she took off her shoes and stockings inside the cabin. While she swept the floor and dusted the shelves, he lit a fire, which made the cabin so warm she removed her sweater. She was wearing a summer dress with a plunging neckline, and when she saw him gazing at her bosom, she blushed.

"You're an attractive woman. I know it's not polite to stare, but it's difficult for any normal man to resist looking at someone as beautiful as you."

"You're making me blush."

"I'll try to control my impulses, but I can't make any guarantees. I've never had the privilege of having company like you in here before."

"Please, Tony, I'm not wearing my manure boots."

He laughed.

"Beautiful and piquant. How do you expect any man to resist you?"

They had lunch in the cabin, and he made a pot of coffee. He had brought beer, wine, and a liqueur that was home made. She took a taste of the liqueur.

"That's good! What is it?"

"Anisette. Made from aniseed. That's where licorice comes from. It's strong. You can easily get drunk on it. I prefer it in coffee."

"In coffee? Which can get you drunk?"

"Quickly, so just sip on it and enjoy the aroma."

"And I thought for a moment you were trying to get me drunk."

"A drunk woman isn't much fun."

"A sober woman is?"

"Depends on the woman."

She poured more than a triple shot of anisette into her glass.

"I've warned you," he said.

"What will you do if I get drunk?"

"Let you sleep it off right here."

She got on the bed, propped up a pillow, placed it behind her, and sat back on the bed, stretching her legs out, her dress barely covering her thighs.

"You'd let me sleep with you, right here?"

"Look, this conversation is going to get provocative, because you're, well, you're making yourself seem vulnerable. Why?"

"I'm wondering why you brought me here."

"You asked me if I wanted company."

"And?"

"I do. I want your company."

"What does that mean to you?"

"Well, since you've offered me your company, that means, obviously, that you know I'm attracted to you, and, apparently, since you're here, the feeling's mutual."

"Does that mean you think I want to fuck you?"

He gaped at her.

"Wow! You're blunt."

"I require honesty in a man I'm attracted to, but I know that's not a major characteristic in most men. If you were me, would you trust you, or any man?"

"No, I wouldn't. I wouldn't even let him know I was attracted to him."

"Why not?"

"I wouldn't trust him, even if I knew he meant well."

"You're saying I shouldn't trust you then?"

"Even though I'm hoping you will."

"Because you want to fuck me."

He nodded.

"Of course, I do. You're sexually attractive."

"You understand, then, why I'm making myself seem vulnerable. I am. We both are. But I'm also afraid of getting pregnant. Even though I'm attracted to you, I'm not going to do anything foolish, anything I'm going to regret later. I don't pretend I'm a virgin, but I want one boyfriend only. If I get involved with you, it's you and me exclusively."

"Fair enough. And if you get pregnant, I'll marry you."

"Talk is cheap."

She took a swallow of anisette.

He got on the bed and sat beside her.

"The most sexy woman in the world, who's been living in my neck of the woods for the past year without my even knowing it, suddenly appears to me and lets me know she wants me to make love to her, but only if I marry her if she gets pregnant. How lucky can any guy get?"

"Sex isn't enough, not in marriage."

"No, but it's a good start. I wouldn't expect you to marry me until we got to know each other, unless, of course, I got you pregnant."

"Do you want to get to know me?"

"Of course. You're an intriguing woman!"

3

"Remember that first day in the cabin?" Tony asked Joy. "We were on the bed, like this, and we got each other so damn excited. That whole summer last year was so great, and then, somehow, everything seemed to deteriorate."

"Things weren't working out the way we had hoped."

"They seemed to be working out perfectly, until winter, at least."

"And then I was saddled with motherhood and with the restaurant, and with your mother. If I'm not as romantic and as sexy as I was, blame reality."

"To me, you're still romantic and sexy. And, you're still intriguing."

"I know I take all my frustrations out on you, that I use you as my whipping board. I lean on you, because I don't have the strength to cope by myself," she said, taking his hand and pressing it to her bosom.

Her pregnancy had begun to show in the middle of August when they were married in a civil ceremony. She said she had been raised in an orphanage in Tennessee, so *The Tennessee Waltz* had become their favorite song. And she had worked her way through college, and had ended up in New Hampshire. After one year of teaching, she quit, and Dante, who had just graduated, had taken over her teaching job. Everyone, except his mother, had seemed happy with the situation, and even his mother would have been happy if they had been married by a priest. Joy had wanted to concentrate on writing, which she had been able to do. He had even encouraged her, at first. Before Rusty was born, they had lived in Gorham, but his mother had the house in Cascade Flats renovated so that he and Joy could live downstairs. And, gradually, Joy became involved with the business of the restaurant. In the middle of winter, Rusty was born. He became Russell Valentino. "Rusty," she said, goes with his hair." He had been conceived, according to her calculations, on that first mating in the cabin, which had made his birth at least a month premature.

During the day, he, his mother, and his Aunt Maria prepared the food for the restaurant, but he had time to look after the baby while Joy concentrated on writing. At night, there would be enough help in the restaurant, especially when Dante had been there, so that Joy would be free to continue writing. And after midnight, he would enter the house and read what she had written while she would take a shower. Then, sometimes, he would take a shower while she would go to bed. Occasionally, she would stay up to talk with him, usually about her script, and have a few drinks together on the couch of the front room, until they would become aroused, and they would get into bed together to satisfy their passion.

One night, after he had taken a shower, and she had gone to bed, he crawled into bed beside her, her back against him, and as he snuggled against her, feeling her warm, soft flesh between his thighs, he became aroused. He slid his hand under her nightgown, moved it up her smooth leg, and touched her hip. When she felt his hardness against her, she recoiled.

"Dammit, Tony! I hate it when you sneak up on me like that! I'm not just a piece of prime roast waiting to get devoured. If you can't practice some restraint, find yourself a brainless slut whose only purpose in life is to get fucked to death."

Screwing, she said, drained her creative energy. And being a mother, and a wife, and a house maid, and working in the restaurant, and trying to appease his mother, who was too damned demanding, had exhausted all of her energy.

"And if you had any brains and feelings, you demented shit, you'd understand."

And she moved into the other bedroom that night, where the baby slept. And that had become her bedroom.

But three weeks or so later, before the end of winter, during a blizzard when the restaurant had closed a few hours earlier, she made him aware that she was feeling the dart of passion penetrating her. They had been sitting on the couch and had been sipping wine. "What a shame," he grumbled; "I don't feel like doing anything. I have a headache." Without saying anything, she got up, took his glass, poured more wine into it, and, bending down in front of him, making sure he could see down the front of her blouse where she had unbuttoned it, she offered him the wine. After he took it, she sat beside him again, placed the back of his head against her bosom, and massaged his temples. "My poor man, being henpecked by his shrew who's unworthy of him. You deserve better, I know. And I'm too impatient. But I really do appreciate you even if I don't show it." She slid her hands down to his belt buckle, unbuckled it, and unzipped his fly.

Later, she smirked, "It'll take more than a cold day in hell to stop my man from fucking me."

But she slept with him in his bed that night, with their arms around each other, and fell into a deep sleep together.

The next night, he wanted her again.

"I'm not in the mood tonight. When I want you to screw me, I'll let you know."

If she had been asked to help in the restaurant at night when it had become busy, she had demanded to spend the next morning and afternoon writing, undisturbed. And she wanted all day Sunday to write. She had agreed to spend Sunday night with him, to do whatever he wanted. And today was Sunday. Tonight they would sleep together, if she would be in the mood, and if she had been given a few hours to write.

At least once a week, usually twice, his mother would come downstairs and say, "Let's go to Berlin." She had become dependent on Joy, especially when transportation was required for shopping, and his mother was a meticulous shopper who enjoyed it, turning it into a consuming affair, and Joy hated it. "If I'm in an ugly mood," she'd say, "blame your mother. She's ruined my whole day!" And his mother would come downstairs almost every morning for coffee and sometimes to have her hair done and would say to Joy, "You're just like Dante, wasting your time and dreaming. Put that aside for a while."

Dante would come downstairs occasionally, and he and Joy would read each other's writings and encourage each other, feeding, thought Tony, each other's fantasy of becoming published writers. Joy, he thought, stood a better chance of becoming a bitchy sex goddess in the movies. She was a talented actress, he thought, but all she'd have to do was flaunt her physical attributes. She preferred to think of herself as a writer rather than as an actress, because writing, she thought, was more intellectual. Writing, to her, he thought, was an escape from reality.

During the past year, she had taken charge of the restaurant, doing all the paper work, figuring the taxes, ordering the supplies and increasing the profits. And, on busy nights, she had worked in the kitchen and, occasionally, had even worked as a waitress, always making huge tips. Men, Tony knew, were attracted to her, hoping she would wait on them, and if they were big tippers, she'd even allow a little flirting, smiling always for the biggest tippers, but ridiculing them and putting them down quickly if she thought they were going too far. She had a way of handling people, and she had made a good teacher, always acting sure of herself even when she had doubts about herself, according to Minnie Birch and Dante. His mother said that Joy had a good head and that he was lucky in finding her. Joy's only flaw, according to his mother, was that she wasn't Catholic yet.

On the bed that Sunday morning, she was becoming affectionate, he thought.

Dante and Rose would be there later, and she wouldn't have a chance to do much writing, but she enjoyed their company, so that would be no problem. That might even put her in a better mood.

His hand was on her breast, and her eyes were closed. He slid his hand inside her pajama top.

"Antoine!"

His mother was banging on the kitchen door.

Tony bounded from the bed, entered the kitchen, opened the door, and encountered his mother in a dark blue bathrobe that shook over her slender frame as though it couldn't contain her agitation. Her lips were quivering as she cried out, "Did you hear what Dante did?"

Her voice, straining, was high.

"Did you?"

"Calm down, Ma."

"Calm down! How can I calm down?"

Grasping the back of a chair near the table, she was almost in tears.

She was a nervous wreck, anyway, he thought, who constantly burned up so much energy that everything in life, to her, was a crisis that required immediate attention. Five minutes with her when she was upset was enough to commit anyone to the nuthouse in Concord.

"Black John's wife just called me," she uttered rapidly, "and I had a hard time understanding her with her accent, but she told me that Black John told her that you told him last night that Dante married Rosie!"

He nodded.

"Did he or didn't he?"

"Yeah, Ma, he did."

"Ohmygod!"

She sank onto the chair, leaned against the table, and groaned.

Joy, in a crimson bathrobe, entered the kitchen.

Tony went to the counter and stirred the pancake mix in a bowl.

Joy snapped, "How can you think of eating at a time like this? The smell of food will only make your mother sick to her stomach. How can you be so insensitive?"

She turned to his mother, put a hand on her shoulder and said, "Come on, Ma. Go in the living room and lie down for a while."

Joy, holding her by the elbow, led her to the couch. His mother was groaning.

Tony followed, as far as the doorway.

His mother, lying back, seemed bewildered.

"Why did he do it? God help us!"

"He is," Joy said, kneeling beside her and patting her hand. "God understands."

"But people won't. They'll ruin us."

"God will protect us. In the eyes of God, Dante and Rose are married now. She's part of the family. She's Dante's wife now. Your daughter."

"God's punishing us."

"Don't be foolish. God's using you."

"What do you mean?"

"Didn't you have the courage to oppose your own mother to marry a Jew?"

"That's different."

"No, it isn't. God's using you."

God, thought Tony, don't pour it on too thick. Joy, an avowed atheist, maybe even a communist who has uttered the slogan "better red than dead," was getting carried away.

"Maybe," his mother said, "they weren't married in church."

"Of course they were. They're good Catholics."

Damn!

"Why doesn't Antoine marry you in church? God has given you a beautiful baby."

"Yeah," Tony said, "and maybe God will call him into the priesthood to straighten his folks out."

Joy shot a dirty look at him.

"Don't poke fun at your own mother, you heathen!"

"Who?" he sputtered. "Me?"

"Maybe Antoine will break down and take you to church, Ma."

Shit, he muttered to himself.

"I can't go," she moaned. "I feel too sick."

"That's okay, Ma," he said. "God understands."

"You can go next Sunday," Joy said, "with Dante and Rose. That'll be nice, won't it?"

His mother groaned again.

"Rest now, Ma. I'll make you breakfast later."

"I can't eat. I'm sick to my stomach."

"What can I get you?"

"Nothing. You go eat. I'll be okay."

"Rest, then," Joy said, patting her hand.

She stood up, grinned at Tony as she brushed past him, and gave him a quick kiss on his cheek. She went to the counter and whispered, "Let your loving wife cook breakfast for you."

He poured himself a cup of coffee and then sat down at the table. A few minutes later Joy plunked a dish of pancakes and sausages in front of him, sat beside him, and lit a cigarette.

"Aren't you going to eat?" he asked.

"I'm not hungry."

He shrugged, spread butter on the pancakes and then poured maple syrup on them.

"Rusty," whispered Joy, "is not going to be brought up Catholic."

"Our Russell," he whispered, "is going to be a priest."

"Fuck you."

She thought she was being so damn sophisticated, using the vernacular like an important modern writer.

He shoved a large forkful of pancake into his mouth.

From the other room, his mother groaned.

"Take it easy, Ma," he said, raising his voice. "Everything's going to be all right."

"Don't talk with your mouth full. It's disgusting."

"Go to hell."

"Antoine! Don't talk to her like that!"

Joy grinned at him.

"Listen to your mother, Antoine."

She blew smoke into his face.

"What a friggin madhouse!" he muttered.

"Ma, Antoine's being nasty to me."

"What's he doing?"

"Cursing me in Italian with his fists."

"Antoine!"

"I'm not. She's lying."

Joy crushed the cigarette into an ashtray.

As he finished eating, his mother dragged herself into the kitchen.

"Well," he said, "you're looking better."

"I don't feel better. I have pains in my chest."

She sat down at the table and put her hands to her bosom.

"Antoine will drive you to the hospital, Ma. And if he won't, I will."

"I'll be all right."

He was seething at both of them, at Joy for manipulating his mother so damn easily, and at his mother for being so damned blind.

He lit a cigarette.

"Do you have to smoke now, in front of your own mother when she's not feeling well?"

"Damn you! Sometimes I feel like strangling you."

"Antoine, why are you so mean to her? You don't know how lucky you are, having a woman like Joy."

4

"I can still feel you inside of me," Rose said, grinning.

He was driving north of downtown Gorham, following the Androscoggin River on their right, on the way to Cascade Flats. Before seeing his mother, they had decided to go to the house of his Italian grandparents first. He'd probably go alone to face his mother. Then he and Rose would go to High Mass at eleven.

"It feels strange," he said, "to have sex, hop out of bed, go to church, and even receive communion."

"I know. The other night, having sex would been a mortal sin, condemning ourselves to hell for eternity; now, we're not only permitted to have sex, but we have the sanction of our religion to enjoy it, although according to the Jansenists, we're not permitted to enjoy the act, but to submit to it only to propagate the species, to go forth and multiply. But now that we're married, I feel that we're in heaven together. If I had known it would have been like this, I would have wanted to make love with you years ago. Come to think of it, deep inside of me, that's the way I had actually felt, but I had subdued the feeling. Now we're free to really enjoy sex together without feeling guilty. I really enjoyed last night, Dante. I had no idea it would be so fantastic, especially after the first couple of times. And you were worried you couldn't satisfy me! You're fantastic! I tingle all over, just thinking about it. You don't think we, well, overdid it, do you?"

"I don't think so. I mean, we had to get it right, so we had to try several times. We have to try again tonight."

"We don't have to." She smiled at him. "We don't have to have any fun in our lives either, but it will be a lot more fun playing with each other before we go to sleep. And that's a great way to put each other to sleep, isn't it?'

A mile before the Berlin line, he took a right turn and went down a hill, into Cascade Flats.

A smell, like rotting cabbage, came from chemicals in the river behind a row of houses on their right. On the other side of the river, Cascade Mountain was a huge wall. On the north, where the houses ended, was a high chain link fence with barbed wire across the top. On the other side, in a wide yard of a mill, where logs were piled high among mounds of sulfur, continuous smoke surged from a brick tower. To the west, where most of the houses faced, was Sugar Mountain; and to the south was the Presidential Range, which included Mount Washington, the highest mountain in the Northeast.

"Living here," Rose said, "you don't even notice, but the scenery, the mountains, is really beautiful."

"Just fifty years ago, this was untouched by modern civilization."

"Most people wouldn't call it modern civilization."

A few people on the sidewalk and on front porches waved at them, and Rose waved back.

"I wonder if they know we're married," she said.

"Do you feel married?"

"I definitely do, especially after last night."

At the upper end of the flats, at a beer joint, he turned right, down a small hill, where the road turned left onto a back street, a predominantly Italian neighborhood of nine houses in a row on their right. The houses on the back street had smaller back yards than the houses on the main street. Almost every house had a barn behind it, with a chicken coop and a pigpen, and a garden over a steep river-bank. Every spring, the river, which always ran swiftly, would swell, but its steep bank protected it from flooding. At the end of the back street, the road turned left at the fence of the mill, making a loop to the main road. Dante's grandparents lived in the third house from the fence. The second house, a long yellow house with four apartments, had been a millhouse, which had boarded the first immigrant mill workers, mostly from Quebec.

Dante's grandfather, at thirty-three, had migrated from Italy in 1908, having left his family behind for two years on a small farm in Lettomanoppello, a village in the mountains of the Abruzzi, and had boarded in the millhouse. After making a down payment on the house next to it, he sent for his family. The house had brown clapboard siding, a narrow front porch behind the sidewalk, and a wider side porch with a stairway on the right leading to a porch of an apartment upstairs.

Dante pulled up to the sidewalk and stopped. As soon as they stepped onto the porch, his grandmother opened the front door and embraced Rose in the doorway. They kissed each other on both cheeks, and after Rose entered the front room, his grandmother embraced Dante. She was a small woman, seventy-two, who had attended a woman's college in Rome where she had studied literature.

His grandfather, taller than average, with thick white hair, entered the front room and embraced them.

They went into the kitchen, a room towards the back, which was the same size of two bedrooms opposite it. The front room and the kitchen were on the south side, on the porch side. On the north side were three bedrooms. At the back, facing the river, was a bathroom and a shed.

"Have you eaten yet?" his grandmother asked in Italian. She understood English but was more comfortable speaking in her native tongue.

"No, Nonna," Dante answered; "we're going to church, to communion."

"Have you seen your mother this morning?"

"Not yet. Rose and I were married yesterday."

"We know. By now, everyone knows. Your mother needs time to accept it. Wait until later today to see her. Sit down."

His grandfather had gone into the shed, and then he went downstairs, to the cellar.

As Rose sat at the end of the table near the kitchen door, Dante sat between the table, covered with a red and white checkered oilcloth, and a window of the side porch. His grandmother, sitting near Rose, smiled at them. Her silvery hair was combed back and rolled into a thick bun at the back of her head. "I am happy for you," she said, and lifted the hem of her apron to wipe her eyes. "You remind me of own wedding day, fifty-two years ago. Fifty-two years!"

Rose turned to Dante and smiled at him.

His grandfather returned with a bottle of chokecherry wine, placed two cups on the table, poured the wine, offered a cup to his wife, and raised his while standing before them. "Your grandmother and I, long ago, drank wine as a symbol of love and of union with each other as husband and wife. We drink now, to you, Rosa and Dante, to a long life as husband and wife, filled with the blessed fruit of your love, under God." He tapped his cup with the other, and he and his wife drank the wine. "We have a gift for you." He went into his bedroom, returned with a large manila envelope, opened it, withdrew a sheet of paper, and placed it on the table. It was a document, printed in Italian. "This is a deed to our small farm in Lettomanoppello. It now belongs to you."

Dante and Rose stared at the document.

"Whenever you want to claim your farm, your grandmother and I will pay for the journey."

Dante reached out and touched Rose's hand.

Last winter, when she had been with him, Dante had told his grandmother of his intention to marry Rose this summer, and his grandmother replied that they had waited long enough. "The winters," she had said, "do not grow warmer with age. Love gives warmth. Others may refuse to understand, but you must live, first, for yourselves, doing what your hearts tell you. Believe what is in your hearts; have courage, and have faith in each other."

And then she had told them that she had married before she had graduated from college.

And she had told them of Lettomanoppello, a village on a hill with a view of surrounding mountains with other villages nestled on top, and in a wide valley below the village, a river, abundant with fish, flowed slowly through the land that bordered their farm.

Since childhood, Dante and Rose had enjoyed her descriptions and had imagined the thrill of being there, seeing the grapevines and the olive trees and, although they had never seen and tasted a ripe fig, they had imagined a fruit of the size and shape of a purple pear with a sweet juice of a pulpy, seedy interior, and they had imagined oranges with red juice, and wild blackberries that grew on their land, and wild rose bushes, and poppies. Their house was made of stone, originally, and an addition to the side, with an upstairs, was made of stucco. Vines with large green leaves grew against the house and provided a shady archway that led to a patio with a waist high stone wall overlooking a gently sloping field of a garden stretching to the bank of the river.

The site was similar in some ways to the one in Cascade Flats, but without the row of houses. In Lettomanoppello, the river flowed slowly, and the valley was much wider, much more open, and the mountains were more distant and much bigger, with peaks covered with snow, even during most of the summer. Although snow fell on the village in the middle of winter, and skiing was a popular sport on the higher sites, the snow usually melted quickly because the climate in Abruzzo was much milder, and, from spring to autumn, the climate was drier. In Abruzzo, except along the seacoast, there were no screens on windows, because mosquitoes were rare. You could hike through the woods or go on a picnic without being eaten by mosquitoes.

And just as you can see the Atlantic Ocean from the top of Mount Washington on a clear day, from the top of Mount Amaro, you can see the Adriatic Sea.

In the village, which the natives called Lu Lette, the buildings were close together, especially the shops, which touched each other as one structure three stories high with balconies. From early spring through late autumn, the balconies were decorated with multitudes of various flowers.

Last winter, she had told her story to Rose. To conceive of Dante's grandparents as students in Rome, not as eternal fixtures of the flats, was as fascinating to Rose as the farm, a plot so distant from Cascade Flats that it sounded imaginary.

Rosa Romano (descendant of Jewish poet Manoello Romano, contemporary of Dante Alighieri) daughter of Giuseppe Romano and Eva Pipperno, had been born in 1880 in Rome, in what is still called the Ghetto, although the wall had been taken down by then. Her father, a former soldier who had considered himself a patriotic Italian when Italy had not yet been unified as a country, had allowed his only daughter to study at The Royal Institute for women.

During her first month of college, while waiting in the Piazza Mattei to meet a female companion at the Fountain of Turtles, she met (either by chance, or by destiny, as she chose, later, to believe) a young man, slim, with black curly hair and dark bright eyes. On a large pad of paper he was drawing the four young men pushing the tortoises up the basin to drink the water. In a gentle voice he asked her if she lived here in Rome. A half hour later her companion had not appeared, and she and the young man had talked. Unlike her, he had said, he was not a Roman, but a simple mountain boy of the Abruzzi.

The history of Rome fascinated him, and he talked about the religion of the ancients. She, too, became fascinated, asking him questions. And then, since her friend had not come, she and he walked together, leisurely, and continued talking. After a while, he asked, "Are we in the Ghetto now?" She nodded. The history of the Hebrews in Rome, he said, was vague to him.

"Do you know," he asked, "that the oldest Jewish culture in the western part of the world is right here, in this community? That the Jews were here long before the Christians?"

She smiled.

"But in the middle of the sixteenth century," he said, "the Pope built a wall around the community to confine the Jews, and the wall remained, until the day of my birth."

"What did your birth have to do with the wall?"

He smiled.

His smile had, somehow, touched something tender deep within her, and his heart seemed to open, to invite her inside of him. And, as they walked together on a crowded street, they seemed, for a few moments, to be alone together. He, too, she thought, had felt that same feeling, and, he, too, must have felt as astonished as she.

He shrugged, saying, "I would like to see the synagogue. Is it nearby? Do you know?"

She smiled, answering, "You know I'm Hebrew. How could you know?"

"I did not know for certain. I thought, perhaps, you are, only because you live here. Will you take me to the temple?"

"It is near the river, opposite the Tiberina Isle. I will take you there."

As they approached the temple, he said, excitedly, "I would like to go inside. Am I allowed?"

"You are not Hebrew."

He said, "No."

"I will take you inside."

He was called Dante. Dante Valentino. He was studying for the priesthood. When he told her that, her heart sank. Why had she felt that way? They had barely met, yet she had been disappointed. She knew little of priests and thought that most of them opposed liberty and the unification of Italy.

But Dante, she later learned, was of the people, the son of peasants who toiled over land under the ownership of an oppressive priest. Dante, she learned, could never tolerate the exploitation and suppression of the people, or to say to them, "Your world is in the next life," a message his people had heard through centuries. "The meek," they would say, "will inherit the earth, in death, when they will be buried in it."

When Dante was ten, his village priest, aware of his keen mind, had persuaded his father to give him to the Church. His father, an atheist, hated priests, but he had said to Dante, "Go, and let them teach you to read and write. You will enjoy a clean, comfortable life, and there will always be enough food on your table and people to serve your needs."

Dante, five years older than she, had a gift, she felt, not only for drawing, but for writing. They met at least once a month that year, dining together, and attending concerts, and talking, talking about everything. His warmth, and his poetry, had stirred her deeply. In her bed, she dreamed of him. In her heart, she knew they had been created for each other, although he had denied it to himself.

Occasionally, he would return to his village in the mountains to spend a few days with his family and to help them on the farm even though his father would say, "I sent you away so that one of us, at least, could escape the miseries of this life. Your visits are welcomed, but not in servitude to the landlord."

When the school year ended, Dante rented a two-room apartment where they spent part of their time earning money by tutoring.

"If you become a priest, you'll be forced on the side of the aristocrats, because that's where most of your money comes from. The priesthood will never satisfy you."

"As a priest, I'll help the people from within."

He insisted that the true revolutionaries, such as Thomas Aquinas and Francis of Assisi, had, from within, been the most effective and beneficial to the whole Church.

"And others," she argued, "were condemned as heretics."

They were sipping wine at a table of an outdoor restaurant that evening, after dinner, during the summer of 1898 when riots had been erupting in streets throughout Italy. Farmers were paying less than subsistent wages to oppressed peasants who worked the soil while the price of bread soared, and journalists and parliamentary members who spoke out in behalf of the poor were arrested and sent to prison, and money of cooperative societies was seized to crush socialism, but others continued to rebel, until the government accepted some of their demands. That year had been memorable for Rosa; she had become more aware of politics and had met a writer for a magazine, Del Popolo (Of the People), who, under the name of Giovane (Jo-vanay, meaning Youth), wrote stories of the peasants and of their dreams. The writer was he, Dante.

In Italy, Catholics were prohibited by their clergy from participating in politics, even in elections, but he, Dante, as a priest, would encourage them to participate in their government.

"Your convictions are not religious, but political."

"My commitment is to the people. That's my religion. Religion is true only if it benefits mankind, if it fosters justice and freedom, improves the conditions of the people, and gives meaning and dignity to our lives."

"The Catholic Church has been powerful for centuries, yet it exploits the people."

"If more priests in Italy had the faith and the determination of a Francis of Assisi, preaching love, and freedom and responsibility and justice that stems from love, Italians would follow, and Catholics, Jews, Protestants, Muslims, and people of all faiths, or none, would live in harmony in our country and share a bit of prosperity and happiness. To me, that, and nothing less, is Italian."

"I've never heard Catholics speak as you speak. When they know I'm Hebrew, they seem to think I'm peculiar."

"They take your religion and then condemn you with it."

"Precisely."

Surely, she thought, Dante was too radical to become a priest; and she tried to persuade him to change his mind before next spring when he would take his vows.

"Everything owes its existence to that which is eternal, but, in particular, my existence comes from the blood and sweat of the people. Under God, I owe them my existence."

His words stung, almost evoking her tears.

"I love you, you foolish man!"

He had deluded himself into thinking their relationship consisted exclusively of intellectual companionship, not of physical attraction and of emotional involvement with each other.

"After you take your vows, what will happen to us?"

"I hope we will continue our friendship," his voice faltered.

The fool! The utter fool! She was tempted to splash wine in his face.

"Our feelings for each other go much deeper than friendship."

He stared at her.

"You have your parents to consider," he said. "You wouldn't do anything that would hurt them."

She felt herself sinking, like a rock, to the bottom of the Tiber.

"Does that satisfy you?"

He sighed, as though expressing pain, and touched her hands. And his eyes held hers, reaching into her, suspending time and activity. And she felt bound to him, within an invisible circle, and squeezed his hands, feeling his anguish.

They were, she felt, linked together, yet so far apart.

Her father and her grandfathers had fought many years for the independence and unification of the Italic speaking people, who speak many dialects of Italian and often have difficulty communicating with each other. One of her grandfathers had left his family in Rome to fight against the Austrians in the north, and another grandfather had fought against the French in the northwest, and her father had fought under Giuseppe Garibaldi against the French in the south until a treaty with France was signed. Parts of Italy had become unified, with Torino as the capital city, but Garibaldi was unhappy with the treaty, because many areas of Italian speaking people remained under control of France, such as Nice, home to Garibaldi, which, ironically, continued to make him and his family, officially, French citizens, and Corsica, where the people spoke the dialect that had become the official language of Italy, where Napoleon Bonaparte, an Italian speaking native, had originated and whose descendant, Louis, had become emperor of France. And the central region of the Italian peninsula, the Papal States, including Rome, was controlled by the Pope under protection of French troops. On September 20, 1870, Rosa's father had been among the patriots who had liberated Rome from the Pope.

Dante's father and his grandfather had also fought against the French and the Papal troops, but his grandfather had been captured, and, subsequently, shot. At that time, his family had owned the farm on which they now labored as peasants. According to Dante's father, his family had gone into debt, and the local priest had given a small amount of money to the family, "Out of Christian charity, as a loan," the priest had said, persuading the grandmother, who couldn't read, to sign her name to a sheet of paper. Several weeks later, when the loan hadn't been repaid, the local authorities removed them from the stone house to a hovel at the end of the field, next to the river, and the priest had placed his brother, a bachelor, in their house. Dante was born in the hovel. His father now waited for his son to enter the priesthood, to return to Lettomanoppello in dignity, and not request, but demand, the return of the farm to them, the rightful owners, whose ancestors through the ages had owned it.

When Rome had become the capital of Italy, and the government had divested the Papacy of its temporal powers, that did not include private property owned by members of the clergy, as long as they paid their taxes as everyone else did, but the Pope, to this day in 1898, was opposed to the Italian government, calling it the usurper of the territories of the Church. The majority of the clergy, Rosa thought, was waiting for the collapse of the Italian government. How, then, could Dante join them?

After the unification of Italy, his father had unsuccessfully sought the return of the farm. The argument by the local priest had been that he had legally purchased the land after the family had gone into debt. Dante's father, with neither enough capital nor education, had not had the resources to present his case effectively, though the judge had been sympathetic to him; but, to have a priest stand before a magistrate and prove that another member of the clergy had, through deception, seized the land of an Italian patriot who had been captured and then shot by troops of the Pope, would cause a sensation, which would be an advantage to the family. The disadvantage, of course, would be the accusation by the local priest that the family had sent a son into the priesthood solely to perpetrate revenge. But, according to Dante's father, the priest had agreed to return the farm one year after Dante would enter the priesthood, an agreement, his father had suspected, the priest would fail to honor.

"If you should somehow gain back the farm," Rosa asked, "would you then leave the priesthood?"

"I will become a priest, a good priest, who will use the priesthood to benefit others."

"Can't you benefit them in other ways? Through writing?"

"Writing isn't enough."

Seeing the torment in his eyes, she said, "I've never felt anyone else's feelings before, but I feel yours; and it's painful."

He squeezed her hands, saying, "I've never felt this close to anyone else. How is this possible? I feel you, inside of me."

"I feel the same way, as though I've always felt it. Dante, what will become of us?"

"I don't know."

His voice, barely audible, quivered, and a lump, she thought, moved in his throat. She felt it in her own.

The street suddenly seemed crowded and noisy.

"Dante, take me to your room."

He was staring at her. Finally, he stood up, took her by the arm, and led her through the crowded street.

When they entered the dimness of his apartment, she turned and leaned against him, putting her arms around him, her face under his, and felt his lips brushing her cheek. Never before had either of them experienced the joys of physical contact, but when his mouth touched hers, drawing her against him, a flame within her leaped up, mingling with his.

At that moment, she knew she would give herself to him, if he, too, would be willing to give himself to her.

"I love you, Dante. If you won't say it, I have, for both of us."

"If only our circumstances were different!"

That moment had given her the courage to speak of him to her mother, but her mother became upset and warned her to stay away from him.

"And don't mention him to your father. Understand?"

When she told him what her mother had said, he asked, "Shall we stop seeing each other?"

"No!"

"I could never tolerate the condemnation of you, especially by your own family."

They were sitting at the table of his scantly furnished apartment late at night. They would be sharing a small bed, sleeping on it with their clothes on. From where she was sitting, part of his bed was visible in the dimness of his small bedroom, the floor cluttered with books. Often, during that past summer, while he had been writing at the table, she had taken naps on the bed. His apartment had become their retreat from the world outside.

"My mother knows I'm seeing you. She doesn't approve, but she doesn't condemn me."

"She trusts you."

"It's not a matter of trust."

"She knows you won't do anything foolish."

"To her, my relationship with you is more than foolish."

"But you won't do anything to hurt her."

"Knowing that I see you, hurts her."

"I don't want to be a thorn to you and your family."

"You are not a thorn! The thorn is in their eyes, not in you. Religion should bring us closer to each other, not separate us. The Catholic faith is the offspring of the Jewish faith, but mother and child have become antagonists."

"This has been the happiest year of my life," he said, "being with you. I don't want it to end."

During their second year together, they spent more time with each other, staying in his apartment and falling asleep together through the night, several times, and though they had seldom spoken of their passion for each other, they had felt the intensity of their desires. Several times, she had expected him to fulfill their desires.

Spring came.

In another month, he would be taking his vows. Neither of them had wanted to think of the reality of their situation. He had rented the apartment for another year so that, he had told her, she could use it to tutor.

They were sitting together on the bed.

"The next time I see you," she said, "you will be an ordained priest."

"I know," he murmured, clasping her hand.

"I have a fear of never seeing you again."

"You will! Not for several more months, perhaps, but we will see each other for the rest of our lives, I promise. I can't even think of living without ever seeing you."

"Can you see yourself as a priest, sitting with me like this?"

"I know," he whispered, wrinkling his brow.

"Dante, is it shameful for us to love each other?"

"No!"

"I love you. I will always love you. I want to hear you say you love me. But if you can't say it," she said weakly, "I understand."

"I do! Rosa, Rosa Romano, I love you!"

"When you become a priest, you will change."

"No, Rosa, my feelings for you will never change, not even after you take a husband."

"A husband! There will never be anyone else!"

"Rosa!"

"And you! You will have to pretend to embrace the priesthood. Your pain will become intolerable, and you will do more harm than good!"

"I don't want to think about it."

She reached up, pushed her fingers through his curly black hair, and whispered. "I want you. I want you to make love to me, tonight."

"Do you want to take the chance of baring a child?"

"I don't want to think about it."

She raised her mouth to his, and as they kissed, she sank back on the bed, pulling him down, on top of her. A tremor, she felt, came from deep within him and sent quivers through her. She pulled his shirt up, slid her hands under his shirt and felt the warm flesh of his back.

"Rosa!" his voice shook. He withdrew suddenly, and sat up, on the edge of the bed, his feet on the floor, and buried his face in his hands.

Her bosom heaved. Tears blurred her vision of him. Light from a lantern on the kitchen table seemed to transform him into a shadow of himself, flickering.

She raised herself up, put her hands on his shoulders, knelt on the bed, and leaned against his back, putting her arms around him and pressing her breasts against him.

"Dante, with you I have no shame, only the shame of not admitting to the world my feelings for you."

"Rosa, you know I want you, for my own self."

"Take me, then, for yourself as well as for mine."

"You may regret it later."

"I would only regret my emptiness, of never having held you inside of me. To feel you inside of me, to actually feel you inside of me, if only for a few moments, would give me something to cherish for the rest of my life."

"Someday, when another man enters your life, what then?"

"This is my life, and you are that man."

"You say that now because we are together."

"Then, let us be together."

"Don't say anything more."

"Is it evil to feel as we feel for each other? Or shall we be false to ourselves? Shall we pretend you have a calling to the priesthood? Or shall we be true to ourselves, at least, in spite of everything that we will encounter later?"

"Rosa, please, we must look beyond tonight."

"Yes!"

She drew back, sat in the middle of the bed, and removed some of her garments, making herself naked to the waist.

"What are you doing?"

As she lifted her hips and pushed the rest of her garments down, he turned away.

She pushed her clothes to the floor, and she lay back.

"Dante," her voice quivered, "look at me."

He turned slowly and looked down at her, tenderly, she felt, and painfully.

"If," she said, "you are tempted now, you will also be tempted after tonight, if not by me, by other women who will be eager to seduce you. Will you reject each one each time? Or will you, eventually, taste the forbidden fruit? Will you allow me to share it with you? Or will you deny me, now, and humiliate me?"

The night became oppressively silent.

Finally, he spoke: "Get under the covers."

She did not move.

He stood up, saying, "With you, I should not be shy, but tonight I am, and I will feel more comfortable, I think, under the sheet."

"I understand."

"Do you want the light or not?"

"Whatever you prefer."

"The lamp on the table remained lit," Rosa said to Rose, "burning itself out late into the night, the most beautiful night of my life, yet the most poignant."

They had not become devoured by passion, for Dante had been slow and tender, and, at times, somewhat awkward, but she, not knowing what to expect, had felt a security that she had never experienced with anyone else, not even with her own parents when she had been younger; yet, when she thought of their circumstances and of the possibility of losing him, of never seeing him after this night, she had been consumed by poignant anxieties. Somehow, after feeling him explore her body with his mouth and warm hands, after expecting him to become incited by uncontrollable passions, after feeling him enter her, not with a thrust, but entering her gradually, with tenderness, she thought of nothing except him, of feeling nothing except him inside of her, feeling him moving and growing inside of her, penetrating deeper and deeper inside of her, and a deliciously warm tranquility enveloped her, lifting her into him, until the barriers between them had been irrevocably penetrated.

And, she felt, they had been joined together within an inviolable circle, she and Dante, as one, under the Supreme Being.

And that night, together, in the bedroom lit by a kerosene lamp on the kitchen table, she felt secure, lying together, fortified against the forces of the world.

He said, softly, "I don't want to feel separated from you, not ever."

"We're thinking and feeling the very same thoughts. I don't want this night to end, not ever."

Late into the night, he murmured, "I don't want to fall asleep. I want to stay awake with you, at least until noon."

But, cuddled to each other, they were succumbing to an intoxicating drowsiness, and they fell asleep, into deep sleep.

He was shaking her.

He, fully dressed, was sitting on the bed, and daylight pouring through an opening between shutters, made the room bright.

"I have to leave."

"Why didn't you wake me earlier?"

"You seemed so peaceful, I didn't want to disturb you."

"But I wanted us to be together before you leave."

She pushed the covers down, uncovering herself, and lifted herself to him. He clasped her and eased her down on the bed and kissed her gently.

"I will think of you," he said, "of holding you, as I did during the night. I must go now."

"One more hour."

"I don't want to leave, but I must. It is almost noon."

"Let me serve you breakfast at least."

"There isn't time. Stay in bed and rest."

"Ten more minutes."

"Please, Rosa. I've stayed as long as I could. Don't make this more difficult."

He kissed her on the mouth.

"I love you, Rosa. Write to me soon and as often as you can."

He stood up, turned, and quickly went into the kitchen.

She jumped out of bed, and as she dashed naked into the kitchen, the door to the hallway closed.

He was gone.

"Dante!"

She grew cold, feeling life draining out of her, and she stared at the door.

He was gone!

The apartment grew gloomy, as though even the sunlight had left with him.

She turned, slowly, went into the bedroom, dropped to the bed, pulled the covers over her, and lay, face down, wanting to feel his warmth.

But he was gone.

And she wept.

A lump in her stomach swelled to her throat. What had he proven by leaving?

Why, why had she become so damned involved with him? Why? Why? She had known he would leave. Damn him! Deep down, she had known he would attempt to live the life of a priest; he would have to try, at least, until he would discover for himself his own true path. In time he would come to that junction in which he would have to decide to remain a priest, or to defect from the priesthood. Neither alternative, she thought, appeared feasible. But she would be waiting for him. Now, she would be waiting for him to decide if their relationship would become platonic, which no longer seemed likely, or if he, as a priest, would continue to express his love physically, violating his vows and making them both hypocrites. Damn him! A priest! She hated them! She hated religion. All religions, tearing them apart. He was gone. Gone!

And she wept, as though tears would wash away the pain, but the tears only dug the pain deeper into her.

He had entered her life, having appeared suddenly before her as though he had materialized from the air, and he had swept her from her mundane existence, having breathed into her life itself, and, suddenly, he was gone!

She hated the pain, but she knew that he, too, was feeling the pain. And she became frightened that he, now, was resenting the pain, the pain that she was causing him.

She clutched the pillow.

Dante! Dante, do not let the pain make you resent your love!

Nothing mattered to her anymore, except Dante. Nothing! If she would become his mistress, mistress to a priest, so be it! Yet, that was not Dante. Not her Dante. Would she see him again, ever?

She would see him again. This summer. In spite of the pain, their relationship would endure. They had become part of each other. He was her Dante, the Giovane, who wrote of the suffering of the people and of their dreams. He would return here, as he had promised, and he would make love to her again, here, in this bed, in their private world, insulated from the world outside.

She closed her eyes, driving away all thoughts of the outside world, and felt him penetrating her, soothing her with the warmth of his desire as he moved slowly and tenderly inside of her, and she felt herself drifting away with him.

An hour, perhaps two, passed, and she opened her eyes, and then she forced herself to get out of bed, but the pain returned and made her aware that the barriers between them would not be easily penetrated. Only with him, inside of her, she thought, would she ever feel the barriers melting away. But after he would take his vows, what then? She did not want to think of him as a priest. She could not!

Dante would return to her here. Somehow, he would return as himself.

Yet, the pain of losing him burned within her. And a feeling, of never seeing him again, persisted.

She dressed, and, without eating, went outside. The sun was shining, but a gloom seemed to be cast over the street. The buildings, which had seemed so real, and the people so alive when he had walked down this same street with her so often, seemed distant and unreal now. In a daze, she walked down the street, turned onto another, and then up another, and returned to the apartment. Everything evoked his image, bringing the past two years to the present. Two years ago, she hadn't even known of his existence; yet, she felt that she had always known him. And now he was gone. And the past two years was like a dream.

In the apartment, she busied herself, cleaning, picking up his books from the floor, and examining them as evidence of his existence. She made the bed and thought of them together during the night, the long night of making love into the early morning, the long night which had passed so quickly. And then she sat on the bed, lay back, closed her eyes, and thought of the past two years. Now, she would be waiting for him, waiting for Dante, but nothing would seem alive again, not with the life she had felt, not until they would come together again. For him, she would be forced to oppose her own parents, her religion, and most of her friends and her relatives. She would have to go against her former way of life, against most of what had been familiar to her, against that which she had never been prepared to oppose. His life and hers had become one life woven together, inextricably. Would they find the fortitude and the courage and the wisdom to endure and to maintain their dignity? What could they possibly do? He would do, she knew, what he must do. And she must also do what she must, but, she thought, she was blind, groping in the darkness, and, without him, she would not be able to persevere.

The only way to endure, she decided, was to believe he would never abandon her, that, in spite of everything, he needed her as much as she needed him, and that he would return to her, to life, together.

But the pain, that she would become his mistress, persisted. She, mistress to a priest! Under such a situation, they would never be free, never be able to live with dignity, never be able to truly respect each other or even themselves.

To think of him, of her Dante, as masquerading as a priest, or as anyone else, was intolerable, making her too sick to even think of it. And the thought of remaining in the apartment, especially of spending the night in the same bed, became oppressive.

The fear of never seeing, or even of hearing from him again, swelled inside of her.

She locked the door to the apartment and left, wondering if she would ever see it again.

Three days passed, and she had heard nothing from him. Nothing! And school, where learning had seemed so vital because she had shared so much of her learning with him, became irrelevant. Tedious.

But the next day, a letter from him arrived. Her heart pounded. It was post-marked here, in Rome. She trembled as she opened it. "My dearest Rosa, without you, existence has been painful. The deepest part of me has been torn away, staying with you for its nourishment," the letter began. They were experiencing the same feelings! He compared their predicament to a path in a dark place that was covered by stumbling blocks, but, in studying the terrain, the darkness would gradually be penetrated by an inner light that would reveal the stumbling blocks that should be removed, and, with time and effort, the biggest stumbling blocks would be removed, and the path would be cleared. That was the belief they shared, the belief in the inner light in each of us, the divine love. "With love, everything is possible. Pray with me, my dearest Rosa." She pressed the letter to her bosom. In spite of the pain that would persist, her spirits had been uplifted, and she would pray for them. She would pray with more fervor than she had ever prayed before.

That night she answered his letter, telling him how happy she was to receive his, and that she would write to him often.

The following Saturday she returned to the apartment, placed his letter on the table, and wrote to him again. And she spent the night in his bed.

They wrote frequently. He complained of having little time for himself, that he was trying to finish a story for Del Popolo, but he wrote little of his religious duties and activities except when she asked him specific questions. He would, he answered, be ordained soon, and his family would be there, and then he would be going to his home village to conduct a service.

Summer came. After his ordination, he continued writing to her frequently, but his letters were brief and seemed impersonal, as though his feelings for her had changed, but he assured her that his feelings had not changed. As a priest, he wrote, he had taken a vow of chastity, and although that had failed to diminish his carnal desires, he had not yet notified that fact to any of the attractive ladies who wanted to seduce him, so she need not be concerned that he would soon be involved in any clandestine affairs. She told him that his joke was not amusing. She wanted to see him. Why was he avoiding her? The path, he answered, was not yet clear.

Late in July, he sent her a story that he had sent to Del Popolo, a supposedly fictional account of Giovane, who was entering the priesthood to fulfill an agreement between his father and a priest. As soon as she finished reading it, she replied, "Not even Del Popolo would dare publish it."

The next day, she read his script again, and this time she was able to read it with more objectivity. In his letters he had mentioned very little of his religious activities, knowing that she couldn't tolerate the thought of him as a priest, but, in his script, he wrote of his studies as a student and of his ordination, and, as Giovane, he wrote of his experience of conducting his first Mass in the church of his village.

During that week, the choir and the brass band had rehearsed the music for the Mass, and his family and his many cousins had cooked in preparation for the feast that would follow the Mass in the fictional village of the newly ordained priest. That week, many had come from neighboring villages, commencing the celebrations, even though some of the men never attended church except for weddings and funerals, and Giovane, aware of their distrust of priests, wanted them to know that he hadn't forgotten that he was one of them. The Mass would be sung in Latin, and many of the congregation, who were uneducated, could not understand the words in spite of the similarity to Italian. Giovane had arranged for a young woman to stand at the side of the altar during the Mass to explain the symbolic movements of the priest to the congregation. The parish priest, although he had not been obligated to attend the service, having conducted a Mass at an earlier hour, would probably be near the choir, observing.

At the vestibule, to the right side of the people, Giovane sent a young acolyte to the altar to light the candles to indicate that the Mass was about to begin. When the boy returned, he said that the church was crowded. Many people were standing.

Giovane, with folded hands, went to the doorway and looked at the people. As he took a step towards the altar, he chanted in Latin: "I go to the altar of God. To God, the joy of our youth!" And the band began to play as he approached the altar, and two acolytes followed him, and the congregation stood up to follow the drama of the Mass, the sacrifice of the lamb, the passion of their Christ in Jesus.

The outer vestment of the priest, the chasuble, was green, the symbol of hope.

As Jesus had gone to the garden to pray, the congregation knelt, and the priest, bowing before the altar, sang the Confiteor. "Confiteor Deo omnipotenti!" I confess to almighty God, that I have sinned, "mea culpa, mea culpa, mea maxima culpa," through my fault, through my fault, through my most grievous fault. And the choir responded.

And then the priest, turning to the congregation as Jesus had looked to the disciples, chanted to them, "Behold the hour has come, and I will be betrayed into the hands of sinners. Let us rise." They stood up, and the priest ascended the three steps to the altar and kissed the altar stone. "Coming to Jesus, he said: Hail, Rabbi. And he kissed him." And "Judas, repenting himself, brought back the thirty pieces of silver to the chief priests and ancients. Saying, I have sinned in betraying innocent blood. But they said: What is that to us? Look then to it. And casting down the pieces of silver in the temple, he departed, and went and hanged himself."

When Jesus had been taken away by the Roman soldiers, Peter had denied Him three times, and the choir sang the Kyrie. "Kyrie eleison! Kyrie eleison! Kyrie eleison!" Lord have mercy. "Christie eleison! Christie eleison! Christie eleison! Kyrie eleison! Kyrie eleison! Kyrie eleison!"

And the sorrow of Peter had been followed by hope through divine mercy, to salvation. And Peter had written in his epistle: "Be steadfast in the faith." And the choir burst into the Gloria. "Gloria in excelsius Deo!" Glory to God in the highest.

Jesus had been taken to the Roman administrator, Pontius Pilate, and the trial had begun.

The congregation sat as Giovane stood at the front of the altar and thanked them for attending his first Mass, and he told them that it was a privilege to serve them and to be with them on this special occasion. "This church is yours, and I, as a priest, am your servant. I am not merely uttering words that have no meaning. I am telling you what I have been taught in Rome by our own Church. I am telling you that as a child of God, you have certain rights, that by the simple act of your birth, by the highest laws of all, the laws of nature, that you have a right to be free. That means you have a right to life. Under the laws of God, no man is better than you. Better behaved, perhaps, or better educated, or better looking, or wealthier, or has more talents, but in the eyes of God, he is not better by nature than you. That means, he does not, by nature, have more rights than you.

And it is the duty of a priest to make you aware of your rights. That is the mission of your Holy Church, to set you free from the darkness. For too long, we as a people, as peasants, have been subjected to the belief that it is the will of God that we must accept our fate to serve our superiors, our masters, who, by their birthrights, were created less ignorant than the rest of us and have a clearer understanding of the mysterious laws of nature, laws that are so simple to them, yet so difficult for us peasants to accept. Why? Why are the laws so convenient to the masters? Does a master of slaves fulfill the will of God? A voice crying in the wilderness is not enough, but the voices of all of us become the voice of our government, the laws, the laws that protect our rights to the basic necessities of life." And Giovane promised to take an active part with them in their government, to enforce their rights.

The old parish priest suddenly stood up, and as he was walking quickly to the rear of the church, leaving it, Giovane continued speaking.

To participate in their government was a right, but with every right came a responsibility. "Husbands, you have responsibilities to your wives. Wives, you have responsibilities to your husbands. Fathers and mothers, you have responsibilities to your families. Children, you have responsibilities to your parents. Priests have responsibilities to their flock. And all have responsibilities to their neighborhoods, to their countries, and to the world. Before the unification of Italy, the Church had provided schools, but the new government had declared such schools unlawful and had placed the sole responsibility of education upon local governments. However, local communities, such as ours, have had neither the money nor the resources to fulfill their obligations, and we have been deprived of our right to develop ourselves, of our right to knowledge, of our right to know that which we need to know in order to live, to govern ourselves. I am your servant. I, as a priest, have been trained to teach you. The Church is yours!" Also, Giovane made clear to his flock, "The State is yours!" The separation of Church and State, according to the young priest, was to clarify the responsibilities of each institution, to "Render to Caesar that which is Caesar's, and to God, that which is God's." The Church and the State ought to be complimentary, not incompatible.

Following the sermon, the congregation stood again as the choir sang the Credo, "I believe in God, the Father almighty," acknowledging their faith, and the trial of Jesus had ended.

The priest went to the right side of the altar, and washed his hands. And Pontius Pilate had washed his hands before the people, saying to them, "I am innocent of the blood of this just man."

The priest returned to the middle of the altar and, with outstretched hands, turned to them, singing, "Orate, fratres." Pray, brethren.

And the priest and the choir chanted the Preface: "Dominus vobiscum!" The Lord be with you.

"And stripping him, they put a scarlet cloak about him. And a crown of thorns they put upon his head and a reed in his right hand. And bowing before him, they mocked him, saying, Hail, king of the Jews. And spitting upon him, they took the reed and struck his head. And after they mocked him, they took off the cloak from him, and they put on him his own garments and led him away."

An acolyte, kneeling, jingled a bell, and the congregation knelt. Jesus had been condemned to crucifixion. And the choir sang the Sanctus. "Sanctus! Sanctus! Sanctus!" Holy, holy holy. "Hosanna in excelsius!" Hosanna in the highest.

When the Sanctus ended, the church became silent.

The priest blessed the bread and the wine. The soldiers had nailed Christ to the cross. And, with both hands, the priest raised over his head a wafer of unleavened bread. Christ had been raised on the cross. And the faithful bowed their heads and prayed silently. "Lord," Jesus had pleaded, "forgive them, for they know not what they do.'"

Jesus, at the Last Supper, "took bread, broke it, and gave it to the disciples, saying: Take, and eat this, for this is my body. And he took the cup, and gave thanks, and gave it to them, saying: Take, and drink this, for this is my blood, the blood of the new testament. As often as you shall do this, you will do it in commemoration of me." And the priest, with both hands, lifted over his head a chalice of wine. And the congregation bowed their heads and prayed. And Giovane prayed, "Let us come together in the joy of living, leaving forever the shedding of blood to our dark past."

And darkness had descended upon the earth for three hours as Christ had hung on the cross. And the priest sang the Pater Noster, and the choir and the congregation joined him. Our Father, Who art in heaven.

And "Jesus cried out with a loud voice, saying: My God, my God, why hast thou forsaken me?"

And the priest broke the consecrated wafer in half.

"And Jesus again crying with a loud voice, yielded up the ghost. And behold the veil of the temple was rent in two from the top even to the bottom, and the earth quaked, and the rocks were rent."

And the choir sang: "Agnus Dei, qui tollis peccata mundi, miserere nobis." Lamb of God who takes away the sins of the world, have mercy on us.

And the priest genuflected, saying, "Panem caelestem accipiam." I will take the Bread of heaven. And he consumed the bread.

The bell rang three times: for humility, sorrow for sins, and hope of pardon.

And the priest consumed the wine from the chalice.

And the congregation stood up, and they lined the middle aisle, approached the altar rail, and knelt.

The priest, facing them, lifted a wafer from the chalice and held it up, saying, "Behold the Lamb of God who takes away the sins of the world." And he went to the altar rail, and to each one he gave the Bread, and they, taking it, came into communion with Life.

Communion took much longer than usual, and the brass band played selections from *Capriccio Italien*, which the priest had not expected, but the music, though secular, seemed in harmony with the spirit of the people.

When the music stopped, the priest went to the middle of the altar, faced the congregation, and chanted, "Dominus vobiscum." The Lord be with you.

And the congregation stood up.

Christ had risen from the dead and had appeared to them, saying, "I am the resurrection and the life. Go, you are sent forth: teach all nations to observe all things whatsoever I have taught you: and behold I am with you all days even to the consummation of the world."

The congregation knelt, and the priest blessed them.

And they stood up again, and the priest departed from the altar, and as the band played and the choir sang, the congregation filed into the aisles, leaving the church.

"And while he blessed them, he departed from them, and ascended into heaven. And they, adoring, returned into Jerusalem with great joy."

5

"Tattone, then, had actually been a priest," Rose had said to Rosa, "and yet, he married you. But he had not left the Church. Or had he?"

"Of course not."

"I am very confused. He could never have left the priesthood, and he could never have married, I thought, not if he would remain Catholic."

"But you have been raised Catholic. Do you think God is unreasonable? Or that your religion is? Our situation was very complicated. And at that time, I, too, had thought that religion, all religions, could be unreasonable at times and had lacked compassion, as though human beings were inhuman. The history of mankind seems to support such a supposition. But let me continue with the story."

After she had read the account by Giovane, Rosa tried to clarify her thoughts, but they remained muddled. Why hadn't Dante visited yet? Was he avoiding her because he was thinking of what they would do together? In reply to his story, she wrote that there was so much to discuss that she couldn't express all her thoughts and feelings in a letter. Why could they not meet for a few hours? "How often," she wrote, "during the past few months have we almost met each other here in Rome?"

He wrote back saying that his story was not yet finished, but, the part she had read, the first part, would be published in October. "Please," he wrote, "be patient with me. Before taking my vows, I had put my life (and in so doing, yours also) in the hands of God. Almost from the moment we met, I have been praying for divine guidance, and now, I think, the inner light is beginning to penetrate the darkness. There is so much to tell you, so much that is happening now, and so quickly. When I see you, I want to spend not a few minutes with you, but many hours."

Summer came to an end.

When the October issue of Del Popolo came out, she looked at it, saw the story by Giovane, and bought a copy.

When she went to the apartment to put the magazine on the table with his letters, there was a note for her. Dante had been there less than two hours ago. She trembled as she read it. He would be going to Lettomanoppello, not knowing for how long, for certain, two or three weeks, perhaps, but he would return here, to the apartment as soon as possible. "I wish I had known I'd be here today. I hope you will have time to be free when I return. I will definitely be here before the end of October, on the last Saturday, at noontime. There is so much to tell you. I love you, and I will always love you."

She could go to Lettomanoppello!

But had he wanted her to join him, he would have said so.

She would have to continue waiting.

A week later she received a letter from Lettomanoppello. It was brief, reminding her that he would be with her the last Saturday of the month. He would be free at least until Monday. She wrote back immediately, saying that she would be waiting.

He wrote almost every day until the last week before he would see her again, and during that week, she was in a state of near anxiety, waiting, unable to concentrate on anything else, and wondering how much he had changed since he had been ordained only a few months before. Would he act like a priest, or as the Dante she had known? She would accept the vows he had made, if she must, but if he would want her in bed with him, she would do it gladly.

An hour before noon on that Saturday, she sat on the edge of the bed and waited. Every time she heard footsteps in the hallway, her heart pounded. She was wearing a white blouse and a crimson skirt and was barefooted. He, perhaps, would be wearing the black garb of a priest. She hoped not. Embracing him, the same Dante who had come together with her in this bed, dressed now as a priest, would feel too awkward. How would he greet her? Would he embrace her, as lover to beloved, or would he look at her as a stranger almost? She clenched her fists to her breasts. Not as a stranger! Not Dante. Surely, here, in their sanctuary, neither of them would let the outside invade their privacy. He, who had taken her in this bed, would feel as he had that night, because he was her beloved, always, in spite of everything else. She was trembling, not only with the excitement of seeing him again, but with fear that his feelings had changed.

At this moment, he was on his way to the apartment, as eager as she. And when he would arrive, they would embrace, clasping each other, letting each other know that their feelings had not changed.

From the bed, she was staring at the hallway door, waiting for it to open. She remembered staring at it when he had left. The painful emptiness. Now, she was waiting for it to open, to let him enter.

Enter, she thought. Enter into her life again. Enter her again!

Any moment now.

Waiting. Waiting.

Footsteps in the hallway.

Knocking at the door.

She jumped up.

"Dante!"

Before she reached the door, it opened. Dante, not dressed in the black of a priest, but in a blue jacket and a white shirt unbuttoned at the neck, entered, closing the door, dropped a small suitcase to the floor, stared at her, and smiled.

She, standing before him, stared back at him.

"Rosa."

The sound of his voice calling her name felt like a warm invitation.

She gasped.

"Dante!"

He squeezed her against him.

Clinging to him, she felt her tears coming.

For several moments, neither of them spoke, and she didn't want him to release her, but after a while she heard his voice, saying, "Rosa, it feels so good to hold you again!"

And she answered, "And it feels so good, feeling you holding me! I've waited so long for this moment! To be separated from you is too painful, yet this moment is almost too good to seem real. If I am dreaming, do not wake me. Let me enjoy this moment. Let me enjoy this dream."

She cupped his face, kissing it, and he kissed her on the mouth, firmly, and, like the first time he had kissed her, she felt the inside of her opening to him, wanting him to enter her.

When he withdrew his mouth from hers, she leaned against him and closed her eyes, feeling as though she had no strength to move, and he held her a long while.

"Rosa, let me look at you."

She stepped back a little, and they gazed at each other, smiling.

"I can't believe you're actually here," she said.

"I hope I'm not disrupting your schedule."

"Disrupting my schedule?" Suddenly he seemed distant, staring at a stranger. "Dante, you're all that matters to me."

He didn't answer.

"Let me take your jacket."

He removed his jacket slowly.

"We'll have red wine with our noon meal," she said, "and white wine with our evening meal."

He nodded.

"Let me put your things in our bedroom," she said, and she examined his face to observe his response, but his expression had not changed.

She took his jacket, picked up his suitcase, and said, "The wine is in the icebox."

She placed his suitcase near the foot of the bed and hung up his jacket. Returning to the kitchen while he was pulling the cork out of the wine bottle, she asked, "How long will you be staying?"

"How long do you want me to stay?"

"As long as you want. You've paid the rent. Remember?"

"Only for a year," he said, grinning.

"Seriously, how long are you staying?"

"I don't know yet. At least a week. Much longer, perhaps."

A delicious feeling flowed through her.

"Much longer, I hope!"

He took two glasses from the shelf, placed them on the table, poured wine into the glasses, and sat down, but he grew reticent again, sipping his wine and looking at her.

"Dante, in your letters, you said you had much to tell me."

He nodded.

"So much," he murmured in a tired voice, as though he had come to an end of a long and arduous journey.

"Tell me later. Do you want to eat now?"

"Let me take you to a restaurant."

"I've already prepared our meals for this noon and for this evening. Would you rather go to a restaurant?"

He shook his head.

"You seem tired."

He shrugged.

"Do you want to lie down? I will give you a massage."

"Later, perhaps."

She smiled at him and said, softly, "We'll eat first."

They hardly spoke during the meal but looked at each other, trying, she felt, to feel the feelings of each other.

After they finished eating, she took the dishes to the sink, returned to the table, poured wine into their glasses, and sat opposite him again.

"Dante, I'm anxious to hear what you have to tell me."

"I've come home."

Elation, mixed with bewilderment, swelled in her, but he grew silent again, agonizingly silent.

"Dante, my feelings for you have not changed."

"Mine have, Rosa. When I left here, I didn't think that was possible, but I prayed; I prayed intensely, pleading with God to light the path before me, to remove all obstacles from us. Through you, I have followed a path to God, and through God, answering my prayers, I've been following a path back to you, and my feelings for you, during each moment, grow stronger. I love you now, more than I ever have before, and tomorrow, I will love you even more, if that's possible. And I know now that with love all things are possible. Love never ends; it is eternal. But I need this time just to sit here, to look at you. To realize this isn't just a dream, as you have said. I probably look idiotic, staring at you and not saying much. And there is much to tell you, so much that has happened, that I don't know where to begin."

She smiled.

"We can talk after you've rested. Do you want me to give you a massage?"

He smiled, too.

"First, we should discuss our future, to give us ideas of what will happen to us, to clarify our relationship."

"Dante, I don't think of you as a priest. I can't." But in saying it, his priesthood became a fact, the most painful barrier between them. "I don't dare! I think of you only as Dante, the Dante I've known. Every day and every night, I've thought of you, especially of our last night together. And before you arrived, I trembled at the anticipation of seeing you again. I'm glad you're not wearing the garments of a priest."

"I won't," he said, "ever be wearing the garments of a priest again if you and I are together. I told you, I've come home. I've returned, Rosa, to you, if you will have me."

She stared at him.

"The story of Giovane is my own. I want to write the conclusion."

After the Mass in Lettomanoppello, Dante's mother and father, his brothers, and his sisters, and his nephews, and his nieces, and his uncles, and his aunts, and his cousins, and his friends gathered in the church to embrace him. And the old priest yelled at them, demanding them to leave. And Dante's father said, "This church is ours, and you are our servant." And the priest became furious. Dante's father told the priest that the time had come to discuss the return of the farm according to their agreement, but the priest refused to discuss it.

"Until then, I hadn't been sure that they had actually made such an agreement. Anyway, the priest submitted a complaint against me, stating that I was unfit for the priesthood. And when I returned here to Rome, my superiors suspended me from practicing my priestly privileges in public until they could gather more information about me, even though I had told them everything they needed to know."

"Did you tell them about us?"

"That wasn't the issue. The issue was why I had joined the priesthood."

"Did you tell them you're Giovane?"

"No, but after the story was published, I was requested to meet with the Pope."

"The Pope?"

"I met with him twice. The first time, we spoke for almost an hour. He had read the complaints against me and the reports from my superiors, which included my original purpose in studying for the priesthood, and he became aware that my parish priest had in fact, years ago, taken over the property of my family; and he seemed convinced that the priest had made an agreement with my father, an avowed atheist, to sacrifice me to the priesthood in return of the farm. He seemed astonished by the situation, and very upset. The situation, he said, sounded similar to a story recently published in Del Popolo. I was surprised he had read it. I admitted that I had written it."

He took a sip of wine.

"He asked me if I thought I had a vocation to the priesthood. I told him my purpose was to serve the people, and that the priesthood was the only way I knew. And he nodded as though he understood. Yet, he said, had my advisors known of my circumstances, I wouldn't have been admitted into the priesthood. Even though my intentions, he said, of serving the people, are honorable, my calling, he felt, is not to the priesthood."

"Was he harsh with you?"

"No. He was sympathetic. My writing, he said, is a divine gift, and I should use it to serve mankind, and in serving man, I would be serving God. Writing, he said, can be used as prayer, returning to

God the gift He has bestowed upon me. And although I had spent most of my life studying for the priesthood and know no other life, he said I needed to get away from it, to see myself under different lights, and that he was granting me a special dispensation."

Dante took a gulp of wine, emptying his glass.

"What does that mean?"

"My vows are no longer binding."

He filled his glass again.

"The Pope, then, approves of your writing. But why shouldn't he? It's a beautifully written portrayal of your religion. The celebration of the Mass, I feel, is deeply moving, even to me, a Jew."

"When I met with the Pope the second time, he informed me that an inquiry had disclosed that the parish priest had violated canon laws in taking the farm, and the priest has been removed from the parish. My family will retain the farm and be compensated for our losses."

"Dante, you're free now!"

He didn't answer.

"What's wrong?"

Could he, she wondered, be afraid of his sudden freedom?

"Dante, the Pope has given you an opportunity to live your life freely and openly now. Through your writing, you have the ability to appeal to our deepest feelings, to our humanity. Use your gift, Dante, for the sake of humanity and for the glory of God."

He was looking at her.

She stood up, went to him, clasped his face, placed her mouth on his, and kissed him. His arms slid around her and held her in a long embrace that stirred, she felt, life in both of them. Slowly, she withdrew her mouth from his, sank down, to her knees, pushed herself between his legs and clung to his waist.

"Rosa, I've dreamt of you often, sometimes in fear of losing you."

"You'll never lose me."

"Do I have the right to come between you and your family, to make your own family despise you?"

"You would never make anyone despise me. If they would despise me, it would be through no fault of yours. If anyone should despise me for loving you, so be it."

"Would you break the hearts of your own parents?"

"The deepest part of me is you. If the hearts of my parents are so small that they cannot include me with you inside of me, so be it."

He closed his eyes and held her against him, and they were silent for a while, and, looking up at him, she saw his tranquility, and she felt life rising in him as though trying to emerge from a long night of cold silence and seeking her warmth, and, shamelessly, pressing her bosom against him, said, "Dante, let us lie down together on our bed."

"Rosa," his voice shook as he opened his eyes and placed his hands on her shoulders, "are you willing, then, to marry me, here, and now?"

"Yes!"

They gazed at each other.

"Stand up," he said, "and bring me a piece of bread."

She stood up, went to the cupboard, cut a slice of bread from a loaf, and brought it to him.

He stood up, took the slice of bread, broke it into halves, dipped part of one half into his glass of wine, and raising the soaked bread to her lips, said, "I, Dante, pledge myself to you, Rosa, to become united with you, as God is my witness." She opened her mouth and took the bread and ate it. And he lifted his glass of wine to her lips, saying, "Drink my wine. What is mine is yours, my sorrows and my joys." And she drank from his glass. And then she took the other piece of bread, dipped it into her glass of wine, and raised the bread to his lips, saying, "And I, Rosa, give myself to you, Dante, becoming one with you, so help me God." And after he ate the bread, she lifted her glass of wine to his lips, saying, "Drink my wine; I am your family, and you are mine, so help me God." And, placing his hands over hers, he consumed the wine, and holding her hands, he said, "If any reject us, they reject us together, or, if any accept us, they accept us together, for you and I are we, part of each other."

And the next morning, she went to the apartment of her parents and told her mother that she and Dante had agreed to marry, but her mother became upset.

"She will speak to my father," she told Dante, but the next day, her mother told her that her father would denounce her as his daughter if she would marry Dante.

That evening, she returned to her parents to speak personally with her father.

"My own parents," she told Dante, "have threatened to disown me unless you become Jewish. I asked them how they would feel if your parents demanded that I become Catholic."

Two days later, Rosa and Dante visited a priest who had become a friend of theirs, and they discussed the conditions under which they could be married in the Catholic Church. She had known that she would be required to study Catholicism, to promise to baptize their children in the Church, and to instruct and to raise their offspring in the Catholic faith.

Dante went to Lettomanoppello for a few days. When he returned, he told her that the farm would soon be returned to his family in his name, and that his parents were eager to meet her and were looking forward to attending their wedding ceremony.

The following month they were married in a church in Rome.

The year ended, and they entered the twentieth century.

Dante took Rosa to Lettomanoppello. His parents were living, still, in the hovel because the exchange of the property had not been finalized. A few days later, after they returned to Rome, Dante met with a priest in the Vatican who told Dante that the old parish priest had been reluctant to relinquish the property, but an agreement was imminent.

In the spring, the second part, the conclusion, of the story of Giovane was published, the property was returned in Dante's name, the Vatican sent them enough money to add two rooms to the stone house and enough to pay for the completion of Rosa's education, and Rosa became pregnant.

To supplement his income, Dante became a clerk in a hotel while Rosa continued her studies.

"My schooling," she told him, "will have to end after this year. Our child will be born in December."

"You can finish school the year after."

Summer came. Several times Rosa had gone to visit her parents, and each time, her father had refused to let her enter. She had seen her mother only when her father had not been there, and the last time she had been there, her mother, on the verge of tears, had said, "Your father forbids me to let you come here."

"Tell him to decide, then, if I am carrying his grandchild."

When she told Dante what her mother had said, he replied, "If I must become Jewish to make peace with your family, so be it."

"No, Dante! All I ask of them is that they accept us as we accept them. They're as wrong as your father was when he committed you to the priesthood. Why do parents make unreasonable demands on their own children? Would you demand our children to pretend to be what they're not?"

On the twenty-ninth day of July, Italians were in shock by the assassination of their king, Umberto. During his reign, the Pope and the majority of the Catholic clergy, Rosa thought, had opposed him in every endeavor, fearing, under him, the spread of socialism, and calling him the usurper of the temporal powers of the Pope, who expected, still, that his former territories would be restored to him. Under the reign of Umberto, who was killed because his assassin had considered him too conservative, public hygiene had been provided, protection of the rights of laboring classes had been instituted, socialized insurance against accidents had been established, long working hours for women and children had been prohibited, and a pension bureau had been established.

While Dante and Rosa mourned the death of the king, someone knocked on their door, and when Dante opened it, a man asked to see Rosa. It was her father's voice. Quickly, she went to the door. Her father and her mother stood before her, but before she could invite them in, her father, wearing a black armband, proclaimed the death of his daughter, and then he grasped the hand of her mother, who broke into tears, and pulled her away. Rosa ran into the hallway, grasped her mother, and dropped to her knees. While they wept together, her father, with a hard face, pulled her mother away and forbade either of them ever to see the other. As her parents departed, Dante placed his hands on Rosa's shoulder, and, unable to speak, they clung to each other.

The following week, he took her to Lettomanoppello.

The farmhouse was occupied, still, by the brother of the priest, because, he said, he had not found a house suitable to him. Dante, furious, told him to vacate the house by the end of the summer.

The feelings of the villagers toward Dante were split. Many of the paesani who had depended on the priest to read and write documents for them, turned with confidence to Dante, especially since he refused to accept a fee. But to some, a defrocked priest was one who lacked control over his sexual appetites, and his taking a woman was proof that he enjoyed sex.

One day, while Dante had gone into the village, the old priest on a donkey appeared at the hovel where Dante's father was outside, wondering what the priest was doing here in Lettomanoppello. The priest said he had heard that Dante was married. "It is true," Dante's father replied. And he called Rosa. When she came out, he put his arm about her waist and said, "Is she not beautiful? And would you believe that she, like the mother of Jesus, is Hebrew?" The priest seemed astonished. Dante's father said, "Come, get down off your ass and have communion with us, a little wine." The priest told him that he and his family would burn in hell. And Dante's father said, "Take you and your ass away from here. And take your brother with you." The priest went away, and they never saw him again. But some of the villagers said that the priest had told them that they who would associate with Dante would incur untold calamities.

Dante's mother, who had a fiery temper, became protective of Rosa, and when others stared contemptuously at her, Dante's mother yelled. "What are you gaping at? Do you want us to put a curse on you?" She, unlike Rosa, was anything but genteel.

After they returned to Rome, Rosa began bulging with a child.

Once, her mother came and visited for an hour.

"Your father must never know I came to see you. He forbids me to even mention your name, but he's inflicted terrible pain on himself."

Three days before Christmas, Rosa and Dante returned to Lettomanoppello.

The brother of the priest was still occupying the farmhouse.

On Christmas Day, an hour after midnight, Rosa bore her first child, a son, whom she named Amadeus, because his name, in Latin, was in honor of Pope Leo X, the patriarch of the Latin Rite of the Catholic Church who had freed Dante of his vows. As she had promised, Amadeus would be baptized in the Church, but as the son of a Jewish mother, according to her custom, he would be a Jew, a Jew who would be taught and raised in the Catholic faith of his father, as she had promised.

And during the day, relatives and friends visited, bringing gifts.

"This infant, born of love," Dante's father proclaimed, "born on this day, of all days, when Christians everywhere celebrate the birth of Jesus, is truly from God."

And the paesani were impressed, for this man, until this day, had never acknowledged God.

"Born in a hovel, in the first year of a new century, by a woman, who, like the mother of Jesus, is Hebrew. Can you believe this is merely a coincidence?"

And a neighbor swore he had seen a bright light over the hovel shortly after midnight.

"The precise time," Dante's father stated, "when the infant was born. Think of it!"

And another said he had heard a cock crowing in the night.

"Paesano," smiled Dante's father, "you've had too much wine."

The paesano thought about it, then he said, "I swear I heard a cock crowing, but at the time, it sounded like the crowing of the old priest."

They laughed.

Then Dante's mother said to his father, "You have something to do."

And then she told all the men except Dante to go.

They were gone over three hours.

When they returned, his father said, "Wrap the infant in a blanket, and let's go into the house."

They had removed the belongings of the priest's brother to the church in the village while the old man had protested, complaining that he had not yet found a house suitable to him.

A week later, Dante and his new family returned to Rome.

One day, that spring, while Dante was out of the apartment, there was a knock on the door, and as Rosa was about to open it, her mother entered. And she embraced Rosa. And then her father entered. He, too, embraced her.

Then Dante entered. He went into the bedroom, lifted Amadeus out of the crib, brought him into the kitchen, and presented him to his grandparents, who wept. First, his grandmother held him, and then his grandfather insisted that he hold his grandson.

Rosa, astonished, asked her mother what had brought about the change.

And her mother said that Dante had agreed to a wedding ceremony in the synagogue conducted by a rabbi, and that he, Dante, was willing to convert.

"No!" Rose cried out. Tears flooded her eyes. She took the baby away from her father, who seemed shocked, and she went into the bedroom, and dropped to the bed, face down, holding the baby.

Stunned, Dante, and her mother and her father stared at each other.

"Surely," said Dante, "if we open our hearts, we can find a way to keep this family together."

Now that her mother and father had seen their grandchild and had held it, he thought, they could no longer cling to their pain of denying themselves the joy of being united.

After Rosa had calmed down and the baby had gone to sleep, they talked of their situation and they drank wine.

Dante agreed to be married by a rabbi, and he agreed that, until then, Rosa and the child would live with her parents, but Rosa was reluctant. And then, having seen the joy in her parents who were hoping to be united again, she said that she and their grandchild would live with them for one week before the wedding, and that Dante would be allowed to visit them. Her mother was eager to accept her terms, and her father, who acted as though he was hiding his joy, accepted.

And they were married in the old synagogue, which, she had told Rose, later became a Catholic church with the Star of David over the entrance.

In October, Rosa returned to school to finish her last year of college. After her graduation, they returned to Lettomanoppello and lived on their small farm.

A year later, in 1903, the Pope, who had held the papacy for twenty-five years, died at the age of ninety-three. As time passed, the tension between church and state eased.

But friction was emerging in Dante's family, as though his brothers and sisters had forgotten their past struggles for survival. The small farm could not, as they had known long ago, support all of them, and during the times when employment had become scarce, especially lately when the family was growing, his brothers and sisters wanted money to buy land of their own, but there wasn't enough money to purchase property for all of them. Dante spoke of putting the farm in the name of his parents and of returning to Rome so that his brothers and sisters could do more work on the farm. "No," his father said. "That won't solve our problems. This property belongs to you. Without your effort, it would still belong to the old priest." But Dante returned to Rome to work again as a clerk in a hotel.

Occasionally, Americans would stay at the hotel and talk of great wealth in their country and of unlimited opportunities for all. Another clerk, Giovanni Nero from Calabria (known later in Cascade Flats as Black John) believed everything the Americans had said, and he told Dante he had read pamphlets about the United States where there was so much wealth that the streets were paved with gold, and everyone was a landowner who controlled his own destiny, unlike here, where the aristocracy still controlled everything. Dante was skeptical. "In every civilization," he said to Giovanni, "there has been an aristocracy that has taken advantage of the lower classes." Giovanni insisted that the United States was an exception, that American employers were seeking laborers and paying high wages because the country was growing rapidly. "The Americans," Giovanni stated, "have no peasants. Everyone is in the same class, all created equal." Dante shook his head. "Peasants are everywhere." And Giovanni replied, "Not in the region called New England where the opportunities are unlimited for everyone. As soon as I save enough money, I'm going."

Giovanni went to Lettomanoppello with Dante, and he showed pamphlets to some of the people and spoke excitedly about going to America, hoping others would go with him. Someone remarked, "What can we lose? Our poverty?" Though Giovanni was a stranger from Rome and had some difficulty understanding the lettesi dialect, he appealed to them through his enthusiasm. "Like you," he said, "I've been raised on a farm, but I've traveled, first to Naples, and then to Rome. In the cities, we tillers are the butt of jokes, but in New England, they're respected, and they make money. Everyone does. Not like here. Over there, you can still work the soil, or you can try other jobs. Many jobs."

They asked Dante what he thought of going to America. He shrugged, and when they pressed him for an opinion, he said, "I can only tell you what I've read and heard. Others have gone to America to fulfill a dream of a better life. Americans promise equality and the protection of rights of the people. It's the new promised land. But promises are not fulfillments, always, of our dreams. I've read that in the United States, some of the living conditions are even more squalid than here, that some children of the poor work twelve hours a day in fields, factories, and even in coal mines, that they must either work for small wages or starve, and that some Americans, having been influenced by the Puritans, blame poverty on the poor as proof of their moral inferiority, and praise wealth as a gift from God, as proof of their superiority. To alleviate poverty, the American president has sent young men of the poor into war. Like European politicians, he has been swept up by the fever of imperialism, glorifying war and conquest, saying that warfare builds the moral character of the nation. Such thinking frightens me. Don't be deluded by promises. Delusion is the breeding ground for greed and power."

"Do most Americans," someone asked, "think like their president?"

"I do not know."

"The American writer, Mark Twain, calls him a madman," Giovanni said.

"Yet," said Dante, "you want to go there."

"Why not? What do we have to lose? Many Americans think like we do. I have met some in Rome. Americans would welcome us, because they believe in freedom for all, and as Americans, we could hold the president to the promises of a government for the people, for us. If a president does not agree with us, we can get rid of him by electing another president. The United States gives us a dream, at least. What do we have here?"

Going to New England became the dream of many of the people in that region, but they wanted Dante to lead them. For months, he gathered information on the United States, especially on the region of New England, and he discussed it with Rosa, and they concluded that Americans were divided by the policy of imperialism, that most of them had gone to America, especially to New England, to be free from strife. "Why don't you take a journey there?" she suggested. "You could write about it for Del Popolo and maybe for other publications." He stared at her. "You mean, you want us to go?" She replied, "I must stay here with the children, but this is a great opportunity for you. The experience will be good, and you'll be earning money at the same time, if Del Popolo agrees." But he was reluctant to leave her; they would be separated for months. She said, "We'll never be separated! Go to America! Go to America and write."

The editor became interested in the idea, and he paid Dante in advance for the articles.

"My English," he said to Rosa in English, "is not very good. I wish to speak it better. Speak to me in English."

In the spring of 1908, after bringing her and their children to the farm, he left Italy from Naples and he landed at Ellis Island in New York City.

In his first letter from America, he wrote of a long, rough voyage on a crowded ship. The next time, if there would be a next time, he would travel first class in a cabin. At Ellis Island, there were long lines in which they had to wait hours, sometimes, to be subjected to various questions and examinations. Finally, they were allowed to enter a crowded street in New York, where many people were eager to take them places. The conditions in New York City were much worse than he had expected. He was living on Mulberry Street, among Italian immigrants, in squalor in terribly overcrowded tenements. In the Yiddish speaking section, conditions were as bad. And they were as bad in the Chinese section. The streets were not paved with gold. The only people he met who were becoming, maybe, remotely wealthy were landlords and shop owners who were taking advantage of the influx of immigrants who, unable to speak English, had landed in the city and had been desperately seeking work and a place to sleep.

Every month, his articles appeared in Del Popolo. He spent three months in New York City, and then he spent the next four traveling through New England. In Boston, he met families who had come from Lettomanoppello. Many of them had relatives in Portland. He went north, into New Hampshire, but had not met any Italians, not until he went to Barre, in Vermont and met Italians from Northern Italy who worked in granite quarries. From the mountains of Vermont, he crossed back into the mountains of New Hampshire, where he came upon a small community of French Canadians in a narrow valley with a loud, swift moving river. It was called Cascade. The inhabitants spoke a quaint patois, which, quite different from the French he understood, he was able, somehow, to understand them, for the dreams of peasants, he thought, were universal. They lived in shacks along a muddy road, which led to a paper mill.

When Dante told the owner of the mill that he was writing about America for an Italian magazine, the owner became friendly, gave him a tour of the area, and took him to dinner in Berlin. Berlin had begun as a fur trading post, Dante was told, even much smaller than Gorham, but was now growing into a city. When it had been named, there were no Germans living there, and there were no Italians in the town north of there, although it was named Milan (pronounced Mylin). The towns in that state had been given British names, but in defiance of the home country before the Revolution, the Yankees gave the towns foreign names. At dinner, the owner told Dante that he needed many workers, that there was so much work to be done in the paper mill, workers who were willing to work hard and steadily could become prosperous.

"The people I see here are poor," Dante said.

"That will change," the man said. "Money makes more money, but there are not enough workers to keep up with the demand. In a few more years, the mill will be huge, and the workers will be making enough money to own their own homes. This is a beautiful place to raise a family, here in these beautiful mountains. Have you ever seen such beautiful scenery?"

Dante, smiling, replied, "In Italy, but people need more than beautiful hills."

"And I'm willing to pay good wages for good workers."

Because Dante could speak French and could understand English, the man wanted him to supervise the workers.

"Try it, at least part time. It won't interfere with your writing. It will actually help it, giving you more experiences to write about. And I'll pay you high wages."

Gradually the mill expanded, and the owner asked Dante to invite workers from Italy.

One day Giovanni arrived at the farm and showed Rosa a letter he had received from Dante. A job in the mill was promised Giovanni if he wanted it. A year ago, he had married a young woman, Flora, from a neighboring farm, had taken her to Rome, and had promised her that they would be living in New England. When he received the letter, he could hardly contain his excitement. In the spring, he and Flora and their infant daughter, Anna, moved to Cascade.

Dante asked Rosa to join him in Cascade. "We can live here a few years, save money, and return to Lettomanoppello."

The idea appealed to her, and she began making arrangements for the journey.

Amadeus, who was almost ten, kept on his bedroom wall two huge maps: one of the Unites States, and the other of New Hampshire, which his father had sent him, and he pointed to the location above

Gorham, and below Berlin, and he said to his grandmother, "This is where we will live, in Cascata." And his nonna said, "When you return from Cascata, the maps will still be here in your room."

In the spring of 1910, a month before their departure, Rosa and her three children stayed in Rome with her parents near a new synagogue. On the opposite side of the road from the Tiberina Isle, along the east bank of the river, stood the great temple, not as huge as St. Peter's in the Vatican, but an imposing symbol to Rosa of her ancient heritage. A wide flight of stairs ascend to a high vestibule, supported by four columns, to three entrances into the hall of worship, and on an upper level, three huge windows are framed behind four more columns, and near the top, in the center of a cornice, the Tablets of the Ten Commandments with the Hebrew inscriptions emanate from golden rays of the sun; and above, on the peak of the cornice, extends the candelabrum with seven branches, the Menorah, representing the seven days of the Creation. And then a huge, gold colored dome rises skyward. In the spacious hall of worship, the dome, with rows of many colored segments converging toward the sun, is soaring into the heavens.

During that month, Rosa took Amadeus through the city to impress upon him their heritage. From the synagogue, she took him to the other side of the river, to the west bank, into Trastevere, where thousands of Hebrews had settled at least a hundred years before the birth of Christ; and then she took him a short distance north, to the Vatican and into the church of San Pietro with its magnificent altar by Bernini. "Pietro," she reminded her son, "was Hebrew. Most of the early Christians here in Rome were Hebrews, and their religion spread rapidly throughout the Roman Empire." They climbed a long flight of steps to a balcony, and they looked down, from a dizzying height, upon the hall of worship. Even from that height, the massive dome extended high above them. They went into a hallway and climbed a very narrow flight of stairs, one person behind the other, leaning to their right as the steps curved around the dome. At the top, looking down from the belvedere, the city of Rome was spread out below them.

In the Sistine Chapel, Amadeus seemed stunned by the frescoes of Michelangelo.

"How beautiful!" he said, gazing up at the middle of the ceiling, at God creating Adam.

They crossed the river again and returned south to their apartment. A short distance north of the apartment was the Pantheon with its high open dome, an ancient Roman temple that had been converted to a Catholic church. And a narrow street west of the Pantheon opened to the spacious Piazza Navonna. East of the apartment was the center of the ancient city, the Forum and the Colosseum. Closer to the apartment was the Portico of Octavia, erected a hundred years before, the entrance, since the middle of the fifteen hundreds, to the Ghetto. Nearby, in the small Piazza Mattei, she said to Amadeus, "This is where your father and I met, here, at the Fountain of Turtles."

That was the month of April when a huge comet blazed across the sky, the comet that appeared when the American writer Mark Twain died, ten days after their departure from Rome. Rosa and her three children and her younger unmarried brother, who had practiced medicine in Rome and was going to America to study more medicine, had left Rome for Naples, where they would embark on a ship to Boston. In Naples, they had met several others from Lettomanoppello who would be taking the same ship. And during their journey, the comet had appeared for several nights. As Dante, and her brother and her mother and her father, had insisted, they traveled first class, taking two cabins. Rosa and the youngest, Maria, occupied one cabin, and her sons and her brother occupied the adjoining one. And in the evenings, they sat on the deck and watched the comet.

That was the year that gave them promise of another beginning, a new life in a new world, a promised land, for she and her children were descendants of Hebrews, meaning: "They who came across the river."

They disembarked at Boston, and according to instructions Dante had sent her, she requested to be taken to North Station for a train to Portland. When they arrived at Portland, Dante was at the station to meet them, and he took them to a house on Fore Street, near the waterfront, where they stayed for two nights. There she met many relatives and friends from Lettomanoppello, for Portland had also been a port of disembarkation. And, within walking distance of the house was a train station where they boarded a train to New Hampshire. They got off the train in Gorham and took a trolley to Cascade. After they got off the trolley, they walked down a gradual slope along the border of the mill until they came to the house that Dante had purchased.

Her brother had stayed with them for a month, then he went to Portland to study and to work in a hospital. Two years later, when the first world war began, he returned to Italy to serve in the army.

After Amadeus graduated from high school, he, too, served in the war, in the American army, and he fought in France.

"After the war," Rosa had said to Rose last winter, "Amadeus returned to Lettomanoppello, and then he lived in Rome with my parents for five years while he attended college. During the following years, he traveled back and forth from here to Italy and tried to persuade us to go, for a visit, not to return there to live, he warned us. The small gains that the peasants had achieved under an independent Italy had been stripped away by the fascists. Amadeus was there, and he witnessed the rise of fascism. After the first world war, the success of the socialists in the elections incited fear among the bourgeoisie, and Mussolini saw an opportunity to exploit that fear. From socialism, he turned to the Italian nationalism that had been inspired by the Risorgimento, the resurgence that had resulted in Italian unity, and he appealed to the middle class, promising to maintain its economic and social status, and then he turned to the industrialists and big land owners. In spite of their suspicions of him, they were willing to pay the price to have someone control the workers. And people in the middle class were willing to acknowledge a hierarchy above them, because it meant that others were below them, and they conveniently blinded themselves to the barbarities of the fascists. One evening, after Amadeus came out of the synagogue in Rome, he was confronted by blackshirts and beaten. When he reported it to the police, they did nothing. Fascism was accepted and even praised here, in this country. People saw in it what they wished to see: law and order in a strong government opposed to communism. Nationalistic pride in Italy was necessary for the success of the Risorgimento, and in the United States it was necessary for the success of the Revolution. The music of Giuseppe Verdi, and our pride in the achievements of art and literature and philosophy has inspired pride in the Italian. But who is the Italian? And what is nationalism? Nationalism focuses on certain characteristics of people and exaggerates them, excluding all the others, and at times, it stereotypes them, even distorts them. For example, some American Protestants think an Italian is a biased, superstitious, ignorant Catholic who blindly worships the Pope and devotes his life to the Church, but some American Catholics think an Italian is a renegade Catholic who's too stubborn to listen to priests or to attend a church. And, during the war, when I had to fill out a long form because I am an Italian alien, a woman in the office told me that if I am Italian, my religion could not possibly be Jewish."

As the fascists rose to power in Italy, Rosa had said, most Americans expected Italians to feel proud of the new regime. Many Italians had faith in Mussolini, but Amadeus had warned that the fascists were ruthless in their power, that Il Duce was a tyrant, not a benevolent dictator. Communism and crime had been effectively suppressed, and the trains ran on time, and the unification of Italy would be complete by bringing Corsica and Nice and Malta and parts of Dalmatia into the union, but at what price? Blackshirts had replaced the former thugs of crime syndicates and were given a license to terrorize the lower classes.

Mussolini was an atheist, and one of his antagonists was the Pope, but Mussolini found a way around him, Rosa had told Rose. Mussolini declared Catholicism as the state religion, thus ending, for a time, the separation of Church and State, on the surface, at least. And the Vatican was declared an autonomous state; therefore, it no longer was required to pay taxes to the Italian government. The Pope thought that he could control Mussolini and that, together, they would end the threat of communism in Italy.

No one really knew what fascism was, perhaps not even Mussolini, warned Amadeus. It was a government controlled by the State. And Mussolini was the State. It was nationalistic and patriotic, somehow, Il Duce wanted the people to believe. Italian liberals thought there were too many obstacles in Italy for fascism to succeed and that it would quickly burn itself out, but when the Pope refused to support the Popolari, the Catholic political party, and told priests to get out of politics, the biggest obstacle to fascism was removed, and it cloaked itself in militaristic religious terms, implying that fascism was essentially Catholic and patriotic, though, according to Rosa, some of Mussolini's closest supporters were Jews.

Another obstacle was the monarchy, but the strength of fascism was too much, the king felt, to oppose it without bloodshed, so Mussolini, the prime minister, became a virtual dictator of a hierarchy, with the peasants, as usual, at the bottom, suppressed, not by a foreign power, but by a government, which, to them, was a foreign power. And like a foreign government, it was resisted by the grandchildren of the Risorgimento.

Mussolini was never able to completely control Italian society or the papacy and the monarchy, which often stood in his way. He saw that the Nazi ideology was more effective than his, and he tried to implement stronger policies, policies of aggression, foreign and domestic, of imperialism in the name of patriotism, to instill in Italians a feeling of superiority. The antagonism between Christian and Jews, stretching back to the history of Christianity, nearly two thousand years, was the key, he thought, to inciting patriotic fever that had made the Nazis so efficient; and, like Hitler, he began to campaign against the Jews, blaming them for internal conflicts and the rise of communism.

And Mussolini formed an alliance with Berlin. But his policies were strongly opposed in Italy. Catholic journals condemned the alliance and the persecution of the Jews as Nazi neopaganism creeping into fascism. The Church, in fear of a proletarian revolution, allowed the suppression of the peasants but not of the Jews.

In one of his stories, Dante compared Christianity to a tree that had sprung up from the soil of Judaism. To hate the Jew, the story showed, is to hate the Christian. Yet, the haters take from the Jews their traditions and distort them to fit into the confines of a twisted world. And in a similar story, he wrote: "Even if the thorns pain you, do not destroy the bush if you want the roses to survive." Both stories showed that to suppress the peasant, yet taking from him the fruits of his labor for our own profits while denying him the fruits of his own labor, is to crush our own humanity. The editor of Del Popolo sent the scripts to a Catholic journal and wrote to Dante saying that criticism of the regime had been banned but that Catholic journals could get away with it, infuriating the hard core fascists.

The editor added in the letter that he was concerned that Mussolini would plunge Italy into a world war on the side of the Nazis, cutting open deep internal wounds.

"I wrote to my parents," Rosa had said, "pleading with them to come here, but they wrote back saying that they felt safe in Italy. Dante and I finally decided to go there to persuade them to come here, but we were too late."

Corsica and Nice had become annexed to Italy when Mussolini sent troops into that part of France, and President Roosevelt, who had spoken admirably of Italy, because Italy had been an American ally during the first war, now called Mussolini a backstabber, but Italians, Rosa had told Rose, had not been prepared to fight for Mussolini and the axis powers. He could not believe that factory workers would actually go on strike during wartime, especially since strikes had been declared illegal long before the war had started. After some of his blackshirts had begun to intimidate some workers, more workers protested and went on strike. They were aware that Mussolini needed them for the war effort. He had no choice but to accede to their demands for higher wages and to better working conditions.

Rosa had not learned until the war had ended what was happening to the Jews, but she feared the worse. In the Italian occupied areas, Jews were safe, although the official fascist policy was to cooperate with the Nazis.

Mussolini was losing support of his fascist council. When Sicily was invaded, the council met, and a new prime minister, Badoglio, a fascist who was loyal to the monarchy, was appointed. Mussolini was taken into custody, sent to an isolated hotel on a mountain peak on Campo Imperatore of the Gran Sasso of Abruzzo, and the king sent the new prime minister to meet secretly with the western allies to negotiate a joint action against the German troops in Italy before Hitler would send in reinforcements, but there were serious complications. The allies had committed themselves to an unconditional surrender of Italy. Badoglio wanted an allied invasion at Genoa, or as far north, at least, as Rome, which was held by Italian troops, but Eisenhower didn't trust him and saw Italians as poor fighters. The talks dragged. The conquest of Sicily was swift and easy. Mafiosi from America, calling themselves American patriots, soon took over Sicily, again. Convicted criminals, such as Lucky Luciano, had been released and sent to Sicily to aid in the invasion, and they had been rewarded by the American government to remain free, labeling it as "deportation."

Badoglio signed the surrender and requested that the announcement be delayed long enough to redeploy the Italian troops, but Eisenhower immediately announced the surrender of Italy, and the German troops occupied Rome. The allies quickly moved from Sicily into Calabria, but at Salerno, south of Naples, they encountered opposition. German troops had replaced the Italian troops and were pouring into Italy. During the first month of the Nazi occupation, over a thousand Jews in Rome were deported to the death camps, never to be seen again; another thousand took refuge in the Vatican. The people resisted the German occupation but suffered severe reprisals. The allies took ten months to move from Salerno to Rome.

Long before then, Mussolini had been rescued by the Germans in the Gran Sasso, a few kilometers north of Lettomanoppello. A small plane, with a squad of soldiers had landed on a small strip of land at the hotel entrance, and the soldiers rushed in, took Mussolini from his room, and somehow lifted off at the edge of a cliff.

The war continued two more years.

"A fifth of the Italian Jews were apprehended by the Nazis and sent to the death camps. We never thought that could happen in Italy, and rightly or wrongly, we felt betrayed by the Italian government, because it had associated with the Nazis. And yet, as an Italian, I'm proud to know that the Italian people had tried to protect the Jews and had aided the Jews who had escaped from Nazi occupied territories. That had been possible only because Italy had been an ally of Germany, I know. But the Jews had felt safe in Italy, at least until Italy had surrendered. And then Germany saw Italy as an enemy. If Italy had declared neutrality at the beginning of the war, I think the Jews in Italy would have been safe."

Winston Churchill was supportive of the king and believed that the fascist government was better than a communist one, but the Italians, especially the grandchildren of the Risorgimento who had resisted fascism from its inception and then fought the Germans, felt betrayed by the government, and they required nothing less than the abdication of the king and a new government.

"Imagine if you could," Rosa had said, "the shame of decent people, Italian and German and Japanese and others, when the rest of the world expressed the shock and the horror of the atrocities committed in the name of a love that no decent person can oppose, in the name of patriotism, but in a form of nationalism that's exclusive of world citizenship and of respect for the rights and cultural heritage of others. People say that cannot happen here. But during the war, a fascist element forced you and your family from your home."

"During the war," Rose had asked her, "did you and Tattone, as Italians, have to report someplace?"

"At the post office, once a week, until the war with Italy ended. We were not allowed to travel without permission."

"Even though your two youngest sons were killed in the war, fighting for our country!"

While Rose and Dante were looking at the deed to their small farm in Italy, she asked his grandparents, "When we go, will you come with us?"

They both smiled.

"Of course," Rosa said. "That would make us very happy."

Rose squeezed Dante's hand.

"When shall we go?" she asked him.

"Next summer, as soon as the school year ends."

The elder Dante said, "We can stay at least a month, maybe two. First, we will show you Rome, the places your Nonna and I knew. And then Lettomanoppello. The house is occupied now by my youngest sister and her family, but the house is more than big enough to accommodate all of us. You will enjoy meeting the rest of the family. So will we."

"Would they," Rose asked hesitantly, "think of me as strange?"

"They are family," Rosa answered. "They know who you are. They have pictures of you. How beautiful, they write, is the grand-daughter of Flora and Giovanni Nero! Your family in Italy is waiting to meet you."

6

The porch reverberated under quick steps. The kitchen door swung open.

"For crysakes!"

Tony, in gray trousers splotched with old flour stains, approached Dante who stood up, and they embraced.

"Schmuck!"

Tony turned to Rose.

"You crazy kids!"

He pulled her up from the chair and squeezed her against him.

"Oh, Rosie! I can't say I'm surprised, but I wish the hell we were celebrating in New York."

"Have you eaten yet?" his grandmother asked in Italian.

"As soon as you walk in here, she wants to feed you. She's afraid we'll all starve to death."

"Sit down," his grandmother said, pointing to a chair to her left.

"I want to sit right here, next to Rosie."

He pulled the chair out, dragged it behind his grandmother, and placed it at the corner of the table, between her and Rose.

"You don't mind if I sit next to you, do you? Even if you do, I'm sitting here anyway."

Rose grinned.

He sat down. He looked at Dante, then he looked at her again.

"What the hell do you see in him, anyway?"

She didn't reply.

"How come you're so quiet? I bet you're exhausted from last night. Didn't you get any sleep at all?"

She blushed.

"For crysakes, Rosie! You're going to wear out my poor little brother!"

"Here," his grandfather said, placing a mug of coffee on the table in front of Tony. An aroma of homemade anisette, almost a hundred proof, ascended from the mug. His grandfather plunked an ashtray in front of Tony, who lit a cigarette.

"How did Ma react?" asked Dante.

"Whadid you expect?" Tony muttered, and he took a swallow from his drink.

Rose looked from Tony to Dante, and then her eyes met Rosa's, as though both of them were thinking of the reaction of Rosa's father, fifty-two years earlier.

"Give her time to come to terms with the situation," Tony said, flicking ashes into the tray. "It's just that she's so damned scared for you guys. And you can't blame her for that, but now that you're married, she's going to accept it. That doesn't mean she's not going to worry like crazy. Hey, you know she's thought about you two getting married, and you know how she reacted to that idea, so, give her time now to get used to it."

A momentary silence annoyed him. He took another sip from his drink, and then he puffed on his cigarette.

"I told Black John last night that you were married. He happened to come in the restaurant. He was happy as hell. Everybody's happy for you. Except Ma, of course."

"I should go see her," Dante said.

"That won't do any good. Wait till you come back from church. Maybe by then, she'll calm down a little."

"But I don't want to give her the impression that we're ignoring her."

"Too late for that. You got married without telling her. That, to her, is ignoring her. And she won't accept any explanations. To her, the fact that you got married was like pouring salt into her wounds."

"Several times, I've told her I was getting married, but she didn't want to listen to me. Well, anyway, I think it's better if I see her now rather than a little later. At least that'll show we don't want to exclude her from our lives."

"Do you want me to go with you?" asked Rose.

He was thinking.

He heaved a deep sign.

"I think it's better if I go alone."

"Take your brother with you," said the elder Dante in Italian. "The two of you together will strengthen your appeal, especially since your brother has already experienced a similar appeal."

"If she's accepted Joy so easily, she'll accept your marriage, but let me finish my coffee first."

"And while you are there," his grandfather said to Tony, "change into a suit."

"Why?"

"You are going to church with us."

"Who? Me?"

His grandfather stared at him.

"Come with us," his grandmother said softly, "to show reverence for your brother and his wife."

Tony lifted his cup, held it up in front of him, and said, "To you, Dante and Rosie, to a long life filled with happy children," and he took a big swallow.

"Maybe," his grandmother said, "the church will fall on us, but at least we'll be together."

Tony noticed the deed to the farm on the table.

"A wedding gift," his grandfather said, "for Dante and Rosa. Next year, we will all go there, together."

"Oh, that would be great! I can't wait to go back! Did Nick tell you about it?" Tony asked Rose in English.

"He said he enjoyed meeting the people, especially our relatives."

"They love him. They'll love you, too. It's been seven years already, since I've been there. Hey, our relatives are the friendliest in the world, but they're poor. They don't have the comforts and the conveniences we have, not most of the people. They don't have electricity and indoor plumbing and telephones, and very few people have cars, and the cars are old. And they don't eat as well as we do. They're at least fifty years behind us, but our relatives are the warmest and the sincerest people in the world. They live in villages on tops of mountains with roads small and curvy along the edges of cliffs in some places. There's a lot to discover there. You'll find it interesting."

"And Nick's ordination will be in Rome next summer," said Rose.

"We have a lot to look forward to," said Dante.

They grew silent.

"Well," Tony said after he had stubbed his cigarette and had finished his drink, "I'm not looking forward to the confrontation with Ma, but let's get this over with."

Tony and Dante stood up.

"Do you want me to wait here?" Rose asked Dante.

He nodded, and then he and Tony went out.

On the other side of the road, in warm sunlight, four elderly men wearing shabby derbies and puffing on Italian stogies were sitting around a folding table and playing cards as though their lives depended on the outcome of the game. Two of them were laughing, and the other two were cursing in Italian as they each slammed their cards on the table. One sounded as though he yelled in English, "Bah fun ghoul!"

Dante and Tony walked passed them, onto a short dirt road to the paved main road. On the other side of the main road was a parking lot for the mill workers. When they got to the road, they turned right onto a sidewalk that led to the gate of the mill, walked a few steps, and then crossed the road to a green house with white trimmings.

"Ma's downstairs," said Tony, "with Joy."

They followed a paved driveway between the house on their left and the restaurant on their right, approached the house at the side entrance, near the back, climbed a few steps, walked across the back end of the porch, passed a stairway that led upstairs, came to the kitchen door, and as Dante opened it, his mother, in a blue housecoat, stared at him from the kitchen table where she was sitting with Joy.

Dante entered, with Tony behind him.

As Dante approached his mother, she put her hands to her face.

"Ma," said Dante, and he leaned over and kissed her forehead.

"Where's Rosie?"

"She's with Nonna and Tattone."

"I don't want to see her now. I can't."

"It's okay, Ma."

"Damn it, Ma! How can you refuse to see her?"

"Tonio," Dante said, "calm down."

"Calm down," muttered Tony. "I'm going to get dressed."

"Why?" asked Joy.

Without answering her, Tony went into his room.

"We're all going to church," said Dante as Joy approached him.

"Congratulations," said Joy, and she embraced him.

"Thanks."

"Do you want coffee and something to eat?"

"No, thanks. I just stopped in for a few minutes to see how Ma's doing."

Joy withdrew from him, went to the other side of the table and sat down again.

"Ma," he said softly, yet firmly. "I understand how you feel. Rose understands, too. But we have to live our own lives; we have to live for ourselves, first. Please try to understand how Rose and I feel. We know that life isn't going to get any easier than it has been, and we've all been through a lot, together. Rose is strong, Ma, and she has a lot of faith. We're not going to let ourselves be controlled by a bunch of bigots. Together, we can, and we will, cope with our situation. We've spent our lives together, Rose and I, and we're prepared to spend the rest of our lives together, but we need you now, Ma, more than we've ever needed you. We're begging you for your support. No matter what happens, we'll always have each other for a family, and this family has always been strong, because we've always been together, no matter what. That's the way we've always been. That's the way you and Papa have always wanted us to be."

"Of course, I'll support you! What's done is done. Just give me a little more time to recuperate. I'll see you and Rose after church. I'd go with you, but I'm feeling a little sick to my stomach. Is your brother really going with you?"

"Yeah, Ma."

"How'd you persuade him?"

"He wants to come with us so we'll be together as a family."

"He does?"

"Of course."

She raised her right hand and waved it.

"I hope the church doesn't cave in."

Dante laughed, and Tony, from his bedroom, laughed.

"That's what Nonna said!" Tony yelled.

"Is she going, too?"

"Nonna and Tattone," said Dante.

"If the church caves in, she'll have to take you to the synagogue. Maybe that'll cave in, too."

"Not today, anyway. Maybe next Saturday."

"Well, Ma," Tony said as he entered the kitchen, "you're looking better, and you act like you've recuperated already."

"Well, look at you! All dressed up. You can look like a human being when you want to."

"Let me do your necktie for you," Joy said to Tony.

"Wow. I'm being treated like royalty, and from my own wife."

"Well," she said, "it's not everyday that I see you all dressed up like this. And on your way to church, no less. Oh, hell! I'm going, too."

"If you're going with us, be ready in an hour."

Tony and Dante left the house, walked quickly over the driveway, crossed the road, stepped onto the dirt path, passed the elderly men playing cards, crossed the back street, and as they approached the side porch of the house, the back screen door swung open.

"Dante!"

His Aunt Maria embraced him. She was his father's only sister, short and plump, and full of life, who was living upstairs. He called her "Zizi" for "Aunt" in the lettesi dialect.

She pulled Dante into the kitchen, close to Rose, who was standing.

Maria, between them, put her arms around them and said, "You're a beautiful couple! When you get back from church, we'll take lots of pictures."

Rose asked Dante, "Did you see your mother?"

He nodded.

"For godsakes," Maria said, "let's not let anything spoil this beautiful day. I'll go talk to her right now."

"We just talked to her," Dante said. "She'll be okay."

"Oh, good! She's going to church with you then."

"Well, no."

"No! Why not?"

She looked from Dante to Tony.

Tony shrugged.

"She's going to church with you, so don't leave without her. I'm going to talk with her, right now. And after church, meet me in the restaurant. I'm going to make a big bowl of gnocchi."

She kissed Rose on the cheek, then she kissed Dante on the cheek.

"See you kids after church."

7

"You look like Adam and Eve!"

Dante and Rose were naked, bathing waist deep in the brook in front of their cabin as Tony approached them from the thick forest. In gray corduroy trousers and a white sweatshirt, he came to a narrow strip of beach and grinned at them.

"This must be the Garden of Eden."

Rose, having crossed her arms to cover her breasts, groaned, sinking deeper into the water until it was up to her neck.

"Hey, Rosie! You have a beautiful body!"

"Damn you, Tonio!"

"Hey, don't let me interrupt anything. I'll just stand here and watch."

He lit a cigarette.

"Will you do something about your brother?"

Dante splashed him.

Tony jumped back, but not in time.

"Hey, you got my cigarette wet!"

"Turn away," Dante said, "so we can come out."

"You don't have to come out."

Dante splashed him again.

"Okay! Okay!"

Dante grabbed a huge towel from a big rock near the shore and held it up for Rose as she emerged from the water. He wrapped the towel around her, and then she dashed into the cabin. Dante grabbed another towel, tucked the ends in at his waist, and moved onto the shore, his small body moving lithely.

"I just want to remind you, the family is getting together this long weekend," Tony said.

Dante nodded, murmuring, "That's right, today is the Fourth of July. You're not opening the restaurant tonight, are you?"

"Ma thinks we should, because Friday's are so busy, but I decided to close. As a matter of fact, I decided to close for the whole weekend. I won't have to work now until Monday. So, I can really enjoy the next couple of days. We can celebrate your marriage again."

Twelve days ago, all their friends and relatives in the flats had celebrated the marriage and had spoken of celebrating it again on this Fourth of July.

Tony said, "Get dressed, will you?"

"I'll get you a beer."

"Get dressed first."

Dante went inside.

Birds were chirping in treetops, and the flow of the brook was making a pleasant sound, accentuating the tranquility of the forest, but at the end of this summer, thought Tony, Dante and Rosie would have to leave this wilderness to encounter the rest of the world.

He sat on a rock in the sunlight and puffed on his cigarette. It was soggy, like the front of him. He grinned at himself and tossed the cigarette away. It landed near a chipmunk who seemed to take a whiff of it, scrambled away, turned towards Tony, and ran up to his feet and sat on its hind legs.

Tony gaped at it.

"What the hell do you want? A good cigarette?"

It was looking back at Tony.

"I don't believe you! Are you really begging for a cigarette? Shame on you! This is for me," he said as he reached into his front pocket and pulled out a pack of cigarettes. He lit one.

The cabin door opened, and Rose came out. She was wearing dark blue slacks and a white blouse with short sleeves. She moved gracefully towards them, sat on a rock next to Tony, and held a peanut above her lap.

"Come on, Chippy."

The chipmunk leaped onto her knee, moved quickly over her lap, sat on its hind legs, placed its paws on her hands and took the peanut.

"I'll be damned! No wonder it seemed so damn friendly. But why am I so surprised? Francis of Assisi and Santa Clara, living in the wilderness."

The chipmunk slid the peanut, shell and all, into its mouth, pushing it to one side of its pouch, and looked up at her. She smiled, opened her hand and uncovered two more peanuts. The chipmunk seemed to hold her hand open, took another nut, slid it to the other side of its pouch, took the last peanut, holding it at the front of its mouth, and seemed to study her for a moment, and then it turned, leaped to the ground, and scrambled away, disappearing into brush on the other side of the cabin.

"That looks like fun. Why don't you let me do that?"

"You want to feed the chipmunk?"

"I mean, let me sit on your lap, and you can put peanuts in my mouth, if you promise to shell them first."

"I don't have enough peanuts," she said, grinning.

"Are you saying I've got a big mouth?"

She smiled.

"Damn you, Rosie! What've you and Dante been doing the past two weeks besides playing with wild animals and bathing naked?"

"Doing what comes naturally."

"Oh!" he howled. "That sounds like fun! Lucky you. And lucky Dante! You really are like Adam and Eve. And in your Garden of Paradise. But in a few more weeks, you'll have to return to our so-called civilized society. Doesn't it get boring, though, communing with the wilderness?"

"Not at all. We've also been reading. And, of course, Dante's been writing."

"On your honeymoon?"

"Why not?"

Tony shook his head, and then he said, "When he's writing, he tends to forget everything else."

"He doesn't!"

"I mean, you have to expect him to write, I guess. He's done that all his life, but you need to be together, really together, this summer, while you have the time and the chance. Do you know what I mean?"

"We are. We are really together. He's happy, and so am I. This past two weeks has been so wonderful, it really is a honeymoon!" she said, looking at him with eyes that could melt the heart of anyone, he thought. "Don't worry about us, for godssakes. He has to write, now, while he has the chance, and I want him to write."

"I guess you have to accept him the way he is."

"I wouldn't want him any other way."

"But people change, especially after marriage. How would you want him to change?"

She stared at him.

"I never want him to change! If he changes, he won't be he; he won't be Dante."

"Change is inevitable."

She stared at him.

Finally, she said, "Maybe for you, and maybe for me, but he's Dante, and he will always be Dante."

"There's a saying, that love is blind. That means, I guess, that when you're blinded by love, you see only the good things in someone you love, the things you want to see, but when you live with *him*, you get to see the things you never saw before, the things you never wanted to see."

"And familiarity breeds contempt!"

"Right!"

"And you've lived with Dante all your life. Are you contemptuous of him?"

"But we're not talking about *me*; we're talking about *you*."

"Well, I've known Dante all my life, too, although not quite the way I know him now. I think I know him better than anyone else knows him. I don't think love is blind. Infatuation is. I think love enhances the ability, provides the insight, to see things that are unseen by others. It gives us the light to understand things that oth-

ers can't. When we love, I think that means we see the good in someone; we see the divine. But that's not the same as being physically
attracted to someone. Were you physically attracted to Joy when you
married her?"

"I still am. Do you think I was blinded by physical attraction?"

"Well, I think attraction can, and should be, related to love, but
when it isn't, it can be blind, and if it's blind, then it isn't love; it's sexual, without love, a blind force. Love, I think, makes sex more exciting than the forbidden fruit, although I can't honestly compare. But
I think love is what provides the ecstasy in sex. What do *you* think?"

He drew a puff from his cigarette, exhaled the smoke, and said,
"That's something I've been thinking about for years, but I've never
actually drew a conclusion. I've never discussed the ecstasy in sex
before, not with anyone."

"Not even with Joy?"

"Especially not with her."

She stared at him.

"Why not?"

"Have you talked about it with Dante?"

"Of course!"

"Before you were married?"

"No, not until we were married, until we actually had sex
together."

"You mean, you didn't have sex until you were married?"

"Of course not."

"You're kidding."

"Why would I kid about it?"

He took another puff.

"I guess Dante's been too busy writing."

"What! Of course not. That doesn't mean he's, well, if he's any
example, writers are deeply passionate. I bet Joy is, too."

"Not when she's writing. It drains her energy. She's just chasing
rainbows, feeding her fantasies and wearing herself out."

"You don't encourage her."

"At first I did, to write as a hobby, as enjoyment, or at least to
vent her frustrations, but not all day, every day, sitting on her ass

and pretending to be an important, famous author. Dante, at least, is talented."

"You don't think her writing is good enough?"

He shrugged.

"Not compared to Dante's. I can even write better than she does."

"You've never shown me anything you've written, so I can't comment."

"I don't want to encourage her. Writers are a dime a dozen, and very few of them can earn a living at it. I don't think they should be encouraged. Would you encourage someone to be a Hollywood movie star?"

She frowned.

"You sound bitter."

"Well, maybe I am, a little, I guess, but I'm realistic. I mean, when you're married, especially with children, certain things should have priority over others. I mean, you should fulfill certain commitments, or else the relationship is doomed to failure."

"What do you mean by commitments?"

"Connecting with each other, and satisfying each other's basic needs."

"Why not feed her fantasy? If you satisfy her needs, she might respond to yours."

"I don't want to deceive her more than she's already deceived herself. I'd be seducing her by using something that's already seduced her, encouraging her to chase grand delusions, chasing something that promises her the ultimate orgasm."

"You can't be serious."

He puffed on his cigarette.

"Why not?"

"To Joy and Dante, writing is as instinctive as breathing."

"A truly gifted person doesn't need encouragement. Think about it. You're the one who encourages Dante, but even if you didn't, he would write. As you've said, with him it's as instinctive as breathing."

"Everybody should be encouraged! Even someone as gifted as Dante. Besides, I look forward to reading Dante's stories."

"But the person he has to impress is the guy in the publishing house who wades through mounds of scripts, day in and day out, and says, 'I can't take much more of this shit!'"

Rose sighed.

"I know, but I'm going to make damn sure that I never discourage Dante, no matter how tough things get. I'll keep reminding myself, if I have to, that your grandmother still encourages your grandfather, and that Dante, like his grandfather, won't ever fail, not for lack of trying, because I'll always be right behind him, pushing him up towards that damn rainbow."

Tony stared at her.

Dante, wearing a white shirt with short sleeves, dark blue trousers, and sneakers, came out of the cabin with two bottles of beer.

"Rosie tells me you've been writing."

Dante, offering a bottle to Tony, nodded.

"What have you been writing about?"

Dante shrugged.

"He's been writing about your last year in high school," Rose said. "Tell him about the last chapter you've finished."

"No," muttered Dante.

Smiling, she turned to Tony and asked, "Who's Sheena?"

"What!" Tony exclaimed. "What the hell did you write?"

Dante shrugged again.

"About your seduction," Rose said, "of your Sheena, queen of the jungle."

Tony's mouth dropped open.

"You didn't!"

"It's only fiction."

"You dumb shit! Let me see it."

"Naw. You don't want to read it, not now."

"The hell I don't! And I'm going to sue you for defamation of character."

"Do you really think I'd write what really happened?"

"That's exactly what I think."

"No one would believe it, anyway."

"Go get the damn script! And bring me another bottle of beer."

8

"Doesn't he make you angry, Rosie, when he writes stuff like this?"

She grinned.

"Why should that make me angry? Does it bother you when he writes about us?"

"If this gets published, it'll bother the people he's writing about. It'll embarrass them.

"Do you remember that year?"

"Of course not."

She smiled at him.

"How can you not remember your white sex goddess?" she said.

Dante said, "Long before that I had written a story about the scariest part of growing up."

"Really?" Tony asked. "What's the scariest part of growing up?"

"The two biggest subjects that grownups don't want to talk about in front of kids, yet the most popular subjects for movies."

Rose said, "I remember the day when you wrote it into a story."

"I remember the night before," said Dante, "because we had been talking about evil with my father. Do you remember that?"

"We were right here that night," Rose said, "sitting by a fire."

"All of us. Do you remember?" Dante asked Tony.

"There were a lot of times, not just here, when Pa used to discuss ideas with us."

"I remember your father telling us that night," Rose said, "how we're all connected with everything in the cosmos, that we're a part of these woods, with the trees and the animals and with the moon and the stars."

They had been sitting outside around a fire on a cool summer evening, roasting marshmallows, when he was telling Dante and Rose that the stars were suns millions of millions of millions of miles away and that they were seeing the lights of the stars traveling through space, that some of the lights had come from the stars thousands of years ago.

"If you could travel a hundred and eighty-six thousand miles in just one second, the same speed of the lights, you would have to travel years just to reach the stars closest to us."

"Wow!" Rose exclaimed. "How long would it take to get to the stars farthest away?"

"We're near one end of the Milky Way Galaxy. Traveling at the speed of light to the other end of our galaxy would take us over a hundred thousand years. And beyond our own galaxy are probably thousands of other galaxies. Maybe more. We don't know yet."

"Can God be way out there, that far?" Rose asked.

"What does it say in your catechism?"

"God is everywhere. But that's so far away!"

"To us, it is, because we're such tiny specks in the universe. Even our earth is a speck compared to the whole universe, yet it seems so huge to us, we call it the world. But there are many worlds, and our sun is an average star. Look at one of the stars, any one. Do you have a star picked out?"

"Yes," she said.

"The star is so far away, it's difficult to imagine how far away it is. Yet, you see its light. And seeing it, you feel that it's much closer to you; and, in a sense, it is, because it's within your vision. Imagine that the light is the eye of the star. Do you feel it looking back at you?"

"Yes!"

"As the light comes from the star, life comes from God, and that life is what makes you. And you can feel it. If you concentrate hard enough, you can feel it deep inside of you, glowing."

"I can feel it!"

"I can, too!" Dante said.

"You can, whenever you let your deepest feelings reach out."

After a while, Rose asked, "How old is God?"

"What does your catechism say?"

"God always is, always was, and always will be."

"So, something that always is has never been created and doesn't age. Everything else has been created from something else. Everything else that exists comes from something that exists. Something comes from something else. Something does not come from nothing. So we know there must always be something. That's what God is. Always something. We call that eternal existence. And you are part of that something. You are part of something, which is eternal."

"Do you know why God made us?" she asked.

"Why?"

"God made us to know Him, to love Him, and to be happy with Him forever in heaven. That's what it says in the catechism."

"Yes, I know."

"Is that true?"

"What is?"

"What it says in the catechism."

"As far as I know, it is."

"Is the Catholic religion the true religion?"

He grinned at her, picked up a thick stick that he was using for a poker, pushed the end of it into the fire, and said, "For you and Dante, it is, otherwise you couldn't believe in it." He moved the stick a little, stirring the ashes, and made the fire blaze. "Your religion is true, if it helps you to know God, but to know is only the first step, as your catechism says. How can you know anything?"

"By studying," Rose answered.

"You mean, reading about something? Like studying your catechism to know about God?"

"But," Dante asked, "how do we know that grownups know about God?"

"Good question, Dante. How can we know anything about anything?"

"I guess we have to believe what grownups tell us."

"But sometimes," Rose said, "grownups are wrong."

"When you believe what someone is telling you, what do you call that?"

"You mean, faith?" Dante said.

"Faith, yes, that's what it's called. Faith. Suppose I tell you that if you put your hand in the fire, it will burn your hand?"

"That's true," Dante said.

"How do you know?"

"I just know."

"But how? Can I convince you, somehow, that there is a way that you can put your hand in the fire for a whole minute without burning it, without even hurting it? Can I convince you that I know how to do it?"

"You would have to show me."

"Good. You want a demonstration; you want proof. I'm going to hold the end of this stick in the fire. What will happen to the end of this stick?"

"It'll catch on fire."

"How do you know?"

"I just do."

"But *how* do you know?"

"It's on fire now," Dante grinned.

"How do you know?"

"I can see it."

"Are you saying you know from experience?"

"Yes! We know something when we experience it."

"And once you know, what's the next step?"

"To love," Dante said.

"You both know the catechism well."

"And to serve God and to be happy with Him forever in heaven," added Rose. "That's why God made us."

"So, is that your purpose in life? Happiness?"

"That must be," she said, "because that's what it also says in our Declaration of Independence."

"What do you mean?"

"It says that all men are created equal, that we all have a right to life, liberty, and the pursuit of happiness."

"So, your purpose in life is happiness, but the first step is to know, to know God. But how can you know God?"

"How can we experience God?" asked Dante.

"Good question. I was just going to ask you that. How can we experience God is the same as asking how can we experience everything good."

"That's impossible!" said Rose.

"You're right. Only God is God. Only God experiences everything good, because all things good come from God. But we can experience, and we can know, something about things close to us. To really know something, you have to experience it; you have to feel it. You have to understand it deep down. You know something is true when you discover it for yourself, not just believing what someone tells you to believe. So, to know God is impossible, but we can know some things about God by knowing some things close to us. And the more knowledge we have, the more we know God. So, even when you get older, you'll have to continue studying everything, including religion. Believing in a religion is called faith. God gave us the ability to experience and the ability to think, to put our experiences in a logical order to give meaning to them. Using our ability to think is called reasoning. And God gave us something that connects our reasoning with our faith. It's the feeling that glows deep down inside of you, the light that come from God. To really know anything or anyone, even yourself, you have to use your faith and reasoning, and you have to use the light."

"What's the light called?" Rose asked.

"It's your deepest feeling. What do you call your deepest feeling?"

Dante said, "It's the second step."

"Love," she said.

"Love. Just as your faith and your reasoning grow the more you use them, the more you use the light within you, the stronger it grows."

Rose smiled and turned to Dante, the flames shining on her face.

"Dante's going to be a priest, and I'm going to be a nun."

Dante whispered in her ear, "Then I won't be able to kiss you anymore."

"Aren't you going to be a priest?" she asked.

"I don't know yet."

"Why are you thinking of being a priest?" his father asked.

"Ma thinks I should."

"What do *you* want to do?"

"I want to write stories."

"A priest can write stories, too," Rose said.

"I know."

"You should do what your own light tells you, Dante, not what others want you to do."

"If you don't become a priest," Rose said, "I won't become a nun."

"Writing," his father said, "can be a form of praying. Don't be afraid to pour yourself into it. Let your deepest feelings do your writing for you. What's inside of you is inside of others. Sometimes people are ashamed or afraid of their thoughts and feelings, and they think they're different from others, and they're afraid to admit, even to themselves, who they are, so they never understand themselves. To know anyone, you have to know yourself. Writing honestly about yourself will help you to know who you are. And others who read it will be able to see and know something about themselves."

His insights had always amazed Dante, who was aware that he was ashamed and that he was confused by his own feelings, especially by his sexual thoughts and feelings, and he thought that he was different from other people, that others could cope better with their human natures. There was something about his nature, he felt, that was inherently evil. Ever since Adam and Eve had eaten the forbidden fruit, the human race has been attracted to evil, he thought, although he had never really dwelt on that thought. He had simply accepted it. Sometimes, he had wondered why they were so attracted to evil. What was there about evil that had made it attractive? Fun? Maybe, evil, such as screwing girls, might be fun, but most evil, such as hate, was ugly. Killing other people, even during wartime, he thought, was ugly; war was evil. Even though playing war games, like playing cowboys and Indians, was fun, the real thing was ugly, not fun.

That night, as he lay in his sleeping bag, he was facing Rose who smiled at him. Her smile gave him a warm feeling. And he wondered if his affection for her was really good. Since they enjoyed kissing each other, maybe their feelings were really evil, but he could never even think of her as evil. The thought seemed so stupid! Everything about her seemed so pure. That's why he liked her so much. And the devil undoubtedly hated her.

She was gazing at him, and Dante smiled back at her. He had a feeling that his smile made her feel good. Their deep feelings for each other, he felt, was something special, something that neither of them could explain, much less understand, and the joy that they gave to each other in kissing, although he felt that it was sexual in a way, could not be adequately expressed in words. As his father had said, it had to be experienced, to be felt, to know it. Although kissing might be sexual, it was nice, not dirty, not like fucking. He had never thought of doing anything like that to Rose; it was too ugly even to think of doing something like that to her.

"Good night," he said as the flames in the fireplace were crackling, and he fell asleep.

And he had a nightmare.

He and Rose were playing on the sidewalk of the back street when they were suddenly approached by older faceless boys with chalky white flesh who were yelling at Rose and him, calling them niggers and wanting to kill them. Rose, screaming, ran, and he ran with her, but they were suddenly in a haunted house as though they had been chased into it, and a woman, who seemed dead, was lying naked on her back. She, in flesh as white as snow, sat up, and her tits began to swell, and he was trapped between them. Evil spirits, all in white, were coming out of her, and he was struggling, having difficulty moving, trying to break away from her.

He woke up.

He became aware that he was in the sleeping bag. Rose was in hers, sleeping peacefully, the flames from the hearth shining on her face. Tony and Nick were playing checkers, and his father was reading.

Dante sighed in relief, and after a while, he closed his eyes and fell asleep again.

In the morning, after breakfast, he sat outside in bright sunlight and began to write about the nightmare, putting it into a story.

"What are you writing, Dante?" Rose asked him.

"An ugly story."

"Why an ugly story?"

"I just am."

"Why?"

"I don't know yet."

She looked at him quizzically.

"Will you let me read it?"

"I've just started it."

"I mean, after you've finished writing it."

"I don't know. Maybe."

He kept writing, and she, aware that she was disturbing him, went away.

He kept writing without stopping, concentrating only on the story and withdrawing from everything around him, until his father touched his shoulder and said, "Take a break for a few minutes and eat lunch."

He did.

A few minutes later, while the others were picking raspberries, he continued writing. He had barely finished writing his story when they returned. He looked up and saw Rose gazing at the ground.

"What are you looking at?"

"Nothing," she mumbled.

"Why don't you sit with me?"

He was sitting on a boulder.

"Do you really want me to?"

"Of course I do."

"I wanted to, before, but you were busy writing."

"I've finished writing my story."

She smiled, sat next to him, and asked, "Will you let me read your story?"

"You won't like it; it's ugly."

"I don't care."

"If you really want to, I'll let you."

She smiled again, but after she began to read it, her smile left. After a while she said, "It's scary."

"I warned you that it's ugly."

"I hate being called a nigger."

"I know."

"I wish I were like you."

"You don't."

"I do!"

"You'd hate being so small."

"No, I wouldn't. I'm smaller than you."

"If you were a boy, you'd hate it."

"You don't look small. You look older and bigger, the way God wants you to be."

"How do you know?"

"I just know. Jesus was small, too."

"He wasn't."

"He was, but He seemed big."

"How do you know that?"

"I just do."

"Why would you want to be like me, anyway?"

"I wish I looked white."

He stared at her, imagining that her flesh was white.

"I like you the way you look now. Some people sit in the sun just to get tanned, wishing they could be dark like you. Skin that's too white means it has too much color in it."

"Well, I don't want skin that's too white. I want skin like yours."

"Skin like yours is the best."

"Then why do the kids call me nigger?"

"Only the kids who don't know any better, who are jealous of you because their skin isn't dark like yours."

"What do you mean, white skin has too much color in it?"

"It makes people look scary, like the evil spirits in my story. Sunlight is white, but do you know what happens when it separates?"

"What?"

"The colors in it, in white, separate, making a rainbow. That means white has many colors in it. But God doesn't want us to be too white. Not in living people. He wants us to have less color. That's why the sun makes us darker. So we don't look dead all the time. Just in winter. When everything else seems dead. Except certain things, like Christmas trees, and you."

"How come I'm dark even in winter?"

"That's how God made you, because you look prettier that way, like a flower that grows even in winter, when all the others are buried in snow."

She seemed to be thinking about it, and then she smiled at him.

"Are you glad I'm dark?"

"Of course I am."

"I'm glad you're small."

"Why?"

"I just am. You're much nicer than the bigger kids. I hate them when they make fun of you. They seem so stupid."

Late that afternoon, before supper, when his father was sitting outside, at a picnic table, and was reading a book, Rose sat beside him and said, "Dante wrote a scary story today."

His father asked to read it. Afterwards, with Rose sitting on one side of him on a wide picnic bench and Dante on the other side of him, his father asked, "Where did you get the idea for this?"

"From a nightmare I had last night."

"You've written it well. Rose is right; it's scary. Is this the way it happened in your nightmare, or did you add to it?"

"I added a lot to make a story, but the ending isn't good."

"What's wrong with it?"

"I didn't know how to end it, so the boy dies. In my nightmare, that's when I woke up."

"You end it well. The boy is trapped by evil forces, and his dying of fright completes the scene."

"But I don't know what happens to the girl."

"You have her screaming because she's seeing evil destroying life. That's what makes the story so scary. It comes from deep inside of you, so deep you're probably not sure what it really means, but the feeling, the fear of evil, seems real."

"Yes!" Dante cried out. "Why do people do evil things? Does that mean they have evil spirits in them?"

"In a sense. But people are not just 'they;' they're 'we,' too."

"But we wouldn't do the evil things evil people do."

His father stared at him.

"When we plant seeds," his father asked, "why do some grow better than others?"

He waited patiently for their answers as Dante and Rose were silent, thinking,

"Sometimes," answered Dante, "weeds will stop them from growing. That's why we have to pull the weeds out. Are they like evil spirits?"

"That's good thinking, Dante."

"Maybe," Rose said, "some of the seeds are bad."

"That's good thinking, too. We have two good thinkers here."

Rose looked at Dante and smiled.

"But," his father asked, "if God created some people good and some people evil, would good people be able to do evil, and would evil people be able to do good?"

Dante and Rose thought about it.

"We have free will," Dante said.

"What do you mean by free will?"

"We can choose to be good or bad."

"Are you saying, then, that we aren't created good or evil?"

"We couldn't be created evil," replied Dante, "because God wouldn't create evil. We're evil when we refuse to obey God."

"Would you, either of you, refuse to obey God and choose to be evil?"

"No!" they both exclaimed.

"Why not?"

"I don't want to go to hell," said Dante.

"Suppose God told you that you wouldn't go to hell. Would you then choose to be evil?"

"Of course not," Rose said.

"Neither would I."

"Do you think some people choose to be bad?"

"Yes," said Dante.

"Why would they want to be bad?"

Dante shrugged.

"Maybe," Rose said, "they don't know how to be good."

"Why don't they know how to be good?"

"They don't know what it is."

"That's excellent thinking, Rose. You're saying that to be good, we have to know what good is. A great thinker said that evil comes from ignorance."

"That's what Dante said!"

"When?"

"Today. He said that kids call me nigger because they don't know any better."

His father nodded, saying, "That's true, Dante."

Dante smiled.

"Another great thinker, a Catholic priest, a saint, said that evil means that something is missing."

"God!" Rose exclaimed.

"Good," said Dante, "is knowing and doing what God wants us to do."

"You kids are amazing! You think well together."

Dante and Rose grinned at each other.

"But, how can we know what God wants us to do?"

"By praying," Rose said.

"And through faith and reasoning," said Dante, "and love."

"What do you mean by love?"

"Our deepest feeling. The light inside of us."

"That's God," Rose said.

"But how can we know there's a light inside of us?"

"We can feel it," she said, looking at Dante.

"Why doesn't everyone feel it?" Dante asked.

"Because," she said, "not everyone knows about it." She looked at Dante's father. "A baby doesn't know about it."

"Can a baby feel love?"

"He can feel it," Dante said, "when someone loves him, but he doesn't know what it is."

"When does he know?"

"When someone tells him," Rose said.

"You mean, you didn't know your mother and father loved you until someone told you?"

"Of course I did!"

"When?"

"I don't know, but I did."

"From the moment you were born?"

She laughed.

"Why are you laughing?"

"Because you're trying to confuse me."

He, too, laughed.

"I'm not trying to confuse you. I'm trying to learn from you."

Dante grinned at him.

"Why are you smiling, Dante?"

"When Rose was a baby, she knew that her mother and her father loved her, because she could feel it, but she didn't know what it was. She knew it like she knew she was hungry and was fed, but she didn't understand what it was until someone told her. Babies feel they need food, but they don't understand what that feeling is."

"Food," Rose said, "makes our bodies grow, and love makes the rest of us grow."

His father smiled.

"But maybe something," said Dante, "like weeds, stops our feelings from growing."

"And what do we call that something?" his father asked.

"Evil."

"And where does evil come from?"

"Ignorance."

"And ignorance breeds fear. And fear breeds hate. And hate destroys life."

"That's what your story is about, Dante! Evil destroying life," Rose said, gazing at him. "Your story is scary, but it tells the truth."

The light inside of her was glowing through her dark eyes, and he felt it, entering him.

"We have to let our deepest feelings reach out," he said, "and feel the light of someone else inside of us."

As he was staring at her, his father asked, "Have you ever felt the light of someone else inside of you?"

"Yes!"

And she, looking into him, said, "I have, too!"

9

"After you wrote the story," Tony asked Dante, "did your nightmares about death and sex end?"

"Actually, they did."

"Well, writing can be therapeutic, I guess."

"Oh, God!" Rose groaned.

"Anyway, nightmares about death I can understand. But how can anyone have nightmares about sex?" Tony asked Dante.

"All the horror movies combine not only our fears and fascination with death, they also include our fascination with sex. When I entered high school and wanted to write a book report on *Oedipus Rex,* I was warned that the subject matter was not fit for school kids."

"Well, those damn Greeks," muttered Tony, "writing stories of their damn kings who killed their own fathers and slept with their own mothers, and then that damn Jew, Freud, claiming that was only human nature, what can you expect?"

"What can you expect from a horny brother who plans to study for the ministry?"

Before Tony's senior year in high school, a cousin, Giuseppe Valentino, who had changed his name to Joe Valentine, a professor of theology at Yale, had somehow obtained a scholarship for Tony. "What can he lose?" Joe had insisted. Tony would get a good education, he'd meet prominent intellectuals, and if he'd want to join the ministry, it would be better than the priesthood, because celibacy wasn't required. Their mother, Dante remembered, hadn't approved of it, but, "If you Protestants are willing to pay for his education," she said, shaking her head in disbelief, "why shouldn't we accept it?"

Dante had been sitting at a desk in the front room of their house that summer before the new school year had started while Tony had been reclining on the couch, and they had been discussing the scholarship,.

"That's a whole year away," Tony had said.

"I still think the situation is weird."

"And you think I can't exercise any restraints?"

"You're not exactly the epitome of chastity."

"What the hell do you think I am, anyway?"

"Superman, who's convinced that females have been put on this earth solely for your enjoyment, who thinks the whole world's just one grand whorehouse and that you've been granted a free pass."

"You schmuck!"

But Tony wasn't without scruples, not entirely, thought Dante. He didn't approve of adultery. "Married people," he had said, "should face each other with their problems, not sneak behind each other and break their vows. That's the most contemptible level of deceit; that's ultimate greed. And it destroys relationships and family unity."

"It's just as bad to fool around before you're married. That's being unfaithful to the woman you'll marry someday."

"Don't be such a sap. Most women prefer guys with experience. They want a man who knows how to keep them satisfied. Like anything else, to be an expert, you have to practice."

"What kind of girls should you practice on?"

"Decent girls you can respect."

"That's crazy!"

"I wonder why I bother to share my wisdom with you?"

"I'm afraid you're going to tell me."

"Because I can't tolerate ignorance, especially in my little brother."

Dante shook his head.

"Can you think of anything," Tony asked, "that can grow properly without getting all the proper ingredients?"

"Don't tell me that you should screw as many girls as you can just so you can be an expert on making love."

Tony, with a look of exasperation, glared at him.

"Can you develop your intellect without nourishing it with good reading?"

"How can you compare that to screwing?"

"How can you be such an idiot? Can you nourish your intellect by reading trash? It's quality that counts. I don't go around screwing all the girls who want me. I give myself only to girls I can respect."

"Oh, well, that makes a lot of sense."

"When you make love, you leave part of yourself with your lover, and she becomes part of you. You share your feelings and everything else, and you develop good relationships, if you go into it with the right attitude."

"Oh, I see now. Of course."

"Guys talk about the nicest thing that can ever happen between two people, and they twist it into something contemptible, accusing the girl of being dirty, right after screwing her, for cryinoutloud, and then they brag about it. If you don't respect the girl, you don't respect yourself; you don't respect what you've done to her, and your relationship with her is dirty. Guys like that are hypocritical, greedy shits; the same guys who want to marry virgins, only virgins, because they're afraid of being compared to guys who are better than they are."

During his senior year of high school, Tony had found the woman to whom all of his experiences could be given. She was a real woman, not just a girl, Tony had said, an intelligent, interesting woman whom he could screw with respect, if only she would let him, but she was modest and reserved.

Immediately upon seeing her, Tony had fallen in love, but he couldn't admit it to anyone except Dante, who was sworn to secrecy, because she was not only seven years older than Tony, she was his English teacher, a graceful, dignified woman who wore spectacles when she read. She was fresh from Boston that year. Her name was Minnie Birch. She had long beautiful hair, the color of honey, and her eyes were bright green. "Like the ocean," Tony had said, "under the surface, with a fascinating, mysterious depth." Dante had replied,

"The depth of the ocean is dark." Tony had answered, "She has emerged from the dark depths like a goddess, more beautiful than the Venus of Botticelli's painting."

She was the editor and the advisor of the school paper, and she admired writers. So Tony became a writer. Sometimes he'd take Dante's writings, and he would submit them under his own name, but usually he'd write something, and then he'd say to Dante, "I'll let you polish this." Dante didn't mind. "But tell me honestly. Is this an endeavor to seduce her?"

And Tony, in a tone of disgust, replied, "I really respect her."

"I suspected that. I wonder why?"

"Besides, she's Protestant. She'll be very valuable to me as a minister in helping me to understand and to treat Protestants."

She was very religious, beginning each class by reading a passage from the Bible, and she always wore prim and proper garments with dark stockings that detracted, Tony said, from her sensuality. And Tony said that she was built better than any of the high school girls who flaunted their bosoms in tight sweaters.

"And to be loved by a woman like her would be the greatest thing that could ever happen to me."

He'd volunteer to stay after school to help her with the paper, and he even thought of quitting the basketball team just to spend more time with her, but the coach became upset and begged him to be sensible, telling Tony how important basketball was becoming in New Hampshire, especially since Dartmouth College had come so close to winning the national championship. Tony couldn't understand what that had to do with him. He was planning to go to Yale, anyway, not to Dartmouth, and to study for the ministry, not to play basketball. The other players and the cheerleaders, unaware of the cause of his sudden insanity (as they called it) to write, tried to persuade him to remain on the team, especially since he had access to the family car. And when she, who was the cause of his insanity, questioned him about quitting basketball, he replied, "Running up and down a floor to toss a ball through a hoop seems rather silly, don't you think?" She said she didn't know much about basketball but had heard he was an exciting player and that she would like to watch him play. And he said, "Of course, intelligence as well as skill is needed to play the game well, just like anything else in the course of human interplay. And playing the game is not just an individual endeavor; it's being part of something bigger than yourself and knowing how to relate to others."

It was almost nauseating, Dante thought, how Tony was pouring the bullshit and how she, with a drooling tongue, was lapping it up with a syrupy smile. She told him how marvelous he was, that he was such a brilliant student and a gifted writer.

And she was just thrilled, she said, that he would be entering Yale. And he was just thrilled, too, he told her, to have her for a teacher. And he remained on the basketball team.

Sometimes, after school, while talking with Tony, she would fold her arms and stand behind her desk, pressing the lower part of her abdomen against the desk, and she would smile at him, gazing at him, thought Dante, with her bright green eyes, as though she actually admired him and was interested in anything Tony had to say. He had read a book on literary criticism just so he could discuss literary forms and styles with her, and she told him that his ideas were fascinating and that he was one of the few people with whom she could enjoy an intelligent conversation.

"Have you noticed," he asked Dante one evening, "that when she talks with me, she squeezes her beautiful tits together and rubs herself against her desk? I make her horny, and that's her way of communicating her feelings to me."

"Yeah, I noticed," he grumbled.

"It's obvious how much she's attracted to me, isn't it?"

"And your attraction to her is even more obvious. Why don't you just come right out and tell her how much you want to screw her?"

"I can't tell her that, you idiot!"

"Why not? Tell her it's the nicest thing that could ever happen between two people, and that you respect her so damn much that you're willing to show her how much."

And Tony, as though he were actually considering it, nodded.

"She's probably afraid, though, of taking any chances. I mean, she might be concerned about her reputation and all that. You know how people like to twist things into something dirty to gossip and destroy a respectable person's reputation. I have to let her know, somehow, that I'm mature, really mature, and that she can trust me."

After a while, Tony said, "If I'd write a story about it, she'd get the message."

And Dante said, "I wouldn't touch a story like that with a ten foot pole."

And Tony said, "You're probably right. I should be direct and honest. A mature man isn't a coward. But being seen together is a problem. We would have to meet someplace where we'd be alone, in absolute privacy."

"Why don't you ask her to invite you to her house?"

She lived way out in the woods in an isolated cottage in Shelburne, a few miles east of the Gorham town line near the Maine border.

"But how can I get her to invite me to her house?"

"Tell her you'd like to look at her boobs. Whoops, tell her you meant her books!"

Tony thought about it.

"Yeah," he muttered, "I could, but that sounds a bit corny. We have to think of something better."

"Well, not only would you like to look at her books, you want to discuss personal issues with her, in private, not in the school where someone could overhear you, because you can't discuss these issues with anyone else, only with her."

"Good idea! But she'll ask me what the issues are. What do I tell her?"

"Use your imagination. That's why God gave you a brain."

Twice, Tony had waited to talk with her after school, but she had been busy with other pupils, and he had lost the courage to express his feelings to her. Disappointed with himself, he asked Dante to help him plan a better strategy on how to propose a relationship with her. His worst fear was not rejection, because he was certain of her attraction to him; he was afraid of sounding uncertain of himself, of sounding foolish and immature. He had to present himself as man enough to know exactly what he wanted. He would have to inspire in her the confidence in his ability to know how to cope with their situation. He would have to show her that he was more mature than the average man.

"Superman," Dante suggested. "Clark Kent sheds his inhibitions and becomes Superman pursuing Lois Lane."

"Be serious, for cryinoutloud."

"I am. Unless you approach her with supreme confidence, she'll think you're a fool. Act like you're her Tarzan, king of the jungle, and that she's your Sheena, queen of the jungle, and let her know how hot you are for each other, and that the inevitable course is your coming together, transcending the mundane conventions of our society."

So, on his third attempt, Tony finally told her.

That had been on a Friday in December, three years and a day after the sneak attack on Pearl Harbor, and the immediate effect on Tony was so devastating that he nearly lost faith in the efficacy of true love.

After the other pupils had finally left, and she had been stuffing papers into her briefcase on her desk, Tony approached her nervously, and she looked up at him and smiled, encouraging him.

"Hi," he said softly, but firmly. "I've been wondering if we could spend some time together to discuss some personal issues somewhere in private. As you know, I've planned to go to Yale next year to study for the ministry, and you, being, well, religious, too, and friendly, can advise me not only about the books I should be reading to nourish my mind, but how I can best cope with some personal issues primarily of a moral nature."

"Of course." she said, putting her briefcase on the floor on the other side of her, "I'm delighted to speak with you anytime. Grab a chair and sit down here."

"Well, you probably want to go home now."

"No, this is fine, Tony."

"Well, I don't want anyone to overhear us. It could be embarrassing, for both of us."

"I'll close the door."

As she went to the door, he said, "If you don't have time now, I understand. I'm willing to wait until it's more convenient for you and to meet you somewhere in private."

She closed the door.

"For goodness sakes, Tony, I told you I'm delighted to spend time with you. Now grab a chair and sit beside the desk, facing me. I'm in no hurry to go home."

As he dragged a chair to the front corner of her desk, she sat in hers again, pulling the chair closer to his, folded her arms, making an emphatic bulge of her bosom, and smiled at him.

Sitting as close to her as he could without creating any suspicion from anyone in the hallway who might happen to observe them, he gazed at her and imagined how exciting making love to her would be.

"Well?" she prompted.

She knew, he thought, feeling the warmth in her green eyes.

"Well, what I want to discuss with you is of such an intimate nature that, well, feeling the way I do about you, with utmost respect for you, for your kindness and for your intelligence, I hope you don't take it the wrong way if I don't express my feelings for you and my intentions clearly and honorably and as delicately as I should."

"You've aroused my interest," she said, smiling again.

He nodded to let her know that he grasped her meaning.

"I promise I won't take it the wrong way. I think I know you well enough by now to know that your intentions are honorable."

"I want to share my feelings with you, only with you, not with anyone else. I trust you. To me, you're special."

"I'm flattered, Tony."

He sighed with relief.

"If you could be objective, like Solomon, how would you advise a young man like me, planning to study for the ministry, who meets a woman in her middle twenties whom he respects, who want to, well, as in the story of Adam and Eve, to share the fruits of the tree of life, which is forbidden to them by our society, but deep down, he feels that would be the nicest thing that could ever happen to him. Now, consider that neither one is promiscuous, that they're both intelligent and mature and have high moral standards and deep respect for each other, and that, if not for the mundane conventions of our society, their relationship would be, well, ideal."

She was gazing at him, her face getting redder, unfolded her arms, picked up a pencil, her hand trembling, and pressed the tip of the eraser to her bottom lip.

"Does she want you," she asked nervously, "to have, well, sex with her?"

"Well, that's why I'm here now, to know what you think and feel about our situation."

"And you're thinking of getting involved with her, sexually?"

"I'm willing to commit myself, that is, if you think that's right. I know it's a difficult situation."

"That is, indeed, an understatement. She wants to have sex with you," she said huskily, "at the risk of becoming pregnant!"

Her candor astonished him.

"Do you think it's worth it, Tony?"

"Well, to tell you the truth, I hadn't even thought about the pregnancy part."

She was staring at him in disbelief.

"Don't you see the problems?"

"Well, not all of them. That's why I need your advice."

"I don't think that you've given this enough consideration."

"That's why I came here. I've been thinking about our situation. I assure you I wouldn't give myself to anyone I don't respect. I'm aware that, like anything else that's good, it's so easily twisted and perverted."

"I suspect that you're infatuated, sexually attracted to her."

"Well, I was under the impression that we have a lot in common, that we liked each other a lot. Does our situation frighten you?"

"Frankly, it does. I've become very fond of you. I didn't think of you as a person willing to jeopardize your future just to satisfy a whim."

"A whim! Do you think this is just a whim? I don't consider love as just a whim."

"Not to you, but to a capricious woman who wants to use you to gratify her lust, it is."

"Well," he stammered, dismayed, "if, well, if that's how you really feel," his voice dropped. "But, anyway, I had to, to hear it from you, to know your feelings."

"I have to warn you, Tony, that a woman can be a dangerous plaything. You're playing with fire. You really are."

He was too astonished to reply.

She was staring intently at him, and the way she was twisting the pencil and then pressing the eraser to her mouth was making him uneasy. She rolled the tip of the eraser over her bottom lip, provocatively, he thought, and squinted at him.

"I suppose you've already decided," she said, "what you're going to do."

"Why do you refer to yourself in the third person? Do you play pathological games with people's feelings? I'm sorry," he muttered, and stood up. "I don't want to get involved with a woman who wants to use me to gratify her lust. I'm disappointed, because I thought there was something special between us. There's so much about you that I like, but, under the circumstances, I just can't give myself to you."

Her mouth opened, and the pencil dropped.

"I'm sorry," he murmured, "I really am. Please forgive me."

He turned away from her and went to the door.

"Wait. You, you don't understand."

As he opened the door, he looked back.

She was standing, staring at him.

"I," she stammered, "I didn't," she said, dropping her voice, "understand."

Shit, he thought, turning away, and he left.

During the following week in class, he would hardly look at her, though she would stare at him, making him uneasy.

Christmas vacation came.

The world seemed to turn upside down. In the war, which had seemed to have been going well since the invasion at Normandy earlier that year, the Germans turned things around by launching a surprise counterattack, and the allies were quickly retreating. Before the year ended, the counterattack stalled, and the allies resumed their march again on Germany.

During the vacation, Tony had written something, which, in form, looked like poetry. He called it "World Inverted" and thought of it as his last testament to Minnie Birch.

"Read it," he said to Dante.

Dante read it.

It didn't make any sense.

Dante shook his head.

"Can't you figure it out?"

"No," Dante muttered, and he read it again as Tony was grinning from the chair in front of the desk.

Dante sat on the couch, and he read it a third time.

> Insanity
> beyond step one
> himself taking
> empathy above selfishness
> and
> love above lust
> and
> knowledge above ignorance
> and
> good above evil placing
> out inside world that turned
> and
> good perverting
> creation inverted man
> and
> unfulfilled was creation
> incomplete but
> good was man
> and
> man created God

"Well?" Tony asked.

"I like the first word; it's an apt description of the poet who wrote this."

"Read it out loud."

"The first word?"

"The whole poem, idiot."

Dante did. When he finished, Tony laughed.

"On the first day back to school, I'm going to hand it to her and tell her it's for the school paper."

"She won't print it."

"I know she won't."

"Then, why bother with it?"

"I guess I'm just upset enough to want to upset her, too."

"I don't know how upset this will make her, but it will certainly confuse her."

"Read it again, backwards."

Dante did, then he burst out laughing.

"She's really going to think you're nuts."

A new year had begun.

On the first day back, Minnie Birch said to Tony in class, "Please see me after school."

After classes, while other pupils were still in her room, he approached her desk where she was sitting.

"Do you mind waiting so that we can discuss your situation?" she asked.

"That won't be necessary. Here, I've written a poem for the paper."

He gave it to her, turned, and left.

The next day in class, she told him she wanted to discuss his poem after school, but, again, several other pupils were with her after school, and she said, "Please wait a few minutes. We really need to discuss your situation."

He replied, "Just make any comments or suggestions and return the poem to me tomorrow during class."

Before she could reply, he turned away.

And the next morning, a Friday, before classes had even begun, she handed him a sheet of paper folded in half, and she walked away. He opened it immediately. It was not his "Insanity" poem; it was a note.

"The poem," she wrote, "(as life itself, I suppose) is very confusing, but anger and bitterness emerge. Considering the situation, that's understandable. When you had begun to relate the situation,

I had assumed that you had been referring to someone else, causing a misunderstanding, and my immediate concern was so grave that it might have sounded like anger, because the situation had been so upsetting to me. After you had made me aware, finally, of the actual situation, I was deeply moved by mixed emotions, and after I had time to review what you had said, I realized that the misunderstanding was not your fault, but mine. I had been completely unprepared for such a revelation. Now that I have had time to reflect upon the actual situation, I can imagine the distress I have caused you. I beg you for your forgiveness and understanding. And, yes, I agree that we need to clarify the situation, to relieve the anguish it is causing."

"Wow!" he thought. "Happy New Year!"

He pressed the note against his chest, feeling that her heart had suddenly opened to his. And then he folded the note, kissed it, and put it into his shirt pocket. He couldn't wait until the end of the school day to be with her. He was in love. In love! No one could possibly be any happier than he was at this moment. Life, for him, for both of them, would never be the same. His task, now, would be to convince her that, together, no barrier would ever be too difficult for them to overcome.

At noontime, he met Dante at lunch.

"I have something to show you, but I can't show you here. Let's go sit in the car."

Tony had brought the car to school, because he would be late returning home after basketball practice. He had parked the car next to hers.

A wind was blowing, whipping up gusts of snow that had been falling during the past hour or so.

"Looks like a storm is coming," Dante said.

"Nothing can dampen my spirits now."

In the car, Dante read the note.

"Wow! What an interesting situation! She knows, now, how you feel about her. I wonder how she's going to handle the situation."

"It's obvious that she's attracted to me. Right? And that she really wants me."

"Don't jump to any conclusions. Even if she's attracted to you, don't expect her to jeopardize her career."

"We should try to anticipate what she's going to say so that I'll be prepared to answer maturely and affirmatively."

"Put yourself in her place. You're the teacher. An attractive female student tells you that she wants you, but you think she's talking about another man, and you give her the impression that you want her, too, but only to gratify your own lust. Disappointed, because you're not the ideal man of her dreams, she walks out on you, crushed. Now that you understand the situation, you must not only defend your honor, feeling so embarrassed and so stupid, you must let her know you're not a monster. She's seems sensitive, sincere, and deeply in love with you. Just think of how much agony the poor girl must have endured, approaching you, and confessing her attraction to you, and how much more pain you caused her in perverting her feelings for you. Would you want to hurt her even more?"

"No, of course not!"

"You'd have to be very delicate with her not to hurt her feelings or to make her feel rejected. If she were clever, she'd know you were in a predicament and that she was really in command of the situation now. She could make you feel flattered, giving you the impression that she wants you so much, yet she could be wringing out your heart, squeezing all the compassion out of you, making you want so desperately to satisfy her. What a great scene that would make!"

"You can be devious, you little shit!"

By the middle of the afternoon, a couple of inches of fresh snow had fallen, and more snow was falling heavily, and the wind was blowing. Basketball practice had been cancelled. After classes had ended, Dante had told Tony he would wait to ride home with him.

Tony, full of confidence, went to Minnie Birch's room. She was sitting at her desk and seemed to be alone as he stood in the doorway.

"Oh," she said, standing up, "I was afraid you had already left, due to the storm."

She was wearing a gray, unbuttoned jacket over a white blouse, a long gray skirt, and black shoes with low heels.

"After reading your note," he replied, after he had closed the door and was drawing close to her, "I've waited anxiously all day to be alone with you."

Her beautiful green eyes seemed to absorb him, and her lips, her voluptuous lips, moved slightly as though she was trying to suppress a smile.

"I should apologize," he said, "for that crazy poem. I was in agony when I wrote it."

Staring at him, she leaned forward against the corner of her desk, pushing, he thought, the lower part of her body against it, closer to him. They were no more than two feet apart, where anyone in the hallway could observe them.

"We have to talk about it."

"Forget it. I should never have written it."

She sank down, onto her chair.

"We need to talk," she said, "about, well, our situation."

He put his hands on her desk and leaned closer to her.

"In your note, you said you thought I was referring to someone else."

"Yes," she murmured.

"I feel so embarrassed," he said before she had a chance to say something else, "and so stupid. You can't imagine how I felt, trembling with anxiety, because I was so afraid you wouldn't understand, but I had to unburden myself. I worship you, and I just had to tell someone how I felt, but you're the only one I could tell. Yet, I was afraid you would think I was young and foolish, that I was no better than any of the other guys who had expressed the same feelings to you. And then, when you gave me the impression that you were downgrading yourself as a capricious female, a dangerous plaything bent on using me just to gratify your lust, my spirit drained out of me. I was crushed. I know, now, after reading your note, that the misunderstanding was my fault, that my own stupidity had caused it. Your reaction makes sense to me now, but at the time, I was confused, and hurt. I'm sorry. I'm sorry I turned the situation into such a mess and made it so unpleasant for you. I feel so utterly stupid and embarrassed."

"Stop it! Stop it right now," she said, looking into his eyes.

He drew back a little.

She sighed.

He had gone too far, he thought, making himself too obvious.

"You mustn't feel that way, Tony."

"No? But I do. I realize, now, how stupid it was of me to come right out and tell you how I feel. If I had any intelligence, I would never have done that."

"Stop that! You came to me with a pure heart, filled with faith in me, with hope, and with love, and I was too blind to recognize it, too unworthy of you."

"Don't say that!"

"Tony, believe me, you are not stupid. What you told me was, well, it was," she stammered, "beautiful. It took a lot of courage to express your feelings, and a lot of trust in me. After I had a chance to think about it, I realized how beautiful it was."

"Really? You don't really think that was stupid of me?"

"Of course not! I'm flattered. It's nice to know that you, well, that someone, like you, well, feels that he," she said, pausing for the proper word.

"Loves you."

"Appreciates me."

They became silent, looking at each other.

"More than appreciate," he said softly.

She nodded.

"When you thought that I had been thinking of someone else, did that really upset you?"

"Yes," she whispered.

"Did it make you angry?"

She bit down on her bottom lip, sighed, and then she nodded.

"I don't ever want to upset you again. I never want to make life unpleasant for you."

"I know. No matter what happens to us, I will always be fond of you, Tony."

"And you know how I feel about you. You know why I came to you for advice. What do I do about my feelings for you?"

"You're tremendously important to me, Tony, and I want us to have a good relationship." Blood flushed through her face. "I mean, as teacher to student."

"I know what you mean. And you know I want us to have a good relationship, too, but under different conditions. Until then, what do I do? And what do you do?

What do we both do? Do we do what we want to do? Follow our hearts? Or do we succumb to the dictates of convention?"

"That's why we have to talk."

"You know that my feelings for you are not only spiritual; they're also physical."

She blushed.

"I know," she murmured.

"Should I acknowledge them, or should I feel ashamed of how I feel about you?"

"You shouldn't be ashamed of your feelings, not if they're sincere."

"I know they're sincere. You don't feel that it's wrong, then, the way I feel about you?"

"No, of course not."

He sat on the edge of her desk, one foot touching the floor, the other leg dangling, and looked down at her. His position, he felt, gave him a psychological advantage, a dominance, over her.

"And the way you feel about me, then, isn't wrong. You're not ashamed, are you, of your feelings for me?"

"Of course not."

"So, the only predicament we have to face is the teacher and student relationship. Do you agree?"

"Yes."

"So, we have to agree, now, on the type of relationship we should have, based not so much on our age difference, but on the difference of our status. Right?"

"Right."

"That's what we'll have to think about, together. I don't think we can come up with a definite solution here, this afternoon. In the meanwhile, we'll follow the dictates of our hearts."

She sighed.

"Tony, you're a wonderful person, and I'm deeply touched by your feelings for me. I really am. I feel good about us, because I'm very fond of you, but our circumstances make it impossible for us to become involved romantically."

"And you think I'm so naïve, I'm unaware of our circumstances?"

"No, of course not."

He leaned closer to her, gazed into her eyes, and said, "That's why I was in such agony. Wanting to study for the ministry and feeling the way I do about you. A very emotional student attracted to his wonderful teacher, an ideal woman, to him. An impossible situation. And it filled me with anxiety. I had to tell you. I know, now, how selfish and unfair it was to share my agony with you."

"No, it wasn't!"

"If our circumstances were different, and I was a few years older, do you think you could possibly become involved with someone like me? Romantically, I mean."

"Of course I could."

"You do? You really do? I mean, you're not just saying that to make me feel good about myself, are you?"

"No, of course not."

"I believe that you really mean that!"

"Of course, I do. I'm very fond of you. I could easily become involved with you."

"Romantically?"

"Romantically," she said softly. "I mean, if circumstances were different. I've never met anyone quite like you. You're an exceptional person."

He slid himself off the desk and stood over her.

"Hearing that from you makes me feel great!" He smiled at her. And when she returned the smile, he said, "I'm glad, now, that I came to see you. You've relieved me of my agony."

"I feel good about your coming here, too."

"Do you, really?"

"Yes, I do!"

"You don't mind, then, if I continue seeing you after school?"

"Of course not. I enjoy your company."

"And I enjoy, well, just being with you, and looking at you. It would be nice, wouldn't it, if we could see each other outside of school, if circumstance were, well, different?"

"Yes," she said softly.

"I enjoy imagining us under different circumstances."

She was gazing at him.

He leaned a little closer and whispered, "I love you."

Her face was getting red again. Freckles, he noticed for the first time, had formed on the bridge of her nose and under her eyes. And in that moment, as he looked into her eyes, he felt her vulnerability. She picked up a pencil from her desk, her hand, trembling. She turned away, towards the window, and said, "My goodness, the storm is getting worse."

He drew back.

She turned again, looking up at him, and as she was about to say something, she sighed.

"I know how difficult this is for you, and I don't want to make our situation even worse. God has a sense of humor, bringing us together at this awkward time in our lives."

"Yes," she said. "Perhaps we're being put to a test."

"It isn't easy, though, is it?"

"No," she murmured.

"Well," he said, "thanks, anyway, for being you, and for making me feel so good about myself."

He turned away.

"Tony," she said before he was halfway to the door.

He turned to her.

"Thank you for coming."

"I'm glad I came. You've lifted my spirits."

She stood up, smiled, and said, "And you've lifted mine." She crossed her arms, making her bosom rise against her white blouse. "Thank you for being you, and for feeling the way you do. You're a wonderful student and a wonderful person, and you make me feel good about myself, too." And as he stared at her, her face became red again, and she leaned towards him, pressing the lower part of herself against the desk.

Damn! He turned away. He opened the door, and when he entered the hallway, he felt like yelling with joy.

Dante was standing in the hallway.

"What are you doing here?"

"Waiting for you. I was going to wait in the library, but it's closed. Almost everybody has left early, due to the storm."

Outside, they dashed through the snow, against a wind, and began to clear the snow from the car and from hers, too, the only cars left in the parking lot.

"How did the meeting go?" Dante asked.

"Perfectly. I'll tell you all about it the first chance we get."

When Tony was between the two cars, he looked around, faced her car, turned the handles at the side of the hood, pulled the hood up, yanked the coil wire from the distributor, closed the hood, and turned to Dante who asked, "What are you doing?"

"I'm taking her home."

"What? What are talking about?"

"We're going to take her home in our car. I'll explain everything later. For now, just do as I tell you. Get in our car, sit behind the wheel, and when I tell you to start it, start it."

Dante stared at him.

"Will you just do as I tell you?"

Dante got into the car, and he slid behind the wheel, and Tony opened the hood, and then he stood with his hands in his coat pockets and waited.

"Will you tell me what's going on?"

"I'm waiting for her to come out. She doesn't know it yet, but we'll be taking her home."

"How come?"

"Just be patient."

Heavier snow was falling, and the wind was blowing harder and colder.

Finally, she came out. As Tony pretended to be looking down at the motor, he saw her pull up the collar of her coat. A purse was swinging from her shoulder, and she was carrying her briefcase as she was walking briskly towards them.

He straightened up, waved at Dante, and yelled, "Okay, try starting it again."

The car started.

Tony closed the hood.

"What's the matter?" she asked.

"Nothing serious. The wind blew snow under the hood, and the car wouldn't start."

He went to the door of the car, opened it, told Dante to move over, and as Dante slid to the passenger side, he got behind the wheel, and, slowly, very slowly, he began to back up the car until Dante rolled the window down, and yelled, "What?"

"My car won't start!"

"She says her car won't start."

"I know; I heard her."

Tony stopped the car, got out, walked quickly past the front of the car, to her window, and she said, "It won't start."

He turned to Dante and said, "Help me get her car started."

Dante got out.

"What do you expect me to do?" he asked, after Tony had opened the hood and had ducked under it.

"Nothing," he whispered. "Just put your hands under here and pretend you're trying to fix something."

"The wires are disconnected from the distributor," Dante whispered.

"Keep quiet."

"And you tell me I'm devious. You could give the devil lessons."

After Tony had told her several times to turn the key, and the car hadn't started, he sighed, opened her door, and asked, "Do you mind if I try it?" As she started to get out, he said, "Just move over," and he pushed himself against her, forcing her against the shifting stick. As his hip and leg pressed against hers, he pulled on the choke to make sure it was all the way out, reached across her lap to check the shift, which was in neutral, pumped the gas pedal, and turned the key. "This car refuses to start," he mumbled. "With all this snow, blowing so hard, there's moisture in the engine, probably."

"What do you think I should do?"

"You shouldn't worry about it. We can always drive you home, if we have to. We can try wiping off the moisture, but it's going to take a while."

"Do you think it will start?"

"I'm sure it will, eventually, when the wind dies down."

She sighed.

"Are you uncomfortable?" he asked, feeling the warmth of her leg against his. "Am I pushing you against the shift?"

"I'm fine; I'm not uncomfortable."

"I'm sure you'd rather be home now, in front of a fire, warm and comfortable."

"Do you want to take me home?"

"Yes, you know I would. I'd enjoy taking you home."

She blushed.

"My knight in shining armor."

"I would like to be your knight in shining amore."

She smiled.

"Let me have the pleasure of driving you home, please."

"I'd really appreciate it, Tony. I noticed you cleaned the snow from my car. Thank you for the effort."

"How do you know I did it?"

"Who else would have done it?"

"My brother. Actually, he did, while I was cleaning mine."

"Do you always drive to school?"

"No, only when I'm planning to stay late. Fortunately, fate is smiling upon us today."

"Try it again!" Dante yelled.

He did.

"It's no use. Pull the hood down," he said as he got out of the car. "We're taking her home. Sit in the back so that she can sit in the front."

In the car, as he started to drive away, she said, "This could create a scandal."

"Nah, don't worry about it. We have a good reputation."

"I know you do, but good reputations are destroyed by scandals."

"Well, I know you're right, but we shouldn't let people with small minds control our behavior. If our greatest minds had allowed others to control them, they would never have created the greatest ideas."

After he drove out of the school grounds, he turned left onto the main street and drove through town, which seem deserted with the wind sweeping snow across the street.

"Looks like were in for a bad storm," she said.

He drove past the park and continued south, straight to the Shelburne road, into woods where snow drifted over the road and made the car swerve occasionally in spite of the chains on the rear tires.

"You're a good driver," she said, pulling her skirt up, above her knees, so that she could cross her legs. "I'd be a nervous wreck driving through this."

Even in dark brown stockings, she had nice legs, he thought, damn nice, like the rest of her. Only she and he, together, he imagined, deep in the woods, snowbound inside her cottage, facing each other in front of a blazing fireplace, and kissing passionately. He looked at her and smiled, asking, "Are you comfortable?"

"Yes," she murmured, "very. You have a nice heater."

"I know. It's nice to have, especially in this kind of weather."

"Do you mind terribly if I smoke?"

"No, of course not. I didn't know you smoked."

"Does that shock you?"

"I've never thought about it before, you, smoking, but a lot of sophisticated women smoke. It just isn't fair."

"What do you mean?"

"It isn't fair that some women have so much: sophistication and intelligence and compassion, plus extraordinary beauty. It's not fair to the other women."

As she laughed a little, Tony thought he heard Dante groan.

She leaned forward, pushed the cigarette lighter in, leaned back again, stretching her legs closer to his, opened her purse, withdrew a cigarette, and waited for the lighter to spring back.

Lying on her back, naked upon a soft carpet in front of her fireplace, she gazes up at him, having intensely gratified her passion, and asks, "Darling, do you mind terribly if I smoke?"

The lighter popped back. She lit her cigarette, replaced the lighter, blew smoke against the windshield, and opened her window a little.

"Are you getting a draft on you, Dante?" she asked.

"No," he muttered.

"It's been a hectic day. I shouldn't be smoking in front of you, but I just couldn't wait any longer."

"No need to apologize," Tony said. "Dante and I are not the type to blab. You can trust us."

"You seem so mature, especially for your age, both of you. And so intelligent. Most men, twice your age, don't have your maturity."

"You mean men so egotistical that they think all women have been put on this earth solely for their enjoyment?"

She laughed again.

From the back seat came a deep sigh.

After a while, Tony turned onto a secondary road between thick woods. The narrow road was covered with snow, and he could feel the chains digging through drifts on a gradual incline.

She stubbed the cigarette into the ashtray and said, "I hope you don't get stuck."

"That would be terrible. We'd have to spend the night with you."

She smiled.

From second gear, he shifted into first, turned into her long driveway, and felt the chains digging through snow up a hill.

"Strange," she murmured, "how the hill seems so steep under snow. I don't think I could have driven my car up here."

He approached her garage, which was behind her small house.

"Drive to the back of the house," she said, "so you'll have room to back up."

He did. And then he stopped.

"Well," she said, "riding with you in a snowstorm is quite an experience. I'm impressed by your skillful driving."

"Thank you. The pleasure is all ours."

"I should invite you in for a hot cup of cocoa to thank you both."

"That's not necessary," Tony said.

"But I really want you to come in and relax for a while."

"That would be wonderful, but I think we should go back to the school and start your car. We'll return here in an hour or so. That's a promise."

"The storm is getting worse, Tony."

"Don't worry about it. Have faith in us."

"How will you manage both cars?"

"I'll drive yours, and my brother will drive this one."

"Are you sure? I'd feel terrible if anything happens to either of you."

"He's a better driver than I am. He's driven this car a lot."

"Not in a blizzard," said Dante,

"Tony, leave my car at the school. I appreciate your concern, but you've done more than enough for me as it is. Come in and have a cup of hot cocoa with me before it gets dark."

"I wouldn't feel right."

"But I want you to come in, please."

"We will, after we bring your car."

"That's not necessary, Tony."

"Don't argue with me, please."

His tone surprised her, and she stared at him.

"The longer you sit here and argue with me, the worse this storm is getting. See you later."

She sighed.

"Okay," she murmured. "See you in a little while. I'll have hot cocoa ready for you."

She opened the door, got out, and as she dashed to the back entrance of the house, Dante slid into the front seat and closed the door. As she entered the house, she waved to them, and Tony backed up the car, put the gear into first, and drove down her driveway.

"She loves me! She wants me! Oh, what a beautiful storm! This is great!"

Dante groaned. "You seem so mature!" he said, imitating her. "And you're such a skillful driver. I could never have driven my car up here."

"If she could hear you now, she'd be disappointed in your immaturity."

"She's supposed to be educating us, not playing the helpless little femme fatale appealing to your ego."

"In the classroom, she's a teacher, but outside, she's a female, a beautiful, sexy woman who's strongly attracted to me. Besides, she's not used to driving under these conditions."

"If she ever forgets that she's a teacher and that you're her student, other people will remind her, but not very kindly."

"Other people! Hell! Don't be so damn conventional."

"You know something? You use convention to support your unconventionality, and vice versa. Always rationalizing."

"You're talking gibberish."

"I'm talking to my brother who writes poetry backwards."

After a while, Dante asked, "Doesn't she think you're strange? A Catholic studying for the ministry, for the Protestant ministry?"

"No, she thinks it's marvelous, that someday I'll be her spiritual advisor."

Dante groaned.

Before they arrived at the school, Tony told him to wait an hour before driving back. "So that I can be alone with her for a while."

"What am I supposed to do for an hour?"

"Go to a restaurant. Buy yourself a sandwich or something. I'll pay for it."

"I can't sit in a restaurant for an hour and nibble on a sandwich."

"Be resourceful."

"What will you tell her when I don't show up for an hour?"

"When you arrive, I'll ask you what took you so long, and you say you had a flat tire."

"No, you'll have to think of something else."

"Like what?"

"Be resourceful."

"You don't have to go in the house, then. Just blow the horn."

"Why don't you just tell her you want to be alone with her?"

Tony was thinking about it.

"I do, but I shouldn't tell her. Why don't you just drive home and stay there?"

"And what should I tell Ma?"

"That I'm staying with a friend. And after you're home for a while, call me and say you can't pick me up because the driving is so bad. Okay?"

"Does she even have a phone?"

"She must have. How would she contact the school in case she's sick or something? Call the operator to connect you to her phone."

"And if the operator is nosey, she'll listen to the call, and she'll know you're there, and everybody in New Hampshire will know about the reputation of our Miss Birch."

"You're right. But I still want to be alone with her for a little while."

"Okay, but not a whole hour. I'll go get some gas, and maybe I'll grab a sandwich. I have enough money. Ma thinks you have basketball practice, so she won't be expecting you home until later, anyway. And if she asks, I'll just tell her that I waited for you."

At the school parking lot, after starting her car, Tony let it warm up while Dante drove away. He cleaned the snow from her car, and after a few minutes, he drove it slowly through town.

"Here I am," he thought, "actually driving her car, and driving it to her house to be alone with her. Wow!"

Snow was blowing against the windshield, and although the wipers were pushing the snow aside, the visibility was poor, but he couldn't remember ever feeling so happy, even happier than he had been earlier that day, and so eager with anticipation. If only he could spend the night with her! The woods at night. There was something about the woods, especially at night, that evoked deep passions. Being alone with him, in a cozy house deep in the dark woods during a blizzard, a fire blazing in a fireplace, would make them so damn horny, they'd forget everything about the outside world, giving themselves completely to each other. He moaned.

He entered her long driveway. As he approached her house, the windows were lit, like a beacon of a lighthouse penetrating the swirling snow. He drove the car inside of the garage, got out, dashed through a gust of wind and snow, and knocked on the door. It opened immediately.

She was wearing tight gray slacks, and her hair, which was usually pinned up into a bun at the back of her head in class, was flowing like honey over her shoulders, to a snug white sweater with two stags leaping over her bulging bosom.

He gazed at her, handed her the car key and said, "She wasn't so stubborn this time. I told her I was going to spank her if she'd refuse my command, and lo and behold, she turned over and started."

She smiled, saying, "Come in."

As he entered a small, narrow hallway, she asked, "Where's Dante?"

"He said he had to get gas, and then he was going to call home to let our mother know that we won't be home for a while, and he said he was hungry, so he probably went for a sandwich."

"I would have given him something here."

"Well, you hadn't planned for us to be here, so we don't want to impose."

"You're not imposing. Take your coat off and hang it in the corner."

He removed his coat, hung it on a hook next to her coat, and as he turned to her again, he noticed that she was wearing slippers lined with wool and that her shoes and her boots were under the coat rack. He untied the laces of his leather boots. After he removed them, he placed them next to her shoes, and he looked at her again.

"I have a pot of hot cocoa for you."

"You're so beautiful!"

She blushed.

"You really are, the most appealing woman I've ever seen."

Her face grew redder.

"Well, you are!"

She turned away, saying, "Sit down near the stove and get warm."

He followed her into a kitchen. It was small and narrow with wide floorboards. Along the same side of the entrance was a porcelain sink under a large window covered with frost. On the opposite side of the kitchen was an entrance to another room, and at the farther side, along the wall, was a large, wood burning stove with a deep oven. On the stove was a pot of cocoa.

He went to the other end of the kitchen and sat in a chair between a small table and the stove.

She put her hands on her hips, gazed down at him, and said gently, "I don't know what I'm going to do with you."

She turned away, went to some shelves above the left side of the sink, next to a refrigerator in the corner, withdrew a mug, went to the stove, and poured cocoa into the mug. His eyes followed her, observing her buttocks under her tight slacks, the slight swaying of her hips, and the undulations of the bucks on her bosom. With each movement, her breasts quivered a little.

"I can't believe I'm actually here, in your house. If I'm dreaming, don't wake me up. Let me go on dreaming about you."

"You haven't forgotten, have you, that I'm your teacher?"

"Let me enjoy my dream. In my dream, you are not my teacher."

"I wish I could."

Immediately, as soon as she realized what she had just said, her face grew red again. He decided not to reply.

As she placed the mug next to him on the table, her hands trembled, almost spilling the cocoa.

Without saying anything more, she went to the side of the table close to him and sat, facing him, and she lit a cigarette.

"I'm acutely aware of our situation," he said, "and I don't want to do anything that will make you uncomfortable or nervous. I can't help the way I feel about you, and you can't help the way you feel about me; but we can control our reactions to our feelings. I know we must be discreet, but we must not be ashamed of our feelings for each other, as you said earlier. Our feelings are good; they're beautiful; they're tender, and they're growing, helping us to become better persons. Why can't we enjoy our feelings? If I were a little older, and you weren't my teacher, we would be celebrating life together."

"You sound so much older than you are, and to be honest, I'm frightened, because I'm also fascinated by you. I enjoy talking with you. I enjoy being with you. I don't even want to think of our age difference, but we can't change our circumstances. It's impossible for us to become romantically involved."

"I know," he murmured.

He sipped the cocoa, and she puffed on her cigarette.

"Your feelings for me will change," she said, "and you'll look back at this someday and probably laugh about it."

As he shook his head and said, "No, never," she smiled weakly at him, flicked ashes into an ashtray, drew the cigarette to her mouth, and took another puff.

"You're afraid of repercussions, of people condemning us," he stated. "I can understand that, but when we're alone, like now, in the privacy of your own home, no one else will know about us, about how we feel for each other."

"None of your friends will know?"

"Of course not!"

"Doesn't your brother know about us?"

"He thinks I have a crush on you, but my secrets are safe with him. You can trust us, both of us. He likes you, almost as much as I do."

After a few more puffs, she put her cigarette out. And then she poured him more cocoa. Her hands were still trembling, but not as much.

"Well," he asked, "how did you find this place?"

"It was a summer place for my folks. They bought another cottage on the cape, and they gave this one to me. Last year, after spending Christmas here, I decided to live here."

"You spent Christmas here with your folks?"

"No," she said hesitantly, and sat down again.

"You wouldn't come up from Boston, alone, to spend Christmas here."

Her face was starting to get red again.

"Why wouldn't I?"

"You just wouldn't," he said softly.

She withdrew another cigarette from a pack on the table, and her hands trembled as she struck a match against the cover. She lit the cigarette, waved the match until the flame went out, dropped the match into the ashtray, and, turning away from him, she said, "Actually, I was with a friend."

"A male friend."

She turned to him and took a puff.

He was staring at her.

"Why should you assume that?"

"I can't explain it; it's a feeling you convey."

She lowered her eyes.

"Is he, whoever he is, part of our circumstances?"

She looked at him, stood up, went to the entrance of the other room, turned to him again, puffed on her cigarette, and said, "Come in here."

He followed her into the other room. To the right of the entrance, on the other side of the wall of the kitchen, a huge bookcase, built into the wall, was crammed with books, and a huge stone fireplace, which formed the other wall, filled the small room with the warmth from a blazing fire. Facing him, against the wall of a wide window, was a couch. To the left, at the corner of the room, was a front entrance. And, to his left, at the near corner of the wall, was a stairwell. The floor was made of knotty pinewood, covered in the middle by a rug.

"Interesting. It's small, but beautiful and cozy. Almost the way I imagined it. I wouldn't mind living here. Dante would like it, too, I bet, but it needs a desk, a place to write."

"Upstairs," she murmured. "I have a study upstairs."

"A perfect place for a writer."

She went to an end table next to the couch, grabbed a photograph in a frame, and thrust it at him.

It was a picture of her and a soldier.

Except for the uniform, he was not impressive, and Tony sighed with relief.

"Is he part of our circumstances?"

"Yes," she murmured.

"The guy who spent Christmas, here, alone with you?"

Without answering, she replaced the picture on the end table.

"He's a lucky man. I envy him. Where is he now?"

"In France."

"Why don't you tell me about him?"

"What can I tell you?"

"Whatever you know about him."

"Isn't it obvious?"

"What is? That you're trying to make me jealous?'

"Of course not!"

"Well, that's good, because some people enjoy playing silly games."

She stared at him.

"I have a gut feeling," he stated, "that you're not in love with him."

She hesitated before she replied, "Because you don't want to believe it."

"True. Why don't you convince me?"

"How?"

"If you were really in love with him, you'd be anxious to tell me all about him."

She sighed, moved towards the hearth, and puffed on her cigarette.

"I met him in Boston through a female friend of mine whose boyfriend, a soldier, introduced me to him. That was over a year ago, a week or so before Christmas. They were going overseas, and," she said, flicking ashes into the fireplace, "they wanted to spend Christmas here in New Hampshire to go skiing, and they wanted us to accompany them, so I invited them to spend Christmas here."

She stared into the fire.

"How long were they here?"

"Just a weekend, two nights. A few days later, they shipped out."

"So, you didn't know him long. Had you slept with him before those two nights?"

"No."

"Have you been writing to each other?"

"Yes."

"Have either of you made any commitments?"

"I told him I'd be waiting for him, here."

"Did he tell you he wanted to marry you?"

"How could he? Who knows what will happen to him?"

"Where's he from?"

"California. Near Los Angeles."

"What's the name of the town?"

"I don't know."

"You didn't go skiing, and neither did the others."

"No."

"He wasn't interested in skiing. What's he interested in?"

She turned away and looked into the fire again.

"Do you know anything about him? His family? Education? Job? His wife? His girlfriends?"

She looked at him angrily, drew another puff, and said indignantly, "This doesn't really concern you, Tony!"

"Of course, it concerns me! I love you! You don't know anything about him. You've been swept up by the damn war, by someone in a uniform!"

"How dare you!"

She turned away from him and flung her cigarette into the fire.

He grasped her by the back of her shoulders.

"I dare because I have strong feelings for you! I dare because it hurts me to think that someone has taken advantage of you. I dare because, right now, I feel so damn insignificant and so inferior to someone in a uniform that I want to join the army. If that's what I have to do, I'll do it!"

"No!"

She turned to him and grasped him, pressing herself against him, her head against his shoulder.

He slid his arms around her, holding her hips against his, and said softly, "I love you."

"Even now that you know I've slept with someone else?"

"He took advantage of your compassion for a serviceman, and you were probably drinking with your friends, and your girlfriend probably wanted to go upstairs to make love with her boyfriend, so you and the other soldier were left alone down here, on the couch, and, things happened."

"That's exactly how it was. You're very perceptive."

"Just because you spent a couple of nights with him doesn't mean you owe him anything. He was lucky to have you. I envy him, because you allowed him to, well, to make love to you."

Very slowly, while pushing herself against him, she rubbed his back as though she wanted him to make love to her, and he became aroused.

He drew back a little, and he cupped her face, gazing into her warm eyes, and as she began to smile, he kissed her on the mouth. Her mouth opened under his, and as she clung to him, pushing herself against him, he felt her desire intensifying, her mouth sucking on his. And he slid his hands under her sweater, feeling the smoothness of her warm flesh. He pushed his hands up her back until he touched her bra, but as he tried to unhook it, she moaned, "No!" and tried to withdraw from him. He clung to her, and she leaned her forehead against his shoulder.

"This can't be happening to us!"

"It is," he murmured, holding her hips to his so that she could feel his desire. "And it feels so damn good, to both of us. I feel like, well, like touching you, all of you, and holding you inside of me. I want to get inside of you, deep inside of you, and never let you go."

"Don't say anything more. Just hold me gently, Tony, until the storm within us passes," she said, almost whimpering.

They became silent as he held her.

After a while, he pushed her hair back, uncovering her face, and brushed his lips across her warm forehead, kissing it.

"I'm so confused," she said, "I can't think straight. I have the impression that you know what you want, and that you're doing exactly what you want to be doing, as though a higher power is guiding you, but I don't have that kind of faith, especially in myself. In the classroom, I act as though I do, but in the actual world, I'm unsure of myself. I don't even trust myself. I'm afraid my feelings will get me into trouble."

"You shouldn't be afraid of your feelings. You should ask yourself why you feel the way you do, because your feelings are trying to tell you things that you can't otherwise know. Trust your feelings. If they come from the heart, they can be your best guide."

"You're an incredible person. I can't believe you're so young. You seem older than I am, and that scares me, too. I really don't know what to do with you."

"Let's sit on the couch and talk about it."

"I need another cigarette."

As she went into the kitchen, he sat in the middle of the couch so that she would be forced to sit close to him.

When she returned with a lit cigarette, she also had his mug of hot cocoa, which she had refilled. As soon as she sat beside him, she said, "Promise me something, Tony."

"What?"

She took a puff, exhaled, and said, "That you won't do anything that either of us will regret later."

"I promise that I won't do anything that I'll regret later."

"Promise me that you won't, well, go all the way with me."

"I won't make a promise that I can't keep."

"You can't, or you won't?"

"I can't, so I won't, and I won't, so I can't."

"Promise me, at least, that you won't seduce me."

"I solemnly promise, as a gentleman and a scholar, that I won't try to seduce you."

"Does that mean if you seduce me, you can deny that you even tried?"

"That means, we should talk about something else. We should trust each other completely. We should be candid. We should try to know as much as we can about each other, although I admit there are things about me that I'm too ashamed to let anyone know. There are things about my own self that I don't even want to know, so sometimes I deny things about my own self, but that's not very rational. So, if you want to know me better, you'll have to do it without my consent, because I ain't goin to tell ya. Seriously, though, we have to trust each other. If we're going to have a good relationship, we have to believe that we're never going to do anything to hurt each other, that whatever we do, we do with the knowledge and the consent of the other."

"Fair enough."

"You make me feel very comfortable, especially now. What about you?"

"In all candor, I wish I could say the same. Strangely enough, I enjoy being with you, but at the same time, I can't feel comfortable about, well, my attraction to you. I feel a little nervous, but that's me, not you. Do you know what I mean?"

"Well, according to the law, I'm still a minor, and an affair with me is illegal. I think that's what's bothering you."

"Precisely. Yet, there's a part of me that refuses to accept that, a part of me that sees you as older than me. And that can be scary, especially since you're really so reluctant to follow social conventions."

"The only thing I can suggest for now is that we proceed slowly, getting to know each other better, before we become romantically involved."

"Easy to say, practice restraint, but we just experienced a sample of our raging attraction to each other. That's why I don't trust our feelings. And, no matter how we feel about each other, you're too young for me, legally."

"How old do I have to be to love you? Legally."

"Good question. But the other aspect is that you are my student. You shouldn't even be here now."

"But in a few more months, I won't be your student anymore. If we can wait that long, we can become romantically involved, as soon as I turn eighteen."

"But you'll be studying for the ministry. If we become romantically involved, I think you know where that will lead. I don't want to have the dubious honor of being the scarlet lady that tainted your innocence."

"Are you saying you prefer that I have experience?"

"Of course not! Is that what I said? I told you, you make me so confused, I can't think straight."

A horn blew.

"My brother!"

Minnie Birch had insisted that Dante come into the house for hot cocoa.

Inside, she, smiling at Dante, seemed composed, which indicated, thought Tony, how sophisticated she was.

"Sit on the couch in the other room, Dante," she said, "and make yourself comfortable. I'll bring you a mug of hot cocoa."

When Dante went into the other room, Tony wanted to remain in the kitchen, to help her, he said.

"I don't need help to carry a mug to the other room."

So he went into the other room, sat on the couch, and drank some of his cocoa while Dante was examining the books in the bookcase.

She entered, bringing him the mug of cocoa.

"You have a lot of Henry James," Dante said as he took the mug. "You must really like him."

"Yes. Have you ever read him?"

"Not much, but I recently read *The Turn of the Screw.*"

"Oh. What do you think of it?"

"I was fascinated. It's so subtle, it's tricky."

"Tricky? How?"

"It forces you to look for implied meanings. The author seems to distance himself from his story, as though he's sitting back and hiding himself in the audience."

She smiled at him, then she asked, "What implied meanings did you get from it?"

"Well, the ghost, I thought, was a projection of the fears of the young woman."

"That's interesting. What made you think that?"

"In the prologue, the author, as the first narrator, stresses the anxiety and the passion of a young teacher who succumbs to seduction."

Her face grew red.

Tony, sipping the cocoa, stared at him in disbelief.

"She feels something in the house, something uneasy, that she feels deep in herself," Dante said, putting the mug on the end table and then pulling the book from the shelf. "Our deepest anxieties stem from our feelings of guilt."

"This is getting morbid," said Tony, standing up.

"This is interesting," she said. "Continue, Dante."

"Well, on the surface, this is a ghost story, but it's really a psychological study of seduction and passion. The young woman, who's inhibited, is sexually attracted to the father of the children who hired her. The origin of the word 'screw' refers to the pudendum, which also means 'shame' in Latin."

Tony said, "We'll have to continue this at another time."

But Dante began reading: "'Christmas eve in an old house.'"

And Tony grabbed the book from his hand. Putting the book back, he said, "We have to leave, now, or we'll be spending the night here."

He looked at her.

She gazed at him, and then she nodded.

In the car, Tony and Dante were quiet as Tony drove slowly down her long driveway, the wind blowing snow against the windshield. On the highway, he said, "She's in love with me, and, just before you showed up, she indicated that she wants me to make love to her. Your timing could have been worse; you could have arrived a few minutes earlier, before I found out for sure how she really feels about me. So, I feel pretty good now."

"Did you kiss her?"

"Yes."

"Wow!"

"But when you started talking about that damn book and the haunted house, I felt like strangling you! I could feel her mood changing, from affection to doubt and guilt. And I began to wonder if her feelings for me are genuine."

"I assume she knows what the book is really about, but I can't help wondering what she thinks of the character, who seems so much like *her*. It's difficult for me to believe that she's willing to become involved with you."

"What do you mean? Why shouldn't she become involved with me? Do you think there's something wrong with me, that I'm a horny monster or something?"

"You're her student! That could ruin her reputation and her career! Doesn't that worry her?"

"Of course it does. We talked about it. We can't become romantically involved right now, not until the school year ends, anyway, but that doesn't mean we can't love each other. For the sake of her reputation, we both have to be patient. After a few more months, we'll be free to let nature take its course. Until then, we can't even think of, well, of doing anything that will ruin our chances for a good relationship."

Over a month passed, and Tony hadn't returned to her house; he had enough pride in himself, he told Dante, to wait until she would invite him. He had made himself available to her, staying after school a few times to help her with the paper, and staying long enough to give her the opportunity to talk privately with him, but she hadn't mentioned anything of their relationship, as though she had pretended that nothing had ever happened between them. But she had attended the home basketball games and had told him how much she had enjoyed watching him play.

On a Monday before Valentine's Day, he asked her if she liked animals, and she said she did. She had thought of getting a dog. The following Saturday morning, he drove to her house and brought her a puppy, a female collie, which had become popular by the fairly recent movie, *Lassie Come Home*.

Three weeks later, on another Saturday morning, he returned to her house with a female Siamese kitten and said, "She needs a home, and your dog needs a companion, especially during the day while you're teaching." She gave him a big smile, and she invited him to stay for lunch.

At the kitchen table after lunch, after the puppy and the kitten had successfully become acquainted, she said, "I appreciate what you're doing for me, for showing me your respect and for not putting any pressure on me. I mean, after you left here with your brother that evening, I wondered if you'd be, well, if you'd be coming here a lot."

"You mean, if I'd be bothering you a lot."

She smiled.

"Well," she said, "I provided you with enough incentive."

"Yes, you did. And I wanted, desperately, to come back here, waiting for you to invite me back. I know that you know how I feel about you, that you know that if you ever want me, all you have to do is let me know."

"I know," she murmured.

"So, why have you acted as though nothing has happened to us?"

"You mean, at school?"

"Well, in school, I understand. But why haven't you invited me here?"

She sighed.

"To be honest, I'm afraid to. I'm afraid of what it will lead to. Right after you had left here that day, I thought about what would have happened if your brother hadn't arrived. I felt as though, well, as though we both knew what we both wanted to do."

He didn't answer immediately. Gazing at her, he felt a stirring of desire deep in both of them.

"I was only following my feelings, responding to yours."

"That's what I just said. You knew what we both wanted to do."

"So? What's wrong with that?"

She stared at him.

She lit a cigarette.

"Well," she stammered, "it's not right, not in our situation."

"I don't understand. I'm in love with you, and I want to touch you, and I know you feel the same way."

"We can't always do what we feel like doing."

"No, of course not. But we shouldn't let others dictate how we should feel about each other."

"Others can destroy us."

He nodded.

"Are you saying, then, that I should never come here?"

"I'm trying to explain my feelings to you, trying to tell you why I haven't invited you here. I'm afraid of getting involved with you."

"Do I make you feel uneasy, being here?"

"You do, even though I want you to be here."

"Why do I make you feel uneasy?"

"You know why."

"Because you know I'm attracted to you."

"Yes."

"That should make you feel good."

"It does."

"But it also makes you uneasy. I excite you. You want, well, you want to take me inside of you," he said, getting more aroused; "You want to taste the forbidden fruit."

She stared at him.

"And that makes you feel guilty?"

She didn't answer.

"When my brother talked about the book, did that upset you?"

She drew a puff from her cigarette, exhaled, and said, "Not upset, no, but he seemed to be warning me."

"Warning you?"

"Yes, warning me."

"He was talking about the book, not about you."

"I wonder. Do you remember how he put it? Our deepest anxieties stem from our feelings of guilt."

"So?"

"He was talking about sexual passion and seduction."

"When we repress our sexual feelings, they emerge anyway, sometimes in the form of guilt. He was talking about people in general, not specifically about you. If you and I made mad, passionate love to each other, right now, do you think you'll develop guilt feelings and suffer deep anxieties?"

She puffed on her cigarette again and grew silent as he stared at her.

"You haven't answered my question," he said.

"What question?"

"If we made passionate love, right now, would you have guilt feelings?"

"Yes."

"Why?"

She didn't answer.

He waited.

"I'd be betraying someone," she finally said, "who trusts me."

"Who? The soldier? Are you still writing to him?"

"Don't ask me to stop, especially now that he's sacrificing his life for us."

"What happens when the war's over?"

She shrugged.

"Do you think you'll marry him?"

"I don't want to think about it, not now."

He stared at her.

"At this moment, am I making you feel uneasy?"

"Yes!"

"Even though we're just talking?"

"We're not just talking."

"We're not?"

"I know what you're thinking."

"You know what I'm thinking? Maybe you're thinking that I'm thinking of what you're thinking."

She stubbed the cigarette into the ashtray and squinted at him, her mouth curving into a slight grin. Her bright green eyes were penetrating him, stirring deep within him an urge to take her, to take her right then and there, not slowly with tenderness, but forcefully, to overwhelm her into submission.

Slowly, he stood up, letting her see how obvious his desire had become, and as he approached her, her grin expanded with anticipation. Her eyes seemed to glow brighter, with more intensity, inviting him to take her. Her blouse, the green of her eyes, was tucked tightly into a black skirt. Her round, full breasts, heaved as he bent down, cupped her face, and planted his mouth on hers, and she, grabbing the back of his neck and pulling herself up to him, opened her mouth, pushed her tongue between his lips, and sucked on him.

He grasped her shoulders and pulled her up from the chair, and, kissing each other, they spun themselves around the kitchen until she was pinned against the sink. He pushed himself against her, pressing his hardness against her and quickly unbuttoned her blouse, yanked it up from her skirt, slid his hands under her blouse, up her back, felt her bra, and unhooked it. He uncovered her breasts, grasped them, and began sucking on a protruding nipple.

She was groaning, holding his head against her, and suddenly she cried out, "Stop! Please stop!"

He stopped.

Her lips were quivering.

She leaned against him, uttered another low cry, and rubbed herself against his erection.

"You don't want me to stop! You want me so damn bad, I can feel it!"

He thrust his hands under her skirt, lifting it above her legs, slid a hand inside of her panties, against the lower part of her abdomen, between her thighs, saying, "You want me to penetrate you deep down here, deep inside of you!" He grasped her. She groaned, and her body stiffened. "But I won't do it! Not until this is free to hold me!"

And he turned away from her and went out the back door, quickly went down the steps, got into the car, and, without turning back, drove away.

He had left her house that March afternoon, frustrated and angry. The war continued, but the end was in sight as the days grew warmer.

When the war would end, she'd be free to decide what she'd really want.

On the twelfth of April, a gloomy Thursday in Cascade Flats, the people mourned the death of President Franklin Roosevelt. His most memorable saying was, "We have nothing to fear but fear itself." People said, "He knew that we've won the war."

On a sunny day on Monday, the seventh of May, Germany surrendered.

The fall of Japan was inevitable.

On the first day of June, a Friday, Minnie Birch was absent from school. She had never been absent until that day. Immediately after classes, Tony drove to her house, the first time during the past three months, since they had kissed each other. When he arrived at her house and parked behind it, her car was in the garage. He went to the back door, and he knocked on it. The dog barked, but Minnie didn't answer. Tony turned the knob, and the door opened. The dog began to wag her tail. "Hello!" Tony yelled in the hallway. He closed the door, bent down, and patted the dog. "Where is she, huh? Is she sick?" He entered the kitchen and yelled, "Hello!" again, and then he went into the other room and yelled out again. And, from upstairs, she said, "I'll be down in a minute, Tony."

The room smelled of stale cigarette smoke. On the end table was an ashtray filled with cigarette butts, a glass that was almost empty, and a fifth of bourbon that was more than half empty. The picture of her with the soldier was missing.

The dog whined and wanted to be patted again, and as he patted her, the Siamese cat, from the side of the couch, peered at them.

"How are you getting along with the kitten, huh? You're getting big, both of you."

He put his left hand on the pinewood floor, thrust his right forefinger under his hand and wiggled his finger, arousing the instincts of the cat who crouched and was getting ready to pounce on his finger as Minnie came down the spiral staircase. She was wearing slippers, a blue bathrobe, and a towel wrapped around her head.

"Hi," she said in a husky tone.

"Hi. Aren't you feeling well?"

As she drew closer to him, her eyes seemed expressionless, as though she were in a trance. She seemed to float up to him, the freshness of a hot bath emanating from her body. Under her bathrobe, her flesh was wet, radiating her heat, and he felt it penetrating him as she leaned against him. He put his arms around her.

"Did you miss me today?" she murmured.

"I was concerned about you."

"That's sweet, Tony."

"What's wrong with you?"

As the softness of her warm, wet body pressed against him, he became aroused.

She grasped his hips and emitted a soft moan, then she leaned back a little and pushed the lower part of her abdomen against his, and smiled at him.

"What's wrong with you, anyway?"

She lifted her mouth to his and kissed him.

"You want me."

"Why were you absent?"

"I had a lot on my mind last night, and I couldn't fall asleep. I was wishing you were with me, just being with me."

"What was on your mind?"

"Our whole situation. So much to think about, I couldn't turn my mind off, not until I got numb, really numb."

"What happened to the picture of you and the soldier?"

"I threw it away."

"Why?"

"Isn't that what you wanted me to do?"

"You didn't throw it away because I wanted you to."

"I threw it away because I wanted to. The war's over."

"Not yet."

"Between you and me, it is."

She turned away, sat in the middle of the couch, pulled the towel from her head, letting her wet hair down, dropped the towel to the arm of the couch, and said, "I'm free now, free to make my decision, and the school year is almost finished. You won't be my student anymore."

"Are you feeling well, right now?" he asked, sitting next to her.

"Right now, with you here next to me, I'm feeling fine. Actually, I was waiting for you. I had a feeling you'd come here. Maybe I was wishing it so hard that you felt it. Anyway, here you are. Just the two of us, free to do what we want."

"What made you decide to throw the picture away?"

"He's married."

"He got married?"

"He already was, before I met him, but I didn't know until yesterday. My girl friend in Boston wrote to me and decided she should tell me. She hadn't known until a few days ago when her boyfriend had written her. She said she hated to tell me, but then she decided she should."

"I'm sorry, for you," he murmured. "I really am. But I'm glad, though, for myself,"

"You really mean that! Even though I let another man use me."

"You didn't know."

"All he wanted was to get me in bed."

"Don't blame yourself for the way some guys are. You haven't lost anything. He did. He lost *you*. He doesn't have any respect for himself or for anyone else. Guys like that don't. In a way, you're lucky."

"Lucky? Because I'm free?"

"Lucky that he's not married to *you*, that he's married to another woman who probably doesn't know anything about him."

She grinned.

"I'm free to hold you. Now you can take me."

"Now? Right now?"

"We've waited long enough."

She clasped his face and pulled him down on the couch, took his hand and slid it inside of her bathrobe, and pressed his hand between her breasts.

"I can't believe this is happening. All of a sudden, it seems so sudden."

"You haven't had time to let it sink in yet. When you feel it sinking into me, hold me tightly for the greatest thrill of your life. I want you to make passionate love to me, if you want me."

"Of course, I want you! You won't be seeing any ghosts?"

"Neither will you. I promise you that, and more. I want you to spend the night with me. Can you do that, tonight?"

"You're not even concerned about your reputation?"

"I'm concerned about feeling you in my bed, tonight, all night long."

"You're not worried that I'll get you pregnant?"

"I want you to get me pregnant."

"Minnie, I love you!"

"I love you, too,"

He pulled the cord of her bathrobe, opening it, and he caressed her breasts.

"Oh, damn," she moaned, "don't wait until tonight!"

He squeezed her breasts, and as she spread her legs, he thrust himself between her thighs.

"Oh, damn!" she cried out. "Do it now! Do it to me now!"

Part Two

Spring, 1957

Last year, after Rosie and I had been reviewing Dante's script again to decide how we should finish it, I asked her, "Where was he going with this?"

"What do you mean?"

We were in the back street, sitting at the kitchen table in the house downstairs where my grandparents had lived until Dante's "accident." They had moved upstairs so that Dante could be moved in and out of the house more conveniently, although we had not moved him from the house during this past two years. He's either been sitting in a big oak chair in the kitchen, or sleeping in a crib in the front bedroom, next to my bed where I can attend to him.

Rosie and I were sipping coffee in the early evening while her two girls were playing in the front room after supper, and her newest baby, Dante, was sleeping in his crib.

Outside, fluffy spring snow was floating down, covering the flats in white shortly after darkness had descended. It gave our isolated community an appearance of purity, of pristine innocence, I'm sure, as in a picture postcard.

But, as in the rest of our country, according to the news on television, paranoia was spreading, planting suspicion and fear and hate and destruction throughout our whole nation. The most popular television program had been the senate hearings, and its most prominent celebrity had been a Republican senator who had been hailed by many as a champion of liberty and patriotism, who had accused President Truman, a Democrat, of Communism, and had even suspected President Eisenhower, also, a war hero, who had been the commander of the allied forces in Europe, even though, like the senator, he's also a Republican. The senator had been quoted as saying (facetiously, I think): "I suspect everybody of Communism, except you and me. And I'm not so sure about you."

The commies, especially in Montgomery, Alabama, had been instigating the Negroes to revolt and to overthrow the government. Over a hundred Negroes had been arrested on charges of boycotting the busses. Two months earlier, an elderly woman, Rosa Parks, had refused to give up her seat to a young white man, a seat in the whites only section of the bus, and after she had been arrested, fined, and jailed, thousands of Negroes boycotted the bus lines, brazenly violating the Alabama laws. Those damn commies were led by a preacher, or by someone masquerading as a preacher, who was called Martin Luther King. He was found guilty. He went to jail, of course. That had been after the first day in March, when the University of Alabama had expelled a young woman, Autherine Lucy, who, by federal law, had been granted admission as the first black student to the school. She had been expelled for her own safety, though. On the first day of school, she had been pelted by rocks and eggs before she could even get to the entrance of the school. The Supreme Court had ruled that segregation in public schools had been unconstitutional, therefore the university had been forced not only to reinstate her but to protect her. President Eisenhower was quoted as saying, "It is somewhat incumbent on all the South to show progress towards racial integration." Opponents of integration called it "an infringement of states' rights." And the governor of Georgia called it "another example of an overt usurpation of the liberties of the people."

On a roadside billboard on the border between Berlin and Gorham there is now a sign in huge letters: "Impeach Earl Warren!" Berlin, although it's in a traditionally Republican state, is heavily Democratic in a poor French-Canadian district. And Cascade, although it's technically in Gorham, a Republican town, is actually a suburb of Berlin. Earl Warren, a Republican, had been chosen by President Eisenhower as Chief Justice of the Supreme Court. Those damn commies had now infiltrated our government right up to, and including, the presidency!

"I mean," I said to Rosie, "why was he writing this?"

"Why? That's what he did. He wrote. He wrote about his experiences to understand them. He did it not only to understand himself; he was trying to understand human nature."

"Well, I know he was writing about us, but each section is a separate story, loosely connected. If anything, he seemed to be comparing, well, one brother to another, comparing himself, actually, to me. Comparing love to lust. his marriage to mine."

"That's not the central theme. Prejudice is. And each section is not separate. They're connected."

"Connected? How? How's my relationship to Minnie connected to you and Dante?"

"If it wasn't for her, Shackle would still be here, terrorizing us!"

I stared at her.

"Dante didn't write about that!"

"He didn't get a chance."

"Did he ever tell you where this script was going? What his plans were? Didn't he write an outline or something?"

"He was writing about what was happening to us. How could he have known where the story was going? But we know! That's why I wanted you to read this again. I want you to finish it for him."

I sighed heavily, and then I shook my head.

"You don't think his story is worth telling?"

"Well, yeah, I guess, but by someone who knows what he's doing, not by me."

"Dante said you did a lot of writing in high school."

"Well, not a lot, and only in my senior year. And that was to impress Minnie. She was my muse, for cryinoutloud. I was a crazy kid, crazy in love with her. That's the only reason I ever did any writing."

"Why don't you go see her? She's still carrying the torch for you. And she doesn't hide it. Maybe she'll inspire you again."

"I don't know," I muttered.

"She's an important part of our story."

"Because she knew Shackle."

"And she had the courage and the integrity to expose him! Write about what happened."

"Shackle never really had much influence. Most of the people in Gorham even laughed at him. They knew how crazy he was."

"Thanks to Minnie! But her warnings came too late to benefit Dante."

I sighed, and I sipped on my coffee.

"Why do you want me to write it? Do you expect to publish this?"

"I want to see it finished," she said softly, "for myself."

"Well, I don't know. I could try, I suppose. With Minnie and you both helping me and encouraging me, I could try, but certainly not for publication. I mean, I don't even want Minnie to see Dante's script. She'd be outraged. Besides, I can't write like he did. The style, the tone, and everything else will be different. So, I'll try to write what happened to him, but it will have to be something separate from this script."

"Why should it be separate? Why not continue what he's started? Why not finish his script?"

I sighed heavily again. I had a feeling she was going to persuade me to continue trying. I wanted very much to please her. Besides, a part of me also wanted to see a conclusion to his story, but I was afraid that there could be no satisfactory conclusion, that I would only end up disappointing myself and disappointing her, too. There will never be a satisfactory conclusion to what had happened to Dante. I could write about what had happened to him and how it had changed our relationships, how it had altered our lives so drastically, but that's hardly a satisfactory conclusion, casting us into limbo.

There was no ending to his story, I thought, not during our lifetime.

"The point of view will be different," I said to Rosie. "It'll seem like a different story anyway."

"So what?"

"I don't know. I can't just continue from where he left off. I have no idea what the next section or chapter is."

She grinned.

"You don't want me to compare your writing to his. That's not important, Tonio. I understand how you feel, because I've thought of finishing his script myself, and then I remembered that Dante had said to me, when he was writing about you and Minnie, that he admired your writing even though you never seemed aware that your feelings were so deep. And he knew that, because of his wounds in Korea, he might not finish his book, but he thought you could if anything would prevent him. I know it's a lot to ask. I've thought of trying it myself, but whenever I've tried, well, I've approached it with trepidation. I'm so much in awe of Dante, I guess, that I don't feel capable of writing his story. Dante always admired you, in everything, even in writing. Why don't you try it, not for publication, but just for, well, for us? For Dante."

"Well, according to Minnie, at the very beginning, the problem should be presented. Did Dante begin his story at the beginning? Well, maybe he thought he did, but I think it began long before that. Anyway, the problem, or the conflict, should be made clear as soon as possible. I mean, what was the conflict? What's the story really about? What's the plot? How is the conflict going to be resolved? So, the story, the plot, builds suspense, leading up to a climax where all hell breaks loose, and the conflict is resolved. *Finito*. I don't think Dante was writing a novel. Short stories, maybe, loosely related, as I've said. If he was writing a novel, he would have written it chronologically, I think, but he hopped around in time. That's why he didn't write an outline. He was recording what had actually happened, each episode as a separate story. If he had been writing the story of his life, such as an autobiography, it would be easier to continue it if it's chronological, but, as you've said, he couldn't, because he had no way of knowing the ending."

"But, now, we know the ending. Why don't you write how it happened?"

"That's what I suggested. But it would be a separate story."

"Of course not! Just add it to what he's already written."

"Do you have any ideas how to do this? How do I even begin the next chapter?"

She didn't know.

"We have to talk about it," she said.

"And where does his story really end? Like this? In limbo? This is how his story ends. He's neither dead nor alive. So, where and how does his script end?"

She shook her head.

For several weeks we talked about finishing his script. It had seemed simple enough. Just write what had happened during the last five years, after Dante and Rosie had married. Yeah, the more I thought about it, the more I wanted to write it, but every time I sat down and forced myself to write something, I became more frustrated, like trying to reach the fruit of a tree that was always a little beyond my grasp.

Late one night, when everyone else was asleep, I actually cursed my brother for having begun this script. He seemed to be sleeping peacefully in his crib. And I cursed him for what had happened to him, as though it had been his fault, because it had happened not only to him; it had also happened to me and to Rosie.

I remember that night well. I had hated myself for having cursed him.

I felt that I needed to get away for a while, but to get away, even for just one day, was unthinkable. Rosie needed me to be with her almost constantly, and I had become acutely aware of how desperately I needed her, too. I had cursed him for having thrust Rosie and me into our situation.

It's been over two years now since Dante had crashed into a tree at the side of the road near the river, after someone in a passing car had taken a shot at him and had made him swerve off the road. The doctors had not expected him to live even a few hours due to the severity of his injuries, but here he is, two years later, not dead yet, but not really alive either, although, apparently, he can still feel pain and pleasure. He can't talk, but he makes guttural sounds when he's in pain. And when we give him warm baths daily, he seems to enjoy them, especially when we put him in his crib and Rosie sprinkles baby powder on him and rubs his chest and belly and genitals. Sometimes I go into another room so she can be alone with him.

She said that when she caresses him, he seems to respond to her, but the doctors doubt that he's aware of his circumstances. Rosie and I wonder about that.

Just a few years before, in Korea, he had experienced a similar situation in which he had come close to death. The doctors in Japan had told him back then that he was lucky to be alive even though he had lost his left arm and would limp for the rest of his life. The rest of his life, or the rest of his conscious life, had become less than twenty months, less than two short years. He had spent those twenty short months recovering from his war wounds and trying to readjust to civilian life.

One night, after I had made another futile attempt to write the next chapter of his script, Rosie suggested, "Why don't you write an introduction to his book? At the beginning, tell about the car crash and the condition it had left him in, and then introduce the main characters and the circumstances of the time."

"In other words, write the ending first," I said. "In an introduction. That would be like telling what the climax is in a novel."

"Why not? And Dante's script, and the part that you'll add, will show how it happened, and how it affected our lives, until now."

I tried writing the introduction.

To my surprise, the words began to pour out of me. I wrote every day, even on Christmas. And I spent most of the winter writing the introduction, and, I thought, I could concentrate, now, on finishing Dante's script. But the question was, still, where do I start the next part? The trip to Italy after I had graduated from high school? But that didn't have much to do with Dante's story. Neither did my close relationship with Rosie when I had gotten married while she was going to college, so I shouldn't write about everything that had happened. I should write only about the events that had made the story move forward.

Rosie was pleased, for the most part, anyway, with the beginning of the introduction, but she had thought it was much too long, and that I had gone too far, especially about Jessica, whom I should not have included, Rosie said, because Dante hadn't even mentioned her. Jessica, I argued with Rosie, is as important as Minnie Birch is in this story, and certainly Jessica is more important than my wife Joy who had left me after only four years of marriage when things had gone, well, for better or for worse, had gone to worse.

Before I had begun my senior year in high school, and Minnie had become my English teacher, Jessica had become pregnant. At the time, I had been unaware of it. She had been certain that I was the father, and she had wanted the baby. A doctor in her own neighborhood had an excellent reputation, so she consulted him. She admitted to him that she was a prostitute, but she assured him that the father was her lover, because, at work, she had always taken precautions to prevent pregnancy, she told the doctor, but never with her lover, because she had wanted to have his child. She made the doctor promise that whatever information she would provide about her lover would be kept strictly confidential. The doctor immediately jumped to the conclusion that her lover was someone of high repute and was probably married. And he agreed never to reveal the identity of her lover to anyone. She was unwilling to provide his name at this time, she said, but she would be willing to provide all the information necessary on the birth certificate at the time the baby would be born. She told him that the father was an Italian who had come from Italy just before the war and had become stranded here. "You mean, here, in Harlem?" She nodded. "What was he doing here?" She told him he had been visiting, but she thought that he had returned recently to Italy, although she wasn't sure yet, because he hadn't contacted her since he had left a little over a month ago. "Was he involved in illegal activities?" No! Of course not! Nothing like that, although he and a friend had been here illegally, due to their circumstances, but were trying to get back to Italy before they'd get caught. The doctor was intrigued by her situation, but she didn't want to risk the chance of her lover getting caught, so she refused to reveal too much information. "I understand. Incidentally, my wife is Italian, too. She was born in Italy. Where in Italy is he from?" She was reluctant to tell him more. "Does he speak English?" She shrugged. "I speak Italian. And my two kids speak it. Do you?" She shook her head and muttered no. "My daughter comes in here sometimes after school, and I think she'd be happy to teach you some Italian, if you'd want." Jessica said she would like that. "So, you've known this Italian since he arrived here, three years ago?" She began to feel uneasy. "I don't want to make you uncomfortable, to make you answer a lot of questions, but I'm so curious. I give you my word that you can trust me. I have the distinct feeling that you have a deep respect for the father, and I assure you that I'll do all that I can to bring your child safely into the world. I know you already love this child, that you see this baby as, well, as a divine gift. And I'm happy to be your doctor. But I have some nagging questions. Does he, the father, know, well, what you do for a living?"

"Yes, he knows. He doesn't like it, but he understands my situation. He really does, and I want him to know I'm going to have his child, but I want to be the one to tell him."

"You love him? The father?"

"Yes, I do. If you knew him, you'd understand."

"And do you think he loves you, in spite of what you do?"

"I know he does."

He nodded.

But she could see the skepticism in his face, she thought.

"He really does!" she insisted. "He's very understanding. He doesn't condemn me, because he knows my situation. I think that's one of the reasons I love him so much."

"But if he knew you were going to have his child, how do you think he'd react?"

"He'd be happy. He's told me he'd like me to be the mother of his, well, he called them, his bambini."

"Do you think he'd marry you or support the child?"

"I don't expect him to marry me or anything like that, and he wouldn't have to support the child."

"You sound like a remarkable young woman."

"Thank you. I wish I were. But he is, he really is. I know it doesn't seem right that he should feel the way he does about me, because, I'm, well, what I am, but he's really a remarkable person, gentle and very intelligent. I've never met anyone like him."

"I'd like to meet him."

"I have a feeling you will."

During the next few months Jessica did voluntary work at the clinic at least every Sunday, and when her pregnancy began to show, and she stopped working at the club for a time, she worked at the clinic several days a week and had begun studying nursing. She was able to recruit other girls from the club to do volunteer work mostly on Sundays, and several times she had seen Rosie who had taught her to speak some basic Italian, but they had never talked about me and had not even been aware, back then, that they had both known me, and, somehow, Nick, who had seldom gone into the clinic, anyway, during his senior year of high school, had never seen Jessica during that period. At the club, Jessica had established a fund for the clinic, in which wealthy business men, not only from the New York area, but from around the world, had contributed thousands of dollars during the past ten years or so. During those last ten years, Jessica has been able to buy the building in which she still lives, had long ago ended her career as a prostitute but had become a major stockholder in the club and had renamed it the Kitty Club and Hotel, had become a supervising nurse at the clinic and had, long ago, obtained a degree from City College of New York.

At the clinic, after she had delivered a boy, she named him Antonio Valentino.

The doctor was flabbergasted.

"I know the father!"

2

As soon as I had seen the new English teacher, Minnie Birch, Eros had smitten me. My heart had already been torn apart so badly by my separation from Jessica that I had thought that never would I recover. I had not mentioned Jessica to anyone, not even to Dante. How could I admit, to anyone, that I had actually fallen in love with a prostitute? I didn't even want to admit it to myself. The thought of how others would react to my feelings had greatly influenced me. But Minnie Birch was an attractive, sophisticated woman whom everybody admired, whom every young woman wanted to emulate, whom every man, young and old, desired. To be loved by such a woman, every guy who knew me would envy me. She was everything, I thought, that Jessica was, and more; she was beautiful, and she was intelligent, and educated, and she was white, a woman with high moral standards, with nothing about her that would shame me. Dante, having noticed my immediate attraction to her asked me if I believed in love at first sight. "Of course," I said without hesitation. I had never pretended, not even back then when I had known almost everything about nearly everything, that I had known what God is, but I knew that there is in nature something that provides us with the ability to know without evidence or reason, something even animals have, which we call instincts, and in humans, which we call intuition. We know that animals, in spite of their instinct to fear death, will sacrifice their own lives in order to save the lives of their young. In humans, we call that love. Yes, I told Dante, I believe that when one soul meets another for the first time, it is possible to feel an attraction other than sexual attraction to another person. I honestly can't deny my sexual attraction to Jessica when I had first seen her, so I won't deny my sexual attraction, either, to Minnie. Without it, I don't think I'd pay much attention to the opposite sex. So, what is the phenomenon that attracts me, if it isn't just sex? My father had called it love. What we feel in the other, his theory was, is the good, the divine. He had not believed that our nature was evil, that we were naturally attracted to evil or to the devil (he hadn't even believed in the devil) as so many Christians believe, especially Puritans, Catholics and Protestants who believe that evil is the consequence of original sin; he believed that we were all born with the ability to love, that we were naturally attracted to our Source. There is a commandment, of course, to go forth and multiply, a natural law that most of us, especially me, are more than willing to obey. Problems, of course, arise from our lack of responsibilities for the little bastards we create, and sometimes some of us make the mistake of labeling sex itself, or even love, as evil. I'll admit how easy it is for us, including me, to make the mistake of confusing sex for love, as when we say, "making love" when we really mean, "just fucking someone for the fun of it." We can take something good, as Jessica has said, such as sex, and even love, and twist it into something degrading. No doubt about it, my initial attraction to Jessica had been very sexual, but as we knew each other and ourselves better, our relationship had become much more than that. By contrast, my relationship with Minnie, which, I had initially thought, was based on love, or on our need for love, had always lacked something. Don't get me wrong. I don't mean we didn't enjoy sex together. Having sex with her has always been, well, a hell of a lot of fun. I mean, she'd get so damn excited that she'd get me so excited, too, that we'd both lose control of ourselves. But with Jessica, we both felt, well, more tender, somehow, and yet, more passionate. Hard on the outside, but softer on the inside, and we'd move more slowly together, yet deeper into each other, letting ourselves float away together into another dimension, becoming one with each other, with the cosmos, with an absolute power embracing us as we'd enter into a state of ecstasy.

Rosie has said that sex is God's way of propagating the species and that love is His method of improving the creation.

I had desired Minnie so damn much that I had wanted, and had expected, her to replace Jessica somehow, but that had not happened. As much as I had enjoyed sex with Minnie, after twelve years now, there's still something that keeps us separate, and she seems to prefer that. I guess we feel the way we feel and that the best thing to do is to understand our feelings in order to control them.

During my senior year in high school, I had written notes to Jessica telling her how much I had missed her and how Nick and I could not leave the ship on the long journey to Italy because we had been without the proper papers even though we had stopped at various ports until we had finally landed at Naples, and even then, we had been taken into custody and questioned, I told Jessica, and had been subjected to a lot of red tape before I could finally mail her a letter from Italy. I hadn't known, of course, that she had given birth to my son, and that Ben John had told her he had even been the doctor at my own birth. Jessica had refused to give him permission to tell anyone, even his own wife, about the birth of my son. She had wanted to be the one to tell me. She had forbidden him, even, to tell Nick about her, so, Nick had known nothing about the situation when we had gone to Italy.

Ben John had tried to assure her that Nick and I were really decent kids and that we'd be able to explain why we had invented such a peculiar tale.

"Don't judge them too harshly until you know them better."

"I know they're decent kids. I liked them immediately, especially Tony. I have the feeling I'll see him again."

"Oh, I'm sure you will!"

And he had kept her informed about me. She had known that Nick and I and my father had gone on a ship from Portland to Italy. And after my father and I had returned, we went to New Haven to visit the Yale campus where I would be attending school, and from there we went to New York. I had called Jessica and had told her I would visit her for a couple of days.

Before that, I had seen Minnie, of course, and had made love to her. I had convinced myself that I was in love with both of them.

My father and I arrived in New York on a Sunday. Jessica was expecting me later in the afternoon.

After lunch, while we were sitting at the dining room table and sipping coffee with anisette, I was trying to think of an excuse to leave. My father and Ben John were talking about the trip to Italy, and Rosie and her mother were in the kitchen washing dishes.

Suddenly Ben John turned to me and said, "You seem restless, Tony. You have a date or something?"

He turned to my father and said, "I think he met a girl here last summer." He turned to me again. "Why don't you give her a call?"

I stared at him.

"Go ahead. Call her."

I did. I told her I'd be there in five minutes.

As soon as I tapped on her door, it opened. She was so damn radiant, and I felt so good seeing her again that I clasped her and held her body tightly against mine, as though our bodies felt so resilient we would melt into each other without even losing our individualities. At that moment our bodies made us aware that we were not separate, that we were, and belonged, together.

And when she took me into her bedroom to show me my son sleeping in a crib, I was so stunned and so overwhelmed that tears actually rolled down my cheeks. She picked up the baby and gave him to me and let me hold him, and I kissed him and kissed him, yet I couldn't believe that I was actually holding my own baby son.

"No one can question that he's your son," she said. "He looks so much like you already."

We sat on the bed, the same bed in which we had conceived the baby, and I remembered what I had said to Jessica: "I wanna you be madre de mi bambini. Much love inside you."

"We are family now," Jessica said. "I'm the mother of your child, and you're the father of my baby, and I'm happy, especially now that we're here, together."

"We should get married."

"I don't expect you to marry me! I feel like I'm already married to you, but I don't want you to ever be tied down to me, not you and not our son. I just hope that some day, before he gets old enough to understand, that I'll have enough money to be, well, not what I am."

Her telephone rang,

We went into the other room, and she picked up the phone.

"Hello." A pause. "Yes, he's here." Another pause. She held the phone out to me and said, "It's my doctor. He wants to talk with you."

"Your doctor?"

I couldn't imagine what he wanted to say to me. As she gave me the phone, she took the baby.

"Hello," I said.

"Tony!"

He sounded like Ben John.

"Who's this?"

"What do you mean? Who does this sound like?"

Jessica returned the baby to the crib.

"Ben John?"

"Your father doesn't know, yet, what's going on. Jessica had sworn me to secrecy. I want your permission to tell him. Ask Jessica if I have her permission, too."

She had just come out of the bedroom, and as she approached me, I said, "Why don't you talk with her?" And I gave her the phone.

"Hi." A pause. "Yeah, that's fine." Another pause. "Are you sure?" She looked at me. "Of course. Are you sure everything's all right?" She nodded. "Oh, of course." She stared at me. "Well, I'm a little nervous about meeting him." She smiled a little. "Of course we'll be there."

She hung up.

"We've been invited to spaghetti dinner this evening. Your father wants to meet his grandson."

We sat on the couch, and she told me about her past year.

"If I remember correctly, it had been Nick, not you, who had invented that story about being stranded here."

"When I saw you that Sunday, I had felt so damn foolish, but I was afraid to tell you the story had just been, well, a sort of stupid joke."

"Why were you afraid to tell me?"

"I thought you might get angry, that you'd think we were, well, just making a fool out of you."

"I can't deny that I was fascinated by you, or, at least, by the person I thought you were. So was Mad." Jessica grinned at me. "Your accent was so endearing! And so convincing." "But there was something else about you that made me feel, well, comfortable, and so close to you. You seemed to understand me. You sounded sincere. You lak a make a funny me?"

"No! I meant everything I said to you. I swear it! I'm really the same person you thought I was. I mean, on the inside."

"But I thought you were older, much older."

"I am! I'm older than my age."

"What?"

"I mean, well, older than I am."

"I know what you mean, Tonio." She put her hand on my knee. "And I know that I mean something to you, because here you are. You've returned. And not because you knew about the baby."

Ben John had told my father how Jessica was supporting her mother and two younger sisters, and she knew that my father had not only accepted her, he had respected her and had welcomed her into our family and had insisted that he'd support his grandson.

My mother, of course, would have to be reconciled. My father knew how to do that. We would never tell her what Jessica had done for a living, and my father asked Jessica if she would be willing to let little Tony be baptized in a Catholic church. My mother, he said, would be greatly pleased. And she was. She had not accepted Jessica as a daughter, but she adored her grandson.

3

During the spring of my first year at Yale, my father was killed. Someone in a moving automobile had taken a shot at him while he was in the middle of a river and was trying to unjam floating logs. He had not been hit, but he had lost his balance, had fallen into the river and had been crushed between logs. Nine years later, a similar incident would happen to Dante. After my father had died, I finished my freshman year at Yale, but my mother had become so ill that I stayed with her and helped her in the restaurant.

Minnie, of course, had been terribly disappointed in me, and although we hadn't ended our relationship, she had made it clear to me that she would never marry me unless I'd finish my education and get into an honorable profession, but I've often wondered if she would ever have married me, because she seemed content with the way we were. Locally, we were seldom in public alone together. And even though we had been in Boston together a few times, I have never met her family. We have been, and we still are, as Jessica and I are, friends, and they both know of the other. It's no secret that Jessica is the mother of my son. On his fifth birthday, she had brought him here, to Cascade Flats, for a week. That had been a year before I had even met Joy, to whom I had been introduced by Minnie.

Until I met Joy, the only two women with whom I've had a serious sexual relationship were Minnie and Jessica. As I've said, I thought I had been in love with both of them. To me, Minnie had been an enigma. I knew I had excited her sexually; other than that, I knew very little about her, yet, I trusted her. Without trust, I thought, there is no friendship. What puzzled me most about her was that although we had been so intimate, sharing not only sex with each other but also some of our thoughts and feelings, a barrier seemed to separate us as though she had deliberately set up a wall around her and had not wanted me to penetrate it. She wanted my body to penetrate hers, but she didn't want me to understand certain things about her. She didn't seem to be jealous of Jessica. Actually, I hadn't been spending that much time with Jessica, anyway, so Minnie had never felt threatened by her. She had even given me the impression that, like Jessica, she had wanted me to impregnate her. "I wish you would," she had said on several occasions. And she really didn't seem worried about her reputation, as though she thought the people in this part of the woods were just a bunch of hicks, anyway, and that she could simply return to the more sophisticated world in Boston. She had given me the impression that she had enough money to be independent.

As I've said, I thought Minnie was an enigma, until I met Joy, who had two distinct and contradictory personalities. I had given up trying to understand her. At times, her sexual desires seemed infinite; at other times, she seemed to loathe sex. Less than a month after I had met Joy, she told me she was pregnant.

After I had decided to marry her, Minnie had called the restaurant. Whenever she had wanted me to go to her house but hadn't wanted anyone else to know, especially the telephone operator, she would order a pizza "with the works" and if she hadn't really wanted the pizza, she would request a home delivery, which I had seldom done for anyone. At midnight, without the pizza, I drove to her house.

As soon as I entered, she lashed out at me.

"You damn fool!"

She was wearing only a bathrobe and slippers. She went into the living room and sat on the couch, and I sat beside her.

Joy had told her we were getting married.

"I was going to tell you."

"A month ago, you didn't even know she existed, and now you're going to marry her? Why?"

"She said she's pregnant."

"So?"

"What do you mean, so?"

"If she's pregnant, do you think you're the one who did it?"

"Yeah, I do."

"She didn't tell you that, did she?"

"Well, when she told me she's pregnant, I assumed I did it. Why would she tell me she's pregnant if I'm not the one who did it?"

"Why? Why do you suppose she'd tell you that?"

"She'd tell the guy who did it to her so he'd marry her, wouldn't she?"

"What if he's already married?"

"Come on, Minnie!"

"You don't know her."

"And you do?"

"Yes, I do. I know her too damn well. Don't trust her."

"So, tell me what you know."

"She's the most pessimistic person I've ever met. To her, everything is negative. She doesn't believe in anything positive. She doesn't even believe in love, in anything good. She's going to drag you so far down and make your life so damn miserable you'll resent her and everything about her. I hate to see her do that to you. Why don't you wait a couple of more months? If she's pregnant, a couple of more months won't make any difference. Besides, I don't want to lose you, especially to her. Are you so attracted to her that you're anxious to marry her? I thought I satisfied you, but, apparently, I'm not enough. One woman isn't enough for you. Not even two. Is she that good in bed? Maybe she is, right now, but after you marry her, you'll get sick and tired of her. She'll never make a good wife, and I doubt if she'll make a good mother. She's too damn selfish. And demanding. She has to be in control of everything. Does she know you have a son? Does she know about Jessica? She'll never tolerate her nor your son. She doesn't have any respect, not for anyone. And you won't be able to tolerate her for long. In a month from now, maybe even less than that, you'll be coming back here, pleading with me to take this," she said, putting her hand on my crotch, "inside of me, deep inside of me, where it belongs."

"I thought you were going to tell me that she got knocked up by another guy who's married."

"That wouldn't surprise me. I told you I don't trust her. I wouldn't be surprised that after the baby's born, she'll dump you and sue you for alimony."

"I think I understand how you feel, but you and I have been, well, sleeping together now for six years. Six years! And you haven't even thought of marriage."

"That has nothing to do with it, Tony! Has it? If she hadn't told you she was pregnant, would you marry her? Would you want to?"

I liked the idea of being married and of having kids around me and raising them. If Jessica hadn't been a prostitute, I wouldn't hesitate to marry her, I thought. It had been a marvelous experience being with her, of sleeping with her, making love to her, and of sharing life with her. And I would have married Minnie if she had wanted to marry me. And I would, I'm sure, be faithful to the woman I'd marry.

Even though I have never thought of myself as particularly religious, unlike my father, who had been writing a philosophy book about religion before he had been killed, and who had been a big influence on me and Dante and Rosie, but, unlike Joy, an atheist, I no longer question whether or not there is God; I question what God is. I don't think God is knowable, but I believe that there are natural laws that govern the universe and that it's wise to know and to follow those laws. And, like my father, I believe in only one God, and that only God, the source of existence, knows everything. So, when I swear anything to God, my oath is sacred. When an atheist swears to God, is that oath valid?

Before marrying Joy, I had wondered if I could be faithful to her. I knew it would probably be difficult for me, at times, and that I'd need something to help me overcome temptations, something stronger than sexual attraction. And I thought about how faithful I would have been if I had married Jessica. Why Jessica? Why hadn't

I thought about how faithful I would have been to Minnie? I wasn't sure, not at first. And then I knew why. If I had to choose between having sex only with Jessica, or with everyone else except her, my choice was easy. Having sex with someone else would not be worth the risk of losing Jessica. I would never take that chance. Yeah, I'm attracted to Minnie and to Joy as much as I am to Jessica. But, with Jessica, there was something more than sex, obviously. What? Why do married people, especially after they've sworn to God to remain faithful, commit adultery? What do we need to help us overcome such desires? We, the people, have a simple answer. Are we willing to risk the loss of someone for a few moments of fleeting pleasure with another? Not if we love that someone. But what is love?

Looking back now to six years ago, when I married Joy, love seemed so simple. And, maybe it is. It's the central theme of all the major religions, the greatest of all the commandments. Love, we have been taught, solves all of our problems. If we all loved each other, we'd all be living in paradise. We assume that we all know what love is. It is so simple to understand. Why, then, is there so damn much evil in this world?

Okay, I have to admit that I had been so damn attracted to Joy that I thought I could easily love her. All I had to do was commit myself to her. Of course I wanted to marry her. Why not? What did I have to lose? My freedom? My individuality? Why not give marriage a try? If it doesn't work with Joy, it will mean that our love wasn't strong enough. Love, I thought, was an act of the will. You plant it, and it grows. How much it grows depends on how much care you're willing to give it. Yeah, I knew that the word had been so overused and distorted that it's meaning is sometimes lost, so you must look for it. So, that's what I was doing, looking for love with an attractive woman whom I could respect enough to marry, I thought.

Actually, the attractive woman whom I respected the most, other than Rosie, of course, (who was a little too young for me and who was in college and wasn't ready for marriage, anyway), was, I thought, Jessica. I visited her to tell her of my circumstances. I made it clear that I wouldn't get married if it meant losing her friendship. She said I would never lose her friendship. But, she said, although she wanted me to be happy and had tried to prepare herself for the day when I would actually get married, she now felt jealous of the other woman. She was trying not to feel jealous. She couldn't help it, she said. I swore that I would never abandon her or little Tony. "I know that! But I don't want us to be a hindrance."

Jessica said she understood my situation and would accept it.

"Of course you should be faithful to your wife. I'd be disappointed in you if you weren't. But I know you. I know you'll be good to her."

I had made up my mind to be faithful to Joy.

Although we weren't married in a church, we both made a vow to ourselves, and to each other, and, of course, to God. I distinctly heard and remember the words to promise to love, honor, and obey each other until death. According to the laws of New Hampshire, we were legally married, and we were given a certificate of proof.

"In the eyes of God, we're not married," Joy said one evening long before Rusty was born. We had gotten into a stupid argument that evening on the meaning of marriage. She enjoyed getting me upset with inane ideas. "According to your mother, we're living in sin."

"What's marriage?" I responded. "We made a promise to God to love, honor, and obey each other."

"A promise to nothing is meaningless."

"We also promised each other."

"A mere formality to give us a license to fuck each other. Did you really mean it when you said you promise to obey me?"

"Of course."

"Bullshit! Do you expect me to obey you?"

"I hope we obey each other unless our requests are unreasonable."

"Suppose I'd forbid you to fuck other women?"

"Come on!"

Minnie was right. Joy didn't believe in love. It was just a euphemism for sex. She could have been any woman in the world, and I, any man in the world, in the same bed at the same time, copulating, and we would have felt the same way, she said, as we would have felt towards each other while having sex with someone else and calling it love. When I asked her what sex is, she said it's a blind force that stimulates us to propagate the species. I asked her where it comes from. From nature, she said.

"What's the difference between nature and God?"

"When people talk about God, they mean an intelligent being who created the world. Nature is not an intelligent being."

"Nature is not an intelligent being, yet intelligent beings, such as scientists, study nature to understand how it works, to understand the laws of nature, because scientists, unlike priests, or I should say, even more so than priests, are so astonished by how nature functions that it takes far more faith to believe in nature, that nature will continue on this incredible, unbelievable course, but everything, you think, that's ever happened, the whole evolution of everything, has happened by accident, by chance, and yet it is so damn intelligible, so far, at least."

"Yes," she answered emphatically.

Nature itself, she said, is a blind force, neither good nor evil; it is impersonal. The history of man is his story to survive, to protect his territory, to kill others who try to take away his territory, to expand his own territory, sometimes by force, killing others if he thinks it benefits him, imposing rules and regulations and inventing religions to enforce the rules and offering rewards to those who obey the rules and threatening punishment to those who break the rules. Man has invented a god to explain the origin and mysteries of life and to impose conformity to the morality of a particular group, decreeing conformity to its morality as good and nonconformity as evil. What is considered by one society as good can be considered by another society as evil, regardless of whether it's natural or not.

"If you were alone with a woman who attracted you and you knew she's attracted to you, and although you both lived in a society which forbids you to touch each other, but you both knew you wouldn't get caught, wouldn't you fuck her?"

"Would you expect me to?"

"Of course I would."

"Would you, if you were alone with another guy?"

"If I was attracted to him. Yeah. Why not?"

I stared at her.

"Suppose he got you pregnant?"

"A married woman doesn't have to worry about that."

"Love, then, wouldn't stop you from being unfaithful."

"Unfaithful to whom? Someone you love? Has that ever stopped you from screwing someone else?"

I didn't answer. I couldn't, because she was right.

"What about that colored girl?"

"What do you mean?"

"The one you got pregnant. The one you visited in New York to tell her you were marrying me."

"She expects me to be faithful to you. We didn't have any sex, not then, anyway."

"Really? She's not a whore then."

"What! Why'd you call her that?"

"Sorry. I just meant a girl who likes to fuck, like me. What about Minnie?"

"What? What do you mean?"

"Have you ever fucked her?"

"I can't believe you're serious!"

"You don't want us to be honest with each other? Do you prefer that we play the respectable husband and wife game?"

"Why did you ask me that about Minnie? Has she given you any indication that she might be, well, interested in me, that way?"

"Oh? She arouses your interests."

"She arouses the interests of every normal guy."

"Answer my question."

"Of course I have. In my dreams. What has she said about me?"

"She told me you're sexy."

"Aw, come on now."

"She really did. She told me you were her favorite student, that you and Dante are gifted writers and that I should meet you, that you're not only interesting; you're sexy."

"She told you I'm sexy? Really? I mean, how did she say it?"

Joy grinned at me.

"After we left the restaurant, the night she introduced us, and she was driving, I said you looked hot, and she said, 'Yeah! I know what you mean.'"

"Well, what else did she say? Did she tell you she was interested in me, sexually?"

"Not in so many words, but she gave me the impression that she wouldn't kick you out of bed."

"Wow! If only I had known. But it's too late now."

"Why?"

"I'm a married man. She wouldn't be interested in a married man, would she? I mean, how well do you know her? Do you think she's, well, vulnerable?"

"So now you're interested. Yeah, I think she's vulnerable. She creates the impression of being prim and proper, but she's inhibited, and if she ever loses her virginity, she'd go wild."

"Her virginity? How do you know she's a virgin? I mean, she must be over thirty."

"I don't. That's what she told me."

"If she's still a virgin, it might be difficult to seduce her."

"She can be seduced, under the right circumstances."

"What are the right circumstances?"

"If we invited her here for dinner, just the three of us, and had a few drinks so that she'd lose some of her inhibitions, wining her and dining her, and playing soft music, and letting her dance with you, and suddenly I pass out, dead to the world in another room, leaving the two of you alone together, it would be easy for you to seduce her. When we talked about you that night, I was wondering how she felt about sex, especially with you. I got the definite impression she's sexually attracted to you, that, under the right conditions, in which she'd feel comfortable enough to shed her restraints, you'd get her so damned aroused she wouldn't resist you. All the locked up passion in her would break loose."

"Sounds like you'd relish that."

"Yeah, I think I probably would."

"Why?"

"She's so damn smug! She thinks she's morally superior to me, that she's morally superior to everybody. Do you know anything about her religion?"

I shrugged.

"I remember that she used to begin each class by reading a passage from the Bible."

"She told me you went to Yale, that you were thinking of entering the ministry, and that you and she used to talk about religion."

"That's true."

Joy laughed.

"You would have made one hell of a minister!"

"I don't understand why you'd enjoy it if she's seduced. I thought you and she were friends."

"We're hardly friends. Yeah, I would enjoy seeing her get seduced. She's such a hypocrite. She ought to be teaching the Bible, not English. To her, modern literature is vulgar; it shouldn't portray reality. The real world should only exist in slums, not in literature, as though literature should be an escape from reality, not an endeavor to understand it. She's a royal prude. She doesn't live in the real world. She can't accept it. I've let her read some of the stories I've written. Big mistake! My writing isn't good enough, not for her. Not for miss prissy purity. Too damn negative. I write about the real world, not about the fantasy world of her religion. She's more negative than I've ever thought of being. Anything pleasurable is evil. The more pleasurable something is, especially sex, the more evil it is. She doesn't like the way I write. She doesn't like the way I talk, the way I think. Friends? With her? I'm not good enough, not for her. I'm not even good enough to be accepted into her religious cult."

"What do you mean, her religious cult?"

"Her body doesn't belong to her. It belongs to God. How can she give her body to a mere mortal? What man is worthy enough to touch her precious body? I'd like to see some man strip her of her pretentiousness. I'd like to say, 'You like that, don't you, bitch! You like to fuck! You're as human as the rest of us.'"

"If she's still a virgin, she'll still be a virgin when she's an old maid."

"Ah, you don't know her like I do. You're just the guy that could cure her."

"Me? Why me?"

"She likes you, and she's revealed enough, although in a round-about way, that she's attracted to you, sexually, not only because you're good looking; you're so, well, so damn inferior to her, socially, and that makes you even more tantalizing. You are *really* the forbidden fruit. And she would really enjoy fucking you, to feel your wild, unrestrained passions burst inside of her, but she can't admit that, of course, especially to her own self."

"Too bad I hadn't known that. I was sexually attracted to her, too, but I had thought she was untouchable. I probably could have married her."

"I don't think so. Even I am out of her class. And if she did marry you, she'd make you miserable."

"Why?"

"She's too damn selfish. You wouldn't be able to satisfy her for long, anyway. No man is good enough for her."

"Tell me about her religion."

"She belongs to The Temple of the Holy Spirit."

"I've never heard of it."

"Neither had I until I moved here. It's restricted to white American born citizens, a fundamentalist Christian religion, and they meet in the house of a member, that creep Shackle. As a matter of fact, I think he was one of the original founders of the group."

In spite of my unstable relationship with Joy, I was determined to remain faithful to her, but she was unable to accept my son, and, after four years of marriage, she used him as an excuse to divorce me, and, as Minnie had predicted, she not only sued me for alimony, she wanted ownership of the house and restaurant.

But I'm jumping way ahead of the story.

4

When I was a kid, two of the most fascinating subjects were inappropriate to discuss in polite society, so I had to learn about them from other kids. The dirtiest word in the English language, I learned, was not *cacca*. What is the dirtiest thing one person could do to another? What is the dirtiest thing a guy could do to a girl? When I was a kid, I asked guys, "What is the worse sin a girl could commit? To kill a guy for no reason, or to let him fuck her?" Most guys said, "Gee, that's a tough question!"

Anyway, when I was a kid, just thinking about the most contemptible thing a guy could do to a decent girl, especially to a girl like, well, like Nick's kid sister, Rosie, sent shivers of guilt through me. She always admired me, calling me "Big Brother." And I loved her too much, I used to tell her, to do anything like that to her. But when we kids used to pile into the back seat of a car, she always wanted to sit on my lap, and she knew how much I enjoyed that, although when we grew older, our feelings for each other would become a serious problem.

When she graduated from high school I was the only one from Cascade who attended the ceremonies. With some of her friends, we went to a club that night and we celebrated almost to dawn. Later, in the middle of July, while her folks were in Italy with Nick, I stayed with her. When her folks would return, Rosie and I would go to New Hampshire, go camping together, spend a week in Quebec City, and then she would enter college.

In Harlem, Rosie had invited a friend, Tina, who had graduated with her, to stay with us one night. After we had eaten dinner, and Rosie and Tina had washed the dishes, Rosie made a pot of coffee. While it was percolating, we went into the front room and sat on the couch. It was a warm evening, and Rosie and Tina were wearing tight shorts and lowcut tops. After a while, Rosie got up and went into the kitchen. When she returned, carrying a tray with three cups, I could smell the aroma of a hundred-proof of homemade anisette rising from the coffee.

After I took a sip and she sat next to me again to my right, I said. "Wow, this is strong! How much anisette did you put in it?"

"Is it too strong?"

"Not for me. It's the way I like it, but for you it's probably too strong."

"I like the taste of licorice. It makes my lips taste sweet."

"After a few more sips, it'll make your lips numb."

"Well, at least they'll taste sweet."

I took another swallow, and then, gazing at her dark, bright eyes, I said, "You don't need to make your lips sweet."

"Why not?"

"Your lips have been made sweet enough by nature."

"Are you flirting with me, big brother?"

"Of course, I am. You know how much I enjoy flirting with such an irresistible woman, a woman with such sweet voluptuous lips, among other delectable assets."

Her lips suddenly touched mine as she planted a quick yet tender kiss on my mouth.

"Your lips are sweet, too."

"That's the anisette," I said, feeling the rush of blood to my face.

"It's not the anisette. It's the man, the whole man. The whole man is sweet."

"Oh!" Tina cried out. "It *is* sweet! I like it, too!"

She took a swallow.

"Don't drink it too fast," I warned her, "just sip on it slowly and enjoy the taste, because this is powerful stuff. If you drink it too quickly, it will make you so drunk that you could quickly lose control over your libido."

She stared at me.

"Is that what happens to *you?*"

"Well, for me, it'll take a lot more than just one cup."

"Do you mind if I ask you a very personal question?"

"That depends on the question, but I don't think I'd mind. So, ask the question."

"How many kids do you have?"

I stared at *her*.

"I'm not married."

"I didn't think so. How many girlfriends do you have?"

Rosie said, "She's wondering about you and Jessica. She was here when Jessica brought the baby here. Remember?"

"I'm wondering why you didn't marry her," Tina said.

"I've been wondering the same thing," said Rosie. "I even asked Jessica about it."

"You did?" I asked. "What did she say?"

"She said you were too young, but she also said that she would never get married, and that you were free to marry anyone, anyone except her, she said."

"What did she mean?"

"She said I'd have to ask *you.*"

"I guess she means I'm not ready to settle down yet."

"She loves you."

"I know."

"Don't you love her, too?"

"Yeah, I do, as a friend, but I love you more."

"Your love for her is obvious. You made her the mother of your child."

"You could be, too," Tina said, "I mean, well, if you were a little older."

Rosie grinned at Tina.

"You're right. I've always been in love with him." Gazing at me, she said, "You know how much I've always loved you. You've always made me feel good, comforting me when I most needed it. Do you remember how you comforted me one night when my folks were out? Right after we had moved here? Do you remember that you taught me about sex that night? And I asked you how big your penis got?"

"What? Are you serious?" I asked as she was almost laughing.

"You don't remember? You and Nick were right here, listening to the radio, after I had jumped out of bed, almost hysterical, because I was bleeding. I was wearing only thin summer pajamas, but I didn't care because I was so frantic. You said to me so calmly that I was growing into a beautiful woman. You actually made me feel proud of being a woman, a woman, you said, who was developing a beautiful body. In my father's library, Nick found a book about sexual reproduction with photos in it. I remember asking both of you if you ever had sex. Nick said he had never had sex. And when I asked you, you told me it was not any of my business, and I knew you had. I wanted you to, well, to tuck me into bed. And you did. You even gave me a goodnight kiss, a *real* kiss. I don't know if you still remember, but I asked you how big your penis got."

"I very conveniently forgot about it, but now that you've mentioned it, I vaguely recall something like that."

"I wanted you to get in bed with me so that I could experience sex with you, but I knew you wouldn't. I asked you if having sex was painful. I was trying to trick you into admitting you had done it. But you cleverly told me that sex was made to be extremely pleasurable so that people would do it, but that I would have to wait until I married a man who could afford to take care of me and my babies. And before I fell asleep, I imagined that you were in bed with me, and that we were making a baby together."

"Now I know why you didn't marry Jessica," Tina said. "You and Rose were made for each other."

"She wants to go to New Hampshire," Rosie grinned, "to meet Dante. She thinks the guys there are sexier."

"There's only one problem with that," I said to Tina. "My kid brother prefers celibacy, not matrimony."

"Really?"

"That's true," Rosie said, "but he's not studying for the priesthood yet. He's not even in a seminary. He's going to the University of New Hampshire."

"You can try to tempt him," I said to Tina, "but, so far, all efforts have failed."

She grinned at me, took a large swallow of her coffee, smacked her lips, and said, "But he's human, isn't he? I mean, he's made of flesh and blood like the rest of us."

"Well, you can try, but he has a strong will and can be terribly stubborn."

"You would like him," Rosie said. "Everybody likes him."

"I like his photos. He's so cute! I bet he's a good kisser."

"He is," Rosie grinned, "almost as good as his big brother."

"And he, like Nick, is going to be a priest? How come you're so different?"

"What makes you think I'm so different?" I asked.

"I know what you want."

"Oh, yeah? Tell me what I want."

She looked at Rosie and grinned, and to me she said, "What you want is so obvious."

"And you don't think that's good?"

"With you? I bet it is! That's what she tells me!"

"You're embarrassing me," Rosie said.

Tina drank the rest of her coffee and wiped her mouth with the back of her hand.

"Why are you embarrassed? I envy you."

"Do you want another cup of coffee?" Rosie asked.

"This cup has already gone to my head. I'm ready for bed." She stood up. "Besides, three is company. So I'll leave you two alone. But," she said to Rosie, "don't do anything with him that I would do."

"And what would you do with me?"

She stared at me.

"Give you the greatest thrill you've ever had." And to Rosie, she said, "Let me know if he does the same to you."

As she entered a bedroom, Rosie said, "She thinks you're so damn sexy! But, like me, she's still a virgin. All talk. No action."

"You're still a virgin?"

"Of course! I've never wanted anyone except you. I thought you knew that."

"Well, I have to admit that if you weren't a virgin, I'd be disappointed, but you're the only girl I feel that way about. And that's because, well, because you're you."

"Nick's kid sister," she muttered.

"You're special to me."

"I've never understood your relationship to Jessica."

I swallowed the rest of my coffee and put the cup on a coffee table.

"As the mother of my son, I'll always be friendly with her, but never as close as you and I are."

"Why not?"

"Why do you and I feel so close to each other?"

"I didn't know you felt closer to me."

"Of course I do!"

She planted a quick kiss on my lips, and then she went into the kitchen and poured us each another cup. And we continued talking about Jessica.

"Do you like her?" I asked.

"Yes. I liked her when I first saw her. I liked everything about her. I thought everybody did. She's so beautiful! She's the sexiest woman I've ever seen, even though she's colored, sexier than Marilyn Monroe!"

"Yeah, she is, almost as sexy as you, even though you're colored too."

She tapped my thigh with her fist. "Stop it," she said, smiling. "I'm serious."

And then she clasped my thigh, pulling it against hers and rubbed my leg gently. Was she unaware that her warm touch was arousing me? But as pleasurable sensations were shooting into my loins and making my pants bulge, I was becoming embarrassed.

I thought, maybe, she would hardly notice it if we continued talking.

"What did you think when you found out I was the father of her baby?"

"Oh! When I saw her with the baby and you coming into the house, I couldn't believe it! I was crushed, thinking I had lost you forever, and yet I was awed by you as the father of her baby. The funny thing is, Tina said that Jessica was so lucky! Tina remembered you from the summer before. She would tell me how lucky I was because you were staying with us. She had even asked me if you had ever, well, kissed me, and I said of course you had, many times, even more than kissed, just to make her envious."

"I don't believe that! You're the one now who's flirting."

I'm not sure why she pulled away a little, but she did, as if she had suddenly become aware of my condition, that our flirting, as much as we were enjoying it and as much as we respected each other, was beginning to cross the line that we could later regret. Even though we have always trusted the other explicitly, I think that both of us were aware that, under certain circumstances, even the loftiest of humans could be vulnerable to the temptations of the flesh, especially a man like me with a woman as voluptuous as she was. We had always been very close to each other, especially after she had developed into a stunningly beautiful woman, and long before I would even meet Joy, we had both been aware of our physical attraction to each other, and by the time she would begin college, we would even think of getting married. Well, she would anyway.

She took a sip from her coffee, and then she took a large swig.

We became silent for a little while.

As I was gazing at her, admiring her bosom, she grinned at me, took another large swig, and put her cup on the coffee table.

"Do you want more coffee?" she asked.

"I still have half a cup."

"You're slow. How come you're so slow?"

"You haven't finished yours already, have you?"

"Yes. Now I'll finish yours so I can refill it."

She pushed her sandals off with her feet, and then she pushed herself up to kneel beside me, leaning against my shoulder and pressing her breasts against it. She took my cup and swallowed the rest of my coffee.

"Should you be drinking anymore?" I asked.

She put the empty cup on the table.

"There's only enough left for you, and I want to give you everything I've got."

I pulled her against me.

"Are you trying to get me drunk?"

"Of course," she said softly, "I want you to stay with me tonight."

"I'm not going anywhere," I said, brushing my lips against hers, "but if you give me more anisette, there's no telling what I'll do to you."

Her dark eyes were bright, her voice sultry: "What will you do to me?"

As I continued to stare at her, my heart began pounding. She was almost smirking.

"Don't you know," I said, "what anisette does?"

"It makes your lips numb, like mine are now, but it also makes your lips taste sweet, so sweet," she murmured, brushing her lips against mine. The front of her body slid over mine, and her right leg pushed between my thighs, pushing against me.

As her breasts were yielding so pleasurably against my chest, and her thigh was pushing against my crotch, I thought, surely, she could feel my hardness swelling. She wasn't just flirting with me now; she was actually tantalizing me. I could hardly believe it. She had become intoxicated enough, I thought, that she wanted me to satisfy the throbbing in her womb.

As I clung to her, I wanted to thrust myself deep inside of her.

"I like your sweetness," she moaned. "Can you taste how sweet my lips are?"

And as her lips were rubbing mine, I slid my hands under the back of her shorts, down her smooth, warm flesh, and I grasped her buttocks and yanked her tightly against me.

"Damn! I want you so much!" I blurted. "You're making me so damn horny, I can't stop!"

Her head snapped back. "You wouldn't go *that* far! Would you?"

"I can't help it!"

"You wouldn't!"

"How do you think Jessica got pregnant?"

As she emitted a guttural sound and drew back a little, I withdrew my hands.

"I'm sorry," she whispered.

She was still kneeling in front of me and was gazing down at me. She seemed to shiver a little.

"I'm sorry," I said, "that I talked to you the way I just did, but you really are exciting me so damn much that I can't resist you, not anymore. Sorry if I'm upsetting you."

"Well, I deserve it. I wasn't thinking about, well, what you did to Jessica. I mean, I wasn't thinking about, well, about us too, doing *that now*. Well," she said, pausing as though she were reflecting upon her deeper feelings, "maybe," her voice dropped, "maybe," she murmured a little above a whisper, "but that word, *horny*, well, I wasn't thinking about *that*. I was just, well," she stammered, "if you hadn't said what you did, that, my making you so horny in that tone, who knows what we would have ended up doing?" She paused, studying my reaction. "But you would have stopped before we had gone that far."

I shook my head. "No, I wouldn't have stopped. You're making me so damn excited that I want to go all the way with you! I can't help it."

"And it would have been my fault, not yours." Her bottom lip seemed to quiver. "But you *did* stop."

"It would have been the fault of both of us. Think of how we would both feel if we would ever go all the way together."

"It could draw us closer together."

"Not if you'd get pregnant, if it prevented you from continuing your education. We'd be feeling so damn guilty we'd be blaming each other and probably resenting each other. I want you so damn badly, right now, but if I really love you, I'd wait a few more years, and if we'd still feel the same way about each other, well, we'd be together for the rest of our lives."

"You want us to wait until we get married," she said.

"Don't you?"

Her eyes seemed to be imploring me to be gentle, to forgive her for having acted so damn sexy, for having tempted me, but neither of us wanted to withdraw from the other. Staring at her enticing lips and at her voluptuous bosom, I was still so damn aroused that I wanted to forget everything else, to caress her breasts, to push her back onto the couch, and to ram my erection deep inside of her, and if she had been anyone else, I thought, I would not have hesitated. Yet, from my conscience, guilt was swelling, overcoming the gall of my lust.

"I'm willing to wait," she finally said, "if you can, but I know that I can give you so damn much pleasure you would never need to touch any other woman, not even Jessica! If you want, take me, but promise that you won't do it with anyone else, just with me."

Slowly, reluctantly, I released her.

"Your folks trust us, but if we ever betrayed their trust, we'd feel terrible. As for Jessica, I can't tell you about her without her permission, but I want you to know that she and I didn't, well, we didn't ever feel like we were just, well, fucking each other. I was young at the time, going into my senior year in high school, but I wasn't a virgin. I guess you'd say I was just discovering the world and getting experienced. But that wasn't the way it was with Jessica. Even though we were so young, we admired and respected each other. We still do, even though we've gone our separate ways. We were, well, each other's first love, really."

"That sounds beautiful, Tonio, how I wanted to think of us, of you and me, ever since, well, ever since I was becoming a woman. I want to think of you as my one and only, but as much as I've loved you, and as much as I thought you wanted me, you never would allow me to go all the way with you no matter how excited we would get."

"Well, there's something else I want you to know." I held her against me. As she gazed at me, I said, "I love you too much to even imagine myself ever, well, doing it to you, ever, well, ever fucking you, though you really are such a tantalizingly sexy-looking woman."

"I love you so much! And I want you to, well, to make me the mother of your babies."

"I do, too, but I want us to do it the right way. We have to wait a few more years, and if we still feel the same way about each other, we'll get married."

"But I'm afraid you won't wait."

"Well, in that case, if you get pregnant, we'll get married."

"I meant, I'm afraid you won't wait for me, that you'll get another girl pregnant."

"Don't be ridiculous."

Two years after North Korea, a Communist country, had invaded South Korea, Dante and Rosie were married. The United Nations, led by our country, the United States, had sent in troops to repel the commies, but war had never been declared, so, officia4lly, it was only a police action. We had expected the fighting to last no longer than a couple of months. The world war had ended less than five years earlier, and people, we Americans included, had been sick and tired of war, even though the world had become divided into two camps: the free world under God, led by the most powerful nation in the world, our United States, and the atheist world led by the Soviet Union. Although the issue seemed simple enough: good versus evil, as in the big war, most people I knew didn't want to be affected by any more fighting. Patriotism, it seemed, was no longer promoted as a virtue to support our troops who were sacrificing their lives to keep us free.

I had become exempt from the draft because I was not only supporting my mother; I was also supporting two other women (my wife and my mistress) and my two children. Jessica had contacted a lawyer here in New Hampshire who had submitted an affidavit to my draft board stating that I was the sole support of her and of our son. Later, when Dante would be drafted, Jessica would offer to help him, also, by contacting politicians who could pull the right strings to exempt him too, but he would refuse. He was terribly idealistic and stubborn. He thought it was an honor to serve his country, to know, love, and to serve God and country, which included his family and his neighborhood. He also thought of himself not only as a citizen of the United States of America; he thought of himself as a citizen of the whole damn world, of the whole damn cosmos; he thought of himself as a son of God.

That year, the Fourth of July was on a Friday, the beginning of a long weekend in which we celebrated the wedding of Dante and Rosie. Friends and relatives from Quebec City to New York City had come here for the celebration. Ben John and Anna and Nick, a student on vacation from the Vatican who had been a year away from his ordination, had arrived the night before. Later that afternoon, after I had gone to the cabin to get Dante and Rosie, we sat at the dining room table at my house and drank coffee with homemade anisette. Ben John raised his cup and said, "Salute to Dante and Rosie!" And we raised our cups, clicking them together, and said, "Salute!" then we sipped our drinks.

Ben John looked at Dante.

"If your father could speak to you now, he would tell you he's happy, because we're together." He looked at my mother, who nodded. "Together, we enjoy remembering the good times, and when we remember the bad, we console each other, but in solitude the bad times frighten us. We did a lot of talking last night, about the good times and the bad. Your mother said she reacted against the marriage of you and Rosie, because she's afraid, for both of you."

"We understand," Dante answered, turning to my mother.

She smiled weakly at him, her blue eyes reflecting the anxiety she was trying to suppress, and looked softly at Rosie, who put her hand on Dante's knee.

"We're together as a family. Your father and I," Ben John said to Dante, "became brothers as soon as we met. Who were we? What was our family?"

They had been born during the first year of the twentieth century, and they had migrated to this country almost at the same time. Ben John was born in Canada four years before his father had died. When he was ten, his mother, a nurse, took him to Cascade Flats, near the gate of a paper mill, in a neighborhood among recent immigrants from a small village in Italy. He and his mother lived in a small green house on the back street next to the Valentino family who had adopted him almost immediately. "They spoke a little English and a little French, and I quickly learned Italian from them. Who were we? What were we becoming, this new family of ours? I knew my people had been taken here from Africa as slaves, against our will, that my grandfather had escaped from a plantation in Louisiana." In Quebec, the new France, his people mixed with the French from Normandy and with the aboriginal Americans who were called Indians by mistake, but the label stuck. And he crossed the border into New Hampshire, an English speaking state of New England, named after a region in England where the people pronounced the name, Hampshire, the same way as the people in Cascade pronounced it. Who were these people in Cascade? The town of Gorham built a school at the southern end of the flats and hired a teacher who understood neither French nor Italian and tried to discourage them from speaking anything except English, so that they could grow into, she told them, good Americans. "The poor woman," Ben John said, "became so discouraged with us. She always pronounced our names in English and even changed the spellings. Giuseppe Valentino became Joe Valentine long before he became a minister. Because your father and I could speak French, Italian, and English, we tutored the other kids. When your mother moved here to the flats, your father was assigned to her as her tutor." In high school in Gorham, Ben John and my father, at the age of seventeen, became American citizens. "I had to denounce my Canadian citizenship, and your father had to denounce his Italian citizenship. What were we, your father and I? And your father said, 'Now, we are as American as Daniel Webster! You, whose ancestors came from Africa, as slaves, and I, an Italian and a Jew from Italy, whose ancestors had gone from Israel to Rome at least a hundred years before the birth of Jesus, are as much American as Daniel Webster, Thomas Jefferson, Abe Lincoln, George Washington or any other American with an English name. We are developing a new culture, helping it to grow into an American culture!'"

After graduation from high school, my father went into the army, the infantry, and fought in France, and Ben John went to

Howard University where he had studied under Thomas Wyatt Turner, a biology professor who had established the Federation of Colored Catholics to protest discrimination outside and inside of the Catholic Church. He was also a founding member of The National Association for the Advancement of Colored People. "I'm trying to convince the Catholic hierarchy," Turner had said to Ben John, "of the opportunity to convert millions of Negroes in this country by desegregating our churches, but they're afraid of repercussions and the loss of our white brethren because there's already so much discrimination here against Catholics. What would we lose if certain Catholics leave the fold because the Church refuses to follow unjust laws in an unjust society? They say we have to move slowly and cautiously within the framework of our society, but I'm convinced that our strength would emerge from doing what's right, not what's politically expedient. Imagine being able to say that Catholics don't condone bigotry anywhere, that we all believe we're brethren under God, as we've always been taught by our priests and nuns."

After becoming a doctor, Ben John returned to the flats, married Anna, and moved a few years later from the small house on the back street to a bigger house on the main road, with his mother living upstairs.

A year after the attack on Pearl Harbor, and many of the young men had entered the armed services, a squad of Negro soldiers was stationed in Cascade, between the flats and the hill, in the waiting room of a trolley stop under the post office, across the street from the new public school. The soldiers had appeared suddenly, and the inhabitants, dumbfounded, wondered why the soldiers were here. There were eleven of them and one white officer, a southerner, who slept in a hotel in Berlin.

"The military," Ben John said, "hadn't done anything to prepare the people here, to promote public relations, and the soldiers knew nothing about the people or the culture here. The soldiers felt like they were in a foreign country, and to most of the people here, the soldiers seemed like foreigners. None of them were Catholic. At first they were surprised by the hospitality they were receiving, because they had met only people who had been friendly, curious, or fascinated. The others had been avoiding them. Two weeks or so after their arrival, I pulled out of my post office box an invitation to attend free lectures and films across the street at the public school. The subject was the nature of the Negro." Ben John sighed. "The invitation was from a supposedly Christian group of renown biologists, whom I had never heard of. The nature of the Negro." He grinned, and he sighed again. "There I was, in a stuffy, hot, crowded little hall, being told, right here in Cascade, who I was and what I was. It was hell."

The invitation had warned that the subject was suitable neither for ladies nor for children; it was only for mature men.

That evening, the middle of winter, was bitterly cold as Ben John and my father walked on the sidewalk up a slight incline next to a tall chain link fence of the mill that curved gradually to their right. To their left, on the other side of a road, a dirt driveway dipped down into a parking lot of the mill, and at the farther end of the parking lot, under flood lights, was an ice skating rink where some of the soldiers were skating, or learning how to skate. They seemed friendly with some high school girls.

The road from the flats connected to a highway from Gorham to Berlin where railroad tracks crossed the road and entered the mill. The sidewalk crossed the tracks and ascended a small hill until it came to the highway, and it curved to the right, to the post office, a brick building. The building had been built against the slope of the hill. At the main floor was an entrance from the sidewalk to a grocery store, and past the store was an entrance to the post office. On both sides of the building were steps that descended to the bottom of the building to a concrete platform. Under the store was a barbershop; under the post office was the waiting room of the old trolley stop, which had become the barracks for the soldiers.

Across the road from the post office, at the bottom of a steep hill, Cascade Hill, was the public school, also a brick building. It had only one floor. Most of the kids went to the Catholic school on the hill.

My father and Ben John crossed the highway, climbed concrete steps to the front entrance of the school, entered it, walked down a vestibule, entered a small assembly hall, and sat in the first two chairs in the back row. The seating capacity was only fifty, and although all the seats were occupied, there were only eighteen other men from Cascade. More than half of the men, thought Ben John, were strangers, and, he noticed, none of the soldiers were there. Surely, he thought, they must have known of the meeting. Maybe none of them had been invited.

The hall suddenly became dark, and, except for a few men coughing, they became quiet. A light behind them shined on a curtain, which opened slowly, showing a movie screen. To the right of a small stage, four men in suits were sitting in folding chairs. Another man, of average height and slim, with thick glasses emerged from the left side, walked briskly to a podium on the left side of the screen, stepped up on the podium and said, "Good evening, gentlemen, and welcome to our special presentation of the ethnic origins and nature of nigro societies. I am the reverend Jed Shackle, a biologist at the high school, as you probably know, and the pastor of the local chapter of The Temple of the Holy Spirit, a Christian denomination. You are undoubtedly wondering why you were invited here and what our society is. It is composed exclusively of educated scholars dedicated to the pursuit of truth and Christian values. Our guest speakers tonight, I'm proud to say, are four eminent biologists from our society who are currently teaching at our most prestigious universities. 'The truth shall set you free,' as we're told in the Bible. And freedom is what our brave soldiers of our country are fighting for today, for you and for me, for all of us. But we will not be free while atheists insist on distorting the truth. We cannot be free if we insist on listening to the devil and succumbing to his lies. We will begin this meeting with the pledge of allegiance to our flag. Please stand and remain standing for our National Anthem and for a recording of Onward Christian Soldiers."

When they sat down again, the auditorium became dark, and a movie came on the screen. It was an introduction to the various races of mankind. The screen showed a globe of the world rotating, then it showed North America, then the white inhabitants of Jamestown Colony performing a folk dance and music of that period, and then it showed American Indian warriors doing a war dance, and then white teenagers doing a jitterbug, black teenagers jitterbugging, a parade through a street in a Chinatown, Andalusian Gypsies dancing a flamenco, an Indian Hindu playing a sitar, South Sea Islanders singing and dancing, Australian aborigines dancing and singing, and the movie showed scenes of North Africa, of the Sahara Desert and pyramids, and of an attractive Egyptian woman performing a belly dance, and, near the end of the first film, the movie finally showed various black African tribes singing and dancing to the beating drums of their pulsating music. And that segment ended by begging the questions: "What is the black race? What does it have in common with the other races? And how does it differ?"

The lights came on, and Shackle introduced the next speaker, a biologist from the University of South Carolina, and the producer of the next film. The speaker went to the podium. "Good evening. How you all doing? I'd like to tell you I enjoy being up here, in this mountainous part of the country, but man, it's sure cold up here! Before we answer those questions, we'll examine the history of the nigro race here in the United States, because there are far too many misconceptions being taught in our schools, especially here in the north. We've included excerpts from several historical documentaries and from the classic historical movie *The Birth of a Nation*. The movie was based on a novel, *The Clansman* by a prominent historian, novelist, and minister of the Southern Baptist Church whom I have the honor of knowing as a personal friend. His name is Thomas Dixon. Incidentally, his books and other books will be on sale for as little as one dollar when this presentation is finished, and hot chocolate and donuts will be served as our thanks for listening to us. Enjoy the show!"

The next film, in black and white, at night, depicted black men, covered in paint, with white bones shining through their noses, chanting and dancing around a huge pot of boiling water while a narrator was speaking of his experiences "with black savages in the deepest part of the African jungles who were still using young virgins as sacrifices to their pagan deities, and were still resorting to cannibalistic rituals of captured enemy warriors, and of raping the women of other tribes, in spite of the laws and the efforts of white colonists to civilize them. What happens when members of the black race are removed from the jungle and come into contact with civilization?"

The small auditorium was beginning to feel uncomfortably warm.

The film depicted the white traders in Africa as saviors, actually, of the blacks, males and females, who had been captured by other tribes. The captured blacks were sold to the traders, but their lives were spared, and they were imported to civilized countries, and although they were sold into slavery, they were, according to the film, quite happy, contrary to the beliefs of the misinformed abolitionists. They were, for the most part, treated kindly by their masters, because their masters had enough sense to know that creatures that were treated kindly would perform their tasks more efficiently than creatures that were miserable. The slaves were, of course, fearful at first of the unknown, but as they became aware of their circumstances and felt secure under the guidance of their masters, their fears evaporated and many became devoted to their masters. Many of the slaves even forgot their African families. The slaves, you see, like wild animals, had only superficial attachments to their original families, but after they had landed in America, they found security under the rule of their white masters. The slaves were given food and clothing and shelter and love, bonding into a large, supporting family; and they found their place in the divine order, as servants to their masters who did their thinking for them. And here, in the land of the free, they found God. They were happy, until slavery was abolished.

The introduction to the film, *The Birth of a Nation*, began with: "The bringing of the African to America planted the first seed of disunion." The movie showed the chaos that had followed after slavery had been abolished. Without the guidance of their white masters, the Negroes reverted to their natural state of savagery, killing their former masters and raping their former mistresses. Like animals tasting blood again, they became wild. In many areas in the former Confederate States where the blacks outnumbered the whites, the blacks were able to vote but had made it almost impossible for the whites to enjoy the same rights, and many of the blacks had gained control of the legislatures of their states, until, finally, an organization of white men, called the Ku Klux Klan, was formed in retaliation against the oppression foisted upon them by the black majority and to protect the rights of the white population.

When the film ended, Ben John was sweating.

The next speaker was from Harvard University who had produced the next film. In the introduction of the film, *The Nature of the Negro*, he had personally interviewed two of his colleagues from Harvard and two from Stanford University who had all made the same claims: the intelligence of the Negro is inferior to the intelligence of the Caucasian, and the nature of the Negro is closer to that of the animal nature than to that of human nature, and that it's virtually impossible for Negroes to control their sexual urges, even under the most civilized conditions, and that the government of the United States, having recognized the mistake of having abolished slavery, had imposed segregation in the states with the highest Negro populations, because studies had proven that savagery was so imbedded in the nature of the Negro that it dominates the blood even of part Negroes who look white.

Ben John pulled out a handkerchief and wiped his brow.

The next part of the film provided an historical explanation, which had been suggested in the Old Testament, but had not been developed.

Man had been the last creature that had been created. According to the calculations of a prominent biblical scholar and theologian, which had been widely accepted and never refuted, humans were created six thousand years ago in the Garden of Eden, and were given dominion over the whole Earth. They were called Adam and Eve. Flora and fauna had been created before man was, and some of the animals have become extinct. Scientists, according to the film, have fairly recently discovered bones of a creature that resembles man so closely that he is mistakenly called man. Neanderthal Man. We do not know how many other species of "man" were created, but they are, obviously, not human. They are animals. They do not have souls.

The small auditorium had become hot and stuffy as the film continued.

Various small primates with tails were shown hopping around in trees in a jungle and screeching at each other. Their resemblance to man was undeniable. Even more so was the resemblance of small primates without tails, and the resemblance of larger primates, of gorillas, especially of apemen, such as the Neanderthals, who could easily be mistaken for human, but only the children of Adam and Eve were human, with a human, not animal, nature, having an immortal soul and intelligence vastly superior to the other races. God had never intended the children of Adam and Eve to copulate with the other races. He had specifically forbidden it. It was the forbidden fruit, the original sin, and man, knowing evil, saw his nakedness and was ashamed, and he was expelled from the Garden.

Apemen, such as the Neanderthals, had existed side by side with the children of Eve and had fought with them and had raped some of the human females, and the children of apemen, and the children of their children through the ages had also been born without souls. And many of the tribes of apemen had become extinct by the white men in battle and by their inability to adapt to nature. Even so, some of their descendants, without souls, are among us tonight.

Ben John had become uneasy, but the worse was yet to come.

On the screen, was a cartoon image, in color, of a black man, really black, with huge red lips, as though dripping with blood, and his black, beady eyes were staring at a voluptuous, naked, blonde woman lying back on a bed. A bolt of lightning flashed on the screen as the black man's long, erect penis penetrated her, and his sperm, like tadpoles, were swimming into her womb. The cartoon suddenly changed into a black and white documentary style a hundred years later of the descendant of the woman, who was also blonde, who was being treated for nymphomania. Only after her ancestry had been traced back could she understand, with the help of a psychiatrist, where her insatiable lust had come from. Although each person in that lineage had mated with a white person, and the physical features of each generation looked whiter, the savagery of that black ancestor, the narrator said, could not be bred away.

The film reiterated, again and again, that the intermingling of the white race with other races was a threat to civilization. "God," the narrator stated, "created the white race of Adam and Eve to be separate from the other races. Had God wanted only one race, only one race would have been created."

The film finally ended. For a few moments, the auditorium became pitch dark, and Ben John felt that all hell would suddenly burst, but no one so much as cleared his throat. It seemed as though no one was even breathing. And then a spotlight shined on Shackle. He didn't seem real. He was standing behind the podium, but the light circled his face as though he were bodiless, and he spoke so softly at first that he seemed to be whispering. The auditorium had become so quiet that Ben John thought that he could hear the frost crackling against the windows. He felt sweat running down his forehead and into his eyes, making the image of Shackle, with his bright red hair, waiver under the light like a spirit emerging from the depths of hell.

"What are soldiers doing here?" Shackle asked in a low tone. "What are they doing here while our brave American soldiers are fighting for our freedom, dying for us? What are the nigro soldiers doing here? Are they protecting us? That's what I've asked our state representatives. They were evasive, telling me that they're testing winter clothing on top of Mt. Washington, but that doesn't make sense. The fact is, the government doesn't know what to do with them, so they're here, playing soldiers. Playing soldiers until the duration." He raised his voice. "Until the duration!" He lowered his voice again. "You know what that means. They could be here for years. For years! Unless something is done about it. Before the end of this year, young girls in this area will be having nigro babies. Nigro babies! Think of it!" His voice dropped. "Nigro babies. Think about it," he said in a soft voice.

A murmur went through the crowd.

"Suddenly," Ben John said, "your father stood up, and said, 'Excuse me, sir. I have a question.' And Shackle said, 'Please reserve your questions for the end of the presentation.' But your father said we couldn't wait that long, because Shackle had presented an issue that was far more important to us than just the nature of one race."

Although most of the inhabitants of Cascade were just as American as Daniel Webster, my father said, they were descended from the French and the Italians, so, rather than being concerned with only one other race, they had to know to which race they belonged. Are they children of Adam and Eve? Do they even have souls? If not, why should they even be here listening to this presentation?

A few of the men began to laugh.

"By their fruits you shall recognize them!" quoted Shackle.

"Yes!" my father agreed. "And if we listen to them, we could be listening to the devil. The devil would try to influence us with his lies; he'd want us to hate each other, to keep us separate, to spread his hate. Does the devil have a soul? Do you, sir, have a soul? You said only one race has a soul. But if you and I are not of the same race, why should I listen to you?"

"By now," Ben John said, "the emotional effects of the films had lost some of their intensity, and Shackle seemed aware of it, and he was obviously annoyed by your father."

Shackle asked someone to switch on the lights. Apparently he wanted to get a good look at the man who was addressing him.

"Now, what is your question?"

"Well, my first question is: is there really, in the natural order, such a thing as a white race? Or, is that only a theory invented by you?"

"I assure you I didn't invent the theory. It's a scientific fact based on irrefutable evidence. Blacks don't think or feel the way we do. They have no sense of morality, of spirituality, of love."

"Thank you! That begs the next question. According to this presentation, there have been many races, many of which, such as Neanderthal Man, have been virtually wiped out, probably by the white race, the only human race, descendants of Eve. You have just used the term, 'the way we do' when you said that blacks don't feel and think the way we do. Are you testifying that you are a member of the white race?"

"Of course! That's obvious."

"Can you tell us to which race most French and Italians belong?"

"The white race, also,"

"And God created the white race to be separated from the other races. If He had wanted one race, he would have created only one race. Is that so?"

"Yes, of course."

"And not all the races are equal. I mean, one race, such as the white race, is more superior, more intelligent than the other races."

"That's true."

"And if I understand correctly, the natures of each race are somewhat different."

"That's also true."

"Each with its own nature."

Shackle agreed.

"And if God had wanted only one nationality, He would have created only one nationality, but when God saw that man was creating the tower of Babel to build a structure to heaven, separate nationalities, more than a hundred of them, had been created, each with its own language, created to keep us separate. And, as one race is more superior to another, one nationality is more superior to another, each nationality with it's own laws of nature, which means that there are no laws of human nature that apply to all of us. Would you agree, sir, that we Americans are superior to our enemies, the Japanese?"

"Of course! What's your point?"

"I'm coming to that, I think, with your help. Would you agree that we Americans are superior to the Germans?"

"The Nazis? The Huns? Of course! They're barbarians! Come to the point."

"Which nationality is the most superior?"

"Ours is, of course!"

"So, Hitler is wrong. The Germans are not members of the master race. We are. We Americans are. We're superior to the Germans. But who is more superior, the Germans, or the black Americans?"

There was a long pause.

"Who is more superior," my father asked again, as some of them began to chuckle, "the Germans, or the black Americans?"

"What do *you* think?"

"I don't know. That's why I'm asking you."

"I don't understand the relevance of your question."

"I just want you to clarify your views so that we can understand them. I'm trying to put your ideas in a logical order, with your help. As Americans of French and Italian ancestors, we want to know how we fit into your hierarchy. As Americans, are we equal to you? Or are we inferior?"

"That's irrelevant!"

"If that's irrelevant to you, your ideas are irrelevant to us."

6

On the Fourth of July after Dante and Rosie has been married, we enjoyed a celebration with family and friends. We began on Friday morning and celebrated into late Saturday night. On Friday afternoon we began roasting a couple of pigs while the women made spaghetti for the big meal. In the afternoon, we had a clambake with lobsters. And, of course, in the afternoon and in the evening, between meals, we danced to lively folk music on the back street, and when darkness fell, we lit up the sky with fireworks.

A year later, the fourth fell on a Saturday. We closed the restaurant that day and had the usual fireworks in the flats that evening, but we didn't have the pig roasts or the dancing in the back street or anything like we had the year before. Neither Dante nor Rosie was here. By that time, she had given birth to their first sibling, Angela, and was living in Harlem with her folks who had gone to Italy with Nonna and Tattone to witness Nick's ordination at the Vatican. That trip would have included Dante and Rosie and me if Dante hadn't suddenly been drafted. But on this Fourth of July, he was in Korea. And he was feeling damn lucky that he hadn't been in combat yet.

He had landed at Inchon in a troop ship in the early part of spring when there had still been snow on the ground, had been put on an army truck, and had been taken to a train station on the outskirts of the city. Waiting to board a train, the troops, with rifles slung on their shoulders, had been greeted by undernourished kids shivering in the cold. Before boarding the train, a troop train, the soldiers gave the begging kids candy bars.

The train, which was old, moved slowly, even more slowly than the trains in Japan, and chugged mile by mile into the interior, north of Seoul, making several stops to unload soldiers who were put on trucks and taken away. They passed villages and farms with mud huts and people in shabby clothing, who seemed cold. The soldiers were wearing parkas. Most of the snow had melted. The snow that remained was covered by black soot and dirt. The mud season was just beginning.

Before night fell, Dante had joined his unit, the Second Infantry Division, which was called the "Indianhead" Division. It had recently come off the front lines and was in reserve. By the fourth of July, he had been with the unit for over three months, having moved several times from one location in the Kumhwa Valley to another, digging another trench across Korea behind the front lines. Occasionally, at night, he could hear the fighting in the distance, and there would be flashes of light in the sky, like a thunderstorm. The mountains looked much like the White Mountains. Sometimes, even an occasional stench, like the odor of dead flesh, had reminded him of the rotten eggs smell in the flats. Most of the soldiers, though, were blind to the natural beauty of the country. To them, it was the asshole of the world. But it was better, of course, than where they had been. They had been in a pit worse than hell. They had been in the real Korea.

In the real Korea, they had been paid a dollar a day more. In reserve, they were forced to sacrifice their "combat" pay. But Dante had never heard any of them complain, not about that. Actually, in reserve, they seldom complained. The only ones who seemed to complain were the ones who had never been on line, who seemed bored with everything. Dante had even learned to recognize some of the soldiers who were fortunate enough to stay behind the lines. Not only did they seem bored, they seemed to resent the combat veterans.

When Dante had arrived at Fox Company, of the 9th Infantry Regiment, he was taken to the tent of the company commander, Captain Rossi, a stocky man who was getting bald and was not much taller than Dante, who saluted, but the captain had lowered his head to read a document. He looked up from the papers on his desk, grinned at Dante and said, "Dante Valentino! From New Hampshire. I've been there. Several times. Beautiful place, but I didn't know there were any paisans there." He told the company clerk to bring Corporal Napolitano to the tent. Less than three minutes later the clerk returned with Napolitano, who wasn't wearing any insignias.

Neither of them saluted, Dante noticed.

"He's from Boston," the captain said.

"Brockton," Napolitano said.

"Whatever. You've been to New Hampshire, though? Right?"

"Yeah, a couple of times."

"So it's not far from where you're from. Do you know any paisans there?"

"No. Why?"

"This is Dante Valentino, from New Hampshire. He's in your squad. So, you're his padrone, for now."

"Good enough. Have you eaten yet?" he asked Dante.

"At division headquarters, before they sent me here."

"You should have eaten good then. Okay, let's go. I'll get you set up."

Napolitano was the assistant squad leader.

On the way to the supply tent, he said to Dante, "Rossi ain't no West Pointer. He got his commission in battle, when we got overrun. He earned it. He won't send you out on any stupid patrols like our last company commander did, sending us out to get him some fuckin souvenirs. And he never got a chance to enjoy them. He got hit, and none of us gave a shit, and that's when Rossi took over. He's one of us."

"In what way?"

"In every way. He knows who we are. He came up from the ranks. He's a paisan from Brooklyn who fought in France."

In the supply tent, Napolitano picked up a folding bunk and carried it out. He wasn't carrying any weapons or ammunition. Dante was carrying a rifle and a duffel bag and was wearing a helmet; everyone else was wearing caps. They were in a large field in a valley on the east side of a dirt road. Not far from the road, soldiers in combat fatigues were playing baseball. Some were playing basketball on a hard dirt court. Large sleeping tents were spread out to the slope of a mountain. Behind the third squad tent, woods covered a steep incline all the way to the top of the mountain. A stream ran down the side of the woods.

"This reminds me of New Hampshire," said Dante.

"Yeah, it does look a lot like New Hampshire. It could be beautiful. Too bad there's a fuckin war, though."

The tent was set on slabs of wood, which could be seen as they approached it.

They entered the tent. It was heated by an oil burning stove fed from an oil drum at the back of the tent. There were four men inside. Next to the entrance, lying on his bunk, was a Korean named Ahn Bong, who was also called A Bomb. Hanging from his neck with his dog tags was a small wood carving of Buddha.

"I'll set your bunk right next to A Bomb. Maybe you can teach him English."

"Well, that's what I did before I was drafted."

"What do you mean?"

"Teach English. In high school."

"You're shitting me!"

"No."

"What the hell you doing *here*?"

"The same thing everybody else is doing."

"Holy shit! Wait till Tiny hears about this!" he said to the other guys. And to Dante, he said, "Tiny's our squad leader. You probably won't like him at first. He's a big bastard, who sounds like a prick, but when you get to know him, you'll see he ain't so tough. His bark is much worse than his bite, but in a fight, he's the guy you want to be with. He doesn't seem to get rattled and seems to know how to deal with the situation. He's like a mother hen trying to protect her chicks. He's a lot like Rossi in some respects. He won't ask us to do anything stupid."

As darkness descended, other members of the squad gradually entered the tent. There wasn't much to do after chow time. They went to a beer tent to drink beer that had been too diluted, or they went to a movie, or stayed in the tent and played poker, or read, or wrote letters, and, of course, they bullshitted a lot.

Tiny finally entered the tent. Napolitano, who was also called Nap, or Nappy, introduced him to Dante. Tiny was tall, broad shouldered, with blond hair, of Polish descent who had lived in the Pittsburgh area and had been a coal miner. Around his neck he was wearing rosary beads.

As Dante stood up from his bunk to shake hands, Tiny said gruffly, "Naw, don't bother getting up. I ain't no fuckin officer. Fuckin rank don't mean shit in this place anyway." And to Nap, he growled, "I don't know why you wops want to be in this shithole."

"To make sure you fuckin polacks don't take it over."

Tiny said to Dante, "Don't get too fuckin chummy with this dago."

Nap said, "He's really serious."

"You bet your fuckin ass, I'm serious! Don't get too fuckin chummy with any of us guys, if you want to survive. The price is too fuckin high!"

"He means, when you see one of your buddies get blown to pieces, it'll tear you apart, and you're no fuckin good to yourself or to anyone else."

"And I hope you ain't no fuckin John Wayne. I don't want no fuckin heroes in my squad. Any guy who's gung ho should be in the fuckin marines."

According to Tiny, the fuckin infantry had nine fuckin men in a fuckin squad, and the fuckin marines had ten: nine fuckin riflemen and one fuckin cameraman.

The weather in Korea was much like New Hampshire weather. In early spring, cold rain fell for several days in a row, and the troops (in Fox Company, anyway) were usually allowed to remain in their tents to remain warm and dry while the trenches they had been digging turned into mud, and when the sun came out, the days were warm and pleasant. After basic training, and being behind the lines, life in the army was much more relaxing.

One bright morning, when they were chopping down trees to clear an area for the trench, Captain Rossi, with his carbine slung over his right shoulder, came by and said to Dante, "Hey, paisan, you really know how to cut down a tree. You must have done a lot of that in New Hampshire."

At noon time that same day, after they had been given their noontime chow, which, again, had been short on everything, especially on coffee, and what little coffee they did have had been bitterly black, Tiny called the squad together.

"We're striking," Nap said to Dante.

"What? What in hell are you talking about?"

"On line, sometimes, it can be difficult to reach us, but there's no damn reason, now, that they can't bring us what we need. So, we're going on strike."

"Isn't there a law or something?"

"What the fuck are we fighting for? Don't do it if you're really against it, but we should stick together. What the fuck can they do to us?"

Tiny had talked to the other three squad leaders in the platoon, and then they talked with the platoon sergeant, Master Sergeant Wells, a Negro who had been a regular army man who had fought in Italy, and had, during the past year, been transferred from a segregated unit to an integrated unit. He said he agreed with their grievances but not with their threat to go on strike. "Not yet, anyway." Wells brought them to the platoon leader, a young West Pointer, Lieutenant Parks, who had joined the outfit only two days earlier. The troops had finished eating and were relaxing, sitting on the grass ground or walking around and talking with each other. After one of the squad leaders had told the lieutenant they wanted to talk with the captain to complain about the lack of enough food, especially coffee, he, Parks, did not even bother to discuss the issue; he simply denied them permission. The squad leader warned him that the troops would no longer work until their grievance could at least be heard by the captain. The young lieutenant angrily ordered the squad leaders back to their duties.

"Are you fuckin serious?"

"What! Soldier, do you know how to address an officer? Stand tall when I'm talking to you!"

That outbreak had been loud enough to draw the attention of many of the troops.

"You *are* fuckin serious! You think you're still in the fuckin academy."

"Sergeant, put him on report. He's insubordinate!"

Wells sighed. "Sir," he asked softly, "can I talk with you, in private?"

"After I'm finished with this, this man, Sergeant."

That man was Tiny.

"Soldier, you have a button missing on your shirt!"

"Yeah, I know. I told the fuckin shower boy I needed a new fuckin shirt. Maybe you can talk sense to that fuckin asshole!"

"And your boots are filthy! When's the last time you polished them?"

"And that's another fuckin thing. If you can get me a new fuckin pair, one without holes made by shrapnel," Tiny said, showing him a hole over the heel, "I'd be glad to polish the fuckin things."

"I told you to stand at attention!"

By this time most of the troops around them were grinning at seeing Tiny being chewed out by the young officer. Some had even burst out laughing.

"Lieutenant! Get over here!"

Yelling at him from a short distance was Captain Rossi.

"On the double!"

Lieutenant Parks ran up to him, stopped, stood tall, and snapped a salute.

The captain sighed, casually returned the salute, and then they turned and walked away, and almost everybody in the company watched Rossi give a tongue lashing to the young officer. No one could hear exactly what he was saying at that distance, but the scene was obvious. After he dismissed Parks, he approached the squad leaders, and they discussed the complaints. The company commander agreed that until some attempts from division headquarters had been made to solve the problems, they would cease work. When Tiny said they'd march back to their tents, almost five miles away, Rossi said,

"Why walk? We can ride back. If we're going to do this, we should do it like pros and take advantage of the situation."

So, after Tiny called the squad together, they marched down to the dirt road with the rest of the platoon. While they waited for the other three platoons, Tiny said to the lieutenant, "No hard feelings, *sir*. Okay?"

"Okay," Parks grumbled.

Wells grinned at them.

The rest of the company joined them.

The trucks came and drove them back to their tents, and they were free for the rest of the afternoon. The beer tent opened that afternoon. Some of the troops stayed inside of their tents; some of them dragged their bunks outside and lay in the warm sun. And in the early evening, there was no shortage of food, and there was plenty of coffee with lots of sugar, even, and powdered milk.

In the tent, later that evening, Dante said to Nap, "You'll never see anything like this in the movies. I can't believe that we actually went on strike. Soldiers, in war, in a war zone, going on strike! Even the company commander!"

"You're an English teacher. You should write a book about us."

"I will, when I get back home."

"If we stay in reserve long enough, maybe there'll be a truce soon, and we won't have to fight anymore."

"There never will be a fuckin truce!" Tiny yelled from his bunk. "The fuckin gooks want to keep fighting."

"They're talking about swapping prisoners now," said Nap.

"Maybe Tiny's right. The president, Syngman Rhee, doesn't want the war to end until Korea is united."

"You bet your fuckin ass I'm right. The only fuckin way to end this war is to nuke this hellhole!"

"Yeah, you dumb polack," snapped Nap, "that'll end the fuckin war alright!"

"Well, who the fuck wants to read about us fuckin guys in this shithole?"

"A lot of fuckin people," said Nap.

"You dumb dago, nobody gives a flying fuck about us! Yeah, the fuckin brass tells you you're the star of the show, that the whole fuckin world is watching you. Bullshit! And you eat that shit! The only ones who give a fuckin shit about us is our fuckin mothers."

"And our wives," added Dante.

"Well, maybe some wives," Tiny said, "but I ain't married, and I've seen too many fuckin guys get too many fuckin dear John letters. Are you really thinking about writing a book about us?"

"Of course he is!" Nap said. "He's an Engllsh teacher."

"I hate fuckin teachers! I don't mean you, Dante. You're alright."

"You mean you hate nuns. Right, Sarge?" Nap said. "Because when you were in school, they wouldn't let you fuck them."

Some of the guys laughed.

Tiny didn't answer immediately. He was lying on his bunk, thinking and staring at the top of the tent.

"Hey, Nap, what the fuck does horse shit sound like when you throw it up against a brick wall? It goes: *WOP!*" And he burst into laughter.

Most of the guys snickered.

"Oh, damn you!" Nap snarled.

Dante said, "Hey, Tiny."

Again, Tiny waited a few moments before he finally muttered, "Yeah, what do you want?"

"I want to ask you a very important personal question."

"You want to ask me a very important question?"

"Yeah. Do you mind?"

"Naw, I don't mind."

"Do you happen to know what cow shit sounds like when you throw it up against a brick wall?" He paused. "It goes: *PO LOCK!*"

Everybody in the tent roared, except Tiny.

"Oh, shit! You son of a bitch, Dante!"

"Great comeback, paisan! You fell right into your own bucket of shit, Sarge!"

"No hard feelings, Sarge," said Dante. "Okay?"

"Okay, Teach. You should have been a fuckin officer. You're a lot brighter than that fuckin Parks."

The next morning, for breakfast, they had not only pancakes, they had eggs, scrambled, made with real eggs, not with powdered eggs, which had been purchased from local farmers, and that morning they had more than enough hot coffee. The air was chilly in the long shadows of early morning, but the soldiers sat on the ground, which was still covered with dewdrops, in the warm sunlight to enjoy breakfast.

The strike had ended. On that bright, warm day, some of them chopped down trees while others dug the trench. And that afternoon, after they returned to their tents and received mail from home, Tiny was called over the loudspeaker to report to supply to pick up his new pair of boots, which had been requisitioned by Parks.

While Tiny was proudly polishing his brand new pair of boots that evening, Dante was teaching Ahn Bong English. Until Dante had arrived, the only English words and phrases Ahn had known were: "number one" which meant *good*, "number ten" which meant *bad*, and "fuckin" which not only meant *very*, as in "number fuckin one" which meant *very good*, and "number fuckin ten" which meant *very bad*, it had numerous other meanings also, which could take the place of almost any word that an English speaker could not remember. Now that Ahn was not only learning English, he, apparently, thought it was appropriate and fair to teach Dante Korean and Japanese.

"Why the fuck do you want to learn that gook talk?" Tiny asked.

"Why not?"

"What good is it? Why do they send these fuckin gooks to us without teaching them English? And why the fuck does he wear that pagan thing around his neck? Does he think that fuckin thing is going to protect him?"

"That's strange, Sarge. He asked me the same thing about you, once, about why you wear rosary beads around your neck. When I told him I thought you wear it for protection, he laughed."

"He laughed? Well, that shows how ignorant these heathens are."

"What makes you think he's ignorant?"

"Because he don't know fuck about religion."

"He's a Buddhist. Do you know anything about Buddhism?"

"No, and I don't want to know any fuckin thing about it!"

"Anyway, when I told him you wear the beads for protection, he told me he doesn't expect his icon to protect him; he wears it because it makes him feel better."

"To me," Nap said, "that makes a lot more fuckin sense."

"If that thing doesn't protect him, why the fuck should he feel better?"

"The icon reminds him that he's not alone, that God is with us, always."

"He thinks that fuckin thing is *God*?"

"No, of course not! Not the thing itself, no more than you think that Christ is actually on that little cross at the end of your rosary beads. It's a representation. Ahn believes that the man we call Buddha, which means the Enlightened One, was searching for God, the same God you and I believe in. And Ahn believes that God revealed himself, somehow, to the Buddha. Anyway, he doesn't wear the icon for protection; he wears it to remind himself that death isn't the end of his existence, that death really means, well, that we return to, well, to a sort of place similar to what you call heaven."

"No shit! Buddha ain't mentioned in the Bible, is he?"

"No, he ain't, I mean, isn't."

"It's your duty to tell this gook the whole fuckin truth!"

"The whole fuckin truth? I mean, the whole truth? What the hell are you talking about?"

"Fuckin Sarge," said Nap, "has you talking just like him now!"

"The whole fuckin truth so he can make it into heaven."

"What do you mean, the whole truth?"

"You know what the fuck I mean. You're Catholic, too, ain't you?"

"What makes you think I'm Catholic?"

"You're a wop."

"So was Julius Caesar."

"I know!"

"He was Catholic?"

"He was a fuckin wop, wasn't he?"

"Yeah, I guess. So was La Guardia."

"Who the fuck was that?"

"Fiorello La Guardia, the mayor of New York City. Didn't you listen to him reading the funny papers on the radio every Sunday morning during the depression and during the war?"

"So what?"

"He was a wop, even more so than I am. I'm only half wop."

"What the fuck does that have to do with anything?"

"He was a Jew."

"No! Fuck no! A atheist, maybe, but a wop ain't a Jew."

Dante sighed.

He wanted to know if Tiny really wore the rosary beads for protection, but he decided not to pursue that conversation.

"You still gotta tell him the fuckin truth," insisted Tiny.

"The truth about what?"

"You know! The whole fuckin truth about God. It's for his own fuckin good!"

"I'm sure he knows at least as much as I do about God."

"I doubt that!"

"We've already talked about it. I agree with him that God is unknowable, that we can only know some things about God from His revelations to us and from our experiences of His creation, which we can know through the intelligence we've been given, and through faith. To know the whole truth about God you'd have to be God, and only God is God. Ahn told me an interesting story. It turned out to be a story about knowing God. Before he was inducted into the army, he took his wife and two children to the seashore, and as he was walking along the beach with his family, Ahn was thinking about God and wondering about the future, wondering if he would survive the war, if he'd see his family again, and wondering why people waged war, wondering about all the things I've wondered about and that you have wondered about, too, I'm sure. Suddenly, he noticed this kid, a boy, about ten years old, with a small bucket. The kid filled his little bucket with sea water, ran back a little ways on the sandy beach, stopped, bent down, and dumped the water into a rather small hole, ran back to the ocean, filled the bucket again, ran back to the hole on the beach, and filled the hole again. Ahn, grinning at him, asked, 'Boy, what are you doing?' And the boy said he was putting the sea into the little hole, and Ahn told him that it was impossible. The hole was too small to contain the whole sea. And the boy answered, 'That's what you're trying to do, but your mind was never created to undertake such a task.'"

"Holy fuckin shit!"

"Wow!" said Nap. "You sure had us! Hook, line, and sinker. You *are* a fuckin teacher!"

7

"Get ready to teach English to another recruit, a spic this time," Tiny said as he entered the tent, followed by someone a little taller than Dante and a little darker with olive brown eyes and black curly hair. He seemed bewildered as he entered.

Tiny, carrying a portable bunk, walked past Ahn, past Dante, and muttered, "I'll set his funkin bunk next to yours."

Dante, standing, asked, "De donde?"

"Puerto Rico," he replied quickly, smiling.

"Como se llama?"

"Chico. Y tu?"

"Chico? Boy? Soy Dante. Dante Valentino."

Chico lowered his duffel bag, pushed his rifle higher on his right shoulder, and extended his right hand to Dante.

"Amigo," Dante said, shaking his hand, "hablas ingles?"

"No, amigo mio. Lo siento."

"Entiendes italiano?"

"Un poco!"

"Ah, poco."

"Si," he said smiling.

"You can even talk his fuckin lingo. You ought to be fuckin president," Tiny said to Dante, "of the United Nations."

The three of them, Ahn, Chico, and Dante, quickly became what Tiny had warned them not to become: the three amigos of the third squad. Ahn and Chico, who were both farmers, had small, attractive wives and two small children, a girl and a boy, and they both talked about their families and showed each other family photos, so Dante took his wallet out and showed them his photos.

They were sitting outside on the grass on a warm, sunny day, forming a triangle.

Chico asked, "Su esposa?"

Dante nodded, and then he said, "Su padre es negro; su madre es italiana."

"Ella es hermosa."

A few weeks later, after the company had hiked to the near top of the mountain, which had taken almost three hours, and they had taken positions to assimilate an attack, the three of them were assigned to the right flank of their squad with Nap at the end. Although it was late spring, and the sunlight was getting hot, the thick forest was shady and cool, but it wasn't infested with mosquitoes and black flies as it was in the woods of the valley, near the tents, when the nights were warm and damp. In the assimilated attack, while they were lying on their stomachs against the ground, and bayonets were attached to the front of their rifles, Nap ordered, "Move out!" The three of them leaped up, dashed a few yards up the steep slope, reached the top, and dropped to the ground.

Their mission had been accomplished.

While they sat on the ground and waited to return to the compound, they became involved in a lengthy discussion about what they were doing there, about how they'd feel about being forced to kill each other if they had been enemies instead of allies, about how inconceivable that seemed now that they have met and have become friends, now that they knew each other as ordinary people, the same in so many ways, but from different parts of the world with different cultures and different languages. Suddenly Dante said, "Here we are, the three of us," pointing to his mouth, "talking." He made a circle with his arms. "Together, talking, Chico, Ahn, Dante, together, talking."

Ahn and Chico looked at each other; they looked at Dante, and they laughed together. And Ahn said they had come here, into his country, in the war, to kill people, but that was number fuckin ten, and the rest of the people didn't seem to know that ordinary people like them are the same as them and that they can find a way to communicate and learn from each other and learn about each other if they tried. "Talking," Ahn said to Chico, "number fuckin one!"

"Si!" Chico said, "si!"

But talking was not always number one in Panmunjom.

There were many rumors floating around, and most of them were too good to believe or sounded too ridiculous to believe. Someone usually knew a rumor was true because he had a friend who knew a friend who knew a reliable source, a clerk at division headquarters, who had heard the general telling someone that certain information was absolutely reliable. The most important information was that of the peace talks at Panmunjom. The fact that the sick and wounded prisoners were already being exchanged had been verified in *The Stars and Stripes*. So, soon the truce would be signed. The troops became very hopeful. They had been expecting a major spring offensive from the Chinese, but it had not happened. And, it had become apparent that neither the United Nations nor the Chinese had been willing to sacrifice the lives of so many when the fighting was about to end. Besides, the new American president, who had been the Supreme Commander of Allied Forces in Europe, had promised, if elected, to end the fighting in Korea. Overwhelmingly, he had won the election. And the troops had faith in him. "I like Ike" had been his campaign slogan, and no one liked General Dwight Eisenhower more than the American soldiers liked him, with the possible exception of Tiny, who called himself "a fuckin Democrat," and even Tiny said he would not only like Ike, he would worship the fuckin general if there was a fuckin truce. "But you fuckin guys are just fuckin dreaming if you think a fuckin general, even though he's the fuckin president now, can make those fuckin bastards stop fighting."

Napolitano suddenly entered the tent and yelled at Tiny, "You fuckin polack! You're fuckin right! That fuckin president!"

"What fuckin president? Eisenhower?"

"No, the fuckin Korean!" He looked at Dante. "What's its name?"

"You mean, Syngman Rhee?"

"Yeah! He released the fuckin prisoners so we can't exchange them!"

They were gaping at each other.

"Why the fuck did he do that?" someone cried out.

Tiny said, "To keep the fuckin war going like I told you in the first place."

"That fuckin son of a bitch should be given a fuckin rifle and sent to the front!"

A few minutes later Captain Rossi announced over the loudspeaker that the prison, which had held Chinese and North Korean soldiers, had released the prisoners. "So we've been asked to remain alert to anyone who seems suspicious and may try to cross back into enemy lines."

"If you were a Chinese or North Korean prisoner of war and you were suddenly released," Dante asked Nap, "where would you go?"

"Good question! I certainly wouldn't try to get back to my outfit. I'd try to stay here for the duration."

"And if they fed me enough and gave me a place to sleep, I'd tell them to keep me here and treat me as a prisoner according to the laws of the Geneva Convention."

"You're damn right."

"And if you were Ike, what would you do now?"

"I'd be pissed as hell! I'd say to the Chinese, 'Let's sign a fuckin peace treaty right now so we can both get the fuck out of this shithole and let these people fight it out by themselves if they want.'"

The fourth of July that year fell on a Saturday, a pleasantly warm, sunny day in the Kumhwa Valley where the Indianhead Division was still in reserve despite the severe losses in lives along the front lines during the past few months while the peace talks by the stubborn negotiators were grinding to a halt. Apparently, some of the negotiators were willing to sacrifice the lives of many fighters to gain a few more yards of territory before the ceasefire. Why? Dante wondered. Would they have been willing to sacrifice their own lives or the lives of their own sons? And the fighting continued, and each day more soldiers died.

Ahn had gone home on a ten day furlough and had returned the afternoon before. He had brought back six quart bottles of rice wine, called *saki*, which he and his father had made. Ahn had given one bottle each to Dante, Chico, Nap, Tiny, and to Captain Rossi in honor of the independence of the United States. And, by coincidence, a shipment of whiskey had arrived, and by that evening, and on Independence Day, many of the soldiers (in Fox Company, anyway) had been sufficiently inebriated in honor of the birthday of our homeland.

And, as Ahn had said, there was now another reason to celebrate: Dante had become a father for the first time; he had recently begun waiting for the war to end so that he could return home to see his daughter for the first time.

That night, they who had not passed out already, enjoyed a variety of dances, singing and clapping their hands. Chico had showed them how to dance the flamenco. And Dante led them in the Mexican Hat Dance. He put his helmet on the ground, began to clap his hands, and chanted, "Tatata tatata tatat! Tatata tatata tatat!" He stomped his feet and danced around his helmet while others were doing the same, clapping their hands hard. They had been outside of their tent, celebrating. When it was time for them to go to sleep, to walk into the tent, every time they tried to take one step forward, Chico and Dante took two steps backwards. Ahn got between them and tried to push them towards the tent, but they pulled him backwards and landed on the ground, laughing at each other. Finally, they decided it was much easier just to crawl back into the tent, which they did. When they got to their bunks, they climbed on top of them and fell asleep immediately.

And the next day, after the celebration of the Mass, Dante, Ahn, and Chico and several others in the company were given one day passes to Seoul. A truck from their company took them, with their rifles, into the center of the city, to a huge PX, where they were told to meet the truck for the return trip at 1700 hours. The first place they visited was the PX, a huge building with a huge dining hall where Dante met two former buddies with whom he had trained in basic training in Kentucky. They had become combat veterans who mentioned the names of some of the others who had been killed. Dante felt fortunate, indeed, that he had been in reserve during that time.

After an hour or so, they went outside and explored the city, crowded with refugees. Most of their time had been spent trying to avoid the kids who were pulling on their shirts and begging, "Hey, Joe, you wanna sheebee sheebee my mother? She a number fuckin one virgin." Some of their "mothers" were teenage "virgins" smiling at the soldiers and waiting eagerly and hopefully to lead them to nearby shacks to trade a few moments of pleasure for a few dollars. The young girls simply wanted enough money to buy food for themselves and their children. The three amigos gave what they could afford (without the sheebee sheebee), but as soon as they gave it away, other young "virgins" and their children suddenly appeared from nowhere until the usually gentle Ahn yelled: "Go away!"

A week later Sergeant Wells went to Seoul, and he returned with a white puppy with black spots, so he called it "Spots." It was, Wells said, going to be served as a delicacy at one of the restaurants, so he decided to buy it while it was still uncooked. Spots seemed happy that he (yes, it was a male) was still alive. And, yes, to him, being alive, still, at his age, undoubtedly seemed perfectly natural. He had been unaware that after just one week in reserve (as a drafted recruit) he would be transported to the front lines, in spite of his young age and lack of training, with the rest of the division.

For two days, the troops of Fox Company waited to move out while others of the division had begun to move up on line. No one seemed to know to what hill they would be going or whom they would be relieving. Anyway, one hill was as bad as another. No hill seemed safer than another, not on line.

The weather in July had been rather warm so far in the Kumhwa Valley, with no mosquitoes, because the compound had been sprayed frequently with insecticides. During the last night in reserve, they watched a Marilyn Monroe movie called *Niagara*. Unless it rained, the stage shows and movies during the summer months were held outside. Occasionally neighboring kids from near-by farms would sneak in but nobody paid much attention to them. Some of them even worked occasionally in the compound. The only ones who were strictly forbidden from the premises were mooses, and that, of course, included all teenage girls and young women, because the army prided itself on its high moral standards. It wanted warriors who were not only chaste enough to kill as many enemy soldiers as possible, but were also chaste enough to stay away from girls, because, according to the army, not all girls in the whole world were as scrupulous as refined American girls who had been raised in a proper moral environment; some of the girls in the rest of the world even participated in sexual intercourse. That made them, in some respects, even more deadly than the enemy soldiers. At least once a month, in reserve, company commanders were required to arrange special meetings for the troops on the evils of sex and venereal diseases. And, of course, each squad was required to patrol its own tent and the area around it, not so much because the enemy was so stupid that he would pull a sneak attack behind the lines, but the army wanted to make sure no mooses were being sneaked into the tents during the night. None of the guys had actually thought they had been guarding the area to stop the mooses. If they had been lucky enough to encounter any, most of the guys would have probably been first in line to accommodate them and then they would have encouraged them to expand their enterprise. American moms, of course, would have thrown a fit to know that their young sons, on the threshold of manhood, had been taken from them to be trained to kill with glory, had been squandering their time playing with mooses. In many ways, the army was not only a substitute father; it was a substitute mother.

Each man in the third squad, including Tiny, pulled guard duty every other night usually, for one hour. Most of the time, each man patrolled outside of the tent, getting together sometimes with the guard from another tent. It was the duty of the last man on guard to switch the lights on in the early morning and yell out: "Rise and shine!"

The next morning, a long row of army trucks with soldiers sitting in the back, were moving down the road.

Someone said, "Looks like our replacements are here." But the trucks did not stop.

A few minutes later other trucks appeared. This time, they turned and entered the compound, stopped, and the soldiers jumped down from the trucks. They were in the Third Division. They had been relieved from Outpost Boomerang. They had been hit hard, especially during the past month, and had suffered heavy casualties. Some of the Second Division, including the Thai battalion, had relieved them during the night, but the rest of the Third Division was still waiting to be relieved.

After chow, late in the afternoon, the members of Fox Company were put on trucks, and one truck after another followed the road north.

The weather had been sunny and warm when they had mounted the trucks, but soon clouds covered them, and after a few miles north, rain began to fall, and when darkness had settled in, the rain fell steadily, and the weather became much cooler.

No one had spoken much as they had been taken closer to their destinations. Each one had been wrapped in his own thoughts, mile after mile. After darkness had settled, Dante, sitting at the end of the truck, had noticed that the trucks following them did not have lights on. Apparently they had been close enough to the front lines that the enemy would have seen them. And the trucks, moving through the darkness, had been moving slowly but steadily, and had not seemed to curve much, if at all, and had not climbed up any hills or had gone down any. In the mountains of Korea, that was unusual. They must have been moving directly north on the floor of the Kumhwa Valley.

The truck went slower, and then it stopped. A door of the cab opened and closed.

Footsteps approached the rear of the truck.

"Okay," Wells said, "dismount and line up on the road."

They jumped down from the truck and got into formation.

Wells, cradling the puppy, said to Dante, "We'll be there in less than an hour. Take the dog with you, please, until we get into position."

Rain was falling.

Dante opened his flack vest, unbuttoned part of his shirt, took the dog from Wells, put it against his chest, buttoned his shirt and hooked his flack vest.

"Ah, good," Wells said. "He looks comfortable and secure. I think he'll sleep."

In double file, they began the hike along the road, past the long line of trucks, and stayed close behind the guy directly in front, because it was so dark. The rain continued to fall, and although Dante was wet, the dog seemed comfortable under the cover of the flack vest and the shirt and the heat from Dante's body. The dog, unaware of any danger, slept.

After an hour they began to climb a steep road. A short while later, the road seemed to narrow, and they stopped. A few minutes later, they continued in single file. When they stopped again, Dante heard Wells, at the front of the column, say, "Second platoon to the right." And a few minutes later, they stopped again. Tiny informed the squad that they were at the platoon command post, called the CP. In the dark, Dante couldn't see what it looked like. All he could see was a faint light at the bottom of what was, apparently, a doorway. Tiny said they would follow a path to a trench to the reverse slope, to their bunkers.

They walked up a path, which became the entrance to a trench at the top of the hill, walked down the trench and came to a fork. The third squad turned to the right, passed a bunker, which seemed empty, came to another, stopped as three men entered, one with a Browning automatic rifle, and two men emerged. The first one said, "I'm so fuckin glad to see you guys!" And they took off towards the command post. At the next bunker, which was empty, Nap said, "A Bomb, Dante, Chico, take this one." Dante followed Ahn into the bunker. "Oh, big step!" Ahn warned. Dante stepped down and then took another step down to the floor of the bunker. "Dos pesos," he said to Chico. "At least it's dry in here. Seco." Dante walked with his hands in front of him. He touched Ahn who was standing at the aperture, but it was too dark to see anything. There couldn't be anyone attacking now, Dante thought, it was too dark. But that didn't mean they couldn't strike with artillery. He continued to feel his way around. He walked into something. His thighs touched something, and he touched something with the palms of his hands. He felt a blanket with his hands. The blanket felt like it was covering strands of rope. At his thighs, his hands were feeling another blanket. There was a double bunk, at least. He reached higher, but he couldn't feel anything. He reached down to his thighs and tried to feel the size of the bunk. There seemed to be more than enough space for one person. He slid his backpack off, put it on the ground, and sat on the bottom bunk. He thought of the dog. The dog had the right idea. Just relax and sleep if you could, but he wouldn't be able to relax and sleep. Not right now, anyway. He would make his mind blank, somehow. Or he would pray. Or he would imagine holding his daughter on his chest, as he was holding and comforting the dog. Or he would close his eyes and imagine he was in bed with his wife, with their arms wrapped around each other. It would be so great to be with her again!

"Home, with wife," he said to Ahn, "Number one!"

Suddenly the area lit up. Instinctively, Dante leaped up and looked out the aperture. So did Ahn. Dante had closed his left eye and looked out with his right eye. A flare was floating down slowly, lighting up the whole area to the front of them. Just below the aperture he could see rolls of barbed wire all the way down to what seemed to be the bottom of the hill. At the bottom, to the right, was a scrawny tree with a few leaves on it. And that was it for vegetation, except for a little grass. For anyone who was down there, there was no protection. He would become a target. There seemed to be a valley below, an open field that provided no cover, no protection. He felt a little better now, a little more secure, even. If anyone would attack from the valley below, and tried to come up this steep hill, it would be almost suicidal, even in the dark. There was hardly any possibility that the Chinese would be foolish enough to attack during the day.

Dante took a quick look inside the bunker. It looked like a little room that had been dug into the earth. If it hadn't been in a war zone, it would have looked like a quaint underground camping spot. Directly behind him, up a step, was an open doorway and a trench that connected to the main trench. And there were two bunks on each side.

Everything was black again.

"You guys okay in there?"

That was Nap.

"Yeah," Dante answered. "I can't remember it ever being this dark before."

"I know!"

"Hey, Dante. This is Wells. Do you have the pup?"

"Yeah, he's still sleeping."

Wells took it.

"He knew I gave it to the right guy. Thanks."

Morning finally was coming, and Dante became aware of how the Chinese could attack at daybreak. The rain had stopped, but thick fog was covering everything.

By the middle of the morning, the fog had gradually lifted. In the early morning, Dante had seen only what he had seen during the night; later he saw that on the left, in the west, the open field of the valley stretched for miles between mountains. No way would an attack come from an open field, but directly in front of him, less than two hundred yards, not even the length of two football fields, as the fog slowly lifted, it was revealing the foot of a hill steeply rising. That must be, he thought, no-man's land. But how big, he wondered, was the hill?

Nap had returned to check on them, but he didn't have any information on where the enemy lines were. Neither did Tiny, who said he was trying to find out. He hoped they would know more after the fog would lift. "At least the fuckin chinks can't see us in this fuckin fog."

After the fog had lifted more, the hill to the northeast continued to rise, but it was no ordinary hill like the hill they were on. It was a mountain.

Then Captain Rossi, who, like the others, wasn't wearing any insignias, showed up with Tiny. Dante was in the trench with Ahn, looking up at the mountain.

"I was going to ask you, sir, where the Chinese are, but I'm afraid you're going to tell us they're way up there where they can piss down on us, and that the top of the mountain goes even higher than what we can see now."

"And I'm afraid to tell you that you're right, but at least you can maintain a good sense of humor, and that's helpful."

"Now I know what they mean when they say that being a little crazy helps you to get through life."

Rossi chuckled.

"How can we possibly attack them? That mountain looks impenetrable."

"Again you're right. I've been told that, inside that mountain they have a small city, like the ones you have in New Hampshire. But we could never attack it. We'd have to go around it, and that's never going to happen. They've had two years to dig in. We're actually on a foot of that mountain. It's called Papasan, because it's the biggest hill around here. This is Boomerang. An outpost. We have to hold on to it, with only one regiment."

"Why?"

"You can't see it from this side, but from the other side you can see the beginning of the Kumhwa Valley. We're here to protect the valley. The Chinese want this, but they'll have to go through us to get it. After the ceasefire, both sides will have to pull back two miles to create a demilitarized zone. So, they will lose Papasan, unless they can get at least two miles past us."

"We can't attack them, but they can easily attack us. So we're here to defend this little hill, not to advance. They won't be attacking us on the left flank; they'll come down the mountain and hit us on the right."

"Yeah, except they won't be coming down the mountain, not the first wave, anyway. They're already down here."

"What are you talking about? How can they be down here? Where?"

"We're right at the point of Boomerang. The Thai battalion is on our left flank. Our regiment has the rest of it. Straight ahead and to the right, going up the finger of the hill, you can see the enemy trench. Here," he said, removing binoculars from his neck, "you can get a good look at their positions."

Dante took the binoculars, looked through them, and clearly saw a trench and began to follow it up the finger of the hill. Suddenly he could see two Chinese soldiers in soft caps talking to each other. "Holy shit! They're so close to us! I think they're standing on something to look over the trench. There are at least two others walking down the trench. Shouldn't we be firing at them?"

"Don't get too fuckin gung ho," said Tiny.

"You fire at them," Rossi said, "and they'll fire back. How would you react if they fired at *us*? Do you think we're invisible to them? Maybe their eyes are slanted, but their eyes can see at least as well as ours."

"But if they attack with enough men, how can we possibly stop them?"

"We'll probably find out soon enough. Others have stopped them. So can we. And we'll have to. That's why we're here. We're at full strength now. That's why they've moved us back on line. We can take a good beating, yet we can still survive. Remember, the enemy is just like us; they're only human, and to them, we are monsters, out to kill them. They get scared. And they panic and run away to save themselves. When any animal feels trapped, it fights back. And we'll fight back. We'll have no alternative."

Captain Rossi stepped inside the bunker, went up to the aperture and looked out. On the way outside, on the floor near the entrance, he noticed a small box with a few grenades.

"They were left here, sir. Do you think I can get enough to fill the box?"

"Of course. Good idea. You should pick up another box at the CP. Right, Sergeant?"

"Yes, sir."

"In an attack," Dante said, "I don't think I can toss a grenade effectively from the aperture, so I was wondering if I can throw one from the trench to see if I can make it explode at the bottom of the slope."

"Sure. Try it."

Dante picked up a grenade from the box, went into the trench, held the grenade in his right hand, squeezed the handle, put his left index finger in the ring, pulled it out, released the handle, waited a few seconds, and heaved it. The others watched it as it flew through the air, and just before it hit the bottom of the slope, it exploded.

"Perfect!" yelled the captain. "You must have played baseball, in the outfield!"

"Hey, let's go get some grenades."

Just as they got into the trench, Nap was headed towards them. "Where you guys going?"

"First, to get some grenades, then we were going to take a little tour of the area, to see if you have a hotel with a heated swimming pool. Money's no object."

"Don't tell me you don't like the accommodations."

"Well, I travelled a long way to get here. I expected something a little better."

"Well, you get what you pay for. This is what happens when you take a cheap trip."

"Cheap, hell! I even gave up my job to come here."

"Now you know you got fucked! Anyway, you should familiarize yourself with the area. I'll show you our platoon area."

They followed Nap along the trench. In the bunker next to them was Henderson, a tall, lanky redhead from Minnesota with a Browning automatic rifle and two other riflemen. The next bunker belonged to Nap and two fairly new recruits. And then they came to the trench that led to the platoon command post on the reverse slope. "After you see the rest of the platoon's positions, we'll go to the CP to get the grenades. We'll continue, straight, following the trench past the second and first squads."

At the end of the platoon's positions, at the mid point of Boomerang was a machine gun bunker. They entered it. Nap showed them a wide, narrow aperture. At the left, looking straight, they could see the valley. To the right, was Papasan. And to the right, where the barrel of the machine gun stopped against a pole, was the position of the machine gun when the enemy would attack, especially in the dark. With the machine gun at the other end, where the third squad ended, a wall of fire would form to protect the whole platoon.

They followed Nap back through the trench, to the fork, followed it up the peak of the hill and down the other side, to the opening of the trench.

"This is the back side of Boomerang," Nap said.

They were near the top of the hill. Below them was a winding road, and even though it was winding, they could see that it was also steep, especially at the curves, as it zigzagged to the bottom of the slope, which they couldn't see. But they could see a road along the middle of a wide valley floor, about three miles long. The road disappeared into hills behind them.

"How can they get supplies to us?" Dante asked Nap.

"Well, not during the daytime, obviously."

"We walked across that valley last night! The trucks must have stopped behind those hills. You know something? If the Chinese had sent up flares last night, we would have been sitting ducks for them."

"Fuck! Don't even think about it!"

"How long do you think it will be before they start shelling us?"

"Your guess is as good as mine. Let's pick up your grenades and continue the tour. I'm not doing this for nothing, you know. I expect a big tip from you guys."

The platoon command post was near the opening of the trench. It looked like a shed with wood door, which was ajar. A medic was sitting behind a desk. Nap tapped on the door and entered.

"I want to get some grenades."

The medic, a Quaker from a farm in Pennsylvania, and a conscientious objector to killing, who wore thick glasses with a rubber band to keep them securely to his head, pointed to a stack of boxes in a corner near the door.

"And can you bring a box of C rations to your squad? Two cans for each one."

"C rations?"

"Well, you can't expect them to bring us chow during the day."

"Hell, they could have brought the chow last night."

"So, let's submit another grievance. It worked a few months ago."

"Yeah, very funny."

As they passed each bunker in their squad, they left the rations, and at their own bunker they put four boxes of grenades on the floor near the entrance, and they went to the next bunker and then continued to the last bunker of the third squad. Then they arrived at a small bunker, called the checkpoint, where Tiny was. There was barely room in it for three men to sit. There was a post inside with a telephone on it, and a telephone line ran to the platoon command post. The aperture was small. Looking through it, at the left, Dante could see all the positions of the second platoon, including the bunker with the machine gun. At the right, a trench ran down a finger of a hill and ended, Nap said, at the listening post. From the checkpoint, Dante had a complete view of the platoon as it faced the enemy lines.

Directly across the trench from the checkpoint was the other machine gun bunker of the fourth squad. Three men were inside. Baker, from Atlanta, who spoke with a thick southern drawl, was the machine gunner. He invited Dante to sit behind the gun. He did. He was looking down the trench to the listening post, which was less than fifty yards away. Baker told him to look to his left. In an attack another machine gun to their right formed a wall of fire with the other machine gun.

The main trench continued to the third platoon.

"Down this way," Nap said. "This goes to the listening post."

They followed Nap down the trench, down the finger of the hill, until the trench ended. "This is it. This is the listening post." They followed him up one step, high enough so that they could easily see over the top of the ground, or they could step up a little higher and sit, and look over the top of the trench. The position was carved out of the ground to accommodate three men. The man in the middle would look straight to the front, the one on the right would cover the right side, and the one on the left would cover the left side.

"You can't see that much from here," Dante said. "You can see more from a little higher up, in the bunkers. And there's no protection at all here."

"That's right. And this is where the chinks hit first, where there is less barbed wire, because this is where the patrols go to no-man's land."

"Can't they see us now?"

"I'm sure they're watching us. They're probably wondering what we're up to, thinking we're damn fools for not setting off smoke screens, but if we did that, they would probably shell us. This way they think we're four fuckin idiots that can't harm them. Come on, I'll show you the break in the barbed wire."

Nap climbed out of the trench and stood up, and he walked up to the barbed wire. The Chinese would shell the wire to break it apart, or they would cut their way through it or throw thick pads on it and walk over it. Nap unlatched a gate and pulled on it. The gate opened. It was holding a roll of barbed wire. Nap stepped inside, unlatched another gate holding barbed wire, and he pushed it open. "Now," he said, "we can follow a path into no-man's land." He pulled on the gate, closing it, latched it, pushed the other, closing it, and as he latched it, he said, "This is where the chinks want to enter, where there is less barbed wire, but, as you can see, when they do, they face the machine gun."

That was the end of the tour.

"We'll return here tonight," Nap said to Dante, "you and I and Tiny, on the first night of duty at the listening post. Tiny is the only squad leader I know who takes duties like the rest of us. He'll never tell you to do something that he doesn't do, too."

When they returned to their bunker, each of the three spent most of the rest of the day inside the bunker, thinking, but not saying much to each other. What was there to say? What was there to talk about? They were on the front lines. Dante had wondered what it would be like, and he was still wondering about it. Ahn and Chico were writing letters. What were they writing? Were they telling anyone they were at the front? But why make your loved ones worry? He would write a letter to Rose, but what would he tell her? He asked about their daughter, how he wished he could hold both of them. Nothing he had written was new, but when she would read it, she would know he was still alive and unhurt. After he wrote the letter, he put it into his backpack, withdrew a notebook in which he was recoding his memoirs, and wrote a description of Boomerang.

He had given his notebook a title: *Who Am I?* He had gotten the title from a notebook his father had kept. His father had gotten the title from Tattone, who had written in his own *Who Am I?* that one can borrow an idea from someone else, a wise man, perhaps, but a borrowed idea might not belong to you, and therefore you might not have a deep understanding of it, and you might not grasp its meaning. An idea that comes from your own mind belongs to you even if that idea is shared by many others. And the ideas that belong to you have profound meanings for you.

And as Dante wrote: "We seek understanding of life and try to convey it honestly, hoping that we can change things for the better, for we feel things we cannot see and believe in things we cannot understand. We believe that existence is more than just an accident, that our experiences are meaningful. And so, I ask now: What in hell am I doing here?"

"What are we doing here?" he asked out loud.

The three of them, sitting on the two lower bunks, looked at each other.

"Number fuckin ten!" Ahn said.

Children of God, thought Dante, but when will we grow up?

The front lines had become stationary during the past two years and had been pounded so much with shelling that Boomerang was almost like a sand dune.

"No birds! There are no birds here," he said, flapping his arms like wings. "No trees here, on this side, and no birds. No butterflies. Certainly, no flowers, and no berries, and no birds flying around. That doesn't even seem natural. No birds. No mosquitoes, though. That's number one. Flies, though. Enough flies. What are they doing here? No garbage here. Wait a minute. I can smell it now. Dead flesh. The rain during the night washed some of it away. That's what the flies are waiting for. Damn! What are we doing here? Not even wild animals are stupid enough to stay here." As soon as he had said that, a pair of huge rats sauntered into the bunker, stopped, and looked up at them as though they were expecting to be fed.

The rats, he would soon learn, had made nests between sand-bags, and they lived by eating pieces of flesh of soldiers that were scattered through the trenches.

"Look at them!"

They had become so accustomed to soldiers that the rats had no fear of them.

Ahn and Chico grinned at them.

"Sorry," Ahn said. "No chow."

"You can give them a can of beans and franks."

"No way! You give."

"I'm going outside to enjoy the sun while I can."

"Good idea," said Chico. "I go with you."

"Me, too," Ahn said.

They went into the trench, but they couldn't enjoy much light from the sun unless they'd get out of the trench. Not that they needed the heat. The sun was bright and the sky was blue. The day was warm, but not hot. If they had been somewhere else, thought Dante, it would have been a beautiful day. Still, if both sides could maintain the attitude of, "If you don't shoot me, I won't shoot you," the war would be a lot more tolerable.

They were at the checkpoint.

"What the fuck are you fuckin guys up to?"

Tiny was sitting alone in it.

"Just wondering what we should be doing."

"Not a fuckin thing. Just fuckin relax, if you can, when they let us."

"Is it usually like this?"

"That fuckin depends. You can never figure them; it's like they don't want to fuckin die any more than we do. But then you know that fuckin dying don't mean a fuckin thing to them."

"Why don't they attack us then?"

"Who the fuck knows? They don't think for themselves, you know. They just follow fuckin orders. Maybe they're told not to bother us for a fuckin while, and just as we let our fuckin guards down, bang! They fuck us up."

"They're just like us, then?"

"What the fuck are you talking about?"

"We see them walking though the trenches, but we don't shoot at them so that they won't shoot at us. It's an unspoken agreement on both sides. And, as far as we're concerned, that's fine, until we're under orders to attack."

"Yeah, that's fuckin true."

"I know Ahn doesn't want to die. He wants to get back to his family."

"You're a fuckin good influence on him. But you never fuckin know what the fuck they're really thinking."

Dante decided to change the subject.

He asked Tiny what he knew about Boomerang.

According to Tiny, Boomerang was about a mile long and less than a half mile in width, and that, at the moment, all the positions had been adequately reinforced with at least five thousand troops.

"Oh, by the way, did Nap tell you we're going out to the fuckin listening post tonight?"

"Yeah, he did. Can you tell me what that's like?"

"Well, sometimes not a fuckin thing happens, and sometimes that's so fuckin boring, you have trouble keeping awake all night, but it's the most dangerous position in an attack. It's usually the first fuckin place that gets hit. You saw that there's no fuckin protection at all. We're there to warn the others that there are fuckin chinks in the valley. As soon as we know, we run back here, yelling, 'Chinks in the valley!'"

"So at night it's the most important position in the platoon."

"You bet you're fuckin ass!"

"You'd think that the listening post would have some protection though."

"Yeah, you'd fuckin think so."

"It's incredible how we're so damned exposed, and how the Chinese are, too. They know damn well they've got the upper hand and don't have to worry about us attacking them."

"That's the fuckin way it looks, to us, and maybe that's the way they want it to look, but they know fuckin well that our brass can easily order us to attack them to keep them on edge, and they know what to do when we do."

"But we'd lose too many men and hardly make a dent in their defense."

"That's what fuckin war is, killing each other. And no fuckin defense can stop a fuckin offense forever. It's a big fuckin game that the fuckin brass plays. It's like a checker game played with real fuckin people. Let's sacrifice this fuckin group and that fuckin group, and wham! We move in for the big fuckin kill, and the winners celebrate the big fuckin victory. It's the biggest game of all. You like baseball, or boxing, or football? Fuck, man, those fuckin games ain't shit compared to this one!"

"But people are sick of war. Nobody back home is interested, not in this one."

"That's only because this fuckin war is so fuckin limited to this little fuckin hole in the ground that nobody ever heard of before. I mean, after a great fuckin world war, who the fuck gives a shit about this fuckin place?"

"You don't think that people really want world peace?"

"I don't really understand most fuckin people. I know some fuckin people really want world peace, but if most fuckin people really wanted it, you and I wouldn't have to be here. So, what the fuck are we doing here? Even religious people, who say to love each other, tell us it's our patriotic duty, to God and country, to fight and win fuckin wars. That's what makes a fuckin country great. Winning all the fuckin wars. Look at the fuckin Romans, the greatest people in the world years ago. And then Mussolini wanted to make you fuckin wops great again. But what the fuck did he do? He embarrassed all you fuckin wops the same way the chinks are embarrassing us fuckin yanks, the greatest fuckin people who ever lived, who even embarrassed their own forefathers, from one of the smallest fuckin countries in the world who conquered half the fuckin world, the fuckin rulers of the greatest fuckin empire that ever existed until their own fuckin kids told them to get the fuck out, we're taking over our own fuckin country and keeping our own fuckin money, and our army ain't drinking any more of your fuckin tea; we're switching to coffee, to Colombian coffee. Now, here we are, we became the greatest fuckin country in the world that never lost a fuckin war, but we ain't going to win this one, because the fuckin people back home don't even think of this as a real fuckin war!"

Dante grinned.

"So what the fuck do you think, Teach? Am I wrong?"

"I'm not going to argue with you, but if they declared a cease fire, I'd be happy."

"Me, too, but I ain't counting on it. Don't get me wrong. I don't like fuckin war, especially this one. You know I ain't gung ho, but, like you, I've been called to stop the fuckin commies, and here I am. I just hope the fuck I survive it."

"Of course. And when you get back home, you'll want to say proudly that you served your country, and you'll want others to appreciate and respect you for what you've done."

"Yeah. Exactly. When it starts getting dark, Nap will get you. I'm not going to tell you not to get nervous. It's only fuckin natural."

"Thanks, Sarg. See you later."

"Have you gotten any fuckin sleep today?"

"No, not really. Too nervous to get sleepy, I guess."

"Lie down for a fuckin while even if you can't sleep. It's could be a long fuckin night tonight."

As soon as Dante retuned to his bunker, he opened a can of rations and ate beans and franks, and then he laid back on one of the lower bunks, thought of Rose on their wedding night when she had said, "Make love to me in Italian," then he closed his eyes, remembering making love to her, and he felt relaxed, much to his own surprise, as he had always felt when he had thought of making love to her. "I'm always making love to you, cara mia, even when I'm not making love to you."

When he woke up, it was still daylight. Across from him, Ahn seemed to be asleep, and so was Chico in the upper bunk. Dante closed his eyes. And he knew he had returned to sleep when he thought he had heard footsteps outside of the bunker.

Nap entered, tapped him on the shoulder gently, and said, "It'll be getting dark soon."

As Dante stood up quickly, Ahn and Chico sat up. Dante looked around, "I guess I've got everything I need. Oh, yeah, my helmet." It was on the bunk. He put it on. He had his rifle, ammo, and flack vest. "It won't get chilly during the night?"

"Nope, and it ain't going to rain either. The sky's clear. Should be a nice night."

"I'm all set then. See you guys later. Buenos noches."

He followed Nap through the trench, to the checkpoint, where Tiny was sitting on a crate and smoking. He was sitting on a folded poncho.

"What the fuck is that for?" Nap said.

"Well," sputtered Tiny. "You know."

"No! No fuckin way! You can pull that shit with others if they're dumb enough to let you, but you know fuckin well what I'll do to you." Nap turned to Dante. "He takes his fuckin poncho out there to get under it to smoke a fuckin cigarette. He knows if he does that while I'm out there, too, I'll blow his fuckin brains out."

"And he's fuckin crazy enough to do it!"

"You bet your ass! If I got to depend on you to protect my ass, I'd expect the same from you if you depend on me to protect *your* ass."

"Yeah, I know, I know."

"I appreciate your going out there with us, I really do." Nap turned to Dante again. "He doesn't have to do this, you know."

"I got a small fuckin brain."

"Bullshit. You got a big heart, well, for some fuckin things, and good instincts. You're a natural leader. I'm glad you're the squad leader. When shit happens, you don't fall apart. You're more concerned for getting us through it."

"Listen to this fuckin wop! He's piling up fuckin brownie points."

"And another thing. No fuckin sleeping on us."

"Well, I don't have much fuckin control over that."

"I'd rather have you get up and walk back here, to this checkpoint, and even have a cigarette or two, and when you'd return to the listening post, you'd be wide awake and alert."

Tiny nodded.

He informed them that a patrol from Easy Company, which was in reserve on the reverse slope behind them, would be coming through a little later.

As soon as a replacement for Tiny arrived to man the telephone, it had become dark enough for them to proceed to the listening post.

"Good luck, guys. I hope it's quiet tonight," someone from the machine gun bunker said.

Tiny went first, followed by Nap. As they walked quietly in the deep trench down the finger of the hill, the sky was clear and stars were out, but the night seemed unusually quiet. As Dante tried to listen to the night air, he couldn't even hear a whisper of a breeze. When they reached the end of the trench, Tiny sat in the front, in the center, facing directly to the front. Nap sat a little behind him and faced to the left, and Dante sat opposite Nap, facing the other way, and listened intently.

After a little while, Dante became aware of a deadly silence. It was, as Tiny had probably meant, a most dangerous situation, when he had said earlier: "Not a fuckin thing happens, and that's so fuckin boring, you have trouble keeping awake; it is the most dangerous position." The silence was unnatural; it was eerie. The usual night sounds of nature did not exist. The sound of crickets was conspicuously absent, and a sudden shiver darted through Dante. Death was natural; this silence was the absence of life; it was nothingness. But he would not succumb to the terror of nothingness, because, deep within him, life was growing. He would not succumb to the inclination to sleep, to despair, for he was not alone; he was not living only for himself. Deep within him was the determination to overcome the nothingness; deep inside of him was the flame inspiring him, making him aware that he was never alone. "Make love to me, mi amore; make love to me, always, and keep me inside of you as I hold you inside of me, always."

The landscape lit up suddenly, making everything even brighter than it had been last night. Even the lower part of Papasan became as bright as it had been at noontime.

"Where is that coming from?" asked Dante.

"That's ours. It's coming from a spotlight behind the Thai battalion, I think."

"Wow! That's one hell of a spotlight! Will they keep it on all night?"

"Fuck no. The fuckin chink artillery would pound at it all fuckin night until they'd fuckin hit it."

A few seconds later, the light went off, and everything was dark again.

"The fuckin patrol should be coming through here pretty fuckin soon."

"It's early yet, Sarge."

"I fuckin know, but I fuckin figure if the fuckin patrol is out there and the fuckin chinks are out there, then we'll fuckin know if the fuckin chinks are out there."

"Yeah, Sarge, that makes a lot of fuckin sense."

They heard Dante chuckle.

"What the fuck are you laughing at?" Tiny asked.

"You guys."

"Ain't you fuckin scared?"

"Of course."

"Well, I ain't ever heard anybody laugh out on the fuckin listening post. They're too fuckin scared. You got a good fuckin attitude. I think you'll do okay without being fuckin gung ho. You think so too, huh, Nap?"

"Yeah, I think so, too. I think it's good we're talking like this. Not too loud, and keeping alert at the same time."

"Yeah, I think we make a good fuckin team."

Someone was coming down the trench.

"Hey, Tiny, the patrol is here."

Tiny's replacement at the checkpoint led the patrol leader to Tiny, and then he returned to the checkpoint. The patrol leader said that there were ten of them and that he had left their names at the checkpoint. They were wearing soft caps, not helmets, which meant that they had not planned to engage the enemy in combat. They would only fire their weapons in defense, if necessary. They would be out there most of the night reconnoitering the area, and they would return an hour before dawn. Tiny said, "There are a couple of fuckin steps to get the fuck out of here. Follow me." He climbed out, approached the gate, unlatched it, pulled it open, stepped inside, and he unlatched the other gate and pushed it open. And after they walked past him, he returned.

An hour or so later, Nap jabbed the barrel of his rifle into Tiny's back.

"Open your fuckin eyes!"

"How did you know his eyes were closed?"

"By the way his breathing changed. Why don't you take a fuckin walk, Sarg?'

"Yeah, okay. It was getting too fuckin quiet. I'm going to have a smoke."

A few minutes later, while Tiny had left to return to the checkpoint for a smoke, the sound of someone blowing a bugle suddenly came from the top of Papasan. It sounded like a cavalry charge. Nap said it was coming from a loudspeaker. The Chinese did that, sometimes, he said, especially at night. A bugle would blow, followed by sound effects of hoof beats and neighing of charging horses. It sounded as though the horses were about to trample them. When they did that, Nap said, they usually wouldn't attack, although you never knew for sure.

"They sure as hell have my attention," Dante said, actually feeling a horde of horses coming towards him.

"Yeah, it does sound kind of scary even when you know it's not real."

The sounds ceased.

And the oppressive silence engulfed them again.

After a few minutes, a recording of *You Made Me Love You* was played with noises in the background, like chatter and the clinking of wine glasses in a nightclub.

Tiny returned.

"Some fuckin entertainment," he muttered.

"Do you think you can keep your fuckin eyes open for a while now?"

"No fuckin problem."

When the music stopped, a soft, sexy, sweet, inviting voice of a temptress with an endearing accent entreated them to join their party. "We are young, very beautiful women waiting with open arms for all of you, Joe, not only for your own pleasures but to experience the thrills of making love to all of you handsome strangers. If you are willing to come to us in peace, we could spend the duration living together and loving together. We want to make love to you, Joe, not kill you."

She spoke for over an hour, between musical selections, and then a friendly male voice, with hardly an accent and whose English sounded almost American, implored them to drop their weapons and to forget the war, that the business tycoons back home didn't give a damn about their lives, that they were out, enjoying themselves while brave, patriotic soldiers were here, fighting and sacrificing their lives. And the big business men and politicians were profiting from the war. Big business men, the voice added, were exploiting the poorer classes, inducting them into the armed services. "How many of you soldiers are from the wealthy class?"

The sexy voice returned, and more music was played.

Nap said that sometimes the Chinese would sneak up and stick pamphlets to the barbed wire, and by morning a voice over the loud-speaker would invite the soldiers to pick up the pamphlets. Some of the soldiers would.

At the end of a musical selection, the sexy voice said they had only one more hour to enjoy their party.

"In another fuckin hour we can get some fuckin sleep, you fuckin cunt, and you can get laid if you ain't getting laid now."

"Hell, I was thinking of going over there and fuckin her myself. I thought you would, too."

"Oh, you fuckin dumb wop, you think they'd really let us fuck them? I don't understand why they tell us such shit. Do they really think we're dumb enough to fall for that fuckin bullshit?"

"Well, I know one fuckin guy who's horny enough to want to believe that shit."

"Aw, go fuck yourself."

"You don't really think those broads would fuckin lie to you, do you, Sarg?"

"Hey, wop, fun ghoul."

The patrol returned.

"Nothing out there," the patrol leader said.

After the patrol had passed the listening post, Tiny heaved a big sigh and said, "Now we can fuckin relax a little. It'll be daylight soon and it won't be too fuckin foggy this morning. Every fuckin time I see morning coming, I thank God I'm still here to see the fuckin sun. I hate this fuckin place! I hate this fuckin war!"

"Just don't close your fuckin eyes yet."

"Yeah, I know, I know."

Fifteen or twenty minutes later, Tiny said, "Hey, Nap, I'm going back to the fuckin checkpoint to have another fuckin cigarette."

"Yeah, I think that's a good idea."

Tiny stood up and returned to the checkpoint.

"It's a strange thing," said Nap. "It gets so fuckin quiet and so fuckin scary that, instead of keeping awake and keeping alert, which seems so damn normal, I reach the point that I just want to close my eyes, and, I don't know, I just, well, sort of, well, want to forget I'm even here. I can't explain it, but I think that's what Tiny feels sometimes, and I almost fall asleep, too."

"I know."

"But you kept alert all night, which seems more normal. I mean, when your own fuckin life depends on it, you'd think you'd be so fuckin scared you wouldn't be able to sleep; that fear would keep you alert. And don't tell me our experience makes us different. I don't think that has anything to do with it. And you can't ever get used to it, whatever it is."

"And I think you're right. There's so little we know about our nature and how our nature works. We know that something in our nature warns us when we're in danger. We feel pain to let us know that something is wrong with us, but when the pain gets too intense, we pass out. That's also how nature protects us. Fear, when it's rational, keeps us alert, but, maybe, when it gets so intense we can't control it, we want to, well, as you implied, to escape from our situation. Maybe that's why we want to sleep."

"How can we control it?"

"I wish I knew."

"But you kept alert. Tiny asked you if you were scared. And you said you were."

"I was. I still am."

"But you didn't get so scared that you wanted to close your eyes."

"Actually, for a while, I did. I think I understand that feeling."

"But you didn't close your eyes. How did you keep your feelings under control?"

"How do *you* keep yours under control?"

"I don't fuckin know! That's why I'm asking *you*!"

"Will power."

Nap stared at him.

"I ask you a fuckin question, and you answer me with the same fuckin question. Now you say will power. How the fuck do you control will power? If the pain gets too intense, you pass out. Right? Can you will yourself to stay awake?"

Dante grinned at him.

"Good question. We need something beyond ourselves."

"Beyond ourselves. You mean, God?"

"Well, maybe it sounds corny."

"Hey, if it helps you to control your fear, I'll take corny. You mean, you pray?"

"Well, yeah, prayer helps. Do you pray?"

"I heard there ain't any atheists in foxholes. Do you think that's true?"

"I don't know, but if that's true, then the worst mistake the communist leaders could possibly make is to send their troops to war."

"Huh! I never thought of that!"

"Well, we don't think of the enemy as human. To us he's a monster, a killing machine. And that's the way they see *us*."

"So you think they're just as afraid as we are."

"Yeah, I'm sure they are."

"So, you think they pray, too?"

"I don't really know. I can only go by my own experiences."

"Well, you make a lot of sense. And you do a lot of thinking, man, a lot of deep thinking."

"I'm going to tell you something, for whatever it's worth. Almost as soon as I came out here, I felt something strange about the silence. Almost everything here has been destroyed. Virtually nothing is alive. To say I felt death itself, well, that's an understatement. And, like Tiny, I wanted to close my eyes, not to overcome my fear, but to, well, I don't really understand why."

"To get away from, well, whatever you were feeling?"

"Well, something like that. Anyway, I felt something inside of me, deep inside of me, something stronger than fear, something that, well, as you've said, something that prevented my fear from, well, from knocking me out. I felt, well, my wife, deep inside of me. I mean, *I felt her love*. I felt her love, keeping me going. I really did!"

"Wow! Man, she must really be something!"

"Oh, man, she really is! I knew that when I was just a little kid. My mother had wanted me to be a priest, and for a while, I thought I would be, but I always knew she's special, that, to me, she's the personification of love. So, when I say I feel her love inside of me, I'm saying that I feel the love of God. And I thank God. I thank God for making me the luckiest guy in the world."

"Holy shit!" Nap cried out, raising his rifle and pointing it directly at the gate. "Who the fuck are you?"

"A Chinese officer. I want to surrender. I'm alone."

A white piece of cloth, like a handkerchief, was waving over the barbed wire.

Nap and Dante were both standing, looking over the trench, and were pointing their rifles at him. It was still too dark to get a good look at him, or to see if he was actually alone.

"I heard you two talking. I was here a little earlier when you had someone else with you, and he said he left to have a cigarette. If I had wanted to kill you, I could have tossed a grenade at you, except I didn't bring any grenades with me."

"Do you have any weapons?" asked Nap.

"Yes, but only a gun that I'm using at the end of the barrel to wave this white flag of surrender."

"And you say you're alone?"

"I know it seems foolish to ask you to trust me, but I give you my word. I'm not a communist. Like your buddy there, whose mother wanted him to be a priest, I'm Catholic, too, and my mother also wanted me to be a priest. I have my reasons to surrender."

"I'm going to trust you," Nap said, "but please raise both hands as high as you can, and under no circumstances drop them until I give you permission, or I and my friend will both be forced to shoot you."

"I understand, and I thank you."

"I'm going to let him in. If he tries anything smart, don't hesitate to kill him."

"You can trust me," Dante said with confidence.

Nap climbed out of the listening post and, carrying his rifle, he walked up to the first gate, unlatched it, and pulled it open. He went to the other gate, unlatched it, and pushed it open.

"Walk through here and when you get to the other side of the barbed wire, stop."

"I'm a little nervous. You seem calm, and I'm grateful for that."

"If you've come peacefully, you've got nothing to worry about."

As the officer walked through, Nap pulled the gate shut, then he latched it. When the officer passed the other gate, he stopped and waited. His hands were still raised.

"You can put your hands down now and let me take your gun."

Nap took the gun, took a few short steps, and he gave it Dante.

"Is this a burp gun?" Dante asked.

The officer said, "Yes, it is."

"It's a lot like a carbine," Nap said.

He closed the gate and latched it.

"I'm sorry, but I have to search you."

"Of course."

Nap said to Dante, "Take my rifle while I search him."

While he was being searched, the officer said, "You were having an interesting conversation. I wanted to join in. You're right about us Chinese soldiers being as scared as you are and seeing you as monsters. And yes, some of us are devoutly religious, and we pray. And some of us, like some of you, are atheists. We're as human as you, just as good and just as bad." He said to Dante, "When I heard you talking about your wife being inside you as the personification of love, I felt a lot easier about wanting to surrender to you."

"Are you frightened?" asked Dante.

"Yeah, I still am; I'm still trembling. Wouldn't you be, too, in my place?"

"Of course."

"I can't find any weapons on him," Nap said.

The Chinese officer seemed unreal as he stood on the ground above Dante in the dimness of early dawn, bathed in a thin white mist. He was wearing a soft cap and a thin jacket with no insignias on it. He was not wearing a flack vest. Even though it was the middle of summer, he was wearing quilted fatigues and felt boots.

Nap told him he could sit on the edge of the trench and slide into the listening post, and when he was in the trench, he could either stand or sit. He sat on the edge of the trench and let himself drop into it. And he decided to sit at the front center, where Tiny had been sitting, and the officer was facing Dante.

Nap sat down, facing both of them, and said, "We'll wait here few more minutes, until it's light. I'm curious as to why you're surrendering."

"Yeah, me too," said Dante.

"I know this sounds incredible. I'm really an American citizen, but I was born in China, and I want to get back to the states. This is the only way I can do it. I was in the Chinese army in the last war, after a couple of years of college, and as soon as the war ended, my parish priest, a Maryknoll missionary from San Francisco, helped me to apply to the university there, a Jesuit institution where a brother of his teaches. Anyway, in my freshman year I met a wonderful American girl, who also is Catholic, and was studying nursing, and in my sophomore year, we married. We have two children, a girl and a boy. As soon as I became an American citizen, I returned to China to visit my parents. Not knowing the conditions here since the communist takeover, my wife and kids stayed in the states. Almost as soon as I returned to China, I was inducted again into the army. And here I am. I figure my best chance to see my wife and kids again is to surrender. At least my wife will know where I am."

"Wow! What a story!" said Nap.

"So, after you got married, you became an American citizen?"

"Yeah, as soon as I could. It was extraordinary to hear you talk about your wife the way you did, feeling her, the personification of love, inside of you, the love of God, sustaining you, giving you the strength to cope with fear. Hearing you talk that way inspired me. It really did. It gave me the courage to do what I just did."

"What the fuck is going on?"

Tiny suddenly popped up in the checkpoint, noticed the Chinese soldier and pointed his rifle at him. The fright in both of them became obvious.

"Point your fuckin rifle away from him, Sarge; he's surrendered. He's a prisoner of war."

"I can see what the fuck he is! He's a slanty-eyed fuckin commie!"

"He ain't a fuckin commie. He's a Catholic."

"A fuckin Catholic! Are you fuckin guys crazy? You can see he's a fuckin chink!"

"Some fuckin chinks, as you refer to us, even believe that you and I were created by the same God, although it may not be expedient for you to affiliate yourself with any of us, or with any Catholic either."

"I know a fuckin commie when I see one!"

"He ain't a fuckin commie, I told you. He don't want to fight us. He's been to the states. He even has a family there, and he surrendered so he can go back to them."

"Them's the worst fuckin kind of commies. We treat them decent, and they turn around and stab us in the fuckin back. Them fuckin red bastards been in the states and learn their fuckin propaganda shit for their loudspeakers."

"I must admit you're right. I'm guilty of that."

"That was you on the loudspeaker?" Nap said.

"Mea culpa. Mea maxima culpa. That was I, doing what I could to survive, just like anybody else. I did that to get here."

"Wow! The brass is going to be happy that you surrendered to us!" said Nap.

Dante asked, "What is your rank, sir?"

"Major. Major Li at your service."

Dante, standing up, saluted him and said, "I'm honored to meet you, sir!"

"Why the fuck are you saluting a fuckin chink?"

The major stood up.

"I doubt," he said to Tiny, "you would ever understand." And to Dante he said, "The honor is mine." And he saluted Dante.

"You fuckin guys are crazy! Move your slimy fuckin ass up the fuckin trench. I'm takin you in."

"Sacred Heart of Jesus!"

"Shut your fuckin mouth! You have no fuckin rights talkin like that, you mother fuckin chink commie!"

The major was looking at Dante, pleading, "I don't want to go alone with him."

Dante looked at Nap.

"We're all going in together," Nap said.

"I'm taking the mother fucker. I can handle him."

"Dante, you can lead the way to the checkpoint. Major Li, you follow Dante. I'll be right behind you."

"Dante? Are you Italian?"

"Dante Valentino."

"I was named after an Italian. Francis of Assissi."

As Dante started up the trench, the Chinese officer said to Tiny, "I notice your display of the rosary beads, and I know you wear it as a decoration, but Catholics, such as myself, are embarrassed and offended by your blatant hatred because it is so unworthy of *any* religion. I know that fear blinds us. I've been guilty of reacting to my fears, too, so I shouldn't be judging you, but please try to remember that when people see your beads, hanging from your neck like that, they mistake you for Catholic, and they judge all Catholics through your speech and actions."

10

Dante had slept a few hours in the morning. The night on the listening post had now seemed like a dream; almost like a nightmare.

"You're finally awake," said Nap as he entered the bunker.

"Yeah, I'm awake, but for a second I had a feeling I was on the listening post, still, and that I was waking up from it, feeling, well, relieved, I guess. Where are the guys?"

"Outside, enjoying the sun. We have coffee this morning, nice hot coffee, if you want some. And we'll be having hot chow for supper. They even brought supplies during the night. And guess what. They brought you, not one, but two love letters."

He dropped them on Dante's chest.

Dante sat up, his feet on the ground, and opened the envelope. A photograph was enclosed.

"A photo of my wife and my baby daughter. Have I ever shown you a picture of them?"

"No," Nap said as he sat in the other lower bunk. He took the photo as Dante handed it to him, looked at it, and said, "Wow, she's beautiful! But she looks, well, dark."

Dante didn't answer. He had begun reading her letter. As soon as he finished it, he eagerly opened the other letter, and he read it. When he finished it, he smiled at Nap and said, "She's a mulatto, half Negro and half Italian. Her mother was born in Italy."

Nap stared at him.

"You told Tiny you were only half wop. Remember?"

"Yeah, of course I remember." Dante took the photo, inserted it into the envelope, and he put it into his backpack. "That's when I asked him why he thought I was Catholic. I don't think I ever told him I am."

"He knows you are, but he had a hard time believing that the Italian mayor of New York was a Jew, and that the Chinese officer is Catholic. Even I was surprised by that. I mean, that he's Catholic. The Chinese major. You can't always tell just by looking at people."

"And now you want to know what my other half is?"

"Well, yeah, I'm curious."

"My father, of course, was born in Italy, in Abruzzo."

"No shit! So was mine."

"How'd you get the name Napolitano?"

"I don't know. Do you know where in Abruzzo?"

"It's a small village near Chieti."

"My father came from a small village near Chieti!"

"Have you ever been there?"

"No. Have you? In Italy, I mean."

"No, not yet, but I own a little farm there that my grandparents gave me. I would have been there this summer if I didn't have to come here."

"Wow! That's really something. Would you have taken your wife?"

"Of course!"

"Well, I mean, will they accept her?"

"I know what you mean. They have to, don't they? I mean, she's family."

"Yeah, but you know how some people are."

"I know. And under the skin, we're all the same. We all belong to the same race."

"Well, I don't know. I think a lot of colored people are just as prejudiced as a lot of white people."

"What did I just finish saying? Do you expect us to be better than white people? Why do you hold us up to a higher standard?"

"I don't know! I never thought of that!"

"Besides, I don't accept the different species that man has invented. I mean, where can we draw the lines between white and black and red and yellow? I've read somewhere that the Ethiopians are really white, not black, that they only look black. According to whom? Who decides? No reputable scientist will even talk about the various races of man. We don't have any scientific knowledge of various races. My father is Italian, but he's much darker than my mother. My mother, who looks white, has an ancestor who was an escaped black slave from Louisiana."

"Wow! No shit! Then that makes you, well, not all Italian, but you're an all American."

"So is my wife. Her mother is Italian, born in Italy. Her father, born in Canada, is the son of runaway slaves, too."

"Sounds like you come from an interesting family, but don't you run into, you know, problems with the rest of society?"

"Yeah, my mother didn't want me to marry my wife, because although she loves my wife, as a decent woman, she was afraid for us, for how people would react."

"She was speaking from experience, probably."

"That's true. My mother and father really loved each other, and they had a great marriage, but they had problems with racists."

"I know of a guy in my hometown whose father is Italian and his mother, I think, is Puerto Rican, and all his life he keeps getting beat up, because he's, you know, mixed. He has a beautiful sister, too, who I thought of dating, but, you know, a lot of people don't think the races should mix because their kids suffer for it."

"Yeah, that's another reason my mother was afraid for us."

"You don't think she's right?"

"Do you?"

"Well, I think she has a point. It's something to think about."

"How can any Catholic think that way and still be Catholic?"

"What do you mean?"

"Well, didn't Jesus say that the greatest commandment was to love others as you love yourself?"

"Yeah, but that doesn't mean if you don't marry someone, you don't love that person."

"Are you saying that just because you love someone doesn't mean you should marry that person?"

"No, that's not what I said, but, well, yeah. That depends on the circumstances."

"Suppose your sister wants to get married, because she's so much in love with some guy, but your father tells her not to marry him, because he's not wealthy enough."

Nap grinned.

"That wasn't my father; that was my mother."

"So, it's okay to love him if he's not wealthy, but only up to a point. Don't love him enough to marry him."

"Okay, I get your point. I never thought of it that way. But your mother has a point, too. We have to live with other people, and not everybody is Catholic."

"And not every Catholic is Catholic."

"It's interesting talking with you, but let's go get some coffee."

Dante grabbed his helmet and his rifle and he followed Nap through the trench.

The sun was shining and others were casually strolling through the trenches.

They came to the fork, followed it up the hill to the top, and went down the reverse slope. On a dirt road, near the platoon command post, was a large pot that had been filled with hot coffee. Dante and Nap refilled their canteens with water, held their tin cups out while someone poured hot coffee into them, added powdered milk and sugar, walked away and sat upon some rocks and soaked up the sun while they drank their coffee.

After a little while, a tank climbed up the road, went past them, and climbed up a steep road to the top of the hill, to a level ground and stopped. Its big gun raised a little, and a round went off. The tank backed down the road, behind the slope, and stopped.

Nap said, "Did you see that?"

"Yeah. What are they doing?"

"They fired a fuckin round, and then they got behind the slope, because the Chinese are going to fire back."

Less than fifteen seconds later, the enemy artillery fired back six rounds.

The tank climbed to the top of the hill again, stopped, fired another round, and retreated again. This time the Chinese fired back with at least a dozen rounds.

Nap quickly went into the command post, told Wells what the tank had done, and Wells called the captain and reported it.

Just as the tank reached the top of the hill, Nap and Dante saw Rossi waving at the tank. A tanker came out of the hatch and spoke with the company commander. Not only did the tank retreat behind the slope, it turned around and went past Nap and Dante, and disappeared down the road.

Nap said that, apparently, the tankers were trying to zero in on an enemy position in case of an attack. An observer from a distant bunker would report where the rounds had landed.

On their way back to their bunkers, Nap and Dante saw fewer soldiers in the trenches. They had taken shelter inside of the bunkers. When Dante arrived at his bunker, Ahn and Chico were sitting inside.

Dante wrote a letter to Rose, telling her he was happy, because he had received the photo. Then he lay on the bunk, closed his eyes, and slept for an hour or so.

He was standing in the trench and was reading *Brave New World* when Nap came by again and stopped to talk with him.

They heard a whistle in the distance followed by an explosion, and they continued talking. A few moments later there was another whistle and an explosion not far behind them, just below the crest of the hill, and Nap said, "That was too close. We'd better go inside."

As he entered the bunker, Dante placed the book on the trench and followed him inside. Just as he stepped into the bunker, a round landed, and dirt poured down into the entrance, spreading some on Dante.

Nap turned around, saw Dante standing behind him, and they both burst out into laughter. Ahn and Chico stared at them as though they thought: "Two crazy guys laughing in the face of danger!"

Dante said, "We're laughing to keep from crying."

Nap looked out the aperture as more rounds were dropping along the trench. A minute or so later, the explosions stopped.

Nap said, "I think they're zeroing in, preparing for an attack for later, maybe for tonight."

The Chinese officer had warned them to prepare for a major offensive before the truce would be finalized.

As Nap left the bunker, he cried out, "Wow! The book got hit. Pages are all over the place."

Dante stepped out into the trench. The book was scattered.

"Sorry, Huxley, I'll probably have to wait until I get home to read about your brave new world. I guess I got too careless bringing it with me into a war zone."

No more rounds dropped during the next hour as dusk began to descend.

Tiny came through and announced that hot chow was being served at the command post area.

"Nap," he said, "will get you when it's our turn to go."

A few minutes later, Nap came to get them. They followed him through the trench, up the fork, and down the reverse slope, to the command post area. They were served hot turkey, sweet potatoes, peas, and even cranberry sauce as though it was a special feast day. All Dante could think of was the Last Supper. He took his tray to a rocky area, found a boulder, sat on it, and stared at the food. He had no appetite.

It would be a shame, he thought, to throw such good food away, but he didn't even want to look at it. He felt that if he would force himself to eat it, he wouldn't be able to keep it down. He looked at the others. No one else was eating. All of the third squad was there and some of the rest of the platoon. No one was even talking.

Someone stood up and walked away without eating. Others began to follow him.

Dante stood up, got into the small line, and, as the soldier in front of him did, he emptied his tray into the waste barrel. One of the cooks, he noticed, was looking at them, watching them as they dumped the food.

Dante didn't even stay to have coffee. Neither did Ahn, nor Chico who followed him back to the bunker.

A few minutes later, Nap entered.

"How you guys doing?"

Dante asked, "Did you eat anything?"

"No, but I tried. I know how you feel. Everybody feels the same way. We're all thinking the same thing, but nobody wants to say anything, because, somehow, that makes it sound more real. I don't think anyone can really prepare for an attack no matter how much experience you have, but try to remember that when the rounds are coming in, the Chinese won't be coming in, not until their artillery lifts. I'll be checking on you guys."

Almost as soon as he left, Dante could hear the artillery whistling over him and to the sides of him and exploding all around him. He was standing in the middle of the bunker. From the flashes of the artillery explosions, he could see Chico looking out the aperture. To the right of him was Ahn, but Ahn didn't seem to be looking out; he seemed to be using the bunker for cover.

"You see anything, Chico?"

"No. Nada."

A flare lit the area.

Quickly, Dante stepped up to the middle of the aperture, between Chico and Ahn, and looked out. He could see no one in the valley.

"Nada!" he cried out.

There was sporadic rifle fire from the bunkers, but nothing more.

The artillery barrage continued as the flare burnt out.

"We wait," said Ahn.

"Yes," answered Dante, "we wait."

Even if the Chinese had started running across the valley immediately after the flare had died out, it would take them another minute to reach the barbed wire at the foot of the hill. The barrage was undoubtedly breaking up the wire, but there was still enough barbed wire to slow them down.

Dante was listening to the enemy artillery pounding them, but as long as it was coming in, their soldiers were not. He was waiting to hear the artillery lift from them, but it seemed to be taking forever. At this rate, he thought, the Chinese could wait all night before attacking with troops, eventually knocking out the bunkers with artillery.

Their most vulnerable spot, he thought, was at the listening post. When the Chinese would reach the listening post, that's when the artillery would probably lift.

Just when that thought had occurred to him, someone was running through the trench and was yelling: "Chinks in the valley! Chinks in the valley!"

The barrage was lifting, falling behind them, nearer to the crest of the hill to stop reinforcements, he thought.

"Why don't we send up another flare or turn on the spotlight?"

A flare suddenly went up.

"Look at them!"

The enemy soldiers hadn't even reached the bottom of the hill yet. The first wave must have been at least fifty yards away, and they seemed to be running as fast as they could just to get to the bottom of the hill where they could, at least, hug the ground. As soon as the flare had gone up, some of them had hit the ground. The spectacle seemed unreal. The whole second platoon, except them, seemed to start shooting at them.

"Okay?" Chico asked Dante.

"Sí!"

Ahn, the veteran, had already put his rifle on the aperture and had started firing it as Chico placed his rifle on the aperture, and as Dante placed his rifle in position, he heard artillery whistling over them. It was going out. Dante was fascinated. It was unbelievable to think that human beings had actually been sent out like that to be slaughtered. The valley floor seemed to be covered completely with thousands of soldiers. The rounds were dropping randomly, making the ground erupt and killing several at one time. And the soldiers leading the charge were being picked off. Dante took aim, squeezing the trigger, and quickly a clip ejected. He couldn't seem to be firing fast enough, but he could see he was hitting his targets. There seemed to be so many that it seemed enough of them could eventually reach the trenches. But they had been stopped before, Rossi had said. "They're not coming up here!" He said out loud.

The flare died out. The only way to tell where they were was from the flash of their weapons but Dante didn't think any of them had yet reached the bottom of the slope.

"Come on! Send up another flare!"

He looked through the sight of his rifle and as soon as he saw a flash of light, he squeezed the trigger.

"I think I got him," he muttered.

The flashes seemed to be coming from automatic weapons, probably from burp guns, he thought.

Another flare went up.

"They're at the bottom of the hill!"

Chico was shooting at them.

"Ahn, the grenades!"

As Ahn stood at the entrance, Dante went into the trench and heaved the first grenade. Ahn tossed him another grenade, and he heaved it.

Chico turned around and yelled, "Ah, bueno! Number fuckin one!"

Dante heaved one grenade after another. When the flare died out, he went into the bunker and looked out of the aperture."

"Wow!"

Only one machine gun bullet out of six, he had been told, was incandescent, but the machine guns had formed a wall of fire that seemed impossible to penetrate, and small arms fire was pouring out incessantly while the ground everywhere in the valley was erupting.

Imagine, thought Dante, actually being down there! Human beings slaughtering human beings!

Man is a rational animal!

And yet, to him, they were monsters below, thousands of them, who existed only to annihilate him. And he had to stop them.

Another flare shot up.

"They're running away!"

They were all running away. Some of them at the bottom of the hill had left, and as far as Dante could see, almost to the other end of the valley, to their own trenches, they were being shot down as they were trying to retreat.

Almost as soon as the flare died, another shot up.

Dante wished he had binoculars. Many soldiers were still on the ground. He wanted to see if they were dead or alive. Perhaps many of them were wounded and had been left behind, but not one enemy soldier seemed to be advancing towards them.

"I think we stopped them!"

"Number fuckin one!" Chico grinned.

Ahn laughed.

"For now," said Dante as he noticed that the incoming rounds had stopped.

The machine guns stopped firing, and as the flare died, the outgoing rounds and the small arms fire ceased, and silent darkness descended.

The three of them sat on the bunks and did not speak. Dante knew that each of them was praying silently, thanking God to be still alive and hoping to survive not only this night, but to live long enough to return home to their loved ones. And yet, he thought, history, the story of mankind, the story of human beings slaughtering other human beings, the story that so many had experienced, and yet, instead of seeing war as evil, mankind has glorified it and has even celebrated it as a standard of greatness, especially, he thought, by those who have never experienced it. Even he has not yet experienced it. He had only been a brief witness to those below him, who were trying to kill him, to kill him in the name of patriotism to their own country. Had the Chinese officer, who had fought to defend his country in the world war, been unpatriotic to his own country? Our schools, perhaps schools everywhere in the world, have glorified war in the name of patriotism, and even our religions have glorified it, in spite of our religious leaders such as Jesus. And now, many Americans are still reluctant to end the war, to make it the only war we have not won.

Nap entered.

"Just checking to see how you're doing."

"We're okay."

"You and Chico are officially combat vets now."

"We didn't do much."

"I saw somebody firing out this aperture. And who was tossing the grenades?"

"I was."

"Well, you stopped quite a few. We all did well tonight."

"So far."

"You're right. So far. But I don't think they'll hit us again, not until morning, anyway. And I'll be surprised if they hit in the morning."

"Why?"

"They had a lot of casualties. We put out a lot of firepower. They'll think twice before they attack us again."

"I was really impressed by the firepower. Who decides when to open fire and to stop fire? Do you know?"

"Usually the leader of the fourth squad, because he controls the machine guns, but right now, Tiny is handling the check point, and he has a good view of things, so he's calling it. Anyway, most guys know when to fire when their lives depend on it."

"There must be a lot of wounded Chinese soldiers down there."

"Yeah, of course. The Chinese don't usually leave them behind, but they were under such a barrage that they had no choice. They had to bug out quick to save their own asses, but in the morning they'll be back to get them."

"How can they do that?"

"What do you mean?"

"Won't we shoot them?"

"Of course not! Not while they're getting their dead and wounded."

"What!" He stared at Nap, who was serious. "By morning, most of the wounded will be dead. Why don't they pick them up now?"

"If they come back now, we'll shoot them. We've got patrols now, down there, making sure there are no chinks in the valley. If there are, they could end up in a firefight. In the morning, unless one side or the other decides to attack, we let them pick up their dead and wounded, and they let us pick up our dead and wounded."

Dante shook his head and said, "I can't believe how stupid this whole situation is! How can we be such intelligent creatures and so stupid at the same time?"

"Hey, as Tiny says, war is a fuckin big game played with real people who don't make the fuckin rules."

"I wonder if most people understand what war really is."

"Of course not. If they did, none of us would be here. We don't understand the Chinese, and I doubt if they understand us, but I'll tell you one thing; they have a lot more respect for the dead than we Americans do."

After a while, before Nap left, he told them to try to rest if they could, because the Chinese would not attack until an hour or so before dawn, and even then it would probably be only to harass them, but they should expect heavy artillery fire.

As Nap had predicted, before dawn a voice in the trenches cried out, "Chinks in the valley!"

A few seconds later, the Chinese artillery began pounding them again, but this time, as Nap had not predicted, the incoming rounds lifted much earlier, and as a flare lit up the valley, the Chinese had already reached the barbed wire and had begun firing at the bunkers, and the platoon retaliated. The crossfire from the machines guns set up a wall of fire, and the outgoing artillery and mortar rounds were pounding the valley.

As Chico fired his rifle from the aperture, Dante was heaving grenades from the trench.

When the incoming rounds stopped, and another flair lit up the area, the Chinese had begun retreating again, and the machine guns and small arms began to spray the valley.

When the flair went out, the firing continued until another flare revealed that the enemy had left the area.

Nap entered the bunker again.

"Everybody all right?"

"Fine," Dante answered. "You think that's it for tonight, or for this morning?"

"I think so. Stay put until it's light. I'm going to check the rest of the squad."

As they sat on their bunks and waited for daybreak, several men passed by. They were carrying stretchers. They were going towards the checkpoint. Dante stepped into the trench. As the darkness lifted, the valley seemed to become thick with fog.

Nap appeared again. He had just come from the checkpoint.

"Not a single casualty in our squad, but the rest of the company wasn't quite so lucky."

"The fog in the valley is awfully thick."

"That's not fog; it's a smoke screen. The Chinese are picking up their dead and wounded, like I told you they would. You don't have to worry about them. Now we have to check the area around the listening post. Why don't you come with me? Tell Ahn and Chico to stay here and relax and not fire if they happen to see or hear any Chinese moving around down there."

Dante did tell them, but Ahn didn't have to be told not to shoot at the Chinese while they were attending the dead and wounded. Chico, however, was astonished. He said he did not understand.

Dante followed Nap through the trench. It was daybreak, but partially cloudy. Tiny was alone at the checkpoint. Nap told him he was going to check out the area with Dante.

"Just the fuckin two of you?"

Nap went into the machine gun bunker and told them to cover him, just in case.

Dante followed him through the trench, down the finger of the hill, to the listening post, where they stepped up to the ground. Nap opened the gates, and as they got to the other side of the barbed wire, he closed the back gate. They were in no-man's land. Nap checked the damage from the shelling. "Not enough to be concerned about," he said.

"Who put up the smoke screen?" Dante asked.

"They did."

"We could meet them here then."

"We could hear them. They're not very quiet. Sometimes they even yell at each other. And they can hear us talking, too."

"Why bother with the smoke screen then?"

"I don't know. Maybe they don't want to see us. Maybe it makes them feel safer if they can't see us. If you were the enemy, would you want to see someone like Tiny staring at you?"

"Hell no!"

Nap grinned at him and said, "Some of them Mongolians are big bastards!"

"What would you do if you suddenly saw some?"

"Just wave and say good morning."

They were walking along flat ground, not far from the barbed wire.

"Listen," Nap said suddenly. "You can hear them talking now. They've already been here and picked up their dead and wounded. Let's go back."

"How do we find our way back in this smoke?"

"Just stay close to the barbed wire. Follow me."

When they returned to their bunkers, the sun was shining, and the clouds were wispy. And the smoke screen in the valley had lasted for almost two hours that morning.

During the rest of the day it was quiet. They wrote letters, and they talked with each other. And, of course, though they tried to occupy their minds, and were reluctant to even mention it, they were dreading another night.

There was no hot food for supper. They had rations, but no one complained, not even the smokers. They each had ten cigarettes with their rations, even those who did not smoke, so they shared their cigarettes.

Darkness came again, and they waited. And waited. And after a long wait, some of them got out of their bunkers and walked along the trenches, and stopped, and visited others. Dante, too, left the bunker, and he went out to the trench where he felt a little breeze. To be back in New Hampshire now, sitting on the front porch with Rose and the baby! Although at this time, he thought, it was not yet noon in Cascade, more than a half day behind them.

He went into the next bunker where the Browning automatic rifle was set on the aperture. The three men inside were silent, waiting intensely for the attack to begin. Dante decided to see Nap at the next bunker. He was with two others who had both arrived in Korea after Dante had. One was big, but gentle, with a soft voice. He looked liked Joe Louis. He was from rural Mississippi. He was called Barlow. The other one was shorter and slimmer, who was called Eddie. He was from Harlem.

When Dante had first met him, he had said his wife, Rose, was now living in Harlem.

"You must mean *East* Harlem," Eddie had said. "No, not far from St. Luke's Hospital. Her father is a doctor who operates a clinic there." Eddie said, "You don't mean the clinic for colored people?" And Dante said, "I thought it was for everybody." And Eddie said, "Yeah, but there's one in Harlem that my mother goes to." Dante said, "They're the only two doctors there, unless another was added recently. So, your mother must know my wife's father." "Doctor Jourdan?" "That's him! That's her father. So, you know him!" Eddie said, "Yeah! I do! I know who he is. But that means, well, that means, she's colored." "Yeah, I guess so. We both are, and we're both Italian, too." Finally, Dante had opened his wallet to show Eddie a picture of her. "Yeah, she sure is colored, but I've never seen her before. I would have remembered *her*. She's beautiful."

When Dante entered the bunker, Nap was looking out the aperture. Barlow was sitting on a bunk, and Eddie was standing near the entrance. Eddie was saying, "Man, when I get back home, *if* I ever make it back, I would never send anybody to a mother fuckin place like this! And I thought my neighborhood was so fuckin bad!"

"We used to brag about the gang warfare in my city," said Nap, but we never killed anyone."

"Do you think Brockton is as poor as Harlem?" asked Dante.

"I don't know. I've never been to Harlem."

"Brockton?" asked Eddie. "The same Brockton that the heavy-weight champ is from?"

"Yeah, the same neighborhood, actually."

"Do you know Rocky Marciano?"

"I've seen him a few times, but I don't know him personally. We went to the same high school, but he's a little older than me. My father and his father, though, both know each other. They both came from the same place in Italy, the same place that Dante's father came from."

The ground shook as a round exploded, and Dante felt the debris falling on him.

"Everybody okay?" Nap cried out.

Rounds were whistling around them, and the earth trembled.

"I'm okay!" Dante answered.

"Me, too!" Barlow and Eddie yelled out.

"I've got to get back!" yelled Dante.

He dashed back to his bunker as artillery fire filled the sky and the earth was erupting.

Both Chico and Ahn were near the aperture trying to see whatever they could from the flashes of the explosions. From the bottom of the hill was a long stretch of flashes from burp guns, and from the bunkers poured the small arms fire into the wall of fire from the machine guns, but there wasn't any artillery fire going out.

Chico put his rifle on the aperture.

"Okay, Chico. Bueno! Ahn, the grenades!"

Finally, a flare lit up the valley.

The Chinese, thought Dante, seemed to be attacking with more forces on the left flank, which looked like an endless sea of troops in the open valley. He suddenly became aware that there had been no warnings of "chinks in the valley" as there had been in the previous attacks. The warnings had come from the right flank, but this time the Chinese had advanced, undetected, from the opening in the valley.

Just before he was about to go into the trench to toss grenades into the bottom of the hill, an artillery shell exploded a short distance behind them, and another shell exploded below the aperture. At the same time, debris came in from the entrance and from the aperture.

"Chico, como estas?"

"Number fuckin one!" he cried out, firing his rifle.

"No grenades now," Ahn said. "We wait."

As the three of them were firing their rifles, Dante thought he heard some rounds going out, and then he saw flashes of lights from explosions in the valley floor.

A few moments later, the incoming rounds lifted.

"Okay, Ahn! Now the grenades!"

Another flare lit up the valley again.

The three of them looked out.

Artillery and mortars were pounding the valley so hard, and the small arms fire continued, having formed such an impregnable firewall that the three of them had become almost hypnotized by the awesome display of human annihilation.

So this, thought Dante, is war. And, at any moment, the tables could be turned. This was the biggest fucking game of all, as Tiny had said. This is what we, the people, glorify and praise. This is what makes any country great. The country that could cause the greatest devastation becomes the greatest country in the world!

Ahn said, "The grenades! Now?"

Dante nodded. He grabbed a grenade, stepped into the trench, pulled out the pin, and heaved it.

Again, after devastating losses, the Chinese retreated.

About half of the night had passed. Would they attack again before morning?

The three of them remained in the bunker for the rest of the night. Just before dawn, they waited for another attack, but everything was quiet, and finally the darkness seemed to be ending, and with daylight approaching, they began to feel grateful that they had survived another night. And they lay on their bunks and closed their eyes, and they were able to relax and to succumb to the desire to sleep.

Dante had slept for about two hours. While Chico and Ahn were sleeping, he looked out the aperture. A smoke screen was covering the valley. It was obvious that the Chinese were carrying away their casualties. He decided to check on the rest of the third squad. Their bunker, he thought, needed to be reinforced. He could actually see daylight through a hole at the top of the bunker. He went into the trench. He noticed that where the trenches had been hit, dirt had fallen into it. He went into the next bunker. The three of them were sleeping. He went into Nap's bunker. Nap was out, checking on the rest of the squad, said Eddy, who was sitting on his bunk and smoking a cigarette. Barlow was lying in the bunk over him.

Eddie said, "I didn't know Nap was from the same neighborhood as Rocky Marciano."

"To tell you the truth, I didn't know either. It's a small world, as they say. I knew that Nap's father and my father had come from the same area in Italy, but I never knew that Rocky Marciano's father had been from the same place. Yep, it's a small world alright."

"I have a buddy in the first squad who's from Camden, New Jersey, who lives near Jersey Joe Wolcott. And here's Nap who lives near Marciano, and the two boxers fought each other twice for the heavyweight championship."

"And you meet me from New Hampshire, and although you never knew me, you know my wife's father. Our paths could have crossed before, several times, and we never even knew."

"Yeah. That's strange."

"If we could make a ball the size of a building, and put one ant at each end and trace their movements, you can imagine how their lives crisscross. It's the same with any two people on this earth. Like the Chinese officer, our lives could have crossed with his before. It's really a small world, and like it or not, the fact is, we are all part of one organism."

"Yeah, that's true, I guess."

"And you've probably crossed paths with my wife's brother hundreds of times. He has been studying in the Vatican, although he's back home now, in Harlem, on vacation, after having been ordained as a priest."

"A priest?"

"You're not Catholic, are you?"

"Me? Fuck no! I mean, no, I'm not."

"You mean, you're not like, well, like Sarg. You don't pray like he does."

"Are you fuckin serious?"

"Naw, I'm not. But I'm serious about human relationships. Two people meet. Any two people, and although they think they have nothing in common, when they get to know each other, they'll discover they have quite a bit in common."

"Any two people," Eddie murmured. "Like you and me, who seem to have nothing in common. We could have passed each other on a street in Harlem. And if we had, you would have meant nothing to me. You don't even look colored; you look, well, almost white, but here we are, in the middle of this mother fuckin shithole, on the same side, trying to protect each other. But, for you, for someone like you, when someone like Marciano fights Walcott, who do you want to win, and why?"

Dante stared at him.

"Being here, a boxing match, even a big one like that, doesn't seem important enough for me to consider whom I'd want as a winner. Does a boxing match really seem that important to you now, while we're here?"

Eddie shrugged, and he said, "No, not really. I understand what you're saying."

"If we had the luxury to indulge in mundane issues, yeah, I'd probably pick the winners I'd want, as I did when I was a kid. My favorite baseball players, I admit, were not Ted Williams or even Babe Ruth; they were Joe Di Maggio, and Roy Campanella, and Jackie Robinson. And in boxing, my favorite was Joe Louis, and, yeah, I like both Rocky Marciano and Jersey Joe Wolcott, and for the obvious reasons. I identify more with them. But what's wrong with that? Especially for a kid. A kid should have heroes to emulate, especially a kid who's been subjected to prejudice. So, don't worry about it. The problem is not so much whom you love more, the problem is whom you hate more, and why. So, if you love everyone more than you love me, don't worry about it, but if you hate me," he said, grinning at Eddie, "because I'm part honkie, then you've got a problem."

"Hey, man, I don't hate you! I could never hate someone like you."

"I know that. Because you know me a little now. I was just using that as an illustration. A woman who saw me with my wife in Harlem, said to my wife that she was betraying her own people, and my wife said, 'My own people? Who are my own people?' And the woman said, 'We are.' My wife said, 'I don't even know you, but I know my own husband.' My brother and my wife's brother went to high school together. Do you know what the other kids called them? Nigger wops!"

"Oh, man! Them mother fuckers!"

"Well, I wouldn't go so far as to call them that."

Nap entered the bunker. Again, he said, there were no casualties in the third squad, but the rest of the platoon, he had heard, had lost seven, four of which had died already.

"I'm going to go check them out. Do you want to come with me?" he asked Dante.

"I'm right behind you."

He followed Nap through the trench. Quickly they came to the fork, which had been hit. They had to climb over the dirt that covered much of the trench on their way to the first bunker of the second squad.

"Oh, shit!" Nap cried out as he looked inside the bunker.

The second squad leader was inside.

"I thought you were the stretcher bearers," he said. "The three of them are gone. An artillery shell must have come in through the aperture."

Where the aperture would have been, it was covered with sandbags, and below the sandbags, there was a hole big enough for anyone to crawl through. There were three dead bodies, sitting up, covered with sand, with blood, and with dollar bills. Money was scattered all over the inside of the bunker. Nobody even seemed to notice the money. At the top of the bunker was a hole big enough for the sunlight to enter.

Some men with stretchers arrived.

"Let's get out of here," said Nap, "to let these guys do their work."

Dante followed Nap through the trench. The rest of the second squad seemed fine, but the first squad leader said he had lost four men. Three had been wounded, and one had been killed. Dante asked him if he knew someone from Camden, New Jersey, who lived near Jersey Joe Walcott. "Ball, yeah. He was the one who got it."

When they got back to Nap's bunker, Dante told Eddie that Ball had been killed. Eddie cried out that he couldn't believe it, and he started shaking.

"You better believe it!" said Nap. "This is fuckin war! That's what happens. That's why we shouldn't get too fuckin chummy with each other. Compared to the Chinese, we've been pretty fuckin lucky so far! We ain't seen nothin yet!"

A little later, Korean civilians, who were too old to be in the army, entered the trench to dig it out more and to reinforce the bunkers. When Dante talked to Nap about it, saying they could have been spying for the Chinese, Nap said, "What can they tell the Chinese that they don't already know? Look up there. They can see everything that's going on. Let the gooks clear the trenches and fortify the bunkers. They do a good job. And they can use the money."

Shortly after the Korean civilians had left, smoke was filling the valley below.

"It may not mean anything much," Nap said, "but the machine guns are going to be spraying the valley every once in a while, just in case, so hold your fire for now. We're going to be sending out patrols."

Less than an hour later, voices cried out, "Chinks in the valley! Chinks in the valley!" And small arms fire broke out in the smoky valley. And artillery fire came in as fast it went out.

Dante could hear the explosions, and he could feel the earth trembling all around him, and he could see steady bursts of fire erupting throughout the valley. Whistles from the incoming rounds did not seem to be lifting, so Dante did not attempt to go into the trench to throw any grenades. The Chinese, he thought, would not come in under their own fire, and as their smoke screens became thinner, he could see that they had not been close enough yet to cut the wire. They were scrambling to retreat.

The wall of fire from the machines guns suddenly stopped as the bullets began to spray the whole valley, cutting down the fleeing enemy.

The Chinese exploded a couple of more smoke screens to protect the retreating soldiers, but it was too little too late. The Chinese had been exposed too long; the outgoing rounds of artillery were falling on them.

The incoming rounds finally stopped. But the outgoing artillery continued for a few more minutes. Then, suddenly, the day became quiet as the smoke lifted. And, Dante noticed, the sun was shining.

The three of them sat on the bunks and closed their eyes as though they were praying. And then they tried to let their minds go blank. There was nothing to say.

Everything was silent.

In spite of, and in contrast to the bright sun, there was a faint, sweet, nauseating smell of death lingering in the air. Not even the sunlight was enough to dispel the effects of the destruction of the natural world, and the three of them sat listlessly, not wanting to move as their leaders were busy inspecting the damages.

Although the enemy had not even reached the barbed wire, and the allied nations had won another battle in which, according to their leaders, they had admirably decimated the communist forces, the barbed wire had been damaged enough by the artillery shells that it should be reinforced before another attack. And several more bunkers had been destroyed, and, although the casualties were light among the allied forces compared to the casualties of the offensive forces, how much more damage could the defenders take? The damage had been inflicted by the artillery of the Chinese.

"Even I can see that!" Dante said to Captain Rossi. "Don't we have superiority over their air force? Can't our air force damage their artillery enough during the daytime so that they won't attack during the day?"

"I don't see why not," Rossi answered. And he went away.

About an hour later, in the middle of the afternoon, Captain Rossi returned. He had returned with engineers who were carrying rolls of barbed wire. They had entered the trench, stopped, and waited. Dante thought they were waiting for smoke screens.

Tiny said, "If we put up fuckin smoke screens now, they'll pound the fuckin hell out of us."

They waited.

They heard fighter planes approaching from the west. The planes seemed to be flying from the bright sun, so that the troops on the ground, and the Chinese, had to be looking up into the sun to see them. The planes were high, until they were over the Thai positions. There were six navy jet fighters from an aircraft carrier off the coast of Inchon, Captain Rossi said. The first plane took a nosedive as anti-aircraft guns fired at it, and then, as it got closer to the ground, it dropped a bomb as it began to climb again. The bomb exploded, and fire, like fire from a flamethrower, shot a long distance along the ground.

The plane had dropped napalm.

Captain Rossi suddenly stood up on the trench and put his binoculars to his eyes.

Tiny and Nap also stood up on the trench.

"What are you guys doing?" Dante asked.

"Didn't you see what the fuck they dropped?" Tiny asked him. "That's fuckin napalm! Don't you know what the fuck napalm is?"

"Of course!"

Nap said, "If somebody was dropping that stuff on you, wouldn't you try to get the fuck out of there? Every chink there is running like hell to go as deep into that fuckin mountain as they can. They're not going to stay out to fire at us. And their field artillery is running inside to save their asses, too. They ain't going to bother us, not with those jets flying over them."

The rest of the platoon climbed out of the trench and stood on top of it, and the engineers lowered the barbed wire to the trench and also stood on the trench as though they were an audience watching a free show.

As the next plane descended, the anti-aircraft fired a few shots and stopped, and as the plane dropped a bomb, it climbed again. This time the napalm dropped into the trench at the lower part of the mountain. The next plane followed the same route except this time, it pulled up a little quicker and dropped the napalm higher up on the trench. No anti-aircraft had even made an attempt to shoot it down.

The first airplane, according to Captain Rossi, had flown to the back of the mountain and had dropped napalm, he thought, on the field artillery, and then the plane was circling back to get to the rear of the formation.

"Okay, engineers," Rossi yelled, using his right hand and point-ing down the trench, "go lay down the barbed wire! You've got one hour!"

"Okay, third squad," yelled Tiny, "let's show them where to go!"

Tiny led the way through the trench on the way to the listening post. There were two others behind Tiny, then Ahn, Dante and Chico. Behind Chico was Henderson with the Browning automatic rifle, two others, then there were Barlow, Eddie, and Nap. Following Nap were four engineers. Two each were carrying a heavy roll of barbed wire with a round stick used as a handle through the middle of it. They went past the listening post and through the gates of barbed wire.

Tiny assigned Nap and Henderson and two of the engineers to reinforce the barbed wire at the gate and to roll the rest of it in front of the first two bunkers.

"And we'll start at the other fuckin end, at the end of the second squad. And we'll meet in the middle."

Dante and the others followed Tiny until they came to the second squad area.

From the bottom of the slope, Dante looked up at the fairly steep incline covered with barbed wire, and under the barbed wire, the ground was covered with mines, and he tried to imagine what it would be like to have to attack the positions. It was too high to throw grenades into the bunkers. They'd have to use grenade launchers, or try to hit the bunkers with artillery and mortars.

As the two engineers laid down more barbed wire, Dante looked up and watched the planes drop more napalm on the Chinese positions, and he wondered where the Chinese air force was. Why hadn't they been called out? He asked Tiny.

"How the fuck should I know? They ain't got the fuckin air force we got."

"Then why in hell don't we use our air force when they attack us?"

"They don't usually attack during the fuckin day."

"Well, even if they attack us at night, we can light up the area, and planes can drop napalm on them."

"Good fuckin question! I don't know!"

When they met Nap, most of the barbed wire had been used.

"Okay, that's pretty fuckin good," said Tiny. "I bet you fuckin engineers will be pretty fuckin glad to get the fuck out of here now."

Nap said, "I don't see the jets, and I don't hear them."

They listened.

"Oh, shit!" yelled Tiny. "Let's get the fuck out of here! Back to the fuckin listening post! Nap, lead the way!"

Tiny was making sure everyone else was running out in front of him.

If the jets had left, Dante wondered, why hadn't anyone thought of protecting them with a smoke screen? The Chinese would have pounded them with artillery, anyway. That's true, but now, especially in this bright sunlight, they would become easy targets as soon as the Chinese would become aware that the jets had gone.

By the time Nap had reached the listening post, burp guns opened fire, spraying bullets into the ground covered by the barbed wire. Pieces of dirt were sprouting up all around them. And before they could reach the listening post, the two men in front of Tiny went down. Ahn and Dante had jumped into the listening post, and as Chico was about to leap into the listening post, he had somehow seen someone drop behind him. He turned around quickly, grabbed him, and dragged him down into the hole. And Tiny quickly grabbed the other one who had dropped to the ground, scooped him up, and carried him into the listening post.

"Are you okay?" Nap asked.

"Yeah, I think so."

"How the fuck could they have missed you!"

"God don't want me in fuckin heaven! Not yet. He wants me to put up with fuckin wops like you to punish me for my fuckin sins."

"You dumb fuckin pollack, let's get the fuck out of here!"

Explosions erupted on the other side of the barbed wire.

"Those are ours," Nap said. "Smoke screens."

"How bad are these fuckin guys hit?"

They were both alive and had, apparently, been shot in the legs.

With help, the two men stood up, and each one, leaning between two others, were taken up the finger of the hill through the trench. At the checkpoint, Tiny called for stretchers. And then he demanded to know why the fuckin jets had left so fuckin early. Rossi had been told that the jets had used up all their napalm, so they had left.

As the two wounded men had been taken away, incoming artillery fire began pouring down, and the rest of the third squad, with the four engineers, went into the bunkers.

"Great," said Nap, "now the Chinese can use the smoke screens we had set up."

But, directly in front of the bunkers, the smoke was not thick, so Dante hadn't expected them to attack again, not until dark, anyway.

Three of the engineers went into the bunker with Henderson, and the other one followed Dante into his.

"I don't think the Chinese are going to attack," Dante assured the engineer, "so they'll let up soon on the artillery. They're just harassing us because we dropped the napalm on them."

Less than two minutes later, one of his buddies popped his head in and said, "Do you want to get the fuck out of here, now?"

He looked at Dante as if to ask if he should take that chance.

"You're welcome to stay here until this blows over. It's probably safer in here than it is out there."

"The others have already left. Come on! Let's get the fuck out of here!"

Almost as soon as he had gone out of the bunker, a shell hit, and the explosion made the bunker shake, sending sand down on them. Dante quickly went into the trench. The engineer was face down in the trench and was groaning. The other one was standing and staring down at him.

Dante knelt down and asked, "Where do you hurt?"

The fallen soldier moaned, "My hips, and the back of my legs."

Dante could see blood oozing through the fatigues on the back of his thighs.

The other engineer knelt on the other side of him.

Ahn and Chico came out of the bunker.

As the rounds continued to fall around them, Dante said, "I think he's going to be number one." He pointed to the bunker. "It's okay, stay inside."

Ahn and Chico quickly returned to the bunker, and Dante asked, "Do you feel any pain in your stomach area?"

"No, just in my legs."

"Turn over, if you can."

He did.

The other engineer held his head up to keep it off the bottom of the trench.

Dante said, "We can try to carry you out of the trench, to the reverse slope, or your buddy can ran there to get a medic while we keep you in the bunker. What do you prefer?"

"The bunker."

"Go now," Dante said to the other engineer, "you pass two bunkers, and on your left the trench will take you to the reverse slope. Chico, ven aca!"

They carried the wounded soldier into the bunker and lay him face down on one of the lower bunks.

"I should have listened to you," he moaned.

"Are you kidding? Just think," Dante said to him, "as soon as it gets dark, you'll be on your way to the rear, inside of a hospital, lying on a nice, clean bed, and, if you get any luckier, you'll have pretty nurses to take good care of you. Hey, man, what more do you want? And it's all free. Socialized medicine, just like the Chinese are getting. And you'll even get paid, except you'll be sacrificing a dollar a day. But what the hell, the military doesn't want to over-burden the tax payers too much."

The wounded soldier was almost laughing.

"I feel better already just thinking about it."

"Where you're going, you won't be needing your carbine. Do you mind giving it to me?"

"Fuck no! I'll be glad to get rid of it. And I'll give you all the ammunition I've got. It's a lot lighter and fires a lot quicker than your rifle."

Dante held it up to show it to Ahn and Chico. They grinned. He took out the banana clip to show it to them, and he inserted it into the weapon again.

"It's nice and light," he said, "that's why all the officers carry these, and, of course, you guys."

"It's a lot easier to carry around and to work with them than with a rifle."

Just before the medics arrived, the shelling had stopped.

"I don't envy you fuckin guys in the infantry. I thought it was bad enough being in the engineers. I hope all you fuckin guys make it."

They lifted the engineer out of the bunk and placed him, face down, on the stretcher. The Quaker with the thick glasses told him he had a million dollar wound because, he said, by the time his wounds would heal, the war would probably be over.

On both sides, it had been a long, tiring day, thought Dante. Surely, the Chinese would not feel that they were in a position to attack again soon. Not tonight, he hoped. To defend against them was one thing. But for them to go on the offense, attacking with foot soldiers again before their artillery could do more damage, seemed crazy, especially after they had lost so many men. Maybe Tiny was right about the brass; they were willing to sacrifice so many of them to gain so little, using them as though they were merely pawns in a chess game. Was it cheaper to lose lives than to use up artillery shells?

That night, Ahn, Chico, and Eddie were assigned to the listening post. For both Chico and Eddie, it would be their first time.

Later, Tiny would tell Dante that Nap had volunteered to take Eddie's or Chico's place, because among the three of them, there was not enough experience, but Tiny had said no, definitely no, because it had been much too soon for Nap to go out to the listening post again, and that he, Tiny, had enough confidence in the three of them, especially in Ahn.

Just before darkness had set in, Nap entered the bunker while Eddie waited in the trench.

"Ahn," Nap said, putting a hand on Ahn's shoulder, "tonight, you number fuckin one! You take care of Chico and Eddie."

"You two," Ahn answered, grinning, and pointing two fingers at Nap, "number fuckin one! And you, Dante."

Dante, standing before him, touched the small, wooden icon, and said, "Buddha goes with you."

Ahn reached into the top pocket of his jacket, pulled out the photo of him with his wife and two children, held it up for Dante to see, smiled, and put it into his pocket again and patted it as though he were patting his heart.

"And love is with you."

Dante turned to Chico and said, "Vaya con Dios."

Chico reached into his top pocket also, showed Dante the photo of him and his family and said, "Love is with me, too."

Chico followed Ahn into the trench, and Eddie followed them.

12

"Chinks in the valley! Chinks in the valley!"

Dante was with Nap and Barlow when the crier was running through the trench with the warning.

Within a half hour after the three had arrived at the listening post, a patrol had passed though, and only a few minutes later, the patrol, on reconnaissance, had met enemy troops. As the patrol had begun to retreat, they had become engaged in a firefight with the Chinese.

Nap darted into the trench to intercept the crier.

"I'm from Easy Company. Our patrol got hit by the chinks!"

"Where's the rest of the fuckin patrol?"

"Fighting them off!"

As the crier ran off yelling, "Chinks in the valley!" a flare burst into the air.

Dante and Barlow joined Nap who said, "I'm going to the checkpoint."

As they followed Nap, they couldn't see anyone in the valley.

Before they reached the checkpoint, incoming rounds began to pour down on them, and Tiny screamed at them because there was no room left either in the checkpoint or in the machine gun bunker. Tiny told Nap to take cover in the empty bunker that had been occupied by the two soldiers that had been wounded earlier.

Dante and Barlow followed Nap into the empty bunker, and they sat inside while the incoming rounds continued to pour down.

Just as the flare burnt out, they heard four men in the trench. The men stopped between the checkpoint and the machine gun bunker. Nap said he was going out to check on the situation. He saw two wounded men being put on two stretchers. They were carried away, going past him. He ducked into the checkpoint. Tiny was alone.

Tiny told Nap that Ahn, Chico, and Eddie hadn't come in yet. There were ten men in the patrol. Two wounded had just been carried away. The two who had carried them to the checkpoint had gone back to the listening post to help the others. And Tiny had sent the first one, who had reported in, to warn the rest of the second platoon.

Nap asked, "Has there been much fighting at the listening post?"

"Not a fuckin lot, especially from the fuckin chinks."

"Then why the fuck don't we get as many as we can from the listening post to here where it's a little safer at least?"

The incoming rounds were pounding them as steadily as before, but there were no indications that their infantry would attack them as another flare lit up the area.

"I fuckin agree, but how the fuck we going to do that?"

"I'll go down there and tell them to come in."

"Like fuck you will!"

Suddenly Nap bolted out and went running down the trench, where, under the flare, he was exposed to everyone.

Tiny rushed into the machine gun bunker and yelled, "Cover him! Fire over his head to keep the fuckin chinks down! Those fuckin guys didn't have enough fuckin sense to come in, so that fuckin dumb wop risks his own fuckin life to save theirs!"

A round landed in the trench behind Nap, and the machine gun stopped firing.

Smoke and debris prevented the gunner from seeing what was happening.

"Oh, fuck!"

A few seconds later, someone, emerging from the smoke, was carrying someone else up the trench, piggyback style. As he was slowly coming up the finger of the hill, it became dark again. The incoming artillery suddenly stopped, but mortar rounds were dropping in the area of the listening post.

Tiny went into the checkpoint, cranked the phone, and asked for more medics and stretchers.

As soon as he hung up, Dante and Barlow popped in.

"That fuckin Nap went down to the listening post to bring in A Bomb, Chico, and Eddie. Someone's coming in now."

It was Nap, carrying Eddie, who was wounded. He set Eddie down gently at the entrance of the machine gun bunker.

"Ahn and Chico have both been hit. Chico, not too bad, I don't think, but I couldn't get him to leave Ahn. And there are a couple of others from the patrol. I've got to get them."

"You're staying here! That's a fuckin order!"

"I left my rifle there."

"Fuck your rifle!"

"Fuck your own rifle, you horny pervert!"

And he bolted down the trench, past someone who was limping up the trench and was leaning on someone else. They were both from the patrol.

Without saying anything, Dante ran down the trench.

Barlow took off after him.

And Tiny, yelling "Fuck!" followed.

A mortar round had seemed to land into the listening post before Tiny arrived there. Dante had picked up Chico and was carrying him back. Barlow had picked up Nap who was groaning. Tiny saw the two soldiers who had been on patrol. They were dead. He saw Ahn. He, too, was dead, but Tiny picked him up, and as he carried him up the trench, the fire from the mortars stopped.

When they made it to the checkpoint, the medics were there. Eddie had already been put on a stretcher and had been carried away with the two wounded men who had been on patrol. Chico was conscious and was asking Dante about Ahn. Dante told him he did not know yet. But the medic said Ahn was dead.

And Nap, who had been badly injured, was still alive, and he was placed next on a stretcher, and before he was carried away, Tiny yelled, "Look, you fuckin wop, I told you I didn't want no fuckin heroes in my fuckin squad! You'd better recover, because I ain't finished with you yet! You cappish, you fuckin wop!"

After the others had been taken away, Tiny and Dante returned into the checkpoint.

Tiny was breathing and sighing heavily as they sat across from each other, as though he were on the verge of crying, and he took out a handkerchief and blew his nose.

"Do you understand now why I told you not to get too fuckin chummy with each other!"

"Hey, Sarg, I know," Dante answered softly, "I know, but it's not a weakness to get chummy with each other. It's only natural."

"I don't give a fuck how natural it is! It fuckin hurts too fuckin bad! And if war is fuckin natural, too, I don't give a shit! Why the fuck don't we learn something from our fuckin wars? Why the fuck do we have to be killing each other? One fuckin war after another! What the fuck is wrong with us?"

Sergeant Wells appeared suddenly at the entrance.

"The people back home pay us a dollar a day extra just so they can have parades and shit and brag about us winning all their wars for them, but civilians like you are always complaining about serving them in this man's army."

"Fuck you and them and this man's army! I want to get the fuck out of here!"

Spot appeared at the entrance and pushed his way past the legs of the sergeant to enter, wagging his tail and smelling Dante, who picked him up.

"Ain't he fuckin scared being here?" asked Tiny.

"Yeah, and although I told him it's only thunder and lightning, he asks me where the fuckin rain is."

"Do you think you should have brought him up to the fuckin lines?"

"Better than where the fuck he was, about to be served as a delicacy."

"So, what the fuck is up?"

"That's why I'm here, to find out. The left flank has been rather quiet tonight, but on the right flank, the third platoon got hit hard.

A few Chinese even made it into the trenches, but things are under control there now. And to the right, the South Korean division is getting clobbered. The brass, apparently, is concerned that the Chinese may be planning to surround us. What happened to the patrol on the listening post?"

"They didn't all make it in. Only seven of the ten did. Three of them didn't. Of the seven who did, two of them died. They're still on the fuckin listening post. Two wounded, and three okay came in."

"And what about your squad?"

"A Bomb was killed, Nap, badly wounded, and Chico and Eddie wounded. We're down to six, including me."

"Okay, sergeant. I can't imagine the Chinese hitting again tonight. They hit us hard in some places, but they paid a much higher price."

"They just seem to keep coming and coming like they don't seem to give a fuck how many they lose."

"I know. They're overpopulated."

"And so fuckin poor."

"And that," added Dante, "is what makes them so damn dangerous!"

"That's true," Wells said. "Somebody told me you were a teacher."

"He still is! A fuckin English teacher. He taught Ahn and Chico how to speak fuckin English."

"Really? Couldn't you have gotten a deferment?"

"I didn't try. Maybe I had something to prove."

"What do you mean?"

Dante put the pup down.

"Well, the high school where I taught for a year is, well, lily white, and the people there apparently thought I was white enough to teach their teenage kids. Now, they're not so sure."

"Because you're eyetalian?"

"And I married a beautiful woman whose skin is much darker than mine, maybe even darker than yours."

"Not a colored girl, though."

"Are you colored?"

"Are you serious?"

"Yes, I am. Where I come from, people call us nigger wops, and I want to prove to them that nigger wops, if that's what we are, are as American as they are, and that we belong in America as much as they do. Maybe we belong there even more than they do because we believe in the American ideals, and, apparently, they don't. You fought for our country in the second world war, and now you're serving our country again. Haven't you proven to the American people that you have as much right as any of them to live there? Does anyone there have any right to tell you to go home to Africa where you belong?"

Wells didn't answer him.

Dante said, "My wife and I live in a white community where we are both labeled as Italian and Negro, but I want to return there and to be labeled as American, both of us."

"I know what you mean, and I'm sure you know that you don't have to prove a damn thing to them."

"And neither do you."

"I bet she's damn proud of you. I understand what you're doing, and why."

"I remember when you said you were only half wop," Tiny said.

"And you wondered what the other half was. Well, the other half of me is red, white and black. How many Americans can say that?"

They became silent for a little while.

"I've got to put somebody on the fuckin listening post for the rest of the night," Tiny said, "so I'll need a couple of stretchers to bring in those two bodies."

Wells said, "I'll have the medics bring in the two bodies. Come on, Spot."

"Oh, one other thing. We're going to need some fuckin water soon."

"Yeah, I know, if they can bring supplies in. Unless things quiet down soon, we'll have to get by on the water we have now."

"Yeah, and if they did bring us more fuckin water, they'd probably make us shave with the fuckin stuff so that we can look real fuckin nice to the fuckin enemy."

"Damn, Sarg, you really love the fuckin army! Why do you hate to admit it?" He turned to Dante. "He never had it so good! If this damn war hadn't come along, he never would have travelled so far, never would have eaten so well, never would have had such thrilling adventures, or fucked so many damn sexy broads, and never would have worn such pretty clothes, never would have slept in such exotic places. Some people are never satisfied no matter what. Always complaining."

"And if I ever get the fuck out of here I ain't ever going to complain again. You bet your fuckin ass I'll be satisfied! Nothing can be this fuckin bad!"

"What about the wounded?" asked Dante. "Is there transportation for them?"

"Yeah. They were being transported just before I came out here."

After the bodies had been removed from the listening post, Tiny went into the bunker where Henderson, with the automatic rifle, was, and Tiny assigned him and the other two to the listening post.

Barlow joined Dante.

It was silent for the rest of the night as Dante stood at the aperture and looked out and listened, but the same feeling of the unnatural silence, as he had experienced that night at the listening post, had returned, and then, from deep inside of him, as though he had almost fallen asleep and was dreaming, yet he was aware that he was still standing at the bunker, Rose was embracing him. He let himself drift with her through space and time, and, for a few moments, it seemed, he felt that they were hovering above the silent darkness.

"Another fuckin night in hell has past," said Tiny as he entered the bunker, "and we've lost more than half of the platoon."

Tiny saw Barlow sleeping in a lower bunk.

"Didn't you get any rest?"

"I'm not tired," said Dante.

"How the fuck do you keep going?"

"What do you mean? How do *you* keep going?"

"On fuckin nerves, but I doze off once in a while, and I still feel like a fuckin zombie. But, you, you look like you had a good night's sleep!"

"Have they come in from the listening post yet?"

"They're waiting for us now. I just came from there. Come on, we're going to be looking for the rest of the patrol. Barlow, rise and shine!"

When they arrived at the listening post, medics and stretcher bearers from both Fox and Easy Companies were there. The third squad led them into no man's land to look for the missing three men.

They did not find them.

Although the sun had been bright, the smell of death lingered late into the day. And as the day had become warmer than usual, an unfulfilled craving for water had seized Dante.

"Just think," he said to Barlow as they sat on the bunks, "the folks at home can just go to the kitchen sink and turn on the faucet and drink all the water they want. I've never thought of that before. There are so many little things we take for granted that we don't appreciate the nice little things we have, not until we're deprived of them. Most of us want to make things better than they are, and that's the way we ought to be, to want to make things better, for everyone. God, or nature, or whatever anyone wants to call it, gave us this world to live in, and gave us the intelligence to develop it, just as a seed develops into whatever it's supposed to be, but I don't think we've been using our abilities to develop it. Do you?"

"No, I don't think so either."

"Do you really think we can ever make this a better world?"

"I sure hope so!'

"Me, too, but what's taking us so damn long?"

"What do you mean?"

"Well, how many thousands of years have we been on this earth, and what else have we've been doing besides killing each other?"

"Six."

"What?"

"Six thousand years. You asked me how long we've been on this earth. Six thousand years."

Dante stared at him.

"Six thousand years," Dante murmured. "You're not required to believe that, are you? I mean, some Catholics believe that, too, but that's not a requirement of the faith."

"Are you Catholic?"

"Yes, I am."

"You're not really an atheist, are you?"

"An atheist? A Catholic? Of course not!"

"Well, the pope's an atheist, ain't he?"

"No, the Pope is the head of the Catholic Church, the successor to St. Peter. Who told you he's an atheist?"

"I don't know. I was taught that."

"Well, you've heard of Martin Luther, haven't you?"

"Yeah, of course."

"Well, a little over four hundred years ago, he was a Catholic priest who got into an argument with the Pope at that time, so the Pope excommunicated him, and the protesting priest wrote that the Pope was an anti-Christ, a Satanist who believed in God and hated God, but never an atheist, and their hatred of each other actually led to persecution and killing of Protestants and Catholics, all in the name of God, and ever since then, some Protestant denominations have been teaching that the Pope is an anti-Christ. War has always been the solution to our arguments. Ever since man was created, there have been wars on this planet. Tell me something. Do you really believe in segregation?"

"Well, yeah. But I guess you don't because, well, because you and your wife are both mixed."

"You don't think slavery was wrong?"

"Well, yeah, slavery was wrong."

"But you think integration is wrong. Why?"

"It ain't natural for us colored folks to mix with whites."

"Why isn't it?"

"It just ain't. It just don't seem right."

Dante sighed.

"I like you," he said, "I really do. You're a gentle person, and I can't see you hating anyone unless someone really hurt you, but tell me what Jesus meant when He said that the greatest commandment was to love thy neighbor as thyself."

"To love each other. I like you, too, man, I really do."

"Is it natural for Catholics and Protestants to love each other?"

"Well, they shouldn't hate each other."

"What about being integrated in the army? Does this bother you?"

"Well, it did, at first, a little, but I'm used to it now."

"You mean, when you get used to something, then it seems natural."

"Yeah, but I never thought of it that way before."

"Tell me now. Do you still think that Catholics are atheists?"

"No, I don't. Not all of them, anyway. I mean, you say you're Catholic, but you ain't an atheist."

"You know that a Catholic is a Christian, right?"

"Well, to tell you the truth, I didn't. Not until now."

Tiny entered the bunker.

"Try to get some fuckin rest. I think it's going to be pretty fuckin quiet, at least until tonight. And tonight, we've got the fuckin listening post, the three of us."

"Okay," answered Dante.

That afternoon he wrote to Rose and told her, again, how much he missed her.

For supper he had cold beans and sliced frankfurters, and from the can he drank the liquid, but it did almost nothing to quench his thirst.

"I wouldn't complain about a little rain now," he muttered to Barlow.

At dusk he and Barlow went to the checkpoint where Tiny was waiting.

"No poncho tonight, right?"

Tiny grinned at him.

"No fuckin poncho."

"What are you talking about?" Barlow asked.

"We ain't going to get no fuckin rain tonight."

As soon as it was dark, Henderson replaced Tiny at the checkpoint. He had left his automatic rifle with Finnegan, because Henderson had taken over the position as assistant squad leader

At the listening post, Tiny took the front, center position, Barlow took the left, and Dante took the right. He had taken the carbine with him.

In less than a half hour, a patrol from Easy Company, with only seven men with soft caps, went through.

Less than twenty minutes later, shots burst out in no-man's land.

"They ran into fuckin chinks!"

Tiny leaped out of the listening post and opened the gates and waited for the patrol to come in.

Quickly, all seven of them came running in, and mortars started dropping on them.

"Let's get the fuck out of here!" Tiny screamed to Barlow and Dante, and he followed Dante up the trench, to the checkpoint. The patrol ran through the trenches yelling, "Chinks in the valley!"

At the checkpoint, Tiny called for a flare. No enemy troops could be seen. The mortar rounds had ceased.

Dante and Barlow had returned to their bunker, and they waited.

After a few minutes, another flare burst out. Still, they saw no enemy troops.

It was silent. Too silent, somehow, Dante felt. Where the hell were they?

Suddenly, as the ground shook, artillery rounds poured in, but there was no one in the valley below them, no one to shoot at. Now, thought Dante, would be the time for the jets to fly behind the mountain and to drop napalm on the enemy field artillery. Why, he wondered, couldn't they do that? Couldn't they somehow stop the enemy field artillery?

Was there nothing they could do besides staying in their bunkers and waiting out the barrage? Eventually, each bunker would get hit directly and each one of them would be killed or wounded without any casualties to the enemy soldiers, but the Chinese, Dante thought, wouldn't wait that long. They would be coming again.

The flare went out, and the incoming rounds kept pouring in.

"Do you think they'll come?" Barlow asked.

"Yes, they will! I have a feeling they will."

The spotlight came on.

"Do you see them?" Dante yelled out. "The skirmish in front of the listening post was nothing compared to what's going to happen out there!"

"I see them!"

As soon as the spotlight revealed them in the distance, most of them went down, hugging the ground.

Machine gun fire went out, spraying the area, and other small arms fire went out.

"Let's wait until they get a little closer," said Dante. "Imagine if the jets were out there now with the napalm! We have air superiority. Why in hell don't we use it?"

Finally, Dante heard the artillery rounds going out. Just as he saw the explosions from the artillery falling among the enemy troops, the spotlight went out.

The incoming rounds were still falling around them, but the sound of outgoing rounds seemed to be at least twice as much.

"I'd rather be up here than down there," he said.

"I'd rather be home!"

Another flare burst out.

"Oh, they're getting closer now!" Barlow cried out.

Although the platoon had lost more than half of its original manpower, they were still pouring out a lot of fire.

"The Chinese are going to be lifting their artillery soon," Dante said, "but I don't think they're going to make it up here; we're pounding the hell out of them."

Just as he had predicted, the Chinese lifted their artillery.

"Keep firing," Dante said, "I'm going to drop grenades on them."

He placed a box of grenades in the trench, and one by one, he tossed grenades down. Then he became aware that not only had the

Chinese stop dropping their artillery, but that the outgoing rounds had also stopped.

He went into the bunker and looked out. A steady wall of fire was keeping the Chinese away from the barbed wire, but the Chinese were firing back. In the dark it was difficult to see how many were out there, but there seemed to be too many. And it was difficult to see how much damage was being inflicted upon them. And in the dark Dante could not tell how many reinforcements they were getting.

"Why don't we send up another flare? And why has our artillery stopped? I'm going to see Tiny to see if he knows what's going on. Are you going to be all right here alone for a while? Or do you want to go in the other bunker with Henderson?"

"I'll stay here and wait for you to come back."

Dante took off down the trench with his carbine.

Tiny was alone in the checkpoint.

"The fuckin phone is dead!"

"I was going to ask you why we aren't sending up any more flares, and why our artillery suddenly stopped."

"I don't fuckin know!"

"I'm going back to find out."

"Good fuckin idea!"

"If I'm asked how long we can hold out like this, what shall I say?"

"If the fuckers keep coming, we can't hold out all fuckin night. I doubt if we have enough fuckin manpower and enough fuckin ammunition."

Dante took off.

At least, he thought, there weren't any rounds falling along the trench now; there was only an occasional round falling near the top of the hill, so he was running through the trench without being stopped. As he drew closer to the fork in the trench, a round landed next to the trench going up to the top, to the reverse slope. He dashed up the finger, made it to the top, and was on the reverse slope. A round missed the top of the hill and whistled harmlessly, it seemed, until it landed near the bottom of the hill and exploded.

He approached the platoon command post, knocked on the door, opened it, and entered. Parks was sitting at the desk and seemed to be peering at a map, and Wells was standing beside the desk and also seemed to be studying the map. The puppy, wagging its tail, ran up to Dante and expected to be patted. Dante put his carbine against the wall, squatted down to pat the pup, looked up when Parks asked, "What's the situation?" and said, "First, the phone at the checkpoint is dead. And second, right now we're stopping the Chinese, but Tiny thinks, and I agree with him, that we can't stop them all night long, and unless we inflict more damage on them, they look like they're going to be here all night long. We're not only short on manpower, we will, unless we get help, run out of ammunition before morning. Are you aware that the support we were getting from the field artillery has suddenly stopped?"

They stared at him.

"What do you mean," Wells said, "that it's stopped?"

Dante stood up.

"We're under attack, and our artillery was firing on them, slowing them down, but suddenly our artillery stops. Can you call someone," he asked Parks, "to inquire why they suddenly stopped firing while we're being attacked?"

Parks looked at a bulletin board on the wall in front of him and dialed a number.

Dante noticed an empty chair between him and the desk, and he sat in it, and he pushed his helmet back a little.

"Parks from Fox Company! We're under attack, and suddenly you stopped supporting us. Why?" A pause. "What?" He looked at Dante. "He said they've used up the quota for the month."

Dante stood up.

"What! That's absurd!" He looked at Wells. "Have you ever heard of such a thing?"

"No!" Wells looked at Parks. "I never have."

Dante raised his voice at Parks: "Tell him to start on next month's quota! Immediately!"

"Start on next month's quota! Immediately!"

"We're under attack! Tell him!"

452

"We're under attack!"

Parks looked at Dante and nodded.

"He said okay!"

"Tell him to stay on the line until we hear the rounds going out!"

"Stay on the line until we hear the rounds going out!"

He covered the mouthpiece with the palm of his hand and looked up at Dante.

"He wants to know who I am."

"Tell him, Parks from Second Division!"

"Parks from Second Division!"

Parks looked up at him again and nodded again.

"He says he's already given the orders; we should hear the rounds going out."

They listened.

And they heard the rounds whistling over them.

"Tell him not to stop until you give him the orders to stop!"

"And don't stop until I give you the orders to stop! Out."

And he hung up.

Parks looked at Wells, and they both looked at Dante and grinned at him.

"Do you want me to call for reinforcements?" Parks asked Dante.

"That wouldn't hurt. We could use a couple of more squads for the firepower. And that's why they're in reserve, in case we need them. And the Chinese look like they're making their big push tonight."

Dante sat in the chair again, and he heaved a deep sigh.

Parks used the phone again to call for reinforcements. Wells recommended a platoon with at least twenty men. He told Dante he'd go out with them and that he'd bring plenty of flares with him.

A few minutes later a platoon was outside of the command post. Dante and Wells went out to lead them.

"How many men do you have?" Wells asked the leader of the platoon.

"Twenty. That includes two machine guns."

"Good. Follow us. Lead the way," he said to Dante.

Dante, with the carbine slung over his shoulder, knew that the others would mistake him for an officer, not a private, even though, under such circumstances, it didn't make any difference, not to Wells, anyway. So, he got in front of the column and said, "Stay in single file."

"Okay, saddle up!" barked the platoon leader.

Dante entered the trench and began to walk up the steep slope. At the top of the hill, no rounds seemed to be coming in, so he moved quickly down the reverse slope. When he got to the main trench, Wells said to the platoon leader, "I'll take the first ten men this way." And to Dante, he said, "After I get these guys settled in, I'll meet you at the checkpoint. I'll bring the flares."

Dante and the platoon leader waited as the first ten men followed Wells.

"Don't get so close to each other!" Dante yelled. "One round will get all of you."

"Okay, you heard him! Spread out!"

After the ten men followed Wells, the others followed Dante.

The first bunker, which had been Nap's, was now empty.

"Three men can go in here."

Dante continued to the next bunker.

He said to the platoon leader, "Wait here a few seconds."

He entered the bunker and said to Henderson, "I've brought reinforcements."

"Oh, great. And we're getting support from the artillery again."

"Yeah, I know. Parks called them. They said they had run out of their quota for the month."

"What the fuck are you talking about?"

"I'll explain later. I have to put these guys in bunkers."

He returned to the trench, and they followed him.

"One guy can go in here. Hey, Barlow, we've got company. I'll be back in a few more minutes."

He continued to the next bunker. Not counting the platoon leader, there were six men left with two machine guns.

"This bunker is empty. So, you can stay here until we find a place to put the machine guns."

As they took cover in the bunker, Dante continued to the checkpoint.

Tiny said, "The fuckin artillery finally woke up."

"Yeah, Parks called them. They said they had used their quota for the month."

"What?"

"I told Parks to tell them to start on next month's quota."

"You gotta be shittin me!"

"I kid you not. And it worked."

A flare shot up.

"That's got to be Wells. He said he's bringing you a bunch of flares. And I've brought twenty guys and their platoon leader to reinforce us. They brought two machine guns."

"Look at those fuckin chinks! They brought their whole fuckin army right here! We'll be fuckin lucky to hold all those fuckers back! Let's set up those two fuckin machine guns."

They went into the next bunker. The reinforcements had already mounted one of the machine guns and were firing it.

"Okay, good," said Tiny.

"Why don't we set up the other machine gun in Nap's bunker?" suggested Dante.

A few minutes after the flare had gone out, Wells found Tiny in the trench with Dante and the platoon leader and two other soldiers. They were tossing grenades at the enemy below. Wells fired another flare.

The Chinese now seemed to have given up trying to attack them. All the way to the other end of the valley, to their own positions, they were retreating, and as they were trying to escape from the artillery and the small arms fire, they were being slaughtered again.

Wells said to Tiny, "Did Dante tell you what happened? When Parks called the artillery, he was told that they had used up their quota for the month, and Dante said, 'Tell them to start next month's quota!' And that's why the artillery gave us support again."

"Unfuckinbelievable!"

Again, the Chinese had been forced to abandon their dead and wounded on the battlefield of the valley floor, and long after the small arms had ceased fire, the field artillery had continued to pound the valley, until Wells had told Parks to call the artillery again. For the rest of the night, the Chinese had not attacked Boomerang.

And the reinforcements had returned to their reserve positions on the reverse slope, but not for long.

Less than two hours after the break of dawn, after the Chinese had dropped smoke screens into the valley, and the stench of death was permeating the warm air, Fox Company was being relieved. It was changing places with Easy Company. The news sounded too good to be true, but the men who had reinforced them had now returned to relieve them.

They went to the other side of Boomerang Hill, on a slope a little below their command post, to a sleeping bunker that had been dug into the side of the hill. It could accommodate twelve men in six double bunkers. Each of them had taken a bottom bunk. And each squad had its own bunker. During an attack, they would be on the alert, of course, and ready to go if the front line troops needed any reinforcements, and every night, at least one squad from the company was required, on a rotating basis, to go out on patrol, otherwise they were free. And, every evening and every morning, if transportation were available, several of them, depending on what type of vehicle would be available, would be transported to the rear for hot showers, and for a change of clothing, and for several hours of rest and recreation. Those who would leave in the evening would return before dawn, and those who would leave before dawn would return after dark.

During the first day in reserve, most of them sat in the sun and relaxed where they could see the road in the valley on which they had arrived. The road ran down the middle of the valley and disappeared between hills. Dante tried to imagine the same view from the top of Papasan. He could imagine the Chinese breaking through to the east of them and easily surrounding Boomerang, but then the Chinese, in the open and unprotected valley floor, would become vulnerable to the Allied troops in the hills behind. The Chinese would have to make a push of several miles in one attack.

Later in the afternoon, Dante, and some of the others, noticed a jeep emerging from the hills. As it moved along the road, it was stirring up a long trail of dust.

Captain Rossi was walking towards Dante who was sitting on the ground with Tiny and Barlow. Rossi stopped. "That damned fool," he muttered, staring at the jeep in the valley. He held his binoculars to his eyes. "The driver is alone. What in hell is he doing?"

Although no one was saying anything, they were all wondering why the Chinese were not firing at him.

And then, when the jeep was about halfway across the valley, close enough to Boomerang so that he wouldn't turn around, the Chinese artillery started to use the jeep for target practice.

Still, no one said anything.

They were watching.

"Suddenly the jeep took off," Dante later wrote in a letter, "like a screaming bitch trying to flee from buck shots shooting up her ass."

And somehow, without getting hit, it came close enough to the hill to use it as a shield. The artillery stopped firing, and the jeep disappeared into the bottom of the hill.

What had impressed Dante was that the others, like him, had been spectators, merely uninvolved spectators at an entertaining event, not normal human beings who would have been concerned about the life of the driver.

"We demonize the enemy as he demonizes us," Dante said. "Does war do that to us? Does war make us heartless?"

"Didn't I fuckin warn you?" Tiny cried out. "If you let it get to you, it'll drive you fuckin crazy."

"He's right," said Rossi. "I could almost hear the Chinese soldiers laughing at the jeep driver. War gives us a license to kill each other. It can drive decent human beings like you crazy. Your feelings get numb to protect you. Otherwise you'd crack up."

"How long does it take to recover from that?"

"Who knows?" Rossi answered. "Unfortunately, some of them never do, and some of the people back home even blame them, the victims, for their wounds, their psychological wounds, for which there are no purple hearts, and the people ask why the fuck can't they pull themselves together now that they're back home. Yeah, you're right. We're fucking monsters."

The jeep was seen climbing the winding road closer to the top. When it arrived at Fox Company, it stopped. The driver was bringing in their mail.

"You asshole," someone yelled at him as he lifted a large mailbag from the back seat and plunked it at the side of the road, "taking a fuckin chance like that with our fuckin mail!"

And someone else said, "I bet you a fuckin dollar you don't make it back."

Captain Rossi approached the jeep and yelled, "Stop harassing the poor guy!" They moved out of the way to let him talk to the driver who was standing near the back of the jeep. "He almost got killed bringing you your mail. You ought to be thanking him! Soldier, is this your first time coming up here?"

The soldier stared at him and didn't know if he should salute or not.

"I'm Captain Rossi, the company commander. No, you don't have to salute. Just answer the question."

"Yes, sir, it's my first time coming up here."

"That's what I thought. No one informed you that you drive up here only in the dark without lights. I think you're aware of that now."

"Yes, sir."

"So, when do you think you'll be driving back?"

"As soon as it gets dark, sir."

"Very good, but wait until l tell you to, because I want you to take back six men."

"Six men? I don't think I can take six men."

"Of course you can. You can take at least one in the front with you, and three in the back. We don't have any gas, so if you run out of gas, you'll need two in the back to push you. Right? Besides, this is your first time here; you're not familiar with the roads, and we don't have any guardrails here, and that's dangerous with no lights at night. So, you'll need two men on the sides of the running boards to guide you." The driver was staring at the captain and wondering, probably, how serious and sane he was. "And when you get back, tell Colonel Ryan that my boys need hot showers and good clean clothes, and that the next time he sends a mail carrier out here, warn him that it could be dangerous because the Chinese enjoy blowing up vehicles on the road."

That evening, as dusk was settling, the first squad of the first platoon was sent out on a reconnaissance patrol, and the six men who were sent to the rear in the jeep was the first squad of the second platoon. Before they returned at dawn, most of Fox Company had moved out. It had been called to support a Thai company that was preparing to attack Papasan.

That first night in reserve had begun quietly. No one had heard a shot from the front line, and there had been no reports that the patrol had encountered any enemy forces. Actually, while the company was walking through no man's land, it met the patrol. The patrol leader told Rossi that there had been no signs of Chinese. Rossi told him to return to their sleeping bunker for the rest of the day and to relax.

Just before daybreak, the company stopped, and they waited. As the darkness began to lift, Dante noticed that they were in a ravine, which, apparently, had flowed with water during the spring but had become dry.

Rossi, from the front of the column, walked past them, to the rear, inspecting the company, and examining the terrain the best he could in the little light that was almost breaking through the cloudy skies. He looked up to the east, and he continued walking.

Dante thought that the attack had been planned to surprise the enemy, but he did not understand what it would accomplish. Even if they would make it into the enemy trenches, they would never be able to hold on to it. A citizen of any country should be willing to die in defense of his fellow citizens, but he should not be ordered to go willingly to be slaughtered, as the Chinese soldiers had been.

A few minutes later, Rossi returned to take a position near the middle of his company. Dante wondered what was going through his mind, and he, Dante, was wondering what Tiny was thinking. The idea of attacking Papasan must have seemed "gung ho" to him, too insanely gung ho.

Rossi looked at his watch. He asked for his phone, and he spoke into it, returned it, leaned against the bank of the ravine and looked at the landscape that was becoming more visible. Parks and Wells were both pacing the ravine. Dante and Barlow were both leaning against the bank and looking to the front of them. Tiny was standing behind them.

As the morning became lighter, Dante could see Papasan looming above them. They were, perhaps, less than a hundred yards away from the Chinese trenches. The bottom trenches on Papasan were not as high as the ones on Boomerang, but they seemed as steep and were protected with barbed wire.

Dante could not yet see the Thais clearly. He thought he had seen movement at a distance to his left front. The silence, he felt, was the same deathly silence he had felt that first night on the listening post. There was a slight, wispy fog slowly rising.

Suddenly, dozens of whistles began screaming over them and were exploding into the trenches of the enemy. The bottom half of Papasan was getting pounded. And the Thais seemed to rise up out of the ground and were advancing, firing steadily as they reached the barbed wire. The artillery rounds began to lift, and quickly the rounds stopped, and the Chinese began to return the fire.

But, out of the west, jets were approaching.

And the small arms fire from the Chinese ceased.

The leading jet began to dive, not gradually, but suddenly.

"Oh, no!" yelled Rossi, "Not yet! Give me that damn phone!"

The jet released the napalm on the Thai troops and climbed up again.

And the next jet went into its dive, closer this time to Fox Company, and it, too, dropped the napalm on the Thais, and climbed into the air.

The Thais, in panic, were quickly retreating to their own lines as the shocked Americans were gaping in horror, feeling the heat from the napalm.

The third jet went into its nosedive, too, but this time, it pulled up without dropping its bomb, and then it dropped the napalm in a trench higher up.

The Chinese had obviously abandoned their positions to take cover inside of the mountain, but the Thais had become too disorganized now to continue the attack. They were running back to their own lines.

"Saddle up!" yelled Rossi. "Let's get the hell out of here!"

As the jets, ten of them this time, continued to drop napalm on the trenches of Papasan and on the backside of it, silencing the artillery, Fox Company trudged back to Boomerang. When they arrived back at their bunkers, most of them dropped onto their bunks and tried to sleep.

They had not spoken of the incident.

What could they say?

That's the way the ball bounces. That's the way the cookie crumbles. In war, shit happens.

15

Supplies had arrived earlier that morning. They were able to fill their canteens with water. And they were told that they'd have a hot meal for supper.

Rossi had announced earlier that their overnight leaves had been extended to a full day, and that evening six men from the second squad were allowed to take the jeep to the rear. They wouldn't have to return until nightfall tomorrow. And in the morning, part of the third squad would go.

The night passed quietly.

Early in the morning, Tiny reported to the command post.

When he returned to the bunker, he yelled, "Rise and shine! We're taking a fuckin truck to the rear! The rest of the fuckin platoon!"

Even Parks had been given permission to go with them. He sat in the cab. Wells sat in the back with the rest of them, including the pup. They were sitting across from Dante, at the end of the seat at the back of the truck. Dante had left his rifle in the bunker and was holding the carbine between his legs. It was a foggy morning and still fairly dark, but everyone was in a jovial mood as the truck moved down the curvy, narrow road. When they got down to the bottom of the hill, the truck moved faster across the flat stretch. Behind them, Papasan was covered in the fog.

When they got into the hills, the truck went a little slower, and when they arrived at regimental headquarters, the driver stopped in front of a tent, which had been reserved for Fox Company. The six men from the second squad were inside, still sleeping. Parks could have stayed at officers' quarters, but he preferred not to wear his insignias and to remain with the platoon.

The first thing they all wanted was a hot shower and clean clothes, but the truck driver, who had led them into the tent, told them to choose a bunk first. They could leave all of their gear there, except their weapons, the truck driver told them. He seemed to be acting, thought Dante, as their tour guide. "It is mandatory that you carry your weapons with you at all times," he said.

"Even in the fuckin shower to protect us from the fuckin perverts the fuckin army keeps in rear echelon. Right?"

The tour guide seemed to ignore Tiny.

"If you have them, you're allowed to wear soft caps instead of helmets, which you can hang on the back of your bunks, but in case of air raids or attacks, you must return here to wear your helmets and then go outside again and to enter an air raid shelter which has been provided for your protection. You will see signs outside marked 'air raid shelter' on bunkers designated as air raid shelters."

"For our fuckin protection. Right?"

With a straight face, the guide asked, "Any more dumb fuckin questions?"

"Yeah," quipped Tiny, "how can I get your fuckin job?"

"You can't. You have to pass an intelligence test first."

Even Tiny burst out laughing, and then he said, "You must be from Pittsburgh."

"Well, it takes one to know one."

Tiny later said they had known each other for years. The truck driver tour guide was regular army now, a staff sergeant combat vet left over from the second world war in Europe.

The showers would not be available, according to the guide, until Fatso, the fat buck private, as the guide called him, would finish breakfast, because Fatso was the one who was in charge of showers. "And Fatso," the guide said, "whose own mother loathed him, even before she had given birth to him in an army stockade, doesn't particularly enjoy the smell and arrogance of combat vets. Wait till he meets you guys!"

The guide said he had to report their arrival to regimental head-quarters, but he would return quickly to take them to breakfast and then to the shower tent.

They leaned their weapons against their bunks, removed their helmets, dropped their knapsacks on the bunks to be used as pillows, and took a rest, and waited.

As he lay on the bunk, Dante, looking down at himself, won-dered why he was still wearing his flak vest. It was covered with dried up blood and dirt. He removed it. How long had he been wearing it? He had put it on when the division had moved up on line, and this was the first time he had taken it off. It had been more than one week, at least. Maybe closer to two weeks. And his fatigues was stained with blood, and felt stiff, especially where the most blood had dried. He closed his eyes, and Rose was lying naked on her back.

"Make love to me in Italian, mia amore."

But he was too filthy to touch her; he was too filthy to even be in the same house with her. He wanted, now, to shed his filthy clothes.

The tour guide returned.

"Let's go get a cup of hot java and some breakfast. You'll feel a hell of a lot better, and then you'll take hot showers."

Dante reached onto the back of his knapsack, pulled out his soft cap, put it on, grabbed his carbine and slung it on his right shoul-der and followed the guys outside, into the sun, which was breaking through the clouds. Without the flak vest, he felt much freer.

In the chow line, Tiny said to the guide, "We're the only fuckin guys with rifles. We stick out like fuckin sore thumbs. Why the fuck do we have to carry our rifles?"

"That's to let us know you guys just came off the fuckin lines. We have to treat you as guests, with respect. We have to give you as much food as you want, and things like that."

"You're fuckin shittin me."

"I shit you not."

"And these fuckin rear echelons are suppose to respect us?"

"But they don't; most of them resent you."

"Why the fuck should they resent us?"

"They're pissed at you, because you get promoted faster."

"Yeah, because we have a fuckin faster turnover! We'd be fuckin thrilled to change places with these fuckin guys!"

"These fuckin guys don't want to go *that* far!"

For breakfast, they were served shit on a shingle.

"What did I tell you? And as much as you want!"

After breakfast, the guide led them into a huge shower tent. They walked over a wood floor, peeked behind some thick, dark curtains where the showers were, but the shower boy wasn't there to turn the showers on. The guide grumbled something to Tiny, walked back to the entrance, opened it, and yelled, "Hey, Fatso, get your big fat ass over here!"

The others leaned their weapons on a long bench in front of the shower curtains. They were facing a long counter. Behind the counter was a large recliner chair, and behind the chair, were shelves of cubicles where clean fatigues were bundled.

The shower boy, a pasty faced chubby kid, finally entered, muttering something about letting a poor guy finish his breakfast in peace.

Tiny snarled, "You should have had your fuckin breakfast three hours ago, Fatso!"

The shower boy removed a bunch of keys from his pocket, and he went behind the curtain. They heard the water come on, and as the shower boy emerged, steam began to rise to the top of the tent. He strolled up to the counter, pushed the top of the table up, went behind the counter, let the top drop, and plopped himself in the chair.

At the long bench, they quickly removed their fatigues, and a few seconds later, they entered the shower, yelling as though they were experiencing the greatest miracle ever. "Ain't this fuckin great! Life is number fuckin one!" They scrubbed soap all over themselves and stayed under the hot soothing water almost a half hour.

"This is the fuckin life, ain't it! And we're going to be here all fuckin day and all fuckin night with nothing to do except relax! And we'll even see a fuckin movie tonight! And drink fuckin beer. Hey,

Pittsburgh," Tiny said as he came out of the shower, "there's only one fuckin thing you forgot."

"No, I didn't forget anything. The brass won't allow any fuckin mooses on the premises. But the cooks have been instructed to add plenty of saltpeter in the food."

When they had gotten out of the shower area, the shower boy had gotten up from the soft chair, had reached under the counter and had stacked a pile of towels on the counter. One by one they picked up a towel, dried themselves off, and returned to the counter to get clean fatigues. The shower boy would turn around, go up to a cubicle, and grab a bundle and place it on the counter. Dante had assumed that the cubicles had been arranged by sizes, and that the smallest sizes would begin at the left. After he had dried himself he stood at the counter and said to the shower boy, "Let me have the smallest you have, please." The shower boy casually reached behind him, and grabbed a bundle at random, thought Dante, and placed it on the counter. Dante took it to the bench. The undershorts would have been too big even for Tiny, and he knew that the trousers would also be too big, but just for the fun of it, he put it on. "If I put water in here," he said, "I could go swimming." Dante took it off. Everybody was laughing, except the shower boy. He was sitting in his chair and seemed to be gloating.

"Okay, no more fucking around. Give me something I can wear."

"You have to take what you get. There's a fuckin war on, you know!"

Everyone else was stunned.

Tiny, who was already dressed, bolted from the bench, pushed the counter top up, picked the kid up by the shirt, pulling him out of the chair so that his feet were dangling, and yelled into his face, "You fat fuckin punk! What the fuck do you know about war! Who the fuck do you think you're talking to?" Tiny pushed him down into the chair. "Dante, give me your dirty trousers!"

"Let him go. I think he's ready to give me clothes that fit."

Tiny, his blue eyes glowing with tears, turned around, opened the counter top again, grabbed Dante's dirty trousers, grabbed his rifle, returned to the shower boy, dropped his rifle at the feet of the shower boy, and shoved the trousers close to the kid's face. "Do you know what the fuck this is? This is fuckin blood! The blood of real fuckin soldiers. Do you call yourself a fuckin soldier? Do you know how he got this blood all over his fuckin clothes? His buddies got hit, and this guy, this real fuckin soldier, risked his life, not once, or twice, but several fuckin times, trying to save their lives. And you tell him there's a fuckin war on!"

Tiny threw the trousers down and picked up his rifle. He jabbed the kid under his chin with the barrel of his M1 and said, "Now, you get off of your fuckin big ass and find him clothes that fit him perfectly, because if you don't I'm going to blow you're fuckin head off! And you know I'm crazy enough to get away with it."

"I'm sorry," the shower boy whimpered, trembling. "I'm sorry."

"Dumb bastards like you who have soft fuckin jobs go back home and tell fuckin war stories."

The others watched silently as the shower boy found Dante clothes that he could wear, but their jovial spirits had been somewhat dampened.

"We owe you an apology, gentlemen," the guide said, "and on behalf of Fatso, I apologize. Although he says he's sorry, I understand if you don't believe him, but I believe him. I know he wasn't thinking of the implications of his casual remark, but I'm sure he's aware of it now. Please don't judge all rear echelons by the attitude of some. I've been on both sides, so I know. Most of us here just want to do our jobs and survive the best we can."

"What the fuck's wrong with us?" asked Tiny. "I mean, as fuckin people. It's not just the fuckin promotions. Is it? The fuckin rear echelon guys shouldn't be resentful of us; they should be grateful."

"Some of them are both, resentful and grateful, like kids on a football team. They're glad to be on the winning team, but resentful of the guys who get most of the glory, the heroes."

"But that's so fuckin stupid!"

"Of course it is. But, as you said, guys like Fatso, who have a soft fuckin job, go home and tell fuckin war stories."

"War ain't a fuckin game."

"But Fatsos envy war heroes and go to the American Legion or, even worse, go with recruiting officers to high schools and tell everybody how great fuckin war is, and how everybody should be glad to fight!"

"Shit," muttered Dante, "why don't we just forget it and enjoy the rest of the day and night?"

The day was sunny and warm, and in clean fatigues, they felt good. And although they had been told to keep their weapons with them at all times, they decided to leave them in the tent. For a few hours, they simply wanted to forget the war and to feel like normal human beings again.

After a hot lunch, Dante sat on the grass ground and wrote Rose a long letter. He wanted to tell her about Ahn and Nap and all the rest of them who felt almost as close to him now as his own brother, but he didn't know how to express himself, not even to her. Some thoughts and feelings could not be adequately understood; they had to be experienced. He did not know how to explain that nature had somehow made his feelings numb. Even the thought of mentioning it implied that his love was never strong enough to cope with the forces of evil, as though evil, as so many people, especially religious people, seemed to believe, was a force as strong, if not stronger, as the force of good, as though Satan was as strong as God, as though infernal hate was as strong as divine Love. He had not felt competent enough, not yet, anyway, to explain the numbness of his emotions, which had made him feel detached, somehow, from his surroundings. He had heard of such writers. To him, they were reporters of scientific knowledge. Write only the facts, man, not your personal interpretation of the facts. How could he tell her that his feelings had become numb and that he had become detached from life, especially after he had written that he had felt her deep inside of him, that, feeling her love deep within him had given him the strength to endure. How could both statements be true? So, he told Rose how much he was missing her and how his love for her was growing so much stronger. When they would come together again, he warned her, he would be making love to her in Italian.

After he finished the letter, he turned onto his stomach, closed his eyes, felt the warmth and the softness of her body beneath his, and he let himself float softly away with her.

16

Before dawn, they had been back on Boomerang. Later in the day, it had begun to rain. They shouldn't complain though, Dante thought; yesterday couldn't have been a more beautiful day, but that afternoon a rumor had spread that the Chinese had planned another major attack that night, in spite of the heavy rain that was expected. And the third squad had been scheduled that night for a patrol.

After Tiny had gone to the platoon command post for a briefing, the others were waiting for him in the bunker. There was always the slim possibility that the patrol would be called off that night due to the heavy rain. That would not have cancelled it; that would have only postponed the patrol, but that had not stopped them from hoping.

The five of them lay quietly, waiting.

Someone had lit a stubby candle and had placed it on the dirt floor. They could hear the wind blowing and the rain coming down hard, whipping the canvas at the entrance, and the rain was splattering in. A rat stuck his head through a sandbag, stared at Dante, turned, and scrambled away. The wick of the stubby candle burned close to the ground, and the flames wavered, and distorted shadows of the men swayed through the bunker.

"Why the fuck don't they do something!" someone cried out.

Barlow, who was in the bunk next to Dante, turned to him, wondering who had cried out, but no one had answered the cry.

Dante closed his eyes and tried to relax. One of his most memorable moments among so many had been when Rose had said, "Make love to me in Italian." He had been thinking of that moment earlier, but he had also remembered when they had been kids in front of the fire in the cabin and they had kissed each other for the first time. He could feel the heat from the fire, and he could see the affectionate smirk on her face as she lay on her back and had prompted him to tickle her, when someone had suddenly cried out.

Dante groped for his canteen, unscrewed the cap, and took a sip. The water was warm and left a tinny taste in his mouth.

The flap opened, and Tiny entered.

"Saddle up! There are only six of us tonight. Stay in this order behind me: Marin, Finnegan, Valentino, Barlow, and Henderson. It's raining fuckin hard, so you can take your fuckin pots. If we meet any fuckin chinks, we turn quickly and come back in. Any fuckin questions?"

Everyone, except Marin, who was directly across a narrow aisle from Dante, had gotten out of his bunk and was standing up, getting dressed for the patrol.

"Come on, Marin," Tiny said gently, "I need you to stick close to me, to protect my fuckin ass."

Marin crawled out of his bunk and stood up.

As the others were putting on their cartridge belts, Marin seemed to be fumbling for something over his knapsack on the ground. He clenched a bandolier of ammo, closed his eyes, and leaned his forehead against the top bunker.

"I'm as fuckin scared as the rest of us," said Tiny, laying a hand on his shoulder, "but a little fuckin prayer helps me a fuckin lot."

"You think that's going to get you back!" Marin snapped.

"Fuck no, that's why it helps. We need each other. Our fuckin lives depend on each other. Don't fuck us up now!"

The only thing Dante had known about Marin was what little Nap had said about him. They had been on Pork Chop Hill when Marin had joined them. One of the first things Marin had said to them was, "Where's the fuckin enemy?" It had been the way he had said it. It wasn't a question; it was a boast. "You're in the wrong fuckin division," Tiny had said to him. "We ain't the fuckin marines, Marine." Marin had said his name was not Marine. It had been on Pork Chop Hill when they had been overrun, and Marin had quickly discovered, Nap had said, that "War ain't a fuckin game; it was real" and the consequences were forever, but Tiny had been convinced that the experience had made Marin a better soldier, that fear had made him cautious. Still, there was something about Marin, Dante felt, which had made him seem more of a loner than the others. It hadn't been just his detachment from them, not even just his aloofness; he had seemed even more contemptuous of people, of all people, than most people had been. Dante had tried to draw him out several times, but Marin had built up a wall around him long before he had been drafted. Dante had suspected that he was from New England, that the name was Latin, not Anglo, probably French, from Quebec originally, but not Catholic, not now, anyway, and that he had been more educated than most of them, but that he had not finished college, and that he had been too good to be in the army, and that he had been arrogant enough, Dante thought, to be unfazed by such a mundane thing as war or the fear of war. Dante had also suspected that the display of rosary beads around the neck as a label to advertise the religion of a vulgar speaking character like Tiny, had alienated Marin, and Dante had even understood how any person, Catholic or otherwise, could be alienated by the unpretentious honesty yet crudity of someone like Tiny without understanding him.

They put on their flak vests, wrapped two bandoliers of ammunition around them, and clipped a couple of grenades to their belts. Marin held his two hand grenades. They shook in his hands. He fastened them to his cartridge belt. He grabbed his rifle, and then he looked at it a moment, and he seemed to curse it. He pulled the bolt back, put the safety on, and then fumbled in the bandolier for a clip. He pressed the clip against the slide. It wouldn't go in. He couldn't hold it still. "Fuck!" He forced it in and pushed the bolt forward.

"Stick fuckin close behind me, Marin. None of us fuckin guys are alone."

Marin glanced around the bunker as though he wondered if he would ever see it again. He stood behind Tiny who was standing at the entrance and was facing them, waiting for them to line up in order.

Dante looked down at the bunk, at his knapsack, at the pouch where he kept the letters from Rose. He reached behind him, against his right hip, and felt his wallet with her picture. "Ti amo, cara mia," he said silently, pulling his helmet down. "I feel you, deep inside of me, mia amore. Take me inside of you, again, mia amore, deep inside of you, and keep me there, always."

Finnegan, with his automatic weapon, stepped behind Marin; and Dante, with his carbine, leaving his rifle behind again, stood behind Finnegan, and, immediately, Barlow got behind Dante, and Henderson, getting behind Barlow, said, "Let's go!"

Tiny pushed the flap aside, and he stepped outside into the wind and rain, and he led them slowly along a path to the platoon command post. Usually, at that time of night, at the back slope of the hill, unseen by the enemy, there were several cigarette smokers sitting on the ground and bullshitting, but the rain was coming down too hard for anyone to do anything except take shelter. Maybe, thought Dante, tonight was the perfect night to go on patrol. The visibility was so damn poor that an attack seemed too damned absurd to even think about. Flares and spotlights would hardly be enough to help much. And the ground was so damned slippery that their footing was unsteady even on level ground. They had to go up a small incline to get to the command post where the ground was fairly level again. They stopped, and they waited while Tiny went inside. Some of them lit up cigarettes.

Tiny entered the shack, dimly lighting the area as he opened the door and stepped inside. When the door shut, a faint light continued to seep under it. They remained silent, waiting for Tiny.

No more than ten minutes had passed when the door opened again, and Tiny, who was smoking a cigarette, tossed it aside and then waved to them to enter.

Inside were Rossi and Wells and Parks, sitting to the left in front of the desk. Tiny went to the right of the desk and stood in front of the bulletin board, which had a map of the area on it. Tiny told them to sit on the floor, facing the map. With a pointer, he showed them the route they would be taking. They would go through the listening post, then go left, parallel to the fighting bunkers they had occupied, until they'd reach the point of Boomerang, and they'd wait there an hour, no longer.

Behind them would be the ravine, which they could use for cover again in case they're attacked. If they are attacked, Henderson will order Marin to lead Dante and Barlow back to the listening post as quickly as possible while Finnegan covers them with his BAR, then Finnegan and Henderson and Tiny would retreat quickly to the listening post. Once they'd reach the listening post, they'd cover the others, and then they'd retreat to the checkpoint.

"Okay, saddle up!"

They followed Tiny outside into the rain and wind again.

They were so close to each other that they could almost reach out and touch each other, yet they could barely see the man directly in front of them.

They entered the deep trench to the top of the hill where they were slipping in the clay that was flowing down the hill. They made it to the top where they could almost slide down the front slope, and some of them put their hands out, trying not to fall against the man directly in front of them.

And they came to the main trench of the fighting bunkers, and they took the trench to the right, where they went past their old bunkers. The soldiers inside were quiet. The trench was muddy, and their boots were making squishy sounds as they trudged towards the checkpoint. At the checkpoint they stopped a few moments and waited as Tiny reported in. Then, they moved down the finger of the hill, to the listening post. They climbed out of the trench, walked between the barbed wire, and entered into no man's land.

Slowly, cautiously, step by step, they moved through the valley.

Suddenly, Tiny stopped, and everybody else pushed against the person in front of him. They had bunched up. One round, thought Dante, would have gotten them all. But it was so dark that if they had spread out, they would not have been able to see each other.

Tiny said, "This is so fuckin crazy! If the fuckin chinks are out here now, they'd be like us, like fuckin blind men."

"You're right," said Dante. "And if we're suddenly attacked, how can we run back to the listening post?"

"I was thinking the same fuckin thing. Why the fuck don't we stay right here?"

They did.

Dante got down on one knee, put the butt of his carbine on the watery ground and used the carbine as a stick between his legs to rest himself.

Everybody else also knelt on the ground, except Tiny. He stepped behind Marin and Finnegan, and he knelt on one knee next to Dante.

"I don't have any fuckin idea where we are," Tiny muttered. "All I know is that we're past the barbed wire and that we began to move parallel with it. So, the fuckin barbed wire has got to be a little ways behind us, and we're in a flat area. So, where the fuck is that little ravine? Anybody have any fuckin ideas?"

Henderson moved a little, behind Barlow, next to Tiny.

"I think we're a little behind it," he said, kneeling down, too. "We're still close enough to the listening post that if we spoke any louder, they could probably hear us."

"So, if we stay right here," Dante said, "out in the open field, and even if it's so damn dark, if the Chinese approach us, we should be able to see them if they're able to see us."

"So?" Tiny asked.

"So, stay right here. Why continue moving? We won't see any better than we do now. We know there aren't any trees in front of us, so, if we see anything, anything at all, any shadows moving, or if we hear anything, we know they're Chinese. I don't think there are any animals here."

"Finnegan," said Tiny, "set your BAR right here. If this fuckin rain lets up a little, we'd be able to see a little fuckin more. But if we can't see them, they sure as fuck can't see us either."

"And if they come," asked Dante. "What do we do?"

"We fuckin bug out of here! If they don't see us, we can get the fuck out!"

"Then, why don't we do an assimilated retreat?"

"What the fuck do you mean?"

"Rehearse what we should do. We don't want to get confused in this dark and go in the wrong direction."

"Good idea," said Finnegan.

"How the fuck do we rehearse it?"

"Why don't we split up? Barlow and I and Henderson go back to the listening post as quickly as we can while you stay here with the BAR and cover for us, and in a little while, you take off, too."

"Do you think you can lead them back to the listening post?" Tiny asked Dante.

"Yeah, I think so."

"Okay. But Henderson stays with us. Marin goes with you. Okay, Marin?"

"Yeah, I guess," he muttered.

"Okay. Get going. Follow Dante."

Dante stood up.

"Try to stay close to me," he said, and he moved away as quickly as he could without actually running. He tried to look down at the ground, but he couldn't see anything. He kept the butt of his carbine in front of him and kept moving. And, somehow, he came to the barbed wire, moved parallel with it, and finally came to the opening, and he noticed that the ground had become more slippery because it was on a slight incline. He went between the barbed wire and said, "Fox Company patrol" as he got closer to the gate.

"That didn't take you long. Did you make contact?"

"No. It's too damn dark to see anything. We just wanted to know if we could make it back here in this dark. We're not coming in. We're going back out there. Could you see us out there?"

"No, I can't see a fuckin thing."

"Nothing at all?"

"I see something moving now," somebody else said.

"Okay. That's the rest of the patrol. We're going back out now."

They met the rest of the patrol a short distance away from the listening post.

"I don't think we have to go as far as we did before," Henderson suggested. "In daylight, we could see the Chinese positions from here."

"Alright, we'll set up our positions here."

Finnegan placed his automatic rifle down, pointing it to the front of them, and the six of them sat on the watery ground and looked in front of them.

"As long as we can't see a fuckin thing, and they can't see a fuckin thing, we can't do a fuckin thing to them, and they can't do a fuckin thing to us. Let's hope that nobody does a fuckin thing to nobody the whole fuckin night. Let it rain the whole fuckin night."

"The whole fuckin week," added Henderson.

"Let's hope we get a flood," said Dante. "I can see the headlines now: 'Korean War Ends Due to Flooding!'"

They were sitting, waiting, peering into the darkness.

After a while, Henderson asked, "How much longer should we stay here?"

"Not much fuckin longer!"

After another long while, Tiny said, "I could fall asleep right here, in the fuckin rain. Maybe we should call it quits for tonight."

Suddenly, Dante thought he saw shadows at a distance forming a long line from left to right, moving. He poked Tiny who was sitting next to him.

"I think I see something."

At first, Tiny didn't say anything. He was peering into the darkness.

"Oh, fuck! I think I see something, too!"

They were staring in front of them. With the heavy rain falling, and the wind blowing, they couldn't hear anything else, but they could see shadows in the distance moving.

"If we don't move," Tiny said, "the fuckers can't see us. But if we move too fast, they might notice us."

"It's too dark to move fast, anyway," Dante said. "They can't see any better than we can, so they're not moving very fast, but they're definitely moving, and they'll be here soon enough. And it's not just a patrol."

"Fuck no! All I can see is fuckin shadows all the way across. It looks like their whole fuckin army! Let's get the fuck out of here! All of us! Henderson, lead the way. Barlow, follow him. Dante. Marin."

Marin didn't move.

"Marin! This is no fuckin time to panic!" Tiny reached down and grabbed Marin at the flak vest at the back of the neck. "If you don't fuckin move, I'll leave you here! Dante, don't wait for us! Get the fuck out! You, too, Finnegan!"

As Marin stood up, Finnegan went past him, tapped Dante, saying, "Move!"

And Dante quickly got behind Barlow, following him. Henderson was moving quickly, not running, but walking steadily.

Above them, dozens of artillery rounds began whistling, one behind the other in a steady stream, and the artillery began pounding the positions on Boomerang.

"Keep going!" screamed Tiny.

On the valley floor, it was still pitch black and raining hard, but they did not slow down, nor did they take any time to look where the Chinese were. The squad, moving steadily, was getting close to the listening post.

Suddenly, above them, a flare exploded.

"Hit the dirt!" screamed Tiny.

Immediately they dropped to the ground. Dante looked to see where the Chinese were. Some of them had hit the ground; others were still going down. They were still too far away to throw grenades at them, but they were close enough to shoot. There seemed to be hundreds of them spread over a wide area. And Dante was certain that some of them had spotted the patrol.

Tiny said, "Don't fire until they do."

But burp guns opened fire.

Dante quickly fired back, spraying them with his carbine, and to the left of him, Finnegan was firing his automatic rifle. A few Chinese decided to advance, but they were quickly cut down or had decided to hit the ground for cover. Everyone in the squad seemed to be firing, except Marin. Tiny screamed at him: "Fire your fuckin rifle!" But Marin didn't move. Tiny rolled over, and he was almost on top of Marin. "Fire, you sonofabitch!" Marin cried, "It's jammed!" Tiny pulled the rifle away from him and fired a shot. "The fuckin safety was on!"

He shoved the rifle back at Marin.

Marin began firing it.

The flare seemed to last forever.

Dante was surprised that more Chinese were not firing back, and he was even more surprised that they were not trying to advance now. He knew that they were waiting for the flare to die out, but the line was waiting for the patrol to return to the checkpoint before opening fire. The line could observe them now in a firefight.

Dante was firing as fast as he could. He replaced the banana clip, and he was firing again. He was suddenly aware that his fear did not interfere with his performance as long as he was active, and he was as strangely thrilled by the display of firepower as he had been in the bunker, even now, as he observed the sweeping fire of Finnegan's automatic rifle flowing with the small arms fire of the rest of the squad. And when Dante inserted another clip, he was surprised to see that his hands were trembling so much.

Just before the flare died out, rounds began to drop around them. Henderson and Tiny both agreed that they were mortar, not artillery rounds. The artillery was still pounding Boomerang.

As soon as the flare died out, Tiny yelled, "Let's get the fuck out of here!"

Henderson cried out, "Go, Barlow!"

"Right behind you. Dante?"

"I'm behind you. Finnegan?"

"I'm following you."

Tiny said, "Marin's here, too. Don't stop! Just keep going."

Mortars were landing between them and the listening post, but there was enough darkness, at least, to keep them going, yet enough light from the explosions to let them see that they were going in the right direction. The problem was that they were moving laterally to the Chinese, while the Chinese were coming straight at them and getting closer. The squad could be seen moving by the flashes of light. Fortunately, so far, the mortars had not landed close enough to stop the patrol, but the patrol would have to move through the mortar fire, which was now falling all around them.

Dante was hoping that neither side would use another flare.

The ground was shaking as he was following Barlow, not running, but moving quickly, and Henderson cried out in front of them, "We're here! I can see the listening post!"

Dante looked to his right. As a round landed, in the flash, he saw the barbed wire, and beyond it, he could see the listening post with men inside. But the ground around him was gushing into the air.

The earth behind him was erupting, and suddenly the earth sprang up and whacked him in the face, and debris came pouring down on him. As he stirred in muddy ground, someone was groaning. And then, screaming over him, someone was running.

As he tried to get up, Dante could feel warm wetness on his right side, from his right hip, down his thigh where his fatigues had ripped open, but his leg was numb.

Behind him, someone was groaning again.

Dante tried to push himself up, but his body slumped down again. He rolled over, placed the butt of his carbine on the ground, pushed down on it, and, leaning on his left leg, he finally pushed himself up.

Tiny, on the ground, was on his back. He was a mass of blood.

Dante got down on one knee to look at him.

His belly was torn open, and his guts were hanging out. In a flash of light, his body quivered. And then it went limp.

His cold eyes seemed to be staring up at the falling rain as though he could not believe that his soul was departing from his body, rising into the darkness, into eternity.

"Dante, where are you hit, man?"

Barlow was pulling him up.

"I don't know, but I think I can stand and I can walk."

"Are you sure?"

"Yeah, thanks. Lead the way. Where's Finnegan, and where's Marin?"

"Finnegan's hit. Henderson's helping him, dragging him to the listening post, but Marin wasn't so lucky."

"Get going, quickly. Don't worry about me."

"You sure?"

"Move, damn you!"

Barlow moved quickly.

Mortars continued falling, but he noticed that Barlow and he had finally reached the opening in the barbed wire. Barlow stopped and looked behind him.

"Don't stop!"

Dante's feet were slipping on the slight incline between the barbed wire, but he stayed close behind Barlow who seemed to move faster across the flat, clear ground past the gate to the listening post. Dante also tried to make a dash to the trench, but his right leg was dragging. He began to hobble frantically to keep up with Barlow. He was gasping, his legs unable to move fast enough; urine oozing down his legs. A voice in the distance was calling, "You can make it," as the earth erupted again and he was hurled into the air.

"Dante! Dante!"

Rose was calling out to him as he lay in a puddle of mud at the bottom of the listening post.

Part Three

Homecoming

What could I say to my kid brother now that the war had ended and he had not only faced Death, he had actually touched it, and he had, somehow, survived? He had barely survived, but he had remained alive, still, in spite of the loss of his left arm and the wounds to his back and to both of his legs, which had caused him to limp. Do I tell him that he must now forget the war? Do I tell him that he was lucky to be alive, still, as the doctors in Japan had told him? Do I tell him that now he had to recuperate from his war wounds and to adjust to civilian life? How does someone forget his most terrifying experiences?

And what should a returning veteran like him expect from his fellow civilians who had sent him into the war? Do they owe him anything for his service? Or had he merely performed his duty, and therefore, he should not expect anything in return? They would allow him to wear his uniform and to display his medals on Veterans' Day parades, and he, in turn, should be thankful that some of them, at least, still allowed him to reside in their neck of the woods with his wife and his daughter. In seventeen other states in our land of the free, he and his wife would be locked up in jail, war veteran or not.

When he had returned home, regular people had expected him to change, but he hadn't. Not really. Not in any way that they had expected him to change. Actually, he had become even more determined and more stubborn than he had been before the war. He had become even stronger in his convictions to know, love, and to serve

485

God, himself, and his family, as though it had not only been his natural rights, but his duty to God Almighty, in spite of the laws to the contrary in some of our states. He had become even stronger in his love and faith, for example, for his wife, to whom God had joined him, and from whom no man could put asunder. He had even become more willing to serve mankind, but to serve mankind in his own way. Now that he had done his duty by serving our country in the war, and having been permanently and seriously wounded in the performance of that duty, he had expected to be allowed to return to teaching, in spite of the fact that the new principal of the school had not wanted to rehire him.

Upon his discharge from the army, Dante had been told that he had been entitled to return to his old job, but regular people here had felt that the federal government had gone too far, forcing its "big brother" communistic principles upon us. Not only had Dante been told he could return to teaching, he had also been told that the federal government would pay all his medical expenses, pay him a monthly income as a compensation for his permanent disability for the rest of his life, regardless of his other amounts of income from other sources, and that he was entitled to receive a loan for the purchase of his first home at a lower interest rate than usual. And, he had been told he was allowed, for a minimal fee, to retain his government issued life insurance policy of ten thousand dollars. How many more benefits could any reasonable combat veteran demand from our government, benefits that had to be paid, of course, from the pockets of us tax payers?

Dante had been in a hospital in Japan for four months. He had been wounded only a few days before the truce had been finalized. Before Christmas, he had been told, he would return home.

When he had been finally discharged, Rosie was staying with her folks in New York City. So, upon his return home as a civilian, Harlem was his first stop. He had left Yokohama harbor on a hospital troop ship and had landed in Seattle where he had been put on a troop train to New Jersey. He had been discharged in the middle of the morning, and by the middle of the afternoon, the first Friday in

December, while I was in the restaurant, preparing the pizzas for that evening, the telephone rang.

"Hi, Tonio." I recognized the voice immediately. "Would you like to say hello to your brother?"

"Rosie! When did he show up, finally?"

"Just a few minutes ago. Oh! I can't believe he's home! I was a nervous wreck, just waiting for him. I'm so damn happy! He's all choked up now. But he wants to say hello to you. He's sitting here in a soft chair, and he's holding the baby now. He's so happy, he's crying! He's really crying."

"Oh, that's great! Put him on, please!"

She held the telephone to Dante's ear.

"Hey, Tonio! How's everybody up there doing?"

"Everybody's great! We're all waiting to see you! How are you feeling?"

"Ah, great! It feels so damn great being here! I now have a beautiful baby daughter. I just can't believe how lucky I am!"

We talked for almost an hour. My mother, in the house, had picked up the phone, and so the three of us talked together.

Dante said that Ben John would drive them here, to Cascade, early Sunday, right after church, so they would be arriving here late Sunday afternoon.

On their first night together after his return, Dante and Rosie had not spoken of his experiences; they simply enjoyed being physically together again. "You feel so damn good!" they said to each other again and again, until, having wrapped themselves into each other, they fell into a deep sleep, drifting together into a land of dreams and fantasies.

He had never even thought of warning her of the nightmares he had been having, though, as if his life would return to normal because he had arrived home.

Almost every time he had fallen asleep, he had been in a bunker or in a trench, and the Chinese had been attacking. Or, he had been in no man's land, and the enemy was surrounding him as he was trying desperately to get back to the listening post. And then, he would wake up and would become aware that he had only been dreaming, and he would sigh in relief and would return to sleep.

On his first night back, sleeping with Rose, he must have been sleeping peacefully for most of that night, because it was daybreak when he woke up, screaming, "Hit it!" and jumped out of bed and landed on the floor.

Almost immediately, he had become aware of what he had done, that he had been having the nightmare again, and that he had thought he had heard an artillery round coming in, and that he had actually yelled out and had jumped down.

When he crawled back into bed, Rose was staring at him.

"I'm sorry," he murmured.

"Are you okay?"

"I was having a dream."

"About Korea?"

"Yeah," he muttered.

"Do you want to tell me about it?"

"If I scared you, I'm sorry."

"Please don't be sorry for something beyond your control. I think you were startled by the alarm clock in the other room."

"Alarm clock? That's what it was? Damn! I was dreaming about the war, which is normal, and when the alarm went off, it sounded like the whistle of an artillery round coming in, and that's why I cried out and jumped on the floor! It's kind of comical when you think about it."

"I'd rather think of something else," she said softly, grasping his face, and she pulled it against her and held it between her breasts. "My mother set the alarm so she could get up early to make us a big batch of pancakes for us because she thought we'd be famished after you'd make love to me in Italian." She reached down between his thighs and grasped his penis and began stroking it. "I want to feel you inside of me again, deep inside of me! You make me feel so good! So damn good!"

That Sunday afternoon, my mother and my Aunt Maria made over thirty pounds of gnocchi in the restaurant while we were waiting for Dante to return home. At that time of the year, just two weeks before the winter solstice, the darkness arrives early, so, by the time Dante had arrived, it was dark, and the celebration of his return home had begun. Officially, the restaurant was closed on Sundays, so we were able to celebrate late into the night.

I didn't get much chance to talk with him that first night, because just about everybody in the flats wanted to welcome him home. Considering how badly he had been wounded, he seemed happy to be surrounded by friends and family. He even joked with the younger kids about having bought himself a modern and a more efficient, but very expensive, left arm, with a clasping hook at the end of it, which he removed every night before going to sleep.

Dante and Rosie would be staying with my mother until they'd find a place to live, but during the next few days, they would be staying downstairs, sleeping in my room, while Ben John and Anna were staying with my mother.

And, that night, for the first time in a very long time, I slept with Joy. She had been happy to see Dante again. Now she had someone with whom she could discuss her writing. She was so happy she even let me have sex with her that night. We were all in a festive mood, of course, eating and drinking and dancing in the restaurant until long after midnight, that by the time Joy and I got into bed, it seemed natural to make love to her. She, of course, wouldn't have said it was making love; it was having sex.

The next day, Pearl Harbor Day, I drove Dante to the school during the middle of the afternoon.

"You're not planning to go back into teaching, are you?"

"I sure am."

"Shackle is the acting principal now. The old principal had a heart attack a few months ago. And, according to Minnie, Shackle doesn't want to rehire you."

"Are you still seeing Minnie?"

"She comes in the restaurant occasionally. So, yeah, I see her, but I'm not still seeing her, not since I got married, if that's what you mean. Besides, I've never told Joy about my relationship with Minnie. Why should I?"

"She's been writing to me, telling me what's been happening at the school. Yeah, she told me that Shackle doesn't want me, but it's not up to him."

"Who's it up to?"

"Me. I'm entitled to my old job."

"I've been thinking of going into insurance. I think you'd be good at it."

"Me? Are you kidding? I'd rather make pizzas."

"I'm serious. You should think about it."

"I don't even want to think about selling insurance."

"It's a good, clean job, and you can help people feel secure. And, if you're willing to put in the time, you can make a good living. People would rather buy insurance from someone like you, someone they can trust, than from some guy who just wants to sell them insurance for the money."

"The only reason anyone would sell insurance is for the money."

"Well, what's wrong with that? The only reason I make pizzas is for the money. That's the only reason most people work. For the money."

"I know," Dante muttered. "It's the only reason why some people live."

"And our American forefathers," I grinned, "the Puritans, thought that wealthy people were favorable to God and were, therefore, highly moral, and that poverty among people was proof of their immorality."

I'm not sure why I had mentioned that, because I didn't really agree with the Puritans, but, I guess, I was trying to say that money itself wasn't inherently evil.

Dante retorted, "And the Puritans also believed in witchcraft."

"And today, some of them still do." But I wasn't grinning when I had said that.

When we arrived at the school, the last class had just about ended.

Dante wanted to see Shackle immediately. I told him I'd meet him in the teachers' room. While he went to the principal's office, I went into Minnie Birch's room.

When I entered her room, she was sitting at her desk. She looked up and saw me staring at her. Her face became radiant as she smiled.

"Hi," I said. "I took Dante down here to see Shackle. My brother came home last night."

"I heard! I want to see him! How's he doing?"

"Well, he was badly wounded, but in spite of that, he seems to be doing quite well."

"Let's talk in the teachers' room. I can use a cigarette."

The first thing she said in the teacher's room was, "Shackle doesn't want to rehire him."

We were alone.

"My brother thinks he's entitled to return to teaching."

"We can certainly use him. Right now. But I suppose he wants time to himself, for a few weeks, anyway."

"I assume he's talking to Shackle now about it."

She lit a cigarette, took an ashtray from a large desk, and then she sat on a couch.

"I don't think Shackle has any influence with the superintendent, thankfully, but if the superintendent asks me about Dante, you know I'll certainly recommend him highly. He's an excellent teacher, too good to be here, actually. He could teach at UNH, or at Dartmouth, if he wants."

I sat down on the couch with her.

She crossed her legs and placed the ashtray between her thighs.

"I suppose." she continued, "he'll be writing about his experiences."

"Yeah, I'm sure he will."

"What about *you?*"

"What do you mean?"

"Have you tried to do any writing lately?"

"No."

"Why not?"

"About *my* experiences? That would be embarrassing. Wouldn't it? Besides, I'm not a writer. I could never make a living at writing."

"You're a much better writer than Joy," she said, smiling at me.

"Thanks, but that doesn't give me much encouragement."

"How are things between you two?"

"Well, that's not something I enjoy discussing, especially now, with you."

"I'm sorry to hear that. I really am."

"Why should you be sorry? You warned me about her. Remember?"

"Yes, I certainly did warn you about her," she murmured, "even though Joy and I had been good friends at the time, I thought."

"You were?"

"She must have mentioned something to you."

"I don't recall her telling me that. If you were good friends, why haven't you ever visited us?"

"I was never invited, not to your house, but I visited you several times in the restaurant."

"Good friends don't have to be invited; good friends can just drop in suddenly."

"Joy and I had been good friends, I thought, until I introduced her to you. Have you ever told her about us?"

"Of course not!"

"Why not?"

"She asked me if I had ever, well, made out with you. She implied that you had said something to her, that you had said that you were attracted to me, and I said that if I had known that, I would have done something about it."

She grinned at me.

"You've never told her *that*!"

"I did, honestly. Did you really tell her that you were attracted to me?"

"I might have implied it. I don't remember if she had ever asked me, but if she had, I never would have denied it. I've always said nice things about you. I've told her, more than once, I think, that you're a great guy. Maybe I even talked too much about you." She drew a deep puff, blew the smoke out, and putting her hand on my knee, she said, "Joy never asked about my relationship with you. I didn't know she had been so desperate to get married until it was too late. I don't think I can ever forgive her for trapping you the way she did. I've never blamed you for, well, for falling for her, although it had made me so damn angry at both of you."

As she slid her hand up my thigh, the heat from her warm hand penetrated me.

"I'd like us to continue to be good friends," she said.

"Even though I'm married now?" I asked, my voice a little higher than usual.

"But are you? Really?"

"Legally, I am." I covered my crotch with my hands. "And I wanted it to work the way it should, whether I had married her, or someone else, like you. And I've never thought of ever being unfaithful to my wife, whoever she is."

"Even if she's unfaithful?"

"Well, I shouldn't have said I've never thought of being unfaithful. I've thought about it, too much, lately," I muttered, "but that's not the type of guy I want to be."

"I know that much about you. And I know what you want. I know that you want her to be faithful to you, too. What would you do if you found out that your wife was having an affair with another man?"

"I'd kick her ass out of the house! Joy knows that."

"What about her son?"

"What about him?"

"Would you let her have custody of him, or would you want to punish her for her infidelity?"

"Why are you asking me these questions? I'm not a complicated guy, am I? I only want what most other people want. I think. Just to love and be loved. I wanted to have that with you. Remember? I haven't changed. For whatever reasons, you didn't want to marry me."

"Not until you'd finish your education."

"But I didn't. Not yet, anyway. I know now that I made a mistake, that I've made one mistake after another, but I have to decide, now, what to do. I need time to figure things out. After all, I'm a married man now, with responsibilities."

"And in the meanwhile, I've been waiting."

"For *me*?"

"No, for Santa Clause!"

I, too, lit a cigarette.

"Do you think," I asked, "that you understand my situation?"

"Yes, I think I do."

"You're aware, then, that I'm letting Joy decide if she wants to continue with the marriage."

She stubbed the cigarette into the ashtray.

"There's no reason why we can't be friends," I said, "the three of us. Is there?"

"Do you remember when I told you that we can't always do what we want?"

"Of course I remember, and we restrained ourselves, and when you were free to do what we wanted, we both enjoyed each other even more. You didn't regret waiting then, did you?"

"Well, I know that *you* can restrain yourself."

"I invite you to visit us, in my house, anytime you want."

"Thanks. And you know, of course, that in my house, I'm open to you, always."

The door opened.

Dante stood in the doorway.

"Goodbye, Mister Valentino," a female student said. "It's awfully nice to see you back!"

"Thank you. Good bye."

He closed the door and faced us.

"Dante!"

Minnie stood up and embraced him, and he returned the embrace.

"It's so good to see you again," she said.

"It's great to see you, too."

She took a step back and said, "Let me get a good look at you. Oh, you look as handsome as ever, but I was expecting to see you in your uniform."

He was wearing his khaki overcoat; otherwise, he was wearing casual civilian clothes. And, what would have been his left arm was tucked to the side of him so that she was unable to see it.

"But I'm out of the army now. I'm home for good."

"Great! Your brother told me you want to get back into teaching. Have you spoken to Jed?"

"Yeah, but he didn't seem particularly happy to see me. As the head of the English department, how do you feel about my returning?"

"I was just telling Tony that we could certainly use you, right now, but, as I've told Tony, Jed doesn't want you. I've talked to him about you, but he won't listen to me."

"I'm going to see the superintendent." He looked at me as I was smoking my cigarette on the couch. "Right now."

"Do you want me to go with you?" I asked.

"No. Do you mind waiting for me? I should be back soon."

"I'll be happy to wait for you, if Minnie will wait with me."

"Of course," she said, smiling. And, turning to Dante, she said, "I have a feeling that the superintendent will gladly hire you. Tell him that I said we need you, right now, and if he has any questions about you, he can call me. Everybody, except Jed, of course, will be so happy to have you back! Good luck to you, Dante."

He turned away, pushed his prosthetic left arm into his deep side pocket, opened the door, and he left.

"He's limping," Minnie said.
"And he lost his left arm."
"Oh, God!"

About a half hour later, Dante returned from the superintendent's office.

According to Dante, the superintendent had agreed that he would get his job back as soon as he wanted to teach. They had both agreed that he would receive a contract in March for the following school year, and that, beginning in January, Dante would be first on the list to be called in as a substitute teacher for the remainder of this school year.

Minnie embraced him again and said how happy she was to have him back.

He then invited her to Sunday afternoon dinner to celebrate his return to teaching, and I, of course, happily agreed, and Minnie accepted.

In the middle of the week, Ben John and Anna went back to New York, and Dante and Rose moved in upstairs with my mother. And, once again, Joy insisted that I would return to my own room to sleep.

I had told her, of course, after I had seen Minnie that Monday afternoon, that Dante had invited Minnie to dinner the following Sunday at noon. To my surprise, Joy had seemed delighted.

"We can continue with our big celebration," she had said in front of Dante and Rosie, "celebrating Dante's homecoming during this Christmas season. We have a lot to celebrate, including his return to teaching. And it will be so nice to celebrate it with Minnie."

To me, that sounded good, and I was happy to see Joy in a festive mood. Usually, she hadn't wanted to bother celebrating our own birthdays, had seemed to forget even our wedding anniversary, and she had always hated all holidays, especially Christmas, when other people seemed happiest, which had seemed to depress her so damn much that she couldn't even write anything, even though she had used writing to express her feelings and to escape from her miserably boring life. So, I was quite surprised to see such warmth glowing in her.

But on that Wednesday night, when we were alone and relaxing on the couch after I had left the restaurant and she had been in the house, writing, she mentioned that she was looking forward to having Minnie for dinner that Sunday.

"Too bad it won't be just the three of us, though," Joy said. "That could be so damn interesting!"

"What do you mean?"

"I mean," she said, "so damn intimate!"

We were clad only in our bathrobes, before getting ready for bed, and we were each smoking a cigarette and sipping on a hot cup of coffee spiked with a hundred proof of homemade anisette. We were sitting so close together that we were almost touching. I stared at her, not knowing how to respond, and wondered what in hell she had really meant.

"On the other hand," she added, slurring her words a little as though she had been drinking a little earlier, and that she was enjoying her thoughts, "with more people here, maybe she'll be, well, inclined to drink more to make herself feel more comfortable and more sociable with your, well, with your family, especially a family like yours, with whom she's not accustomed to having intercourse, if you know what I mean, a family that can be so damn loud and earthy, and so damn overwhelming to someone like her, such a dainty, superior thing, so demure and so far beyond them that they could never understand nor appreciate such a delicate lady with such an elegant demeanor."

"I don't know what in hell you're talking about!"

"Well, anyway, after they would leave, and she's become so inebriated that her inhibitions have become subdued, we can invite her to spend the night with us."

"Spend the night with us?"

"It'll be just the three of us. And maybe we'll be able to get to know the real woman, the real Minnie Birch, the morally upright, or, I should say, the morally uptight, sophisticated school madam, stripped to her flesh."

"You mean, sleep here, with us?"

"Well, she shouldn't drive home when she's intoxicated."

"Yeah, but where's she going to sleep?"

"You wouldn't mind if she slept in *your* bed."

"Of course not."

"That's what I thought."

"And I'll sleep in yours, then."

"Like hell!"

"What are you talking about? Where am I going to sleep?"

"Where the hell do you think you'll be sleeping? Where you're going to sleep tonight. Back in your own friggin bed."

"Are you suggesting what I think you are?"

"What do you think I'm suggesting?"

"That I can, somehow, seduce Miss Birch. That I can get her into my bed."

"You're man enough to do it. Aren't you? For you, it should be easy. This Sunday night should be a good opportunity for you."

"How do I persuade a spinster like her, probably even an uptight virgin, to get into bed with me, especially with you here with us? Are you suggesting we get her so damn drunk that she'll pass out, and that we'll put her into my bed so that when she wakes up, she'll see me in bed with her and will think we had sex even though she'll think she can't even remember? I don't think that makes much sense, and that's too damn cruel to do to anyone, even to someone you despise."

"No, I wasn't suggesting that! Although, that would certainly humiliate her, especially if she thought I had walked into your room and had caught the two of you in bed together!"

"Why do you despise her so damn much?"

"I don't despise her! I've told you before; I just don't like her condescending attitude. She thinks she's so damn superior, to both of us, just because she's so, well, so damn religious, such a damn puritanical Yankee whose ancestors came over on *The Mayflower*! A Wasp! A Brahmin on Joy Street. She assumes that being a virgin validates her purity, that it substantiates her perceptions of her moral superiority to us, that she's had a better upbringing, from a higher class of people. I'd just like to see you pull her down from her pedestal, to strip away her virtuous façade, to prove to her that she'd really enjoy getting laid. She'd enjoy it so damn much, she'd want you to do it to her again and again, and, of course, she would even convince herself that she's madly in love with you. That would become her excuse for wanting you to fuck her so damn much. Tell me the truth now. Wouldn't you like to get her into your bed?"

"Well, at first, when you said the three of us, I thought you meant the three of us sleeping in the same bed."

"A ménage a trois! Are you serious?"

I drew a deep puff, and after exhaling and shaking my head, I grumbled, "Well, it sounded like you were the one who was suggesting it, not me."

"Your mind is twisted!"

"Me? Aren't you the one who suggested getting her drunk and then we invite her here to sleep with us?"

"So that she can have fun playing with you, and you can free her of her damned puritanical inhibitions. You'd enjoy it as much as she would, probably more!"

I put my cigarette out, finished my drink, and put my empty cup on the coffee table.

"But if she gets too drunk, she won't be able to play with me. And if she doesn't get drunk enough, she'll probably get too damned embarrassed to play with me, unless, well, maybe, but just maybe, she sees you playing with me, and if she sees how much fun you're having," I said, sliding my hand under her bathrobe between her thighs, "maybe that will make her get so damned excited, she'll want to have fun, too."

I wasn't serious, of course; I was just talking foolishly and amusing myself, but Joy took a couple of swallows from her cup, took a puff from her cigarette, and she looked up and squinted at me.

"Maybe you're right," she said softly. "Together, we can get her in the mood."

"Get her in the mood? How?"

"By creating an intimate atmosphere, you and I," she said, putting her cigarette out, "like you're trying to do now, with me."

She took another swallow, put her empty cup on the table, and, grinning at me, she said, "We'll give her the opportunity to express her deepest erotic feelings, encouraging her to respond to your own desires. She will see you touching me, like you are now. You're touching me and looking at my body, but you're really seeing Minnie, now, aren't you? And you're aching to feel her up, right now. Oh, I can see you getting a big hard on! You're feeling so damn hot for each other! You can feel how hard her pussy is, opening up to you and waiting for you to penetrate her."

And Joy, stretching back on the couch, reached down and put her hand on mine.

"As Minnie," she said, pressing my hand against her, "sees you touching me like this, she will be feeling you touching *her*, igniting a blaze deep inside of her."

Stroking her fluffy pubis, I could feel the excitement surging in her, pushing my hand and urging me to stroke her harder.

"Turn the lamp off," she said softly.

I did. The parlor became dim. The only light in the front room was coming from the kitchen. The television had been turned off, and the only sound was her deep breathing. She lay back on the couch, urging me to lie next to her. Her bathrobe was open now as she pressed my hand against her. She had become as hard as a rock, and as I continued to stroke her, warm juices were oozing down her thighs.

"Getting a few drinks into her," Joy said huskily, "but not getting her too damn drunk, and playing soft music, with the lights down low, will relax her. And while you're dancing closely and slowly with her, in rhythm to the slow music, rubbing against each other, stimulating your sexual desires," she said, and paused, "well, I'll pass out, here, on the couch." She paused again. "Now," she said in a low, soft tone as I was stroking her, "she has you all to herself. She feels the heat of your body penetrating her; your hands are so damn hot, squeezing her hips against you so damn hard, making her feel so damn horny, feeling your hard prick between her thighs! Oh," she groaned, undulating her hips, lifting it against my hand. She grabbed my arm suddenly and yanked it against her. "I can feel her throbbing!" She opened my bathrobe, grasped my erection, and groaned, "Oh, it feels so damn hard! Do it to her! Do it to her *now!*"

As I crouched over her and thrust my erection between her thighs, she was trying to pull it into her. I slid my hands under her hips as she lifted herself to me, and I grabbed her buttocks, squeezing her, and pulling her against me.

"Ram it into her! Now!"

I lifted her hips up and rammed myself into her, and I began pounding her, striking her pubis with mine, and she was moaning and squirming more than I had ever seen her do before, even though, this time, we hadn't even kissed or expressed any indications of affection.

Her hands were underneath my bathrobe, on the back of my shoulders, holding me tightly against her.

"Oh," she was groaning, "oh, damn it! Do it to her harder! Harder! Oh, oh! Don't stop! Harder, harder! Do it harder! Hurt her! Hurt her!"

And the harder I did it to her, the more intense we became.

Suddenly, her body stiffened, squeezing and pulling on my erection deep inside of her, and as I was ejaculating, she plunged her fingernails into my back, and she pressed her mouth against my shoulder and bit into my flesh.

4

Just thinking about that weekend now, while I'm writing this script, fills me with disgust. Two women, both of whom I loved, I thought, had somehow, with my own cooperation, dragged me down into the pit of darkest night to wallow with them in the perverse pleasures of the flesh.

I was thinking, "I can omit this part; it's too disgusting. But what would Dante have done?"

He, who had once warned Minnie, although he had been so damn young at the time, that our deepest anxieties stem from our feelings of guilt, would not have omitted this part, because this is a fact of life, a revelation of our true selves. It is imperative of the writer, he would have said, to tell the whole truth so that we can understand life. Nothing of importance, no matter how disgusting it seems, should be forbidden as a subject in literature.

I wanted Rosie's opinion. I decided to tell her what had happened that weekend, but first I wanted her to read the chapter I had just finished as an introduction to what would follow. She sat at the table, close to me, to my right, and began to read it. As she did, her dark eyes seemed to grow bigger. A couple of times, she looked up and stared at me, as though she had been startled by what I had written. As she continued to read, I lit a cigarette. It was after midnight, and everyone else was sleeping, including Dante.

"Wow! Is that how Joy really talked?"

"Actually, I toned down the dialogue. As a matter of fact, I toned down the whole damn scene."

"Really? You mean, it was actually sexier than this?"

"Sexier? You mean, dirtier?"

"Well, yeah. Disgusting! Arousing!"

"Arousing? Are you serious?"

"When you were experiencing this, weren't you aroused?"

"Well, yeah, I was."

"And when you were recreating this, weren't you aroused again?"

I stared at her, and I was beginning to feel a little uneasy.

"That's not the point."

"Of course it is," she said, putting her warm left hand on my knee and pressing her leg against mine and smiling at me as though she were suddenly amused and was teasing me. "A good writer arouses the feelings of the reader. That's what you do."

"That's not why I wrote it."

"Why did you write it?"

And I told her what had happened that weekend. As I was relating the lurid details, she seemed shocked, but at first, she did not say anything; she removed her hand from my knee, folded her arms, and leaned back in the chair, as though she wanted to get away from me now. If she had become aroused by what I had written, she had now been repulsed by what I had told her, and she had probably become suspicious of my intentions, and was reluctant, now, to trust me anymore, I thought.

"I wanted to show you the last chapter to help me decide whether to include what had happened that weekend, or to omit it from the script."

After she had thought about it, she felt that if Dante had known the details of my relationships with Minnie and Joy, he would definitely have written about it.

"But I don't like to portray myself that way. I don't even like to portray Joy and Minnie that way, either."

"It depends on how you write it. If you do it to appeal to our prurient interests, it's trash. But if you do it to explore the laws of our nature, it could be fascinating."

She unfolded her arms, leaned towards the table, looked down at my notebook, at the last page I had written, and asked, "Why did you tone down that scene, the way Joy actually talked? You didn't want her to sound too damn sexy?"

"The way she talked sounded too damn vulgar. She thought it made her sound so liberal, so sophisticated and so damn modern to talk in the vernacular, but all it did was make her sound so damn filthy, dirtier than any bestial whoremaster."

She smiled a little and put her hand on my knee again, stroking it.

"Tell me what she really said, please."

Her voice was soft, but her dark eyes were bright.

"Well," I said reluctantly, "she referred to her, to her vagina as her," I sighed, "well, as her cunt, and, she, well, she told me to ram my big, stiff prick into her hot, juicy cunt, because it was throbbing."

She squeezed my knee and burst into laughter.

I was surprised by her reaction.

"You don't think that sounds sexy," I finally stated.

"No, not sexy at all," she said, still smiling. "It just sounds, well, it sounds comical. Actually, it sounds ridiculous."

"Joy never sounded comical to me. Ridiculous, yes, and disgusting, but never comical."

"Well, at least I understand now why you toned it down. You made it sound sexier than it was."

"I toned it down so it wouldn't sound quite so damned dirty."

"And it worked, I think. Anyway, I always thought she was sexy, but I never thought she was, well, so damned wild, or, as you put it, dirty."

"Well, at times she was, and at times she was frigid. I've never understood her."

"Dante gave me her stories to read, to get my opinion. There was ⌐ th flow to her writing, and her sex scenes were quite ne of her characters were ever endowed with any admi- :ept maybe a fierce determination to achieve success, h, if you call that admirable, but they had none of the ove, even though she tried to portray her heroes as supermen, as rugged Granite Staters, 'live free or die' individualists, but they were so damn selfish and possessive. Dante agreed with me. He said that all of her protagonists were extensions of herself, that she had difficulty believing in love."

"He was right, but she admired and respected Dante. She really did. Not that she understood him, but she had a thing for him. It wasn't sexual, I don't think, although she enjoyed teasing me by saying that if he had ever wanted her to sleep with him, that she would never hesitate to accommodate him. I think she felt, somehow, that he was more capable of love than I am, more sincere in his feelings."

"Really!"

"You never had to worry about Dante, though; you know that."

"Did you ever give Joy any reason to worry about *you*?"

"No, not until that weekend, anyway, but she had never trusted me; she doesn't trust human nature. As Dante said, she had difficulty believing in love. I think she saw Dante as a possible exception."

"Because he encouraged her."

"What do you mean?"

"To write," she muttered. "She liked him because he encouraged her to write. She does have a talent for expressing her feelings, for showing how we women really feel, and she's not reluctant to write about it either. Her problem is looking at nature as an evil force, even though she's not religious and is so critical of religion. It's so ironic."

"Ironic? Why?"

"That her ideology is so puritanical and yet so irreligious."

"You know she was so damn jealous of you, don't you?"

"Because Dante married me?"

"No, it had nothing to do with that, I don't think."

"Why would she be jealous of me?"

"I shouldn't be telling you this, but she saw you as so damn sexy! She knew, she used to say, how much guys, including me, of course, were so damn attracted to you, because we imagined how wild you would be in bed."

"What!" she cried out, folding her arms and leaning back in the chair.

"I'm serious. She said that sex, well, what she actually said was, 'Fucking comes so damn naturally to her, that I really envy her.'"

"That's so damn absurd! Joy is the ideal sexual woman." She put her warm hand on my knee again and pushed her leg against mine. "Do you think white women are sexier than, well, sexier than colored girls?"

"Of course not!"

"But you prefer white women. Don't you?"

"Well, I guess I thought I did, when I was younger, because I was influenced by the norms of, well, of the majority."

"But you're still attracted to white women, like Joy and Minnie."

"Yeah," I muttered, "but I'm also attracted to women like, well, like Jessica, and to you, of course."

She squeezed my knee again, leaned closer, and gazed at me.

"You said that, to Joy, I'm so damn sexy, but, well, I'm not, really, not to you."

"Of course you are!"

"I am?"

As her eyes studied me, I quickly became aware of having admitted my sexual desire for her. But I had assumed that had already been so obvious to her, that, as any other normal man, I had become sexually attracted to her ever since she had blossomed into such a voluptuous woman, and that she had understood, I thought, that particularly in our present situation, of having been thrust together almost constantly, the necessity of restraining my desire for her.

"You really think I'm so damn sexy?"

She sounded so damn natural, so spontaneous and innocent, and yet, she seemed so damn provocative the way her eyes, caressing me with such profound affection, were reaching deep inside of me and pulling me into her, arousing in me a deep tenderness, and yet, an intense passion.

"Rosie," I said softly as her face drew closer to mine, and the heat from her hand penetrated my thigh, "Joy had good reason to be jealous of you. She could see that you're sexier than she could ever be, more sexually attractive than she is, that sex, to you, is so natural that you don't have to make any effort to be sexy. You are sexy!"

"But I could never excite you the way she did."

"What are you talking about?"

"Well, you say that sex is so natural to me, but I don't know how to excite you the way Joy did. Sex is a lot more natural for her than for me, otherwise she couldn't have made you so damn excited the way she did."

I stared at her.

"You can't actually believe that! Do you really think you can't excite me, well, even more than she ever did? You know damn well you can! And a hell of a lot more than she ever did!"

"Well, you don't indicate, well, that kind of interest in me, not in the same way as you did with her."

"Of course not! When I say that sex is so natural to you, I don't mean it the same way as she did."

"I know that! With you, it's not something dirty. She was stereotyping us, both of us. To her, nature is evil; it's an uncontrollable, blind force. I told you, that's her problem. She was so damn attracted to you, sexually, and yet, that made her feel so damned dirty, she resented you. And she was so damn envious of me, because, to her, fucking, for us, is so damn natural that we feel free to do it! But we have to be free to love."

"You know more about Joy than I thought you did."

"Well, Dante did. We used to discuss your relationship with her, how strongly you were attracted to her, sexually. I had never mentioned it to Dante, but I was so envious of how you were so damn attracted to her, that I even felt guilty because I resented her. I told myself I resented her because of the way she was treating you, but it was also because you were so damned attracted to her, sexually, but not to me."

"No! You know how I feel about you, that I've always loved you."

"Yeah, as Nick's baby sister," she said, lowering her voice and her eyes. She rubbed my thigh again. "You love me too much to even think of, well, of fucking me. You've provided me with everything I need. Well, with almost everything."

"First of all, you're certainly capable of exciting me, of exciting any man."

"I don't want *any* man. Only you."

"And I don't want you to want any other man," I said softly. "I'd be terribly jealous."

"I'm glad. I'm glad if that's the way you really feel. But I'm afraid of losing you, too."

"And I certainly don't want you to lose me. I want to be with you, not just to take care of Dante. I want to take care of you, too, and the kids. I want us all to be together, but don't let me take advantage of our situation, to use you to satisfy my sexual urges."

She stared at me.

"I know you would never use me just to satisfy your sexual urges. Had you wanted, you could have done to me what you have done to other women, many times."

As she spoke, she rubbed the inside of my thigh and felt my desire swelling.

"Damn it, Rosie! I was never worthy of your love! Don't trust me so damn much!"

Suddenly she put her left hand on the back of my neck, drew us closer together, and planted a kiss on my mouth and let it linger.

"I'm glad I can excite you, and I hope I can satisfy you."

"Have you felt this way, well," I asked, with a weak voice, "all this time we've been living here, together?"

"After what happened to Dante that night, life had drained out of me. Nothing was real. I merely existed, like an automaton, until a few days ago, when I had a dream. It was so vivid! And it seemed so real!"

She clasped my face with both of her hands, and she gazed at me.

"You were making love to me," she said softly, almost whispering. "Everything was so beautiful. It felt like a warm summer evening, around sunset, deep in the woods, next to an isolated lily pond where colorful butterflies were floating from flower to flower. Somehow, it seemed that Dante had brought us there, to a place he knew well, so that you and I could come together, where no one could interfere.

I was lying naked on my back, on a soft bed of grass, and you were naked, too, lying on top of me, and I could actually feel your hot flesh penetrating me, moving inside of me, pushing into the deepest part of me and filling me with your love. It felt so real, and so natural; I was alive again, even though I was dreaming. You felt so good! I even had a climax. You, too. Your whole body became rigid against mine. And I felt my insides bursting into you. We came together. And I woke up in bed. Night had ended. It was the beginning of a new day. I was alive again! I felt great. Every night, I've dreamt of us, and every day, I've thought about us, but I didn't tell you, until now, because now I feel certain about us. We have a strong mutual attraction that includes sex, but it goes far beyond that, although sex is the spice that our nature provides us to enhance our feelings. Sex is our urge to come together to create new life. But for obvious reasons, you were reluctant to act on your feelings for me, and I love you all the more for that. But I've felt your sexual attraction to me. I could never feel this strongly for you unless I felt it in you," she said, stroking my thigh.

"I've always had a tender feeling for you, but I had never wanted to think of it as sexual, the way I've felt with, well, with other women. I had always enjoyed hugging you and kissing you, but my feelings for you felt so tender and so natural until, well, until I became aware of you as, well, as a woman, a sexually exciting and a so very incredibly attractive woman, a woman with needs, whose needs excite my own needs and desires."

"Your affection for me became compounded by sexual desire. And that makes you feel guilty?"

"Yes."

"Why?"

"You know why," I replied weakly. "I wanted to fuck you; I really wanted to fuck you."

"Sex without love for each other, as a source of guilt, I understand. But if all you ever wanted was to fuck me, you would have been doing it to me these last two years."

"Not without feeling guilty."

"But that's not why you've restrained yourself, with me, anyway. Whenever Joy excited you, you've never hesitated to, well, to fuck her. And that's what you were doing to her. Can you honestly say you were making love to her?"

"No," I muttered.

"Imagine us now, if you can," she whispered, "you and me, in bed together. Do you want to fuck me now? Is that what you really want to do to me? Think about it right now. Think about how much you really want to, how much you've always wanted to. Why have we come so close so many times when we were younger, but you would never go all the way, not with me? Think about how much you really want to."

I felt my face getting warm, but she continued.

"What is the source of your feelings? What are your feelings telling you now?"

She didn't wait for me to answer.

"And your brother, from wherever he is now, what is he saying to us? Put yourself in his place. Has he stopped loving us because we're locked into this situation? Has either of us stopped loving him? What is he saying about our situation? Is he telling you that it is better to fuck Joy and Minnie than to make love to a woman whom you love and who loves you? In our situation, what do the laws of our nature dictate? We know what our society dictates. We know that some people are certain that we're committing adultery, simply because we're living together, that, like a bitch in perpetual heat, I'm enticing you, gratifying carnal forces of our nature, because they assume we're in a situation that's controlled by the forces of our nature, which are blind and therefore evil, forces that are too tempting even for them to resist."

I didn't know how to respond.

"During the past two years, our situation has changed drastically. I didn't change it. You didn't. Your brother didn't. Love didn't change it. But it has changed; and it has changed our relationship. And I'm afraid, now, of losing you."

"No, I swear you won't lose me! We didn't create our situation. But we have to overcome it, somehow."

"Whatever we do, I need you. I know that's not the ideal form of love, but that's the best I can do for now. I want you to know how our situation has changed our relationship, how I now feel about you. If you want to sleep with me, I'm more than willing. You give me strength and courage. I want to be, well, a wife to you. Not like Joy was, but a real wife, like I was to Dante. I love you. I love you so damn much; I love you the same way that I love Dante, maybe even more so, because now I need you so much."

"You know that I love you, too."

"And I know that you desire me, that we desire each other, because we know and love each other, and we want to know and love each other more and make each other happy. I know who you are. Big brother of Dante! I want you to take me as your wife. I want to feel you, to feel you moving deep inside of me!"

She rested her head on my shoulder, and I put my arms around her and held her, letting a delicious feeling flow through my whole being as her warmth penetrated my body.

"If we could only understand the laws of our nature," she said. "Sex, for example, is an expression of love, but it's also so much more, somehow, yet I've heard of cases of sex being terribly violent, of being perverted, twisted into an evil force."

"That's what I was trying to show in the last chapter. We can take something good, and twist it into something ugly, which disgusts us and yet promises to satisfy our sadistic impulses, especially our hate. Why do we derive pleasure from such desires? Are we created with such desires? And if so, why?"

"I can't believe that we're born with the desire to be evil. Being in harmony with our nature sounds good, but what is our nature? When Dante returned home from Korea, I had expected our lovemaking to be gentle, the way it had been, and on the first night, he was very gentle, as though he was afraid of hurting me, but after each nightmare, he became, well, intense. He didn't hurt me, but he would thrust himself into me desperately, and he would cling to me, clinging to life. And I enjoyed it. He was using my body to restore life to his, and I became terribly excited, letting him use my body, and he filled my own body with life, with intense passion, and as he clung to me for life, I clung to him. I could never get enough of him. I wanted him more and more. I took from him, yet I gave to him; I gave him all of me, all of my heart and my womb. My whole being was open to him, always. And then, and then," she moaned. And her eyes were filling with tears.

I held her tighter, and I brushed my lips over her face. As she closed her eyes, I kissed them lightly and tasted the saltiness of her tears.

"I love you," I whispered as I kissed her ear.

I felt her hand rubbing the top of my leg again.

Cupping her face, I kissed her mouth, long and hard, sucking on her lips, and I could feel her passion rising as she moved her hand up and slid it inside of my shirt, under my belt, inside the top of my trousers. Her warm hand was touching my flesh, rubbing the lower part of my abdomen, and she reached down and grasped my erection, and, tenderly, she began stroking it.

I gasped.

"I want to feel you inside of me!" she cried out. "I want you to make me feel good again! To be alive again!"

5

After making love with Rosie, I didn't even want to think of having had sex with Joy and Minnie, and I certainly didn't feel inspired to write about that weekend with them almost four years ago, but in the afternoon, after Rosie and I had given Dante a bath, I sat at the kitchen table and, while everyone else was taking a nap, I made the effort to write about that weekend.

On that Saturday morning, one day short of two weeks before Christmas, instead of going directly into the restaurant to prepare for that evening, I had decided to see Minnie to warn her of what Joy had planned for her after that Sunday afternoon dinner.

I drove to the back of her house, and as soon as I got out of the car, her dog, which I hadn't seen in two years, came running through snow, seemed to recognize me immediately, and I patted her. As she followed me to the back door, it suddenly opened.

"Wow! What a surprise seeing you here!"

The dog and I entered the house.

Minnie was wearing tight, black ski slacks and a tight, white wool sweater, and her long hair, like honey draping her shoulders, was clinging to her bulging bosom. She was looking as sexy as ever as she had opened the door. We were staring at each other in her tiny hallway.

"I hope this isn't an inconvenient time to suddenly drop in on you like this."

"That depends. If this is a friendly visit because you want to see me again, this is certainly not an inconvenient time."

"After seeing you last Monday, I couldn't wait to see you again."

"Well, I don't know what to say, except that I'm glad you're here. I hope you stay for a while. I've told you that I'm always open to you."

I nodded and smiled as I removed my coat. I hung it on the clothes rack, and I removed my boots and put them under the rack.

"Have you eaten breakfast?" she asked as she put her arms around me and pressed the front of her warm body against mine.

"Yes, I have," I answered, then kissed her gently on the lips.

"Have you forgotten how to kiss? I thought you said you couldn't wait to see me again."

As I gave her another kiss, she opened her mouth wide and thrust her tongue between my lips. I thought of sliding my hands under her sweater, but my hands would have been too cold against her warm flesh, so I pulled her hips into mine and felt her breasts squeezing against me.

"I'm so glad you're here! Do you want anything?"

"Just you."

I followed her into the kitchen.

"I mean, coffee or anything?"

"No, just you."

"You know you can have me anytime you want. Do you want me here, in the kitchen?" She turned, facing me. "Or on the couch in front of the fireplace, or," she said softly, putting her arms around me again, "upstairs, in my warm bed?"

"Well, that's not exactly why I came to see you."

"What a shame! You make me so damn excited by coming here, and then you disappoint me so damn much."

"Well, I was afraid that my presence would make you feel so uncomfortable that I didn't dare to think of us as I used to, but now, you feel so damn good, like this, that you make all of my old feelings for you rise up."

"Yeah, I can feel all of your old feelings for me rising up and pushing into me, but why do you think I'd feel uncomfortable with you?"

"Because, well, I'm married, and that makes me, or should make me, well, to a woman like you, unavailable."

"A woman like me? But I don't think of you as really married, not to anyone I know, not yet, anyway. I only think of you as a man who's been deceived, but that, eventually, since you're decent, intelligent, and mature, you'll find a solution to your predicament. And the way you're feeling right now, with me, makes it obvious that you desire a quick solution with yours truly."

"That's really why I want to see you, to talk with you, about, well, about Joy."

"Can't we talk about her after we satisfy this desire for a quick solution?" she said, pushing against my crotch.

"Let's talk in front of the fire."

"This feels hot enough to me."

But we went into the other room and stood in front of a crackling fire, and as I put my hands over the fire, I told her how Joy had planned for me to seduce her.

"Joy had even become so damn excited just thinking about me screwing you while you were inebriated, that she wanted me to screw her, too. I had never seen her become so damn passionate!"

Minnie was staring at me. She lit a cigarette.

"Did you? Did you screw her?"

"Yeah," I muttered.

She drew a deep puff and exhaled slowly.

"And you enjoy screwing her so damn much you don't want her to leave you."

"That's not true, well, not in the way you said it. As you've said, she and I are not really married; we seldom have sex, but I didn't come down here to talk about that; I came here to warn you of what she has planned for you. Do you know why she wants to do that to you? She had asked me if I had ever had sex with you, because she said you were sexually attracted to me. What have you told her?"

"I would never tell her we've had sex! I would never trust anyone that much, especially her!"

"What do you know about her?"

"Not much. I know that she's very cynical, that she doesn't believe in much, not even in love."

"That much I know. Do you know anything about her background?"

"She told me that she never knew anything about her parents, that she had been raised in an orphanage in Tennessee and had been yanked from one foster home to another when she was younger, until she was finally adopted. Even before high school, she, well, she became involved, sexually, with her adopted father, a real estate tycoon with a wife and several children, and a leader of the Klan. She told me that before she had graduated from high school, he got her pregnant, and that he paid for her to have an abortion. And he knows Jed, who's also a member of the Klan. She said that Jed had recommended her to come here to teach."

"Shackle? She never told me she had known him, not before she had taught here. Is he from Tennessee, too?"

"He told me he's from South Carolina, that he had never known her, and that he had never been in the Klan. And when he had heard that she had married you, he called her white trash."

"Rusty," I said as an ugly thought had suddenly popped into my mind, "has red hair. Shackle has red hair."

Minnie laughed.

"No," she said, "I can't even imagine her being remotely attracted to him. When you told me she was pregnant, I immediately thought of her adopted father. Maybe he has red hair, too, or maybe red hair is recessive in her genes. Anyway, she had given me the impression that her sexual relationship with him was ongoing, because she was using him for his money. Now, apparently, you're her source." She flicked ashes into the fireplace. "I'll make an effort to know her better. She's interesting. And it's interesting that she wants me to have sex with you. I wonder why."

"Not sex with me, necessarily; she said she wants to see you dragged down from your pedestal. When she asked me if I ever had sex with you, I told her I think you might still be a virgin. That's why she'd like me to seduce you."

"So, what do you think we ought to do?" She took another deep puff, and then she blew the smoke out. "Shall the three of us get drunk together, and then should I let you screw me in your own house, right in front of her, while she's gaping at us?"

"Of course not!"

"Why not?"

"It's so stupid."

"Of course it is, but it's her own idea. I'm curious to see how she'll react."

"I'm afraid she'll become even more excited than when she had only thought about it."

"I think so, too. I think she'll get so damn excited, she'll want you to do it to her, too, for me to see you doing it to her. But why did you say you're afraid?"

"Because it seems so unnatural for any woman, especially for a wife, to feel that way. Doesn't it seem unnatural to you? Do you want to see me screwing another woman? Do you think that would excite you?"

She flicked her cigarette into the fire.

"Oh, damn! Why the hell don't you divorce her? I don't want to wait for you any longer."

"You mean you want us to get married? To each other?"

"As soon as you'd finish your education and get a decent job. You know I'd wait for you. I've waited this long."

"And what would you do if you suddenly got pregnant?"

"I know damn well you'd marry me, and then I'd nag you until you'd finally finish your education."

"So, you want me to divorce Joy, pay alimony for her and for Rusty, and return to college. Are you going to pay for my expenses?"

She stared at me. After a while she said, "Let me think about it."

She invited me to stay for lunch. After lunch, I drove home, went immediately into the restaurant and made preparations for the evening, and then I went into the house and took a nap.

6

Two hours before midnight, Dante came into the restaurant and said to me, "You have company."

"Who?"

"Minnie Birch."

She had arrived at the house almost an hour earlier. Joy had called Minnie to remind her of the invitation to the Sunday afternoon dinner, and during the conversation Joy had invited her to come to the house and to sleep over. Needless to say, Minnie had been delighted to accommodate Joy.

A few days later, Minnie would tell me of their conversation. While both of them had been drinking and becoming sufficiently inebriated to confide in each other, Joy had admitted that two years ago, when she had married me, her adopted father had impregnated her again, but this time, according to Minnie, Joy had not wanted another abortion. And now Joy, having felt somewhat guilty for having deceived me, hadn't really wanted to remain married either, because marriage had made her feel too damn restricted, especially by the insufficient amount of money I had allowed her. That had surprised me because Joy had been in charge of the books for the restaurant and had taken responsibility for all its finances. Anyway, Joy had also told Minnie that she hadn't wanted to hurt or to deceive me, because, for the most part, I had been good to her and to Rusty. Minnie had been clever enough, in spite of having become somewhat tipsy, not to admit that she had ever had sex, but she had confided to

Joy that, during the past few years, especially, she had become more sexually attracted to me and had, at times, even thought of having sex with me, and she had asked Joy how it had felt having sex, especially with me. Joy had grinned at her and had told her that I was the most passionate man she had ever known, and that if Minnie had really wanted to experience the most intensive sex ever, she could not select a more suitable partner than me. And, together, they had plotted to seduce me, there, in the house, that very night. And it wouldn't be difficult, Joy had assured Minnie; Joy had known for sure how eager I would be to fulfill their sexual fantasies.

"They want a pizza," Dante told me, "with everything on it except anchovies."

While I was making it, he told me that they were getting drunk.

"They're drinking tequila, straight. Joy poured us each a double shot." He really sounded concerned. "Why don't you go in the house and entertain your company?"

I told him I couldn't leave the restaurant now because it was too busy, but my Aunt Maria said that she and my mother didn't need me, that they were in control.

"I'll bring the pizza in when it's ready," Dante said.

So, I removed my apron, hung it up, left the restaurant through the back door, dashed through the cold night, and entered the back of the house.

Joy and Minnie were sitting on the couch in the front room. They were both in snug pajamas. Joy was wearing pink pajamas, and Minnie was wearing blue, and soft music was coming from the record player. They were sipping on margaritas, Joy said. They both smiled at me. Joy, who was sitting closer to the entrance, said, "Why don't you quit for the night and join us? We're having a pajama party. Just wear pajamas and slippers. Nothing else."

I went into the bathroom and took a quick shower, and I put on my pajamas and slippers, and as I was about to join them in the front room, Dante banged on the back door, entered, approached the kitchen table, stared at the three of us in our pajamas as we entered the kitchen, and placed the box of hot pizza on the table.

"We're having a pajama party," Joy told him, slurring her words a little. "Why don't you join us?"

"Thanks, but Rose and I are busy right now with the baby. I have to get back to them."

"You know you're welcome to join us," Joy said.

"Thanks, anyway, but we're going to bed early tonight."

"Well, let me make you a margarita."

The ingredients were on the table. A bottle of tequila was more than half empty. Another bottle had not yet been opened.

"Another time. Thanks. Rose is alone with the baby."

"Won't you even have another shot of tequila?" she insisted, drawing so close to him that he instinctively put his right hand up and put it on her shoulder to prevent her body from touching his.

"I will, tomorrow. We'll have a big feast tomorrow."

He was gazing bashfully at her conspicuous bosom jutting out of her tight fitting pajama tops, and he seemed cognizant of her state of intoxication that was encouraging her to boldly display the availability of her flesh to his. She was smiling provocatively.

"Well, girls," he said in a somewhat ironic tone, "relish each hot piece, and have a delightful night, and remember me in your prayers tonight."

Joy suddenly embraced him, thrusting her body against his. He looked at me, rolled his eyes up, and said, "And you, too, Superman," and he gently, but firmly, pushed Joy away, quickly turned, and left.

"Why did he call you Superman?" Minnie asked.

As though I didn't know, I shrugged.

After we had eaten the pizza in the kitchen, Joy made me a margarita, with a little too much tequila in it, and we went into the parlor and sat on the couch. I sat between them.

After a few minutes, Joy stood up and turned off all the lights except the lights on a Christmas tree in the opposite corner from us. In another corner, an automatic record player, containing several long-playing records was playing soft dance music.

After a little while, Joy, on my left, who had been rubbing the inside of my left thigh while Minnie had been rubbing my other thigh, asked me to dance with her. By this time, of course, my desire had become so damn obvious that when Joy had touched it, she had looked down and had laughed at me, and she had grasped it, pulling it through my fly to make sure that Minnie would also notice it, which, of course, she certainly had, especially when I stood up to dance. I danced with Joy for a little while, closely and slowly, and we were rubbing against each other, trying to move to the rhythm of the music. And then I danced with Minnie for a much longer time, holding her buttocks with both of my hands, and rubbing the front of my body against hers, and feeling her pushing against me, holding me tightly and pulling me against her, and her breathing grew so heavy that I thought she would have a climax right then and there, directly in front of Joy. And then we sat on the couch again and drank and talked.

"So," Joy said to me, "you actually considered becoming a minister. You would have made one hell of a spiritual advisor! Reverend Tony," she moaned, "I need you to help me, please. My husband doesn't love me anymore. Can you help me?"

After we had drunk several glasses of margaritas, Joy was sitting on my left lap, and Minnie was sitting to my right side, and both of them were leaning against me and rubbing me.

"Oh, Reverend Tony," Joy sighed, "I hurt so damn much, right here," she said, opening the top of her pajamas. "My heart is broken. Feel it," she said, grabbing my right hand and placing it on her bosom. "Heal it with your touch. Your hand is so hot! I can feel the fire in you burning me all the way down here." She pulled my hand down her belly, inside of her pajamas, between her thighs, and held it against her. "Oh, yes! I feel your fire penetrating me!"

And Minnie was staring at both of us.

Joy said, "Let us pray to Reverend Tony."

She slid down from my lap and knelt on the floor, pushing herself between my legs and covering my hardness between her breasts. As Minnie was gazing down at her, Joy put her hand over Minnie's and asked, "Do you want to feel his awesome power?"

"Oh, yes, I do!"

Joy grabbed Minnie's right hand and put it on my erection.

"How does that feel?"

"Oh, it feels so hot and hard!"

"Squeeze it a little."

Minnie was holding it tightly.

"Stroke it gently and you can feel it getting even bigger."

And then Minnie began to stroke it.

"If you want him to ram it into you, deep inside of you, you can feel its power surging through your whole body. Would you like to feel it, ramming deep inside of you?"

"Oh, yes, I do!"

"Do you want him to fuck you?"

"Oh, yes!"

"Take off the top of your pajamas and pull his face to your breasts. You have to get him so excited that he wants to fuck you."

Even through the fog of my intoxicated brain, I thought I could feel the reluctance in Minnie. To her, I thought, this had become too degrading. But, to my surprise, she complied. She unbuttoned the top of her pajamas, quickly removed it, and tossed it to the floor, grabbed the back of my head and pulled my face to her naked bosom.

"Do you feel an intense throbbing for him deep inside of you?"

"Oh, yes."

"Do you want him to fuck you?"

"Yes."

"Tell him!"

"Yes! Oh, yes!"

"Say it!"

Minnie's lips were quivering.

"Say it!"

But she was obviously too embarrassed even though she was so damn intoxicated.

"Say it!"

"Fuck me."

But she did not sound convincing enough. And as I could feel her disgust, I was ready to stop.

Joy, exasperated, said, "Lie back for him, and let him do it to you." And Joy reached up and grabbed Minnie's lower part of her pajamas.

Minnie raised her hips to let Joy pull the bottom of the pajamas down her legs, and Joy removed it, uncovering Minnie's body completely.

And as Minnie turned a little, lying back, she spread her legs, opening herself up to me. Her green eyes were opened wide, gazing up at me, waiting for me to get on top of her as Joy was kneeling over us and staring down at Minnie's full nakedness.

"She's waiting for you! Do it to her, now!"

Minnie, her face distorted, was lying silently on her back, looking up at me as though she was really expecting me to get on top of her and to actually penetrate her then and there, while Joy was eagerly observing us.

"She's waiting! Get on top of her, now, and ram it into her!"

I was staring down at her, but she seemed unreal, almost as though I were dreaming, and somehow I crouched over her and planted my knees between her legs, and as I tried to focus on her body, her white belly seemed to rise and float away. I was trying to grasp her hips.

"What are you waiting for? Fuck her! Now!"

But as she lay on her back and waited for me, the room slowly began to spin around and around and from side to side and up and down, and I knew I was about to throw up.

Somehow, I was able to get up from the couch, to push Joy aside, and to stand up on the floor, and to stagger out of the parlor, resisting, somehow, the almost uncontrollable urge to vomit, and I bumped into the kitchen table and almost stumbled to the entrance of the bathroom, flicked the light on, dropped to my knees, and threw up into the toilette bowl, wanting to empty my guts out, again and again and again to get rid of all of the terribly disgusting things that I had allowed to enter me. Sweat was running down my face. After a while I was able to stand up, lean against the sink, turn on the water faucet, and to push a handful of cold water onto my face, and I was able to stagger through the kitchen, somehow, into my bedroom, and to crawl into my bed, and to fall into deep, deep sleep.

A week after that disgusting Saturday night, Minnie told me she wanted to spend Christmas week with her folks in Florida. She had come into the restaurant that Saturday morning as I was preparing the food for that night. First, she had gone into the house, but Joy had been so busy writing that she hadn't wanted anyone to disturb her, so Minnie quickly left her and came into the restaurant to be with me, she said. I told her that she could stay with me for as long as she wanted. "Well," she said, smiling and hugging me as we were standing together in the middle of the kitchen, "I want to stay with you all day and all night." And she kissed me on the mouth.

I told her to remove her overcoat, and I asked her if she wanted a cold drink to cool down. She was wearing a snug, orange, woolen sweater and tight, blue slacks. As she hung her coat on a rack near the back entrance, she said she wanted coffee. I poured each of us a steaming cup of coffee with a shot of anisette, and we went into the dining room and sat next to each other in a booth. That's when she told me she wanted to go to Florida. She asked me to watch her house while she would be gone, to go to her house each day to let the dog and the cat out for a few minutes and to feed them.

"So, that's why you came in here. You need me to do you a favor. And I thought you came in here because I was alone and you wanted to make me warm."

"No, not to make you warm," she replied. She was sitting on the inside of the booth, to my right. She rubbed my knee. "I want to make you hot."

"You're succeeding."

She grinned and gave me a quick kiss on the side of my face.

"But remember that I'm a married man."

"A married man with a hot and cold wife," she grumbled. "I tried to be friends with her, well, sort of a friend, anyway, but I can't."

"Why not?"

"I hate what she's doing to you. If she really had any feelings for you, I'd keep away from you, probably. Well, maybe not, but she doesn't give a damn about you. She's just using you until something better comes along, and you're letting her use you. Why?"

I reached into my shirt pocket, took out a pack of cigarettes and a book of matches, put them on the table between us, and lit a cigarette.

"Because I married her, for better or for worse."

She, too, lit a cigarette.

"You thought you married her, but she never married you. When you realized she had deceived you, and you continued the relationship, you gave her the power to manipulate you."

"She can't manipulate me, and that makes her angry."

"She certainly does manipulate you, but you don't want to admit it. She uses sex to control you, but you're too blind to see beyond that. That's how most men are, I suppose, especially with women like her. When you got sick last week, she wasn't even concerned about you. When I told her I was going to see if you were okay, she said you were disgusting. Disgusting!"

"I am disgusting. The whole situation was disgusting. Sickening."

"That includes me, too, then."

"You don't think that what we were doing was sickening?"

"Yes," she murmured, and puffed on her cigarette.

"We knew that it was, and yet, we continued to degrade ourselves and each other. What does that tell you about us? Not just about you and me. The whole damn human race! Well, maybe not everybody. And what can we blame it on? Nature? Booze? Free will?

Determinism? You know what I really feel like doing to you right now? Ever since I first laid eyes on you? Way back, since high school? Back even then, when Dante told me I wanted to seduce you, I got so damn mad at him because I refused to face what had been so damn obvious to him. I told him I respected you so much that I could never do that, not to you, but when you told me you let the soldier fuck you, I got so damn mad at you, and so damn jealous of him, that I became aware of how much I, too, wanted to fuck you. I wanted to fuck your brains out!"

She stared at me.

"But you didn't, not at first. You knew you could have, yet you restrained yourself. The day that you walked out on me, after you had gotten me so damn excited, you made me feel so disgusted with myself, yet, I knew that your feelings for me were so much deeper than just wanting to, well, to fuck me, and I wanted you so damn much more! And if that's what you really want now," her voice dropped, "you can."

"But we both know that isn't love."

"Tell me what it is."

"You don't really want to know; it's a desire to degrade you. I know, now, that when I first saw you, I was sexually attracted to you, and that, of course, is natural. But when I thought of you letting the soldier fuck you, my sexual attraction intensified. Why?"

She stubbed her cigarette into an ashtray.

"All I know is that when you fuck me," she said in a voice so soft that it was filled with deep emotion, "you give me the greatest satisfaction I could ever experience."

She was gazing at me.

As I put my cigarette out, she slid her hand under my apron and unzipped my fly.

"Stop."

"Why should I stop? You know that what we feel for each other is much stronger than your relationship with Joy. What's really stopping you?"

"Not like this. Not here." I put my hand on her wrist. "Later. This afternoon. At your house." I pulled her hand away, and I zipped up my fly. I sighed. "I warn you, though, I'm going to fuck your brains out, but it has nothing to do with love. We both know that now. And we both know you don't want us to get married, not to each other, anyway."

She glared at me.

"We're not only sexually attracted to each other," she said; "we've become, well, attached to each other, and that's a form of love. You and I are more in love than you and Joy are, that's for sure, and sex with you means more to me than sex between you and Joy means to Joy. She doesn't even have as much right as I do to be jealous if you do it to another woman, and apparently, she doesn't even care if you do. I think that the mere thought of it excites the hell out of her."

"Yeah, I know," I muttered.

"She's sick. I don't know why you trust her. The way she threw herself at your own brother was so sick! And it wasn't as though she was too drunk to know what she was doing!"

"I'm not worried about my brother; he can take care of himself."

"Yeah, but can *you*? Does she get you so damn excited that you can't free yourself from her? Why do you let her have so much power over you?"

"You think she has power over me?"

"You really don't think so? You're really that blind?"

"I admit that sex has power over me and that she uses sex sometimes to seduce me to do certain things, but you have more power over me than she does."

"Me? I've never had any power over you. You were the one who was always in control. And that's why I was always so fascinated by you. I guess that's why I'm so damn jealous of her! It's as though she's cast a spell over you, as though she's drugged you. Is she really that good in bed?"

"No, not nearly as good as you. Since I've been married, my sex life has been virtually nonexistent."

"Your choice or hers?"

"Hers, of course. And when we do have sex, it's somehow perverted."

"Maybe that's the secret to her control over you. I'm too eager to have sex with you, the good old fashion way."

"And that's the way I prefer it."

"But I'm too easy. I don't lure you with the excitement of the chase."

"Well, to each other, we're still the forbidden fruit."

"I've missed you during these past two years."

"It's too bad you're going to Florida next week. After tonight, we're closing the restaurant for the next two weeks. After tonight, I'll be free, for a while, anyway."

"I'm not leaving until Wednesday. I'm free now. But will you be free? Really free? You're in the same situation as I had been with the soldier. You don't owe her a thing. You owe it to your own self to break free from her."

"That sounds familiar. Isn't that what I said to you years ago?"

"And you were right. And you made me feel so good, being there for me. You were so much older than seventeen! You made it seem so easy and so natural to want to give myself to you and to take you. You made me feel so free, yet wanting you so much. Without Joy, you and I can start over again, maybe; maybe it will lead to something permanent this time. Who knows?"

"I've thought of that, but when you said I'm blinded by sex, you're right. I think we both are, especially me. They say opposites attract. That's us. And they also say familiarity breeds contempt. Maybe that's us, too; maybe we feel the depravity in each other, and we enjoy wallowing in it. We're strongly attracted to each other, but not enough for you to make a lifetime commitment to me, because what you see in me is not good enough to overcome the obstacles we'd have to face, the same obstacles Joy and I are facing now. To each other, you and I, we will always be the forbidden fruit."

"So? What will it be for us? Feast, or famine?"

I shoved my right hand behind her, and grasped her buttocks, and I slid my left hand down the front of her, between her legs.

"You know how I hunger for your sweet, succulent flesh."

She drew her face closer to mine, our lips almost touching, and gazed at me with her bright green eyes.

"And you know," she responded, "how my sweet, succulent flesh reacts to the intense heat of your penetrating hardness. Come home with me, now, and snuggle up to me in my warm bed and ram your rod into my hot juicy womb."

She grasped the back of my head and pulled my mouth onto hers, sucking me so hungrily that I wanted to plunge myself deeply into her.

"Wait here, I'll be right back."

Without even removing my apron, I leaped up, bolted through the swinging doors, through the kitchen, out the back door, dashed across the driveway and leaped onto the back porch and ran up the steps. Dante was in the upstairs kitchen. I asked him to take my place in the restaurant to prepare the food and then to make the pizzas that night in case I wouldn't show up. He didn't ask me any questions. He simply agreed.

Quickly, I returned to Minnie. I took off my apron and said to her, "Take me to your house in your car. I'll leave my car here in case Joy needs it. I'm not even going to tell her I'm leaving."

We went to the back entrance and put on our coats, and we left the restaurant, got into her car, and she drove away. I lit a cigarette. I looked at her. She grinned at me. She seemed happy.

I thought of what I had said to her, about fucking her brains out, and I was wondering what she was thinking and how she really felt about me.

"How long have we known each other?" I asked.

"Nine years."

"In all that time, I've never heard you talk dirty, until, well, until this week."

"Joy is a bad influence, on both of us. I don't remember you ever talking dirty either, until now."

"Our perceptions of each other are changing, but after nine years, that's to be expected, I guess. When I told you I wanted to fuck your brains out, well, how did that make you feel?"

"That was a crude way of expressing yourself, but I've always respected you for your honesty, even to the point of such bluntness. You put it that way for emphasis. I know that. And I know that beneath your hard exterior is the real you, a tender, loving human being. And Joy isn't aware of the real you. She's blind. She really is. I think you'd make an excellent minister. She sees you only as, well, as an inferior being. She would never admit that your intelligence exceeds hers and mine. When you told me you, well, wanted to fuck my brains out, I should have felt insulted, but I didn't; I felt, well, excited. Flattered, actually," she said, and she smiled at me.

"Flattered, and excited? Really?"

"When you were my student, and you told me how you felt about me, I felt guilty, because I was so sexually attracted to you, even though I thought I was, well, in love with the soldier, but, as you had said, I had been swept up by the war, by someone in a uniform, and when I found out that he had already been married, I had felt like such a damn fool. And my guilt had been compounded. And, that night, when I had become so intoxicated, trying to drown my guilt, I thought of calling you on the phone. I almost did. I wanted you, as you had so adequately put it, I wanted you to fuck my brains out. And when you showed up at the house the next day, that's how I felt. And you didn't disappoint me. And ever since then, that's precisely how I've felt about you."

"Wow! No wonder you've always excited me! Is that how you're feeling now, at this moment?"

She blushed.

"I can't wait to get you in my bed again. You've never disappointed me."

"You want me for sex, because it helps you to forget your disappointments. It has nothing to do with love, then."

"Love," she said, "is relative."

"What in hell does that mean?"

"That means, I want you. You make me feel good."

"I want to use your body, because it gives me such great pleasure. And that, I used to think, was love."

"And now, what do you think love is?"

"Caring."

"Well, I know that you care about me. I've never doubted that. You don't think I care about you? If I didn't, I wouldn't have bothered to see you today; I wouldn't be so eager to take you home with me, to get you into my bed."

"Are you really feeling so eager?"

"Of course I am. I'm so eager just thinking about it, I can almost feel you doing it to me right now. Aren't you eager?"

"Concentrate on the road."

"I know, but how can I?"

"Think about love, not just about sex."

"What's the difference?"

"The difference? Two men claim they love flowers. Every morning, one man stops at a florist shop, buys a red rose, cuts off the stem, and sticks the rose into the lapel of his jacket, and the other man waters the flowers every morning and watches them grow. Which man loves the flowers more?"

"They both love the flowers for different reasons."

"Which man has more love?"

"Each man loves in his own way."

"But you can't see a qualitative difference in their ways of loving?"

"You're talking about a difference between physical love and spiritual love."

"English teachers! Maybe I'm talking about a difference between relative love and absolute love."

"Absolute love is impossible."

"I thought you were religious, that you believed in divine love."

"Of course I do, but you can't expect love from people to be divine."

"You're beginning to sound like Joy. What, then, shall we use as a guide?"

She glared at me.

"Concentrate on the road, Minnie."

"Well, then, when we get into bed together, I'll just let you stare at me and watch me grow and not let you touch any part of me."

"I told you what I'm going to be doing to you, and you won't resist me, because you want it as much as I do, but love has nothing to do with it."

"In a few more minutes, in my warm bed, we're going to be making such intense love to each other, and loving it so damn passionately, that neither of us will ever want us to stop. And call it whatever you will, our feelings, for ourselves and for each other, will soar to the utmost satisfaction. You have never disappointed me. Have I ever failed to gratify your deepest desires?"

"Concentrate on the road."

8

Minnie and I spent most of that Saturday afternoon upstairs in her warm bed.

Neither of us had been disappointed.

"Haven't you missed this during the last two years?" she asked. I told her I had.

Finally, we got out of bed and took a hot shower together. That was one day before the longest night of the year. And as soon as darkness descended, I lit the fireplace to roast two thick, juicy steaks for supper. We had both worked up a big appetite, otherwise we were both feeling quite satisfied. I told her I was tempted to spend the whole night with her, and then she told me that she wanted to remain with me and not go to Florida, but that she had promised her folks she would go with them. She would return the day after New Year's. To see what her reaction would be, I thought of telling her that I could go with her and her folks, but I had the feeling that she would never be comfortable with me in the presence of her family, so I decided not to even mention it. I suspected that our relationship, if it would continue, would be limited to an occasional sexual tryst, that she would be satisfied with that arrangement and would not demand much more from me, that there would always be something that would separate us. She would live in her own world, and I would live in mine, and never the twain shall meet. Many guys, I thought, probably preferred that type of arrangement.

Anyway, I couldn't leave home during that Christmas week, because Jessica and my son, who was now eight years old, wanted to be here with me, especially since Dante had just returned home, but Joy had told me she had not wanted either my son nor Jessica to stay with us. When I mentioned that to Minnie, she said she'd be happy to have them stay here, at her house.

"That would be perfect," she said, "not only for them, but for the dog and the cat. Your son will love the dog."

They would be arriving late Tuesday afternoon with Ben John and Anna.

I had never told Minnie that Jessica had been a prostitute. Joy had never known either, nor Dante. Not even Rosie, who had met Jessica at the clinic in Harlem, had known until I had written about Jessica in the introduction.

That Saturday night, I didn't stay to sleep with Minnie. I had decided to return to work.

About four hours before midnight, Minnie drove me back to the restaurant. She dropped me off and then drove away. As soon as I entered the kitchen, my mother lit into me.

"You just take off without even telling your wife where you're going? What's wrong with you?"

I tried to ignore her, but when I had not answered her, she became even angrier with me.

A little while later, when Dante could speak to me privately, he told me that Joy, looking for sympathy, has been complaining about me to everybody who would listen.

At midnight, when I went into the house, Joy was in the front room. She refused to talk to me. I sighed with relief, went into my room, and went to sleep.

During the next three days, she had still refused to talk to me. As far as I was concerned, the separation between us was permanent, if not complete. I would take responsibility for feeding, clothing, and providing shelter for her and her son, but marriage, I told myself, although it had been legal, had never united us, therefore I was not morally obligated to love, honor, and obey her as I had promised.

Yet, she knew I didn't have the heart to kick her out, that I had accepted Rusty as my son.

Late the following Tuesday afternoon, as the sun was setting, Ben John drove into the driveway between the house and the restaurant. Most of us were waiting in the restaurant for them, where we were preparing a big spaghetti dinner for them, for Ben John and Anna and my son, Little Tony, and Jessica. Joy was in the house, writing, I presumed. My mother told me to go get her. "She knows where we are," I answered. Jessica and I sat together in a booth as Dante, in another booth, was showing my son how his artificial left arm and hand worked. Jessica asked me if there was a problem. "No, no problem, not for you and me, anyway."

"I mean, with Joy, about my being here."

"If she has a problem, it's her problem; not ours. She should have dealt with it earlier, when I told her you would be here, too. We'll talk about it later. Let's get ready for Christmas; it's time for the whole family to get together and celebrate, and you're part of my family."

It wasn't long after when Joy came into the restaurant with Rusty. Actually, Dante and Rosie had gone into the house and had talked her into joining the rest of us, and she dutifully greeted and embraced (and even smiled) at Anna and Ben John, and she even said hello to Jessica, who stood up in the booth and stepped into the aisle, and embraced her, which seemed to surprise Joy. They had never met, not until then.

"So, you're Joy! I've heard so much about you. I've wanted to meet you for a long time. My name is Jessica. I've been a friend of Tony's since, well, since high school. He's bragged to me about how beautiful you are, and I can see he wasn't exaggerating. And this is, of course, Rusty. He's beautiful, like his mother. I'm really glad to meet you, finally!"

Until that moment, I had never seen Joy struck speechless. She simply stared at me as I sat there, and she stared, with her mouth open, at Jessica, who asked softly, "Would you please sit with us?"

And Joy muttered, "Thank you," and she slid into the booth, opposite me, and left a space for Jessica to sit, and Joy talked with her as though they had been old friends.

An hour or so after we had eaten, I left the restaurant with Jessica and my son to drive them to Minnie's house.

Jessica had become my closest friend and confidante, and she had known of my relationships with both Joy and Minnie, except, of course, of my most recent sexual episodes, which I would discuss with her later in the week. We couldn't discuss any of my intimate affairs in the car with our son present.

At the house, Minnie and Jessica (who had met three years earlier, before I had met Joy) became friendly, and my son and Lassie, as Minnie had predicted, had fallen in love instantly.

There were two bedrooms upstairs, a toilette with a shower, and another small room with a desk.

Minnie led us into the small room, which had a small bed in it.

"This is Lassie's bed," she said to Little Tony, "but she'll let you share it with her, if you want, and if you don't mind if the cat, Thai, shares it, too."

About an hour later, I returned home, but I wasn't quite sure where I would sleep. Dante and Rosie had assumed they would sleep in my room, and that I would sleep with Joy. When I was alone with Joy, I told her that I was going to sleep in her bed that night, but that I would let her sleep there, too. She told me she didn't care where I slept. She had, of course, been drinking.

The next morning, I drove to Minnie's house. I arrived long before Minnie left for Boston, and after she left, I told Jessica about my relationship with Joy. Even after I had told her that Joy had not wanted to sleep with me, Jessica said that she had not planned to sleep with me either, because, legally, I was married, and that I still had moral as well as legal obligations to Joy and Rusty even though Joy refused to acknowledge her own obligations to me. That did not give me the excuse not to honor the vows I had made, Jessica said. I told her I understood her feelings and that I would abide by her wishes.

"It's not that I don't want to sleep with you," she said. "You know I do."

And then she asked me about my current relationship with Minnie.

And I told her that during the past two years, while I had been married, I had not slept with Minnie, not until this past weekend.

"You're certainly making your life complicated, not only for yourself, but for everyone who relates to you, but at least you tried to do right, anyway."

She said she wanted to know about Joy, that maybe she and Joy could spend some time together, just the two of them. I told her that when Joy was busy writing, she didn't like to be disturbed.

"Maybe, or maybe she's using writing as an excuse to escape from you."

Anyway, the primary reason Jessica was there, she told me, was for me and my son to know each other, and another reason was to present a gift to Dante, a check for ten thousand dollars, money that she had collected for him, a fund, contributed and signed by almost a thousand people listed on several sheets of paper stapled together, including their signatures with personal notes, such as "welcome home, Dante" from the mayor of New York City, Vincent Impellitteri, and the governor of New York, Thomas E. Dewey, and signatures of professional baseball players, such as Roy Campanella and Jackie Robinson of the Brooklyn Dodgers, and Yogi Berra and Phil Rizzuto of the New York Yankees. I stared at the list of signatures and the notes and at the check in disbelief.

"How much of this money came from you?"

"That's not important," she replied.

"More than a thousand dollars?"

"That's none of your business."

"This is utterly fantastic! It's unbelievable."

"It wasn't much more than that. I just wanted to round it out to an even ten thousand dollars. Besides, I can easily afford it now."

"Okay, but don't wait until Friday. Give him the check now to see if he can deposit it."

We got into my car. My son wanted to bring the dog, so Lassie got in the back seat with him.

At the house, Joy said that Dante and Rosie were upstairs. Jessica gave me the check with the list of signatures and said she wanted to stay downstairs with Joy.

I took my son and the dog and the check upstairs with me, and I gave it to Dante. Ben John said he had known of the check. He, too, had signed the list. "Jessica," he said, "is a remarkable woman." He was sure the check was valid. It was from her personal bank account.

Dante and Rosie and I went to the bank in Berlin, and Dante signed the check and deposited it into his savings account, and when we returned, we went into the restaurant and celebrated.

Jessica and Joy had been alone together for most of that time, but they joined the rest of us for supper.

An hour before midnight, Joy came into the restaurant and said to me, "Don't let them stay alone in a strange place again. I think you should stay with them. I really do."

"Are you sure? You won't say anything to my mother?"

"Of course not! She'll never know. Don't worry about it. They're waiting to leave now."

I said good night to everybody, and as I left the restaurant, Jessica and Tony and Lassie came out of the house and got into the car.

As I drove away, Jessica said, "Well, that was an interesting day! I'm glad now that I came here. Maybe I should have met her a long time ago."

"Don't keep me in suspense."

"I'll tell you all about it when we're alone. Do you want to sleep with me? So we can talk?"

"Tonight?"

"Of course."

"I can't wait."

"Neither can I!"

And Jessica and I, in bed together that night, talked.

Joy had admitted that, over two years ago, she had become pregnant by a married man and had been desperate to get married, and she had intended to tell me later, to let me divorce her when she'd be able to support herself and the baby. She had been feeling guilty for having deceived me, but she could see no other way out of her predicament, and her guilt had been tormenting her. Joy needed me for financial support, but she also knew how unfair it was of her to expect me to abstain from sex. At times, Joy said, she wanted sex with me, and had enjoyed it, but she knew it was not often enough to keep me satisfied, so she expected me to enjoy sex with other women, too, such as with Minnie. Joy, however, didn't particularly like Minnie, who felt, Joy had said, that I was an inferior being and was only using me for sex. Joy knew that I felt close to Jessica, and that she had given birth to my son. If Jessica and I wanted to sleep together, Joy told her, we should. Neither Joy nor I, Joy had said, felt bound by our marriage vows; we had been forced by social convention to endure the brief ceremony in order to obtain a piece of paper that had given us the official permission to live together lawfully.

"Did she sound sincere?" I asked.

"She sounded sincere, but I don't know for sure. She told me that since you had planted your seed in me, and I had produced your offspring, I'm more married to you than she is. Have you ever told her that I was a, well, you know?"

"Of course not! That's nobody's concern except ours."

"I didn't tell her, but I feel as though I'm really married to you and that she isn't married to you, not really, and that what she said is true, that she should feel guilty, not me, for sleeping with you."

"Do you like her? I mean, do you think you can trust her?"

"I don't really know yet. She seems interesting. I'd like to know her better, but I don't feel guilty now being in bed with you, so I guess I can thank her for that."

"Why should you feel guilty? We're just talking."

"Oh, okay. I just thought that after you'd kiss me goodnight, you'd want to, well, never mind."

"Well, now that you've mentioned it, I should kiss you good night."

"That's not necessary."

"I know, but that would be so damn nice, at least for me before, well, before we go to sleep."

Before we fell asleep together, I told Jessica that I felt married to her, and that I felt happy, really happy that I was with her and my son.

"Me, too," she said. "I've always felt that we're a family. And Tony is so happy that we're together."

"Being with you like this feels, well, so natural!"

"I know! It feels natural to me, too."

"Maybe we ought to think of getting married."

"Maybe you ought to think that, legally, you're already married."

"Let's not think of that now. Let's just enjoy being together again. I don't want to fall asleep right now."

"If you don't want to fall asleep right now," she asked, "what do you want to do?"

"If we put our minds together, I'm sure something will come up."

"Not only putting our minds together. Something big is already coming up; I can feel it in me, again," she groaned.

"How long has it been since we've done this?"

"Too long. I bet it's been at least ten minutes. But earlier I was thinking of the first time. Do you remember that Sunday afternoon?"

"Of course! It was the greatest day of my life!"

"Do you really feel married to me?"

"Yes, I do."

"If we were legally married, would it bother you terribly that I was a, a whore?"

"But you're not! Not anymore!"

"But I was! I can never change that."

"Stop, Jessie! Please. Please, for me, at least, and for our son, think of yourself as the great woman you are now, and the great mother! Being inside of you, like this, I feel a love inside of you that I've never felt in anyone else, and it isn't only physical attraction; it goes way beyond that. You've already made this world a much better place. And I feel so damn lucky to know you, to be so loved by you. To know you is to love you. You know who you really are!"

"I love you!"

"I know you do. I can feel it in you. You make me feel like I'm a better person than I really am, because I know you love me. I feel closer to you than anyone else in the world, and I'm so happy when you're with me."

"And I'm so happy when I feel you inside of me like this. If there's a heaven, it can't feel any better than this! Whenever I feel you, like this, moving inside of me, you fill me with love. I feel your love flowing into me. Whenever we come together, I'm enraptured by love, by a glimpse into eternal life."

"Wow! That's how I feel, too. I've never felt this way with anyone else."

On Christmas Eve we had steamed clams and lobsters in the restaurant, and long before midnight, when Dante and Rosie and some of the others planned to attend church, I drove Jessica and my son, and the dog, back to Minnie's house. After we got out of the car and was walking towards the back of the house, a shooting star flashed across the sky.

"Wow! Did you see that? That must have been Santa Claus delivering his gifts."

Jessica and Tony laughed.

As soon as we went into the house, I lit a fire in the huge fireplace, and then Tony went upstairs to sleep. A few minutes later I went upstairs to tuck him in. Jessica was already in his room.

When I entered, he was kneeling beside the bed, his hands folded, and his head bowed. The dog was sitting next to him. The cat was sitting at the foot of the bed. Tony made the sign of the cross, and then he crawled into bed, and the dog lay down on the other side of him. Jessica kissed him good night. And then, as I bent down over him, he put his arms around my neck and pulled me against him, and we kissed each other good night.

While Jessica and I were returning downstairs, she said, "I'm raising him Catholic. I hope you don't mind. That's what I promised your mother and father, if you remember."

"Yeah, I remember, and I don't mind."

"Your mother asked me about it earlier today. She was happy when I told her that this spring her grandson would be receiving his first holy communion. She asked me if I planned to convert. I'm sorry, but I had to tell her the truth."

"I understand. Don't worry about it. You're doing an excellent job; I told you, you're a great mother."

"Well, she seemed happy when I told her I've been studying the catechism. I've been helping Tony with it."

"Now she'll think you have to convert, because if you don't, you'll be rejecting God."

"Rejecting God? How can she think I'll be rejecting God?"

"By not joining the true religion, especially after studying it."

"But I'm a Christian."

"I know, but I'm not the one you have to convince."

"I don't understand."

We sat close together on the couch.

"Frankly, I don't either. She never told my father that he was rejecting God, maybe because she knew that my father was more like Christ than she was, that he was more like Christ than most Christians were. She would say that my father was more religious than she is. So, when she knows you better, she might see you as religious, too."

"Wasn't your father Catholic?"

"Right after he was born, he was baptized Catholic, and he was raised Catholic, because my grandmother, who's Jewish, made that promise when she married my grandfather, but when my father came of age, he chose Judaism. Someday, I'll tell you his story."

"I liked your father a lot. You remind me of him, in some ways, especially by your gentleness, although you like to think of yourself as so damn virile."

"I think I'm more like my mother, though. I tend to be pessimistic."

"I like your mother, too. She's good hearted, like your father was, but she's awfully, well, awfully nervous, sometimes. And she seems ashamed of her, well, of her own mother, because, well, she's colored."

"My mother wants to think of us as white. She hates to think of us as colored."

"I know. At least all of you in your family, even you, almost, can pass for white. Many of us colored folks hate being colored."

"That's only because we're brought up to think like that, because we live in a white society. We tend to conform to the standards of the majority. That's the 'follow the rest of the herd' tendency. You don't hate yourself, do you, for being colored?"

"I shouldn't, but I've sometimes thought I'd like to be white."

"If you were white, do you think you'd be more beautiful? Sexier?"

"Don't you?"

"Beautiful is beautiful. Sexy is sexy. You couldn't be more beautiful, or sexier. You excite me physically. Dark skin on you looks, well, natural. But the most beautiful aspect of you, and the most important, is what my father would call your soul, the divine in you, the good. And to me, you are the most beautiful person I have ever known. You really are. As Ben John said, you're truly remarkable."

She blushed.

"Let's not think of anything dark or ugly for the rest of the night. Let's talk," she said, "only of things that are merry."

"Let's think and talk," I suggested, "of making love."

"Why think and talk of it? Action is louder than words and thoughts. Why not just practice it? Practice makes perfect."

"Let's drink to that."

"Do we have any wine?"

"Do you want white wine or red?"

"Vino bianco," she said.

"Molto bene."

We drank white wine, and, quietly, we celebrated a white Christmas.

We roasted chestnuts in the fireplace, and then we roasted marshmallows.

And then we sat close to each other again on the coach, and we drank more wine.

"This is so nice," Jessica said, "and so relaxing, and so romantic. Christmas Eve, in front of the fireplace, and we're together. We're together as a family! Mio caro! Buon Natale!"

"Buon Natale, cara mia!"

And we kissed, tenderly, on the lips.

"I was just thinking," she said, "how nice it would have been if we, you and I, could have gone to High Mass at midnight together with the rest of the family, but we couldn't do that. We couldn't be seen together in church, not in your home town."

"We agreed to only think and to talk about merry things for the rest of the night. Remember?"

"Okay. You suggested that we make love."

"That's what we're doing now, making love."

"I thought you meant in bed, together."

"Well," I said, "I thought we'd continue this is bed. I thought we were setting the mood, which would lead to the bed."

"And you should get enough sleep so you can get up early and take your son to church."

"What? I had forgotten about that. Are you sure he wants to go? He'll get bored in church."

"He wants to go to church, with you. He's expecting you to take him. He thinks that will impress you, somehow. His father, taking him to church, to pray to God together. He's only been to church with his mother. Besides, it's a holy day of obligation. He wants the three of us to go together, as a family, but as I told you, I can't go with you. And you know Joy won't go. We should be at the house early for family breakfast before you go to church."

"Have you told him you can't go with us?"

"And he asked me why not."

"What did you tell him?"

"What could I tell him? I told him I couldn't explain it to him now. Maybe I could when he's older."

"He'll probably ask me to explain it."

"I know."

"So, what will I tell him?"

"I don't know."

"If he asks, I'll tell him we're not married yet."

"Suppose he asks you why not?"

"I'll have to tell him I don't know. I'll tell him to ask his mother."

"And what shall I tell him? That you're already married?"

"I should ask Joy for a divorce, but she won't divorce me unless I can provide her with a good settlement."

"I know. I didn't say anything to her, but I can afford to pay her a reasonable amount."

"Of course not!"

"I have the money," she said softly. "Your freedom will be worth it. But I don't expect you to actually marry me."

"If I were free, there's no reason to not marry you. My choice would be either you or Minnie, but I know that with Minnie, it's mostly sex, not really love, that attracts us. I mean, Minnie and I like each other, but not enough to get married. Being with you like this, for the rest of our lives, is appealing, at least to me, but I'm not sure why a woman as beautiful as you would want me for life."

"Of course I would want you for life, but when we first met, I told you I could never expect anyone to marry me. I meant it. But that doesn't mean that I don't love you. I do, and I always will. I know that you love me, in spite of what you know of me, that you accept me as I am. But that's not the only reason I love you. I love you because you're you; you make me feel, well, good. You understand me. When I'm with you, I can be myself. You make me feel comfortable. I love you! And I want you to accept yourself as you are, too. I know you like sex, and somehow you think you shouldn't like it quite so much, but sex is natural; it's good, and like anything else that's good, it shouldn't ever be used to manipulate others. I know that Joy uses sex to control you. That's her problem. Don't let it be yours. She uses sex, but she doesn't know how to control it, so sex controls *her*, and she gets frightened when that happens."

"I could never understand how she could be so cold at times, and so hot at other times. What you're saying is beginning to make sense. When she gets hot, she gets so hot, she loses control, and afterwards, sometimes, she seems to hate herself so damn much that she resents me for getting her so excited."

"We're forgetting that this is Christmas Eve, that we agreed not to think dark thoughts, that you suggested that we make love. Let's not wait until midnight to go to bed."

We went upstairs, and we got into bed together, and we entered another world of our own, filled with bliss and passionate love.

And on early Christmas morning we woke up together, refreshed and ready to join the rest of the world. We had breakfast in the restaurant with the others, and then I took my son to church. In the afternoon we had a big spaghetti dinner in the restaurant. And in the middle of the evening, I drove Jessica and Tony back to Minnie's house, and I slept with Jessica again. We did the same thing on Saturday and Sunday. On Sunday, most of the family went to church again while Joy and Jessica stayed at the house to take care of the babies, Rusty and Angela. On Monday, Ben John drove the others back to New York.

Since I had been gone five nights in a row, I had expected my mother to question me about it, but according to Joy and Dante and Rosie, my mother had been so busy with so much company that, apparently, she hadn't even noticed that I had been gone during the nights. Anyway, my mother hadn't said anything to me. I'm sure that if she had known the situation, she would not have been quiet about it. So, Joy hadn't complained to her, not during that Christmas week, anyway. To say that my mother had enjoyed that Christmas would be such an understatement. Her son, in spite of his war wounds and the loss of his left arm, had returned home and was happy to be reunited with his family. She, too, was happy, and she was proud of him. She was proud of her whole family.

10

I hadn't known, of course, some of the things that Dante had been experiencing after he had returned from Korea over three years ago. After Rosie had read the last part of this script, she told me something about Dante and Joy that stunned me. Had I been more observant, or had I cared more about Joy, I would have seen more beneath the surface, and I would have been prepared for what Rosie had told me.

During that Christmas week I had been so wrapped up with Jessica, that I had pushed Joy and everything about her out of sight and almost out of mind, except when Jessica and I had discussed her. And when Jessica had left, I hadn't even wanted to be in the same house with Joy. I returned to the house, of course, and I slept in my own bed. Dante and Rosie had returned upstairs.

On New Year's Eve, we had a party in the restaurant, and at the stroke of midnight, everybody yelled out: "Happy New Year!" and all the men kissed all the women on the lips.

"Don't you remember that night?" Rosie asked me.

"What's there to remember?"

"How Joy kept wanting to dance with Dante and kept wanting him to kiss her."

"She had a little too much to drink, if I remember right, but that was more than three years ago. I don't recall anything particularly unusual. Besides, you have to remember her situation. Joy and I had virtually split, which made her lonely and vulnerable."

Rosie was sitting next to me at the table. She had been review-ing the script while I had been trying to recall what had happened that year. It was late at night in the early spring when I (with Rosie's help) was recreating this. Several weeks before that, Rosie had told me how Dante had been having nightmares, and how he would wake up sweating during the night, and she'd get a towel from the bathroom and dampen it with cold water and would wipe the sweat from his clammy flesh, and then she would hold him against her warm body. And they would cling to each other and make love pas-sionately. Their need to touch each other had increased dramatically since his return. Even during the daytime when he would look at her, his bright eyes penetrating her, he would reach out and touch her, and his hot touch would ignite a fire deep within her. They would go into their bedroom, close the door, and she would lie back on the bed and let him lie on top of her and penetrate her body. His desperation would stimulate her deepest passions. Feeling his body pressing against hers, and his hardness stroking the inside of her, sending waves of pleasure through her whole body, she wasn't always able to wait for him to reach a climax. She would cling to him and groan with intense passion as her body stiffened against his. And he would continue as though he hadn't wanted to stop, not ever, making her body squirm away from sensations that were almost too great to endure, and he would grasp her buttocks harder, pulling her deeper into him, penetrating her even more. Deep in her womb, his hard-ness, stroking her, sent ripples through her flesh, curving around her pelvis, darting down her thighs, and tingling to the rigid tips of her breasts.

"Don't ever stop loving me!" she had cried out.

I remember vaguely when they had been looking for their own apartment that winter, but I had assumed that they had needed pri-vacy, away from my mother. I had never suspected that it had been to get Dante away from Joy.

"I know Dante had never told you. How could he? And I never wanted to tell you either, in spite of the problems between you and Joy. Now that our situation has changed, I think I can tell you. I don't think you'll resent your brother; I think you'll understand him better."

While we had been in the restaurant, the night before Christmas Eve, Joy had entered and had spoken to me, and after she had left, I said good night to everyone, and I left. When Rosie and Dante went into the house, Joy, in her bathrobe, was in the front room, on the couch. She told them that I had taken Jessica and my son back to Minnie's house, and that she had expected me to return in a little while. She asked them if she could get them anything to eat or drink. Rosie said she was tired and was going to bed. Dante said he'd stay up and wait for me to return, but I would not return that night, as Joy knew. Rosie was asleep when Dante finally joined her in bed.

And on New Year's Eve, Joy was uncharacteristic in her pursuit of Dante.

"So what? We were all celebrating in the restaurant. Dante wasn't acting as though he were interested in Joy."

A week or so later, when Rosie and Dante were alone, and my mother was in the restaurant, they had a chance to talk in private. Dante, she said, had confessed his feelings for Joy; they were sexually attracted to each other.

"Are you trying to tell me they had sex with each other?"

"I don't think they went that far," she muttered.

Dante had told her that on the night while they were waiting for me, Joy fixed margaritas for herself and Dante. After they had drunk a couple of strong drinks, Joy put soft dance music on and they danced, very slowly, and he felt Joy holding him and pressing herself against him, arousing him. And he noticed that she was not wearing anything under her bathrobe. Dante said something about me being gone for a long time. She stopped dancing, put her arms around him, and muttered, "I'm sorry. I don't want to dance any-more. I want to sit on the couch." She sat down in the middle of the couch and began to cry. "He's with Jessica," she sobbed, "I know what he's doing to her." And as Dante sat beside her and put his arms around her, she cuddled against him and said, "I wish I could have you!" She wrapped her arms around his neck, pulled his face down, and kissed him hard on his mouth. As he quickly grasped her shoulders and pushed her back, the top of her bathrobe opened. He stared at her uncovered breasts. She made no effort to cover herself.

"We better go to bed," he said softly.

"Together?"

"Of course not! I love Rose! I never want to lose her! Never! You are a sexy woman. You can have almost any man you want. Please, Joy, don't do this to me."

"I'm sorry. Rose is a lucky woman. You know," she said, almost whimpering, "how I feel about you, if you ever want me."

I stared at Rosie. She was looking blankly at the script on the kitchen table.

"When Dante told you," I asked, "how did you feel?"

"Scared." She grasped my knee. "And angry. I hated Joy. And I resented Dante. I didn't want to believe what he had told me."

I put my hand on her knee, holding her leg against mine, and rubbed her thigh, not to excite her sexually, but to calm her and to comfort her. She had stirred a deep tenderness in me.

"Why do you think he told you about that night?"

"I don't know. Maybe he was feeling guilty."

"Guilty about what?"

"About the way he felt."

"How did he feel?"

"He wanted, well, he wanted Joy. He wanted to, to fuck her."

"As far as you know, did he ever, well, fuck her?"

"No, but he wanted to."

"And you resented him for telling you that."

"Yes. You think I was wrong for resenting him?"

"I didn't say that. When he confessed his feelings to you, I understand how much it scared you, and why it hurt you terribly, and that you couldn't help the way you reacted, but I know that Dante did not tell you because he wanted to hurt you."

"I know, but it sounded as though he was asking for permission to screw her."

"Of course not! Maybe, he shouldn't have told you, or maybe he should have told you in a more subtle way. Anyway, I have two questions. First, why didn't he screw her? Joy was giving herself to him. From the way you told it to me, she was begging him to do it to her. If he really wanted her, why didn't he do it?"

"It made him feel guilty. What's the second question?"

"Why did he tell you?"

"Maybe he needed more sex. Maybe I wasn't enough for him."

"Yeah," I said, rubbing her thigh, "and maybe Joy is a lot sexier than you. Is that what you think Dante thought?"

She didn't answer.

"Did you resent Dante because he was tempted? A man who would not be tempted by a woman like Joy, or a woman like you, would not be a normal man. I don't know about you, but I can't always control how I feel. We say things like, 'You shouldn't feel that way,' as though we choose to feel the way we feel. All I can do is ask myself why I feel the way I feel, so that I can understand my feelings, so that I can control them. Maybe that's what Dante was doing. Maybe he wanted to confide in you, that he looked to you for help, wondering what he should do about the situation, and wondering if he should even discuss it with me. There was always one thing that would have stopped him from screwing Joy. If he hadn't stopped, if he had succumbed to temptation, do you think he really would have told you?"

"I don't know," she muttered.

"You knew him even better than I did. You know damn well he never screwed Joy, and that he never would. His love for you would have stopped him."

She leaned her head against me.

"I'm glad I told you. You make me feel better. I know that Dante loved me, and that I could trust him, but when he told me how he felt, I got scared."

"It seems as though you loved each other from birth."

"I've always loved both of you."

"After he told you about him and Joy, though, did that affect your love-making?"

"Not really. For a little while I was so afraid of losing him, especially to Joy, that I tried to think of ways to satisfy him more, but, somehow, I knew that I satisfied him. He often assured me how great

I was, and I would jokingly say, 'How would you know? How many others can you compare to me?' He certainly satisfied me though."

"I mean, the first time you had sex after he told you about Joy, did that make you feel, well, strange?"

She put her hand between my thighs and said, "Let's continue this discussion in bed. I have something else to tell you."

While we were lying in bed together, naked, under warm blankets, she said, "When he began to make love to me, I couldn't stop wondering if he was thinking of Joy. I didn't say anything to him, of course, but I was feeling uneasy. I was trying hard to pretend how much I was, well, enjoying it, the way I used to enjoy it, and as I thought of him, well, as I thought of him having sex with Joy, I, somehow, became Joy. And I could really feel his, his hardness, pushing in and out of me, pushing in and out of Joy. I *was* Joy! I could feel him, doing it to her. I had become the white sex goddess that Dante was, well, was enjoying so damn much, and although I had been somewhat uneasy, still, I also became excited, feeling the excitement in him, surging, as she grasped his buttocks and held him deep inside of her. And, suddenly, as intense waves of pleasure were penetrating her exquisite body, I became aware that I was capable of giving him more, so much more, than Joy could! I would give him my whole being, not only my flesh. And I began giving him *all* of myself, copulating with him, connecting us with renewed strength and confidence. And he was responding, not only to the flesh; he was responding to *me*! To *all* of me. And then, and then," she said as we lay side by side in the dark, "he wasn't only Dante, not anymore." Her voice faded. Her hot hand touched my thigh. Keen sensations darted down my legs and up into my groin as she continued: "Someone else," she said in a low tone, "was also penetrating me, not Joy; he was penetrating *me*," she said, almost whispering, "not only Dante, but someone else, who felt even more forceful and more desperate than Dante, was also penetrating me, deep inside of me."

She was rubbing the inside of my thigh, making my desire swell more intensely.

"Do you know," she asked softly, "who else I could feel penetrating me?"

"Who?"

I was waiting patiently for her to continue.

Finally, she said, "It was *you!*"

For a few moments, everything became silent.

"You," she said, touching my erection. "I could feel you; I could feel how powerful you were, penetrating, not Joy, not anymore; you were penetrating *me*! And I was making you terribly excited! You and Dante had become one, thrusting yourself deep inside of me." Her hand squeezed my erection, and as she was speaking, she was stroking it, slowly, tenderly. "You were inside of me, deep inside of me, and you were penetrating me so damn desperately, exciting me so damn much, that my, my vagina, throbbing, suddenly lifted, rising up, and it tightened around your penetrating manhood, and I began to squeeze it into me, pulling it even deeper inside of me, so damn much that my whole being began exploding into yours as I felt life shooting into me, again and again! I could feel you inside of me, penetrating me. I could feel the earth shooting out of the sun."

As she paused, I murmured, "You could feel the earth, shooting out of the sun?"

"As though I were experiencing the Creation. When I gave all of myself to Dante, I could feel him penetrating me, and I was no longer Joy, and as I felt his love flowing into me, I felt your love filling me, too, creating new life. Love is the source of the Creation, I could feel the burning earth shooting out of the sun."

As she squeezed my erection, I climbed on top of her, spreading her thighs, and putting my legs between hers, I planted myself into her warm, moist, vagina and felt her hips undulating against me, rising and falling, her body and mine, moving together, and quickly, too quickly, we came together. And her body went limp. She moaned.

And for a long while, I lay on top of her without speaking.

When I withdrew from her, she asked softly, "How are you feeling?"

"Great! You?"

"Deliciously relaxed, thanks to you."

"Me, too, thanks to you," I murmured.

"Are you ready to sleep? Or do you want to fuck me some more?"

I didn't answer immediately.

"Well? Is it something you have to think about?"

"What do *you* want to do?" I asked.

"Whatever *you* want. That's why I asked you."

"What's gotten into you?"

"Just now? I thought that was you. Wasn't that you? Or was that the devil making me feel so damn good?"

Before responding, I sighed, giving me time to collect my thoughts.

"You don't have to emulate Joy, you know, or Minnie. I don't want to do this with them, not anymore. You're the one I want," I said as I turned and got on top of her again. "You're the only one I want. And that's the truth, I swear to God. When I'm, well, when I'm doing this with you, I'm not doing it with anyone else, only with you. With you, this act is sacred; it's the most wonderful feeling we can ever experience, and we should approach it with reverence. Like me, you're reciprocating. You're not just taking; you're giving. You're taking me into you, deep inside of you, and you are giving yourself to me, letting me take you inside of me. We're not just, well, fucking each other. We're transcending our physical selves. When I'm touching you, penetrating your body, you make me feel so damn good. I can feel the love in you flowing into me. I'm plugging my body into yours," I said as I pushed myself into her again, and she moaned, grasping me, "and I feel your love surging into me, the intense sensations in you, rising into me, engulfing us, making us come together, to create new life."

"I love you, so damn much!"

"I know," I said, kissing her lips, "and you know that I love you, too, and that you make me feel so good when I'm doing this with you." I pushed myself deeper into her, and she groaned again as she clung to me, her vagina squeezing my erection and pulling it deeper inside of her. "If this is the work of the devil giving us so much joy (pardon the pun) then we've been worshipping the wrong deity."

"Let me concentrate on what you're doing to me. You make me feel so damn good!"

"I never knew Joy, or Minnie, not really, but I want to know *you*. I want to know you better than I knew you before."

"Now you know me better than you knew me before. Now you know I'm not the sweet, innocent, little, black girl you thought I was."

"I know you're not like Joy or Minnie."

"I've never tried to pretend that I'm better than they are, or even as good as they are."

"As *good* as they are! You really piss me off when you talk about yourself like that. How many people could have endured what you have? What have you and Dante ever done to deserve *this*, this situation?"

"I'm sorry," she murmured, "let's not talk about, well, about our situation."

"Why do you think I love you so damn much?"

"Why?"

"You were a devoted wife to Dante, and even though he can't respond to you, you're still devoted to him; and you're a loving mother to your children, a devoted daughter to your parents, and a compassionate woman and a good friend to many, many others, and to me, you're a very beautiful, sexy, warm woman who makes me feel so damn good, physically as well as spiritually. I'm so fortunate and so happy to have you in my life."

I cupped her face and I kissed her tenderly on the lips.

"I don't ever want to lose you," she said.

I caressed her breasts, and after a little while, when she became more excited and was groaning again, I slid my hands under her hips, pulled her against me, and thrust myself into her again and again and again until her whole body tightened against me.

"I love you so damn much!" she moaned.

"I know, cara mia! I know!"

Slowly, I withdrew from her.

And we lay quietly together.

After a little while, she turned to me, rubbed my belly, put her arms around me and cuddled against me.

She whispered, "Do you want to fuck me some more?"

"What!"

She laughed.

"Were you and Dante, well, so sexually active, like this?"

"I'm just teasing you. Actually, we were, especially during the first few months after he returned from Korea. No matter how often we did it, almost every night, and sometimes during the day, we never seemed to get tired of doing it. It energized both of us, and yet, relaxed us."

"I don't know why, but I had never thought of you and Dante like that. I had always thought of him as my kid brother who needed me. I seem to remember that he did a lot of writing, especially after he returned."

"He did."

"Joy used to tell me that sex drained her energy, that it prevented her from writing. She had to save her energy for writing."

"For Dante, it was just the opposite. He needed more sex to write, and writing gave him more energy for more sex."

"Well, I've been trying to tell you I'm not really a writer."

She laughed.

"You've been doing fine, in both categories, especially since, well, these past few weeks."

"You've been my muse, in both categories."

"Too bad we hadn't been aware of that long before you started working on Dante's script. You would have finished it long ago. Do you think you'll finish it before summer begins?"

"If you keep inspiring me the way you have, yeah, I think so."

"Well, what do you think I'm trying to do now?"

"Is that what you're trying to do? Talking dirty like Joy did, to arouse and to inspire me?"

"She didn't talk to you like that to inspire you to write, though. When she talked dirty to you, did that really arouse you?"

I didn't answer her.

"I admit that when we're copulating, I really enjoy it."

"You enjoy it because it's sacred, yet so often our nature is frowned upon as the work of the devil, and then we wonder why so many of us become so damn neurotic. How can anything that provides such ecstasy be so damn evil? To the Puritans, anything that gives us pleasure is the work of the devil. Anything that gives us pain must come from an opposite source, so, we're required to endure suffering as the will of God. I'm sorry; I'm raving like a lunatic trying to understand life."

"Sometimes, like now, it's helpful to turn off our minds and to feel what's in our hearts. Why don't we just enjoy how we feel being together like this? This is good, for both of us. Isn't it? Feeling so intimate with each other."

"Of course it is. We both know it, because we're both feeling so good about being together like this. But I like to understand our feelings, to understand our nature."

"All I'm suggesting for now is that we stop thinking for a little while and soak up this, this blissful sensation we're experiencing together."

I embraced her and gave her a long, lingering kiss on her lips.

"I know I'm making you feel good," she said, "and I'm glad. That means you need me as much as I need you, so I'm willing to spend half of the night, letting you fuck me, if it inspires you to complete Dante's book. I want you to finish it, for me, just so I'll have it, all of it. I want you to compose it with your deepest passion. And when I read it, I want to feel that passion. I want to feel the spirit of Dante, to feel his love. As I look at each word, I want to be feeling Dante, to feel his love. I want to feel his love penetrating all of us!"

Lying next to her quietly, I didn't know how to respond.

Finally, I mumbled, "Maybe, after I write it, you could pay a professional writer to rewrite it."

"Tonio! You can't pay for love, for passion! Do you remember how your father talked about that church in Assisi?"

"Of course. He took your brother and me with him inside the church. But what does that have to do with the book?"

"After you were in there a few minutes, you could actually feel *love*! Five years or so after Francis had died, the greatest artists in Italy had devoted their time and their love to build the church, without pay, and when you were inside of it, you were so moved that it brought tears to your eyes. Someday, I want you to take us there. But for now, you must finish Dante's book, to express his love for us, so that when we read it, we can feel his spirit."

I felt so overwhelmed, I couldn't respond.

She held my hand and said softly, "You don't think you can do it, but I know that you can. And so far, you have been doing it. You've portrayed us as real people. You write about us with feeling. And you fill me with so much love and with so much hope, that my greatest desire now is not only to take you, to take you deep inside of me, but to give you my whole being, to want you to take me into the deepest part of you, to become one with you. I want to inspire you. I want to help you to make your brother become alive again. Through you, through your work and devotion, I want to feel Dante again, to feel his love. And I *know* you can do it. I have confidence in you. Long ago, Dante told me that if he couldn't finish the book, you could. He used to say that you hadn't even been fully aware of the depths of your own feelings, because you hadn't taken the time so far to explore yourself."

She squeezed my hand.

"I hope, so much," I said, "that I don't disappoint you."

"You won't disappoint me, and I'm not ever going to disappoint you, either. I'm going to keep you so damn close to the fire that, when you write, you'll be filled with so much passion, you'll be pouring it out, and I'll be here, with you, opening up to you again and again, to feel you penetrating me so damn hard and so deep, taking what you need from me to fill yourself with the passion to recreate our story."

The big news during the first month of the new year had been that of the white sex goddess, Marilyn Monroe, marrying Joe Di Maggio. Many men envied him. Not I. I felt sorry for him. If she were anything like Joy, Joltin' Joe was headed for a major jolt. Too bad, I thought, she hadn't gone after someone more white like, well, like Ted Williams. Even in Fenway Park in Boston, when he'd get up to bat, he'd give all of his adulating fans, including the ones watching on television, the finger, and while his fans enjoyed booing and laughing at him, he would get a hit and he'd run, laughing at all his adulating fans, all the way to the bank. Imagine, I thought, if a gentleman like Joe Louis had given American boxing fans the finger, especially when his fight with Max Schmeling had been promoted as good versus evil, even though, contrary to popular belief, Max had not been a Nazi; he had not even been a racist. Actually, Joe Louis, who had become a good friend of his, would have had good reasons to give us Americans the finger. Many "white" Americans saw the fight as black against white and had cheered for Max during the first fight when he had won in a big upset. And after Joe had long passed his prime, he was forced to continue boxing, getting beaten up badly by a young Rocky Marciano, because Uncle Sam, in spite of having praised Joe as an American hero who had quickly and decisively destroyed the Nazi myth of the master race, went after him to pay over a million dollars in back taxes, although Joe had never actually received a total of a million dollars in his whole career. His handlers had "handled"

his money for him. Getting back to Ted Williams, though, the Red Sox star, I can understand why Yankee fans enjoyed hating him, but to be honest, I couldn't really hate him, not after he had served in the world war and then he had been recalled to active combat aviator duty in Korea, which had interrupted his baseball career again. He didn't have to serve as a pilot; as a celebrity, he could have stayed in the rear to entertain the troops, but, as Tiny would have called him, he was a gung ho marine who chose to do his duty again. Anyway, he saw his adulating fans as hypocrites who loved him when he had entertained them with his greatness, which was most of the time, but who were contemptuous of him whenever he had failed, even though that had been seldom.

The other big event for us that month was the passing away of my Zia Maria's husband. She and the rest of the family decided it would be better for her to live upstairs with my mother than to live alone. Dante and Rosie could easily move into her apartment, already furnished, upstairs, over Nonna and Tattone, and Zia Maria would be living next door to the restaurant, which she owned, anyway, with my mother.

During that month, Dante had not been called to substitute in school, although Minnie said she had requested him several times. He didn't really care, because he had been busy writing, and twice that month he had appointments at the veterans' hospital in White River Junction in Vermont.

My mother and my aunt didn't need me to work in the restaurant, but I went in anyway when they were busy, especially on Saturday nights, and I had time to sell insurance, too, when I felt like it. Sometimes I sold insurance to the customers in the restaurant. Some of them came to the restaurant for their appointments, and I offered them free pizzas. That was a virtual guarantee that they would buy a policy.

I was working for an insurance agency in Berlin, but I planned, eventually, to have my own agency, especially if I could persuade Dante to join me. Teachers, I was told, make good insurance agents. Hell, I bet Minnie and Joy could make a lot of money selling insurance. I wondered why more women didn't sell insurance. They'd make a lot more money than they would teaching, or nursing, or waitressing, or doing secretarial work, especially if they were sexy, and they wouldn't have to work as hard. Maybe I could get Minnie and Joy to work for me, too.

As the month passed, Dante was readjusting to civilian life.

Every Sunday was family day. My mother would go to church with Dante and Rosie, and after church we would get together for a big dinner in the restaurant. But my relationship with Joy did not improve, not even enough to hate each other, as though hating each other took too much effort. We were aware of the existence of each other in the same way that we were aware of the existence of the furniture in the house. I guess you could say that she had become my housemaid, not my wife. But she was also unpredictable. There were times when she wanted me to, well, to screw her. She had no better word for it. Before the end of that winter, after we had kept away from each other for weeks, she woke me up in the middle of one cold night by climbing into my bed. She knew I wouldn't kick her out of my bed. And when she'd wake up and find me in *her* bed, she'd get so damned aroused I knew that she wouldn't kick me out of her bed either. But afterwards, she'd get terribly pissed off at me for having taken advantage of her while she had been asleep, of having gotten her so damn excited that she had lost control over herself.

February came and went. Dante still had not been called to substitute in school.

And on the national scene, Senator Joseph McCarthy of Wisconsin continued to accuse government officials as subversive commies, focusing attention now on the military personnel, including generals, who resented being questioned and being treated with disrespect, being called "unfit to wear their uniforms" by the senator, on national television. To many viewers, the senator became a masterful entertainer as well as a great patriot. President Eisenhower tried to remain above the political battle, especially since the French were losing the battle to the commies in Vietnam, but even he had now become concerned with the friction and the paranoia that was spreading throughout the country. It seemed that the more arrogant and irrational the senator was becoming, the greater his popularity

was becoming. In Washington, especially, sickness seemed to precip-
itate more sickness.

Before the month had ended, Dante met with Minnie and
with a representative of the Veterans' Administration in the restaurant one night. Shortly after Dante had returned from Korea, he
had anticipated trouble with Shackle and had called the VA office
in Manchester. The representative who had been assigned to Dante
happened to be a war veteran originally from Berlin and was visiting
his parents who had migrated almost forty years earlier from a small
town in Quebec, and who spoke mostly a French patois. Regular
people, of course, had never approved of them. If they had moved
down from Quebec, they couldn't ever become *real* Americans.

Minnie had verified that Dante had been an excellent teacher,
and she had made it clear that the acting principal had resented Dante,
because Dante's background had not been properly American. The
representative had told Dante not to worry. Even if he did not receive
a contract, he would be paid from the day he had reported that he
was available to teach. "On Pearl Harbor Day," the representative
grinned.

All the other teachers had received a contract for the following
school year, but Dante had not. He had received a letter from his
representative in Manchester. The letter had stated that if he would
not receive a contract by the end of March, further action against
the school would be taken. The superintendent of schools had been
warned. Dante had been advised not to take any action of his own.

March passed. Dante had not received a contract.

May first was on a Saturday. The following Monday morning, I
drove Dante to Manchester to the Veterans' Administration office so
that he could sign some papers agreeing to a contract with the school.
A week or so earlier, his representative had called to tell him some of
the details of the negotiations with the administrators of the school.
For the coming year, Dante would be paid the same salary as he had
been paid in his first year, plus two hundred dollars. And there were
other details that the representative wanted to discuss with him. If
Dante would not be satisfied with any of the terms, he would not
be required to sign anything, and the negotiations would continue.

On the way down, we discussed the film version of *From Here to Eternity*, in which Frank Sinatra, after it had seemed that his acting and singing career had grinded to a halt, had won the Academy Award for best supporting actor in his portrayal of Maggio.

We discussed the use of the "vulgar" language in the novel and the depiction of sex. Was it appropriate to use "dirty" dialogue in literature and to include sex scenes? We both agreed that people were blaming the world war for the changes in moral standards and the collapse of religious values, and that we, the people, tended to gradually accept and to even normalize repeated behavior regardless of how bizarre such behavior was, instead of studying and understanding the causes and trying to change our behavior. The response of we, the people, to immoral behavior was usually and simply: "It's what we choose to do. That's why we do it. Don't confuse us with facts."

"The value of literature," Dante said, "is to help us to understand life. How can we understand life if the writer doesn't, or refuses to depict it? Is it a sin to read or to write about certain subjects, such as sex? Of course, like anything else that's good, a writer can write about it and distort it for shock effects, to exploit the readers just to make a profit."

And then, we discussed the business of insurance. I tried to persuade him to join me in the business. He'd make a great insurance man, I told him. He was a talker, I said, as well as a writer, a convincing talker, who spoke with optimism, humor, humility, good will, and with honesty and sincerity. People trusted him, I said.

"That's why I wouldn't sell them insurance."

That really pissed me off.

"But you're so frigging stubborn!"

He grinned at me.

"Whom would you rather buy insurance from? Some crook, or someone like you who can be trusted?"

"Wow! That's a loaded question. Would you buy insurance from someone like Joe McCarthy?"

That pissed me off, too.

"You sound like a commie."

He grinned again.

"People need protection against financial disasters," I said, "but most people don't know if they're buying what they actually need, because there are unscrupulous insurance men selling insurance policies only, spreading honey over shit, for profits only."

"That's the measure of a successful business: profits."

I ignored his rude interruption.

"Such salesmen don't give a damn about the people they're supposed to serve. They serve only themselves, but they're everywhere, not just in business."

"And you're trying to talk me into doing the same thing?"

"Hell no! I wouldn't even expect you to work for the insurance companies; you'd be working for the people who are buying from you. I wouldn't expect you to be a salesman; I'd expect you to be a professional, counseling your clients on their financial needs, not selling them policies. You'd examine your clients' financial needs and fit them into a program that serves their needs according to the cost that they could comfortably afford. You'd give your clients the most for their dollars. That's the kind of insurance man you'd be; the kind that people need." I thought that sounded pretty good, that Dante was impressed. "There are many similarities," I said, "between insurance and literature."

"Such as?"

"You begin with an effective story of disaster. And the most effective story must be simple but heart rendering. And it must illustrate a truth about life. Literature can be dishonest. The dishonest writer is not an artist; he's a bullshitter. Insurance men can be the same. A good writer is concerned with the quality of his writing, not with the big business of publishing. I'm concerned with the quality of my products, not with the big profits of the insurance companies. But we both want to be rewarded for our services. And the rewards can be excellent. Even the problems are similar. You have to convince the public how valuable literature is, and I have to chase after people when they should be chasing after me if they knew better. Maybe that's because there are too many writers in this country and too many insurance men. Anyway, I think you'd do well at selling insurance."

"There's only one problem."

"What's that?"

"I'm not interested."

"How the hell do you know unless you try?"

"By using your imagination, you can know a lot of things without actually trying to do them. Imagine watching paint dry. Could I interest you in doing that?"

"I thought writers were curious, that they want to try different things, to have various experiences. Why don't you spend one day with me, at least? You might even enjoy it. Selling insurance is like writing a short story."

"I'll probably regret telling you this, but, okay, convince me that I'd enjoy it, that it's like writing a short story."

I lit a cigarette. Smoking seemed to help my concentration.

"The opening statement in a presentation is like the first line in a story. It should grip the interest of the audience, and it should create a disturbing problem that stirs the emotions to such a degree that the audience is eating out of your hand, eagerly waiting for you to solve the problem. You should build upon the emotions through suspense, hinting at a solution until you come to the climax, the signing of the application. You'd be great! And you'd enjoy it. When you convince the applicant to sign the application, you feel a sense of achievement. And you've made a lot of money."

"You astound me."

"And when you're training, you learn a lot of psychological tricks to persuade people to buy things. Some of it even sounds crazy, but research has shown that these little tricks work. For example, if you're selling to Jews, never wear anything brown. I've forgotten why now, but they react against brown. And, of course, on St. Patrick's Day, always wear something green and never wear anything orange unless you're sure you're selling to a Protestant."

"Do you still write poetry backwards?"

"I'm not joking; I'm serious."

"I know. Why can't you logically and rationally show someone what his needs are? Why do you have to scare the shit out of him?"

"If you want people to act, the most effective way is by appealing to their emotions, otherwise they tend to be apathetic. Thinking requires too much effort. If a doctor tells someone to either exercise or to sleep in order to feel better, which will a guy do? If you try to appeal to a man's reason, he'll say, 'Let me think about it,' but he probably never will. That's the nature of the beast."

"Man is supposed to be rational. That's why he was given a brain. My job is to get him to think."

"There's a big gap in what education is, and what it should be. Don't tell me how great education is, not when so called educators like Shackle are telling us that the scientists are wrong, that the universe is only six thousand years old, because his religious authorities tell him so. And speaking of religions, why do you suppose they try to make us behave by telling us we'll be condemned to hell fire for eternity if we don't behave? If you tell people to do what's right because it's rational, how many people will do what's right because it *is* rational? How do you suppose Hitler was able to influence a whole nation of people, supposedly intelligent, rational beings, to commit acts of atrocities? Did he appeal to their reasoning, or to their emotions? Why are we on our way to Manchester? Is it because Shackle is treating you so damn rationally?"

"Hey, if you want to sell insurance, sell it. I think the challenge of selling appeals to you."

"Yeah, it does."

"That's fine. And if you get tired of it, you can always make pizzas. But selling doesn't appeal to me. I'd be glad to go around with you sometimes, but I wouldn't want to sell for a living. I want to teach, for a while, anyway. Getting kids to think really appeals to me. Somehow I feel that I should, and that I can, make somewhat of a difference in this world, that I can do a little something to make this a better world. And, of course, writing, to me, feels natural, even more so than teaching, but now that somebody is trying to stop me from teaching, as incredibly stupid as that is, trying to stop me only because I married Rose, I'm especially attracted now to teaching. And I don't really need the money. Like you, I can always make pizzas, too, if I ever really need to make more money. So, I'll be able to teach the way I want to teach, without being told how and what I *must* teach. I'm excited about that! Teaching with love! With passion!"

"Selling insurance," I said, puffing on the cigarette, then blowing the smoke out, "is like making love."

He stared at me.

"What? You mean it's like screwing someone?"

I tried to ignore his facetious remark.

"When you make love to a woman, you don't try to appeal to her on a rational level. You don't say, 'Hey, babe, be reasonable.' You appeal to her on her most effective level, by stimulating her deepest passions. If you don't, and someone else does…"

"He's the one who'll be screwing her, not you."

I groaned and shook my head.

"English teachers!"

When we arrived in Manchester, we had lunch in a small restaurant on Elm Street, which is the main drag. Then, I drove down farther and took a left turn and parked near the VA office. Almost as soon as we went in, we were taken into the office of the representative, who took us into the office of his supervisor, a much larger office, and as we sat around a desk, they discussed the situation. They gave Dante a check, which was the equivalent to the amount he had received the year before, plus a hundred dollars. The check was for the current school year. If Dante would be called in to substitute between now and the end of June, the school would have to pay him more, even if he would accept the check for his compensation for this school year.

"Is this agreeable to you, so far?" the representative asked. "We could try to get more, if you want."

"This is great! How did you get the superintendent to agree to *this*?"

The rep, a man of average height and rather stocky, looked at his supervisor, an older man with white hair and thick glasses, and said, "Do you want to tell him, or do you want me to tell him?"

"Tell him what you said to the superintendent."

The rep turned to Dante.

"During our negotiations, the both of us, in the superinten-dent's office with, what's his name, the acting principal?"

"Shackle?"

"Whatever. I said, 'Do you have any idea what this young, ide-alistic citizen has done for his country, for all of us, this past year, after, from what I've been told, not only from the head of the English department, but from so many of his students who had him last year? After having done a tremendously excellent job of teaching, and hav-ing fought so heroically in Korea, receiving not only a combat infan-try badge and, as you can see on his discharge papers, not just one, but two bronze stars, and a purple heart, having come so close to losing his life, protecting our way of life, even losing an arm and hav-ing his whole body embedded with shrapnel. And then, he returns to his hometown. You'd .think that the people in his own hometown would be proud and happy to have him return. You'd think that people would welcome him home and would happily want him to return to his old job, especially since he had been so successful at his job and had been such an asset to his community. But no, the princi-pal of his school, where he had studied and later did such an admiral job of teaching, had not wanted him to return to his job. And why not? Because the principal saw that his arm is artificial and is so ugly looking that he refuses to rehire him.' 'That's not true!' Shackle says. 'No?' I ask. 'Why should you refuse to let him return to his job?' Shackle didn't answer. 'Imagine,' I said, 'when this story gets in the news. Imagine the adverse publicity, not only to this school, but to the whole community! To the whole state of New Hampshire! A war hero is rejected by the school in his own home town, because he has an ugly looking artificial arm.' The superintendent glared at Shackle, whose face became red, as red as his head."

"That's true," the supervisor said, "and the superintendent drew up this contract for you. You can sign it now, if you want, or you can hold out for more money."

Dante looked at it.

"This is the contract you told me about on the phone," he said to the rep.

"Does it meet with your satisfaction?"

"Yes."

"Well then, if you sign it, you'll return to teaching this September. And if you encounter any problems, don't hesitate to let us know. I'm sure that Shackle will try to sabotage you, and when he does, don't yield; fight back, and notify us; we'll fight him with you. That's why we're here. The government of the United States of America is backing you up; your government is thanking you for the service you've performed."

"Uncle Sam thanks you," his supervisor said, grinning.

And we all shook hands.

When we went outside, the sun was shining, and Dante said, "Shackle is going to be so pissed off at me."

"Good! Didn't I tell you that you have to stir a person's emotions to get anything done!"

Two weeks later, racial segregation in public schools was unanimously outlawed by the Supreme Court. In the ruling, Chief Justice Earl Warren wrote: "In the field of public education, the doctrine of separate but equal has no place. Separated educational facilities are inherently unequal."

Once again, the political party of Abraham Lincoln had spoken on behalf of racial justice and equality and had defeated the disgruntled Dixiecrats.

On the other hand, some of my drinking companions at the beer joint lamented the loss of the good old days.

"Well, you know the saying," one of them said. "If you can't lick them, you might as well join them. That's what Shackle wants to do now, join the party of Honest Abe just so he can see it crumble."

"Hey, we Democrats are going to be happy to get rid of him."

On Monday, June 21, was Dante and Rosie's second wedding anniversary. On the previous Friday and Saturday, we closed the restaurant and had a big gathering of family and friends. Little did we know then that we would be celebrating their last wedding anniversary. On Sunday, after church, when Ben John and the others from out of town went home, some of us went to the cabin on Sugar Mountain.

During the rest of the summer, I worked occasionally in the restaurant, and I also built up my insurance clientele, and Dante, of course, did a lot of writing. Sometimes we went to the cabin with our families, or we took our families for a weekend or so to other parts of the mountains, or to the sea, and went fishing and swimming. We spent four days of a long weekend in Quebec City. Jessica and my son spent two weeks at Minnie's house while Minnie visited her folks for a few days.

Rosie was pregnant again. The baby was due in November.

Two weeks before the beginning of the school year, Dante received a notification from Shackle in the mail. He told Dante to prepare detailed daily lesson plans for each of his classes for the coming school year, and to submit them to him in one week. Dante had not even been told, yet, which classes he would have. He had only assumed, as in his first year, he would have two English grammar classes, and two literature classes. He didn't want to discuss the issue with Minnie on the telephone, but he called to inquire if they could meet somewhere and discuss it. That had been when Jessica was visiting, and Minnie had returned from Boston. I happened to be at Minnie's house when he called.

"I don't understand why he wants you to submit lesson plans to him. That's not his job. Besides, daily lesson plans for each day, for the whole year?"

Minnie asked Dante to come to her house that afternoon to discuss the letter, and she invited him to bring Rosie to stay for dinner with the rest of us.

After they had arrived, we stayed outside to enjoy the warm, sunny weather, and when Dante showed the note to Minnie, she said, "This is so damned crazy! And he wants you to submit it next week! I can't believe he's doing this. He has nothing to do with your lesson plans. That's between you and me. You can use the same lesson plans that you used before. Just ignore this. If Jed mentions this, just tell him to see me about it. It's obvious what he's trying to do to you. I hate to tell you this, but he's going to try to discourage you."

Dante grinned at her.

"If he does, that could be interesting."

"As far as I know, he hasn't asked any of the other teachers for any lesson plans. He doesn't have the authority; he must know that. Besides, how can anyone make 'detailed daily lesson plans' for each class a whole year in advance?"

"I was told at the VA, that if he gives me any crap, to report him. Maybe you'd be doing him a favor, if you warned him about that."

"Jed and I are not friends. He doesn't listen to me."

"You belong to his denomination, don't you? And it's a small group."

"I've attended his religious services a few times, but mostly out of curiosity. His views are too extreme for me."

"Yeah, I know what you mean. He tries to propagate his views to the kids in his biology classes."

"Incidentally, now that you're back, you won't be teaching four classes this year. We have enough English teachers now so that you'll be teaching only three classes, and you'll have one study hall, and you'll actually have a free period now."

"That sounds good. So, what will I be teaching? English grammar?"

"If you don't mind. You're the best grammar teacher we have. And I know you'd like to teach modern American lit, too. So, I was thinking of giving you the freshmen grammar class, the modern American lit class, and the classical lit class."

"Fine."

The teachers were required to attend meetings at school the day after Labor Day and to prepare for classes, which would begin the next day, on Wednesday, after an hour or so at the assembly hall for student orientation, where all the teachers would be introduced to the students. On the first day, the classes, of course, would be abbreviated so that the students would be introduced to the teachers and to the subjects.

On the day after Labor Day, Dante arrived at the school, went into Minnie's home room, where they greeted each other, "Good morning!" and then she gave him the list of students for the freshmen English grammar class and the classical lit class in the morning, followed by a study period, then lunch, and in the afternoon he had the modern American literature class.

"The last period is your free period. So is mine. Is that okay?"

"Yeah, that's fine."

"And your home room is next to mine."

"Okay, good. I'm going to the office and check my mail now."

"We have to meet in the biology room in a half hour."

He went downstairs to the secretary's office to check his mailbox. It was full. There were some advertisements for school supplies, and several applications for Horace Mann insurance policies. He grinned. He could compare the prices to the prices of Tony's policies. And there was a list of forty names of pupils on a large sheet of paper: ten freshmen, ten sophomores, ten juniors, and ten seniors, who were assigned to a remedial reading class for his last period. He stared at the list.

"Is Shackle in?" he asked the secretary, a middle aged woman with thick glasses who was typing.

She looked up, at an opened door directly in front of her, and she could see into the office of the principal.

"He's in, but he's very busy right now."

As Dante limped gruffly past her desk, she cried out, "You can't go in there now!"

"What the hell is this?" he demanded, waving the sheet and shoving the roster under Shackle's nose.

Shackle, sitting behind a big desk, glared up at Dante.

"An experiment."

"An experiment! An experiment in what?"

"A special class for slower pupils to separate them from the rest of the student body so that they can compete on a lower level. It was a last minute decision, but I know you can handle it. I have confidence in you. I thought you'd welcome the challenge. Seventeen of the pupils are from the flats. I'm too busy to discuss it now. Why don't you, at least, think about it? You'll have to excuse me now. You're going to make me late for our meeting."

Dante left the office, returned to Minnie's room, and showed her the list of his new assignment.

"What!" she cried out. "This is outrageous. Right after the meeting, I'm going to show this to the superintendent. This is so unfair!"

"Let me think about it first. This really sounds like it could be a good idea. And I don't need a free period."

"Of course you need a free period! Especially you, with all the writing you assign them. You can certainly use a free period to correct some of the papers. And forty pupils in a class like this! That's almost impossible! We'll discuss this when we get back from the meeting."

They went into Shackle's room, and Dante and Minnie and the others stood around and greeted each other and waited for Shackle. Most of the teachers welcomed Dante back, and when Shackle entered and stood beside his desk, they all sat down behind students' desks and waited for Shackle to speak. He welcomed them back for another year. He would be the acting principal, he said, again this year. And then he introduced a new teacher, a young man from South

Carolina who had recently graduated and would be teaching biology in his first year of teaching. No other new teachers were introduced.

"I thought Jed would announce your return," Minnie said on the way back to her room. "I think the other teachers expected it, too. By not even acknowledging your return, he has made his attitude towards you so conspicuous, as though, well, as though you're a threat to him, somehow. He really hates you!"

A week later she would inform Dante that the new biology teacher had majored in English in college, and that he had been hired by Shackle to teach English, and that he was also a member of the Temple of the Holy Spirit.

When Dante and she had returned to her room, they discussed the new class that had been assigned to him. If he was willing to take the class, she suggested that he should reduce the class size in half, at least. She recognized, she said, several pupils as troublemakers who, she suspected, had been planted there by Shackle to disrupt the class.

"I have the distinct feeling that he doesn't want you to succeed. He is actually hoping that you fail. I don't understand his reasoning. If you do well, if we all do well, and you've already proven you're an excellent teacher, he'd take credit for doing a good job as principal. That might even get him the position permanently."

"If you're familiar with his beliefs, especially about the human species, you should understand why he wants me to fail."

"Yeah," she murmured, "but it's so stupid."

"Prejudice is stupid. People who are prejudiced aren't even aware of their own prejudice. That's one of the reasons it can be so damn irrational and seditious."

Her bright green eyes were staring at him, but she didn't say anything.

"Seventeen of the pupils on this list," Dante said, "are from the flats. I want a chance to teach all of them, especially the three seniors. If they're going to graduate this year, they should, at least, have *some* education."

After an hour or so, Minnie decided that the seventeen of them, twelve boys and five girls, would be big enough for the size of the special class.

"And," she said, "we'll teach the class together. I'll be your assistant." She grinned at him. "This will really be a special class. I think I'll really enjoy working with you. But I'm still going to report this to the superintendent."

Another thought occurred to her.

"If we're going to be teaching in our free period," she said, "occasionally, one of us can sneak into the teachers' room for a quick smoke."

"It won't even have to be quick. Since I don't smoke, you can take time to smoke at least two cigarettes. On some days, you'll be able to spend most of the period just smoking one cigarette after another."

The next morning, during the first period of the freshmen English class, after he had distributed to each student a sheet that listed the eight parts of speech, he said, "I promise you that this, grammar, is the easiest subject you'll ever take, because English grammar is so logical, not like English spelling, which is so confusing. Grammar has rules, easy rules, and once you know the rules, which won't take you long to learn, maybe a day or two, a week, at the most, you won't have any trouble with English grammar for the rest of your lives. That's a promise. And I also promise you, I won't give you much homework, not at first, at least, not until you become adjusted to high school, and even then, it won't be much, but for every hour you spend in class, you should be willing to spend at least one hour a night doing homework outside of class. Actually, you should spend more than two to three hours on some nights." He paused to let them absorb the idea. Distressful looks were darkening their faces. "But I won't give you any homework over vacations, and that includes weekends. After all, we've been told that even God rested on the seventh day, and so we mortals, not as strong as God, need to rest more than God needs to rest; that's why we mortals need at least two days off a week. Right? You don't have to go to classes on weekends. So, you'll have plenty of free time as long as you're still in high school. Take advantage of all the free time you'll have. Use it to advance yourself. Think of all of the poor kids in all of the poor countries around the world who don't have all of the advantages you have, who can't afford to spend at least four hours a night to study. But you'll be free every Friday night and all day and all night on Saturdays and Sundays, and you'll have at least one national holiday every month, and you'll have a fairly long Thanksgiving vacation, a long Christmas vacation, and a long spring vacation. And, of course, the very, very long three months of summer vacation. Goodness! You'll have hardly any homework at all when you stop and think about it, but you can't learn much if you don't study much, so you'll have to spend some time studying when you have so much time and opportunity to study. The assignment for tonight, since this is only the beginning of the school year, and we'll gradually increase your productivity over the next few days, is to write an introduction of yourself, in other words, a synopsis of your life, an autobiography that includes your interests and your dislikes, especially what you expect from this class and what you'd like to learn about writing, whether you'd like to be a reporter for the school paper, or whether you'd like to act in schools plays and even if you'd like to write plays, or simply would like to write. But you don't have to make your composition too long; keep it under a thousand words, because you'll need time to study the eight parts of speech tonight. You'll be tested on them tomorrow. I know that after you study the parts of speech, which, even though you've been taught them before, some of you won't remember all of them perfectly. That's why I'll be testing you, to see how well you remember them. As I've said, after you know them, you won't have any trouble remembering them for the rest of your life. That's how well you'll know them, even if we have to spend the rest of the week on them. We can't advance if we don't know the rules well. To write well in English, to be understood, to communicate clearly, we must know all the rules. And if we make the effort to know all the rules, we will know them; we all will. But before we know the parts of speech, we must know what a sentence is. Can you tell me what a sentence is? At the top of this paper," he said as he distributed more sheets to the class, "write down, 'A sentence is a group of words that express and complete an idea.' You know, when we think of primitive people, we have a tendency to think of them as stupid, because they're not familiar with modern technology. But just stop and think of one of our greatest creations: language. It's amazing! We've taken sounds we can make with our voices and created words. There are times when we can't understand one other, when we don't follow the same rules, but if you and I follow the same rules, we can easily understand each other. And we've created ways of making language so easy that even babies can learn to understand it." He went to the blackboard, drew a stick figure of a man pointing a rifle at a round target with a bull's eye at its center. The drawing was similar to a drawing at the top of each paper he had distributed. Under the drawing was the sentence: "The man hit the target." Dante said, "As you know, of course, every complete sentence must have at least two parts that tell us who or what is doing or being whatever. What are those two parts? Someone or something is doing or being something. Under the first part, write an S; under the second part, write V." On the blackboard, under the word, man, he wrote an S, and under the word, hit, he wrote a V. On the drawing, he made a dash from the barrel of the rifle. "This is the path of the bullet," he said, making several dashes until the last dash ended at the bull's eye. "Sometimes, to complete a sentence, we also need a target. The bullet hit something. So, to make a complete sentence, we use a subject and a verb, and sometimes, an object. But before we talk about objects, concentrate on subjects and verbs, and remember this rule: the verb always depends on the subject, no matter what, no matter how stupid it sounds. I'm not talking about how we talk to each other; I'm talking about English grammar. If you're taking a test, and you're required to use the correct verb, always go by the rules; not by the way I talk when I'm in the flats. Notice the box on my desk. How many of you like big chocolate chip cookies? These cookies are really big. And they're all homemade. And I'm going to give them away." He took one out of the box and he held it out. "They're all this big." He took a bite and chewed it. "It's so tasty! And if I give you a cookie, you can eat it, right here, in class. I'm going to give you a quick test, and if you pass it, I'll give you a cookie. I want you to humor me, just for a minute. Some of you might think this test is strange, but I just want to see if you've been paying attention to what I've just said. What did I just say I'm going to give you?" When they answered "a cookie" in unison, he said, "Right. A cookie, not the whole box. You seem to have paid attention. Good. If you look at the sheet again, you can see the test. It says, 'The box of cookies is are on the desk.' What I want you to do is cross out the verb that does not belong in that sentence. Do it now. Cross out the verb that does not belong. Cross it out completely so that we can't even see what it was. Now, show it to your neighbors. All of you who crossed out 'are,' raise your hands." No hands went up. All the students were looking around. "I said all of you who crossed out 'are,' raise your hands." Finally, three hands from three girls were raised, reluctantly. "Three out of thirty," Dante said, and he gave away three of his cookies. He said to one of the girls, "Tell the other ninety per cent of the class what the rule is that you followed." And as she was eating her cookie, she said, "The verb always depends on the subject." He nodded. "And when I said, 'Notice the box on the desk,' you knew I was giving you a clue, didn't you?" She nodded, too, and she smiled. "How many of you actually thought of the rule, but thought that the subject was cookies, not the box?" Most of the others raised their hands. "Ah, I think I know what you were thinking; you were eager to eat the cookies, not the box. You could argue your case, but after you know all the parts of speech, you won't have any problems with picking the correct subjects. A complete sentence must always have a subject and a verb, so, before we study all the parts of speech, let's concentrate on complete sentences. We'll finish that today, in a few more minutes, because it's so easy. Subjects and objects are always nouns, which are simply words for people, places, and things, and their proper names, or they are pronouns, which are simply substitutes for nouns. Examples: People eat food. Write it down, and label the subject, verb, and the object. We eat food. The pronoun 'we' is the substitute for the noun. We eat. That's a complete sentence. We don't always need an object." He took a cookie from the box, held it up and wrote on the board, "Eat it." He turned to the class and said, "I'll give this cookie to the first one who can label the subject, the verb, and the object to this sentence, if it's, in fact, a complete sentence." He waited for a response. Some of the girls were giggling a little. "Well, what's the verb?" Several said, "Eat." Dante asked, "Is there an object?" Someone asked, "It?" Dante said, "Yeah, the object is a pronoun. 'It' means this cookie." Someone said, "There's no sub-ject. That's not a complete sentence." Dante said, "it's a complete sentence; it's called a command. If a father says to his son who doesn't like his dinner, 'Eat it!' what's the subject? *Who* eat it?" Dante began to eat the cookie. As he was eating it, he was writing on the board, "(You)" and he said, "The subject is implied, so you write it in paren-thesis. 'You' is the subject of the sentence. If you say to your dog, 'Sit,' that's a complete sentence. So, every sentence has a subject, a verb, and sometimes an object. A verb can be used to do two things: to denote action, or simply being. If a verb is used as an action word, then the sentence may sometimes need an object. In the sentence we used originally, 'The man hit the target,' the subject, man, is doing the action. What is the object, target, doing?" The class agreed that the target was not doing anything; it was an object. "In this sen-tence," he said, writing on the blackboard, "Jack is kissing Jill. The subject, Jack, is doing the action. What is the object, Jill, doing?" Dante shrugged. The class didn't know. She was an object. "Did you ever hear anyone say that a man should never treat a woman as an object?" Dante asked. "Let's just assume," he said, "that Jill is happy." He wrote that on the board. "Now Jill is the subject of the sentence. What's the verb? The verb is 'is.' What does 'is' mean? Does is mean equal? Two and three equal five. Does five equal five? If Jill is Jill, does Jill equal Jill? If a subject is a subject, does that mean a subject is equal to a subject? If the subject is doing something to an object, that means they're opposites. The subject does the action, and the object receives it. If five equals five, that means five is the same as five. Simple enough. Right? So, if subject equals subject, a subject is a subject. Example: Jill is a girl. Girl is not an object. This sentence does not have an object, because the verb is a linking verb. No, not an Abe Lincoln verb, even if it frees the object. A link is a bridge, a connecter; the equal sign is a bridge. Remember that objects, like subjects, are nouns or pronouns, but if they follow a linking verb, they are not objects of the sentence, so in this sentence, Jill is a girl, what is the object of the sentence?" He paused. No one said girl. He took another cookie from the box, and he ate it. "This tastes so deli-cious! I'd really like to give everyone a cookie, but you have to earn it;

you have to pass another taste, I mean, another test. I'm the one who's been tasting them, so far." He wrote on the board: "The box of cookies taste so delicious!" He turned to the class, looked at the board, and read the sentence out loud. "Wait a minute. I was going to have you write the sentence and then have you label the subject, verb, and object, but what's wrong with that sentence? What is that sentence really saying?" He paused as the class responded. "You're right. The subject is box. That sentence is really saying that the box tastes delicious. Even English teachers sometimes make mistakes. In a few more days, maybe less, you'll be picking up a newspaper and you'll be correcting all the grammatical mistakes in it. You'll even be correcting my mistakes." He went to the board again and erased 'box of,' and said, "Write the sentence now, and write S under the subject, V under the verb, and O under the object. I hope you all pass this test and get a cookie. That will mean I did my job as a teacher. When you finish, put your pencils down." After all the pencils went down, he said, "Show it to your neighbors. If you labeled the subject under cookies, that is correct, and even though cookies don't do the actual tasting, taste is the verb used as a linking verb, and there is no object. If you passed the test, raise your hand until you receive a delicious chocolate chip cookie."

And then he told them to write down a sentence using a subject, verb, and object, and to write two sentences without objects. And then he sent them, three at a time, to write their sentences on the board and to label the subjects, verbs, and objects, and their classmates corrected their mistakes.

Dante's next class was classical literature. He decided that his class would begin with the study of the Bible as literature, not as science, although he would compare the six days of Creation in *The Book of Genesis* to the scientific stages to indicate that there are no conflicts or contradictions necessarily between religion and science.

Although there had been some religious groups that had confronted him in his first year of teaching, none of the parents of his students had opposed him when he had taught the same subject three years earlier, especially after he had stated in a meeting with the parents back then that an educated person should have a basic understanding not only of the various religions, especially of Christianity, because it was so important to the understanding of our culture, even though our culture was still evolving, but also of the discoveries of science. "Science," he maintained to the parents, "is knowledge of the physical world. An educated person should be able to understand the theories of science, and when the theories are proven, they become factual, and if a fact is not the same as a belief, an intelligent person must reevaluate his belief. To continue to believe that the earth is flat, or that the earth is the center of the universe, or that the earth is only six thousand years old," he said to them, "is irrational. And I don't believe that intelligence is the work of the devil who's trying to deceive and seduce us. I believe that intelligence is one of the divine gifts, which we're required to use."

He had worked on the course as a student in college, and three years earlier, before he had begun teaching, he had shown it to Minnie, who had agreed to let him teach it as one of his classes, under classical, or world literature.

Before distributing an outline of the course to the class, Dante asked, "How did we get here? What are we doing here? What's going to happen us?" He paused. He looked around the room. "When you got out of bed this morning, when you were having breakfast and getting ready for school, how many of you wondered why it is you have to be here? Is it to learn about life?" He paused again, limped towards a window and looked outside. "But what do we know about life? And what can you learn about life, here, in a classroom? Have you ever noticed, for example, the trees, and then asked yourself what they were doing on this earth?" He turned and moved towards the blackboard. "If this blackboard represented the universe, even just part of the universe that we know about with our great telescopes, this earth would be such a tiny speck that we wouldn't even see it. And yet, here we are. Why are we here? How much do we really know? My job is to teach you, to help you to know. And if that's so, why am I forbidden to teach you some of the things that I know? Some people say we're better off not knowing certain things, such as, well, you know some of the things we're forbidden to even talk about. We can't talk about anything dirty enough that will corrupt us. I'm sure you've heard people say, 'I don't know what it is, and I don't want to know anything about it; all I know is that it's not good, and I don't like it!' Yeah, you've heard people say that. If I even mention a certain name of something in class, I could get fired, even though you've heard the word on television, so I'd better not tell you anything about communism. That's definitely taboo. And yet, there's something deep inside of us that haunts us with a question: why? We want to *know*! Yeah, there's a saying, 'Curiosity killed a cat.' But without curiosity, life would be so boring. Let's be honest with each other. One of the reasons why certain subjects are taboo is because once we accept certain beliefs, and we live a certain way, we don't like to be told that we're wrong, so we say, 'Don't confuse me with facts,' and we tell ourselves that if you don't believe the way I believe, there's something wrong with you, not with me. I don't want to argue with you, because if you show me that I'm wrong, I won't feel right about it, and I might have to change some of my ideas. I tell myself that I have a right to my ideas, to my opinions, even if I'm wrong." He paused. "When I go to bed at night, I like to turn off my brains and go to sleep. Besides, I don't want other people to think I'm a, a, well, whatever they call a person who thinks, a person who's a book-worm and who reads because he wants to know about, well, about everything. Do you know a guy or a girl like that?" He pointed his finger at the class. "If you're one of those, those people, those, those intellectuals, who can think without, well, without even getting a headache, and others call you a weirdo, then you're going to enjoy this class. You're really going to enjoy it."

He distributed a sheet which listed some of the works they would be studying, beginning with the Bible, and continuing with Greek mythology, Plato's *Allegory of the Cave* and some of his other writings, Aesop's Fables and other Roman literature, and the literature, the folk tales, of Africa and of Asia.

"To get some clues to why we're here, where shall we find them? From the study of science? From religion? But this is neither a science nor a religion class. It's a literature class. What is the subject of literature? Everything, of course, especially humanity, is the subject of literature. I've met people who I had thought were more educated and intelligent than most people, but they, even teachers, English teachers, believe it or not, have told me that they read only nonfiction, because fiction, they said is not true; it's only make believe. The value of literature, especially in the classics we'll be reading, is in the insights it gives us into life, into the laws of human nature. Classical literature is the works of prophets and poets who were, or seemed, at least, to be, divinely inspired. They wrote stories, called fables and allegories, to enable us to understand truth. It isn't the plot in a story that makes a story great, although if the plot is suspenseful, it makes the story interesting, and some will say, 'What a great story!' But its greatness is in the truth it reveals. It's great not because it's so unique; it's great because it's so typical of life. All of the arts is valuable, not just because it can be so interesting and entertaining, but because it helps us to mature, to understand life."

He distributed the Bibles to the class, and said, "The assignment tonight is in two parts. The first part is to write a paragraph or two telling me what you think our basic needs are for survival in relation to why we're here and to what you think is going to happen to the human race and to the whole planet. The second part is to read the first ten chapters and to answer this question in writing. He wrote it on the blackboard: "Does the Biblical account of the creation of the earth conflict with the theories of science?" I want your opinion, so tell me why you think either yes or no, regardless of whether you have much or little knowledge of science. What we'll be looking for in this course is the basic need, if there even is a basic need, for the survival of the human race. When we discuss the laws of nature, we'll have to distinguish between physical nature and spiritual nature, and between the nature of animals and human nature. Are there differences of nature, of basic needs? Many people say that war is a law of nature. How does intelligence, or emotions, affect our nature? There are so many questions! Let's hope that by reading, and by using our intelligence, we can gain some understanding of ourselves and of our world."

As they read the first chapter of *Genesis*, Dante asked several questions, such as, "In the beginning of what? The whole cosmos, or the beginning of earth? And did the Creation in the first chapter actually happen in six days? Was that six days, literally or figuratively?"

And he wrote on the blackboard, and the class took notes. He wrote down the events of each day.

On the first day, the earth was covered in darkness. According to science, the earth had shot out of the sun, and when the fires of the burning earth had finally died out, the steam from the earth had been rising, covering the earth in darkness. The clouds had been pouring water on the earth for centuries. At the end of this first scientific "day," as the clouds became smaller and began to disperse, the first dawn appeared. The rays of the sun broke through and "light was made."

"How long was the first Biblical day?" Dante asked the class. "Centuries? Or was it actually twenty-four hours long as some fundamentalists insist?"

On the second day, "God divided the water from the waters." What does this mean? That the rains finally ceased, making the heavens visible? God created a firmament and called it Heaven. And the dry land, called Earth, appeared. And the earth yielded green grass and the fruit trees.

On the third day, the fruit trees bore fruit. "And the evening and the morning were the third day."

On the fourth day, "God said: Let there be lights made in the firmament of heaven, to divide the day and the night." And: "God made two great lights: a greater light to rule the day; and a lesser light to rule the night." And the days and the nights, and the four seasons became fixed.

On the fifth day "the creeping creatures of the sea went on the land, and the birds flew over the earth."

On the sixth day, earth yielded beasts of many kinds. Out of the earth, "God created man to have dominion over the whole earth."

"How was it possible," Dante asked, "that man, smaller, weaker, and slower than some of the animals, could have dominion over the earth? What makes us different from the animals? Yet, how are we the same?" He went to the blackboard again, and he said, "Write down these questions, and we'll try to answer them in this course."

"What did early man spend most of his time doing? What does a wild animal spend most of its time doing? What is the life cycle? How do the plants and animals fit into the life cycle? Man is classified as Homo Sapiens, which means 'the man who knows.' At one time other kinds of man once occupied the earth. They are not classified as Homo Sapiens. Neanderthal man became extinct. Was he wiped out by Cro-Magnon man who was a Homo Sapiens? Animals know exactly what to do, such as build nests. Their nature provides them with that. We call it instinct. What has nature given to us? There is a part of our brain that we call the cerebrum, which we use for thinking. Some of the animals also have a cerebrum, but it is small. Is the brain of man developing or not? Since man has been on the earth, a development of his technology, and of his knowledge, has certainly been ascertained. Most of it has been very beneficial, such as the advancements in medicine, but some of it has been so bad that it can destroy all human life on this earth. Where are we going? And why? According to *Genesis*, man was created to have dominion over the earth. Think of the awesome responsibility that we've been given!" He paused. "I've heard people ask, 'If there is a God, why does He allow us to commit so much evil?' In other words, why does He endow us with so much free will? You know what I find so ironic? I think that we have been given so much intelligence that if we used just a fraction of it the way we were intended to use it, we could create the paradise for which man was created. Most of us use very little of the intelligence with which we have been endowed. We waste it. We don't want to be burdened with too much responsibility. Maybe we've never been encouraged to think. But some of us, for some ungodly reason, having been endowed with extremely high intelligence, have used it, unfortunately for mankind, to make bigger and more powerful weapons, until we have the ultimate weaponry to destroy all mankind." He paused. "When we take something good, and we pervert it, we commit the worst evil, even when we think we're benefitting others. The history of mankind, so far, has been a history of war, and we glorify it. Where will it lead us? Where will hatred lead us? What is man looking for? What will lead us back to the garden of paradise?"

During the rest of the period, the students were allowed to read the next nine chapters silently, or to work on their written assignments.

Dante's right leg was beginning to hurt a little. He sat behind his desk. His next period was a study period, so he was able to sit and relax.

Minnie joined him at lunch in the cafeteria and asked him how he was feeling.

"It feels good to be teaching again."

"I've noticed you've been limping."

"Is it that noticeable?"

"You seem to limp more as the day goes on."

"Well, it's been more than a year since I've been on my feet so much, even though I've been exercising."

"Is it painful?"

He shrugged.

"I'll get used to it. I hardly notice it when I'm teaching."

"How is Rose doing?"

"She's doing great. She's due around the early part of November. Why don't you come up for dinner this Sunday?"

"That sounds good. Thank you."

After lunch, his next class was modern American literature. After he had given out a list of authors and their works to the class, he asked them, "What is the dream of most of the immigrants to this country?"

The class would be studying the various cultures and history of the United States through its literature, beginning with Mark Twain and Stephen Crane, covering the days of slavery, through the civil war, through the first world war, prohibition, and the second world war, until the present.

The last class of the day was the special class, the remedial reading class. Minnie had been a little worried about it because they hadn't had any time to prepare for it.

Dante had said, "I'll think of something."

She sat in a back row while he stood by his desk as the pupils entered.

"Fill the front seats first," he told them.

The five girls sat in the front row. There were six rows with six seats in each row.

"The seniors can sit in the third row."

The three seniors were boys. Dante knew each pupil, and he knew that none of them were disciplinary problems. And he knew that the three seniors could read; he had taught them when they had been freshmen. Why, he wondered, were they in this special class? As though one of the seniors were reading his mind, a boy in the third row, grumbled, "They're putting us bunch of dummies together."

Dante slammed his fist against his desk.

"You're not a bunch of dummies! I had the three of you when you were freshmen, and you did fine. What happened?"

"Shackle and us hate each other."

Dante stared at him.

"Go to the board, Danny."

He went to the sideboard.

"Write done what you just said, but write 'Sam and us,' not Shackle."

He did.

"Draw a line under the subject, two lines under the verb, and three under the object."

"It's a compound subject, and 'hate' is the verb, and 'other' is the object."

"So, what's wrong with the sentence?"

"I shoulda said 'we' but he still hates us. He calls us the brats of the flats. He hates you, too."

Dante sighed. He wasn't sure how to respond. He motioned to Danny to take his seat.

"I guarantee one thing," he said softly, "that the best writers for the school paper are going to come from this class. You have not one English teacher, but two, who will help you. Miss Birch is the editor of the paper. Your English is going to be impeccable. And maybe some of you are going to be acting on the stage in front of the whole school. But before you do any writing, you have to know how to use the rules. Maybe some of you, like Danny, already know the rules. If you do, that's good; you'll help the ones who don't. You'll be taking a diagnostic test tomorrow. That means, you won't be graded on it. The test is for me to know if you know the rules." He distributed the sheets on English grammar that he had given to his first class. "Study this tonight, and write three sentences and label the subjects, verbs, and objects. Do it by yourself. Don't ask anyone to help you. To teach you, I need to know what you know about grammar. How many of you are wondering what this course is?" All the hands went up. "Well, you know that Miss Birch and I are both English teachers, so this is an English class, therefore we'll be reading and writing in English, and since we have all the high school grades mixed together, well, that must make us special. The juniors and seniors will probably be, well, coaching the rest of you, depending on the level you're on. As I mentioned, you will be writers for the school paper and for the plays we'll put on. Now," he said, "we're going to read a story out loud, with each of you taking turns." He distributed the sheets. "As you can see, it's called *The Patrol*. The patrol is a small group of soldiers, in combat, who are selected to patrol the area in front of the front lines called no man's land, between their own lines and the lines of the enemy."

He did not tell them that the dialogue had been edited to remove all of the vulgar words.

The girl in the first desk in the front row began to read.

After thirty seconds or so, Dante said, "You read that well. Next."

Each pupil in the first row read. And then the rest of them took turns reading.

Dante read the last two pages.

The final sentence in the story was: "The earth erupted again, and he was hurled into the air and landed in a puddle of mud at the bottom of the listening post."

"Wow!" some of them cried out.

"Was he killed?" someone asked.

"Of course he was!" someone else answered.

They looked at Dante, who shrugged.

"Who's the author?" someone asked.

He shrugged again.

"He is!" Danny cried out. "Aren't you?"

"What makes you think that?"

"I heard someone say you're writing a book. Is it about Korea?"

Dante didn't answer.

"Can we read the book?" someone asked.

"You want to read the *whole* book?"

"Yeah!" several others replied.

"Can we keep this story?"

"Why do you want to keep it?" Dante asked.

"So I can have it. And I want to show it to my father. He'd like it, too."

"I want to keep mine, too!"

"Okay, keep it if you want it. The rest of you, pass yours down."

Nobody returned it.

"You all want to keep it?"

"Yeah!"

"You like war stories?"

"Yeah!"

"Maybe we can read a book called *All Quiet on the Western Front*, written by a German. After you convince me that you can read and write well, and so far, you have, we'll call this class Literature on War."

"Yeah!"

The bell rang. As the pupils began to get out of their seats, Dante yelled out, "Sit down!" They seemed surprised, but they sat down again. "That bell rings to notify the teachers that the period has ended, but you don't move until I dismiss you. Do you understand? And when I dismiss you, you don't run; you walk out. First row, you're dismissed." He paused. "Second row, dismissed. The rest of you, you're dismissed."

As the pupils walked out of the room, Minnie came up to him and said, "Well, I think we're going to enjoy this class. It went very well."

"Yeah, their reading was pretty good. I certainly don't think that all of them need remedial reading."

"No, I don't either. Some of them need to practice reading out loud, but most of them read your story quite well. They were certainly interested in it. They were fascinated. So was I."

"What's Shackle thinking? Why do you suppose he put them in one group?"

"Some of them, I think, had disciplinary problems. But they seem to respect you. Let's meet in the teachers' room to talk about it."

After he dismissed the pupils in his homeroom, Dante went into the teachers' room. Minnie was already there, sitting at the other end of a couch. She was smoking a cigarette. He sat in a lounge chair, facing her.

"So, do you have any plans for the special class?" she asked.

"I want to test their grammar, especially on the parts of speech, and if they do well, and I have a feeling that most of them will, I'll try to make it a class on the literature of war."

"How much have you written about Korea?"

"No, I don't think I'll give them that."

"Why not? You saw their reaction. They really liked it. Besides, I want to read more, too. I like it, and the kids like it, so now you know it's interesting to your readers."

"I used it today to test their oral reading. The script needs to be polished."

"Will you, at least, let me read it?"

"Later, maybe. Do you have any ideas about the special class?"

"Do you know all the kids well?"

"I know their parents pretty well. Why?"

"I know that Jed has had problems with these pupils. I think that's why he put them all in the same class. What I don't like is why he originally put them in a huge class of troublemakers. I talked with the superintendent yesterday, and I showed him the list of pupils, and he agreed that it was so unfair to you. At least he's aware, now, of your situation with Jed."

"Let's not worry about Jed. Let's focus on these kids. Most kids have trouble with grammar, so tomorrow we'll work on parts of speech. When we see their sentences they have to do for homework, we'll have a better idea of where they're at, and we'll get an idea of their reading ability. I'd still like to do literature on war with them. Can you requisition twenty paperbacks of *The Human Comedy*?"

"I think so."

The next day, shortly after the last class had begun, Shackle's voice came from the intercom: "Mister Valentino, report to the principal's office immediately!"

A startled look appeared on Dante's face. Four pupils were at the board and were writing their three sentences to labels the subjects, verbs, and objects. He looked at Minnie.

"Mister Valentino, report to the principal's office immediately!"

"Go," she said, standing next to him near the desk, "I'll take over. I hope it's nothing too serious."

Quickly, thinking that something at home had happened, he limped downstairs and went into the principal's office. After Shackle told him to close the office door, and Dante closed it, Shackle showed him a copy of his story and asked, "Does this look familiar?"

"What? You called me down here to show me *this*?"

"Do you recognize this?" Shackle demanded.

"Of course! It's mine."

"So you admit it."

"Of course I admit it. How did you get it?"

"I confiscated it from a pupil in the cafeteria. I heard him reading it while the others were trying to eat."

"Do you mind telling me from whom you confiscated it?"

"I didn't ask him his name."

"You didn't have to confiscate it. Whoever it was, I gave it to him. If you wanted a copy, too, all you had to do was ask me."

"I took it away from him because he was annoying the others!"

"Are you sure? I mean, was he reading it too loud?"

"Yes, I heard him."

"Was he reading it well? With expression?"

"That's not the point!"

"Of course it is. Why are we here, Jed? You're the one who put him in the remedial reading class. Remember?"

"When I questioned him, he told me they read this in your class yesterday."

"Yes, we did."

"This," he stammered, "*this* story isn't fit for high school kids."

"Why not?"

"It's unpatriotic!"

Dante stared at him.

"What! Are you calling me unpatriotic?"

"I'm calling the story unpatriotic."

"Are you serious? Why?"

"Because it is!"

"You don't understand the meaning of patriotism. Furthermore," Dante said softly, "you had no right to confiscate this story from that kid. I gave it to him."

"I have every right to know what they're reading in this school. This story is going into your file, with my personal comments. And from now on, you don't give them anything to read unless you consult me first and get my permission."

Dante stared at him again.

"Why are you doing this, Jed?"

Shackle stared back at him.

"I'm doing my job."

"You almost lost your job by costing the school district a year's salary, which it had to pay me for work I hadn't done because you refused to rehire me. And now you're stepping over the line again. Do you want to get yourself fired, Jed? Let me tell you something, in case you don't know. To survive, I don't need this job. Can you say the same thing about your job? Please, just let me do my job. You know I'm a good teacher. And you know, surely, that by doing my job well, I'm helping you in your own career. With my help, you could be next in line for the principal's job. Think about it, Jed. A truce between you and me would be tremendously beneficial to you. I'm going back to my remedial reading class, if you'll excuse me."

He turned around and limped out of the office, and he returned to his class.

Three pupils were at the board and were labeling the subjects, verbs, and objects.

Dante whispered to Minnie and told her about his encounter with Shackle. She was looking at him in disbelief.

After all the pupils had been to the board, Dante said, "You all did quite well. Tomorrow we'll work on the parts of speech. How many of you showed your parents the story we read in class yesterday?"

Almost everyone raised a hand.

"What was their reaction?"

"They liked it!"

"Did any of your parents object to it because it's a war story?"

There was no response.

"Did anyone have a copy confiscated?"

One hand shot up.

"What happened, Bobby?"

"I was reading it to a couple of my friends at lunch, and Shackle pulled it away from me."

"Why?"

"He said it wasn't appropriate for us high school kids. And he said not to bring that kind of trash into the school. I told him it wasn't trash! And he asked me how I got it."

Some of the pupils began to grumble.

"Do you want another copy?"

"Yeah."

"See me after class."

After the class ended, Minnie said, "Jed is going too far. I'm going to report him to the superintendent."

She did. And she showed him the story. He said it was very impressive, and he said he could understand why the pupils were interested in it.

"Is this something Dante wrote?"

"Of course! Do you think it's unpatriotic?"

"No, of course not! It seems authentic. I'm sure it is. I'll talk with Jed."

"Please don't tell him that I reported this to you."

"No, of course not, but he'll think that Dante did. Well, let him think that. At least Jed will know now that I'm aware of the situation and that I'm not pleased by it, and maybe he'll think twice before he gives Dante anymore grief. My god, you'd think Jed would have more sense than that! Why is he treating Dante like that?"

"You don't know?"

"Yes," he muttered. "I do, but Dante's become a hero to this school. If Jed persists, it's going to backfire on him."

Columbus Day fell on a Tuesday, exactly one week after Marilyn Monroe had sued Joe DiMaggio for a divorce, after nine months of marriage. The "remedial reading class" had prepared a play for the holiday, which they presented in the school auditorium that Monday afternoon after lunch.

As the curtain opened, and the smallest girl of the class walked out onto the empty stage, the audience began to quiet down. When she walked up to the front of the stage, to a microphone at the middle of the stage, she spoke into it: "Welcome to the Special Literature Class presentation of this Columbus Day Celebration. All seventeen members of this class, otherwise known as the Brats of the Flats, have participated in this presentation. As you all know, in 1492, when Columbus sailed the ocean blue and was looking for a water route, he knew that it would bring him and his Spanish crew to a land of spices in a far eastern country known as India. As he said to the king of Spain: 'To travel east by land is long and arduous, but to travel west by sea to get to the Far East is short and easy.' The king looked at the queen and said, 'This Italian is a mad man. He wants to travel west to go east.' And she said to the king, 'But if the earth is round, not flat, he could be correct. This is what he showed me.' Taking a parchment of paper, she drew an X near the left edge of the sheet. From the X, which represented Spain, she drew a straight line to the right, to the east, across the Mediterranean Sea, south of Italy and Greece, into, and across Turkey, across the Near East, and eventually into India, where she drew another X near the right edge of the sheet. She lifted the parchment and said to King Ferdinand, 'My dear Ferdie, place your thumbs on the X's, and now fold the paper back so that both X's are almost touching.' He did. 'See how close your thumbs are! If the earth is round, India, by way of the Atlantic Ocean, is not far away. Let us give Columbus not one ship, but three, to carry back many spices. And the king agreed with his wife, the queen of Spain, Queen Isabella. Little did they know, however, that at the other end of the Atlantic Ocean lies a great expanse of land, a large continent, later called North America, which was not even half way to India. When the king and queen later became aware that Columbus had not landed in India, they jailed him and called him a fool for having wasted so much of their money only to discover a new world inhabited by worthless savages who didn't even know how to speak English, even though we all knew, of course, that until very recently, like the Quebecois, they had belonged to the British Empire. But now we're getting way ahead of our story. Let us go back in time to the twelfth of October when Columbus landed on an island that he had thought was India." Turning a little and pointing behind her, she continued talking. "To the rear of the stage is north, past the blue sea behind me, past Cuba, into Florida, up the Atlantic coast of the United States, and into Canada." She turned to the audience. "To my left is east, across the Atlantic Ocean, to Spain and the rest of Europe. Behind you is south, to South America, and to my right is west, the great forest of this tropical island. A short distance away, I can see natives walking down a steep hill. They are coming this way. They should be here in a few minutes. And to my left, I see three ships anchored in the distance. They are named the Nina, the Pinta, and the Santa Maria. A few minutes ago, I saw men in three boats. They were rowing here to the shore. They are now walking on the sandy white beach coming in this direction, so I will leave now on this warm, sunny morning so that you may observe their meeting with the natives of this land." She began to walk off the stage. Suddenly, she stopped and turned to the audience again. "Oh, by the way, since we have no way to know for sure what they actually said, their conversations were, of course, made up by us; we don't pretend that everything we wrote is historically accurate, but we tried to do the best we could under the circumstances. To give you an example, the name of Christopher Columbus, as we call him, is not the way he actually pronounced his name, not in his native tongue, the way they actually spoke in Genoa, which was probably in an eyetalian dialect. And, of course, you know that in real life, none of the characters were speaking English, but none of us knows sign language, and even if we did, you probably wouldn't understand it anyway, so we wrote the play in the language that we know, in English, not in the English we speak in the flats, but in the English that you Yankees speak, because we thought you'd understand it better. We hope you enjoy the play. But if you don't, remember that if it wasn't for him, who, excuse me, *whom*, we call Columbus, you would be in your regular afternoon classes right now, and that tomorrow you wouldn't have a day off just because he came here to America, even though it was sort of, well, sort of a mistake, because he was really looking for India." She exited to the left side of the audience.

On the right side of the audience, someone entered from behind the curtain. It was Danny, the senior, dressed as Columbus. He was carrying a big stick with a white cloth as a token of peace at the top of the stick. He was walking slowly to the middle of the stage, and he stopped. Lined up behind him in a single file were five others who had emerged from behind the curtain.

Columbus turned to the one behind him and said, "Well, America, mi amigo, our journey is a success. We have finally landed in India just as I had predicted. And now I claim this land in the name of King Ferdinand of Spain."

"But ain't this a British colony?" America asked.

"We will meet the redcoats," Columbus replied, "and we will defeat them in battle."

"If you don't mind, Captain Chris, I'd rather defeat them in cricket."

"Cricket? You disappoint me, America. I had thought of changing the name of India to America in your honor. Listen! I think I heard someone cursing. Can you hear voices?"

They listened.

"Yes, I hear voices, too," America said. "Yes, I think they're cursing us. I wonder if they know were from the flats. Do you think they're angry because we're going to change the name from India to America?"

"Why should that make them angry? America is a good Italian name. Don't you like your name?"

"Of course. But I don't think they understand."

"Can you understand them?"

"No, Captain."

America pulled out a pair of binoculars from his breeches, and he looked through them.

"Ah," he said, "I can see them. They're Indians, I assume."

"Let me look, too."

America gave the glasses to Columbus.

"Do they look like Indians to you?" America asked.

"No, I can't see anything with these. Where'd you get them?"

"I bought them the day before yesterday."

"The day before yesterday? On the ship?"

"No. On the long island where we stopped for an hour or so near the German town. I don't remember the name."

"We stopped for an hour or so? On a long island? Where was I?"

"In your cabin."

"I don't remember stopping! Certainly not on an island!"

"You were taking your siesta, sir."

"Why didn't you wake me up?"

"I tried, sir! But you cursed me for disturbing you! So I let you sleep. It was a very cold day, and you were buried under heavy warm blankets, and you seemed so content!"

"The day before yesterday! Don't tell me, America, that since then we've been coasting down the coast of India!"

"Okay, I won't, but the weather became so much warmer as we went south!"

"What was it like on the long island?"

"I told you, sir, it was cold and rather windy. I went into a store called Wool's Worth. And I bought these binoculars."

"By the way, America, where is your rifle?"

"Well, Chris, my captain, and my paisan, you see, I didn't have any Indian money or wool worth the price of these binoculars, so I, well, I traded my rifle for these glasses."

"America! You fool!"

"Yes, Chris, I know. That's why you're the captain, and I'm only the historian. I'll write that you discovered a new route to the Indies. And you'll be honored in all the history books."

"If that's true, America, you can change the name of India to America. And the inhabitants of this land shall be called Americans."

"Oh, thank you, mi amigo!"

"Oh, here they come!"

Two boys, dressed as Indians, entered the stage from the opposite side. The second boy wore a huge head of feathers. The first boy spoke to Columbus: "How!" he said, raising his right hand and drawing close to the explorer.

"Fine," Chris replied, "How do you do?"

"This old man next to me is Chief Heckhow. We're the Heckhowee."

"I'm not sure where we are either. We're just as lost as you are. All I know is that we're somewhere in India. I was hoping you could give us more information."

"Somewhere in India? What are you talking about? You dress funny. And you speak funny. Where are you from?"

"You dress funnier than us, and you speak funnier. We come from a land far far away from here, from the other side of the sea."

The Indian turned to the chief and said, "He said they come from a land far far away from the other side of the sea."

The chief grunted.

"Chief Heckhow asks me if you're tourists from Florida."

"No, we're not tourists; we're explorers. I'm leading an expedition for these soldiers from Spain."

"From Spain? The English warned us about the Spanish. We were told never to trust the Spanish."

"The English must have told you that."

"That's what I just said. Do you know the English? You speak their language."

"Yes, I can understand their language, but I'm not English."

"Ah," he said to the chief, "he says he is not English." And to Columbus, he said, "The chief does not like the English; he hates them. That scoundrel, Captain John Smith (probably a fictitious name, anyway) visited us last year, and after we entertained him and his soldiers one night, the next morning they had disappeared, having taken some of our most beautiful wives with them, including the wife of our chief. She is young and very beautiful, and the heart of our old chief is broken. Her name is Pocahontas."

America said, "You should never have trusted the English. They are even less trustworthy than the Spanish."

The Indian said to the chief, "He said we should never have trusted the English; they are even less trustworthy than the Spanish. Ah, yes, yes, no, no, they are not English, and they are not Spanish." To Columbus and America, he said, "Our chief asks me if you're French."

Columbus asked, "Does he like the French?"

"Do you like the French?"

The chief shrugged, and then he grunted.

"He says he does not hate the French as much as the English."

"Me, too. Ask your chief if he hates eyetalians."

"Eyetalians? Ah, I know he likes eyetalians."

"He does? Are you sure he likes eyetalians?"

"Very much, especially eyetalian movie actresses, like Gina Lolobrigida."

"We are both eyetalians," Columbus said.

"Both of you? Working for the Spanish?"

"The Spanish trusts us."

"Chief Heckhow, too, trusts eyetalians, except the eyetalians who insist on calling us Indians, like the one called Christopher Columbus. Who had ever heard of an eyetalian called Christopher?" And the Indian laughed. "I bet he ain't even eyetalian."

Columbus and America joined him in his laughter.

"You are very funny," Columbus said. "Is he not funny, America?"

"Yes," America agreed, laughing, "Christopher ain't even an eyetalian name."

"No, of course not," Columbus said. "Tell me then. If you do not like to be called Indians, what do you like to be called?"

The Indian stared at Columbus.

"Do all eyetalians have such short memories? Or are you an exception? Maybe you don't understand English well. I told you, we're the Heckhowee. The chief here is Chief Heckhow, the father of us all."

"He is the father of all of you? How many are you?"

"On this part of our little island, there are over a thousand of us."

"How many wives does your father, the chief, have?"

"After the first hundred, we stopped counting."

"Did you hear that, America?"

"Yes, and I thought we eyetalians were prolific!"

"Tell us," Columbus said, "how come you understand English so well."

"Oh, none of us Heckhowee understand English at all."

"What! Of course you do! We're speaking to each other in English now."

"*You* are speaking English. I don't understand a word of it."

Columbus and America stared at each other. They seemed bewildered.

"You are wondering, perhaps, why we are conversing in English if we don't understand it at all? The answer is so simple, if you think about it."

"If the answer is so simple, enlighten us," Columbus said.

"Our father, the wisest of us all, enlightened us. I wanted to be a warrior, but my father said that there are so many tourists coming to our little island, that it would profit us to speak their language."

"By the way, what do you call this island?"

"Guess."

"Bermuda?"

"No."

"Jamaica?"

"No."

"Haiti?"

"No. Give up?"

"Yes."

"We simply call it: Heckhow, after the father of us all."

"Of course! And you call yourselves Heckhowee."

"Precisely."

"But how can you speak English without understanding it?"

"Oh, that. Very simply. The chief said to me that we need an interpreter. So, he made me his interpreter. Whatever tongue someone speaks, my job is to interpret it for the chief."

"Oh, that is indeed so simple!" America exclaimed. "Why hadn't we thought of that? Just hire an interpreter. Even someone like Christopher Columbus of Genoa should understand how simple that is."

"Indeed!" Christopher said. "If you ever record this conversation, America, all the inhabitants of this new world will be arguing about it for the next five hundred years. And none of them will ever believe this."

Danny looked at the audience and said, "Columbus was wrong in thinking he had discovered a short cut to India, but he was correct in assuming that none of us would ever believe his amazing adventure. If you like being an American, thank us eyetalians! And enjoy the holiday in honor of Columbus tomorrow!"

"And remember," the interpreter added, "that Indians live in India." And, looking around him, he said, "We're the Heckowee?"

14

Every month I drove Dante to the Veterans' Hospital in White River Junction in Vermont. Usually, Rosie went with us. In October, when the foliage was at its peak, she came with us again even though she was due to have her second baby in about two more weeks. While we were there this time, a nurse showed Rosie how to use tweezers to remove slivers of shrapnel from Dante's skin, especially from his back and from his hips and the back of his legs. The staff asked her if he had been complaining about his pains. He had never complained, she said. Occasionally, he had taken pills to alleviate some of his pains. And then she asked the nurse if she thought it was painful for him to, well, to make love to her. The nurse smiled at her and said that making love to her was probably his best incentive for staying alive.

On Saturday, November the 6th, Dante drove Rosie to the hospital in Berlin, and that evening she delivered their second daughter, Maria.

Five days later, Veterans' Day that year replaced Armistice Day. Without Dante's knowledge, the members of the special class, with the help of Minnie, had prepared a tribute to Dante on that Wednesday afternoon, the day before the holiday. They presented almost a half hour of readings in the school auditorium by all seventeen members of the class. They ended the tribute by a reading of *The Grass* by Carl Sandberg. The smallest girl of the class added, "But we will never forget our own hero, our veteran, Mister Dante Valentino. And the class ended the tribute by saluting him. He was sitting in the front row with Minnie who later told me that Dante had become so emotional that she actually saw tears in his eyes.

A week later, the first edition of the year of the school newspaper had been printed. All the pupils had been encouraged to express their feelings and ideas and to share them with other pupils through the school paper. The day the paper was published, Shackle scheduled a meeting after school in the biology room.

He said he wanted to discuss a suggestion made by one of the pupils in the school paper that since the pupils are not allowed to smoke on the school grounds, the teachers should not be allowed to smoke on the school grounds either, including the teachers' lounge, where they had been allowed to smoke.

The teachers who smoked stared at Shackle, but none of them spoke.

"Does anyone want to begin the discussion?" Shackle asked. The teachers were looking at each other. "If not, smoking will no longer be tolerated on school property, by anyone, including in the teachers' room."

"I'm not a smoker," said Dante, "so the smoking rule, by itself, will not apply to me, but the repercussions certainly will. What the pupil, and I know the pupil quite well, was suggesting was that not the adults should be the authorities on making the rules, but that the kids, themselves, should be the authorities in the making of the rules. The rule against children smoking is clear and simple. It's against the laws of this state. Our state legislators make the laws, not our children."

"We're not talking about children making the laws," Shackle said.

"That's precisely what we're talking about. If we say that since the children are not allowed to smoke, the adults should not be allowed, either, then, if we follow that logic, we are saying that since children are not allowed to have sex, their parents should not be allowed either. If children are not allowed to drink, neither should adults. If children are not allowed to drive, or to vote, neither should adults. If children cannot be drafted, neither can adults. You think that's rational? If children are not allowed to make the laws, you think adults should not? What's the alternative? Children should make the laws? If a smoking ban goes into effect, we should, at least, support it with a reasonable reason other than if children are not old enough to do it yet, then neither should adults. It is not rational to involve the children in our discussion of whether or not the teachers should be allowed to smoke in the teachers' room. I propose that such a discussion be limited to the people involved in the decision. And, since this does not involve the children, the children should not be involved in the making of rules that involve only the teachers."

Shackle was staring at him stiffly. The teachers stared at Shackle.

"This meeting is adjourned," Shackle finally said, very softly.

After the meeting, Minnie went to the superintendent and reported what had happened. Since the pupils had been allowed by Dante and her to write about their feelings and ideas in the school paper, and Jed had been opposed to it, he had tried to make a rule, she said, to prevent the teachers from smoking on the school grounds. She knew, she said, that Jed had proposed such a rule to blame Dante for it. It had become obvious to her, she said, that Jed had been planning to cause problems not only to Dante; he would cause problems to anyone who would agree with Dante, and that would only disrupt the structure of their educational system.

"I wish I could have been there to see the expression on Jed's face when Dante contradicted him, but we cannot tolerate such friction among the staff, especially among us educators. I'm going to request Jed to have the teachers get together to develop a philosophy of education as a guide to which we can all agree."

"Dante," she said, "would be perfect to chair such a committee."

A few days later, Shackle announced a meeting of the teachers in the biology room immediately after the end of classes.

"The superintendent has requested," he said, standing next to his desk, "that we work together to develop a philosophy of education that will guide and inspire us. He wants us to complete this assignment before the Christmas break so that each teacher and each member of the school board has a copy of it by then."

"I make a motion," Minnie said, "to nominate Dante as the chairman of such a committee."

Immediately, several teachers simultaneously seconded the motion.

Shackle stared at them.

Finally, he said, "As principal, I think I should be ultimately responsible for such a project."

They grew silent.

"I agree with you," Dante said. "We can all discuss a philosophy and agree to how we should write it, and after we agree, you, as the principal can dictate it to your secretary and submit it on our behalf, after we all see the final draft and agree to it. I make a motion to nominate Jed as the chairman of the committee."

The new biology teacher seconded the motion.

Shackle became the chairman of the committee.

"The purpose of a good education," he said, "is to create good citizenship. Do we all agree on that?"

The teachers looked at each other and seemed to agree, but Dante asked, "How do you define 'good citizenship'?"

"Well, how would you define it?"

"I would define a good citizen as someone who is well educated, which means a good citizen knows the society in which he lives and strives to make it better. But that's *my* definition. What's yours? We have to agree on the definitions before we continue this discussion."

"Well, mine is basically the same as yours. We agree with each other then."

"So, the question remains, how do we educate such a person? We're expected to develop a philosophy of education to guide us in the educational process. Does anyone have any ideas to get us started?"

"I told you," Shackle said. "We start with a goal. And the goal of education is to create good citizenship."

"But that becomes a circular argument if we use the definition I just gave, that a good citizen is one who is well educated. *How* do we educate such a person? I think we have to define *education*, too."

"It's very simple. We simply teach him to obey the laws of society."

"Him or *her*. Are you saying that a good citizen is one who obeys the laws of society?"

"Of course."

"Are you saying that we develop a philosophy of education by beginning with a goal of creating a person who obeys the laws of the society in which he or she lives in?"

"Yes, definitely."

"Why bother teaching biology or history or anything? Why don't we just train the pupils to obey the laws of society? But what if we were living in an oppressed state, like Nazi Germany?"

"We're not living in Nazi Germany."

"What if we were living now in South Carolina with its laws of segregation still?"

Shackle stared at him.

"We're not living in South Carolina!"

"If we were living in an ideal society, our educational system might, maybe, also be ideal. But until we are actually in that ideal society, if we're going to develop a valid philosophy, we should be able to apply it universally, anywhere, anytime. Simply obeying the laws of a society, even here in this wonderful town of Gorham, is not enough. My ideal citizen is one who has been ideally educated, who follows the laws of society, which are rational, but strives to change the laws that are not rational. Because such a citizen is educated, and is a thinker rather than simply a follower of the laws that irrational people have made, the good citizen strives, through legal means, to lead the way to change the laws, to lead the way to make our society better. An educator, as the word means, *leads* out of the darkness, out of ignorance, and into the light, into knowledge. And a good educator stimulates the minds of the students and encourages them to *think*."

As Dante spoke, Shackle moved away from his desk to a window, grabbed a cord from a Venetian blind and wrapped it around his index finger, and unwrapped it, repeatedly. When Dante finished speaking, Shackle seemed to have withdrawn from them. Finally, he muttered, "We're taking something simple and making it seem complicated. Our duty is to mold these children into good citizens, to make them obey the laws of our society. All we have to do is write a simple paragraph or two. It doesn't have to be anything complicated. Surely we can do that much. Let's think about it for a few days and we'll meet again next week."

And he dismissed them.

A few minutes later, Minnie said to Dante, "Meet me in the teachers' lounge before you leave."

In the teachers' room, she lit a cigarette and said to him, "You made a fool out of Jed, exposing him in front of all the teachers. He's never going to forgive you for that."

"That wasn't my intention. He never gave enough thought to education. He's not a teacher. You know what he's doing here? He's a true believer who's trying to convert these kids to his religious cult. Maybe you know him better than I do, but I was in his biology class. It wasn't a biology class; it was a perversion of Christianity in the name of Jesus. I'm sorry, Minnie. I know you attend his services, but I can't accept his ideas as Christian, or as truly religious. His ideas are a distortion, not only of religion, but of education and even of ideology. It's, well, it's a sickness."

"I know."

They never did submit a philosophy of education to the superintendent. Shackle had gone to him and had complained that the teachers, under Dante's influence, would not agree on a philosophy. The superintendent called Minnie into his office and asked her about their meeting. After she had told him, he asked, "Do you think Dante would make a good principal?"

A few days later when Dante was called into his office, the superintendent told him that the principal, who had a heart attack almost two years ago, would be retiring a few years earlier due to his health.

"Would you be interested in that position?"

"I, I don't know," he stammered. "I'm happy in the class room. Besides, if I were principal I'd be after you for more books, for more everything, for better standards of education for these kids. I'd be a pain in the ass to you."

The superintendent grinned.

"Yeah, I think you would be. I know how dedicated you are. And how determined. We'll both sleep on it. Okay?"

In December, Dante had been home for a whole year, and it had been a good year for the whole family. In that month, Dante had successfully completed the autumn's season of teaching and was happy in his work. The Senate had taken Senator Joe McCarthy down a peg by censuring his activities as "unbecoming a Senator." The novelist, Ernest Hemingway, had proven he hadn't lost his ability to write. *The Old Man and the Sea* had propelled him to win the Nobel Prize. And in science, the world's greatest astronomers announced the Big Bang Theory of the beginning of the universe, which Dante had planned to discuss with his Classical Lit class when school would resume after the Christmas break.

"Did you know," Dante asked me during the break when I was visiting him, "that Adolf Hitler was a devout Catholic who took orders from the Pope to exterminate all Jews in Europe? And I bet you didn't know that Sigmund Freud converted to Catholicism to spread his psychoanalysis for the Church to brainwash the people. And although Karl Marx was a Jew in Germany, the Pope encouraged him to spread Communism. The true menace to Christianity is not Moscow, a satellite of Rome; it is the Papacy."

"Of course," I replied. "That's common knowledge. And a lot of people don't know that Karl is the oldest of the Marx Brothers."

"Everything you ever wanted to know about the Mark of the Beast, the Vatican, the anti-Christ, is all here in these pamphlets," he said, which were on the kitchen table. There were a dozen pamphlets, all written by Shackle.

"Did you know," Dante said, reading from one of the pamphlets, "that the movie industry is controlled by Rome? Many movies are another form of Catholic propaganda, showing the Church in a favorable light, buying Hollywood stars and making them act in movies such as *The Song of Bernadette* and *Going My Way* to make the Catholic Church look good and the other churches look bad. Did you know that novelists, such as Sinclair Lewis, were commissioned by the Jesuits to write such trash as *Elmer Gantry* to make preachers of Protestant denominations look greedy and crooked and to make Catholic priests look good by comparison? And did you know that the French and the Italians are only one step above the blacks on the intelligence scale? And that all Latinos are at the bottom in Europe? Did you know that if a Catholic ever became President of the United States, he'd be taking orders from the Pope? And the Pope would attempt to make Catholicism the official religion in this country?"

"That, too, is common knowledge. And Italian would become the official state language."

"No, not Italian, exactly. Latin."

"Only for religious services."

"And here it says," Dante said, reading from another pamphlet, "that Catholics and Jews are encouraging the blacks, led by Martin Luther King and the Black Panthers, to join the Communists in an effort to overthrow the government."

"So, what else is new?"

"Did you know that the Catholic Church is trying to outlaw the study of science?"

"Why should Shackle complain about *that*?"

"Did you know that Adam, created in the image of God, was a blue eyed blond, and that after his fall from grace, his children were corrupted by mingling with other races?"

"The other races were undoubtedly Catholic and Jewish."

"There's a lot I haven't read yet. It's fascinating reading."

"Where'd you get these?"

"From Minnie."

"Why did she give them to you?"

"She wanted me to read them. She became aware of how sick Shackle really is. She wants to leave his cult."

"Why doesn't she?"

"She's afraid to. She knows too much about him. He wants to replace the teachers with members of his cult."

"He must really be pissed that you were rehired."

"Yeah, and Minnie told the superintendent about it, and he offered me the job as principal."

"He offered you the job?"

"Yeah, he did."

"Does Shackle know?"

"No, I don't think so, not unless Minnie told him. But why would she tell him?"

"You took the job, of course."

"No. I'm thinking about it."

"What's there to think about? You could get rid of Shackle. These pamphlets alone should do it. There's enough proof here to show that he's nuttier than a fruit cake, and that instead of educating the kids, he's spreading his hate."

"Yeah, Minnie thought of that, too."

"Do it! Take the job of principal and get rid of Shackle. You'd be doing this community a great service. And you'd be improving the quality of education by getting rid of him."

"I want to think about it, first. I don't know if I'd like being principal. I can still expose him without replacing him as principal."

"He's been getting away with his crazy ideas for too damn long. He should have been exposed a long time ago. You know what you should do? Challenge him to a debate. Question the statements that he makes in these pamphlets and demand proof of his statements in a public hearing. Expose his lies and his stupidity. You can do it. You can even use his own ideas as your weapons. Make him defend these ludicrous statements," I said, waving one of the pamphlets.

Dante was staring at me.

"That's exactly what I've been thinking of doing. I've even talked about it with Minnie."

"Do you remember when Ben John told us about the meeting Shackle conducted when the soldiers were stationed here?"

"Yes, I do. It was in the public school house. That's where I'd like to challenge him, just me against him. But how can I persuade him to debate me?"

"Just tell him you want to debate him. He might be arrogant enough and dumb enough to do it. If you can stop him from becoming the principal, you should do it. You'd make a hell of a good principal. The superintendent can see that too. He can see that you're a hell of a lot more intelligent and educated and dedicated than someone like Shackle."

An intelligent, educated person, I think, reads with understanding and compares and contrasts various ideas and forms of knowledge, and constantly increases his knowledge, and such a person writes clearly and effectively, inspiring others, and thinks logically and intuitively. That was Dante. Not only was he intelligent and educated; like my father and my Italian grandfather, he was gifted with intuitive perceptions and insights. As his big brother, I used to like to think I was superior to him in some respects, such as being bigger and therefore more virile, but according to Rosie, she didn't think anyone, including me, could be as passionate, and yet as tender, as Dante. Artists, especially writers, she thought, were incredibly passionate people. I can honestly say I was never jealous of him; I was always proud of my little brother, and I was never reluctant to argue with him even though he'd piss me off sometimes, because whenever I'd become even slightly inconsistent, he would point it out to me. Oh, how I hated it when he used to grin at me and would very gently tell me I was wrong! I wanted to see him do that to Shackle.

Ever since I can remember, my little brother and I had enjoyed arguing with each other. We used to challenge each other's thinking, arguing about such topics as the meaning of original sin, and arguing about why the disobedience of Adam and Eve should be passed down to us. And our father, who would be listening to us, would get sucked into our arguments, and my mother would say to him, "Why are you arguing with your kids?" And my father would grin. Sometimes my mother would get perturbed over the subject of our arguments. To my father, no subject was taboo, not even sex. And my mother would cry out to us: "Oh, you Italians!" How I miss those arguments! How I miss my father and my mother and Dante!

To my father, as well as to Dante and me, the model of a good, logical arguer was Socrates. We used to sit around the kitchen table, my father and Dante and I, and we would read from Plato's *Dialogues*. We used to take turns playing the part of Socrates. Dante had told me that his model of a teacher was Socrates. Dante would ask his students a series of questions, which would logically lead them to a certain conclusion.

The greatest lesson from the philosopher is the first step in the lesson of life: "Know thyself." And my father would add that the next step is: "To love thyself," to grow from thyself as a seed, to grow outward, to know and to love others, as in the divine commandment, knowing, loving, and embracing the All, returning to the Source, to obtain the ultimate happiness for which we were created.

16

On the first day back to school, after the Christmas break, Dante received a note in his box from the superintendent to report to his office that Monday immediately after classes.

"Have you given any thought to taking the job as principal?"

"Yes, I have," Dante answered softly as he sat in a chair at the front of the desk, "but I'm not sure you'll approve of my motives."

"Try me."

"Well, you know that Jed tried to prevent me from returning to teaching."

The superintendent grinned, saying, "I recall something to that effect, but I have to admit that I didn't think he'd really go as far as he did. That's why I did nothing to stop him. I admit my own blame for that. So, are you saying that turnabout is fair play?"

"No, of course not. But by refusing to rehire me, especially after Uncle Sam required him to rehire me, showed that he's not very, well, not very astute, therefore, he's not qualified for the job."

"I agree."

"He's not qualified to teach either."

"And if you become principal, you'd want to fire him?"

"Yes, sir, I would."

"I see. Is that what you mean when you said you're not sure I'd approve of your motives?"

"The thought of getting rid of him would be a major influence in accepting the position of principal."

The superintendent stared at him.

"If someone else, who would fire Jed, was principal, would you be satisfied with that? Would you rather remain teaching?"

"Yes, sir, I think I would."

"And who would you say is more qualified than you as principal?"

"Well, I think Miss Birch is qualified. Yeah, I think she'd be a good principal. She's certainly dedicated to teaching."

"She recommended you as principal. Do you really think she'd be better than you? Don't be modest. I need your honest assessment."

"A good principal is someone who can work *with* the teachers as well as to lead them. Jed can do neither; he thinks he has to boss them. I saw a lot of that in the army. I *know* what I'm capable of doing. I'd make a good principal. So would Miss Birch. We would work with each other."

"If you were principal, what do you think you'd do?"

"You mean, besides getting rid of Jed?"

The superintendent grinned again, and then he nodded.

"Besides getting rid of Jed."

"I like your suggestion: to get the teachers to work together, to come up with a philosophy of education to guide us, a philosophy to which we can all agree, and to which we can all work together to accomplish, something ideal, yet practical, that we can comfortably achieve and take pride in, something that will inspire us and can sustain us. When we come up with something that's good enough, and after we've put it into practice, and we've successfully improved the quality of education, of having enhanced the quality of the lives of everyone in our society, the whole state could follow our lead. That's what I would like us to do."

The superintendent continued to stare at Dante. Finally, he said, "I have a gut feeling that you are the person who can lead us."

"Well, sir, there's something else I should tell you. I don't know how familiar you are with Shackle's ideas, but when I was a student here, I was in his biology class. Not only are his ideas irrational, they're dangerous; they're sick. They are the antithesis of education. They're filled with hatred."

"Some of his ideas have been brought to my attention."

"I know you don't like to see any friction among your staff, but I want to challenge Jed's ideas with him in a public debate. I want to expose his twisted ideas and to let the public judge his ideology, to judge whether or not his ideas should be tolerated in the classroom. I believe in the freedom of speech and of thought to enlighten us, but I don't advocate the freedom of inciting and spreading hatred."

"I'd like to witness such a debate, but according to Miss Birch, you've already made a fool out of him (her exact words) in front of the other teachers by contradicting him and by showing him and everyone else how contradictory his ideas are. I doubt that he'll ever debate you. You know why he hates you so much, don't you?"

"Why?"

"You make him aware that when he compares himself to you, he's so, well, he lacks your acumen, your ability to think, and he's obviously aware that he doesn't have your intelligence nor your knowledge. And I suspect that your dedication and your determination also scare him."

"You really think that?"

"I know that. He's whined about you several times, complaining to me about how you influence the other teachers by making fun of his, well, of his lack of knowledge. Why do you think he hates you so much?"

"Well, I don't want to accuse him unjustly, but he's blinded by his prejudices. We're all blinded by our prejudices, but at least some of us try to understand the feelings of others who think or who look differently than we do. I don't think that Jed tries to understand others. Maybe you're right. Maybe he feels inferior to some of us. But when he teaches, and even when he acts as the principal, he seems to think he's required to act superior to the rest of us. When I was a kid in his class, he used to point to us kids from the flats and he would literally belittle us because our cultural heritage is French or Italian, and Catholic. You probably think I'm exaggerating, but we could actually feel his hatred of us, right there in the classroom as he was, quote, trying to educate us."

"No, I know you're not exaggerating. I've known for a long time how much he hates you, especially since he feels so inferior to you in so many ways. He'll never give you the opportunity to debate him, because he knows damn well you'll tear him apart."

"Why is he still here?"

"Because he has enough influence with enough people in this community who feel the same way that he does."

They stared at each other.

"They must hate going into Berlin to go shopping," Dante muttered.

"Some of them do, but most of them are even more afraid of going into the flats."

"Why the flats?"

"Because you Italians have a reputation of arming yourselves with switchblades."

"In the flats? Are you serious?"

"I'm just telling you what Jed and some of the others say about you."

"Well, my mother isn't Italian; she probably never knew that it's natural for Italians to arm themselves with switchblades."

"Your father was Italian."

"Born in Italy. Yes, and he became an American citizen."

"He was Jewish?"

"How do you know that?"

"Jed mentioned it."

"Oh? What else did he tell you?"

"Besides Italians being criminals and anarchists?"

"And my mother is just as bad. She's a mixture of red, white, and black, mostly French Canadian. The ironic thing is that most of the French Canadians of Berlin, especially the younger people, are proud to think of themselves as Americans, as proud as Jed is, maybe even prouder. Our Canadian relatives don't understand why we think we're so much better than they are. They don't seem to understand that we Americans are the best people in the world. But that's their problem, not ours."

The superintendent was studying Dante's face, because Dante still seemed so serious.

"Do you really think Americans are the best people in the world?"

"Of course. That's only natural. Isn't it?"

"I don't know. Maybe if you were born here that might seem natural, but I was born in Canada."

"Really?"

"I really was."

"Well, not everybody's perfect. But don't worry, I won't tell Shackle where you were born."

"As a matter of fact, I was born in Quebec."

"Wow! You're even less American than I am! At least I was born here. How did you get to be superintendent? You must have changed your last name from LeBlanc to White."

"No. White's my real name. I'm as Wasp as anyone can get," he grinned. "My folks came from England. My father was a university instructor who went to Montreal to teach at McGill. I graduated from there, then I lived in England, got married, moved back to Montreal, finally toured the White Mountains, liked it, and stayed here, in Gorham."

"If your folks came from England, then some of your ancestry is quite probably French."

"Well, Norman, yes. But that was a thousand years ago."

"And since the English and the French continue their family feud, you crossed the border. And here you are. Did you become an American citizen?"

"A citizen of the United States, yes. My wife and I became citizens."

"Is the rest of your family still in Canada?"

"Yes, still in Montreal, as a matter of fact, my mother and father and siblings."

"And they envy you, now, of course, because you became an American. Welcome to joining us. Doesn't it feel good to belong to the best people in the world? Don't worry; I won't say anything about you to Shackle. He probably thinks you're a real American, anyway."

"But he doesn't think you are."

"And he thinks he's entitled to his opinion."

"When I told you I was born in Quebec, you assumed I was French."

"Yes, Quebecois. I jumped to that conclusion. If you had told me you were born in England, I would have jumped to the conclusion that you're English. We're all prejudiced to some extent. Your religion, of course, could have been almost anything, but if you told me it's Anglican, or Episcopalian, I wouldn't be terribly surprised."

"If I told you I were Catholic, would you be surprised?"

"Not really, but I'd probably label you as Protestant."

"Oh, I admit to being a Wasp. Actually, my family and I attend the Episcopal Church, but I think of that as a bridge to Catholicism."

"And, according to Shackle, that's not quite as bad as Catholicism; at least Episcopalian is American. Well, *almost* American."

"Well, at least the English speak English."

"But the English in England speak English that doesn't sound American, which means their English ain't as good as ours and that they ain't as good as us Americans. I know a lot of Canadians speak our English, but they ain't as good as us Americans, either. But, after all, what do Canadians have that would make them feel as good as us, anyway?"

The superintendent grinned at him and said, "For a minute you had me wondering about you. I wouldn't want you as an adversary, so, don't pull out your switchblade." He opened a drawer in his desk and pulled out a large manila envelope, and he placed it on the desk. "I want you to sign your signature on this contract for my records," he said, pulling two sheets out of the envelope. "I want you to sign it now before you change your mood. And I'll sign my signature on this one for your records."

Dante read the contract.

"You're going to almost triple my salary?"

"Well, if you think it's too much, I can always lower it."

"No, this is fine. Just show me where you want my signature."

As soon as he left the superintendent's office, Dante drove home and told Rosie about the meeting. The superintendent went to the school and informed Shackle that Dante had been promoted to principal. Shackle was stunned, and then he burst out screaming that he was quitting, immediately.

When he left the building, he would never be seen in the school again.

On that evening, we opened several bottles of homemade champagne, and the family and many friends came to the restaurant to toast Dante on his good fortune. And we began to make plans for a big celebration, to close the restaurant for that Saturday, to welcome the beginning of a truly happy new year for all of us.

"But don't carry your switchblades," Dante said.

Since we didn't know what he had meant, he had to explain it to us.

"It's just a bad joke," he muttered. "I shouldn't have said it."

Before the week ended, Shackle had disappeared. According to Minnie, he had withdrawn almost all of the bank account of the Temple of the Holy Spirit, which had been over a hundred thousand dollars, and nobody in town seemed to know where he had gone. The money, Shackle had told his followers, had been for the construction of a temple on a hundred acres of forest with many white birch trees. With his disappearance, the idea of debating him, or any other member of his cult now, became, of course, pointless.

Minnie said that all of the members seemed disgusted with Shackle for having disappeared with their money, and they had lost interest in meeting for religious services.

After two months, the worst of the winter had passed, and we were looking forward to an early spring. The people were tapping the maple trees in the flats, and by March, they had begun to boil the sap and were making maple syrup. When I was a kid, sometimes I would drink the deliciously cold sap directly from the bucket. That winter we had an abundant amount of snow, as usual, and during the warmer days, some of the snow would melt, and the roots of the trees would suck up the water and make the sap. Whoever had tapped the trees owned the sap. That was an unwritten agreement to which we naturally abided. And before the end of spring, whoever would dig up a certain portion of the earth and would plant seeds in it, would become the owner of that portion. We called that area "the park." It was across the road from the line of houses. Although each house had a garden behind it, along the bank of the river, some inhabitants also planted a garden in the park, which the rest of us respected without even thinking about it. Maybe we did that because, as a small community, we all knew each other, but I felt that it was natural to respect someone else's property even though someone had no legal ownership of that property. Anyway, a certain section of the park was used for the kids to play ball games, with adults supervising sometimes, for swinging from branches of trees, or for making a bonfire, especially for roasting potatoes, or for picking wild berries all the way to a brook at the foot of a mountain where smaller kids went bathing or fishing.

Near the end of that winter, everything was going well, especially for us in the flats. The weather was getting warmer, and spring was just around the corner. Soon the kids would be playing baseball, and we older folks would be playing bocce.

Maybe, you would probably argue, if we were living in a bigger community with more diversity, we would be experiencing a lot of adversity, because adversity is natural with diversity, you might say. Well, maybe. I don't know. All I know is that we didn't experience much diversity in the flats. When people migrated from the same areas, they tended to stay together. Familiarity made them feel more secure, apparently. Yet, people from other cultures, to me, tend to be interesting, especially attractive women, even though, basically, people are similar. I liked it when Minnie used to take me to Boston, and we'd walk around the North End and eat in an Italian restaurant, or we'd go down into Chinatown to eat, and Minnie and I would spend the night together in a cozy room on Joy Street. Diversity, I think, makes this country so interesting; maybe that's what makes this country so great. I know that some people, especially white Protestants, don't want to change our culture, but it's inevitable; I accept it, hoping it's for the better. I know that our American culture is still evolving, and that some day the Wasps, like the rest of us, will become a minority group whose power and influence will dwindle. I think we're adopting the best that other countries are offering us and making it American. I think that's why our American culture is so unique and so interesting, and it will become even richer with each generation. Yeah, variety is the spice of life.

We Americans had survived a revolution, a terribly bloody civil war, slavery, and even genocide and other atrocities to minorities, a depression, two world wars, and we have recently survived the Korean war, and we have emerged as the most powerful and influential nation in the world, and now, as one nation, under God, we can overcome the ungodly, divisive world of segregation and hatred prolonged by the Shackles, and we can become a role model and a leader of peace, brotherhood, and prosperity to the rest of the world.

Let us remember the words of Abraham Lincoln as our Civil War was coming to an end and we righteous Yankees were screaming to punish the Confederate Rebels for having disgraced our nation with the sin of slavery: "With malice towards none, with charity for all, with firmness in the right as God gives us to see the right, let us strive to finish the work we are in." Let us take down the hateful, divisive flag of the Confederate States for all time and replace it again with the flag of the United States of America, the flag of one nation under God, with life, liberty, and justice for all of us, "to do which may achieve and cherish a just and lasting peace among ourselves and with all nations." Let us pray to God to forgive us, to cleanse our wounds and to help us to help each other to heal our wounds.

During the past two months, with Shackle gone, our lives seemed much calmer, as though Satan, or the anti-Christ, had given up on us and had gone elsewhere to prey upon other unfortunate beings. Life, to us, seemed to have improved, letting us live and let live the way God had intended us to live, to let us adults work hard for a living, and to let our kids study life to learn how to improve it, and to let all of us celebrate life on holidays and on weekends and on vacations.

On Friday, the fourth of March, after I had finished selling insurance early in the evening, I went into the restaurant. It was busy as usual for a Friday, and it was warm in the kitchen. I took off my suit jacket and necktie, opened a beer, and was making myself a small pizza when Dante, with his two year old daughter, came into the restaurant.

Dante went to the refrigerator and helped himself to a beer.

We talked while my mother was waitressing and my Aunt Maria was making the pizzas.

When I gave part of my pizza to little Angela, Dante said to her, "What do you say?"

"Grazie, Zi Tonio."

My mother exclaimed, "You're so adorable!"

A few minutes later, after Angela ate her pizza, my mother took her into the dining room to show her off to the customers. Angela obviously enjoyed the attention.

"Buonasera!" she cried out to the customers.

In one of the booths were two fairly young blondes from Boston who had come up here for the weekend to go skiing.

"Oh, she's so cute!" one of them said to my mother. "She looks so Italian!"

I was curious as to how my mother would respond. Angela had dark flesh and looked like Rosie. But my mother simply looked at the young woman and smiled.

Dante had told me a week earlier that Nick had come home on a one month vacation from the Vatican, and that he would be coming up here this weekend. Dante was expecting him any time now.

"He should be here soon," Dante said, finishing his beer.

A few minutes later, after the phone had rung, my mother handed him the phone and said, "It's your wife."

"Yeah," he said, paused, and then he said, "I'll be right there." He hung up, and he said to me, "Nick just called from Al's Steak House. He wants me to join him. Do you want to go down and have some fried clams?"

"I just ate a pizza. Besides, it's getting busy here. Why don't you bring him in here on the way back?"

"Okay. Andiamo, Angie. Your mother wants to put you to bed. Say good night to everybody."

She gave my mother a hug and a kiss and said, "Bonne nuit, Memere." And then she gave my aunt a hug and a kiss and said, "Buona notte, Zizi."

And when she turned to me, I said, "Dove vai?"

"Vado a dormire."

"Tres bien."

"No," she said, smiling, "you say, molto bene."

As I bent down, she grabbed my neck, pulled it down, kissed my face, and said, "Buona notte."

"Buona notte, cara mia. Dormi bene."

"Come on, you little ham," Dante said.

As they went out the front door, my mother said, "He seems to be limping more. Does he look worse to you?"

"He's tired, Ma. He's been on his feet all day. He'll rest up for a couple of days, and he'll get his energy back."

The night became as busy as I had expected.

About an hour before midnight, I wondered why Dante and Nick hadn't shown up yet. I had expected them at least an hour ago.

As I was in the dining room, talking with some of the customers, a young couple entered and said there had been a bad accident on the road from Gorham not far from Al's Steak House.

A shiver went through me.

They couldn't give me much information. All they said was that they had come up from Gorham, saw lights from local police cars and a state trooper car, and proceeded slowly as a car from the side of the road, which had seemed smashed, was being towed. They hadn't seen any ambulances or any injured people. I asked them if they had noticed any cars with New York plates. The only cars they noticed were police cars.

I think I was the only one in the restaurant who knew that Dante and Nick had gone to the Steak House. I didn't know what to do, but I didn't like the nagging feeling that I was having, and I didn't want to say anything about the accident to my mother, who was in the kitchen.

A few minutes later I decided to call Dante, but then I thought: if he hadn't gone home yet, I didn't want to mention anything to Rosie about the accident either, especially not in front of my mother. I finally decided to walk to Dante's house.

"I'm going to Dante's," I told my mother. "He was expecting Nick to come up from New York tonight."

I seldom stayed to clean up, anyway, so it wasn't unusual for me to leave the restaurant an hour or so earlier, even when a night had been busy.

"Why didn't Nick stop in here?" my mother asked.

"I don't know. It's a long drive, especially in the dark. Maybe he got tired."

I put on my coat but left it unbuttoned, and I went out through the front door. The night was cold with a March wind, which was blowing a little snow around. I pulled my collar up, and then I shoved my hands into my deep pockets as I crossed the road. If Dante or Nick had been in a serious accident, I thought, one or the other would have called. Being in separate cars, it wasn't very likely that they'd both be involved, I reasoned. I took the short, unplowed road to the back street, and I followed a path where the snow had been packed down by the foot traffic. I crossed the back street, went onto the porch of the house, and as I climbed the stairs, I noticed the kitchen light on downstairs. My Italian grandparents were probably watching the late news. After the news, they would be going to bed.

On the landing upstairs, I tapped on the kitchen door. No one was in the kitchen even though the light was on. Rosie appeared from the front room and flicked the porch light on. She opened the door. She was wearing tight black slacks and a white wool sweater.

"Hi!" she said as her dark olive eyes and face suddenly lit up into a warm smile. "Come in," she said softly. "Are you quitting a little early tonight?"

"Yeah," I said as I stepped inside, and I closed the door. "I was expecting Nick and Dante at least an hour ago."

Quickly her expression changed.

"Me, too!"

She seemed alarmed.

"I was starting to worry," she said. "But I'm so glad to see you! Take off your coat. Can I get you anything?"

"No," I said, taking off my coat and hanging it by the door. "I just came to see if they're here."

"They should be here soon. Come and sit with me. Are you sure I can't get you anything? A beer, wine, or anisette?"

"Nothing right now. Thanks," I said as I followed her into the front room.

The couch was directly to the right of the entrance, facing the front of the house on the street side.

On a coffee table at the front of the couch was a manuscript.

"I was rereading about Dante's experiences in Korea," she said, after she sat in the middle of the couch.

I sat down next to her and leaned my left elbow on the arm of the couch.

"It's strange that tonight I felt even more affected by his script than before, when I first read it. When you get a chance, you should read it, too. Just before I heard you knock, I felt that I was with him, in Korea, when he was hit. It felt so, well, scary, as though I felt, well, I felt we were going to, to lose him. I feel much better now that you're here. I really do."

I didn't know what to say.

My right hand reached out and grasped her left hand. As soon as my hand touched hers, I felt hers squeezing mine. Her hand in mine, she touched the top of my right thigh and rubbed it a little, and she said softly, "But I can't stop worrying about them. It's just, well, it's just a feeling I have."

I put my arm around her shoulders, and as she leaned her head against me, I kissed her gently on the lips, and I, too, became more worried.

"What's there to worry about? If anything happened to them," I said, "somebody would call us."

"Where do you think they went?"

"Well, Dante said they were going to Al's for fried clams."

"I know, but that was more than three hours ago."

I heaved a big sigh.

"Maybe they lost track of time. After all, there's a lot for them to talk about."

"I know," she murmured.

"It's getting close to midnight. Al will be closing soon, so they should be here in a little while."

"I'm going to call," she said.

The telephone was on her side, on an end table at the end of the couch, almost touching the wall. She looked in the phone book, which had been under the phone, for the number, found it, dialed the number, said, "It's ringing," but there was no answer.

"Well," I murmured, "at least we know they're not there."

Between long periods of silence, I felt that we were both experiencing the same sense of foreboding, which was becoming too painful to endure, and we were trying to dispel the feeling with small talk. I told her about Angela in the restaurant, about how the woman said she looked so Italian. Rosie grinned. "Whenever she's with her father," she said, "she's so amazing! They make each other so happy!"

"How's the baby doing?" I asked, noticing that her breasts were unrestricted.

"Great. Everything is really great! Maria is four months old already. I want to give Dante a son now."

"Another bambino? So quickly?"

"We've been trying," she said with a broad smile. "It's been almost two months since I've had my last period, so maybe this is it."

"My kid brother lucked out."

"What do you mean?"

"Marrying not only such a beautiful woman, but such a fertile woman."

"Joy lucked out, too. If she ever becomes aware of it, she might even appreciate you almost as much as I do." She suddenly turned away. "I'm sorry. I shouldn't have said that. I should just mind my own damn business!"

"Don't be sorry," I muttered. "I'm aware of how obvious my relationship is with Joy. It *is* part of your business; you're family. Besides, you've always been special to me."

I hadn't even suspected back then, over a year earlier, after Dante had just returned home, that Joy had ever made any overtures to Dante, and that he had told Rosie about it.

"I hope you're not blaming yourself," she said, "for your, well, for your unstable relationship with Joy."

She rubbed her warm hand on the top of my thigh again.

"Well," I replied, "it takes two to tango, you know."

"It helps when the two of them *want* to tango together."

I heaved a sigh.

"My brother is a very lucky guy. You have always made him happy. And I'm happy, too, that you're part of the family."

"I'm the one who's lucky to be a part of this family. I even like the name, Valentino."

"You have so much love in you, I can feel it. And I'm not just flirting with you. I mean it. It's so easy to know why my brother loves you so much! I do, too. I always have. Not only are you so damn sexy looking and intelligent, you're so damn compassionate. You're everything a woman could ever be. You're God's gift to us. How could anyone *not* love you?"

"And I love you, too. You know I always have," she replied, rubbing my leg. "I've always felt so much love in you, too, even though you wouldn't wait to marry me," she said, grinning, "but I'm glad, at least, that you're still our big brother. Dante has always been so proud of you!"

"I'm the one who's proud of *him*. Why should he be proud of *me*? I've never accomplished anything."

"After your father died, you took care of the family, of your mother and Dante. You even sacrificed your education, maybe your whole future, to help your mother run the restaurant, and to help Dante finish college. Don't say you've never accomplished anything. Your life isn't finished *yet*. And, in spite of everything, you've helped Joy. Deep down, she should look into herself, to feel how much you've given to her and Rusty. You've cared for them. That's who you are. And if she isn't aware of who you are, you, at least, should be."

And her dark bright eyes gazed deeply into mine, penetrating the deepest part of me, silently expressing her affection, and then she held my face tenderly, and she pressed her lips against mine, letting her kiss linger just long enough to stir the tenderness deep inside of me. Her warm, soft breasts were touching me, and as I began to respond, she slowly drew back.

"Tell me about Minnie," she said softly, "about how you feel about each other. I know that Joy knows, that she knows about, well, your relationship with her, but Joy, obviously, could care less."

"I don't know what to tell you about her."

"Do you think you love her?"

"Long before I met Joy, when I was still in high school, I thought I did. I was sexually attracted to her. I still am," I muttered. "I don't expect you, or Dante, to approve of my relationship with her, but, well, since I married Joy, Minnie and I hadn't slept together, not during the first two years, anyway."

"Dante and I are not condemning you and Minnie. I think we understand your situation, but if your relationship with Minnie is, well, even if it's mostly sexual, it seems like you'd be wanting to, to see Minnie more, not less. I mean, it seems like, well, like you're trying to do what's right, in spite of a situation which, created by Joy, is not healthy, physically or spiritually, for you nor Joy, and certainly not for Rusty."

I stared at her, absorbing what she had said. And I was wondering how she knew so much about my situation with Joy.

"Is that how Dante sees my situation, too?"

"Yes, but we want to understand your relationship with Jessica, too."

"With Jessica? Why with Jessica?"

"Together, you and she, well, you seem so impressive, like a king and his queen, and you seem so devoted to each other, and to your son. A king and a queen, and their little prince. A modern fairy tale for adults."

"A modern *family* tale for *romantics*."

"Well, I know you were too young, then, to marry her, but that was over ten years ago, and you still seem to love each other so much. Dante and I can't help wondering why you didn't marry her."

I had never even told Dante why. And, apparently, Ben John had never told her about Jessica.

"I hope," she said, "it's not because she's colored."

I sighed. I had thought about what Rosie had said long before she had said it; I had thought about it until this day, more than two years later, while writing this, and the word "colored" as applied to people has always sent shivers through me, like someone scratching a blackboard.

"Years ago you asked me about Jessica."

"I've never understood your relationship with her. Back then she had even told me that you were waiting for me to finish college. She said she couldn't believe that you had married Joy."

"Back then, I was too unworthy of you. And as it turned out, you were much better off marrying Dante."

"Dante was always my best friend. I usually told him everything, but not about us. I thought I was going to marry you, right up until you suddenly married Joy."

"You and Dante seem to be made for each other. You seem so devoted to each other and so happy together."

"We are! We make each other happy, but I know that you and I would have been happy, too. And to see you like this, well, it makes me miserable."

"Hey, it ain't so bad; if it was, I'd kick her out, but my concern, now, is you."

I didn't want to tell her about the accident, because I was feeling her same fear, and I didn't know how to tell her. Just thinking that it could be Dante or Nick, or both, in the smashed car, was horrifying.

"Tony," she whispered, pulling back suddenly, "what's happening?"

"Are you frightened?"

"Yes! Are *you*?"

"A little."

"Where is this anxiety coming from?"

"This feeling," I said, "is going to pass, and then we'll be able to talk about it. When we calm down, and talk about it, maybe things will become clear. What were we talking about before?"

"About you and Jessica."

"How did that lead to this? Rosie, there's a reason why we're feeling this way. And I think it's because we need each other. You need Dante too, of course, more than you'll ever need anyone else."

"I need both of you. You and Dante are like parts of the same person."

I stared at her, and we seemed to become silent for a long time.

She touched my hands.

"Tell me about Jessica."

"Your father never told you anything about her? Even after you had met her in the clinic?"

"No. It's strange that he hadn't even told us you were the father of her baby, that you even knew her."

"Jessica didn't tell him, not until the baby was born."

"Why not?"

"She didn't know that your father even knew me. And when he said he knew me, she made him promise not to tell anyone, not until I heard from her."

"So, the summer you visited us, while you were only in high school, you were, well, you were having sex with her."

"Well, I think that's how she became pregnant."

"Oh, you! What about my brother? Didn't he know?"

"Yeah, but I told him I preferred Jessica."

She laughed a little.

I was happy to hear her laugh.

Suddenly, the telephone rang.

She pulled away from me, reached out, picked up the phone, put it to her right ear, turned to me, and drew close to me again so that I could hear, too, rested her left hand on my shoulder, and said loudly, "Hello!"

"Rosie, this is Nick." His voice sounded shaky. "Is Tony with you?"

"Yes."

"Let me talk with him."

She put the phone against my ear, and as I held the phone, I said, "Yeah, I'm here."

"Thank God you're with Rosie. I just talked with your mother, and she said you were waiting for us at the house. I didn't tell her, but I'm in the hospital with Dante; he was in a terrible," he said, pausing, "accident."

Rosie groaned. She put her arms around me, clasping me, and pressed her mouth against my chest to smother her cries.

I was stunned.

"Is he badly hurt?"

"Yes. I gave him the last rites. He's still breathing, but the doctors don't expect him to last long. They're surprised that he hasn't gone yet. Stay with Rosie. We can't see him now, anyway. He's not conscious. The doctors are doing everything they can to keep him going."

Rosie was shivering.

"What about *you*? Are you okay?"

"I was in my own car, following him. I'll tell you about it when I see you."

"Are you staying there, in the hospital?"

"If he even survives the night, he'll be in the operating room for several more hours. As soon as my nerves calm down, I'll join you. I don't feel like driving right now."

"I'll come up to get you."

"No, stay there. Stay with Rosie. I'm going to stay here and pray for a while. I'll call when I leave. If he should pass away soon, I'll call you. If I don't call, that means he's, he's still breathing. Did I tell you that the doctors are operating on him now? I'll tell you more later. Whatever you do, stay with Rosie."

He hung up.

Part Four

Conclusion

"You should finish Dante's story in just a few more days. It's getting much longer than I thought it would be. It would be nice if you could finish it before our fifth wedding anniversary. You don't think you're going into too many unnecessary details?"

"Such as?"

It was a pleasant June evening, and we were sitting side by side at the kitchen table. We've been working on this script for almost two years now. She had just finished reading what I had hoped would be the final draft of the previous chapter.

"Such as our relationship to each other."

"It explains our reaction to what was happening." I put my hand on her knee and gently rubbed it. "Rosie, our reaction was so deep because our feelings for each other are so deep, even deeper than we had been aware of. Our reaction wasn't just sexual; we were feeling the need to comfort each other, because, being so close to each other, we felt so much pain in the other. And we wanted to alleviate the pain. If we didn't love each other as much as we do, and if what we had wanted was just sex, we would not have gone without it for so long, living together like this, for the last two years. You even said it yourself, that night just a month ago, before we finally, well, before we finally…"

"Came together," she said. "I can't wait to see the finished book."

"And you know what the next scene is. You know that I have to write about it, that I have to explore it, in depth, because we both experienced it, together. I have to write about your own brother, a priest, who implored me to stay with you, even through the night, in bed with you. I'll need you to help me write it, to show it the way it really happened, to walk that tightrope without falling, again, into the abyss of depravity."

"Well, think of it as a challenge. And as you struggle to write it, remember that when the writing, well, meets with my approval, if it's honest and faithful, and expressed with love, you will be greatly rewarded."

"Greatly rewarded? How?"

She clasped my knee, rubbed the inside of my thigh, gazed into my eyes, and said in a soft, seductive voice, "I'll give you everything I have."

She had become sick to her stomach.

When Nick had hung up, I had felt as though a force had wrenched away my guts, leaving me nothing. My legs had become weak, and I had dropped against her as I returned the phone to its cradle. My body, aching from a feeling of nothingness, was draped over hers, my dry mouth touching her moist, cold forehead.

"I have to throw up," she moaned.

Somehow, I stood up and pulled her up to take her to the toilette.

She leaned against me as I led her through the kitchen and into the bathroom where she vomited into the bowl.

She was throwing up until she had nothing left in her stomach, and then she was heaving and heaving, and beads of sweat had broken out across her forehead.

I knelt beside her, placed one hand on her shoulder, and rubbed her back with my right hand.

She flushed the toilette, and then she leaned back and laid her head against me.

"I'm sorry," she murmured.

"For what? For feeling sick? You have good reason for feeling sick."

"Do you feel sick, too?"

"I'm feeling a little sick, too, and I'm worried about you. I only wish I could do something to make you feel better."

"You do! And I don't want you to leave me."

"I'm not going to leave you!"

I slid my hand under her sweater. Her flesh was cold, and I rubbed it gently.

"I wish I could do something to make you feel better, too," she said.

"Letting me touch you like this makes me feel better."

"Your hand is so nice and warm! It feels so good!"

For a long while, it seemed, we remained there, kneeling at the foot of the toilette bowl, and I was rubbing her back and her stomach.

"You're not going to believe this," she said, "but I knew that something horrible had happened to him. It was the same kind of feeling I had when he was in Korea, when he was so badly wounded. About two hours ago, when I was reading his script, a cold shudder went through me and left me with a terrible feeling. I can't describe it or explain it. When you came into the house, I just wanted to embrace you, I was so damn relieved to see you."

Finally, she stood up.

"I want to rinse out my mouth," she said, and she turned on the cold water faucet.

"You'll have to excuse me," she said suddenly, "I have to use the toilette."

"Of course. I'll be waiting behind the door," I answered, not closing the door completely.

She had diarrhea.

A long time seemed to pass.

Finally, the toilette flushed, and I could hear water running in the sink.

I opened the door. She had thrown cold water on her face, and she was wiping it. As she was hanging the towel, I walked up behind her. She looked at me in the mirror, and as she leaned back against me, I slid my hand under her sweater and wrapped my arms around her waist. She was shivering.

"Are you cold?"

"Yes. I wish," she said, her teeth chattering, "you could make me warm."

"Why don't you get into bed?"

"I don't want to be alone."

"I'll stay with you."

"In my bed?"

I hesitated before answering, "If you want. In your bed or on the couch."

"On the couch. Get a blanket from the bedroom."

With my arm around her waist, I led her back to the parlor, and as she lay on the couch, I went into the next room, opposite the parlor, and got a heavy blanket. I covered her body, took off my shoes, slid under the blanket and lay down beside her shivering body. She turned, facing me, and her back was against the back of the couch.

Since I didn't know how long it would be before Nick would arrive, I decided to call Joy to tell her where I was. Our heads were near the phone, so all I had to do was reach over the arm of the couch to pick up the phone. I called. The phone was ringing. I knew she was still up, that she was writing, and I waited for her to answer.

Finally, she answered.

"I'm at Dante's, with Rosie. There's been an auto accident. Dante is in the hospital now, but the doctors don't know if he'll even survive the night."

"What! Oh, no!"

She wanted to know the details.

"I don't know any of the details yet. My mother doesn't even know. Don't say anything to her tonight. Let her sleep. I'll tell her in the morning."

"How is Rose doing?"

"She's in shock."

"Do you want me to go there?"

"There's no need. I'm calling to tell you I'll be here for a while. I don't know for how long. We're waiting for Nick. He's at the hospital now. He said Dante's in the operating room now, and will be there for hours. So, we can't see him now, not until later."

After I hung up, Rosie snuggled against me to get warm. She was still shivering. I put my hands under her sweater, and I rubbed her cold flesh. After a while, I unbuckled my belt, loosened my trousers by unbuttoning my fly and unzipping it, pulled my shirt and my undershirt up, and I pushed her sweater up to her breasts, and as I pressed my belly against hers, she emitted a low, pleasant moan.

Her cold hands slid under my shirt and slowly rubbed my back, and she tried to pull me against her. As our bellies were touching, we pushed against each other.

Under the blanket, my body was warm, and, eventually, hers was beginning to feel warm, too. With my belly warming hers, she seemed to become relaxed enough to fall asleep. And as her body became warmer, it seemed as though our bodies were not only filling each other with more warmth; our bodies, which had felt so empty, were sustaining each other with renewed life as long as my flesh and hers were touching. In spite of the circumstances, however, my desire for her was stirring deep within me.

When I thought she had felt warm again, I closed my eyes, but the urge to get on top of her intensified.

Although she had seemed relaxed, her body was gradually moving under mine, and I became aware that I was on top of her, my legs between hers. I pushed her sweater up and uncovered her breasts. Even though she was on her back, her breasts were raised into a pair of smooth, opulent mounds with protruding nipples, but I was wondering if she had been fully aware of what I was doing. Later, when she would think of what I had done, how would she feel? How would I feel? She was no longer shivering. If I did nothing more, she would probably fall asleep.

I wanted so desperately to thrust myself into her! That feeling had not been new to us. Before she had married Dante, the urge to fuck her had felt so damn natural, but somehow we had always been able to restrain the desire. Why was I having such difficulty now? I loved and respected her as much now, maybe more so than in the past. An agonizing groan rose from my throat. I didn't want to stop what I was doing to her. I wanted to *fuck* her! To *fuck* her! I wanted to fuck her so damned much!

Suddenly, I turned away, and as I lay back, next to her, I bit down on my bottom lip, and I pushed my shirt and my undershirt down, pulled my trousers up, and zipped up my fly.

Her eyes opened, but she said nothing. Although I pulled her sweater down, I put my hand on her belly and stroked it gently.

After a while, she asked softly, "How are you feeling?"

"Were you aware of what I was doing to you?"

"Yes. You were trying to make me feel better, and you did. You always do."

"Do you know what I almost did to you?"

"I know. But I knew you would stop."

"You knew I would stop?"

"Yes."

Someone was coming up the stairs. I thought it was Nick, but he had said he would call. Without knocking, someone opened the kitchen door, closed it, and walked into the parlor. It was Joy. She was still wearing her coat. She glared down at me and Rosie, whose eyes were closed. We were covered together under the blanket.

"Well, that's cute!"

"Keep your voice down," I said, lifting the blanket and getting up, facing her; "she's having a difficult time sleeping."

"So, she needs *you* to sleep with her?"

I didn't respond to that.

"Where's Rusty?"

"Sleeping, in his own bed, where he should be."

"Who's with him?"

"I'm not staying long."

"You left him alone?"

"I just came here to see what's going on."

There was enough space between Rosie's feet and the end of the couch for me to sit, so I sat down there.

"We're waiting for Nick to tell us. I told you, he's at the hospital."

"He's at the hospital, and you're here?"

"He was with Dante when the accident happened. They were in separate cars."

"You'd think *she'd* want to rush to his side."

"For crysakes, Joy! So do I, but we can't see him now."

I looked at Rosie. She seemed to be sleeping.

We were silent for a little while.

"I'll stay with her if you want to go home and get some sleep," Joy said softly.

"Thank you, but I don't want to leave her. We need each other, especially tonight."

Joy stood there, without moving or speaking, for a long time. Finally, she said, "I care about Dante, too, you know. I hope he'll be all right."

"I know," I sighed as my chest heaved, and I struggled to prevent myself from crying. I wanted to lie down with Rosie and to hold her. I closed my eyes and clenched my fists. "If you want," I finally said, sniffling a little, "you can go get Rusty and bring him here, and we can all be together, except my mother, of course. She doesn't have to know now."

Joy seemed to be thinking about it.

"That means disturbing his sleep," she said.

"Well, he shouldn't be left alone either."

Finally, she left.

As soon as the kitchen door closed, Rosie mumbled, "I'm so sorry."

"She must have thought you were asleep."

"I wasn't in the mood to talk with her. I'm sorry."

"What are you sorry about?" I asked as I slid in beside her.

"That she saw us like this. I hope that didn't upset you."

"Of course not, not unless she blabs about it."

She began to shiver again.

"Are you feeling miserable?" I asked.

"And cold again."

I slid both of my hands under her sweater again and gently rubbed her cold skin.

"Does this help?"

"Yes, the heat from your hands feels nice, but I shouldn't be feeling this way with you, wanting you to do this to me, especially tonight."

"We feel the way nature makes us feel."

She stared at me.

"Does that mean there's something wrong with nature and with us?"

"That means there's something wrong with us for not understanding what nature is doing to us. I know that you don't want us to, well, to fuck. Well, at least a part of you doesn't, but we both know that when my flesh touches yours, the life in both of us rises."

"And, right now, I want to feel your flesh touching mine, to make my flesh warm with yours. I want to feel your belly pressing against mine, to feel life again, in both of us."

I unbuckled my belt again, loosened my trousers, pulled my shirts up, and pushed her sweater up. And, as I pressed my belly against hers, we clung to each other.

This time, in a little while, we had become so warm and comfortable, yet so exhausted, that when Nick called back, we had been sleeping together with our arms wrapped around each other.

Dante was still in the operating room. Nick had been told that Dante had received such incredibly severe injuries, which would have killed anyone else instantly, that he would remain unconscious in the recovery room long after they'd wheel him out of the operating room, but there was no guarantee that he would ever again regain consciousness.

"I'm leaving the hospital now. They'll call us at the house as soon as there are any new developments to his condition."

As we waited for Nick, I sat in the corner of the couch, and Rosie sat beside me, her legs folded under her. She rested her head on my chest, and put her arms around my waist. To keep her warm, I covered the front of us with the blanket. Only our faces and my shoulders were uncovered. The top of the blanket was under her chin, and the ends were tucked behind my back against the back of the couch. My right arm was holding her against me, and my hand was under her sweater. I was rubbing her belly.

"Are you warm enough?" I asked.

"Yes," she answered, but it sounded more like a whimper.

I continued to rub her belly in a circular motion, rubbing her flesh very close to her breasts.

After a little while, she cried out, "Why did this happen?"

She grabbed my hand and pushed it up and pressed it against her breasts. "Why?" she whimpered. "Why? Why is this happening to us? To Dante? Why?"

"You want Dante, now," I said softly. "You need him."

"Yes! Oh, God!" she sobbed, pressing her face to my chest and grabbing me around my waist with both hands. "I want him! Oh, God! Please! I want him!"

We were holding each other tightly, and I was rocking her.

And, I thought, I had become a substitute for Dante to relieve her of the pain she had felt earlier, and now, her pain had become too severe to endure. Seeing her in such agony, I could no longer contain my own feelings, and I, too, cried out, "Oh, God!" and clinging to each other, we sobbed together.

We were still crying when Nick entered the house, and immediately, without even removing his coat, seeing us, he knelt in front of us, and without speaking, he reached out and embraced us, and the three of us were weeping together.

"I couldn't tell you everything over the phone," he sobbed. "They had to amputate both of his legs."

The three of us, clinging to each other, cried out, wailing.

Finally, Nick stood up, and he removed his coat, and he hung it by the kitchen door. He returned to the parlor and walked around the coffee table, and he sat on the couch on the other side of his sister. He was wearing his Roman collar. He took her hand.

Rosie was leaning against me again, her legs tucked under her as she was facing him, and the blanket was covering our laps. She removed her hand from his, took my arm and pulled it over her shoulder to make her warmer, I assumed, and then she reached out and took his hand.

Nick told us what had happened.

As Dante had entered Al's, the fried clams Nick had ordered for them were ready. As they were eating, Dante spent most of the time talking about how happy he had been ever since he had returned home over a year ago.

"He loves you and the kids so much!" he said to Rosie, with tears running down his face. "You've made him so happy! He even had me wondering if I had done the right thing, joining the priesthood instead of getting married and raising a family. The greatest thing in life, he said, is the passionate love between a husband and his wife, creating new life. He's convinced he had made the right decision, marrying you, that, through you, it was the easiest way for him to know God."

Rosie withdrew her hand from his, buried her face against my chest, wrapped her arms around my waist, and cried. Her body was shaking.

The three of us were in tears again.

Nick took out a handkerchief and blew his nose.

After a while, he continued talking.

The restaurant had been fairly crowded, as usual for a Friday night. Just before he and Dante had finished eating, three boys had come into the restaurant. At first, Nick and Dante had hardly noticed them as they sat a few tables away, but as the boys began to speak about "papist nigger priests" in voices loud enough that most of the customers had heard, Dante said he thought he recognized one of them as a former pupil, a troublemaker, from three years ago. He seemed a little younger than the other two, who seemed old enough to drink, and all three of them seemed to have been intoxicated. They had become so obnoxious that the waitress approached them and told them to lower their voices and to stop annoying the patrons, or else the owner would be forced to call the police.

Nick and Dante had been ready to leave, anyway. They got up and put on their coats. Nick walked past the three boys first.

"Hey, nigger papist, ain't it too cold for you way up here away from the jungle?"

The three of them began snickering.

Dante stopped and glared at them.

"Do you boys have a problem?"

"No problem we can't fix."

"I remember you now," Dante said, pointing his artificial arm at the youngest looking boy. "Yeah, you have a serious problem. Ladies and gentleman," he said to the other customers, "we have to forgive this boy who has a serious problem, and maybe the other two have the same problem. This boy, you see, calls himself a true Christian. He's a Templar of the Holy Spirit, and he hates Catholics. If you're Catholic, don't be offended; he hates everyone else who he thinks is not a white Christian. He has a serious problem; feel sorry for him."

As some of the others were chuckling, Nick and Dante left.

After Nick had started his car and was ready to follow Dante, he noticed the three boys coming out of the restaurant. There were no car lights on the road, so Dante pulled out onto the road, and he turned left to go north. Nick followed.

After a short distance from the steak house, and they were speeding along the flat highway, a car went racing past Nick, and as it was speeding past Dante, there was a flash and a loud bang, like the shot of a gun, from the passenger side of the passing car. Dante's car swerved off the road and smashed into a tree.

Nick slammed on his brakes, stopped, and rushed to Dante, but he was unable to open the door. Quickly, he returned to the steak house to call an ambulance.

"I told the police I was certain that one of the three boys had taken a shot at Dante." And then he muttered, "The policeman asked me if I had been drinking."

Rosie clung to me and groaned. She was shaking again, not so much from cold, I thought; she was sobbing. I squeezed her against me. I, too, wanted to cry out, to release my grief.

A loud cry burst out.

Rosie looked up at me; her eyes were wet, swollen, and red.

"The baby," her voice shook, as the baby was wailing, "needs to be breast fed. Oh, God!"

"I'll get her," I said, rising up.

Quickly, I replaced the blanket on Rosie, and I went through the kitchen, to the babies' room, and switched the light on. Angela, in another crib, woke up, called me "Daddy" and wanted to get down.

"Your daddy isn't here, sweetheart," I said, as I lowered the bars of her crib. "I have to get Maria. Your mother's on the couch. And your Uncle Nick is here." I picked her up and stood her on the floor. Immediately, she ran to the front room.

As soon as I picked up Maria, her crying began to decrease. Her diaper felt damp. I looked around the room to see where I could change it. Then I carried her to the front room and told Rosie I should change her diaper. Angela was sitting next to her, the blanket covering their laps.

"Everything is in the spare room, on the bed," Rosie said. "I'll change her."

"No, I can do it. Just hold the baby for a minute."

I lay the baby in Rosie's arms, went into the bathroom, wet a washcloth with a little soap and hot water, squeezed the water out, returned to the front room, took the baby from Rosie, went through the kitchen, into the spare room between Rosie's room and the babies' room, placed Maria in the middle of the bed, removed her soiled diaper, washed between her legs gently, sprinkled baby powder on her, grabbed another diaper, and put it on her. Then I took her to the front room to give her to her mother.

Rosie pulled her sweater up, uncovering her left breast, and I placed the baby in the cradle of her mother's arm. The baby immediately opened her mouth and begun to suck hungrily on the nipple, but after a few seconds, the baby stopped sucking and began to wail in protest.

"Oh, God!" Rosie cried, "She knows there's something wrong with me! Get a bottle from the fridge. Get two bottles. One for Angela. And heat them on the stove."

I went into the kitchen, grabbed a pot, and turned on the hot water.

Nick came into the kitchen and asked, "Is there anything I can do?"

"Yeah, get two baby bottles of milk from the fridge and put them on the stove."

I put hot water into the pot and put the pot on the stove. Nick put the two bottles of cold milk, with the rubber nipples on top, into the pot.

"When the water starts to boil," I told him, "remove the bottles of milk."

I went into the bathroom.

In the meanwhile, Maria continued crying.

After I came out of the bathroom and returned to the front room, I sat in a big, soft chair, facing them. In spite of the crying, I felt so tired that I could hardly keep my eyes open.

When the milk was warm, Nick gave a bottle to Rosie, who put the nipple to Maria's mouth, and the baby stopped crying, finally. He gave the other bottle to Angela, who sat beside her mother and contentedly sucked down the milk. And Nick sat at the end of the couch again, near the phone, as though he were expecting a call any-time from the hospital.

I looked at them. Rosie, too, seemed exhausted.

She looked up at me. I could feel her grief.

"Come sit with us."

There was enough room at the corner of the couch where I had been sitting before, but it was a snug fit. I squeezed myself between her and the couch, and I leaned back into the corner. As she did before, she took my arm and pulled it over shoulder. She pulled the blanket over my hand, and under the blanket, she pushed my hand under her sweater.

"I'm beginning to feel relaxed," she murmured. "I actually feel like sleeping. Our whole family seems to be relaxing, finally. Are you tired, Nick?"

"Yeah, I'm getting there."

"You can sleep in my bed. I'm going to stay here."

"You should sleep in your own bed. I want to stay here, near the phone."

In a little while, both babies fell asleep.

"I'll put Maria in her crib," I said.

"I'll take Angela," said Nick.

He followed me through the kitchen and into the babies' room, and we put the babies in their cribs.

Before we had even left their room, Rosie suddenly rushed into the bathroom and was gagging and heaving and trying to vomit. Sweat was rolling down from her forehead.

I stood behind her and held her shoulders, and I could feel her body trembling.

She rinsed her mouth with cold water.

"Can you get me a small glass of orange juice?"

"I'll get it," Nick said.

She swallowed it down quickly.

"I feel I have to use the toilette again. I think I have more diarrhea."

We closed the door and waited for her at the entrance to the kitchen.

Neither Nick not I uttered a word; we looked at each other and waited anxiously for her to come out.

Finally, we heard the toilette flush, and then she turned on the faucet, and a few seconds later, the door opened.

Her lips quivered.

"I'm cold. I want to lie down."

Nick said, "Lie down in bed."

"No! I don't want to be alone!" She leaned against me. "I don't want to be left alone," she repeated in a soft but desperate tone.

"Lie down under the blanket on the couch," I said as I led her to the front room.

"I won't leave you alone, I promise."

In the front room, I released her, and I picked up the blanket.

"Lie down."

She lay with her head near the phone, and I covered her.

"I'll get you each a pillow," Nick said, and he went into her bedroom and returned with two pillows.

I got under the blanket and faced her as she lay on her back. After Nick placed the pillows under our heads, I thrust my hand under her sweater and rubbed her belly, but the shaking would not stop.

"Oh, for God's sake, Tony," Nick cried out after a while, "this won't do! We can't let her get sick now! Take her into her bed, please. I know what you're thinking, but if your brother could speak to you now, he'd tell you to do what's best for her. Do whatever you must to make her warm! She needs to sleep!"

"Heat some milk. Maybe that will help."

Quickly, he went into the kitchen.

I picked up Rosie and carried her to her bed, pulled the covers down, and she pushed herself under the covers, and quickly, I went to the closet, took out two more thick blankets, covered her, got into bed with her, left the lights on, pulled the pile of covers over us, and, although we were under a pile of blankets and were wearing our clothes, she was still shivering.

"Hold me," she mumbled in a shaky voice. "Make me warm."

"I'm going to make you so warm," I said, thrusting my right hand under her buttocks and pulling her against me, "that you'll be begging me to let you sleep."

I was lying on my right side, my mouth near hers. With my left hand, I was rubbing her under her sweater from her hips to her breasts. Her own hands were on my back, holding me against her. And though I tried not to think about how passionate we had become when we were a little younger, stroking her flesh was inflaming our passions. The tips of her fingers were pressing into my shoulders.

As I lifted my body over hers a little, wrapping my left leg between hers, she moved her hands down to my hips and seemed to be pulling me over her. Her eyes were closed, and her mouth was open a little, and her lips were quivering. As my own lips began to brush hers, she murmured, "You feel warm." But she was still trembling. "Hold me tighter." As I was pushing against her, I was aware that I could easily get on top of her, and I became even more aroused. Waiting for her brother to bring her a mug of hot milk, seemed like an eternity. As I was pressing myself against her, she spread her legs, and both of my legs dropped between hers, and I was lying on top of her, and my hands were under her buttocks, lifting them. Her trembling had finally stopped. Her hips began to move, rising up, and she emitted a soft moan as her hips were undulating, sending wave after wave of sensational feelings down my thighs. I had become so damn excited that I suddenly began to ejaculate.

I thought that she hadn't even been aware of what had happened to me. She would only assume that I had stopped pressing and rubbing myself against her because I had become so overwhelmed with guilt. Such loss of control had seldom happened to me before, except with her, years ago. I became aware, now, of how sexually attracted I really was to her, the little sister of Nick, and the devoted wife of my own brother. Although my sexual attraction to her had become so damn intense, the sensation was also so damned scary. How was I, whom she had trusted so damn much, different than Joy? I began to understand, I thought, why Joy had been so afraid of losing control of her sexual passions. But the difference, I thought, in spite of my strong sexual attraction to Rosie, was that I cherished her as a person. Why, then, did I lack such control with her, especially under these circumstances? Maybe it was because I had, somehow, denied a strong sexual desire for her, but that, subconsciously, I was possessed by an irresistible desire to fuck her. Yet, how could I have denied such a strong desire for her if I had never even allowed myself to think about it consciously? And if I had such a strong desire for her, why had I been able to restrain it before but not now? One thing was for certain. From now on, I would have to be more aware of my feelings for her. Even though I had told her that I loved her too much to even think of fucking her, and I had firmly believed that, I had been deceiving myself.

I lay back, next to her, with my arm around her shoulders, and she, no longer trembling, cuddled against me with her head against my shoulder. Her eyes were closed, and she seemed exhausted, as though she would sleep.

There was a light tap on the door, and Nick entered, carrying a mug of hot milk.

"How is she doing?"

"Much better. I think the hot milk will help her sleep."

"Thank God. I'm glad she's better. I was really worried about her."

"I still am. I'm going to stay with her, at least through the rest of the night."

"Of course. She needs you, especially tonight. She's always loved both you and Dante."

"I know. I need her, too."

"I mean," he said, putting the mug on a nightstand next to me, under a lamp, "she's always been in love with both you and Dante, even though she has always felt that you've looked upon her as a younger sister."

"I've always known that's she's not a younger sister."

He stared at me.

"On the way out," he said, "I'm going to switch the overhead light off. You have the light from this lamp. I'll close the bedroom door so that no one will disturb you. Sleep as late as you need to. You both need the rest. The baby girls will be fine."

"Are you sure?"

"I'm not going to tell your mother about Dante. I'll leave that to you, but I'm going to tell your Nonna. I'm sure she and Tattone will understand your situation, and she'll take care of the baby girls. I'll only come in here on occasion to see how you're both doing. And I'll tap on the door first. So, sleep late."

"Thanks, Nick."

"Prego."

After he switched off the overhead light, he left, closing the door behind him.

"Can you sit up and drink some hot milk?"

I propped up the pillow behind her as she sat up, and then I gave her the mug.

She took a sip.

"It's hot, but not too hot." She took another sip. Her hands were no longer trembling. "I can feel the hot milk going down. It feels good. I'm beginning to feel sleepy, now."

"Good," I said, putting my hand on the inside of her knee and rubbing her thigh.

"That feels so good when you do that to me. Thank you, and thank you for staying with me tonight."

"I should be thanking *you* for wanting me to stay with you."

"You're not embarrassed?"

"No, of course not. Are *you*?"

She took a large swallow of milk.

"If you weren't with me, I'd fall apart. I don't know what I'd do without you. I know how much you love your brother, that you're hurting as much as I am, but you're my strength, and I need you. I can't bear to think you'd hate me for feeling the way I do about you, especially now."

She took another large swallow.

"I could never hate you, especially about the way you feel about me. I'm not embarrassed for loving you. Are *you*?"

"Not for loving you. Of course not. I've always loved you."

She took another large swallow of milk.

"Then, what are you embarrassed about?"

She swallowed the rest of the milk, and gave me the mug. I put it on top of the nightstand, and then we both slid under the covers.

"About the way I feel now. You make me feel, well, good, but," she whimpered, "I don't want you to feel guilty for wanting to, well, to be with me. How you feel about me is very important to me. If you ever hated me, I could never bear it."

"I love you so much, I could never hate you."

"Unless I make you feel guilty."

Tears began to form in her eyes.

"I can't blame *you* for making me feel guilty; I can only blame myself."

"But I'm the one who's doing this to you. If it makes you hate me, I'll regret this for the rest of my life, and losing you is too devastating. Why are you feeling so guilty?"

I didn't answer her immediately. I had assumed that my reasons for feeling guilty had been obvious.

"For coveting the wife of my own brother, especially now when I know how much you need me. If that's not the mark of a beast, what is?"

"I could never love a beast! That's not who you are! Until now, have you ever coveted me, the wife of your brother?"

"Well, no, not until now. The thought never occurred to me. I had no reason to think of you that way."

"You had no reason to think of the little sister of Nick that way, not the ripe young woman who had always adored you, whom you could have had any time you wanted, who would become so damn eager to feel you penetrating her so damn deep inside of her that there would no longer be any separation between you and her, who had waited so long and so damn patiently for you to make your commitment to her, until you shattered her dream by suddenly getting married, but not to her, and three years after she married your little brother, you suddenly coveted her!"

Her dark, bright eyes, wet with tears, seemed to be piercing me. I was stunned. A heavy, gloomy silence descended upon us.

"Over ten years ago," she added, "when you made me aware that I, the little sister of Nick, was developing the body of a woman, I used to imagine you planting your seeds deep inside of me, creating new life. So many times you could have done to me what you had done to other women, *if* you had wanted."

She was gazing at me with such deep sorrow!

"I wanted you to," her voice dropped, "to fuck me. I wanted you, so much! Not just to assimilate it, but to actually let me feel the fire of your passion penetrating me so much, and so deep inside of me, shooting your seeds into my womb. I thought that I would have given you so damn much pleasure that you would surely marry me. You wouldn't wait for me to graduate. Even after you married Joy, I wanted you to fuck me, so damn much!"

"You would have let me do that to you, even after I married Joy?"

"You knew I would have! I had made it so obvious to you. Even Joy knew. I made sure she knew, as soon as I saw what your situation was with her, what she was doing to you. I wanted to free you from her! And she knew! She always knew!"

"You would even," I asked reluctantly, "have betrayed your own husband, my own brother?"

"Of course not!"

"But you just said you would let me, well, do it to you, even after I married Joy."

"Before I committed myself to Dante. We could never have done that, not after I married him, betraying your own brother."

"You trust me; your brother trusts me, and he said if Dante could talk to me now, he would tell me to do what's best for you. All I have to do now is to trust myself."

"You have always been able to stop yourself from going all the way. And you would hate yourself and me if we would betray Dante. The evil is not in the temptation, but in the act, in the betrayal. Do you feel that, being together like this we will betray Dante?"

"I hope not."

"If Dante had ever been tempted by Joy, and had almost did it with her but somehow he had stopped himself, would you say he had betrayed you?"

"No, of course not. I know that Joy would. But why would you even mention that?"

"To convince you that you would never betray Dante, either."

"Don't compare Dante to me. I know for a fact that you married a virgin, and that he was always faithful to you. And he assumed you were, too."

"You know I was! Until I married Dante, you know you were the only one to whom I had ever given the opportunity, the only one I ever really wanted, but in spite of all the opportunities I gave you, you would never go all the way with me. With other women you did, but never with me. You loved me too much to do that to me, you said. According to you, I was still a virgin when I married Dante, but I didn't feel like a virgin, not after coming so close so many times with you. When I think of how far we had actually gone, I hardly considered myself a virgin. Being with you, I knew how Eve felt when the serpent tempted her."

"What do you mean?"

"She thought that the forbidden fruit would be good, especially since it had been placed in the Garden of Paradise."

I nodded, saying, "That's why she chose it."

"That's why I wanted you to go all the way with me. If you had, I was sure you would have wanted to marry me, that I would have made you so damn happy, you would never even think of making love to any other woman."

"Making love and creating life *is* good, under the right circumstances."

"That means making a lifetime commitment. And that involves choosing the right woman for you, even if she's colored."

I stared at her.

Finally, I asked, "Have you ever told Dante how close you had come to, well, to going all the way with me?"

"Of course not! You advised me not to. Remember?"

"So much is happening so fast and so unexpectedly. I have to stop and think."

"Yes, I know. And I need you to think for both of us. I feel too disquiet to think clearly. And I'm afraid of losing you, too."

"I don't want you to feel that you're losing me. You're not. I think you know how much I want you and how desperately I need you, but we have to stop and to think."

"Yes, I know."

"We can't do anything that we'll regret later. And I need you to help me to be strong. We have to think of Dante, and the rest of the family. *We are not alone, you and I*; we're part of something much bigger than us."

"I know. I don't want us to do anything, either, that would later make you feel guilty, that would make you hate me."

She gasped, grabbing my arm, and then she heaved a deep sigh.

"I love you," she whispered. "I'm so afraid of losing Dante, of losing both of you." Tears began to stream down her face again. "How could anyone hate him? Why would anyone want to hurt him? Why?"

As I embraced her, she turned onto her side, facing me, putting her arm over my belly and pushing herself against me.

"Do you think you'll be able to sleep?" I asked.

"I'm feeling sleepy now, and warm. I love you so much!"

"I love you, too. Sleep now."

I switched the light off, and we began to drift away into silent darkness.

When I woke up that first Saturday in March, twenty-seven months ago, and saw Rosie cuddled up to me and was still sleeping, I quickly thought of what had happened during the night. Through the drawn shades of two windows in the room, enough daylight had entered the room to indicate that dawn had arrived hours ago. A painful emptiness in the pit of my stomach had become lodged there as the reality of what had happened to Dante was sinking into my brains again, but, feeling the warmth of Rosie as she was sleeping against me, tenderness was also stirring in me. I held her face gently, and I planted a soft kiss on her forehead. But as I recalled how I had wanted to use her to gratify my desires, I became filled with guilt and disgust.

Almost as though she could feel my thoughts, her eyes opened, and she gazed at me. She seemed to be looking at me a long time, but she didn't say anything. I gave her another kiss on her forehead.

"Buon giorno," I whispered, but as soon as I had said it, I knew it would not be a good day.

She smiled a little, as though she had forced a smile, but still she said nothing.

"What are you thinking?" I asked.

"About what happened." And then she added, "To Dante."

After a long while, I finally said, "I need you to help me to cope with its reality."

"And I need you, too. And thank you for staying with me. We need each other. But I don't want you to hate us for the way we're

661

feeling. I know you're feeling the way I'm feeling, that you can't help the way you're feeling. And hating each other doesn't solve our problems."

"I just want to stay here and sleep with you, to escape from the world."

"That's the way I feel too, but there are people who are depending on us. As you've said, we are not alone. But you are my strength. Without you, I don't even have the will to survive. I need you!"

"I need you, too."

Finally, we got out of bed. She put on a bathrobe and slippers. I opened the door to the parlor. The younger baby, Maria, was crawling in a playpen, and as Rosie and I entered the kitchen, Angela cried out, "Momma!" and hugged her mother's legs. Nick was sitting at the table and was drinking coffee. The first thing he said was that Dante was in the recovery room but had not regained consciousness. Nonna was also in the kitchen. As soon as she saw us, she wiped her hands on her apron, burst into tears, extended her arms to us, and the three of us put our heads together and wept. Then she hugged Rosie and whispered in her ear, "You must find the strength now to be strong, to hold the family together." And Rosie, gasping, embraced her, and, together, they cried. The presence of Nick and my grandmother that morning was a great comfort to both Rosie and me. Neither of them condemned nor judged us for having spent the night together.

I went into the bathroom and showered, and as soon as I entered the kitchen again, Nonna poured me a hot cup of strong coffee and insisted that I stay there for ham and eggs with home fried potatoes served with onions and lots of garlic. Nick joked about her serving us ham. While she was cooking for Rosie and me, Rosie was taking a shower.

While Rosie and I were eating breakfast, or *attempting* to eat, we talked about going to the hospital in the afternoon. And, of course, I still had to tell my mother about Dante.

After breakfast Nick went with me to tell my mother. I had thought that my mother and my Aunt Maria would probably be in the restaurant to prepare for that evening. The restaurant, of course, would be closed now until further notice. They were in the house, downstairs, and they were talking in the kitchen to Joy, who had already told them about Dante.

At noon, Nick called the hospital to inquire if Dante was allowed visitors. He was still unconscious, but members of his family could visit him for a brief period. In the middle of the afternoon, while Joy stayed behind to care for the baby girls, thirteen of us gathered in the waiting room for permission to see Dante. One of my uncle's wife, sniffling and holding a handkerchief to her face, made the inevitable remark, "Why him? He wouldn't hurt a flea." But, of course, Rosie knew. I had been with her in her room for a few minutes while she had been getting ready to go to the hospital. She had burst into tears.

"If he hadn't married me, this probably would never have happened to him."

"How in hell can you even think that! What would Dante say? Even if he had known what would have happened to him, and if he could choose again whether or not to marry you, what would he have done? And if he did refuse to marry you, he would have done so only to prevent you from getting hurt. Rosie, you gave him so much happiness! Don't ever forget that. Promise me that you will never forget that. Promise me."

When she had embraced me and had mumbled her promise, I had thought back to almost two years earlier on a July morning when I had told my Tattone that Dante had been wounded in Korea. Tattone had been in the back of the house, working in the garden, and I had thought that the news would have upset him, but he had seemed calm. He looked across the river, up at the sky above Cascade Mountain.

"Beyond the gods that most people of this world have created, gods created in our image, there is God that has given me a few more years to serve here, but both you and your brother have a life yet to live. There is a place waiting for him, here. He will return. My son, your father, is with him now. I know of only two people in my lifetime who have spoken with God. I understand if you doubt me, but one of them is your father. Your brother will return here, I know he will."

"Who," I asked, "is the other one? The Pope?"

He stared at me before he answered, "Even if I told you, you would believe me? Do you believe me when I tell you that your father is with your brother now? Do you believe me that, more than once, your own father has spoken with God? There are things of this world that we will never understand, things that we know with our feelings, which our minds can never fathom."

"Anyone," I said without thinking, "can speak to God. Even I have spoken to God."

His dark blue eyes penetrated me.

"I did not say *to* God; I said *with* God."

I stared back at him.

"If you know that my father has spoken with God and that he is with my brother now, and that Dante will return here, then, you also have spoken with God."

He was still staring at me.

"And," he finally said, "until you, too, have spoken with God, and God has answered you, you will not believe me. It would not surprise me to know that the wife of Dante, Rose, knew that your brother has been seriously wounded even before she had been notified by the government. Would that surprise you?"

This time, however, when Tattone had gone upstairs and had embraced Rosie, he had wanted to say something, but was unable to speak. They clung to each other. Words had not been necessary, anyway.

In the waiting room of the hospital my memere, leaning on a cane, approached Nick, who was wearing his collar, and she asked him if he was now an ordained priest, and he said yes, that he had been a priest for almost two years now. He had been ordained when Dante had been in Korea, and this was the first time since his ordination, he told my grandmother, that he had seen Dante.

"Why is God doing this to our family? Hasn't this family suffered enough?"

"This isn't God's doing; it's man's."

"Why does God allow such evil?"

"He gives us the ability to choose to do good or evil, and He does not interfere with our choices. We have the ability to improve our lives, or to destroy it."

"Why do white people choose to be so cruel?"

Nick looked at me as if to say, "Do something to take me away from her."

To my grandmother he said, "It has nothing to do with being white."

"I think it's because the devil is white."

"We priests do not have all the answers."

"I was taught that you do."

"If that was what you were taught, you were misled. Not even the Pope has all the answers."

"Not even the Pope?"

"No."

"Does he not take the place of God on earth?"

"No man can ever take the place of God."

"That can't be! What kind of priest are you?"

"The Pope is the religious and spiritual leader of our Church, and he is as human as you and I, which means that he is not above sin and is prone to making mistakes, such as the Pope who had condemned Galileo, and the Pope who had condoned the Inquisition, and the Pope who had excommunicated the priest, Martin Luther, before trying to understand the situation, causing a great schism within our Church, and so many other Popes who have made so many serious misjudgments."

"That can't be!"

"It is. I'm sorry to disappoint you, but the Pope is infallible only when God speaks to him on matters of our faith, which almost never happens. Otherwise, the Pope, himself, must rely on the authority of the teachings of the Church just as the rest of us mortals must do. The Pope does not take the place of God. His purpose is to lead us to God. Whenever a Pope, or even a teacher who, in the name of our Church, or in the name of God, misleads us, his sin is even more grievous than the sin of a nonreligious person."

"These Italians," she grumbled to my French Canadian grandfather, "have a different religion than we do."

"And the Pope," Nick reminded her, "like most Popes, is even more Italian than I am."

My grandfather put his hand on Nick's shoulder.

"You make a good priest. You tell the truth."

"Yes, a good priest," my grandmother grumbled, "for someone who is part Italian."

We were in St. Louis Hospital, a Catholic hospital in which most of the nurses were French Canadian nuns. It was the only hospital in the area, for all the people.

A nun approached Rosie, took her hands and said, "I remember you, Rose, from only four months ago when you were here to deliver a baby. We're so sorry about Dante. We're all praying for him. If you follow me, I'll take you to him now, but he's still unconscious. You may bring three others with you."

Rosie nodded to me and to my mother, and then she looked at Nonna.

Nonna said, "Bring your brother. I'll go later." And she whispered into Rosie's ear, "Remember, you must be strong, now, stronger than the rest of us, for our family."

We saw a body that was, apparently, sleeping in a hospital bed, but it could have been anyone. His face was covered with bandages. Rosie and I sat next to each other, and my mother and Nick sat opposite us, and we hardly spoke. For several minutes we sat there and stared at him, at the tubes going into his right arm. None of this even seemed real, not to me, anyway. I wanted to leave, to escape from this oppressive situation, to go outside, to return to familiar surroundings, yet I didn't want to leave Dante behind, not in this oppressive room.

Rosie stood up, and very carefully, she put her face near his, and said softly, "Ti amo, marito," and she gave him a kiss on his lips, and kept staring at him.

Eventually the nun came in and told us that someone would have to leave so that the others could see him. Rosie didn't want to leave immediately, and she grasped my hand to stay with her. My mother and Nick left, and my Italian grandparents were allowed to take their place. When Nonna and Tattone left, Rosie and I left with them. Rosie had seemed stunned the few minutes we had been with him, staring at him, and none of us even knew what to say.

Instead of staying with the others in the waiting room, Nick drove us back to the flats.

For the rest of the day, I didn't leave Rosie's sight for more than a few seconds. As soon as we returned to her house, and Angela went with Nonna and Joy and Rusty to the restaurant, Rosie changed into more comfortable clothes, removing her stockings and was wearing a skirt and a blouse. We, including Nick and Tattone, had a cup of coffee with anisette, and a little later, when everyone else was either at home or in the restaurant, and Rosie and I were together, the baby, who had been sleeping, woke up. When Rosie was breastfeeding Maria, we were sitting on the couch. I was gazing at her with deep admiration and affection.

"Having you here, with me," she said softly, "looking at me like that, feels so natural that you make me feel proud that I'm a woman and a mother. I feel as comfortable with you sitting here with us, and as intimate with you, as I've felt with Dante, as though you *are* Dante. I don't understand why Joy, especially since she's lived with you, can't appreciate who you really are. Maybe she feels guilty for having deceived you."

"Deceived me? How?"

"For making you think you were, well, the biological father of Rusty."

"How do you know that?"

"What do you mean?"

"Well, you seem to know a lot about my relationship with Joy. How do you know so much about us? I didn't know that you and she were friendly enough to know her that well."

"Dante must have told me things about you and her, I guess."

"How would Dante know?"

"He's talked with her. He's very perceptive. He could ask someone a question in such a way that sounds so casual, and he'd get an answer to five other questions."

"Yeah, that's true."

"Sometimes," she said, "his insights have even been scary, as though he could read my mind. I could be sitting here like this and be thinking of something, and he'd make a remark about what I'd be thinking. He did that to me so often! He used to say that he could do that to me because we love each other so much. But he could really do that to almost anyone."

"Maybe that's because he has so much love in him, so much empathy."

She smiled. Suddenly her eyes filled with tears.

"He used to say that when you were with me," she said, "you were a different person, a much better person."

"That's true. With you, that's the way I've always felt. You've always brought out the best in me."

"He used to ask me about our trip to Canada, just you and me, the summer after I had graduated from high school. I don't think he ever knew how I really felt about you, about how eager I was to spend a whole week alone with you. I remember telling him that I trusted you completely, and that my folks trusted you, too. And they did. I told Dante that I knew that you would never do anything to hurt me, that, with you, I felt perfectly secure, that I thought that when I'd finish college, I'd marry you, and that by going away with you, especially for a whole week, just the two of us, we'd get to know each other much better. He was concerned, of course, that I'd lose my virginity, that I'd fall under your spell," she grinned, "which, as you well know, I didn't, (lose my virginity, I mean). Technically, I remained a virgin. Do you remember what you told me, even back then? Well, you told me I was still too young for you, too young for having sex, period, being only seventeen, and that I had four years of college before I should even consider, well, going all the way, but you also said you loved me too much to, well, to actually fuck me." She paused. "I've never told Dante how sexually attracted I was to you, how much I had always wanted you. By not telling him, was I intentionally deceiving him?"

"No," I muttered, "of course not."

I was feeling too embarrassed to say anything more.

"The baby has finished," she said in a high voice, as though she suddenly had trouble speaking. "Can you take her for a few seconds? She's ready to go to sleep now."

As I took the baby, Rosie pulled her bra down, covering her breasts, and then she buttoned her white blouse.

"I'll put her in her crib," she said, taking the baby.

About a half hour later, Nonna, returning with Angela, tapped on the door and entered the kitchen. She said that if we wanted to eat in the restaurant, she would stay with the babies.

We went into the restaurant to join the others, and later when we returned to the house, Nick and I had a cup of coffee with anisette. And that evening, after Rosie fed Maria again, I tucked Rosie into bed, stayed with her on top of the bed while she was snug under the covers, and when she fell asleep, I went into the parlor and talked with Nick for a few minutes, and then I went home.

I was tired, so I had no trouble falling asleep alone in my bed and hearing the clicking of a typewriter by Joy in the front room.

And I had a dream of Dante and Rosie sitting at the other side of a table from me. Dante had both of his arms, I noticed. "I need you, too," he said softly. Rosie was gazing at me, but she didn't say anything. "What do you need me for?" I asked. He gave me a sheet of typewriter paper, but it was blank. And I woke up. It was still dark, and I fell back to sleep. In the morning, that little scene was the only part of any dreams that I remembered.

3

Later in the morning, at Sunday Mass, one of the two local parish priests announced that Nick would be conducting the daily Masses during the next two weeks each morning at seven to pray for Dante. My mother and Rosie would be attending the services every morning, and I would be attending with them most of the time. I think that helped me to restrain my impulses, for a little while, anyway.

On that Sunday afternoon and evening, the restaurant was crowded. Late in the afternoon Ben John and Anna, and Jessica arrived. Ben John and Jessica would leave in the middle of the week, but Anna would stay indefinitely with Rosie. Minnie, who had visited Dante (who had not yet retained consciousness) during the afternoon, was at the restaurant when Jessica arrived, and she invited Jessica to stay with her. She also told Jessica about Shackle, who, Minnie suspected, had something to do about having inflicted the injuries to Dante. Minnie had reported her suspicions to the police. She had also submitted the twelve pamphlets, which Shackle had written, to the local newspaper. Each pamphlet would be printed each week for the next twelve weeks, but, for her own protection, her name would be withheld. She had planned, with permission of the superintendent, to dedicate the graduation ceremonies that year to Dante.

The next day, on Monday, we visited him, but he hadn't regained consciousness.

Early that evening, in the restaurant, as we began to eat, we received a call from the hospital. I answered the phone. Dante had regained consciousness. He had not spoken, but he had opened his eyes and had looked around, and had made guttural sounds that had indicated that he had felt pain, and his pain medication had been increased and had put him back to sleep.

Apparently, he was gradually improving.

The next day, Rosie and I and my mother and Nick and Ben John were allowed to see him when he was awake, but he didn't seem to recognize any of us. Rosie kissed him and talked to him, but he wouldn't speak. He looked at her as though he were bewildered. Ben John thought that his brain had been severely damaged, and the local doctors agreed.

After two weeks in the hospital, although he could not communicate, he had gained enough strength to be transferred to the White River Junction veterans' hospital. A round trip from here was about five hours, so we didn't visit him every day. Twice Rosie and I had made unplanned overnight trips due to inclement weather. The second time, my mother had been with us, so that had not been much of a problem, but the first time, only Rosie had been with me.

After we had left Dante late in the afternoon, sleet was falling. The ground had been so icy that we could hardly walk. We didn't go far by automobile. We stopped at the first motel we saw. The room had one bed.

"Well," I muttered, as soon as we entered the room, "shall I flip a coin to see who gets the bed? Or shall we get another room?"

"We only need one room. And I don't want to sleep alone, anyway. It's a small room, but at least it's warm, so let's make ourselves comfortable."

"I noticed a restaurant not far from here. Maybe we should eat now before it gets dark. And we should call home."

As soon as we went into the restaurant, which had a telephone booth in it, we both went into the booth, and she called her house. Her mother was still there, taking care of the babies. Her mother said it was snowing there and that she had been worried about us, but she said she was glad we were staying here for the night.

Then I called Joy.

"Just you and Rose?" she yelled. "Well, I hope she gives you the best fuck you've ever had!"

And she hung up.

Rosie was staring at me.

"I'm sorry," she said.

"What are you sorry about? She got all excited just thinking about you and me together. It'll probably inspire her to write a thrilling sex scene. Besides, she hopes you give me the best, well, the best."

"Yeah, I heard."

But we didn't talk much about sex in the restaurant. We talked about Dante. He did not seem to be getting much better; he still slept most of the time. And when he was awake, he remained in bed. To prevent a bedsore from spreading on one of his hips, a nurse rubbed an ointment on his skin. Rosie thought she could take better care of him at home, that she could give him more attention, and that it would help him to improve his overall condition, but the doctors thought that he had been so severely brain damaged that there was little hope that he would ever respond to us, and that he could not live much longer, not with a body that been inflicted with such injuries. Tears would come to her eyes when she heard them talking about him that way. She did not want to accept the fact that he would never embrace her again, that he would never kiss her again, that he would never make love to her again, and that she would never again feel him moving inside of her. He would never again write. He would never again do anything for himself, not even eat; he would only sleep and soil himself.

I thought of the hateful remark that Joy had made, and my blood began to boil, and then, after we finished eating and were sipping hot coffee, the thought came to me of how much I wanted to make Rosie feel good, how much I wanted to caress her, and, as she was gazing at me, as though she were feeling what I was feeling, I was staring at her, looking deeply into her dark eyes and thinking of how much I *really* wanted to fuck her.

"What?" she suddenly asked.

I touched her hand, and I said, "Maybe I shouldn't be admitting this, but, just, well, just thinking of spending the night in bed with you, is, well, making me terribly excited."

Her eyes lit up.

She squeezed my hand.

We left the restaurant and returned directly to the motel room. As soon as we had hung up our coats and jackets and had taken off our shoes, we got on the bed together. She was wearing black slacks and a yellow blouse. Her head was on my right shoulder, facing me as her arm was around my waist, and my right arm was around her, holding her close to me.

"Are you comfortable?" I asked.

"Very. Are you?"

"Holding you like this, how could I not feel comfortable?"

"I'm thinking of that remark that Joy made."

"She really is a bitch. She's just being hateful. She knows that I know that I don't really mean a damn thing to her, but for some reason, she wants to play the role of the abandoned housewife."

"Anyway, I keep hearing her words."

"And that's upsetting you?"

"No. Well, at first it was upsetting, but now it makes me think of, well, of us, doing what she said, as though it's, well, inevitable. I mean, this situation, the way things are happening, makes it seem inevitable. And I don't even want to be thinking about Joy anymore."

"Neither do I."

"I just want to think of you and me, together."

I gazed down at her voluptuous mouth and at her full breasts bulging under her yellow blouse, and I had the urge to reach down, inside of her blouse, and to caress her.

Her dark eyes were questioning me as though she were wondering why I was taking so long to initiate the inevitable.

We were staring at each other, waiting for the other to do or to say something to persuade the other to make the first move, to do what we both wanted to do, what we had both expected by now to be the inevitable. Actually, I was feeling quite shy, like a virgin, I guess, on his wedding night who, in spite of his strong desire, became more concerned about satisfying her than gratifying his own passion.

Sharing a bed to sleep together was not new to us, of course. During her college years we had spent several nights together, but the situation back then had been different.

"In a way," she said, "this reminds me of one of your visits to Harlem, except that it was summer then, and it was hot in my bedroom. You were on my bed with me, telling me about sex. I told you not to cover me with the sheet. I was too hot, especially in my pajamas, even after I had unbuttoned the top part. Do you remember that night?"

"Is that when you were having your menstrual period?"

"No. I had just finished my first year of college, and my folks had gone on their annual trip to Italy. I told you that I wanted your advice, because I felt uncomfortable with the boys in school who had expected me to put out for them. You always gave me good advice. You said the boys would respect me more if I maintained my moral values. You told me I had developed into a beautiful woman with a body that was so ripe, so tempting, that it would drive men wild. The way you described my body, you made it sound so exciting, that I often thought of how much I wanted you to touch it. Do you remember how you described my body?"

"No."

"You called my body the Garden of Paradise, and the entrance, you said, is here, where the man who will father my children will enter me and plant the seeds of life deep inside of me, where it's warm and moist, to create new life. When I feel him penetrating me, my body will tremble with so much pleasure, you said, that as the pleasure becomes even more intense, the inside of me will feel like it's erupting. That's called coming together, you said, with my lover, creating new life. I can't make it sound as wonderful as you did, but the way you described it made me want you to do it to me, to make me feel complete as a real woman. A man and a woman were not yet complete, not until they would experience the coming together to create new life, spectacularly, as the Creator had created the earth, having made the earth shoot out from the sun."

"Is that really how I described making love?"

"You called it sacred, an act of devotion, one of the many gifts with which we had been endowed, but, you also said, too often many ignorant people abused their gifts, twisting it into something dirty, as though nature is dirty, the work of the devil, and could be used to take advantage of others, to have power over them. I was fascinated by you. Don't you remember anything about that night?"

"Yeah," I muttered, "but whenever I thought about that night, it filled me with so much guilt that I pushed a lot of it out of my mind."

"Really? I've thought about that night a lot. You were making me feel like a real woman."

"You were lying back, next to me, on your bed, I remember, and making me, well, horny as hell, especially when I tried to cover your body with the sheet, but you said you were too hot, and you even unbuttoned the top of your pajamas. Even though you were Nick's little sister, I wanted to fuck you right then and there. Were you that innocent? That naïve? Or were you enticing me?"

"I was trying to get you to notice me as a woman, a *real* woman. I wanted you to see how ripe my breasts had gotten; I wanted you to touch them."

"I certainly noticed you!"

"I could see how big your penis was getting, bulging through your trousers, and I even asked you how big it got when you wanted to, well, to fuck, but you wouldn't tell me. I knew, though, that you were getting so excited that you really wanted, well, that you really wanted to fuck me."

"I really did. I wanted you so damn badly!"

"I wanted you to be the one to plant your seeds in my garden. That's why I had opened my pajama tops, to make sure that you would notice my breasts. And you did. You called my breasts the sweetest, succulent, nourishing fruit of the garden. Do you remember?"

"You're making me so damn horny again just thinking about it. Do you remember what I did to you?"

"You grabbed me, and suddenly you got on top of me, and I could feel you pushing against me as though you wanted to, well, to penetrate me, and I grabbed you, wrapping my arms around your back, and I pulled your head down until I felt your mouth pressing against mine. I had never been kissed like that, or had ever experienced a feeling like that before. I was so surprised by how much a kiss could get me so excited. You made me feel so damn good, like a real woman! You knew how much I worshipped you, and after that night you knew how much I wanted you, and you told me how much you wanted me, too, but you told me that I was still much too young for you, even though you were so attracted to me and loved me so much. We would have to wait several more years, you said, and then, if we still felt the same way, we could enjoy making love to each other. I assumed you meant getting married. But," she said, her voice dropping, "you seemed more interested in other, in older, experienced, sexier women. Suddenly, you were married. You married Joy."

We were silent for a long while. I didn't know how to respond.

I finally asked, "Were you a virgin when you married Dante?"

"Of course. I had never even thought of having sex with anyone, except with you."

"Not even with Dante?"

"Not even with Dante, not until I married him. I had thought, as everyone else had, that Dante had been destined for the priesthood. I was the one who probably persuaded him to marry me. If he hadn't married me and had become a priest, what had happened to him never would have happened."

"Don't say that! Never blame yourself for what happened to him. You enriched his life. You made him a wonderful family. Besides, until recently, I wasn't ready for you. I thought I was so damn superior to Dante just because I was bigger than he was. And I resented him a little because he looked white. But he was a lot more courageous and wiser than I'll ever be. When I was younger, especially, I was ashamed of being Italian, and Negro, and French, and as much as I admired my father and my grandmother, I was even ashamed of them just because they were Jewish. And by the time I graduated from high school, I wasn't proud of being Catholic, either. A few years ago, I never would have married you for the same reason I never married Jessica."

"Because she's colored?"

As she was staring at me, I nodded.

We became silent again for a little while.

"Since we were kids," she said softly, "I used to tell Dante I was in love with both of you, and he used to say he hoped I would marry you, because he would become a priest, and he and I would be brother and sister."

"Marrying him was a wise choice. You seemed so happy together, so much in love."

"We were! He was so good, not only to me; he loved everyone! He would have made a good priest."

"Don't ever regret marrying him."

"Of course not. I'm proud that he's the father of my children. I know I shouldn't still be feeling the way I do now, about you, but that's how I've always felt, ever since I can remember, and I know you feel the same way about me."

"The question now is, how will we feel afterwards?"

"Feeling you inside of me can only make me feel stronger, but how will *you* feel afterwards?"

"If you'll feel stronger, that will make me feel better, but if you'll feel worse, I'll feel worse, too."

"We can never feel good when we think about what happened to Dante. That will always pain us. We'll never be able to change that, but together, we can give each other the strength to endure the pain. I know that, with you inside of me, I'll have the love and the will to prevail. I only hope that I can provide you with the same love to make you stronger, too."

I brushed my lips over hers, and then I opened my mouth a little and sucked on hers. Tenderly I brushed my lips over her face and kissed it. And as I moved my lips down her neck, I began to unbutton her blouse. I opened it and uncovered her white bra. The tops of her deep breasts were bulging over the top of her bra. Kissing her warm, soft, smooth flesh, I slid my hands under her blouse, up her smooth back and unhooked her bra, pushed it up, and began to touch her magnificent breasts.

"You have such a voluptuous body!" I said tenderly. "The most beautiful breasts I've ever had the pleasure of seeing and touching. Just by letting me look at you and touching you like this, you make me feel so damn good!"

She was staring at me.

"Why don't we take our clothes off," I suggested, "and get comfortable under the covers?"

She let me undress her. I did not turn the light off, because I wanted to see her naked, and later I'd want to see the expressions on her face as I'd be making love to her. I was filled with utmost confidence and determination to give her the greatest pleasure any woman could endure. As she lay naked on the bed, she was gazing up at me. I stood at the side of the bed and quickly removed my clothing. I crawled into bed and lay beside her.

Gusts of late March winds were blowing snow and sleet against the window, but being naked together under the covers of the bed was making me warm and cozy. Tenderly, with my hands and mouth, I began to explore her beautiful body, kissing her breasts, not only with intense passion, but with deep tenderness. I decided not to penetrate her too soon; I would wait until she could no longer wait. To prevent myself from becoming too excited, I relaxed my thighs and listened to the howling of the wind and the beating of the sleet against the pane of the window. I sucked on her mouth, squeezed the flesh of her opulent breasts, took her rigid nipples into my mouth and sucked on them, and I rubbed my lips down her belly, sucking and kissing it. When her hips began to undulate, I slid my hands under her buttocks, grasped them, and pulled her against me.

For the past few minutes, her mind, like mine, I thought, had been focused only on her and me. We had transcended the outside world, locked together into our own world.

As she felt my hardness between her thighs, ramming against her, she began to moan and to lift her hips, wanting, I thought, to feel my hardness entering her. But I did not enter her, not yet. I pushed myself down, grasped her buttocks, and I buried my face between her warm, soft, smooth thighs, kissing and sucking on her flesh, and feeling her thighs tightening and squeezing my face as her pelvis was rising up, rubbing against my lips.

"I have to throw up!" she cried out, pushing me away.

As I withdrew, she jumped out of bed and dashed into the toilet, leaving the door ajar, and I could hear her retching.

I got out of bed and went into the toilet and stood behind her as she was looking down into the bowl. She had not yet vomited.

"I'm sorry," she whimpered.

"You can't help feeling the way you do."

She turned, facing me.

"The feeling has passed. Just give me a few more seconds."

She put her arms around my waist and pressed the front of her body against mine, making my erection rise up again almost to its fullness.

"Oh!" she cried, "I want so much to make you feel good! I wanted to give you the best, the best fuck you've ever had! I really did!"

"I know, I know you do, but not tonight," I said, holding her. "Listen to what something deep inside of you is saying. You've been badly wounded, and you need time to let your wounds heal. We both do. Let's help each other. Let's get back into bed and let's just relax together. Nothing else. Cappish?"

"Could I at least give you the best hot shower you've ever had?"

4

As soon as Rosie had finished reading the last chapter, she said, "After we returned here, our relationship seemed to change again." When I didn't respond, she said, "Besides, this part doesn't really fit into Dante's story. Why don't you just write the ending?"

I stared at her. The sex scenes between us, I thought, apparently embarrassed her as she thought that someone, especially her own children, would come across this someday and would read it, as she and I had come across my mother's diary.

"What we did," I replied, "I don't regret. As I told you that night, I was happy. I've thought of us, together, that night, giving us the best shower we've ever had. It was fun. And it relaxed us that night,"

She put her warm hand on the top of my thigh as we sat close together. It was still early in the evening, in June, more than two years after Dante had been in the car crash. Darkness had descended, and Dante and the three babies were sleeping. "But I don't understand why it had taken you so long after that to make love to me. More than two years! And I was the one who had initiated it. I even thought that I hadn't interested you in that way, not after, well, after my panic attack in the motel."

"Well, before I answer that, I want to discuss something else with you. I've reread part of Dante's script. The first thing I noticed is that he called it *Rose of the Flats*, which refers to you, of course. He begins with your wedding night, and then he tells the story of my grandparents, and he even tells the story of me and Joy and of me and Minnie. So, he wasn't just telling his own story. He was writing about all of us, and the theme is prejudice and how it affects us, how it divides us with fear and hatred. So, what happens to you and me, especially as the consequences of racism, is part of this story. Do you agree with that?"

"Yes," she admitted softly, "I do. And what has sustained us, even strengthened us, you and me, is our love for each other. Do you agree with that?"

"Yes," I answered. "And I wanted to prove to myself that I was motivated by love, for you and for Dante, and not by wanting to satisfy my sexual urges for you. But I had become aware of how strong my sexual attraction for you is. And, wisely or not, I made a vow."

"A vow? What was the vow?"

"Well, you've heard of Faust, selling his soul to the devil. If I had believed in the devil, I would have sold my soul to him, too, but you could say that I tried to make a deal with God, in spite of what Tattone had told me of God."

"What did he tell you?"

"When I told him that Dante had been wounded in Korea, Tattone said there is God beyond the gods we have created in our image."

She grinned at me.

"Actually, I tried to bribe the god I had created in my image by promising that I would not touch you again for at least six months. I had thought of making it much longer, but I wanted to make sure I could restrain myself for a reasonable amount of time. I had promised my god I would restrain myself if Dante had miraculously made some improvement, and after six months, after Dante seemed to have improved a little, I renewed my vow. And every six months, I renewed it until, well, until a couple of months ago."

"Dante was religious, but I never knew that you were."

"And when it came to enjoying sex, we had opposing views. Sex to him appealed to our animal nature, which we had to learn how to control. But to me, sex has always been my greatest pleasure, and I had to enjoy it whenever I could."

"I always knew that about you, and when it seemed that you were no longer attracted to me, I just let myself withdraw from everything, just going through the motions, until I dreamt of you making love to me. And after I had read that ugly sex scene between you and Joy, I knew how, well, how much you really needed me, and how much I needed you, too. But why did you wait two whole years? A year, even six months, would have been proof enough that you wanted me out of love, not just for sex."

"Well, anyway, to restrain my desires, I tried to channel them, and I began having dreams, too, dreams about morality and religion. I read *Dark Night of the Soul* by John of the Cross, and I studied the book about the history and evolution of religion that my father, like Dante, hadn't quite finished writing. Since the restaurant had closed, and I hadn't the incentive to sell insurance, and in spite of driving you back and forth almost every day to Vermont, I studied my father's book, and I even had a dream about the latest prophet he had written about, the prophet who had died before the twentieth century, just a few years before my father was born."

I had always thought of my father as being more Catholic than a lot of people I know who call themselves Catholic. He was more Catholic than my mother or my French Canadian grandparents were. As an infant he had been baptized in the Church in Italy, but when he became an adult, he decided that he was more Jewish. To be truly Catholic, he thought, there were certain doctrines that one had to accept. My father could not, in good conscience, accept the doctrine of the Trinity, that there are three persons in one God, as there are three leaves to one clover, the analogy that St. Patrick, the Roman missionary who had converted Ireland, had used. To most people, that's not important, that it's merely a play on words. Nevertheless, it's a concept, a belief that is required to be Catholic. And a Christian, my father believed, is someone who believes that Jesus is, also, in fact, not simply a Manifestation of God, but God, and had become man—true God and true man. My father had been unable to see the necessity for God having literally become truly human for thirty-three years, a man that was, by definition, omnipotent, and was, therefore, unable to choose evil even though He had been tempted by Satan. Jesus was divine, of course. What we call love, my father believed, was seeing and being attracted to the divine in others, of seeing the divine, the good, in everything that has been created. And everything that is, that has existence, has been created by the Creator. Jesus was, perhaps, the most divine of any person, more divine than Moses, perhaps, closest to God, perhaps, than any other man. But if Jesus is literally God, why hadn't that been stated explicitly in the New Testament? Does God not want us to know? Jesus is also the Son of God. But are we not all children of God? And is the son equal to the father? A Catholic is required, according to the laws of the Church, to accept certain doctrines on faith, such as believing that Jesus is, in fact, God, and had died, and on the third day, had been resurrected, and that Mary, the mother, had been a virgin (the miracle of the Immaculate Conception), and a Catholic is required to go to confession to a priest and to receive Holy Communion at least once a year. To deliberately reject the requirements, a Catholic is automatically excommunicated. If a Catholic cannot accept any article of faith in good conscience, then he must, according to Catholic doctrine, abide by his own conscience, the ultimate guide and authority. My father had never actually disavowed Catholicism. Before he had married my mother, he had gone to a local priest, not in the confessional, but directly to the house of the priest, next to the church, and had told the priest his situation, that he had been raised Catholic by his Jewish mother, but he could not believe that because he had expressed love physically to a woman to whom he wanted to marry that if they had suddenly died before confessing their "mortal" sin, they would both be condemned forever in hellfire. He had believed, he told the priest, that heaven was a state of closeness to God and that hell was a state of relative separation from God, and that in the afterlife we would continue to know and to love God more. The priest had known that my father knew more Catholic theology and doctrine than he did, and wisely, the priest asked my father, "If you were in my place, what advice would you give?" My father thought for a few moments and said, "Even though sin is an act that is contrary to the laws of God, and is therefore evil, because the consequences of such an act is destructive, not creative, I don't feel, according to my conscience, that I'm guilty of committing evil. On the contrary, I've made the woman I love joyful, therefore I cannot be sorry, but if I were a priest I would advise me to go to confession anyway, especially since I want to marry a Catholic woman in the Church, to be joined together, she and I, by God, and I would advise me to go to Holy Communion with her, and to let God be my judge." And the priest said, "Interesting," and he told my father he would hear his confession immediately. Afterwards the priest suggested they have a glass of white wine in celebration of his coming marriage.

"By the way," the priest asked, "why did your mother, a Jewish woman, choose a Latin name for you?"

"What better name could a Jewish mother, who was born and raised in Rome, give to her son, who, according to Jewish tradition, is also Jewish, and is a gift from God, and who is about to be baptized into the Latin rites of the Catholic Church? The Latin name, Amadeus, means the love of God."

In the preface to his section on Judaism, which my father titled *Who I Am*, he wrote:

> *Tell me something. Can there be anything wrong with me? I know there are some people who are reluctant to blame themselves when something is not quite what it should be, because I'm one of them. If I tell you something that I think is profound, I don't enjoy your reaction a bit if you tell me I'm full of it. On the other hand, if there's nothing wrong with me, that definitely means there's something wrong with the world. But, I've been taught, the world was created by an intelligent, loving, omnipotent God, and that everything He created was very good. Now, I know I didn't create myself, that I came into the world that was already here, so there's no question, to me, that existence has a source, which is uncreated and eternal. My question, then, is "Who is God?" As in Genesis, I speak of "Him" not as a bearded old man floating on a cloud above us, but as a person-*

ified "Other" to Whom I can relate a little easier than to a What. *Not that I expect to truly understand Him, for my finite intelligence can't contain the infinite. So, God created nature, including human nature, making man in His image, "a little lower than the gods," and gave man dominion over the earth, and everything He created is very good, including me. Yet things are not always what they ought to be. If I have been given dominion over the earth, then that makes me responsible, and if there's something wrong, I guess God expects me to change it. He made me, then, to take part in the Creation. An animal does what it's supposed to do by its very nature. But how can I be responsible if, like the animal, I'm confined to that order and lack the ability to understand how it works? So, when God created Adam and Eve, He endowed them not only with the ability to know, but with the freedom to act as they will. In the psalm: "I was born guilty, a sinner when my mother conceived me," doesn't mean we are naturally attracted to evil; it simply means that we haven't developed our potentials, the* amore, *the* imago dei *in each of us, our divinity, and, as such, not having perfected ourselves, as in exercising our free wills, we are prone to making mistakes, to sin, which means, in Hebrew, "to miss the mark," which is not quite the same as saying we are inclined, through our nature, to evil. But, if those mistakes are harmful, they are not good, they are sinful. And the first, or original sin was depicted in the story of Adam and Eve, who, in choosing to eat the forbidden fruit and not knowing the consequences of their action, though they were tempted by the serpent, by their curiosity to know, they had the alternative not to eat the fruit. But, thinking it might be good, they ate from the tree of life, and then they knew good and evil, and they were expelled from Paradise, in the same way that a person who, in committing, as he is bound to do, sin for the first time, must be held responsible, because he is the agent of his actions even though he acted in ignorance. But God has endowed us with intelligence and with the ability to love. That's what makes us truly human.*

So, who am I? According to Jewish tradition, a Jew is anyone whose mother is Jewish, or anyone who has converted to Judaism or who has been brought up in the Jewish faith regardless of whether that person continues to practice the faith or not. As a Jew, I will never be excommunicated. I am not required by any authority to believe in any particular doctrine. Even an atheist can claim to be a Jew. But to me, that's like an acorn claiming to be an oak tree. The more one embodies the Jewish faith, the more Jewish one is.

5

When Rosie and I had become sexually intimate, our relationship, of course, changed, and we had felt much closer to each other, but still, I wanted to prove, at least to myself, that I had acted out of love, not out of lust, although I had not told her of the vow I had made until two years later, because I hadn't been sure that I'd be able to keep it. It had not included all women, however, and I thought that would make it much easier to keep. Anyway, when I had made Rosie my one temporarily forbidden fruit, I hadn't really had that much interest in other women. I had thought about that back then, even though the only other woman who had been available to me was Minnie, and since she had become the acting principal, she had become quite busy, especially as she had been preparing the graduation class. The only one with whom I had discussed my vow was Jessica, and she had told me that she understood how Rosie felt, that Rosie had always loved me and had been sexually attracted to me.

Jessica said that she had read somewhere that there is an ancient Jewish law, in the book of Deuteronomy, that an unmarried brother is required to marry the widow of his dead brother.

First of all, I replied to her, that I was not technically unmarried yet, and that Rosie was not yet the widow of my dead brother, and furthermore, neither Rosie nor I were Jewish. And, according to Jewish law, the widow can refuse to marry her husband's brother.

"All I'm saying is that, if you were both Jewish, she would be foolish to refuse to marry you, especially since she's so attracted to you and so close to you and trusts you so much, and she knows that your technically lawful, civil marriage will not last much longer. And, as you both well know, Dante is expected to die at any time now. You and Rosie have to be prepared for that."

"Rosie says that she and Dante couldn't understand why I hadn't married you a long time ago, especially since, well, since I had gotten you pregnant."

"Have you ever told anyone what I had done for a living when we had met?"

"No."

"That's understandable. I'm not proud of it either. Besides, I told you I had never expected you to marry me."

"But they're right; I should have married you."

"We were both too young."

"But it would have worked."

"Maybe, and maybe not. If we had gotten married at that time, you would have needed more time to accept what I was. You've never told anyone what I did, because you were too ashamed of it. I was, too. So, I know how you felt, and how you still feel."

"Maybe we should still get married."

"Except that you're already married, and that Rosie needs you now. I mean, she really needs you, not for sex, but for someone to be with her, to provide her with strength, someone in whom she has faith. And she has always trusted you. She really needs you now, to be with her."

"So, what do you think of the vow I made?"

"As a vow to God? Not much. I can understand praying to God for guidance, but not trying to bribe God, telling Him that if He performs a miracle, which is what it would take to make Dante better, that you will abstain from having sex with Dante's wife. It's commendable of you to abstain from having sex with her simply to prove to yourself that you love her enough to support her without her repaying you with sex. Make a vow to yourself, and maybe to her, to prove not only to yourself, but to her, that you're acting out of love for her, supporting her, because you love her, not because you want, well, to fuck her."

Jessica had driven up alone from New York on a Friday to accompany me and Rosie to visit Dante at the hospital in Vermont. Afterwards, she followed us to Cascade. Later that evening in early June, Jessica and I had gone for a ride to talk. I would return her to Rosie's house where she would spend the weekend with Rosie and her mother.

"What if," I asked while driving leisurely, "Rosie wants me to have sex with her?"

"Are you asking me what you should do if she wants you to have sex with her even though you made the vow?"

"Yes."

"I assume you want to have sex with her, so you want me to convince you that it would make her feel so much better than if you would deny her. But the question is still, are you doing it to her out of love for her, or out of lust? The only way to prove you're acting out of love is to deny yourself."

"How would you feel if I told you I made that vow with *you?*"

"Interesting question. I'd might enjoy seducing you, to feel that I can entice you to do something that you can't resist."

"I get your point."

"Why don't we go parking?"

"Jessica, you know I've always loved you, and that I've always respected you. And that's never going to change, but my relationship with Rosie, well, that's different. We were practically raised together. I need to talk about her, seriously."

"You really love her!"

"Yes, I do."

"I mean, you *really* love her. You always have. Ever since I've known her, she seemed to worship you so much. And you've known, deep down, how she's always felt about you, but, for some reason, you've denied it to yourself. Why?"

I didn't answer her.

After a brief silence, she said, "I've never seen you like this before. You and I never had any problems exciting each other, until now, anyway."

"Well, that hasn't changed."

"Yes, it has. And that's fine. Our relationship goes way beyond sex. You're the father of my son, and I'm the mother of your child. And, I'll always be able to say that. So, you and I are special to each other. I may even like you better this way. At least I know your attraction to me is more than sexual. And I've always liked Rosie. But I can't help thinking of her as the wife of Dante, which she still is. Anyway, I like the idea of you abstaining from sex with her. But, please, don't try to bribe God. I've always given you credit for being wiser than that. Just make up your mind that your love for her is much greater than your sexual attraction is, that you will do what is most beneficial to her. That's the Tony I love."

"I knew you'd give me good advice. You always do. You really are a remarkable woman. And I'm not going to mention anything to her about a vow; I'm simply going to do what I should do, to do what's right because it's right, to follow my conscience, to abstain from sex, all sex, just to prove to myself I'm acting out of love and not out of lust."

We became silent again for a little while.

"Did she ever ask you why we hadn't married?"

"Yeah," I answered. "She said she hoped it wasn't because you're colored."

"What? What did you tell her?"

"I don't remember. I think I told her we were too young."

"If you gave her the impression that you wouldn't marry me because I'm colored, she must think you would never want her, either, that you prefer someone like Joy. Maybe she thinks that's why you married a white woman."

"That's ridiculous!"

6

In the middle of April, the greatest scientist of our time, Albert Einstein, died. Due to anti-Semitism (if *he* was inferior, what does that make *me?*) he had been driven out of Germany in 1933 and had immigrated to the United States. On speaking of faith, he has been quoted as saying, "I believe in the brotherhood of man and the uniqueness of the individual. But if you ask me to prove what I believe, I can't." And then he added: "There comes a point where the mind takes a higher plane of knowledge but can never prove how it got there. All great discoveries have involved such a leap."

Rosie had wanted Dante to return home by the Monday of June 20, on their third wedding anniversary. Nonna and Tattone had agreed to move upstairs for what we had thought would be a temporary arrangement so that Rosie and Dante could occupy the downstairs apartment. We hadn't even bothered to change most of the furniture. The doctors had warned us that Dante would not continue to live for more than a few more months. Rosie had wanted him at home when he would die.

On that Monday, almost two years ago, Dante had returned home.

Three nights before that, had been graduation night, and Rosie and I had been invited by Minnie to attend the graduation ceremonies. The high school seniors from Cascade Flats gave a special presentation in honor of Dante, telling the audience who he was and how devoted he had been to them and to education. And then

Minnie gave her presentation. She began by telling the audience who she was. She was a woman who was proud that her Pilgrim ancestors had come over on *The Mayflower*, and she was proud to refer to them as the Founding Fathers of America, and she ended up by telling the audience who Dante was.

Shortly after she had moved up here from Boston to teach English, she had heard of a religious group called the Templars of the Holy Spirit, an exclusively white Protestant group, whose purpose was to unite to make America pure again.

She had truly believed that her Pilgrim ancestors (although they had received very little formal education) were superior beings who had been looking for the promised land so that they could freely worship God according to their own beliefs. At first (according to her testimony) they had tried to reform the politically and morally corrupt Church of England, which, until the previous century, had been part of the Roman Catholic Church (and as corrupt and false) with its display of decorative garments and statues and music, but her ancestors, reluctant to conform to the rules of the Church, had suffered terrible persecutions by the other members of the Church, and finally, wanting to separate themselves entirely from the English Church, some of them had fled from England to Holland, where they were allowed to practice their religion. However, there was so much freedom in Holland that even the Jews were allowed to practice their religion.

So, they left Holland on *The Mayflower*, which took them to New England, to Plymouth Rock, where, free from the corrupt authorities in England, and in the rest of Europe, they were free to practice their Christianity according to the rules of their own beliefs.

The only other people using the nearby land in the new world, if in fact, they could be called people, were very simple. They obviously knew nothing about religion and morality and civilized society, and not only did they know nothing about becoming wealthy as individuals, sharing the land and the food with each other, like a pack of wild animals, having no concepts of ownership of private property, and although they lived separately from the Pilgrims, they actually taught the Pilgrims how to survive during the frigid conditions of the wilderness. And, in the beginning, the Pilgrims followed the communistic way of the Indians, sharing the work, and the land, and the food with each other, until they had become firmly established and successful, but what really made the Pilgrims superior to their new neighbors was, obviously, their pure religion, especially their belief that human nature is evil and had to be suppressed.

Those few among the Pilgrims who were filled with pride and other sinful inclinations and were stubborn and would refuse to conform, to attend religious services regularly, and to follow the moral laws, disrupting the unity and the harmony of their religious community, were punished. Their way of life was strict, but the path of righteousness was indeed narrow. Thus the colony grew and prospered into the greatest country the world has ever known, in the promised land, in the only country that has ever known freedom.

"The freedom," she said, "which we have inherited from my Pilgrim ancestors, the first Americans."

She paused to let that sink in.

"Of course I'm proud of my ancestors! I'm proud to be an American! I eagerly joined the Templars of the Holy Spirit. I, too, wanted to make America pure again. You're probably wondering what this has to do with Dante Valentino."

In her first year of teaching here, she had the privilege of teaching one of her most brilliant students. He had questioned her on what and who was an American. Why had she thought of the English Pilgrims as Americans, the first Americans, and not the indigenous people as Americans also? And she had told her student that an American was a citizen of the United States of America, and that did not include the indigenous people, because they did not qualify as American citizens. But, the student had replied, neither did the Pilgrims; the United States had not yet become a country. But their descendants, she answered, children of the Pilgrims, had become citizens; they had inherited their ideals and their country from their founding fathers.

"You are saying, then, that the original Americans were the Pilgrims, who were also Puritans from England, who were superior to others, that they believed that human nature is evil and had to be suppressed, and that the people who had lived here for centuries were not Americans."

"Yes," she had replied. "Our country had been founded on the highest ideals of the Puritans, on their Christian ideals."

"But," the young student had argued, "the wealth, including the slave plantations of the property owners, according to the Puritans, was proof that they had been looked upon favorably by Divine Providence, and that in countries in which the population was predominately Catholic, and poor, was proof of the falseness of their religion. Yet you accuse the Catholic Church of being excessively wealthy, and therefore, of being corrupt. How can this be?"

"The wealth of their Church, I informed the student, had been extracted from the followers of the Church, not to the benefit of its followers, but to make the Church, the institution, its leaders, more powerful than its followers, and more influential, giving them control of its followers. It was the same situation that Jesus had encountered two thousand years ago with the Jews. This concept had been recognized by the Puritans, who had seen the merits in the ideas of some Roman Catholic priests, such as Martin Luther and John Calvin, who sought to purify the Church, and to return to the roots, to the origins of Christianity. And now, ten years later, as I look back on the short life of that student, Dante Valentino, who had become a devoted teacher whose love deeply touched not only each of his students, but all who had come into contact with him, I see another side of the Temple of the Holy Spirit, a dark side, of which I am terribly ashamed; I see Satan, with whom we have made a deal, to whom we have sold our souls, who has twisted our minds with blinding hatred, who has tempted us with the belief that we are the only worthy, righteous children of God who must distance ourselves always from others, to condemn them, to preserve our own purity. It was I," she told the audience, "a member of the Temple of the Holy Spirit, who submitted the pamphlets of our insidious hatred of other people to the local newspaper. And I have reported to the police that a member of the Temple had taken the shot in an attempt to silence Dante Valentino, as someone had done also to his father just nine years earlier."

A gasp rose up from the stunned audience.

Why, I wondered, had she announced that publicly, at this grad-uation ceremony, putting herself in such jeopardy? At that moment, Rosie grasped my hand and squeezed it, and I felt her deep admira-tion of Minnie.

During that weekend we prepared the downstairs for Dante's return. The floor plans of the rooms downstairs were the same as the rooms upstairs.

On the following Monday afternoon, an ambulance stopped in front of the house, and Dante was put on a stretcher and taken through the front door, through the front room, and to the front bedroom facing the street. We put him in a crib. Next to the crib was a bed in which Rosie would sleep. She said she would sleep better now with Dante sleeping in the same room. Opposite the kitchen was the middle bedroom where her mother would sleep, at least until she would return to New York near the end of summer.

The routine for Rosie and me to take care of Dante had begun on that day, on their third wedding anniversary. He could sit in a chair quietly for hours, sometimes. He even seemed to notice Angela most of the time as she would give him her dolls or other toys, espe-cially something with bright colors. In the morning, we'd bathe him in the bathtub. Rosie had purchased a special tub, one in which he could sit in one section, and we could push a barrier down so that his body would not slide down into the deeper part of the tub, and we could shower him, or we could let him soak in hot water at the other end of the tub. In the deeper end, he seemed to enjoy splashing the water. Whenever we'd let him in the deeper end, Rosie would wear one of my white undershirts so she could remove it after we'd bathe him. I would act as though I would hardly notice that her beautiful breasts were showing through the undershirt and was stimulating my desire for her. After a year or so you'd think I'd no longer get aroused, especially in the presence of my brother, even though he hadn't been aware of what was happening, but trying to restrain my urges hadn't become any easier. One time when she was wearing only a bra to cover part of her bosom, somehow Dante had grasped her bra with his right hand. Instinctively I reached out to remove his hand, but his grip was strong. He pulled on her bra, and one of her breasts popped out. I grabbed it, held it, and I didn't want to let go of it. Her dark eyes penetrated me, and a craving deep inside of her was stimulating mine. Dante finally released her bra and, as she tucked her breast inside of her bra again, we both felt in the other what we wanted to do with each other. I could almost hear her saying, "I want you! Now!" The way she was looking at me, I swear she could hear me thinking how much I wanted her, too. And I knew she was wondering why I had gone so long without even attempting to find a way to be alone with her. At that particular time in the afternoon her daughters were taking a nap, and her mother and my mother had gone shopping in Berlin. As soon as we'd finish bathing Dante, he, too, would take a nap, and if we'd want, Rosie and I could easily get into her bed together while Dante would be sleeping.

After we had put Dante in the crib, Minnie, who had been shopping in Berlin, stopped to visit us on her way home. By the time she left, it was almost time for Rosie to prepare our evening meal. So, thanks to Minnie, the temptation that day had come and gone.

After Dante had returned home from the hospital, I had stayed with them most of the day even though my mother had told us to eat in the restaurant, which had been closed to the public during Dante's first four weeks in the hospital. My mother, who had seemed pale and listless during that time, had decided she'd feel better being occupied. Joy seemed happier that my mother had resumed working, too, because she had more free time away from my mother. I returned home each night to sleep in my own bed. Taking care of Dante had become a full time job, and after we'd put him in his crib to sleep, I'd stay with Rosie for a while, and then I'd kiss her good night and go home, but after I'd kiss her good night, neither of us wanted to part. However, while her mother was staying with her, I didn't think we had much choice.

Two weeks after Dante had returned home was the Fourth of July. That was on a Monday, and the restaurant was closed. The next day Rosie and I went to the restaurant for a spaghetti dinner. It was a fairly slow evening. While Rosie stayed in a booth in the dining room, I went into the kitchen to see how my mother was doing. As soon as I went through the swinging doors, I saw my mother sitting in a chair under an opened window. She seemed paler than usual.

"Your mother is tired," my Aunt Maria said. "I told her to take the night off. We don't need her, but she's so damn stubborn!"

I felt her forehead. It was so cold and clammy that it frightened me.

"Ma, you don't look well. I'm going to drive you to the hospital."

"Don't be crazy! I'll be fine. I just need to rest."

"It won't hurt to check you out. Just to take your blood pressure, at least."

"No! I'm not going to the hospital."

"Just for a quick check up. We'll come right back."

"I said no!"

"Well, go in the house, at least, and lie down."

"Toni," my aunt said, "go in the house and rest, please. You'll make us feel better."

"Suppose it gets busy in here?"

"I'll go get you. I promise. Go in the house and lie down."

My mother nodded, and she stood up. I took her by the elbows to steady her.

"I don't need your help. I'm not that old yet."

Rosie entered the kitchen.

"My mother is going in the house to lie down."

"Do you mind if I come, too, Ma? Let me hold on to you."

"Hold on to me? Why?"

"So I won't fall."

"You? Fall? You're the strong one in this family. You're the one who's keeping us going."

We didn't take her upstairs; we kept her downstairs, on the couch, where Joy could keep an eye on her, and then Rosie and I returned to the restaurant to eat. After we finished eating, we went into the house to see how my mother was doing. She was sound asleep on the couch.

Rosie and I returned to her house.

Her mother had bathed the babies, and they were sleeping in their cribs. Maria, like Angela, was now at the stage where she, too, would usually sleep all night. And Rosie's mother had fed Dante.

"There was certainly nothing wrong with his appetite tonight," she said.

He could only eat soft or grounded up food. We kept a grinder clamped onto the edge of a smaller table between the kitchen table and the sink where we would turn a crank to grind meat and other foods. That evening Anna had fed him hamburger cooked with scrambled eggs with lots of fried onions and garlic and several other spices.

"I even cooked enough for myself."

Dante was sitting quietly in the front room facing the television. The final task of the day for Rosie and me was to give him a bath. After he would fall asleep in his crib, he, like the kids, would usually sleep all night. I've often wondered if he had ever dreamed anymore. Sometimes Rosie and I would look at him while he was asleep, and we would look for any indications, any movements, of dreams he could have been having. To even think that he could possibly be having any dreams stimulated our imaginations.

There were times when her mother was not with us that Rosie would try to elicit a response from him when he had been awake, especially after a bath, by touching his genitals. Sometimes he even seemed to be on the verge of getting aroused.

"If I thought I could make it get hard again," she had once said to me, "and that it would give him pleasure, I wouldn't hesitate to do it to him. Imagine getting pregnant by him again! If he could respond to me," she murmured, but she didn't tell me the rest of her thought.

I imagined Dante in bed with her, and that somehow her body was stimulating his, that it was giving him pleasure, but although he was still her lawfully wedded husband, the thought of them indulging in such an act, now, somehow seemed grotesque. Why? I wondered. Maybe, I thought, the circumstances would be so unusual, and therefore seemed unnatural. Even the thought of me fucking her, not out of love, but just doing it to gratify our sexual desires, the way it had felt with Joy, and even with Minnie, seemed less perverse. It even seemed more natural. I wondered about that.

Joy used to call me a sex maniac, never in an endearing way, though. She really meant it. Maybe she was right. I had even thought I was, sometimes.

During the hot summer days when Rosie would be wearing tight shorts and a snug blouse with a low neckline but no bra, uncovering most of her tantalizing flesh, I could hardly look at her without wanting to grab her, drop her on her bed, pull her shorts down, undo her blouse, suck on her beautiful breasts, and to plunge myself deep inside of her hot, voluptuous body. My desire for her would become so damn intense that she had surely felt it, I thought, especially when we would bathe Dante, and her scant clothing had become soaked. I longed to feast my eyes on her completely naked body again and to caress every part of her. Whenever she would see me gazing at her body, I would feel that she knew what I was feeling, because she, too, felt the same craving, I told myself. A part of me didn't want to think of her that way, of thinking of me fucking her, but I *did* think of it, and the thought of her letting me fuck her, of wanting me to do it to her because it also gave her so damn much pleasure, excited the hell out of me. I had often thought of that hot shower we had taken together in the motel. We have always known each other, and we have always loved each other, of course, but at the same time, we had been, and we still are, strongly attracted to each other sexually, and that alone was enough to make our passions swell up and explode. Yet, I didn't want to think of either of us acting only out of lust. When I had thought even of Jessica having sex with other men, I couldn't tolerate the thought. I certainly could not stand the thought of Rosie being promiscuous, of letting other guys have sex with her, too. I didn't even want to think of her as wanting to have sex, even though I knew, of course, that my feelings were so absurd. Sometimes it's difficult to accept things as they are, as though we don't have the strength or the faith in ourselves to cope with reality. When I thought of it, I didn't want to think of her as *not* wanting to have sex, either. Oh, well. My ideal woman is a sexy woman who only wants, and likes, to have sex with *me*, only with me.

Back then, even her mother had asked her if she and I had been sexually attracted to each other. Rosie had been too embarrassed to admit it to her own mother, who had known that Joy and I slept "American style" not "Italian style" because Joy did not want more babies, and her mother knew that whenever I said good night to Rosie, she and I would always sneak off to a dark corner so that her mother would not see how I would kiss her good night. I was a man who needed a woman, her mother said, and she, Rosie, would soon need a man, if she hadn't already needed a man now. I was a man who was taking good care of my brother, and taking good care of his children as their own father would, and, her mother said, I was a good man who wanted to take good care of Rosie. If her own mother had suspected anything between Rosie and me, I thought, surely others would suspect the same. What could be more natural in our circumstances than for us to want to be, and to sleep, with each other? But I had to prove to myself, if not to Rosie, that I wanted her for *herself*, for love, not only because I wanted so much to make love to her. So often I have mistaken a strong sexual attraction for love. So often I had felt that it was so easy to love an attractive, sexy woman. The ideal, I thought, is for me to be sexually attracted to the woman I love. To love, then, precedes sex; love is stronger than sex. When we love another person, we love the good in that person; we are attracted to the divine in that person. And to be sexually attracted to the person I love is the ideal. You can also say, "I love the person to whom I am sexually attracted, because I am sexually attracted to the person I love." But if I think I love a woman to whom I am sexually attracted, because she's sexually attractive, sex is stronger than love. And I am attracted to the physical beauty of that person, which is fine, but my feelings are directed only to the superficial aspects of her, not to the whole person.

If I love Rosie, and if I love my brother, I should have the strength that is stronger than my sex urges. I should have enough strength to abstain from sex for a lot more than only six months, and I had become determined to prove it. Taking care of Dante would occupy my time and my thoughts long enough to remind me of my determination to fulfill my vow, and it would strengthen my resolve to remain on the straight path.

But I needed a better way, I thought, of controlling my passions without losing my passions. When I thought about it, I became aware that I didn't have to worry too much about losing my passions, not my sexual passions, anyway, not unless I became sick. All I had to do was think of Rosie. I didn't even have to think of anything sexy with her. If I just imagined that I was kissing her tenderly on the lips, that little tyrant down below would suddenly pop up. "You have something you want me to do for you, master?" That little part of me, of course, was appealing to my vanity, calling me master. It knew damn well what my biggest influence was. I had been given enough intelligence to govern myself, but that always took a little effort on my part, and even though the tyrant, in size, was nothing compared to the serpent that had seduced Eve, it boldly asserted itself, rising up to its greatest strength. "Let me take her for you, master. She can't resist me. I'll make her want to give you the greatest pleasure of your life by letting you do to her, that beautiful, sexy looking woman, whatever you desire to do to her." If I would let that little tyrant control me, what chance did she have? What chance did any woman have, no matter how morally upright she was? And, what chance did I have?

7

After we had given Dante a bath and had put him in his crib, he went to sleep almost immediately, and as Rosie and I sat on the couch to watch television, her mother heated a pot of coffee, and we relaxed with coffee and anisette.

Even though it was after the fourth of July, almost as soon as the sun went down, the night became chilly, and we closed all the windows and the doors to the outside.

After a while, Anna said, "I think the anisette is making me sleepy. I'm going to leave the two of you together, so behave yourselves. I'm going to bed. Buona notte."

"You're going to bed so early? Are you okay, Ma?" Rosie asked.

"I'm fine. I told you, I'm just sleepy."

She had been sitting at the other end of the couch, and Rosie was between us. As soon as her mother left us, I, sitting near the entrance of the kitchen where I usually sat, reached out and put my hand over Rosie's shoulders. Immediately, she drew against me and leaned her head on my right shoulder.

She was at least five months pregnant, and her breasts and her belly were getting bigger.

"It feels so good to relax like this," she said. "You make me feel so comfortable, that if I close my eyes, I'll fall asleep immediately. I wish," she whispered, "that we could sleep together again. Don't you?"

I planted a kiss on her forehead.

"You know I do, but we shouldn't even be thinking about it, especially with your mother here."

"My mother," she whispered in my ear, "knows we love each other. She even thinks we, well, you know, want to be alone. That's why she's gone to bed so early. We don't have to do anything in bed, you know. Just be comfortable together and sleep."

"We couldn't do anything else, anyway, not now."

"What do you mean?"

"Well, when Joy got pregnant, we had to wait at least six months before the baby was born, and at least six months after he was born."

"Of course not! Dante and I use to do it whenever we'd want. Besides, I know what I look like now. I know I don't appeal to you, anyway, not looking like this."

"This still appeals to me," I said as I kissed her long and tenderly on her mouth.

"Let's get in my bed," she whispered, "at least until I fall asleep."

"If I get in your bed with you, I won't want to leave; I'd want to spend the whole night with you."

"Let's do it then. Let's sleep together, the whole night."

When I seemed hesitant, thinking of her mother in the next room, Rosie whispered in my ear, "You don't have to be amorous, you know; just sleep with me."

"If you want us to just sleep together, I'm willing."

We stood up. As she flicked the light on in the bedroom, I turned off the television. She stood beside the crib and gazed down at Dante, who seemed to be sleeping peacefully with his mouth opened a little.

"He seems to be, well, normal," she said, "when he's sleeping like this, especially with the blanket covering him, as though he still has both of his arms and legs, except, of course, for the scars on his face."

"I know," I muttered, drawing close to her and putting my hand over her hips and rubbing her a little.

His crib was near the front window to the street. A shade had been pulled down, and red drapes had been drawn, covering the window. On the other side of the room was an average sized bed near the wall of the middle bedroom.

"I want to go to the bathroom first," I said.

I went through the parlor again, through the kitchen, past the middle bedroom, past the babies' room, and into the bathroom. When I returned to the front bedroom, Rosie, in her pajamas, was in bed and was waiting for me. The covers on my side of her bed had been pulled down, leaving a space for me, and she was smiling at me. She was radiant. As she lay on her side, facing me, her body covered by red pajamas, and she was gazing at me, I could feel the deep warmth of her love penetrating me. She was so damn beautiful! She had become the closest person in my life, the one person I wanted to be with. For us to be together seemed so damn natural!

I sat on the bed and gazed back at her, admiring her. She took my right hand in both of hers, pulled it to her lips, and she kissed it. She unbuttoned the top four buttons of her pajamas, and she held my hand against her breasts.

Someone was at the front door, pounding on it, and the door opened.

I jumped up, put on my trousers, entered the parlor, and turned on a light.

It was my Aunt Maria.

"Sorry to barge in here like this, but I have to give you some bad news. Your mother passed away! Oh, I knew she didn't look good. I told her earlier. Oh, I wish she had let you take her to the hospital! She's so damn stubborn! Why didn't she listen to you?"

I put my hands on her shoulders.

"Calm down, Zizi."

She leaned against me. She was sobbing.

"I can't help it!" she cried. "I closed the restaurant immediately. I can't work anymore tonight."

Anna, in a bathrobe, and Rosie, in her pajamas, came into the parlor.

"She died in her sleep. Joy is with her. She came in the restaurant to tell me, and she called the ambulance. They're there now, waiting for you. They're going to take her to the hospital so a doctor can officially pronounce her dead, they said. The medics tried to revive her, but they said she had been dead for too long. They're waiting for us now."

"Go now," Rosie said to me. "I'll be there in a few minutes. Ma, stay here and watch the babies."

"Let's go," I said to Zizi.

As soon as we stepped outside, I could see red lights flashing.

We ran along the path to the front street where people were lingering. An ambulance was parked in front of my house. We ran across the street, to the front door, which was open.

As soon as we entered the house, a stretcher with my mother on it was almost blocking the entrance. I looked down at my mother's face. She didn't seem real. Nothing about that scene seemed real. I was in a daze. Joy dutifully came up to me, put her arms around me, and said, "I'm sorry." I don't remember if I nodded or if I even responded to her. I kept looking at my mother. I couldn't believe that she was dead. Before I knew it, someone spread the cover over her face, and she was carried through the doorway and pushed into the rear of the ambulance. I was following the stretcher out of the house. The back doors of the ambulance closed, and a little while later, the ambulance, with it's red lights flashing, pulled away, turned left on the road, went past the entrance of the mill, and disappeared.

Someone grabbed my right arm. It was Rosie. She led me back into the house, into the front room. We stood together near the front entrance. She was holding my arm against her breast. For some reason, I didn't want to go any farther into the house. Joy was sitting on the couch. My Aunt Maria was standing between me and the doorway of the kitchen. I don't remember seeing anyone else in the house, although others were there, too.

"I don't want to stay here, not tonight," I said in a low tone to my aunt.

She looked puzzled.

"I mean, I don't feel comfortable here, not tonight. I can't sleep here."

"I understand. Go back to the house now and take care of Dante. I don't think I can sleep upstairs tonight, anyway. I'll sleep down here tonight. I have to go back into the restaurant now. I didn't want to kick the customers out until they finished eating, but I'll come and see you in a little while, then I'll come back here."

As Rosie and I left, the people who had been lingering in front of the restaurant had left, too. We were silent on the way back to her house. It seemed very late, and I was tired, but it was more than two hours before midnight.

In the house, Anna had heated the coffee so that I could drink it with anisette, but I had only a shot of anisette, and then I sat on the couch. A few minutes later, Rosie sat at the other end of the couch and told me to lie down and to use her lap as a pillow, which I did. She made me feel comfortable, rubbing my head and my hair with her fingers, and I began to drift off into sleep.

After a while, my Aunt Maria came into the house. She told me not to get up. She sat in a lounge chair, facing us. Anna gave her a hot cup of coffee with anisette, and the three women talked while I was almost falling asleep. Rosie didn't stop massaging my scalp, and soothing voices were coming from a distance as the warmth of Rosie's body was penetrating mine.

Suddenly Rosie was shaking me a little.

"Sleep in my bed," she said, "You'll be more comfortable."

"Huh?" I managed to utter. "Where are you going to sleep?"

She whispered in my ear, "With you."

As I stood up, she put my left arm around her shoulders to help me walk into her bedroom. Someone stood to the right side of me to help her. It was her mother. Half asleep, I let them help me walk into the bedroom. They lowered my body onto the bed. Rosie unbuttoned my shirt, and while she was removing it, her mother was removing my socks.

"Okay, Ma, thanks. I can take care of him now."

After her mother left us, Rosie unbuckled my belt, told me to lift my buttocks as she pulled my trousers down, leaving my under-shorts on, and she removed my pants, and she pulled the covers over me. She went to the crib, lowered the side, gave Dante a kiss on the forehead, raised the side again, turned off the light, and after she removed her clothes, she got into bed with me. She was naked. She cupped my face, held it between her smooth, soft breasts and said, "Relax now and go back to sleep. You'll never have to be alone again. I'll always be here for you, if and whenever you want me."

That night, I don't remember dreaming of my mother or of anyone else except Dante. I asked him what it was like being in the state that he was in. He had never even thought about it, he said. He simply existed, as though he were dreaming. Sometimes he had felt a little pain, but he had never known where in his body it had come from, and sometimes he could feel mild, but pleasant sensations, but most of the time he just wanted to sleep. When he had been in a deep sleep, he had felt nothing, nothing that he could remember, anyway. "Well, what about now?" I asked him. "Do you know who I am?" Of course, he knew who I was. "Who am I?" "You don't know who you are?" I told him I knew who I was, but I wanted to know if he knew. And he said, "I'm part of you. We're part of each other." I wasn't sure what he meant, but I asked him how he felt about me and Rosie being together. "You mean Rose. She's not just Nick's little sister now; she has blossomed into a beautiful, caring woman. You need her as much as she needs you, but you also need to know who you are. You ask me if I know who you are, but you should ask yourself, not me. And you should know yourself enough to control who you are, not only for your own sake. Make yourself known to her and prove that you are worthy of her." He began to disappear into darkness. "Hey, wait. How do I do that?" But he disappeared. I was in bed with her. She was sleeping, and she seemed unaware that I was talking with Dante. And then I knew that I had been dreaming.

I got out of bed and slipped on my pants, and in the darkness I could see Dante sleeping in his crib. I went to the bathroom.

When I returned and got back into bed, Rosie asked softly, "Are you okay?"

"Yeah, I just went to the bathroom."

"I should go, too."

She got out of bed, put on a bathrobe, and left.

I didn't want to fall back to sleep until she'd return.

When she returned, she removed the robe, got back into bed and cuddled up to me.

"You feel so nice and warm!" she said as I put my arms around her and held her against me.

"You do, too. It feels so good just sleeping with you!"

Almost immediately, we both fell back to sleep.

When I woke up, it was daylight.

Rosie was so beautiful with her black hair against the white pillow. Her eyes opened, and she looked at me.

"Did you sleep well?" she asked.

"Yeah. With you, I always seem to sleep well."

"Am I that boring?" she grinned.

"Not boring. Fascinating. You are so fascinating that you hypnotize me, putting me under your spell. And you can do anything you want with me. You can drive me wild, or you can put me to sleep."

"Really!"

"Really."

"Then, why aren't you kissing me good morning?"

"Don't ask *me*. Ask yourself."

We kissed, tenderly, on the lips.

"And why aren't you making passionate love to me?" she grinned.

"That's what I'm wondering. You have me under your spell, but I guess you have to be concerned with the rest of the family."

She slid part of her body onto mine, pressing her naked breasts against my naked chest.

"Do you want to get up now," she asked, "or do you just want to relax like this for a few more minutes?"

"Relax like this for a few more minutes, but your mother will be getting up soon."

"She's already up. She's waiting to make breakfast for us. She asked me what she should get us. I told her eggs, sunny side up, and toast. The coffee is ready."

"She saw us in bed together?"

"Maybe she thought you were someone else."

"You're not embarrassed?"

"Well, at first I was, when she asked me who you were, but when I said it was only you, she said, 'Oh, only him. I thought it was someone else.' I wonder who she thought you were."

"Very amusing."

"Well, she helped me to carry you to my bed, so she knows you're here, but when she was going to pull your pants off, I sent her away. I didn't know if this was erect or not," she said, reaching between my thighs. "I guess I didn't want her to see it if it was. My goodness! Doesn't this ever get smaller?"

"Well, what do you expect when you touch me like this?"

"Can't you make it go down?"

"Not if you're touching it. I can't train it like a dog, you know."

"You won't be able to get out of bed," she said, grinning and holding it. Then her face became somber. "Seriously, though, if you want to stay in bed longer, I understand. I know you're going through a tough time, and I want to stay here with you. We don't have to get up now."

"Just a few minutes longer. Being with you like this feels so good!"

"I'm glad I can make you feel good. I want so much to comfort you! I'm willing to do anything to make you feel better. Does this make you feel a little better?" she asked, stroking me gently.

"Of course it does," I said, "if we were, well, someplace else, in private. I appreciate your sentiments, but, somehow this doesn't feel quite right, not under these circumstances. I feel good just feeling you next to me."

She withdrew her hand and put it on my hip, and we lay silently together for almost another half hour.

After breakfast, Rosie and I bathed Dante. While we were bathing him, Joy called and told Anna that she had taken care of all the funeral arrangements for me, and that if I had wanted to make any changes to let her know. The visiting hours for my mother would be on Thursday and Friday, for one hour on each afternoon and one hour each evening, and the funeral would be on Saturday morning. Later that afternoon I went to the house and thanked Joy for being so efficient and helpful. I was really surprised that she had been so considerate. For a long time, I had been ignoring her.

During that time, I had become aware of how much time I had to spend taking care of Dante. I had to dress up in a suit to go to the funeral home in the afternoons, then rush home to take care of Dante, then get dressed again to return to the funeral home, and then rush home again to get Dante ready for bed. Then I'd go home to get some sleep, and in the morning, I'd give Dante another bath. That Saturday night, after the funeral and the reception, I was exhausted. The reception was in the restaurant. Relatives and friends from Quebec City to New York City had gathered in the restaurant. The presence of so many loved ones expressing their sympathy to me had alleviated so much of the sorrow of having lost my mother that I can appreciate someone else's experiences when I try now to express my own sympathy for the loss of someone else's loved one. I used to think that my simple words had meant so little to someone in pain. Now I know better. How powerful words can be! How good they can be, and how destructive when words are used to hurt others!

Life marches on.

That night, with Rosie's help, of course, I gave Dante his bath, and then I said good night to her and to Ben John and Anna, and I went home, and immediately, I went to bed and slept.

The restaurant had been closed for the rest of July. My Aunt Maria wanted to open it again In August. She did, but Joy had wanted nothing to do with it, especially after she had learned that I had not inherited it. My mother and my aunt had owned it jointly, so now the restaurant was owned exclusively by my aunt. I told Joy not to expect any money from the restaurant unless she would work for it. I told her I had not planned to work full time for a while either in the restaurant or by selling insurance because I would be too busy with Dante. He (and Rosie) and I became joint owners of the house. My mother had invited my aunt to live with her, so Maria had not been required to pay rent. She had offered to pay Rosie and me rent after my mother had died, but we had both refused. We would, I told Joy, have to cut back drastically on our expenses. We had owned two fairly new, and very expensive, cars, one of which, I had thought, I would sell.

Before the end of August, Joy had taken one of the cars and Rusty to visit her adopted father in Tennessee, she had told me. She hadn't told me the address, or how I could contact her. And she had not known for how long she would be gone.

She has not returned.

A few days after she had left, I discovered that she had taken more than two thirds of our savings from our banking account, which, her lawyer had said, was her and Rusty's share. And I received papers in the mail from her lawyer to inform me that she had petitioned for a divorce. I would be required to give her half of my property and to pay alimony for her and Rusty.

Jessica had not liked the way the police had been investigating Dante's so called accident, so she had hired private investigators in New York City to find Shackle. Before the end of the year, they found out that he had disappeared to South America. They also found out that Shackle was the illegitimate son of a Robert Russell, the foster father of Joy Russell, of whom he had adopted, but his wife, who had fairly recently been deceased, had kicked Joy out of the house. And her foster father, the biological father of Rusty, had invited Joy to live with him, and to take care of him. Jessica, also with a lawyer, had flown to Tennessee and had met again with Joy. She had persuaded Joy to drop the divorce proceedings, to declare the marriage null and void, to admit that she had deceived me into thinking I had been the biological father of Rusty, and to return half of the money she had taken from our savings account. Joy had agreed. Jessica had been convinced that Joy had nothing to do with what had happened to Dante, that Joy had actually been devastated by it.

"Wow!" I had thought. "Joy should write a book about her own life."

She had even sent me a Christmas card to ask for my forgiveness for the problems she had caused me. She had married me because she hadn't known what else to do. She knew that she had often acted like a bitch to me, that she had used me to release all of her frustrations upon me, and after what had happened to Dante, she had been so

711

upset that she had felt on the verge of cracking up. Her foster father, she had written, forbids her from contacting me again, but if I would ever need to contact her for anything, she gave me a number of a post office box to contact her. She said she did not want us to be enemies.

By September, when it had become obvious that she had left me, I could see no reason to return to my house to sleep at night, so I stayed with Dante. I slept in the bed in his room, and Rosie slept in the middle bedroom, and her mother returned to New York. I knew that Rosie could see no reason why we shouldn't sleep together, especially since we had been so intimate with each other, and everyone else would assume that we would be sleeping together, anyway, even her own mother, but Rosie respected my wishes, and she no longer questioned me about our separate sleeping arrangements.

"What about if I cuddle up to you on the couch?"

"Fine," I said. "I would like that. And I would like kissing you. But I want to prove to myself that I'm acting out of love for you, and not because I want to fuck you."

"But I want it, too. Do you want me to prove to you that I'm acting out of love for you, too?"

"No, of course not. I know you would do it out of love, that you wouldn't do it with anyone else."

"Are you saying you want to prove to yourself that you, well, wouldn't do it with anyone else either?"

"No, of course not!" I answered quickly without thinking.

"Well, I know you wouldn't either."

Suddenly I had become aware that I had just committed myself to abstaining from sex with other women, too, when she had said she knew I wouldn't do it with anyone else either.

On Halloween night Rosie gave birth to little Dante.

On Thanksgiving, the restaurant was closed for the whole week. Ben John and Anna had come up from New York that Wednesday night and had brought Jessica and my son with them. Ben John and Anna slept upstairs in my house, and Jessica and my son, Tony, slept downstairs. I explained to Jessica that although Rosie and I were staying together, we were not sleeping together. My vow of chastity, I told Jessica, included all women, not just Rosie. Legally, I was still married to Joy, and Rosie was married to Dante.

"I will honor your vow," Jessica said. "I'm proud of you. Is it difficult to keep your vow?"

"Yeah, but I knew it would be."

It was the evening before Thanksgiving, and we were in my house while I was checking it to see if it was clean and warm enough for them.

I told Jessica how happy I would be seeing them again for the next three days, and that I was looking forward to seeing them again during Christmas vacation.

Rosie and I didn't often leave the house, taking care of Dante and the three kids, but my grandparents and hers and my Aunt Maria and others offered to take care of them and kept telling us to get out of the house and to go bowling or to go to a movie or whatever. "Just get out of the house and do something," they'd say, "even if it's just to visit other people." We went to the restaurant, of course, and always saw someone we knew. And occasionally we visited others. One afternoon we visited my Aunt Maria. She said she hated to throw out anything that belonged to my mother. I already had what I wanted from my mother and from my father, but we went into my mother's room again and looked at her things. Rationally, I knew that she was gone, but almost everything upstairs still seemed to belong to her, as though she were still living there. On the wall of the front room was a wedding photo of her and my father standing together. She was in a bridal gown, and my father in a dark suit. That photo had been in the house all of my life. It didn't seem right to take it down, even though the past had been irretrievable. Everything in the apartment seemed suspended from the past. Sometimes we associate material things with a person, such as her old television set, yet we know that life is not in inorganic material. Such a simple fact, yet we cling to our possessions as extensions of ourselves. Our furniture, our clothes, our house, our car, our land, are all symbols of us. And the cliché, "You can't take it with you," is so damn true!

Yet, when Christmas came, and once again, friends and family gathered together, I thanked God and joined them in the restaurant, and I indulged myself in the food and drinks in the celebration of life with them. Thank God for friends and family!

Earlier in the month, both Jessica and Rosie had suggested that I mail a Christmas gift to Joy and Rusty. I had no idea what to send them, but they did. The gift included a bouquet of mixed flowers of red, white, and blue from their local florist, signed by me, Jessica, and Rosie, and it was sent by us to the home of a leader of the Klan. Joy knew we would be in the restaurant on Christmas afternoon, and she called to wish us a merry Christmas, and, she said, even her foster father had been touched by the gift.

That was the Christmas that Rosie had given me a copy of *The Prophet* by Khalil Gibran. The prophet, she thought, probably referred to Baha'u'llah, who founded the Baha'i Faith, even though Gibran was a Catholic. And, of course, she asked me to read Dante's story, and tried to persuade me to help her write the ending to his story.

1955 had ended, and we all looked forward to the new year, hoping that it would be better than the old year.

1956 had come and gone, and half of 1957 had almost gone, and I, with Rosie's help and inspiration, of course, had almost completed the task of finishing Dante's story.

Almost. Rosie kept telling me that we would know the ending when we'd come to it. Actually, the ending had come to me in a dream about a month ago, as most of my ideas have been coming to me lately. During the past two years, ever since I've been taking care of Dante, reading and studying a book, *A Brief History of Religion*, which my father had written, and poring over Dante's writings, and writing the last half of his book, many of my ideas have been coming from dreams. I don't feel that I should even take credit for them because they were emerging from my subconscious, and I had no control over them. How much control do we have over our dreams? Sometimes I wake up while I'm dreaming, and I want to fall right back to sleep to find out what happens, as though I'm watching myself in a movie. Sometimes I know when I'm dreaming. A few months ago, for example, in the middle of last winter, I had a dream that I was on top of Mount Washington. Not only was the view from there utterly fantastic, it was so warm and sunny that I was wearing a shirt with short sleeves, and I was warm. I asked myself how I had gotten there, and why it was so warm in the middle of winter. And I became aware that I was dreaming. The colors were so bright and so beautiful! There were colorful birds and butterflies flying over a various assortment of flowers. I had read that pollution of the atmosphere would eventually cause the earth to become warmer, but this was too much of an exaggeration. In the dream, I even asked myself why I was dreaming this. But as soon as I had asked myself that, I woke up.

It was daybreak. We were having a blizzard.

Rosie reminded me that we had just one week left before her and Dante's fifth wedding anniversary. They had celebrated their anniversary together only once. I had written the story of how he had become incapacitated, and of how that had changed our lives. Officially, he had been injured in an automobile accident. No perpetrators had been arrested. No crime had been committed.

"The end of his story?" I asked her.

"How else can we end it?"

"Maybe something will happen between now and next Thursday," I uttered.

"There will never be an ending to his story, will there?"

"Not in our lifetime, no. Whose story is this? Dante started writing this. You wanted us to finish it for him, but this story isn't just about him. It's about all of us. With no ending. It's so frustrating to think that we human beings will go one hating and killing each other, that we are so damned irrational that we can't get together and get along with each other."

We were sitting close together on the couch. We hadn't turned on the television. Dante had been given a bath and was now sleeping in his crib, and the three children were asleep. And Dante's typewritten manuscript was on the coffee table, as well as my father's unfinished history of religion, which Rosie and I had both been studying.

"When we look back over the last few years, though," Rosie said, "some things have changed for the better."

"Such as?"

"Minnie, especially since Dante started teaching. She's changed quite a bit. Her religious cult, if you call it religious, seems to be gone since she's exposed it. And I think Joy has mellowed. Well, at least she sent us another Christmas card. Anyway, if it hadn't been for you, I couldn't have survived the last two years. And although I always knew you loved me, I had thought that after we had slept together in the motel, well, I was afraid you were having guilt feelings, and I didn't know what to do about it. I had wanted you so damn much that, eventually, I began to dream about you. I was afraid that I hadn't attracted you that much, yet I knew that you couldn't have been seeing anyone else, because you were always here with me. You had been so busy taking care of Dante and the rest of us, and trying to finish writing the book, that you must have been too tired to, well, to do anything else."

"Actually, I wasn't that tired. Writing the script and having you help me and giving me compliments and suggestions, and, well, just keeping me company, kept me going. And yes, there were times, plenty of times, when I wanted to hop into bed with you, or just grab you on this couch and caress those nice breasts of yours, but that gave me the energy to write."

She stared at me, inviting me with her bright, dark eyes to embrace her, and I did, and I kissed her tenderly.

"I'd like to make a baby with you, to try again, right now, but we can't," she said. "I've started my period. We'll have to wait until our wedding anniversary."

"If you get pregnant again, everyone will know for sure it's mine this time."

"I don't care. I want to be the mother of your children. Don't you want me to be?"

"Right now, let's think about how we should end the book. We can't end it by me getting you pregnant tonight. And I don't want to end it by showing how hard we work all day keeping this family together. I'd like to end it with an upbeat. If we can't do anything about making a baby tonight, we can discuss the ending to the book in bed together."

"Right now?"

"Not this minute. When we go to bed."

"Let's talk about it now."

As we talked about the ending of the book, without reaching any conclusion, our discussion somehow turned to my father, and how, like Dante, someone had ended his life before his work had been completed.

"My father," she said, "respected him so much! He thought that your father was such a brilliant man, such a great thinker. He and Dante. It's so ironic that your father was writing a book about how the religions must unite to solve our greatest problems, yet the religions are dividing us instead of uniting us! The worship of God, including our own religion, seems to encourage us sometimes to hate others in the name of God, in the name of love."

"Perverting religion, like perverting love, is one of our most grievous evils."

"That's why people like Joy," Rosie added, "see religious institutions as evil."

We talked about my father's book until long after midnight, talking about all the major religions, including the most recent one, which was less than a hundred years old. That would have been the last chapter of his book if he had been alive to finish it.

Finally we went to bed together. And quickly, with my arms around her, I fell asleep.

Somehow I was walking along a shady narrow street, similar to a side street in Rome, except that the buildings were much smaller, and they all seemed to be residential. They were more like huts with one or two rooms, and quite shabby, at least in the twilight. There were no sidewalks. I was walking in the middle of a narrow street, which was unpaved, packed down, hard dirt. There were no vehicles or any signs of modern life. How in hell did I get here? It was beginning to look like an ancient Near East section of a city or a village. I really had no idea where I was, and that frightened me. I had no memory of how I had gotten here. Could I be dreaming? But this place seemed so real. I was wearing shoes. A few men around me were all wearing sandals, and everyone seemed to be going in the same direction I was going. I was looking around me, desperately trying to figure out where I was and how I had gotten here. I could not see the sun. It seemed to be late in the afternoon or early evening, and rather warm. I had no idea whether it was summer or not. I was wearing a sports shirt and khaki pants. And everyone was male. Why weren't there any females? And everyone seemed as dark or almost as dark as I was. They reminded me of Arabs, but certainly not wealthy. Peasants, I thought, all going in the same direction. Why? To my right, I heard a door open. Someone was emerging from one of the huts. He pushed the door, closing it behind him. It was a squeaky wooden door, but it didn't even have a window on it. Like the other men, he was draped in a shabby robe. He began to walk beside me. Even though I felt somewhat dazed and a little nervous, everything around me seemed so real, and nothing was out of proportion or seemed vague, so I decided I could not have been dreaming. Everything was too concrete and tangible.

"Pardon me," I said to the middle aged man beside me, hoping that he spoke English, "but where is everyone going? Do you know?"

He stared at me.

"To listen to the prophet."

"The prophet? What prophet?"

"Baha'u'llah!"

"Baha'u'llah? He died about sixty years ago!"

He was gaping at me, looking at my clothes.

"He's in the square now," he replied, and he turned away from me and began to walk faster as though he wanted to distance himself from me.

Overcome by curiosity and bewilderment, I, too, followed the crowd down the street.

After taking a right turn, we were entering what was apparently the village square. The buildings forming the square were bigger than the buildings on the street where I had been walking. In the middle of the square, in the shape of an oval, were concrete steps that made the oval look like a small outdoor arena, and we were entering the oval from the top, or the back of it. Around the oval was a walkway that gradually led down to a stage. The stage seemed to extend from a second floor of a building, where three men were sitting. There were steps at the back of both sides of the stage that led up to it. The stage wasn't much higher than an average man. Men were walking below the stage level without obstructing the view on the stage. From there, small concrete steps gradually led to the back of the oval, where I was. Men were sitting on the steps. There was enough space between them to allow many others to sit with them, and above me, I could finally see the sky, which was covered with gray clouds. The day seemed to be coming to an end soon. As one of the men on the stage stood up and approached the front of the stage, the crowd of about two to three hundred grew silent. To get a better look at the man who was about to talk, I decided to get a little closer. Others had the same idea. The man on the stage was waiting for us to get settled. When I got quite closer, almost directly in front of him, I sat down.

I was reminded of the Spanish Steps in Rome where tourists would gather and sit, except I wasn't among tourists. I was the only foreigner here, an uneasy, yet terribly curious bystander, lost in a mysterious, old place, looking at a man who had a long dark beard that was beginning to turn gray, a middle aged man who desperately needed a shave and a haircut like the other men around me who were dressed as though they were at least a hundred years behind us modern Yanks. I was almost expecting someone to yell at me: "Yankee, go home!" People around me were calling the man who was waiting to preach to us a prophet, a Manifestation of God, who had died about sixty years ago. I was, of course, skeptical, but intrigued. I had read about the prophet Baha'u'llah in an unfinished book that my own father had written. How could this possibly be the same man? Where were we? And how did I get here?

He began to speak, finally.

Without a microphone, his voice was so loud, it surprised me, but I didn't understand what he had said. Even from a distance, his eyes seemed dark and penetrating. I felt him looking directly at me as though he knew who I was. Whoever he was, he had a rather strange but serene look. And I wondered if he had the same effect on the others as he had on me, that he was looking and speaking directly to me as though we had known each other. Suddenly he looked upward, to the sky. I didn't know what he was saying; he wasn't speaking English, but the sounds just flowed out of him like honey. I looked at the faces of those around me. It was obvious that they were reacting to his words. Their eyes were glued to him. They seemed fascinated, I felt, by images which his words must have been casting upon their minds. I wished I could understand his words, too, but, somehow, I could feel his spirit rising as he was gazing up, his spirit connecting with the Spirit that penetrated him, and as he gazed down at us, the Spirit that had penetrated him, was penetrating us, the audience. I felt the Spirit penetrating *me*, anyway. I felt certain that the Spirit united us, that the separation that had divided us had been an illusion, and that our unity was the reality. I was reminded of my father, especially of the summer nights at the cabin when we sat around a camp fire and my father had spoken of being connected with the rest of the cosmos and asking us if we had ever felt the light of others inside of us.

The voice of the man was steady and smooth, and he paced back and forth a bit, not nervously, but calmly. His movements were leisurely, and he expressed himself with utmost confidence. He looked up at the sky again, raised his hands, and uttered something that sounded like, "Thanks be to God!"

And the words ceased. He lowered his eyes and he looked directly at me again. He seemed a bit tired, and the hypnotic look in his eyes when he had been talking, faded. He seemed to have come back down to earth, and the spell he had created in the crowd was also fading, and the crowd, muttering to each other, began to disperse.

I stood up to leave, too, but I had no idea where I would go. A young man, about my age, with a dark beard, and wearing a shabby robe, of course, faced me and asked if I would like to meet Baha'u'llah. To tell you the truth, I was too stunned to reply. He obviously knew I wouldn't refuse. Instead of replying, I looked at the stage and saw the man looking back at me.

"Follow me. He wants to meet you, too."

I followed him through the crowd. At the street where the stage was, the man, whom others called Baha'u'llah, approached us and smiled at me. He extended his hand to clasp mine, and he touched my elbow with his other hand, and said he was very pleased to see me.

"Let us go where we can talk together."

We left the square and followed the young man. This was not the village where the man called Baha'u'llah lived, and he was as unfamiliar with the village as I was, he said, but the young man was an inhabitant here.

"I know you have many questions to ask me," the man said, "but first let me ask you a few questions, if you don't mind. I know you're an American, so you have travelled a long distance. How did you get here?"

"It's strange that you should ask me that question."

"Yes, I know. It's the first question you were about to ask me."

"I have a feeling you know how I got here."

"Perhaps. When you travel, how do you usually travel?"

"I went to Italy once. I took a ship, but I usually travel in an automobile. I certainly didn't drive here."

"I have a feeling that you're a serious young man, but you also have a sharp sense of humor. That's good. Here, an automobile is worthless. I assume you mean a horseless carriage."

I stared at him; he seemed serious.

"Please tell me how I got here."

"That's what I'm trying to do, to help you understand how you arrived here, but if I told you, I doubt that you would believe me."

We followed the young man into a place that was hardly more than a hut. We went into a room that had only a table and a few chairs, and in each corner at the other end of the room were two small beds with a pillow and a blanket.

While the young man went into another room, the man and I sat at the table.

"We will first discuss how you came here. By the way, you must excuse me for not being a good host. You have come here at an unexpected time when I'm on a mission and I am fasting, otherwise I would have prepared a feast for us. You have travelled a long way, and I'm sorry that I cannot accommodate you better."

The young man entered, placed two mugs on the table, and filled them with water.

"Leave us now," he said to the young man. "I will call you if I need you."

The young man returned to the other room.

"You know, of course, who I am, so I assume you want to discuss something."

I was reluctant to tell him that Baha'u'llah had died long ago, so I said, "Well, others have referred to you as the prophet Baha'u'llah."

"You know that's not my birth name, of course, that it means *Glory of God.*"

"Are you Baha'u'llah, the founder of the Baha'i Faith, who had been raised as a Muslim and had died years ago?"

He stared at me. Then he smiled.

"I'm sorry," he said, "I had assumed you knew who I am, that you wanted to discuss something with me. What were you doing just before you came here?"

"I don't remember."

"Your father wrote a book about the history of religion, explaining the beliefs of each of the major religions, but before he could write more of the Baha'i Faith, someone killed him. Have you thought of finishing it for him?"

I didn't want to disappoint him, but I said, "No, I'm trying to finish a book written by my brother."

"Your brother was badly wounded in the Korean war, and a little over two years ago, someone who belongs to a fanatical religious group tried to kill him. Apparently, you want to discuss that with me. And we will, after you understand how you arrived here."

"I don't want to sound disrespectful to you, or to your Faith, but, well, I didn't intend to come here to see you."

"Not consciously, perhaps, but here you are, and you're here for a purpose."

"Again, I don't want to sound disrespectful to you, but I read what my father had written about Baha'u'llah, and I know that my father would agree with me about how impressive the Baha'i Faith is, but that was almost a hundred years ago."

He held his hand up to stop me, and, smiling, he said, "I understand now! You're having difficulty believing I'm actually Baha'u'llah. That's understandable. Did you know that your father was with your brother when he was wounded?"

"That's what my grandfather told me! How could you have known that?"

"If you still can't remember what you were doing just before you arrived here, tell me what you've been doing since the time someone shot at your brother and he crashed the automobile."

"I've been taking care of him."

"Does that require much of your time and effort?"

"Yes. Most of my time and effort."

"Does anyone help you to take care of him?"

"His wife, Rosie."

"Why can't she alone take care of him?"

"That's impossible. She couldn't carry him to give him baths, for one thing."

"So, she's dependent on you. Are you living together?"

"Yes, and now we're sleeping together."

"Now? You mean you weren't sleeping together while you were living together, until now? How long is now?"

"The last two months."

"You have been living together and caring for your brother together for how long?"

"Two years."

"So, during those two years, you were sleeping with other women?"

"No, of course not!"

"Why not?"

I gave him more details of my situation with Rosie, and of my vow.

"And you said you were finishing writing Dante's book, and that you were studying your father's book on religion."

I told him that Rosie and I were doing both together, that we discussed the dissension and lack of unity among the various religions.

"Interesting. And I want to discuss that with you, but first I want you to understand how you arrived here. Have you ever experienced the feeling of leaving your body, or have heard of people badly injured in accidents and had left their bodies for a time?"

"Yes, but that's not why I'm here."

"Why are you here?"

"I don't know."

"You do, but not consciously. The mind is such an amazing thing! Do you remember discussing religion with the wife of your brother?"

"Yes. We were discussing how the various religions were dividing us rather than uniting us."

"And that concerns you deeply."

"From what my father wrote, Baha'u'llah was also deeply concerned about it, too."

"I know," he said, grinning. "Were you having this discussion at night?"

"Yes. Late at night."

"Late at night. Before going to sleep?"

"Yes, I think so. I remember, now, that we, well, we didn't make love, not physically. We embraced each other, and, well, here I am!"

"Dreaming?"

"How else could I have gotten here?"

He was grinning at me. I was staring at him. I was still bewildered. He asked, "Where is your body now?"

I tried to think, but I was too confused; nothing was making sense. I thought that my body was obviously here, that I was touching it.

"If I'm dreaming," I finally said, "my body is in bed, with Rosie. If she wakes up, she could see my body next to hers."

"But where is your mind?"

"My mind? My mind is here."

"Out of your body?"

I thought for a few more moments.

"If this is a dream, my body must be asleep, so I must be in bed in my body dreaming that I'm in my body while I'm dreaming I'm in this strange place. When you look at me, can you see my body? But if I'm dreaming of you, I'm dreaming that you can see my body."

"And if you're dreaming, do you feel you're controlling your dream?"

"No, I feel I have no control, not of *this* dream. Whatever is happening in this dream seems beyond my control. Usually, when I know I'm dreaming, I can control it."

"Let me give you something to think about when you wake up. And then we'll talk more about how religion is often abused, like so many other things that are good but are perverted. In three years from now a Catholic candidate will run for the presidency of your country, and the opposing party will be running ads: 'This Sunday, attend the church of your choice,'" he said, emphasizing *of your choice*. I couldn't see what was wrong with that. Then he pointed out that such phrases very subtly, but certainly, promote individualism and disunity, setting one religion against another in the name of religious tolerance. "In your time, this will be called 'subliminal.' In other words, it appeals not to our conscious minds, but to our subconscious. 'This Sunday' is, of course, a message aimed at Christians, and 'of your choice' implies that Catholics do not have a choice. To the predominately Protestant majority, the hierarchy of the Catholic Church is not democratic, it is dictatorial. If a Catholic becomes president, the implication is that he will be following orders from the Vatican." We were staring at each other. "When you wake up, you will have something to think about. For now, let us talk about the problems that the various religions, which have so much in common, and yet have set us against each other, even killing each other in the name of the Almighty God. From the beginning of the human race, man has strived to satisfy not only his physical needs, but his spiritual needs. The Source of Life is the same Source of Religion. When religion separates us from the Source, it is no longer religion; it is the abuse of religion."

In discussing the history of religion, he said he agreed with my father. He said that my father had not only done much research, but he was convinced that my father had spoken with God. And in this dream, I wondered if I was really dreaming. I mean, I knew that I was dreaming, but through my dream, I felt that my spirit was in closer contact with the Spirit of God. And the man, who somehow knew my thoughts, said, "Yes, through your soul, your spirit is connecting with the Almighty Spirit."

We had been discussing the lack of unity among the religions for five hours, which had gone by remarkably quickly. Anyway, Baha'u'llah said it was getting late and that he wanted us to get a good rest to greet the next day.

"But if I'm dreaming now, and I return to sleep, I will wake up in my own bed."

"No, I'm hoping you will stay with me for a full day. I have to preach before noon, but I'll be free for the rest of the afternoon. We have much more to talk about. Before we go to sleep, we should use the outhouse."

"The outhouse?"

"To urinate."

"But if I'm dreaming, I don't need to urinate, and if I urinate, I will go in my bed."

"I can't explain it to you," he grinned. "You'll have to trust me. You may not need to urinate, but it will make it easier for you to sleep if you follow your usual routine."

He took the lantern from the table, and I followed him out the front door, to the side of the hut, through an alleyway, to the back of the hut, to another hut, and went inside. At the other end, near the wall, were several seats. When I was about to urinate, I half expected to wake up in a wet bed, hearing Rosie screaming at me, but I didn't. I sighed with relief.

When we each got into the beds in the pitch dark, Baha'u'llah said, "I don't think you'll have any trouble sleeping, but if you do, pray, and soon you will fall asleep."

I was surprised that I felt so sleepy as soon as I got into the bed.

After a little while, someone was wakening me. It was Baha'u'llah. He laughed a little, saying he hoped I enjoyed my long slumber, which seemed like a few minutes, but he had been awake much earlier, praying while waiting for me to wake up. He said I had slept half of the morning, but soon we had to be going, and he couldn't wait for me much longer. It would take at least an hour, he said, to go where we were going, near a neighboring village, to the rural home of a farmer.

Quickly I got dressed, and he went with me to the outhouse, and I urinated again.

The sun was out, and it seemed like a clear, autumn morning. The air was brisk. I felt that this was no dream. It felt too bizarre to be real, to be in this strange place, yet too vivid not to be real.

When we returned to the room, the young man put a bowl of warm water and a small piece of soap, and a hand towel on the table for me to wash my hands and face. And then he brought me a plate with a couple of pieces of bread on it, and a cup of juice.

We left the hut. After fifteen or twenty minutes, we left the narrow streets and followed a dusty, dirt road into the countryside. We went past several small farms where we actually saw some females.

The day was getting warmer as it got closer to noon.

Finally we came to an estate with a large wall around it. In the middle of the wall was an iron gate through which we could see a large green field to the left of a huge house. A man with a dark beard opened the gate for the three of us. I, of course, in a white sports shirt and khaki pants, even though I was a little darker than most of them, stuck out like a sore thumb. We were inside a large courtyard, which had a large picnic table with fruits and pastries on it. A small crowd of men, not more than a hundred, who were mostly merchants, I was told, had gathered, apparently waiting for Baha'u'llah to preach to them. The young man tugged at my arm, and I followed him towards the house, almost to a patio where the table was, and we ate some of the pastry and fruit. Several young women were near the table, not all of whom had their faces covered.

"They are servants," the young man said. "They are attracted to you."

"Because I seem strange to them. It's my clothes. They all have beautiful dark eyes, especially with their faces covered. It makes them look mysterious and sexy. Is that why they cover their faces?"

"Baha'u'llah is ready to talk," he said. "Let's sit close to him."

We quickly went through the crowd, and we drew close to him, at the front of the crowd, and we sat on the grass. Baha'u'llah looked at us, turned away, and as he took a few steps back, then turned and faced the crowd again, I noticed at a short distance behind him, a white object, like a huge rock. It was moving, as though it were growing out of the ground. It stood up. It was a huge, white dog with thick hair, like a beautiful Italian sheep dog, facing us. For a while, it just stood there, motionless, and seemed to be studying us as Baha'u'llah was waiting for the crowd to be silent. He closed his eyes and bowed his head. As he was silently praying, the dog was slowly approaching him, and most of the men became silent, waiting for the prophet to speak. The huge white dog did not stop until it stood next to Baha'u'llah and seemed to glare at the crowd. A few men were still talking, and others were hushing them. Baha'u'llah, immersed in prayer, did not seem to notice the dog.

Even as a few men continued to talk, despite the hushes, the prophet opened his eyes and looked up at the sky. It was a clear day with a few wispy clouds. Even though I did not understand the words, the loud voice of Baha'u'llah was chanting as though his sounds were rising into the distant sky.

There were a few jeers and heckles from the crowd. It seemed that some had come not to listen to him, but to ridicule him. I could not understand such rudeness. If they did not want to listen, why had they even bothered to come here?

The dog seemed to glare at the agitators. It turned and looked directly at me, as though, somehow, it was expecting me to do something about the hecklers. Others, who were annoyed, were telling them to hush, and the huge dog began to bare its powerful teeth and to growl at *me*, as though it were threatening me to do something about them, or else. Why, I wondered, had it not threatened the hecklers? The dog could have easily frightened them away.

Why hadn't the owner of the estate told them to be more respectful of the other guests?

Baha'u'llah did not seem to notice the jeers. And, quickly, I became aware that he hadn't. He had entered another state. As he continued to talk, the jeers died out, and the crowd became attentive. And the words flowed steadily and smoothly out of him.

In spite of the calm that had now prevailed, the growling dog suddenly lunged at me and grabbed my pants with his teeth and began shaking and pulling it, tearing it. The dog was growling so viciously that it seemed to want to tear me apart. It had suddenly gone mad, scaring the hell out of me. Somehow, I had gotten my arms around its neck, in a headlock, and had wrapped my legs around its body, and I was able to prevent it from biting me as long as I kept putting pressure on it, but as soon as I'd release a little pressure, it would growl again and try to move. I hung onto to it tightly, and I was wondering why its owner, or the young man with me, or some of the others, had not tried to get the mad dog away from me, but no one even paid attention to the dog or me. If they were afraid of the dog, you'd think they would have gotten up and moved away, but no one was a bit concerned. Everyone was ignoring us. I was bewildered.

I couldn't relax a bit; I had to concentrate on the dog and not on Baha'u'llah. When I thought the dog had calmed down and I could release it, a growl quickly formed in its throat. It took all of my strength and attention to hold it down. How could anyone not have noticed how this mad dog had reacted to me?

Eventually, the dog seemed to have finally fallen asleep. A little at a time I released some of the pressure, and the dog continued to sleep between my legs.

All this time, Baha'u'llah was preaching. I had noticed how he had looked while he was preaching, but I had been too distracted by the dog to notice anything else. And now, as his eyes lowered, I knew that he was coming to the end of his sermon. He was coming out of the strange, hypnotic state he had been in.

Slowly, carefully, I stood up, and the dog stood up, and, like a cat wanting attention, the dog rubbed against my leg.

Baha'u'llah stepped towards me. Immediately, I apologized that I hadn't been able to concentrate on him due to the incident with the dog. He smiled. I told him how the dog had gone mad, biting my pants and tearing them. He seemed amused.

He told me to meet him at the table and to eat something while he said goodbye to the men. It would only be a few minutes, he said. The young man and I returned to the table. The dog followed me.

A few minutes later Baha'u'llah joined us.

"Let's go someplace where you and I can continue our talk."

What we had talked about last night, he said, had merely been an introduction to something more important and more personal to me, particularly in my situation. I was wondering what he meant about my situation.

We walked past a flower garden, Baha'u'llah and I and the white dog, to an orchard, to sit in chairs where we could lie back if we wished, out of the bright sun, but I didn't think I should allow the dog to follow us in case its master wanted it. I didn't even know if the dog belonged to anyone on the estate. So, I turned around and told the dog to leave us. It stopped, and it gazed at me as though it could not believe I did not want it.

"Take the dog with you," Baha'u'llah said, "it's so beautiful, and it seems so devoted to you now, and it obviously knows it belongs to you. You deserve such a beautiful dog!"

"What! I don't understand."

Baha'u'llah began to explain, and while he did, I was intrigued by his explanation. Here I was, dreaming, I thought, and someone in my dream was interpreting the dream for me. That would save me time and trouble after I would wake up to interpret it myself, consciously.

"This beautiful dog," he said, as we were walking towards the orchard behind the huge house, "is your impulses, all of your passions. Your task was to subdue the dog before it had gotten too wild, to control it, to become its master, and not the other way around, before the dog would tear you to shreds. And in so doing, you became master of the dog. That was your purpose for coming here, to discuss your present situation. That's really what we should be discussing this afternoon. That's part of the situation you're in now, or have been in during the past two years. Incidentally, the whiteness of the dog represents its purity."

We became silent for a few moments as I let this thought sink in.

"But," I said, "I thought that was an incongruity in your philosophy. Impulses, per se, in this case, would be basically good, with white representing purity. In reading your ideas, I had interpreted impulses as basically evil."

"What is the source of your impulses? Of your passions? What is the source of your nature? Whatever God has given you, is good," he said, "provided you do not abuse it. This beautiful white dog is your gift."

"That is the argument I would have used against you."

He grinned at me.

In the orchard, under the shade of trees with a soft breeze refreshing us, we each sat in a large wooden chair covered by a cushion, and we stretched our legs. The dog, standing near my feet, stared at me and whined, asking for permission to share the chair. I tapped the cushion next to my hip, and it leaped onto the chair and put its head and its huge paws across my thighs.

"Tell me why I have come here, to you," I said, "and not to, well, to someone else."

"To someone else? Such as Jesus?"

"Now that you've mentioned it, yes. It seems to me that a Christian would want to talk with Jesus."

He grinned at me again.

"Good question! I don't know. Do you think it would have made much difference?"

"I don't know either. There are many more Christians than Baha'is. Maybe Jesus is too busy."

He burst into laughter.

"So, Jesus sent you to me. I told you that you have a good sense of humor. Satan must really hate you. He hates comedians. To get back to your question. When you were studying the history of religion from your father's book, he wrote about the Baha'is last. Maybe that chapter was the freshest in your mind, so you thought of me. Or maybe your father wants you to finish that chapter. And who would be your best consultant? Anyway, here you are. If you have any particular questions about the Baha'i Faith, this is your opportunity for me to answer, but remember, I think you're here particularly to answer questions about your present situation and the ending to your brother's book."

"My biggest question is your claim to infallibility."

"Of course. And, for me, that's the most crucial question. Everything hinges on that claim. Whenever a prophet claims infallibility, he is saying that God is speaking through him, directly through him. The only definitive answer I can give is: I don't know. If I have ever implied that I know everything about God, then that is misleading. Only God knows everything about God. Buddha is right. God is unknowable. To know everything about God *is to be God*. But only God is God. We can only know some aspects of God through Revelation, through the Manifestations of God, through the Creation, through science and religion, through our intelligence and feelings, through love. No matter how much I may try to accept something on faith, to make that great leap, if I cannot accept something with my whole heart and mind, I must, in good conscience, reject it. For example, I cannot understand the concept of the Trinity, so I reject it. Perhaps it's just a problem of semantics, but your own father wrestled with the same problem. Yet, he was as much Catholic as he was Jewish."

"I'm still confused about your concept of infallibility. I know that doesn't mean you're infallible in everything."

"That's what I'm attempting to explain. I think I'm getting there. Whenever I begin to preach, I let myself go, deeply emerged in prayer, to God, just as you do, when you get involved in writing your book, shutting your mind off from everything else around you and concentrating all of your being on the book and letting your subconscious emerge. I concentrate on God."

He comes into contact with the Holy Spirit, which pervades all existence, the universe. He refers to the Spirit as Eternal Being, of which everything is part. "Just as your father and Dante and you refer to God as Eternal Existence. 'The essence of God,' your father wrote, 'is existence.' God always 'Is' without past or future, without time. God is the Source of existence. To say there is no God is to say there is no source of existence, an extremely difficult position to defend rationally."

Baha'u'llah claims to be among the succession of the major prophets. From time to time, a prophet appears to revitalize the old religion. A prophet is an extremely sensitive being who, when immersed in the fervor of prayer and contemplation, enables his spirit to come into contact with the Holy Spirit. A prophet is necessary, because religion has a tendency to become distorted by mediocrity and materialism. Providence, however, has provided us with a few sensitive souls who are able to transcend the flesh aspect of their human nature through their spirit. I asked Baha'u'llah if he is a reincarnation of Jesus, Mohammed and the other great prophets. The spirit of Jesus and the others, he said, is alive and partakes of the Eternal Being, and when Baha'u'llah's spirit comes in contact with the Holy Spirit, he is also in contact with the spirit of Jesus, Mohammed, and the other prophets. And when Baha'u'llah is preaching, he is in communion with the Holy Spirit, and it is the Holy Spirit speaking through the spirit of Baha'u'llah. In this particular instant, the Word, made flesh, is infallible. How does Baha'u'llah know for sure? He doesn't, not in any empiric sense. But his conviction is rooted in faith. He feels his spirit in union with God. He experiences God. And he believes he is a man of Destiny, one of the few sensitive men chosen by God to preach the Word.

"Is it remotely possible," I asked, without trying to offend or challenge him, "for you to be deceiving yourself, and therefore deceiving us, too?"

"Of course! I would expect a sincere, rational person, such as you, to examine the words carefully. At times, I, too, am amazed at the thoughts that have come out of me, that I would know things that I hadn't known that I knew. On the other hand, it is possible to think our spirit is in contact with the Holy Spirit when it is not; it is very difficult at times to discern. One must rationally examine what is said, which is not a very easy task. By its fruits will you know it."

It was in prayer and in contemplation when he actually felt in contact with the Holy Spirit. At this moment, while talking with me, there were vague doubts, but doubts that were easily washed away through faith. He claimed infallibility while preaching; while conversing with me, he was not speaking with infallible authority.

As impressed by Baha'u'llah as I was at this stage, I thought it would be interesting to push him a little, so I told him that I thought that Jesus was always sure, that Jesus was infallible, always. Baha'u'llah simply shrugged, saying he didn't know, that, perhaps that was so, but he had said it in such a way that suggested that he wasn't concerned about it; he knew only, and was concerned only, that the spirit of Jesus is in union with God, and that God spoke through Jesus.

"You know," he admonished me, "that I don't question the veracity of any of the true religions. The purpose of my mission, as you well know, is to unite the religions. As the Hindus say: 'All rivers lead to the sea.'"

"I believe that, too."

"I know. And I have to tell you what happened to me when my soul left my body."

"You mean, while you were preaching?"

"No. When I died, and my soul ascended into heaven. Do you want to hear it?"

"Of course!"

"When I reached the Golden Gate, Saint Peter, the first Pope of the Catholic Church, opened the gate for me and gave me a big welcome as he led me into heaven, and he said he would personally give me a tour." He was speaking with a very somber look on his face, but I suddenly felt terribly disappointed in him, and I seriously began to doubt him. He had sounded so different, so phony, all of a sudden, like an Elmer Gantry, but he was looking at me, observing my reaction, and he continued. "When we came to a huge door, he put his index finger against his lips and told me to be very, very quiet as we tiptoed past the door. 'In this room,' he whispered, 'are the Catholics, and they think they're the only ones up here.'"

I burst into laughter.

"I thought you were serious."

"I know, and in a way, I was, and you laughed because you recognize the truth of that little joke, which could apply to any and to all of the religions."

I finally admitted to him that while he was preaching, I couldn't pay any attention to him due to the incident with the dog.

"On the contrary," he said, "you were the best listener."

His sermon was on controlling our passions, on our spiritual selves, our souls, leading and transcending our natural selves, our bodies. Even though I was not consciously observing his spirit rising, I was elevating my own spirit to the Divine Spirit. During this state, I had subdued the dog. This furthermore gave evidence that I, too, have the Faith. My spirit had transcended my natural self, lifting me into contact with the Holy Spirit. I had the Faith, he said, because I have harkened to the Divine Spirit. It is our spirit that calls, which beckons us to God. I have, he said, devoted much of the past two years to finishing the script that Dante had begun, and in so doing, I have elevated my spirit.

"The spirit of man, that which is pure in man and yearns to be joined everlastingly to God, becomes evident in the devotion you have expressed, caring deeply for your brother and for his family. The spirit of man is manifested in your creation, in your highest aspirations. Although you rose up from the depths of human depravity, your depiction of depravity will offend the sensibilities of many who call themselves righteous, who refuse to confront the truth about themselves, to admit their own temptations to taste the forbidden fruit, and they will condemn you. Let your conscience be your guide, and let God be your judge. God is more merciful, more loving and more understanding of your sacrifices and of your devotion to your brother and to his family than any human, including the one who is closest to you and has always loved you deeply, who has seen in you the Divine Spirit."

"You're speaking of the wife of my brother, who loves me, and whom I love. As far as my devotion to my brother and to his family, if our situation had been reversed, I know that he would have done the same for me. Caring for me, I mean."

"And, caring for her and for her babies, you're concerned about how others see her, especially now, in your present situation. 'What God has joined together, let no man put asunder.' Who can say that God, that Love, has not joined you two together? Those who judge you and condemn you cannot even imagine themselves in the same situation, much less would they endure such a situation. Tell her what I have said. But she knows you well, and in knowing you so well, she loves you so much. Incidentally, you don't mention much about how much time and work you put in every day in caring for your brother, how often sometimes you and Rose have to bathe him whenever he soils himself. You can't even leave the house to take a weekend off as other people do. You and Rose have resigned yourselves to the situation because you consider it a duty to be taking care of him. Of course you and Rose cling to each other!"

"I need her," I murmured. "I went two years without touching her, without touching any woman, even though I needed her desperately. I'm not complaining. I'm just, well, I need her. I don't know how I can live without her now."

"She's been your inspiration. You will finish the book soon."

"I wish I could include this part."

"Why can't you?"

"Use this dream as part of my story? Who would ever accept it?"

"Since you have experienced this, I assume others, especially writers who create such stories as you have, have done the same. You're not the only one who ever obtained his ideas from deep within, from the subconscious. I assume that some, if not all, of the greatest insights have emerged from the subconscious."

"Incidentally, when the dog was, well, attacking me, why didn't anyone help me?"

"Remember, this is *your* dream. If this were not your dream, I would think that the others had not been aware of your situation. The struggle with the dog was happening within you."

"This is *so* strange, but it seems more real than reality."

"The mind is amazing! And we use so little of it! So many of us just look at the surface of things and understand so little, but instead of listening to the experiences of others and learning from each other, we are so complacent that we tell ourselves we have the right not to know, the right to be wrong, the right to our own opinions. And yet, when even a child, or I should say, especially the child, who is curious and is eager to know, becomes alive with excitement when he discovers knowledge through his own efforts. That knowledge becomes so personal and so meaningful! You have written that knowledge is knowing God better, and that the first task in life, therefore, is knowing. If we know nothing, we love nothing. If we know no one, we love no one. But, if we know, we can love! Return to your life and finish writing the book. You will finish it soon. Rose is right. The story is worth telling."

"Before I leave you, tell me something. Now that I have spoken with you, even if this is a dream, do you expect me to join the Baha'i Faith?"

He stared at me before he answered.

"There is only one faith. And, like your father, you have that Faith."

He meant that I had grasped the fundamental truths: the Will and the Word of God that lies at the core of religious faith. The mediocrity within organized religion has a tendency to lose sight of this core, and this will happen within the Baha'i religion, as it has happened in all religions. He said he had not intended the Baha'i religion to be a new religion, which some Baha'is, he fears, will make it, thus making another branch in religion rather than uniting religions.

"Before talking with you," he said, "I knew you had strayed from religion, or, as your mother would say, 'living in sin with Joy.'" He smiled again. "Retain the purity at the core within the religion in which you were raised. Religious unity can only be reached through the core of religious faith, the one, true religion of God."

With that, he said it was time for us to depart.

"You have work to do. You must return now, to Erebus?"

"That was the fictitious name my brother Dante gave it, but it's no worse than any other place. I know everyone here, and everyone, well, mostly everyone here is friendly. I decided to use the actual name the inhabitants have given it. Cascade Flats."

"A hamlet, surrounded by mountains?"

"Yes. The houses aren't big and beautiful, but they're functional."

"Please keep in touch. And go with God."

"You, too. I promise to keep in contact with you."

"That would please me very much. I assure you, we will meet again."

I was in bed.

I was fully awake, and Rosie, not the dog, was lying against me with her thigh covering mine in our dark bedroom.

I was so astonished by the dream that my impulse was to wake up Rosie to tell her what I had just experienced. It was utterly incredible! Maybe she wouldn't believe that it could possibly have seemed so real. Of course, it was a dream, but even now, it seemed too real to just be a dream. How could I possibly describe it to her?

I let her sleep, but I was too excited, too joyful to remain in bed much longer.

As I slowly got out of bed, she began to stir, but she did not wake up. In the dark, I slid my trousers on, went through the kitchen, into the front room, and turned on the light from a lamp on the end table. I went into the front bedroom to check on Dante, who was sleeping. Then I went to the bathroom, and as I urinated and thought of the outhouse in the dream, I felt so damn good to be alive. The prophet had implied that I was sacrificing so much to take care of my brother and his family, but I wanted Dante to be here, with us, not in a hospital. And I was happy to be here, with people whom I loved so much and who loved me, with Rosie and the kids down here, and my Nonna and Tattone upstairs, and others of the family so close together. Baha'u'llah, I'm not just giving, I'm receiving!

I felt so good, so rested, and so energetic, that I wanted to write about the dream while it was so vivid in my mind.

I washed my face with cold water.

I went through the kitchen again, into the dark bedroom and put on a shirt, reentered the kitchen, closed the bedroom door to keep the bedroom dark, pulled the chain to the overhead light, and when the kitchen light came on, I noticed that the time was not even four o'clock yet. I had slept only a little more than three hours, but I felt I had slept a whole day at least.

I decided to make a pot of coffee.

After I made the coffee, I filled a mug, took it into the front room, to the couch, where I sat and began to write about the dream in a notebook. I had become so involved that I hadn't even noticed day breaking.

I was startled by a sudden: "Good morning!"

Rosie, in a bathrobe and slippers, and holding a cup of coffee, entered the room. She sat in the corner of the couch, next to me.

"You're up early," she said. "Couldn't sleep?"

"I feel like I had a good sleep."

I told her about the incredible dream. And I read to her what I had written so far during the past three hours, up to the part where Baha'u'llah was about to tell me about the next presidential election when a Catholic would run.

"That's interesting," she said, "but I thought you were writing the ending to the book."

"He told me it would come to me. Let me write about the whole dream, and then we'll talk about it. I might even use the dream to end the book."

"What? How can that fit into the book? The book is already too long as it is. And I think you should cut out most of the sexy parts. I don't want to publish it; I just want to have it so I can read it occasionally."

"If the ideas in it are worthwhile, we should try to publish it. You even said that the story is worth telling. If the religious leaders of the world would unite instead of dividing us, that would be a major step in eliminating prejudice and hatred. That fits in with the theme of the book."

"Does your dream have an ending? I mean, a point to it, unlike most dreams."

"For me, personally, it does. According to the dream, my completion of Dante's book is my spiritual journey. And, you, as my muse, are accompanying me along my journey. That means, we're on this spiritual journey together."

She gave me a big grin.

And then she told me to continue writing while she'd get the kids up and cleaned, and she would get us breakfast before we'd give Dante his bath.

Between my daily tasks of caring for Dante, it took me the rest of that day and part of that night and another day to finish writing about the dream. That was late Saturday night while everyone else was sleeping. I got up with Rosie early in the morning, but I still felt well rested. While she had been in church with Nonna and Tattone, I took care of the three kids who helped me to give their father a bath.

When Rosie returned from church, she read about the dream.

"This is fantastic! I love the part about the white dog! Maybe you *should* use it. It's not just Dante's story; it's *our* story."

In the afternoon, while Nonna was watching Dante, Rosie and I and the three kids went into the restaurant for spaghetti. Rosie reminded me that her fifth wedding anniversary, the first day of summer, was coming that Thursday. Not that we had anything specific planned, but she was hoping I'd finish writing the book by then. That gave me four more days. We still weren't sure how to finish it.

"It's really not that important," she said. "Actually, the book is finished. All I have to do is finish typing it. You've explained how we ended up in this situation. This is how this story ends, without an ending. What more can you say? Life marches on."

"We can leave it just the way it is now, I suppose, but in the dream, Baha'u'llah told me to finish it, that the ending will come to me."

"You talk about the dream as though it actually happened. It was a dream."

"Yes, but the dream actually *did* happen. It happened to me. I mean, it gave me the feeling that the ending will come to me, even if it comes from the subconscious. It will come to me. I can feel it! The mind is an amazing thing!"

She grinned at me.

"*You* are amazing! That's why I love you so damn much."

After we ate, we took a walk to the other end of the flats in the afternoon sun, and when we returned to the house, we took a nap.

On the bed, Rosie said, "When Thursday night comes, I'll let you try again to plant your seeds in me, but even if you should get me pregnant, little Dante will be over two years old before his next sibling is born."

"And people will really talk then."

"They talk anyway. Regular people, Dante used to call them. Regular people will say, 'Well, what can you expect from them black eyetalians?'"

I didn't dream that afternoon while I napped with Rosie, but that night, I did. Well, technically, I did not dream during the night, because when I woke up from the dream, it was daylight. I didn't tell Rosie about it, though. I decided to write it down so that she could read it. The first chance to put it on paper, I did.

I was sitting at the kitchen table, writing. Dante was sitting in the big wooden chair where I had tied him down. He was sitting near the table, between me and the kitchen door, which was open. I had given him a bath a little while ago. Rosie and the three kids had been out, and I had been alone with Dante.

Someone appeared at the screened door, opened it quickly, entered, and stood behind Dante. It was Shackle. I was stunned. I stood up quickly, facing him.

He was wearing a pink shirt with short sleeves.

Dante couldn't turn around, so Shackle couldn't see his face, but he obviously knew that it was Dante.

"Never send a kid to do a man's job," Shackle muttered. "If you want something done right, you have to do it yourself. This time I'll do it myself."

His eyes were filled with hatred.

On the table, close to me, happened to be a butcher knife that I used to cut meat to put into the grinder. As soon as Shackle reached out and grabbed Dante by the throat, I grabbed the knife and put the end of it against Shackle's throat. I was tempted to ram it through his neck. He stepped back quickly and dropped his hands to his side. And then he began to laugh.

He seemed amused, and he laughed louder.

"You think that's going to stop me? Go ahead, cut my throat! You know what's going to happen to both of you. Don't you? You can't stop me. Go ahead and try!"

As he raised his hands, laughing, and took a step towards Dante again, I quickly slit his neck.

He continued to laugh.

The blade had sliced his neck, but no blood had squirted out.

"You can't stop me! There's nothing you can do to stop me."

"You're not even human! What are you?"

He, with his eyes almost on fire, was laughing menacingly.

He was not afraid of the knife.

As he grabbed Dante by the throat again and began to strangle him, I instinctively thrust the knife into the stomach of the inhuman being, but his stomach was like soft rubber. And his laugh grew even louder and more sinister.

Suddenly I became aware of what he really was.

"Are you the devil?"

He continued to laugh, glaring at me.

I became stronger, with the power of my belief, and determined to stop him.

"Yes, you are the devil! You are Satan! You are the opposite of God," I said, raising my voice at him and slashing him. "That means you are nothing! The opposite of God is nothingness!" He withdrew from Dante. "Nothing comes from nothingness. Without me, you have no power. You are nothing! You get your power from me. Without me, you're powerless. Whatever power you have, I give to you. But now I give you nothing!"

As I was talking, I was slashing him to nothing. His eyes were filled with panic as his image was disappearing.

"You are nothing! Go to hell, damn you! Go to hell!"

And as he disappeared, Dante began to laugh.

I dropped the knife on the table, and as I bent down to embrace Dante, he was staring at me and was smiling. His blue eyes were gazing into mine, and he spoke. He *actually* spoke to me. As I was cupping his face, he said in a soft, yet clear voice, "I don't belong here anymore; I want to go home."

"You *are* home. You're home where you belong, with me and Rosie and your three kids."

"No. I mean, home, our *real* home."

"What are you talking about? *This* is our real home."

"Existence here is only temporary, but soon I will be free of this existence; I want to move on to a higher level, to a higher level of reality from which we all came, to which we will all return. That's where I belong now. And when I am free, you and Rose will be freer, too. I have confidence in you that you will continue to care for her and the kids just as you have fulfilled my desire to complete my book."

I wanted to ask him so many questions of what his existence was like during the past two years, but I couldn't think of any specific questions. However, I thought that if I were an atheist with all the answers, I would say, probably, that when we're so sick and close to death, nature protects our psyche by providing us with some sort of narcotic that induces us into thinking that we're entering into a better state. That would explain the experiences of those people who had come so close to death that they had felt that they had actually left their bodies, and then they had returned to life. And that would also contribute to the origins of religion. But that begs another question. What is nature?

To a mystic, Nature confirms faith; to a skeptic, nature raises a question that can't, or shouldn't, be ignored.

Dante, without uttering another word, was staring into me so deeply that in his eyes, I had glimpsed into eternity; time had suddenly stopped, as in a photograph, in which there is neither past nor future; there is only *now,* an eternal timelessness, yet in perpetual motion.

It was daylight.

I was in bed with Rosie. I wrapped my arms around her, and although she was asleep, the feeling of her warm flesh against mine felt so pleasurable, that I closed my eyes and pressed myself against her, and went back to sleep.

THE END

About the Author

Before World War II, Dario Addario was born at the foot of Mount Washington, on the backstreet of Italian immigrants in Cascade Flats in the town of Gorham, New Hampshire. During WWII, he lived in Portland, Maine, where his father worked in the shipyard. In June 1950, Dario graduated from St. John's High School in Concord, New Hampshire when the war in Korea began. In 1953, Dario served in Korea as a rifleman in the Ninth Infantry Regiment of the Second Infantry Division. In July of 1953, when the ceasefire went into effect, he was on Boomerang Hill. After the service, he attended the University of New Hampshire and became a teacher in the Concord area. In 1964 he married Sara Jane Tremblay of Claremont. They have one child, Michael. In 1970, they moved to Claremont, where Dario taught English in the junior high school. He has lived in Claremont for the past forty-eight years. From 1988 until 1998, he worked in the White River Junction, Vermont, postal facility, from which he has retired. He and his wife became frequent visitors to Italy until she passed away in 2006. Dario had become friendly with a priest in Italy, Jean Paul Matoe, from Madagascar, who passed away in 2012. In 2014, Dario spent the whole month of July visiting Jean Paul's family in Ambanja, Madagascar.

CPSIA information can be obtained
at www.ICGtesting.com
Printed in the USA
JSHW020054200722
28263JS00001B/1